W9-ADP-713

PRAISE FOR SARAH J. MAAS'S
COURT OF THORNS AND ROSES SERIES

"Maas transcends her genre. . . . No longer do people ask whether someone has read her; they ask which book started it all for them."
—*New York Times* bestselling author Christina Lauren

"Intensely emotional, wildly sexy, and absolutely unputdownable."
—*New York Times* bestselling author Sarah MacLean

"A viciously vibrant epic."
—*Entertainment Weekly*

"Simply dazzles."
—*Booklist*, starred review

"Passionate, violent, sexy and daring. . . ."
—*USA Today*

"Suspense, romance, intrigue and action.
This is not a book to be missed!"
—*HuffPost*

"Fiercely romantic, irresistibly sexy and hypnotically magical.
A veritable feast for the senses."
—*USA Today*

"Hits the spot for fans of dark, lush, sexy fantasy."
—*Kirkus Reviews*

"An immersive, satisfying read."
—*Publishers Weekly*

"Darkly sexy and thrilling."
—*Bustle*

BOOKS BY SARAH J. MAAS

THE COURT OF THORNS AND ROSES SERIES

A Court of Thorns and Roses

A Court of Mist and Fury

A Court of Wings and Ruin

A Court of Frost and Starlight

A Court of Silver Flames

―――

A Court of Thorns and Roses Coloring Book

‿◦

THE CRESCENT CITY SERIES

House of Earth and Blood

House of Sky and Breath

‿◦

THE THRONE OF GLASS SERIES

The Assassin's Blade

Throne of Glass

Crown of Midnight

Heir of Fire

Queen of Shadows

Empire of Storms

Tower of Dawn

Kingdom of Ash

―――

The Throne of Glass Coloring Book

A COURT OF WINGS AND RUIN

SARAH J. MAAS

BLOOMSBURY PUBLISHING

NEW YORK · LONDON · OXFORD · NEW DELHI · SYDNEY

BLOOMSBURY PUBLISHING
Bloomsbury Publishing Inc.
1385 Broadway, New York, NY 10018, USA
29 Earlsfort Terrace, Dublin 2, Ireland

BLOOMSBURY, BLOOMSBURY PUBLISHING, and the Diana logo are trademarks of
Bloomsbury Publishing Plc

First published in the United States 2017
This paperback edition published 2020

Copyright © Sarah J. Maas, 2017
Map copyright © Kelly de Groot, 2017

All rights reserved. No part of this publication may be reproduced or transmitted in any form
or by any means, electronic or mechanical, including photocopying, recording, or any
information storage or retrieval system, without prior permission in writing from the publishers.

Bloomsbury Publishing Plc does not have any control over, or responsibility for, any third-party websites
referred to or in this book. All internet addresses given in this book were correct at the time of going to press.
The author and publisher regret any inconvenience caused if addresses have changed
or sites have ceased to exist, but can accept no responsibility for any such changes.

ISBN: HB: 978-1-63557-559-0; PB: 978-1-63557-560-6; eBook: 978-1-61963-449-7

Library of Congress Cataloging-in-Publication Data is available

20

Typeset by Westchester Publishing Services
Printed and bound in Great Britain by CPI (UK) Ltd, Croydon CR0 4YY

Visit www.bloomsbury.com to learn more about our authors and books.
Visit www.bloomsbury.com/author/sarah-j-maas to sign up for our Sarah J. Maas newsletter.

Bloomsbury books may be purchased for business or promotional use. For information on bulk purchases
please contact Macmillan Corporate and Premium Sales Department at specialmarkets@macmillan.com.

For Josh and Annie—
A gift. All of it.

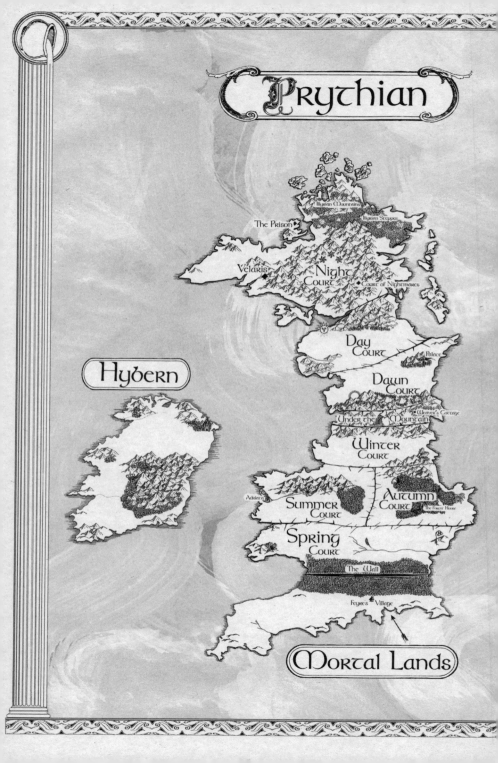

A COURT

OF

WINGS

AND

RUIN

Rhysand
Two Years Before the Wall

The buzzing flies and screaming survivors had long since replaced the beating war-drums.

The killing field was now a tangled sprawl of corpses, human and faerie alike, interrupted only by broken wings jutting toward the gray sky or the occasional bulk of a felled horse.

With the heat, despite the heavy cloud cover, the smell would soon be unbearable. Flies already crawled along eyes gazing unblinkingly upward. They didn't differentiate between mortal and immortal flesh.

I picked my way across the once-grassy plain, marking the banners half-buried in mud and gore. It took most of my lingering strength to keep my wings from dragging over corpse and armor. My own power had been depleted well before the carnage had stopped.

I'd spent the final hours fighting as the mortals beside me had: with sword and fist and brute, unrelenting focus. We'd held the lines against Ravennia's legions—hour after hour, we'd held the lines, as I had been ordered to do by my father, as I knew I must do. To falter here would have been the killing blow to our already-sundering resistance.

The keep looming at my back was too valuable to be yielded to the

Loyalists. Not just for its location in the heart of the continent, but for the supplies it guarded. For the forges that smoldered day and night on its western side, toiling to stock our forces.

The smoke of those forges now blended with the pyres already being kindled behind me as I kept walking, scanning the faces of the dead. I made a note to dispatch any soldiers who could stomach it to claim weapons from either army. We needed them too desperately to bother with honor. Especially since the other side did not bother with it at all.

So still—the battlefield was so still, compared with the slaughter and chaos that had finally halted hours ago. The Loyalist army had retreated rather than surrender, leaving their dead for the crows.

I edged around a fallen bay gelding, the beautiful beast's eyes still wide with terror, flies crusting his bloodied flank. The rider was twisted beneath it, the man's head partially severed. Not from a sword blow. No, those brutal gashes were claws.

They wouldn't yield easily. The kingdoms and territories that wanted their human slaves would not lose this war unless they had no other choice. And even then . . . We'd learned the hard way, very early on, that they had no regard for the ancient rules and rites of battle. And for the Fae territories that fought beside mortal warriors . . . We were to be stomped out like vermin.

I waved away a fly that buzzed in my ear, my hand caked with blood both my own and foreign.

I'd always thought death would be some sort of peaceful homecoming—a sweet, sad lullaby to usher me into whatever waited afterward.

I crunched down with an armored boot on the flagpole of a Loyalist standard-bearer, smearing red mud across the tusked boar embroidered on its emerald flag.

I now wondered if the lullaby of death was not a lovely song, but the droning of flies. If flies and maggots were all Death's handmaidens.

The battlefield stretched toward the horizon in every direction save the keep at my back.

Three days, we had held them off; three days, we had fought and died here.

But we'd held the lines. Again and again, I'd rallied human and faerie, had refused to let the Loyalists break through, even when they'd hammered our vulnerable right flank with fresh troops on the second day.

I'd used my power until it was nothing but smoke in my veins, and then I'd used my Illyrian training until swinging my shield and sword was all I knew, all I could manage against the hordes.

A half-shredded Illyrian wing jutted from a cluster of High Fae corpses, as if it had taken all six of them to bring the warrior down. As if he'd taken them all out with him.

My heartbeat pounded through my battered body as I hauled away the piled corpses.

Reinforcements had arrived at dawn on the third and final day, sent by my father after my plea for aid. I had been too lost in battle-rage to note who they were beyond an Illyrian unit, especially when so many had been wielding Siphons.

But in the hours since they'd saved our asses and turned the tide of the battle, I had not spotted either of my brothers amongst the living. Did not know if Cassian or Azriel had even fought on the plain.

The latter was unlikely, as my father kept him close for spying, but Cassian . . . Cassian could have been reassigned. I wouldn't have put it past my father to shift Cassian to a unit most likely to be slaughtered. As this one had been, barely half limping off the battlefield earlier.

My aching, bloodied fingers dug into dented armor and clammy, stiff flesh as I heaved away the last of the High Fae corpses piled atop the fallen Illyrian soldier.

The dark hair, the golden-brown skin . . . The same as Cassian's.

But it was not Cassian's death-gray face that gaped at the sky.

My breath whooshed from me, my lungs still raw from roaring, my lips dry and chapped.

I needed water—badly. But nearby, another set of Illyrian wings poked up from the piled dead.

3

I stumbled and lurched toward it, letting my mind drift someplace dark and quiet while I righted the twisted neck to peer at the face beneath the simple helm.

Not him.

I picked my way through the corpses to another Illyrian.

Then another. And another.

Some I knew. Some I didn't. Still the killing field stretched onward under the sky.

Mile after mile. A kingdom of the rotting dead.

And still I looked.

PART ONE

PRINCESS OF CARRION

CHAPTER
1

Feyre

The painting was a lie.

A bright, pretty lie, bursting with pale pink blooms and fat beams of sunshine.

I'd begun it yesterday, an idle study of the rose garden lurking beyond the open windows of the studio. Through the tangle of thorns and satiny leaves, the brighter green of the hills rolled away into the distance.

Incessant, unrelenting spring.

If I'd painted this glimpse into the court the way my gut had urged me, it would have been flesh-shredding thorns, flowers that choked off the sunlight for any plants smaller than them, and rolling hills stained red.

But each brushstroke on the wide canvas was calculated; each dab and swirl of blending colors meant to portray not just idyllic spring, but a sunny disposition as well. Not too happy, but gladly, finally healing from horrors I carefully divulged.

I supposed that in the past weeks, I had crafted my demeanor as intricately as one of these paintings. I supposed that if I had also chosen to show myself as I truly wished, I would have been adorned with flesh-shredding talons, and hands that choked the life out of those now in my company. I would have left the gilded halls stained red.

But not yet.

Not yet, I told myself with every brushstroke, with every move I'd made these weeks. Swift revenge helped no one and nothing but my own, roiling rage.

Even if every time I spoke to them, I heard Elain's sobbing as she was forced into the Cauldron. Even if every time I looked at them, I saw Nesta fling that finger at the King of Hybern in a death-promise. Even if every time I scented them, my nostrils were again full of the tang of Cassian's blood as it pooled on the dark stones of that bone-castle.

The paintbrush snapped between my fingers.

I'd cleaved it in two, the pale handle damaged beyond repair.

Cursing under my breath, I glanced to the windows, the doors. This place was too full of watching eyes to risk throwing it in the rubbish bin.

I cast my mind around me like a net, trawling for any others near enough to witness, to be spying. I found none.

I held my hands before me, one half of the brush in each palm.

For a moment, I let myself see past the glamour that concealed the tattoo on my right hand and forearm. The markings of my true heart. My true title.

High Lady of the Night Court.

Half a thought had the broken paintbrush going up in flames.

The fire did not burn me, even as it devoured wood and brush and paint.

When it was nothing but smoke and ash, I invited in a wind that swept them from my palms and out the open windows.

For good measure, I summoned a breeze from the garden to snake through the room, wiping away any lingering tendril of smoke, filling it with the musty, suffocating smell of roses.

Perhaps when my task here was done, I'd burn this manor to the ground, too. Starting with those roses.

Two approaching presences tapped against the back of my mind, and I snatched up another brush, dipping it in the closest swirl of paint, and lowered the invisible, dark snares I'd erected around this room to alert me of any visitors.

I was working on the way the sunlight illuminated the delicate veins in a rose petal, trying not to think of how I'd once seen it do the same to Illyrian wings, when the doors opened.

I made a good show of appearing lost in my work, hunching my shoulders a bit, angling my head. And made an even better show of slowly looking over my shoulder, as if the struggle to part myself from the painting was a true effort.

But the battle was the smile I forced to my mouth. To my eyes—the real tell of a smile's genuine nature. I'd practiced in the mirror. Over and over.

So my eyes easily crinkled as I gave a subdued yet happy smile to Tamlin.

To Lucien.

"Sorry to interrupt," Tamlin said, scanning my face for any sign of the shadows I remembered to occasionally fall prey to, the ones I wielded to keep him at bay when the sun sank beyond those foothills. "But I thought you might want to get ready for the meeting."

I made myself swallow. Lower the paintbrush. No more than the nervous, unsure girl I'd been long ago. "Is—you talked it over with Ianthe? She's truly coming?"

I hadn't seen her yet. The High Priestess who had betrayed my sisters to Hybern, betrayed *us* to Hybern.

And even if Rhysand's murky, swift reports through the mating bond had soothed some of my dread and terror . . . She was responsible for it. What had happened weeks ago.

It was Lucien who answered, studying my painting as if it held the proof I knew he was searching for. "Yes. She . . . had her reasons. She is willing to explain them to you."

Perhaps along with her reasons for laying her hands on whatever males she pleased, whether they wished her to or not. For doing it to Rhys, and Lucien.

I wondered what Lucien truly made of it. And the fact that the collateral in her friendship with Hybern had wound up being *his* mate. Elain.

We had not spoken of Elain save for once, the day after I'd returned.

Despite what Jurian implied regarding how my sisters will be treated by Rhysand, I had told him, *despite what the Night Court is like, they won't hurt Elain or Nesta like that—not yet. Rhysand has more creative ways to harm them.*

Lucien still seemed to doubt it.

But then again, I had also implied, in my own "gaps" of memory, that perhaps I had not received the same creativity or courtesy.

That they believed it so easily, that they thought Rhysand would ever force someone . . . I added the insult to the long, long list of things to repay them for.

I set down the brush and pulled off the paint-flecked smock, carefully laying it on the stool I'd been perched on for two hours now.

"I'll go change," I murmured, flicking my loose braid over a shoulder.

Tamlin nodded, monitoring my every movement as I neared them. "The painting looks beautiful."

"It's nowhere near done," I said, dredging up that girl who had shunned praise and compliments, who had wanted to go unnoticed. "It's still a mess."

Frankly, it was some of my best work, even if its soullessness was only apparent to me.

"I think we all are," Tamlin offered with a tentative smile.

I reined in the urge to roll my eyes, and returned his smile, brushing my hand over his shoulder as I passed.

Lucien was waiting outside my new bedroom when I emerged ten minutes later.

It had taken me two days to stop going to the old one—to turn right at the top of the stairs and not left. But there was nothing in that old bedroom.

I'd looked into it once, the day after I returned.

Shattered furniture; shredded bedding; clothes strewn about as if he'd gone looking for me inside the armoire. No one, it seemed, had been allowed in to clean.

But it was the vines—the thorns—that had made it unlivable. My old bedroom had been overrun with them. They'd curved and slithered over the walls, entwined themselves amongst the debris. As if they'd crawled off the trellises beneath my windows, as if a hundred years had passed and not months.

That bedroom was now a tomb.

I gathered the soft pink skirts of my gauzy dress in a hand and shut the bedroom door behind me. Lucien remained leaning against the door across from mine.

His room.

I didn't doubt he'd ensured I now stayed across from him. Didn't doubt that the metal eye he possessed was always turned toward my own chambers, even while he slept.

"I'm surprised you're so calm, given your promises in Hybern," Lucien said by way of greeting.

The promise I'd made to kill the human queens, the King of Hybern, Jurian, and Ianthe for what they'd done to my sisters. To my friends.

"You yourself said Ianthe had her reasons. Furious as I might be, I can hear her out."

I had not told Lucien of what I knew regarding her true nature. It would mean explaining that Rhys had thrown her out of his own home, that Rhys had done it to defend himself and the members of his court, and it would raise too many questions, undermine too many carefully crafted lies that had kept him and his court—*my* court—safe.

Though I wondered if, after Velaris, it was even necessary. Our enemies knew of the city, knew it was a place of good and peace. And had tried to destroy it at the first opportunity.

The guilt for the attack on Velaris after Rhys had revealed it to those human queens would haunt my mate for the rest of our immortal lives.

"She's going to spin a story that you'll want to hear," Lucien warned.

I shrugged, heading down the carpeted, empty hall. "I can decide for myself. Though it sounds like you've already chosen not to believe her."

He fell into step beside me. "She dragged two innocent women into this."

"She was working to ensure Hybern's alliance held strong."

Lucien halted me with a hand around my elbow.

I allowed it because *not* allowing it, winnowing the way I'd done in the woods those months ago, or using an Illyrian defensive maneuver to knock him on his ass, would ruin my ruse. "You're smarter than that."

I studied the broad, tan hand wrapped around my elbow. Then I met one eye of russet and one of whirring gold.

Lucien breathed, "Where is he keeping her?"

I knew who he meant.

I shook my head. "I don't know. Rhysand has a hundred places where they could be, but I doubt he'd use any of them to hide Elain, knowing that I'm aware of them."

"Tell me anyway. List all of them."

"You'll die the moment you set foot in his territory."

"I survived well enough when I found you."

"You couldn't see that he had me in thrall. You let him take me back." Lie, lie, lie.

But the hurt and guilt I expected weren't there. Lucien slowly released his grip. "I need to find her."

"You don't even know Elain. The mating bond is just a physical reaction overriding your good sense."

"Is that what it did to you and Rhys?"

A quiet, dangerous question. But I made fear enter my eyes, let myself drag up memories of the Weaver, the Carver, the Middengard Wyrm so that old terror drenched my scent. "I don't want to talk about that," I said, my voice a rasping wobble.

A clock chimed on the main level. I sent a silent prayer of thanks to the Mother and launched into a quick walk. "We'll be late."

Lucien only nodded. But I felt his gaze on my back, fixed right on my spine, as I headed downstairs. To see Ianthe.

And at last decide how I was going to shred her into pieces.

⊕

The High Priestess looked exactly as I remembered, both in those memories Rhys had shown me and in my own daydreamings of using the talons hidden beneath my nails to carve out her eyes, then her tongue, then open up her throat.

My rage had become a living thing inside my chest, an echoing heartbeat that soothed me to sleep and stirred me to waking. I quieted it as I stared at Ianthe across the formal dining table, Tamlin and Lucien flanking me.

She still wore the pale hood and silver circlet set with its limpid blue stone.

Like a Siphon—the jewel in its center reminded me of Azriel's and Cassian's Siphons. And I wondered if, like the Illyrian warriors', the jewel somehow helped shape an unwieldy gift of magic into something more refined, deadlier. She had never removed it—but then again, I had never seen Ianthe summon any greater power than igniting a ball of faelight in a room.

The High Priestess lowered her teal eyes to the dark wood table, the hood casting shadows on her perfect face. "I wish to begin by saying how truly sorry I am. I acted out of a desire to . . . to grant what I believed you perhaps yearned for but did not dare voice, while also keeping our allies in Hybern satisfied with our allegiance."

Pretty, poisoned lies. But finding her true motive . . . I'd been waiting these weeks for this meeting. Had spent these weeks pretending to convalesce, pretending to *heal* from the horrors I'd survived at Rhysand's hands.

"Why would I ever wish for my sisters to endure that?" My voice came out trembling, cold.

Ianthe lifted her head, scanning my unsure, if not a bit aloof, face. "So you could be with them forever. And if Lucien had discovered that Elain was his mate beforehand, it would have been . . . devastating to realize he'd only have a few decades."

The sound of Elain's name on her lips sent a snarl rumbling up my throat. But I leashed it, falling into that mask of pained quiet, the newest in my arsenal.

Lucien answered, "If you expect our gratitude, you'll be waiting a while, Ianthe."

Tamlin shot him a warning look—both at the words and the tone. Perhaps Lucien would kill Ianthe before I had the chance, just for the horror she'd put his mate through that day.

"No," Ianthe breathed, eyes wide, the perfect picture of remorse and guilt. "No, I don't expect gratitude in the least. Or forgiveness. But understanding . . . This is my home, too." She lifted a slender hand clad in silver rings and bracelets to encompass the room, the manor. "We have all had to make alliances we didn't believe we'd ever forge— perhaps unsavory ones, yes, but . . . Hybern's force is too great to stop. It now can only be weathered like any other storm." A glance toward Tamlin. "We have worked so hard to prepare ourselves for Hybern's inevitable arrival—all these months. I made a grave mistake, and I will always regret any pain I caused, but let us continue this good work together. Let us find a way to ensure our lands and people survive."

"At the cost of how many others?" Lucien demanded.

Again, that warning look from Tamlin. But Lucien ignored him.

"What I saw in Hybern," Lucien said, gripping the arms of his chair hard enough that the carved wood groaned. "Any promises he made of peace and immunity . . ." He halted, as if remembering that Ianthe might very well feed this back to the king. He loosened his grip on the chair, his long fingers flexing before settling on the arms again. "We have to be careful."

"We will be," Tamlin promised. "But we've already agreed to certain conditions. Sacrifices. If we break apart now . . . even with Hybern as our ally, we have to present a solid front. Together."

He still trusted her. Still thought that Ianthe had merely made a bad call. Had no idea what lurked beneath the beauty, the clothes, and the pious incantations.

But then again, that same blindness kept him from realizing what prowled beneath my skin as well. Ianthe bowed her head again. "I will endeavor to be worthy of my friends."

Lucien seemed to be trying very, very hard not to roll his eyes.

But Tamlin said, "We'll all try."

That was his new favorite word: *try*.

I only swallowed, making sure he heard it, and nodded slowly, keeping my eyes on Ianthe. "Don't ever do anything like that again."

A fool's command—one she'd expected me to make, from the quickness with which she nodded. Lucien leaned back in his seat, refusing to say anything else.

"Lucien is right, though," I blurted, the portrait of concern. "What of the people in this court during this conflict?" I frowned at Tamlin. "They were brutalized by Amarantha—I'm not sure how well they will endure living beside Hybern. They have suffered enough."

Tamlin's jaw tightened. "Hybern has promised that our people shall remain untouched and undisturbed." *Our* people. I nearly scowled— even as I nodded again in understanding. "It was a part of our . . . bargain." When he'd sold out all of Prythian, sold out everything decent and good in himself, to *retrieve* me. "Our people will be safe when Hybern arrives. Though I've sent out word that families should . . . relocate to the eastern part of the territory. For the time being."

Good. At least he'd considered those potential casualties—at least he cared that much about his people, understood what sorts of sick games Hybern liked to play and that he might swear one thing but mean another. If he was already moving those most at risk during this conflict out of the way . . . It made my work here all the easier. And east—a bit of information I tucked away. If east was safe, then the west . . . Hybern would indeed be coming from that direction. Arriving there.

Tamlin blew out a breath. "That brings me to the other reason behind this meeting."

I braced myself, schooling my face into bland curiosity, as he declared, "The first delegation from Hybern arrives tomorrow." Lucien's golden skin paled. Tamlin added, "Jurian will be here by noon."

CHAPTER
2

I'd barely heard a whisper of Jurian these past weeks—hadn't seen the resurrected human commander since that night in Hybern.

Jurian had been reborn through the Cauldron using the hideous remnants of him that Amarantha had hoarded as trophies for five hundred years, his soul trapped and aware within his own magically preserved eye. He was mad—had gone mad long before the King of Hybern had resurrected him to lead the human queens down a path of ignorant submission.

Tamlin and Lucien had to know. Had to have seen that gleam in Jurian's eyes.

But . . . they also did not seem to entirely mind that the King of Hybern possessed the Cauldron—that it was capable of cleaving this world apart. Starting with the wall. The only thing standing between the gathering, lethal Fae armies and the vulnerable human lands below.

No, that threat certainly didn't seem to keep Lucien or Tamlin awake at night. Or from inviting these monsters into their home.

Tamlin had promised upon my return that I was to be included in the planning, in every meeting. And he was true to his word when he explained that Jurian would arrive with two other commanders from Hybern, and I would be present for it. They indeed wished to survey the wall, to test for the perfect spot to rend it once the Cauldron had recovered its strength.

Turning my sisters into Fae, apparently, had drained it.

My smugness at the fact was short-lived.

My first task: learn where they planned to strike, and how long the Cauldron required to return to its full capacity. And then smuggle that information to Rhysand and the others.

I took extra care dressing the next day, after sleeping fitfully thanks to a dinner with a guilt-ridden Ianthe, who went to excessive lengths to kiss my ass and Lucien's. The priestess apparently wished to wait until the Hybern commanders were settled before making her appearance. She'd cooed about wanting to ensure they had the chance to get to know us before she intruded, but one look at Lucien told me that he and I, for once, agreed: she had likely planned some sort of grand entrance.

It made little difference to me—to my plans.

Plans that I sent down the mating bond the next morning, words and images tumbling along a night-filled corridor.

I did not dare risk using the bond too often. I had communicated with Rhysand only once since I'd arrived. Just once, in the hours after I'd walked into my old bedroom and spied the thorns that had conquered it.

It had been like shouting across a great distance, like speaking underwater. *I am safe and well*, I'd fired down the bond. *I'll tell you what I know soon.* I'd waited, letting the words travel into the dark. Then I'd asked, *Are they alive? Hurt?*

I didn't remember the bond between us being so hard to hear, even when I'd dwelled on this estate and he'd used it to see if I was still breathing, to make sure my despair hadn't swallowed me whole.

But Rhysand's response had come a minute later. *I love you. They are alive. They are healing.*

That was it. As if it was all that he could manage.

I had drifted back to my new chambers, locked the door, and enveloped the entire place in a wall of hard air to keep any scent from my silent tears escaping as I curled up in a corner of the bathing room.

I had once sat in such a position, watching the stars during the long, bleak hours of the night. Now I took in the cloudless blue sky beyond the open window, listened to the birds singing to one another, and wanted to roar.

I had not dared to ask for more details about Cassian and Azriel—or my sisters. In terror of knowing just how bad it had been—and what I'd do if their healing turned grim. What I'd bring down upon these people.

Healing. Alive and healing. I reminded myself of that every day.

Even when I still heard their screams, smelled their blood.

But I did not ask for more. Did not risk touching the bond beyond that first time.

I didn't know if someone could monitor such things—the silent messages between mates. Not when the mating bond could be scented, and I was playing such a dangerous game with it.

Everyone believed it had been severed, that Rhys's lingering scent was because he'd forced me, had planted that scent in me.

They believed that with time, with distance, his scent would fade. Weeks or months, likely.

And when it didn't fade, when it remained . . . That's when I'd have to strike, with or without the information I needed.

But out of the possibility that communicating down the bond kept its scent strong . . . I had to minimize how much I used it. Even if not talking to Rhys, not hearing that amusement and cunning . . . I would hear those things again, I promised myself over and over. See that wry smile.

And I was again thinking of how pained that face had been the last time I'd seen it, thinking of Rhys, covered in Azriel's and Cassian's blood, as Jurian and the two Hybern commanders winnowed into the gravel of the front drive the next day.

Jurian was in the same light leather armor, his brown hair whipping across his face in the blustery spring breeze. He spied us standing on the white marble steps into the house and his mouth curled in that crooked, smug smile.

I willed ice into my veins, the coldness from a court I had never set foot in. But I wielded its master's gift on myself, turning burning rage into frozen calm as Jurian swaggered toward us, a hand on the hilt of his sword.

But it was the two commanders—one male, one female—that had a sliver of true fear sliding into my heart.

High Fae in appearance, their skin the same ruddy hue and hair the identical inky black as their king. But it was their vacant, unfeeling faces that snagged the eye. A lack of emotion honed from millennia of cruelty.

Tamlin and Lucien had gone rigid by the time Jurian halted at the foot of the sweeping front stairs. The human commander smirked. "You're looking better than the last time I saw you."

I dragged my eyes to his. And said nothing.

Jurian snorted and gestured the two commanders forward. "May I present Their Highnesses, Prince Dagdan and Princess Brannagh, nephew and niece to the King of Hybern."

Twins—perhaps linked in power and mental bonds as well.

Tamlin seemed to remember that these were now his allies and marched down the stairs. Lucien followed.

He'd sold us out. Sold out Prythian—for me. To get me back.

Smoke curled in my mouth. I willed frost to fill it again.

Tamlin inclined his head to the prince and princess. "Welcome to my home. We have rooms prepared for all of you."

"My brother and I shall reside in one together," the princess said. Her voice was deceptively light—almost girlish. The utter lack of feeling, the utter authority was anything but.

I could practically feel the snide remark simmering in Lucien. But I stepped down the stairs and said, ever the lady of the house that these people, that Tamlin, had once expected me to gladly embrace, "We can easily make adjustments."

Lucien's metal eye whirred and narrowed on me, but I kept my face impassive as I curtsied to them. To my enemy. Which of my friends would face them on the battlefield?

Would Cassian and Azriel have even healed enough to fight, let alone lift a sword? I did not allow myself to dwell on it—on how Cassian had screamed as his wings had been shredded.

Princess Brannagh surveyed me: the rose-colored dress, the hair that Alis had curled and braided over the top of my head in a coronet, the pale pink pearls at my ears.

A harmless, lovely package, perfect for a High Lord to mount whenever he wished.

Brannagh's lip curled as she glanced at her brother. The prince deemed the same thing, judging by his answering sneer.

Tamlin snarled softly in warning. "If you're done staring at her, perhaps we can move on to the business between us."

Jurian let out a low chuckle and strode up the stairs without being given leave to do so. "They're curious." Lucien stiffened at the impudence of the gesture, the words. "It's not every century that the contested possession of a female launches a war. Especially a female with such . . . talents."

I only turned on a heel and stalked up the steps after him. "Perhaps if you'd bothered going to war over Miryam, she wouldn't have left you for Prince Drakon."

A ripple seemed to go through Jurian. Tamlin and Lucien tensed at my back, torn between monitoring our exchange and escorting the two Hybern royals into the house. Upon my own explanation that Azriel and his network of spies were well trained, we'd cleared any unnecessary servants, wary of spying ears and eyes. Only the most trusted among them remained.

Of course, I'd forgotten to mention that I knew Azriel had pulled his spies weeks ago, the information not worth the cost of their lives. Or that it served *my* own purposes to have fewer people watching me.

Jurian halted at the top of the stairs, his face a mask of cruel death as I took the last steps to him. "Careful what you say, girl."

I smiled, breezing past. "Or what? You'll throw me in the Cauldron?"

I strode between the front doors, edging around the table in the heart of the entry hall, its towering vase of flowers arching to meet the crystal chandelier.

Right there—just a few feet away, I had crumpled into a ball of terror and despair all those months ago. Right there in the center of the foyer, Mor had picked me up and carried me out of this house and into freedom.

"Here's the first rule of this visit," I said to Jurian over my shoulder as I headed for the dining room, where lunch awaited. "Don't threaten me in my own home."

The posturing, I knew a moment later, had worked.

Not on Jurian, who glowered as he claimed a seat at the table.

But on Tamlin, who brushed a knuckle over my cheek as he passed by, unaware of how carefully I had chosen the words, how I had baited Jurian to serve up the opportunity on a platter.

That was my first step: make Tamlin believe, truly believe, that I loved him and this place, and everyone in it.

So that he would not suspect when I turned them on each other.

⸙

Prince Dagdan yielded to his twin's every wish and order. As if he were the blade she wielded to slice through the world.

He poured her drinks, sniffing them first. He selected the finest cuts of meat from the platters and neatly arranged them on her plate. He always let her answer, and never so much as looked at her with doubt in his eyes.

One soul in two bodies. And from the way they glanced to each other in wordless exchanges, I wondered if they were perhaps . . . perhaps like me. *Daemati*.

My mental shields had been a wall of black adamant since arriving. But as we dined, beats of silence going on longer than conversation, I found myself checking them over and over.

"We will set out for the wall tomorrow," Brannagh was saying to Tamlin. More of an order than a request. "Jurian will accompany us. We require the use of sentries who know where the holes in it are located."

The thought of them so close to the human lands . . . But my sisters were not there. No, my sisters were somewhere in the vast territory of my own court, protected by my friends. Even if my father would return home from his business dealings on the continent in a matter of a month or two. I still had not figured out how I'd tell him.

"Lucien and I can escort you," I offered.

Tamlin whipped his head to me. I waited for the refusal, the shutdown.

But it seemed the High Lord had indeed learned his lesson, was indeed willing to *try*, as he merely gestured to Lucien. "My emissary knows the wall as well as any sentry."

You are letting them do this; you are rationally allowing them to bring down that wall and prey upon the humans on the other side. The words tangled and hissed in my mouth.

But I made myself give Tamlin a slow, if not slightly displeased, nod. He knew I'd never be happy about it—the girl he believed had been returned to him would always seek to protect her mortal homeland. Yet he thought I'd stomach it for him, for us. That Hybern wouldn't feast on the humans once that wall came down. That we'd merely absorb them into our territory.

"We'll leave after breakfast," I told the princess. And I added to Tamlin, "With a few sentries as well."

His shoulders loosened at that. I wondered if he'd heard how I'd defended Velaris. That I had protected the Rainbow against a legion of beasts like the Attor. That I had slaughtered the Attor, brutally, cruelly, for what it had done to me and mine.

Jurian surveyed Lucien with a warrior's frankness. "I always wondered who made that eye after she carved it out."

We did not speak of Amarantha here. We had never allowed her presence into this house. And it had stifled me for those months I'd lived here after Under the Mountain, killed me day by day to shove those fears and pain down deep.

For a heartbeat, I weighed who I had been with who I was now supposed to be. Slowly healing—emerging back into the girl Tamlin had fed and sheltered and loved before Amarantha had snapped my neck after three months of torture.

So I shifted in my seat. Studied the table.

Lucien merely leveled a hard look at Jurian as the two Hybern royals watched with impassive faces. "I have an old friend at the Dawn Court. She's skilled at tinkering—blending magic and machinery. Tamlin got her to craft it for me at great risk."

A hateful smile from Jurian. "Does your little mate have a rival?"

"My mate is none of your concern."

Jurian shrugged. "She shouldn't be any of yours, either, considering she's probably been fucked by half the Illyrian army by now."

I was fairly certain that only centuries of training kept Lucien from leaping over the table to rip out Jurian's throat.

But it was Tamlin's snarl that rattled the glasses. "You will behave as a proper guest, Jurian, or you will sleep in the stables like the other beasts."

Jurian merely sipped from his wine. "Why should I be punished for stating the truth? Neither of you were in the War, when my forces allied with the Illyrian brutes." A sidelong glance at the two Hybern royals. "I suppose you two had the delight of fighting against them."

"We kept the wings of their generals and lords as trophies," Dagdan said with a small smile.

It took every bit of concentration not to glance at Tamlin. Not to demand the whereabouts of the two sets of wings his father had kept as trophies after he'd butchered Rhysand's mother and sister.

Pinned in the study, Rhys had said.

But I hadn't spotted any trace when I'd gone hunting for them upon returning here, feigning exploration out of sheer boredom on a rainy day. The cellars had yielded nothing, either. No trunks or crates or locked rooms containing those wings.

The two bites of roasted lamb I'd forced down now rebelled against me. But at least any hint of disgust was a fair reaction to what the Hybern prince had claimed.

Jurian indeed smiled at me as he sliced his lamb into little pieces. "You know that we fought together, don't you? Me and your High Lord. Held the lines against the Loyalists, battled side by side until gore was up to our shins."

"He is not her High Lord," Tamlin said with unnerving softness.

Jurian only purred at me, "He must have told you where he hid Miryam and Drakon."

"They're dead," I said flatly.

"The Cauldron says otherwise."

Cold fear settled into my gut. He'd tried it already—to resurrect Miryam for himself. And had found that she was not amongst the deceased.

"I was told they were dead," I said again, trying to sound bored, impatient. I took a bite of my lamb, so bland compared to the wealth of spices in Velaris. "I'd think you'd have better things to do, Jurian, than obsess over the lover who jilted you."

His eyes gleamed, bright with five centuries of madness, as he skewered a morsel of meat with his fork. "They say you were fucking Rhysand before you ever jilted your own lover."

"That is *enough*," Tamlin growled.

But I felt it then. The tap against my mind. Saw their plan, clear and simple: rile us, distract us, while the two quiet royals slid into our minds.

Mine was shielded. But Lucien's—Tamlin's—

I reached out with my night-kissed power, casting it like a net. And found two oily tendrils spearing for Lucien's and Tamlin's minds, as if they were indeed javelins thrown across the table.

I struck. Dagdan and Brannagh jolted back in their seats as if I'd landed a physical blow, while their powers slammed into a barrier of black adamant around Lucien's and Tamlin's minds.

They shot their dark eyes toward me. I held each of their gazes.

"What's wrong?" Tamlin asked, and I realized how quiet it had become.

I made a good show of furrowing my brow in confusion. "Nothing." I offered a sweet smile to the two royals. "Their Highnesses must be tired after such a long journey."

And for good measure, I lunged for their own minds, finding a wall of white bone.

They flinched as I dragged black talons down their mental shields, gouging deep.

The warning blow cost me, a low, pulsing headache forming around my temples. But I merely dug back into my food, ignoring Jurian's wink.

No one spoke for the rest of the meal.

CHAPTER
3

The spring woods fell silent as we rode between the budding trees, birds and small furred beasts having darted for cover long before we passed.

Not from me, or Lucien, or the three sentries trailing a respectful distance behind. But from Jurian and the two Hybern commanders who rode in the center of our party. As if they were as awful as the Bogge, as the naga.

We reached the wall without incident or Jurian trying to bait us into distraction. I'd been awake most of the night, casting my awareness through the manor, hunting for any sign that Dagdan and Brannagh were working their daemati influence on anyone else. Mercifully, the curse-breaking ability I'd inherited from Helion Spell-Cleaver, High Lord of the Day Court, had detected no tangles, no spells, save for the wards around the house itself, preventing anyone from winnowing in or out.

Tamlin had been tense at breakfast, but had not asked me to remain behind. I'd even gone so far as to test him by asking what was wrong— to which he'd only replied that he had a headache. Lucien had just patted him on the shoulder and promised to look after me. I'd nearly laughed at the words.

But laughter was now far from my lips as the wall pulsed and throbbed, a heavy, hideous presence that loomed from half a mile away. Up close, though . . . Even our horses were skittish, tossing their heads and stomping their hooves on the mossy earth as we tied them to the low-hanging branches of blooming dogwoods.

"The gap in the wall is right up here," Lucien was saying, sounding about as thrilled as me to be in such company. Stomping over the fallen pink blossoms, Dagdan and Brannagh slid into step beside him, Jurian slithering off to survey the terrain, the sentries remaining with our mounts.

I followed Lucien and the royals, keeping a casual distance behind. I knew my elegant, fine clothes weren't fooling the prince and princess into forgetting that a fellow daemati now walked at their backs. But I'd still carefully selected the embroidered sapphire jacket and brown pants—adorned only with the jeweled knife and belt that Lucien had once gifted me. A lifetime ago.

"Who cleaved the wall here?" Brannagh asked, surveying the hole that we could not see—no, the wall itself was utterly invisible—but rather felt, as if the air had been sucked from one spot.

"We don't know," Lucien replied, the dappled sunlight glinting along the gold thread adorning his fawn-brown jacket as he crossed his arms. "Some of the holes just appeared over the centuries. This one is barely wide enough for one person to get through."

An exchanged glance between the twins. I came up behind them, studying the gap, the wall around it that made every instinct recoil at its . . . *wrongness*. "This is where I came through—that first time."

Lucien nodded, and the other two lifted their brows. But I took a step closer to Lucien, my arm nearly brushing his, letting him be a barrier between us. They'd been more careful at breakfast this morning about pushing against my mental shields. Yet now, letting them think I was physically cowed by them . . . Brannagh studied how closely I stood to Lucien; how he shifted slightly to shield me, too.

A little, cold smile curled her lips. "How many holes are in the wall?"

"We've counted three along our entire border," Lucien said tightly. "Plus one off the coast—about a mile away."

I didn't let my cool mask falter as he offered up the information.

But Brannagh shook her head, dark hair devouring the sunlight. "The sea entrances are of no use. We need to break it on the land."

"The continent surely has spots, too."

"Their queens have an even weaker grasp on their people than you do," Dagdan said. I plucked up that gem of information, studied it.

"We'll leave you to explore it, then," I said, waving toward the hole. "When you're done, we'll ride to the next."

"It's two days from here," Lucien countered.

"Then we'll plan a trip for that excursion," I said simply. Before Lucien could object, I asked, "And the third hole?"

Lucien tapped a foot against the mossy ground, but said, "Two days past that."

I turned to the royals, arching a brow. "Can both of you winnow?"

Brannagh flushed, straightening. But it was Dagdan who admitted, "I can." He must have carried both Brannagh and Jurian when they arrived. He added, "Only a few miles if I bear others."

I merely nodded and headed toward a tangle of stooping dogwoods, Lucien following close behind. When there was nothing but ruffling pink blossoms and trickling sunlight through the thatch of branches, when the royals had busied themselves with the wall, out of sight and sound, I took up a perch on a smooth, bald rock.

Lucien sat against a nearby tree, folding one booted ankle over another. "Whatever you're planning, it'll land us knee-deep in shit."

"I'm not planning anything." I plucked up a fallen pink blossom and twirled it between my thumb and forefinger.

That golden eye narrowed, clicking softly.

"What do you even see with that thing?"

He didn't answer.

I chucked the blossom onto the soft moss between us. "Don't trust me? After all we've been through?"

He frowned at the discarded blossom, but still said nothing.

I busied myself by sorting through my pack until I found the canteen of water. "If you'd been alive for the War," I asked him, taking a swig, "would you have fought on their side? Or fought for the humans?"

"I would have been a part of the human-Fae alliance."

"Even if your father wasn't?"

"Especially if my father wasn't."

But Beron had been part of that alliance, if I correctly recalled my lessons with Rhys all those months ago.

"And yet here you are, ready to march with Hybern."

"I did it for you, too, you know." Cold, hard words. "I went with him to get you back."

"I never realized what a powerful motivator guilt can be."

"That day you—went away," he said, struggling to avoid that other word—*left*. "I beat Tamlin back to the manor—received the message when we were out on the border and raced here. But the only trace of you was that ring, melted between the stones of the parlor. I got rid of it a moment before Tam arrived home to see it."

A probing, careful statement. Of the facts that pointed not toward abduction.

"They melted it off my finger," I lied.

His throat bobbed, but he just shook his head, the sunlight leaking through the forest canopy setting the ember-red of his hair flickering.

We sat in silence for minutes. From the rustling and murmuring, the royals were finishing up, and I braced myself, calculating the words I'd need to wield without seeming suspicious.

I said quietly, "Thank you. For coming to Hybern to get me."

He pulled at the moss beside him, jaw tight. "It was a trap. What I thought we were to do there . . . it did not turn out that way."

It was an effort not to bare my teeth. But I walked to him, taking up a place at his side against the wide trunk of the tree. "This situation is terrible," I said, and it was the truth.

A low snort.

I knocked my knee against his. "Don't let Jurian bait you. He's doing it to feel out any weaknesses between us."

"I know."

I turned my face to him, resting my knee against his in silent demand. "Why?" I asked. "*Why* does Hybern want to do this beyond some horrible desire for conquest? What drives him—his people? Hatred? Arrogance?"

Lucien finally looked at me, the intricate pieces and carvings on the metal eye much more dazzling up close. "Do you—"

Brannagh and Dagdan shoved through the bushes, frowning to find us sitting there.

But it was Jurian—right on their heels, as if he'd been divulging the details of his surveying—who smiled at the sight of us, knee to knee and nearly nose to nose.

"Careful, Lucien," the warrior sneered. "You see what happens to males who touch the High Lord's belongings."

Lucien snarled, but I shot him a warning glare.

Point proven, I said silently.

And despite Jurian, despite the sneering royals, a corner of Lucien's mouth tugged upward.

✠

Ianthe was waiting at the stables when we returned.

She'd made her grand arrival at the end of breakfast hours before, breezing into the dining room when the sun was shining in shafts of pure gold through the windows.

I had no doubt she'd planned the timing, just as she had planned the stop in the middle of one of those sunbeams, angled so her hair glowed and the jewel atop her head burned with blue fire. I would have titled the painting *Model Piety*.

After she'd been briefly introduced by Tamlin, she'd mostly cooed over Jurian—who had only scowled at her like some insect buzzing in his ear.

Dagdan and Brannagh had listened to her fawning with enough boredom that I was starting to wonder if the two of them perhaps preferred no one's company but each other's. In whatever unholy capacity. Not a blink of interest toward the beauty who often made males and females stop to gape. Perhaps any sort of physical passion had long ago been drained away, alongside their souls.

So the Hybern royals and Jurian had tolerated Ianthe for about a minute before they'd found their food more interesting. A slight that no doubt explained why she had decided to meet us here, awaiting our return as we rode in.

It was my first time on a horse in months, and I was stiff enough that I could barely move as the party dismounted. I gave Lucien a subtle, pleading look, and he barely hid his smirk as he sauntered over to me.

Our dispersing party watched as he braced my waist in his broad hands and easily hefted me off the horse, none more closely than Ianthe.

I only patted Lucien on the shoulder in thanks. Ever the courtier, he bowed back.

It was hard, sometimes, to remember to hate him. To remember the game I was already playing.

Ianthe trilled, "A successful journey, I hope?"

I jerked my chin toward the royals. "They seemed pleased."

Indeed, whatever they'd been looking for, they'd found agreeable. I hadn't dared ask too many prying questions. Not yet.

Ianthe bowed her head. "Thank the Cauldron for that."

"What do you want," Lucien said a shade too flatly.

She frowned but lifted her chin, folding her hands before her as she said, "We're to have a party in honor of our guests—and to coincide with the Summer Solstice in a few days. I wished to speak to Feyre about it." A two-faced smile. "Unless you have an objection to that."

"He doesn't," I answered before Lucien could say something he'd regret. "Give me an hour to eat and change, and I'll meet you in the study."

Perhaps a tinge more assertive than I'd once been, but she nodded all the same. I linked my elbow with Lucien's and steered him away. "See you soon," I told her, and felt her gaze on us as we walked from the dim stables and into the bright midday light.

His body was taut, near-trembling.

"What happened between you?" I hissed when we were lost among the hedges and gravel paths of the garden.

"It's not worth repeating."

"When I—was taken," I ventured, almost stumbling on the word, almost saying *left*. "Did she and Tamlin . . ."

I was not faking the twisting low in my gut.

"No," he said hoarsely. "No. When Calanmai came along, he refused. He flat-out refused to participate. I replaced him in the Rite, but . . ."

I'd forgotten. Forgotten about Calanmai and the Rite. I did a mental tally of the days.

No wonder I'd forgotten. I'd been in that cabin in the mountains. With Rhys buried in me. Perhaps we'd generated our own magic that night.

But Lucien . . . "You took Ianthe into that cave on Calanmai?"

He wouldn't meet my gaze. "She insisted. Tamlin was . . . Things were bad, Feyre. I went in his stead, and I did my duty to the court. I went of my own free will. And we completed the Rite."

No wonder she'd backed off him. She'd gotten what she wanted.

"Please don't tell Elain," he said. "When we—when we find her again," he amended.

He might have completed the Great Rite with Ianthe of his own free will, but he certainly hadn't enjoyed it. Some line had been blurred—badly.

And my heart shifted a bit in my chest as I said to him with no guile whatsoever, "I won't tell anyone unless you say so." The weight of that jeweled knife and belt seemed to grow. "I wish I had been there to stop it. I should have been there to stop it." I meant every word.

Lucien squeezed our linked arms as we rounded a hedge, the house rising up before us. "You are a better friend to me, Feyre," he said quietly, "than I ever was to you."

⊹

Alis frowned at the two dresses hanging from the armoire door, her long brown fingers smoothing over the chiffon and silk.

"I don't know if the waist can be taken out," she said without peering back at where I sat on the edge of the bed. "We took so much of it in that there's not much fabric left to play with . . . You might very well need to order new ones."

She faced me then, running an eye over my robed body.

I knew what she saw—what lies and poisoned smiles couldn't hide: I had become wraith-thin while living here after Amarantha. Yet for all Rhys had done to harm me, I'd gained back the weight I'd lost, put on muscle, and discarded the sickly pallor in favor of sun-kissed skin.

For a woman who had been tortured and tormented for months, I looked remarkably well.

Our eyes held across the room, the silence hewn only by the humming of the few remaining servants in the hallway, busy with preparations for the solstice tomorrow morning.

I'd spent the past two days playing the pretty pet, allowed into meetings with the Hybern royals mostly because I remained quiet. They were as cautious as we were, hedging Tamlin and Lucien's questions about the movements of their armies, their foreign allies—and other allies within

Prythian. The meetings went nowhere, as all *they* wanted to know was information about our own forces.

And about the Night Court.

I fed Dagdan and Brannagh details both true and false, mixing them together seamlessly. I laid out the Illyrian host amongst the mountains and steppes, but selected the strongest clan as their weakest; I mentioned the efficiency of those blue stones from Hybern against Cassian's and Azriel's power but failed to mention how easily they'd worked around them. Any questions I couldn't evade, I feigned memory loss or trauma too great to bear recalling.

But for all my lying and maneuvering, the royals were too guarded to reveal much of their own information. And for all my careful expressions, Alis seemed the only one who noted the tiny tells that even I couldn't control.

"Do you think there are any gowns that will fit for solstice?" I said casually as her silence continued. "The pink and green ones fit, but I've worn them thrice already."

"You never cared for such things," Alis said, clicking her tongue.

"Am I not allowed to change my mind?"

Those dark eyes narrowed slightly. But Alis yanked open the armoire doors, the dresses swaying with it, and riffled through its dark interior. "You could wear this." She held up an outfit.

A set of turquoise Night Court clothes, cut so similarly to Amren's preferred fashion, dangled from her spindly fingers. My heart lurched.

"That—why—" Words stumbled out of me, bulky and slippery, and I silenced myself with a sharp yank on my inner leash. I straightened. "I have never known you to be cruel, Alis."

A snort. She chucked the clothes back into the armoire. "Tamlin shredded the two other sets—missed this one because it was in the wrong drawer."

I wove a mental thread into the hallway to ensure no one was listening. "He was upset. I wish he'd destroyed that pair, too."

"I was there that day, you know," Alis said, folding her spindly arms across her chest. "I saw the Morrigan arrive. Saw her reach into that cocoon of power and pick you up like a child. I begged her to take you out."

My swallow wasn't feigned.

"I never told him that. Never told any of them. I let them think you'd been abducted. But you clung to her, and she was willing to slaughter all of us for what had happened."

"I don't know why you'd assume that." I tugged the edges of my silk robe tighter around me.

"Servants talk. And Under the Mountain, I never heard of or saw Rhysand laying a hand on a servant. Guards, Amarantha's cronies, the people he was ordered to kill, yes. But never the meek. Never those unable to defend themselves."

"He's a monster."

"They say you came back different. Came back wrong." A crow's laugh. "I never bother to tell them I think you came back right. Came back right at last."

A precipice yawned open before me. Lines—there were lines here, and my survival and that of Prythian depended upon navigating them. I rose from the bed, hands shaking slightly.

But then Alis said, "My cousin works in the palace at Adriata."

Summer Court. Alis had originally been from the Summer Court, and had fled here with her two nephews after her sister had been brutally murdered during Amarantha's reign.

"Servants in that palace are not meant to be seen or heard, but they see and hear plenty when no one believes they're present."

She was my friend. She had helped me at great risk Under the Mountain. Had stood by me in the months after. But if she jeopardized everything—

"She said you visited. And that you were healthy, and laughing, and happy."

"It was a lie. He made me act that way." The wobble in my voice didn't take much to summon.

A knowing, crooked smile. "If you say so."

"I *do* say so."

Alis pulled out a dress of creamy white. "You never got to wear this one. I had it ordered for after your wedding day."

It wasn't exactly bride-like, but rather pure. Clean. The kind of gown I'd have resented when I returned from Under the Mountain, desperate to avoid any comparison to my ruined soul. But now . . . I held Alis's stare, and wondered which of my plans she'd deciphered.

Alis whispered, "I will only say this once. Whatever you plan to do, I beg you leave my boys out of it. Take whatever retribution you desire, but please spare them."

I would never—I almost began. But I only shook my head, knotting my brows, utterly confused and distressed. "All I want is to settle back into life here. To heal."

Heal the land of the corruption and darkness spreading across it.

Alis seemed to understand it, too. She set the dress on the armoire door, airing out the loose, shining skirts.

"Wear this on solstice," she said quietly.

So I did.

CHAPTER
4

Summer Solstice was exactly as I had remembered: streamers and ribbons and garlands of flowers everywhere, casks of ale and wine hauled out to the foothills surrounding the estate, High Fae and lesser faeries alike flocking to the celebrations.

But what had not existed here a year ago was Ianthe.

The celebrating would be sacrilege, she intoned, if we did not give thanks first.

So we all were up two hours before the dawn, bleary-eyed and none of us too keen to endure her ceremony as the sun crested the horizon on the longest day of the year. I wondered if Tarquin had to weather such tedious rituals in his shining palace by the sea. Wondered what sort of celebrations would occur in Adriata today, with the High Lord of Summer who had come so very close to being a friend.

As far as I knew, despite the murmurings between servants, Tarquin still had never sent word to Tamlin about the visit Rhys, Amren, and I had made. What did the Summer lord now think of my changed circumstances? I had little doubt Tarquin had heard. And I prayed he stayed out of it until my work here was finished.

Alis had found me a luxurious white velvet cloak for the brisk ride into the hills, and Tamlin had lifted me onto a moon-pale mare with wildflowers woven into her silver mane. If I had wanted to paint a picture of serene purity, it would have been the image I cast that morning, my hair braided above my head, a crown of white hawthorn blossoms upon it. I'd dabbed rouge onto my cheeks and lips—a slight hint of color. Like the first blush of spring across a winter landscape.

As our procession arrived at the hill, a gathered crowd of hundreds already atop it, all eyes turned to me. But I kept my gaze ahead, to where Ianthe stood before a rudimentary stone altar bedecked in flowers and the first fruits and grains of summer. The hood was off her pale blue robe for once, the silver circlet now resting directly atop her golden head.

I smiled at her, my mare obediently pausing at the northern arc of the half circle that the crowd had formed around the hill's edge and Ianthe's altar, and wondered if Ianthe could spy the wolf grinning beneath.

Tamlin helped me off the horse, the gray light of predawn shimmering along the golden threads in his green jacket. I forced myself to meet his eyes as he set me on the soft grass, aware of every other stare upon us.

The memory gleamed in his gaze—in the way his gaze dipped to my mouth.

A year ago, he had kissed me on this day. A year ago, I'd danced amongst these people, carefree and joyous for the first time in my life, and had believed it was the happiest I'd ever been and ever would be.

I gave him a little, shy smile and took the arm he extended. Together, we crossed the grass toward Ianthe's stone altar, the Hybern royals, Jurian, and Lucien trailing behind.

I wondered if Tamlin was also remembering another day all those months ago, when I'd worn a different white gown, when there had also been flowers strewn about.

When my mate had rescued me after I'd decided not to go through with the wedding, some fundamental part of me knowing it wasn't right. I had believed I didn't deserve it, hadn't wanted to burden Tamlin for an eternity with someone as broken as I'd been at the time. And Rhys . . . Rhys would have let me marry him, believing me to be happy, wanting me to be happy even if it killed him. But the moment I had said no . . . He had saved me. Helped me save myself.

I glanced sidelong at Tamlin.

But he was studying my hand, braced on his arm. The empty finger where that ring had once perched.

What did he make of it—where did he think that ring had gone, if Lucien had hidden the evidence? For a heartbeat, I pitied him.

Pitied that not only Lucien had lied to him, but Alis as well. How many others had seen the truth of my suffering—and tried to spare *him* from it?

Seen my suffering and done nothing to help *me*.

Tamlin and I paused before the altar, Ianthe offering us a serene, regal nod.

The Hybern royals shifted on their feet, not bothering to hide their impatience. Brannagh had made barely veiled complaints about the solstice at dinner last night, declaring that in Hybern they did not bother with such odious things and got on with the revelry. And implying, in her way, that soon, neither would we.

I ignored the royals as Ianthe lifted her hands and called to the crowd behind us, "A blessed solstice to us all."

Then began an endless string of prayers and rituals, her prettiest young acolytes assisting with the pouring of sacred wine, with the blessing of the harvest goods on the altar, with beseeching the sun to rise.

A lovely, rehearsed little number. Lucien was half-asleep behind me.

But I'd gone over the ceremony with Ianthe, and knew what was coming when she lifted the sacred wine and intoned, "As the light is strongest today, let it drive out unwanted darkness. Let it banish the black stain of evil."

Jab after jab at my mate, my home. But I nodded along with her.

"Would Princess Brannagh and Prince Dagdan do us the honor of imbibing this blessed wine?"

The crowd shifted. The Hybern royals blinked, frowning to each other.

But I stepped aside, smiling prettily at them and gesturing to the altar.

They opened their mouths, no doubt to refuse, but Ianthe would not be denied. "Drink, and let our new allies become new friends," she declared. "Drink, and wash away the endless night of the year."

The two daemati were likely testing that cup for poison through whatever magic and training they possessed, but I kept the bland smile on my face as they finally approached the altar and Brannagh accepted the outstretched silver cup.

They each barely had a sip before they made to step back. But Ianthe cooed at them, insisting they come behind the altar to witness our ceremony at her side.

I had made sure she knew precisely how disgusted they were with her rituals. How they would do their best to stomp out her usefulness as a leader of her people once they arrived. She now seemed inclined to convert them.

More prayers and rituals, until Tamlin was summoned to the other side of the altar to light a candle for the souls extinguished in the past year—to now bring them back into the light's embrace when the sun rose.

Pink began to stain the clouds behind them.

Jurian was also called forward to recite one final prayer I'd requested Ianthe add, in honor of the warriors who fought for our safety each day.

And then Lucien and I were standing alone in the circle of grass, the altar and horizon before us, the crowd at our backs and sides.

From the rigidity of his posture, the dart of his gaze over the site, I knew he was now running through the prayers and how I had worked with Ianthe on the ceremony. How he and I remained on this side of the line right as the sun was about to break over the world, and the others had been maneuvered away.

Ianthe stepped toward the hill's edge, her golden hair tumbling freely down her back as she lifted her arms to the sky. The location was intentional, as was the positioning of her arms.

She'd made the same gesture on Winter Solstice, standing in the precise spot where the sun would rise between her upraised arms, filling them with light. Her acolytes had discreetly marked the place in the grass with a carved stone.

Slowly, the golden disc of the sun broke over the hazy greens and blues of the horizon.

Light filled the world, clear and strong, spearing right for us.

Ianthe's back arched, her body a mere vessel for the solstice's light to fill, and what I could see of her face was already limned in pious ecstasy.

The sun rose, a held, gilded note echoing through the land.

The crowd began to murmur.

Then cry out.

Not at Ianthe.

But at me.

At me, resplendent and pure in white, beginning to glow with the light of day as the sun's path flowed directly over me instead.

No one had bothered to confirm or even notice that Ianthe's marker stone had moved five feet to the right, too busy with my parading arrival to spy a phantom wind slide it through the grass.

It took Ianthe longer than anyone else to look.

To turn to see that the sun's power was not filling her, blessing her.

I released the damper on the power that I had unleashed in Hybern, my body turning incandescent as light shone through. Pure as day, pure as starlight.

"Cursebreaker," some murmured. "Blessed," others whispered.

I made a show of looking surprised—surprised and yet accepting of the Cauldron's choice. Tamlin's face was taut with shock, the Hybern royals' nothing short of baffled.

But I turned to Lucien, my light radiating so brightly that it bounced off his metal eye. A friend beseeching another for help. I reached a hand toward him.

Beyond us, I could feel Ianthe scrambling to regain control, to find some way to spin it.

Perhaps Lucien could, too. For he took my hand, and then knelt upon one knee in the grass, pressing my fingers to his brow.

Like stalks of wheat in a wind, the others fell to their knees as well.

For in all of her preening ceremonies and rituals, never had Ianthe revealed any sign of power or blessing. But Feyre Cursebreaker, who had led Prythian from tyranny and darkness . . .

Blessed. Holy. Undimming before evil.

I let my glow spread, until it, too, rippled from Lucien's bowed form.

A knight before his queen.

When I looked to Ianthe and smiled again, I let a little bit of the wolf show.

⊹

The festivities, at least, remained the same.

Once the uproar and awe had ebbed, once my own glow had vanished when the sun crested higher than my head, we made our way to the nearby hills and fields, where those who had not attended the ceremony had already heard about my small miracle.

I kept close to Lucien, who was inclined to indulge me, as everyone seemed to be torn between joy and awe, question and concern.

Ianthe spent the next six hours trying to explain what had happened. The Cauldron had blessed her chosen friend, she told whoever would listen. The sun had altered its very path to show how glad it was for my return.

Only her acolytes really paid attention, and half of them appeared only mildly interested.

Tamlin, however, seemed the wariest—as if the blessing had somehow upset me, as if he remembered that same light in Hybern and could not figure out why it disturbed him so.

But duty had him fielding thanks and good wishes from his subjects, warriors, and the lesser lords, leaving me free to wander. I was stopped every now and then by fervent, adoring faeries who wished to touch my hand, to weep a bit over me.

Once, I would have cringed and winced. Now I received their thanks and prayers beatifically, thanking them, smiling at them.

Some of it was genuine. I had no quarrel with the people of these lands, who had suffered alongside the rest. None. But the courtiers and sentries who sought me out . . . I put on a better show for them. Cauldron-blessed, they called me. *An honor*, I merely replied.

On and on I repeated those words, through breakfast and lunch, until I returned to the house to freshen up and take a moment for myself.

In the privacy of my room, I set my crown of flowers on the dressing table and smiled slightly at the eye tattooed into my right palm.

The longest day of the year, I said into the bond, sending along flickers of all that had occurred atop that hill. *I wish I could spend it with you.*

He would have enjoyed my performance—would have laughed himself hoarse afterward at the expression on Ianthe's face.

I finished washing up and was about to head out into the hills again when Rhysand's voice filled my mind.

It'd be an honor, he said, laughter in every word, *to spend even a moment in the company of Feyre Cauldron-blessed.*

I chuckled. The words were distant, strained. Keep it quick—I had to keep it quick, or risk exposure. And more than anything, I needed to ask, to know—

Is everyone all right?

I waited, counting the minutes. *Yes. As well as we can be. When do you come home to me?*

Each word was quieter than the last.

Soon, I promised him. *Hybern is here. I'll be done soon.*

He didn't reply—and I waited another few minutes before I again donned my flower crown and strode down the stairs.

As I emerged into the bedecked garden, though, Rhysand's faint voice filled my head once more. *I wish I could spend today with you, too.*

The words wrapped a fist around my heart, and I forced them from my mind as I returned to the party in the hills, my steps heavier than they'd been when I floated into the house.

But lunch had been cleared away, and dancing had begun.

I saw him waiting on the outskirts of one of the circles, observing every move I took.

I glanced between the grass and the crowd and the cluster of musicians coaxing such lively music from drums and fiddles and pipes as I approached, no more than a shy, hesitant doe.

Once, those same sounds had shaken me awake, had made me dance and dance. I supposed they were now little more than weapons in my arsenal as I stopped before Tamlin, lowered my lashes, and asked softly, "Will you dance with me?"

Relief, happiness, and a slight edge of concern. "Yes," he breathed. "Yes, of course."

So I let him lead me into the swift dance, spinning and tilting me, people gathering to cheer and clap. Dance after dance after dance, until sweat was running down my back as I worked to keep up, keep that smile on my face, to remember to laugh when my hands were within strangling distance of his throat.

The music eventually shifted into something slower, and Tamlin eased us into the melody. When others had found their own partners more interesting to watch, he murmured, "This morning . . . Are you all right?"

My head snapped up. "Yes. I—I don't know what that was, but yes. Is Ianthe . . . mad?"

"I don't know. She didn't see it coming—I don't think she handles surprises very well."

"I should apologize."

His eyes flashed. "What for? Perhaps it was a blessing. Magic still surprises *me*. If she's angry, it's her problem."

I made a show of considering, then nodded. Pressed closer, loathing every place where our bodies touched. I didn't know how Rhys had endured it—endured Amarantha. For five decades.

"You look beautiful today," Tamlin said.

"Thank you." I made myself peer up into his face. "Lucien—Lucien told me that you didn't complete the Rite at Calanmai. That you refused."

And you let Ianthe take him into that cave instead.

His throat bobbed. "I couldn't stomach it."

And yet you could stomach making a deal with Hybern, as if I were a stolen item to be returned. "Maybe this morning was not just a blessing for me," I offered.

A stroke of his hand down my back was his only reply.

That was all we said for the next three dances, until hunger dragged me toward the tables where dinner had now been laid out. I let him fill a plate for me, let him serve me himself as we found a spot under a twisted old oak and watched the dancing and the music.

I nearly asked if it was worth it—if giving up this sort of peace was worth it, in order to have me back. For Hybern would come here, use these lands. And there would be no more singing and dancing. Not once they arrived.

But I kept quiet as the sunlight faded and night finally fell.

The stars winked into existence, dim and small above the blazing fires.

I watched them through the long hours of celebrating, and could have sworn that they kept me company, my silent and stalwart friends.

CHAPTER
5

I crawled back to the manor two hours after midnight, too exhausted to last until dawn.

Especially when I noted the way Tamlin looked at me, remembering that dawn last year when he'd led me away and kissed me as the sun rose.

I asked Lucien to escort me, and he'd been more than happy to do so, given that his own status as a mated male made him uninterested in any sort of female company these days. And given that Ianthe had been trying to corner him all day to ask about what had happened at the ceremony.

I changed into my nightgown, a small, lacy thing I'd once worn for Tamlin's enjoyment and now was glad to don thanks to the day's sweat still clinging to my skin, and flopped into bed.

For nearly half an hour, I kicked at the sheets, tossing and turning, thrashing.

The Attor. The Weaver. My sisters being thrown into the Cauldron. All of them twined and eddied around me. I let them.

Most of the others were still celebrating when I yelped, a sharp, short cry that had me bouncing from the bed.

My heart thundered along my veins, my bones, as I cracked open the door, sweating and haggard, and padded across the hall.

Lucien answered on the second knock.

"I heard you—what's wrong." He scanned me, russet eye wide as he noted my disheveled hair, my sweaty nightgown.

I swallowed, a silent question on my face, and he nodded, retreating into the room to let me inside. Bare from the waist up, he'd managed to haul on a pair of pants before opening the door, and hastily buttoned them as I strode past.

His room had been bedecked in Autumn Court colors—the only tribute to his home he'd ever let show—and I surveyed the night-dark space, the rumpled bedsheets. He perched on the rolled arm of a large chair before the blackened fire, watching me wring my hands in the center of the crimson carpet.

"I dream about it," I rasped. "Under the Mountain. And when I wake up, I can't remember where I am." I lifted my now-unmarred left arm before me. "I can't remember *when* I am."

Truth—and half a lie. I still dreamed of those horrible days, but no longer did they consume me. No longer did I run to the bathroom in the middle of the night to hurl my guts up.

"What did you dream of tonight?" he asked quietly.

I dragged my eyes to his, haunted and bleak. "She had me spiked to the wall. Like Clare Beddor. And the Attor was—"

I shuddered, running my hands over my face.

Lucien rose, stalking to me. The ripple of fear and pain at my own words masked my scent enough, masked my own power as my dark snares picked up a slight vibration in the house.

Lucien paused half a foot from me. He didn't so much as object as I threw my arms around his neck, burying my face against his warm, bare chest. It was seawater from Tarquin's own gift that slipped from my eyes, down my face, and onto his golden skin.

Lucien loosed a heavy sigh and slid an arm around my waist, the other threading through my hair to cradle my head. "I'm sorry," he murmured. "I'm sorry."

He held me, stroking soothing lines down my back, and I calmed my weeping, those seawater tears drying up like wet sand in the sun.

I lifted my head from his sculpted chest at last, my fingers digging into the hard muscles of his shoulders as I peered into his concerned face. I took deep, heaving breaths, my brows knotting and mouth parting as I—

"What's going on."

Lucien whipped his head toward the door.

Tamlin stood there, face a mask of cold calm. The beginnings of claws glinted at his knuckles.

We pushed away, too swiftly to be casual. "I had a nightmare," I explained, straightening my nightgown. "I—I didn't want to wake the house."

Tamlin was just staring at Lucien, whose mouth had tightened into a thin line as he marked those claws, still half-drawn.

"I had a nightmare," I repeated a bit sharply, gripping Tamlin's arm and leading him from the room before Lucien could so much as open his mouth.

I closed the door, but could still feel Tamlin's attention fixed on the male behind it. He didn't sheath his claws. Didn't summon them any further, either.

I strode the few feet to my room, watching Tamlin assess the hall. The distance between my door and Lucien's. "Good night," I said, and shut the door in Tamlin's face.

I waited the five minutes it took Tamlin to decide not to kill Lucien, and then smiled.

I wondered if Lucien had pieced it together. That I had known Tamlin would come to my room tonight, after I had given him so many shy touches and glances today. That I had changed into my most indecent nightgown not for the heat, but so that when my invisible snares in the house informed me that Tamlin had finally worked up the nerve to come to my bedroom, I'd look the part.

A feigned nightmare, the evidence set into place with my thrashed sheets. I'd left Lucien's door open, with him too distracted and unsuspecting of why I'd really be there to bother to shut it, or notice the shield of hard air I'd placed around the room so that he wouldn't hear or scent Tamlin as he arrived.

Until Tamlin saw us there, limbs entwined, my nightgown askew, staring at each other so intently, so full of *emotion* that we'd either just been starting or finishing up. That we didn't even notice until Tamlin was right there—and that invisible shield vanished before he could sense it.

A nightmare, I'd told Tamlin.

I was the nightmare.

Preying on what Tamlin had feared from my very first days here.

I had not forgotten that long-ago fight he'd picked with Lucien. The warning he'd given him to stop flirting with me. To stay away. The fear that I'd preferred the red-haired lord over him and that it would threaten every plan he had. *Back off*, he'd told Lucien.

I had no doubt Tamlin was now running through every look and conversation since then. Every time Lucien had intervened on my behalf, both Under the Mountain and afterward. Weighing how much that new mating bond with Elain held sway over his friend.

Considering how this very morning, Lucien had knelt before me, swearing fealty to a newborn god, as if we had both been Cauldron-blessed.

I let myself smile for a moment longer, then dressed.

There was more work to do.

CHAPTER
6

A set of keys to the estate gates had gone missing.

But after last night's incident, Tamlin didn't appear to care.

Breakfast was silent, the Hybern royals sullen at being kept waiting so long to see the second cleft in the wall, and Jurian, for once, too tired to do anything but shovel meat and eggs into his hateful mouth.

Tamlin and Lucien, it seemed, had spoken before the meal, but the latter made a point to keep a healthy distance from me. To not look at or speak to me, as if still needing to convince Tamlin of our innocence.

I debated asking Jurian outright if he'd stolen the keys from whatever guard had lost them, but the silence was a welcome reprieve.

Until Ianthe breezed in, carefully avoiding acknowledging me, as if I was indeed the blinding sun that had been stolen from her.

"I am sorry to interrupt your meal, but there is a matter to discuss, High Lord," Ianthe said, pale robes swirling at her feet as she halted halfway to the table.

All of us perked up at that.

Tamlin, brooding and snarly, demanded, "What is it."

She made a show of realizing the Hybern royals were present.

Listening. I tried not to snort at the oh-so-nervous glance she threw their way, then to Tamlin. The next words were no surprise whatsoever. "Perhaps we should wait until after the meal. When you are alone."

No doubt a power play, to remind them that she did, in fact, have sway here—with Tamlin. That Hybern, too, might want to remain on her good side, considering the *information* she bore. But I was cruel enough to say sweetly, "If we can trust our allies in Hybern to go to war with us, then we can trust them to use discretion. Go ahead, Ianthe."

She didn't so much as look in my direction. But now caught between outright insult and politeness . . . Tamlin weighed our company against Ianthe's posture and said, "Let's hear it."

Her white throat bobbed. "There is . . . My acolytes discovered that the land around my temple is . . . dying."

Jurian rolled his eyes and went back to his bacon.

"Then tell the gardeners," Brannagh said, returning to her own food. Dagdan snickered into his cup of tea.

"It is not a matter of gardening." Ianthe straightened. "It is a blight upon the land. Grass, root, bud—all of it, shriveled up and sickly. It reeks of the naga."

It was an effort not to glance to Lucien—to see if he also noticed the too-eager gleam in her eye. Even Tamlin loosed a sigh, as if he saw it for what it was: an attempt to regain some ground, perhaps a scheme to poison the earth and then miraculously heal it.

"There are other spots in the woods where things have died and are not coming back," Ianthe went on, pressing a silver-adorned hand to her chest. "I fear it's a warning that the naga are gathering—and plan to attack."

Oh, I'd gotten under her skin. I'd been wondering what she'd do after yesterday's solstice, after I'd robbed her of her moment and power. But this . . . Clever.

I hid my smirk down deep and said gently, "Ianthe, perhaps it *is* a case for the groundskeepers."

She stiffened, at last facing me. *You think you're playing the game*, I itched to tell her, *but you have no idea that every choice you made last night and this morning were only steps I nudged you toward.*

I jerked my chin toward the royals, then Lucien. "We're heading out this afternoon to survey the wall, but if the problem remains when we return in a few days, I'll help you look into it."

Those silver-ringed fingers curled into loose fists at her sides. But like the true viper she was, Ianthe said to Tamlin, "Will you be joining them, High Lord?"

She looked to me and Lucien—the assessment too lingering to be casual.

A faint, low headache was already forming, made worse with every word out of her mouth. I'd been up too late, and had gotten too little sleep—and I needed my strength for the days ahead. "He will not," I said, cutting off Tamlin before he could reply.

He set down his utensils. "I think I will."

"I don't need an escort." Let him unravel the layers of defensiveness in that statement.

Jurian snorted. "Starting to doubt our good intentions, High Lord?"

Tamlin snarled at him. "Careful."

I placed a hand flat on the table. "I'll be fine with Lucien and the sentries."

Lucien seemed inclined to sink into his seat and disappear forever.

I surveyed Dagdan and Brannagh and smiled a bit. "I can defend myself, if it comes to that," I said to Tamlin.

The daemati smiled back at me. I hadn't felt another touch on my mental barriers, or the ones I'd been working to keep around as many people here as possible. The constant use of my power was wearing on me, however—being away from this place for four or five days would be a welcome relief.

Especially as Ianthe murmured to Tamlin, "Perhaps you *should* go, my friend." I waited—waited for whatever nonsense was about to come out of that pouty mouth— "You never know when the Night Court will attempt to snatch her away."

I had a blink to debate my reaction. To opt for leaning back in my chair, shoulders curling inward, hauling up those images of Clare, of Rhys with those ash arrows through his wings—any sort of way to dredge my scent in fear. "Have you news?" I whispered.

Brannagh and Dagdan looked *very* interested at that.

The priestess opened her mouth, but Jurian cut her off, drawling, "There is no news. Their borders are secure. Rhysand would be a fool to push his luck by coming here."

I stared at my plate, the portrait of bowed terror.

"A fool, yes," Ianthe countered, "but one with a vendetta." She faced Tamlin, the morning sun catching in the jewel atop her head. "Perhaps if you returned to him his family's wings, he might . . . settle."

For a heartbeat, silence rippled through me.

Followed by a wave of roaring that drowned out nearly every thought, every self-preserving instinct. I could barely hear over that bellowing in my blood, my bones.

But the words, the offer . . . A cheap attempt at snaring me. I pretended not to hear, not to care. Even as I waited and waited for Tamlin's reply.

When Tamlin answered, his voice was low. "I burned them a long time ago."

I could have sworn there was something like remorse—remorse and shame—in his words.

Ianthe only tsked. "Too bad. He might have paid handsomely for them."

My limbs ached with the effort of not leaping over the table to smash her head into the marble floor.

But I said to Tamlin, soothing and gentle, "I'll be fine out there." I touched his hand, brushing my thumb over the back of his palm. Held his stare. "Let's not start down this road again."

As I pulled away, Tamlin merely fixed Lucien with a look, any trace of that guilt gone. His claws slid free, embedding in the scar-flecked wood of his chair's arm. "Be careful."

None of us pretended it was anything but a threat.

☩

It was a two-day ride, but took us only a day to get there with winnowing-walking-winnowing. We could manage a few miles at a time, but Dagdan was slower than I'd anticipated, given that he had to carry his sister and Jurian.

I didn't fault him for it. With each of us bearing another, the drain was considerable. Lucien and I both bore a sentry, minor lords' sons who had been trained to be polite and watchful. Supplies, as a result, were limited. Including tents.

By the time we made it to the cleft in the wall, darkness was falling.

The few supplies we'd hauled also had encumbered our winnowing through the world, and I let the sentries erect the tents for us, ever the lady keen to be waited on. Our dinner around the small fire was near-silent, none of us bothering to speak, save for Jurian, who questioned the sentries endlessly about their training. The twins retreated to their own tent after they'd picked at the meat sandwiches we'd packed, frowning at them as if they were full of maggots instead, and Jurian wandered off into the woods soon after, claiming he wanted a walk before he retired.

I hauled myself into the canvas tent when the fire was dying out, the space barely big enough for Lucien and me to sleep shoulder to shoulder.

His red hair gleamed in the faint firelight a moment later as he shoved through the flaps and swore. "Maybe I should sleep out there."

I rolled my eyes. "Please."

A wary, considering glance as he knelt and removed his boots. "You know Tamlin can be . . . sensitive about things."

"He can also be a pain in my ass," I snapped, and slithered under the blankets. "If you yield to him on every bit of paranoia and territorialism, you'll just make it worse."

Lucien unbuttoned his jacket but remained mostly dressed as he slid onto his sleeping roll. "I think it's made worse because you two haven't . . . I mean, you haven't, right?"

I stiffened, tugging the blanket higher onto my shoulders. "No. I don't want to be touched like that—not for a while."

His silence was heavy—sad. I hated the lie, hated it for how filthy it felt to wield it. "I'm sorry," he said. And I wondered what else he was apologizing for as I faced him in the darkness of our tent.

"Isn't there some way to get out of this deal with Hybern?" My words were barely louder than the murmuring embers outside. "I'm back, I'm safe. We could find some way around it—"

"No. The King of Hybern crafted his bargain with Tamlin too cleverly, too clearly. Magic bound them—magic will strike him if he does not allow Hybern into these lands."

"In what way? Kill him?"

Lucien's sigh ruffled my hair. "It will claim his own powers, maybe kill him. Magic is all about balance. It's why he couldn't interfere with your bargain with Rhysand. Even the person who tries to sever the bargain faces consequences. If he'd kept you here, the magic that bound you to Rhys might have come to claim *his* life as payment for yours. Or the life of someone else he cared about. It's old magic—old and strange. It's why we avoid bargains unless it's necessary: even the scholars at the Day Court don't know how it works. Believe me, I've asked."

"For me—you asked them for me."

"Yes. I went last winter to inquire about breaking your bargain with Rhys."

"Why didn't you tell me?"

"I—we didn't want to give you false hope. And we didn't dare let Rhysand get wind of what we were doing, in case he found a way to interfere. To stop it."

"So Ianthe pushed Tamlin to Hybern instead."

"He was frantic. The scholars at the Day Court worked too slowly. I begged him for more time, but you'd already been gone for months. He wanted to act, not wait—despite that letter you sent. *Because* of that letter you sent. I finally told him to go ahead with it after—after that day in the forest."

I turned onto my back, staring at the sloped ceiling of the tent.

"How bad was it?" I asked quietly.

"You saw your room. He trashed it, the study, his bedroom. He—he killed the sentries who'd been on guard. After he got the last bit of information from them. He executed them in front of everyone in the manor."

My blood chilled. "You didn't stop him."

"I tried. I begged him for mercy. He didn't listen. He *couldn't* listen."

"The sentries didn't try to stop him, either?"

"They didn't dare. Feyre, he's a High Lord. He's a different *breed*."

I wondered if he'd say the same thing if he knew what I was.

"We were backed into a corner with no options. None. It was either go to war with the Night Court *and* Hybern, or ally with Hybern, let them try to stir up trouble, and then use that alliance to our own advantage further down the road."

"What do you mean," I breathed.

But Lucien realized what he'd said, and hedged, "We have enemies in every court. Having Hybern's alliance will make them think twice."

Liar. Trained, clever liar.

I loosed a heaving, sleepy breath. "Even if they're now our allies," I mumbled, "I still hate them."

A snort. "Me too."

☦

"Get up."

Blinding sunlight cut into the tent, and I hissed.

The order was drowned out by Lucien's snarl as he sat up. "*Out*," he ordered Jurian, who looked us over once, sneered, and stalked away.

I'd rolled onto Lucien's bedroll at some point, any schemes indeed second to my most pressing demand—warmth. But I had no doubt Jurian would tuck away the information to throw in Tamlin's face when we returned: we'd shared a tent, and had been *very* cozy upon awakening.

I washed in the nearby stream, my body stiff and aching from a night on the ground, with or without the help of a bedroll.

Brannagh was prowling for the stream by the time I'd finished. The princess gave me a cold, thin smile. "I'd pick Beron's son, too."

I stared at the princess beneath lowered brows.

She shrugged, her smile growing. "Autumn Court males have fire in their blood—and they fuck like it, too."

"I suppose you know from experience?"

A chuckle. "Why do you think I had so much fun in the War?"

I didn't bother to hide my disgust.

Lucien caught me cringing at him when her words replayed for the tenth time an hour later, while we hiked the half mile toward the crack in the wall. "What?" he demanded.

I shook my head, trying not to imagine Elain subject to that . . . fire.

"Nothing," I said, just as Jurian swore ahead.

We were both moving at his barked curse—and then broke into a run at the sound of a sword whining free of its sheath. Leaves and branches whipped at me, but then we were at the wall, that invisible, horrible marker humming and throbbing in my head.

And staring right at us through the hole were three Children of the Blessed.

CHAPTER
7

Brannagh and Dagdan looked like they'd just found second breakfast waiting for them.

Jurian had his sword out, the two young women and one young man gaping between him and the others. Then at us, their eyes widening further as they noted Lucien's cruel beauty.

They dropped to their knees. "Masters and Mistresses," they beseeched us, their silver jewelry glinting in the dappled sunlight through the leaves. "You have found us on our journey."

The two royals smiled so broadly I could see all of their too-white teeth.

Jurian, for once, seemed torn before he snapped, "What are you doing here?"

The dark-haired girl at the front was lovely, her honey-gold skin flushed as she lifted her head. "We have come to dwell in the immortal lands; we have come as tribute."

Jurian cut cold, hard eyes to Lucien. "Is this true?"

Lucien stared him down. "We accept no tribute from the human lands. Least of all children."

Never mind that the three of them appeared only a few years younger than myself.

"Why don't you come through," Brannagh cooed, "and we can . . . enjoy ourselves." She was indeed sizing up the brown-haired young man and the other girl, her hair a ruddy brown, face sharp but interesting. From the way Dagdan was leering at the beautiful girl in front, I knew he'd silently made his claim already.

I shoved in front of them and said to the three mortals, "Get out. Go back to your villages, back to your families. You cross this wall, and you will die."

They balked, rising to their feet, faces taut with fear—and awe. "We have come to live in peace."

"There is no such thing here. There is only death for your kind."

Their eyes slid to the immortals behind me. The dark-haired girl blushed at Dagdan's intent stare, seeing the High Fae beauty and none of the predator.

So I struck.

The wall was a screeching, terrible vise, crushing my magic, battering my head.

But I speared my power through that gap, and slammed into their minds.

Too hard. The young man flinched a bit.

So soft—defenseless. Their minds yielded like butter melting on my tongue.

I beheld pieces of their lives like shards in a broken mirror, flashing every which way: the dark-haired girl was rich, educated, headstrong—had wanted to escape an arranged marriage and believed Prythian was a better option. The ruddy-haired girl had known nothing but poverty and her father's fists, which had turned more violent after they'd ended her mother's life. The young man had sold himself on the streets of a large village until the Children had come one day and offered him something better.

I worked quickly. Neatly.

I was finished before three heartbeats had passed, before Brannagh had even drawn breath to say, "There is no death here. Only pleasure, if you are willing."

Even if they weren't willing, I wanted to add.

But the three of them now blinked—balking.

Beholding us for what we were: deadly, merciless. The truth behind the spun stories.

"We—perhaps have . . . made a mistake," their leader said, retreating a step.

"Or perhaps this was fate," Brannagh countered with a snake's smile.

They kept backing away. Kept seeing the histories I'd planted into their minds—that we were here to hurt and kill them, that we had done so with all their friends, that we'd use and discard them. I showed them the naga, the Bogge, the Middengard Wyrm; I showed them Clare and the golden-haired queen, skewered on that lamppost. The memories I gave them became stories they had ignored—but now understood with us before them.

"Come here," Dagdan ordered.

The words were kindling to their fear. The three of them turned, heavy pale robes twisting with them, and bolted for the trees.

Brannagh tensed, as if she'd charge through the wall after them, but I gripped her arm and hissed, "If you pursue them, then you and I will have a problem."

In emphasis, I dragged mental talons down her own shield.

The princess snarled at me.

But the humans were already gone.

I prayed they'd listen to the other command I'd woven into their minds: to get on a boat, get as many friends as they could, and flee for the continent. To return here only when the war was over, and to warn as many humans as possible to get out before it was too late.

The Hybern royals growled their displeasure, but I ignored it as I took up a spot against a tree and settled in to wait, not trusting them to stay on this side of the border.

The royals resumed their work, stalking up and down the wall.

A moment later, a male body came up beside mine.

Not Lucien, I realized with a jolt, but did not so much as flinch.

Jurian's eyes were on the place where the humans had been.

"Thank you," he said, his voice rough.

"I don't know what you're talking about," I replied, well aware that Lucien carefully watched from the shade of a nearby oak.

Jurian gave me a knowing smirk and sauntered after Dagdan.

+

They took all day.

Whatever it was they were inspecting, whatever they were hunting for, the royals didn't inform us.

And after the confrontation that morning, I knew pushing them into revealing it wouldn't happen. I'd used up my allotted tolerance for the day.

So we spent another night in the woods, which was precisely how I wound up sitting across the fire from Jurian after the twins had crawled into their tent and the sentries had taken up their watch positions. Lucien had gone to the stream to get more water, and I watched the flame dance amongst the logs, feeling it echo inside myself.

Spearing my power through the wall had left me with a lingering, pounding headache all day, more than a bit dizzy. I had no doubt sleep would claim me fast and hard, but the fire was too warm and the spring night too brisk to willingly breach that long gap of darkness between the flame and my tent.

"What happens to the ones who do make it through the wall?" Jurian asked, the hard panes of his face cast in flickering relief by the fire.

I ground the heel of my boot into the grass. "I don't know. They never came back once they went over. But while Amarantha ruled, creatures prowled these woods, so . . . I don't think it ended well. I've never encountered a mention of them being at any court."

"Five hundred years ago, they'd have been flogged for that nonsense," Jurian said. "We were their slaves and whores and laborers for millennia—men and women fought and died so we'd never have to serve them again. Yet there they are, in those costumes, unaware of the danger, the history."

"Careful, or you might not sound like Hybern's faithful pet."

A low, hateful laugh. "That's what you think I am, isn't it. His dog."

"What's the end goal, then?"

"I have unfinished business."

"Miryam is dead."

That madness danced again, replacing the rare lucidity. "Everything I did during the War, it was for Miryam and me. For our people to survive and one day be free. And she *left me* for that pretty-faced prince the moment I put my people before her."

"I heard she left you because you became so focused on wringing information from Clythia that you lost sight of the real conflict."

"Miryam told me to go ahead and fuck her for information. Told me to seduce Clythia until she'd sold out all of Hybern and the Loyalists. She had no qualms with that. None."

"So all of this is to get Miryam back?"

He stretched his long legs before him, crossing one ankle over the other. "It's to draw her out of her little nest with that winged prick and make her regret it."

"You get a second shot at life and that's what you wish to do? Revenge?"

Jurian smiled slowly. "Isn't that what you're doing?"

Months of working with Rhys had me remembering to furrow my brow in confusion. "Against Rhys, I would one day like it."

"That's what they all say, when they pretend he's a sadistic murderer. You forget I knew him in the War. You forget he risked his legion to save Miryam from our enemy's fort. That's how Amarantha captured him, you know. Rhys knew it was a trap—for Prince Drakon. So Rhys went against orders, and marched in his whole legion to get Miryam out. For his friend, for *my* lover—and for that bastard Drakon's sake. Rhys sacrificed his legion in the process, got all of them captured and tortured afterward. Yet everyone insists Rhysand is soulless, wicked. But the male I knew was the most decent of them all. Better than that prick-prince. You don't lose that quality, no matter the centuries, and Rhys was too smart to do anything but have the vilification of his character be a calculated move. And yet here you are—his mate. The most powerful High Lord in the world lost his mate, and has not yet come to claim her, even when she is defenseless in the woods." Jurian chuckled. "Perhaps that's because Rhysand has not lost you at all. But rather unleashed you upon us."

I had never heard that story, but it seemed so like my mate that I knew the flames between us now smoldered in my eyes as I said, "You love to hear yourself talk, don't you."

"Hybern will kill all of you," was all Jurian replied.

✠

Jurian wasn't wrong.

Lucien woke me the next morning with a hand over my mouth, warning gleaming in his russet eye. I smelled it a moment later: the coppery tang of blood.

We shoved into our clothes and boots, and I did a quick inventory of the weapons we'd squeezed into the tent with us. I had three daggers. Lucien had two, as well as an elegant short sword. Better than nothing, but not much.

A glance from him communicated our plan well enough: play casual until we assessed the situation.

I had a heartbeat to realize that this was perhaps the first time he and I had worked in tandem. Hunting had never been a joint effort, and Under the Mountain had been one of us looking out for the other—never a team. A unit.

Lucien slid from the tent, limbs loose and ready to shift into a defensive position. He'd been trained, he once told me—at the Autumn Court and at this one. Like Rhys, he usually opted for words to win his battles, but I'd seen him and Tamlin in the practice ring. He knew how to handle a weapon. How to kill, if need be.

I pushed past him, devouring the details of my surroundings as if I were a starving man at a feast.

The forest was the same. Jurian was crouched before the fire, stirring the embers back to alertness, his face a hard, brooding mask. But the sentries—they were pale as Lucien stalked to them. I followed their shifting attention to the trees behind Jurian.

No sign of the royals.

The blood—

A coppery tang, yes. But laced with earth and marrow and—rot. Mortality.

I stormed for the trees and dense brush.

"You're too late," Jurian said as I passed him, still poking the embers. "They finished two hours ago."

Lucien was on my heels as I shoved into the brambles, thorns tearing at my hands.

The Hybern royals hadn't bothered to clean up their mess.

From what was left of the three bodies, their shredded pale robes like fallen ashes through the small clearing, Dagdan and Brannagh must have shut out their screams with some sort of shield.

Lucien swore. "They went through the wall last night. To hunt them down."

Even with hours separating them, the royals were Fae—swift, immortal. The three Children of the Blessed would have tired after running, would have camped somewhere.

Blood was already drying on the grass, on the trunks of the surrounding trees.

Hybern's brand of torture wasn't very creative: Clare, the golden queen, and these three . . . A similar mutilating and torment.

I unfastened my cloak and carefully laid it over the biggest remains of them I could find: the torso of the young man, clawed up and bloodless. His face was still etched in pain.

Flame heated at my fingertips, begging me to burn them, to give them at least that sort of burial. But— "Do you think it was for sport, or to send us a message?"

Lucien laid his own cloak across the remains of the two young women. His face was as serious as I'd ever seen it. "I think they aren't accustomed to being denied. I'd call this an immortal temper tantrum."

I closed my eyes, trying to calm my roiling stomach.

"You aren't to blame," he added. "They could have killed them out in the mortal lands, but they brought them here. To make a statement about their power."

He was right. The Children of the Blessed would have been dead even if I hadn't interfered. "They're threatened," I mused. "And proud to a fault." I toed the blood-soaked grass. "Do we bury them?"

Lucien considered. "It sends a message—that we're willing to clean up their messes."

I surveyed the clearing again. Considered everything at stake. "Then we send another sort of message."

CHAPTER
8

Tamlin paced in front of the hearth in his study, every turn as sharp as a blade.

"They are our *allies*," he growled at me, at Lucien, both of us seated in armchairs flanking the mantel.

"They're monsters," I countered. "They butchered three innocents."

"And you should have left it alone for me to deal with." Tamlin heaved a jagged breath. "Not *retaliated* like children." He threw a glare in Lucien's direction. "I expected better from you."

"But not from me?" I asked quietly.

Tamlin's green eyes were like frozen jade. "You have a personal connection to those people. *He* does not."

"That's the sort of thinking," I snapped, clutching the armrests, "that has allowed for a *wall* to be the only solution between our two peoples; for the Fae to look at these sorts of *murders* and not care." I knew the guards outside could hear. Knew anyone walking by could hear. "The loss of *any* life on either side is a *personal connection*. Or is it only High Fae lives that matter to you?"

Tamlin stopped short. And snarled at Lucien, "Get out. I'll deal with you later."

"Don't you talk to him like that," I hissed, shooting to my feet.

"You have jeopardized this alliance with that stunt you two pulled—"

"Good. They can burn in *hell* for all I care!" I shouted. Lucien flinched.

"*You sent the Bogge after them!*" Tamlin roared.

I didn't so much as blink. And I knew the sentries had heard indeed by the cough of one outside—a sound of muffled shock.

And I made sure those sentries could still hear as I said, "They terrorized those humans—made them suffer. I figured the Bogge was one of the few creatures that could return the favor."

Lucien had tracked it down—and we'd lured it, carefully, over hours, back to that camp. Right to where Dagdan and Brannagh had been gloating over their kill. They'd managed to get away—but only after what had sounded like a good bit of screaming and fighting. Their faces remained bloodless even hours later, their eyes still brimming with hate whenever they deigned to look at us.

Lucien cleared his throat. Stood as well. "Tam—those humans were barely more than children. Feyre gave the royals an order to stand down. They ignored it. If we let Hybern walk all over us, we stand to lose more than their alliance. The Bogge reminded them that we aren't without our claws, too."

Tamlin didn't take his eyes off me as he said to Lucien, "*Get. Out.*"

There was enough violence in the words that neither Lucien nor I objected this time as he slipped from the room and shut the double doors behind him. I speared my power into the hall, sensing him sitting on the foot of the stairs. Listening. As the six sentries in the hall were listening.

I said to Tamlin, my back ramrod straight, "You don't get to speak to me like that. You *promised* you wouldn't act this way."

"You have no idea what's at risk—"

"Don't you talk down to me. Not after what *I* went through to get back here, to you. To our *people*. You think any of us are happy to be working with Hybern? You think I don't see it in their faces? The question of whether *I* am worth the dishonor of it?"

His breathing turned ragged again. Good, I wanted to urge him. *Good*.

"You sold us out to get me back," I said, low and cold. "You whored us out to Hybern. Forgive me if *I* am now trying to regain some of what we lost."

Claws slid free. A feral growl rippled out of him.

"They hunted down and butchered those humans for sport," I went on. "You might be willing to get on your knees for Hybern, but I certainly am not."

He exploded.

Furniture splintered and went flying, windows cracked and shattered. And this time, I did not shield myself.

The worktable slammed into me, throwing me against the bookshelf, and every place where flesh and bone met wood barked and ached.

My knees slammed into the carpeted floor, and Tamlin was instantly in front of me, hands shaking—

The doors burst open.

"What have you done," Lucien breathed, and Tamlin's face was the picture of devastation as Lucien shoved him aside. He *let* Lucien shove him aside and help me stand.

Something wet and warm slid down my cheek—blood, from the scent of it.

"Let's get you cleaned up," Lucien said, an arm around my shoulders as he eased me from the room. I barely heard him over the ringing in my ears, the slight spinning to the world.

The sentries—Bron and Hart, two of Tamlin's favorite lord-warriors among them—were gaping, attention torn between the wrecked study and my face.

With good reason. As Lucien led me past a gilded hall mirror, I beheld what had drawn such horror. My eyes were glassy, my face pallid—save for the scratch just beneath my cheekbone, perhaps two inches long and leaking blood.

Little scratches peppered my neck, my hands. But I willed that cleansing, healing power—that of the High Lord of Dawn—to keep from seeking them out. From smoothing them away.

"Feyre," Tamlin breathed from behind us.

I halted, aware of every eye that watched. "I'm fine," I whispered. "I'm sorry." I wiped at the blood dribbling down my cheek. "I'm fine," I told him again.

No one, not even Tamlin, looked convinced.

And if I could have painted that moment, I would have named it *A Portrait in Snares and Baiting.*

⊹

Rhysand sent word down the bond the second I was soaking in the bathtub.

Are you hurt?

The question was faint, the bond quieter and tenser than it had been days ago.

Sore, but fine. Nothing I can't handle. Though my injuries still lingered. And showed no signs of a speedy healing. Perhaps I'd been too good at keeping those healing powers at bay.

The reply was a long time coming. Then it came all at once, as if he wanted to cram every word in before the difficulty of the distance silenced us.

I know better than to tell you to be careful, or to come home. But I want you home. Soon. And I want him dead for putting a hand on you.

Even with the entirety of the land between us, his rage rippled down the bond.

I answered, my tone soothing, dry, *Technically, his* magic *touched me, not his hand.*

The bathwater was cold by the time his reply came through. *I'm glad you have a sense of humor about this. I certainly don't.*

I sent back an image of me sticking out my tongue at him.

My clothes were back on when his answer arrived.

Like mine, it was wordless, a mere image. Like mine, Rhysand's tongue was out.

But it was occupied with doing something else.

⊹

I made a point to take a ride the next day. Made sure it was when Bron and Hart were on duty, and asked them to escort me.

They didn't say much, but I felt their assessing glances at my every wince as we rode the worn paths through the spring wood. Felt them study the cut on my face, the bruises beneath my clothes that had me hissing every now and then. Still not fully healed to my surprise—though I supposed it worked to my advantage.

Tamlin had begged my forgiveness at dinner yesterday—and I'd given it to him. But Lucien hadn't spoken to him all evening.

Jurian and the Hybern royals had sulked at the delay after I'd quietly admitted my bruises made it too difficult to accompany them to the wall. Tamlin hadn't possessed the nerve to suggest they go without me, to rob me of that duty. Not when he saw the purplish markings and knew that if they were on a human, I might have been dead.

And the royals, after Lucien and I had sent the Bogge's invisible malice after them, had backed off. For now. I kept my shields up—around myself and the others, the strain now a constant headache that had any extra sort of magic feeling feeble and thin. The reprieve on the border hadn't done much—no, it'd made the strain worse after I'd sent my power through the wall.

I'd invited Ianthe to the house, subtly requesting her comforting presence. She arrived knowing the full details of what had transpired in that study—letting it conveniently slip that Tamlin had confessed it to her, pleading for absolution from the Mother and Cauldron and whoever else. I prattled about my own forgiveness to her that evening, and made a show of taking her good counsel, telling the courtiers and others at our crowded table that night how lucky we were to have Tamlin *and* Ianthe guarding our lands.

Honestly, I don't know how none of them connected it.

How none of them saw my words as not a strange coincidence but a dare. A threat.

That last little nudge.

Especially when seven naga broke into the estate grounds just past midnight.

They were dispatched before they reached the house—an attack halted by a Cauldron-sent warning vision from none other than Ianthe herself.

The chaos and screaming woke the estate. I remained in my room, guards beneath my windows and outside my door. Tamlin himself, blood-drenched and panting, came to inform me that the grounds were again secure. That the naga had been found with the keys to the gate, and the sentry who had lost them would be dealt with in the morning. A freak accident, a final show of power from a tribe that had not gone gently after Amarantha's reign.

All of us saved from further harm by Ianthe.

We all gathered outside the barracks the next morning, Lucien's face pallid and drawn, purple smudges beneath his glazed eyes. He hadn't returned to his room last night.

Beside me, the Hybern royals and Jurian were silent and grim as Tamlin paced before the sentry strung up between two posts.

"You were entrusted with guarding this estate and its people," Tamlin said to the shuddering male, already stripped down to his pants. "You were found not only asleep at the gate last night, but it was *your* set of keys that originally went missing." Tamlin snarled softly. "Do you deny this?"

"I—I never fall asleep. It's never happened until now. I must have just nodded off for a minute or two," the sentry stammered, the ropes restraining him groaning as he strained against them.

"You jeopardized the lives of everyone in this manor."

And it could not go unpunished. Not with the Hybern royals here, seeking any sign of weakness.

Tamlin held out a hand. Bron, stone-faced, approached to give him a whip.

All the sentries, his most trusted warriors, shifted about. Some outright glaring at Tamlin, some trying not to watch what was about to unfold.

I grabbed Lucien's hand. It wasn't entirely for show.

Ianthe stepped forward, hands folded over her stomach. "Twenty lashes. And one more, for the Cauldron's forgiveness."

The guards turned baleful eyes toward her now.

Tamlin unfurled the whip onto the dirt.

I made my move. Slid my power into the bound sentry's mind and freed the memory I'd coiled up tightly in his head—freed his tongue, too.

"It was her," he panted, jerking his chin to Ianthe. "*She* took the keys."

Tamlin blinked—and everyone in that courtyard looked right to Ianthe.

Her face didn't so much as flinch at the accusation—the truth he'd flung her way.

I'd been waiting to see how she'd counter my showing of power at the solstice, tracking her movements that entire day and night. Within moments of my leaving the party she'd gone to the barracks, used some glimmer of power to lull him to sleep, and taken his keys. Then planted her warnings about the naga's impending attacks . . . after she gave the creatures the keys to the gates.

So she could sound the alarm last night. So *she* could save us from a real threat.

Clever idea—had it not played right into everything I'd laid out.

Ianthe said smoothly, "Why should I take the keys? I warned you of the attack."

"You were at the barracks—I *saw* you that night," the sentry insisted, then turned pleading eyes to Tamlin. It wasn't fear of pain that propelled him, I realized. No, the lashings would have been deserved and earned and borne well. It was the fear of honor lost.

"I would have thought one of your sentries, Tamlin, would have more dignity than to spread lies to spare himself from some fleeting pain." Ianthe's face remained serene as always.

Tamlin, to his credit, studied the sentry for a long moment.

I stepped forward. "I will hear his story."

Some of the guards loosed sighs. Some looked at me with pity and affection.

Ianthe lifted her chin. "With all due respect, milady, it is not your judgment to make."

And there it was. The attempt to knock me down a few pegs.

Just because it would make her see red, I ignored her completely and said to the sentry, "I will hear your story."

I kept my focus on him, even as I counted my breaths, even as I prayed that Ianthe would take the bait—

"You'll take the word of a sentry over that of a High Priestess?"

My disgust at her blurted words wasn't entirely feigned—even though hiding my faint smile was an effort. The guards shifted on their feet at the insult, the tone. Even if they had not already trusted their fellow sentry, from her words alone, they realized her guilt.

I looked to Tamlin then—saw his eyes sharpen as well. With understanding. Too many protests from Ianthe.

Oh, he was well aware that Ianthe had perhaps planned that naga attack to reclaim some shred of power and influence—as a savior of these people.

Tamlin's mouth tightened in disapproval.

I'd given them both a length of rope. I supposed now would be the moment to see whether they'd hang themselves with it.

I dared one more step forward, upturning my palms to Tamlin. "Perhaps it was a mistake. Don't take it from his hide—or his honor. Let's hear him out."

Tamlin's eyes softened a fraction. He remained silent—considering.

But behind me, Brannagh snorted.

"Pathetic," she murmured, though everyone could hear it.

Weak. Vulnerable. Ripe for conquest. I saw the words slam through Tamlin's face, as if they were shutting doors in their wake.

There was no other interpretation—not for Tamlin.

But Ianthe assessed me, standing before the crowd, the influence I'd made so very clear I was capable of stealing. If she admitted guilt . . . whatever she had left would come crumbling down.

Tamlin opened his mouth, but Ianthe cut him off. "There are laws to be obeyed," she told me, gently enough that I wanted to drag my nails down her face. "Traditions. He has broken our trust, has let our blood be spilled for his carelessness. Now he seeks to accuse a High Priestess of *his* failings. It cannot go unpunished." She nodded to Tamlin. "Twenty-one lashes, High Lord."

I glanced between them, my mouth going dry. "Please. Just listen to him."

The guard hanging between the posts had such hope and gratitude in his eyes.

In this . . . in this, my revenge edged toward something oily, something foreign and queasy. He would heal from the pain, but the blow to his honor . . . It'd take a little piece out of mine as well.

Tamlin stared at me, then Ianthe. Then glanced to the smirking Hybern royals—to Jurian, who crossed his arms, his face unreadable.

And like I'd gambled, Tamlin's need for control, for strength, won out.

Ianthe was too important an ally to risk isolating. The word of a low sentry . . . no, it did not matter as much as hers.

Tamlin turned to the sentry tied to the posts. "Put the bit in," he quietly ordered Bron.

There was a heartbeat of hesitation from Bron—as if the shock of Tamlin's order had rippled through him. Through all the guards. Siding with Ianthe—over them. His sentries.

Who had gone over the wall, again and again, to try to break that curse for him. Who had gladly done it, gladly *died*, hunted down as those wolves, for him. And the wolf I'd felled, Andras . . . He'd gone willingly, too. Tamlin had sent them all over, and not all of them had come back. They had gone willingly, yet this . . . this was his thanks. His gratitude. His trust.

But Bron did as commanded, sliding the small piece of wood into the now-trembling sentry's mouth.

Judging by the barely concealed disdain in the guards' faces, at least they were aware of what had occurred—or what they believed had occurred: the High Priestess had orchestrated this entire attack to cast herself as a savior, offering up the reputation of one of their own as the asking price. They had no idea—none—that I'd goaded her into it, pushed and pushed her to reveal just what a snake she was. How little anyone without a title meant to her.

How Tamlin listened to her without question—to a fault.

It wasn't much of an act when I put a hand to my throat, backing up a step, then another, until Lucien's warmth was against me, and I leaned fully into him.

The sentries were sizing up Ianthe, the royals. Tamlin had always been one of them—fought for them.

Until now. Until Hybern. Until he put these foreign monsters before them.

Until he put a scheming High Priestess before them.

Tamlin's eyes were on us, on the hand Lucien put on my arm to steady me, as he drew back the whip.

The thunderous crack as it cleaved the air snapped through the barracks, the estate.

Through the very foundations of the court.

CHAPTER
9

Ianthe wasn't done.

I knew it—braced myself for it. She didn't flit back to her temple a few miles away.

Rather, she remained at the house, seizing her chance to worm her way closer to Tamlin. She believed she'd gained a foothold, that her declaration of justice served at the bloody end of the whipping hadn't been anything but a final slap in the face to the guards who watched.

And when that sentry had sagged from his bindings, when the others came to gently untie him, Ianthe merely ushered the Hybern party and Tamlin into the manor for lunch. But I'd remained at the barracks, tending to the groaning sentry, drawing away bloodied bowls of water while the healer quietly patched him up.

Bron and Hart personally escorted me back to the estate hours later. I thanked them each by name. Then apologized that I hadn't been able to prevent it—Ianthe's scheming or the unjust punishment of their friend. I meant every word, the crack of the whip still echoing in my ears.

Then they spoke the words I'd been waiting for. They were sorry they hadn't stopped *any* of it, either.

Not just today. But the bruises now fading—at last. The other incidents.

If I had asked them, they would have handed me their own knives to slit their throats.

The next evening, I was hurrying back to my room to change for dinner when Ianthe made her next move.

She was to come with us to the wall tomorrow morning.

Her, and Tamlin, too.

If we were all to be a united front, she'd declared over dinner, then she wished to see the wall herself.

The Hybern royals didn't care. But Jurian winked at me, as if he, too, saw the game in motion.

I packed my own bags that night.

Alis entered right before bed, a third pack in her hands. "Since it's a longer trip, I brought you supplies."

Even with Tamlin joining us, it was too many people for him to winnow us directly.

So we'd go, as we'd done before, in segments. A few miles at a time.

Alis laid the pack she'd prepared beside my own. Picked up the brush on the vanity and beckoned me to sit on the cushioned bench before it.

I obeyed. For a few minutes, she brushed my hair in silence.

Then she said, "When you leave tomorrow, I leave, too."

I lifted my eyes to hers in the mirror.

"My nephews are packed, the ponies ready to take us back to Summer Court territory at last. It has been too long since I saw my home," she said, though her eyes shone.

"I know the feeling," was all I said.

"I wish you well, lady," Alis said, setting down the brush and beginning to braid back my hair. "For the rest of your days, however long they may be, I wish you well."

I let her finish the plait, then pivoted on the bench to grip her thin fingers in mine. "Don't ever tell Tarquin you know me well."

Her brows rose.

"There is a blood ruby with my name on it," I clarified.

Even her tree-bark skin seemed to blanch. She understood it well enough: I was a hunted enemy of the Summer Court. Only my death would be accepted as payment for my crimes.

Alis squeezed my hand. "Blood rubies or no, you will always have one friend in the Summer Court."

My throat bobbed. "And you will always have one in mine," I promised her.

She knew which court I meant. And did not look afraid.

✝

The sentries did not glance at Tamlin, or so much as speak to him unless absolutely necessary. Bron, Hart, and three others were to join us. They had spotted me checking on their friend before dawn—a courtesy I knew none of the others had extended.

Winnowing felt like wading through mud. In fact, my powers had become more of a burden than a help. I had a throbbing headache by noon, and spent the last leg of the journey dizzy and disoriented as we winnowed again and again.

We arrived and set up camp in near-silence. I quietly, shyly asked to share a tent with Ianthe instead of Tamlin, appearing eager to mend the rift the whipping had torn between us. But I did it more to spare Lucien from her attention than to keep Tamlin at bay. Dinner was made and eaten, bedrolls laid out, and Tamlin ordered Bron and Hart on the first watch.

Lying beside Ianthe without slitting her throat was an exercise in patience and control.

But whenever the knife beneath my pillow seemed to whisper her name, I'd remind myself of my friends. The family that was alive— healing in the North.

I repeated their names silently, over and over into the darkness. Rhysand. Mor. Cassian. Amren. Azriel. Elain. Nesta.

I thought of how I had last seen them, so bloodied and hurting. Thought of Cassian's scream as his wings were shredded; of Azriel's threat to the king as he advanced on Mor. Nesta, fighting every step toward the Cauldron.

My goal was bigger than revenge. My purpose greater than personal retribution.

Dawn broke, and I found my palm curled around the hilt of my knife anyway. I drew it out as I sat up, staring down at the sleeping priestess.

The smooth column of her neck seemed to glow in the early-morning sun leaking through the tent flaps.

I weighed the knife in my hand.

I wasn't sure I'd been born with the ability to forgive. Not for terrors inflicted on those I loved. For myself, I didn't care—not nearly as much. But there was some fundamental pillar of steel in me that could not bend or break in this. Could not stomach the idea of letting these people get away with what they'd done.

Ianthe's eyes opened, the teal as limpid as her discarded circlet. They went right to the knife in my hand. Then to my face.

"You can't be too careful while sharing a camp with enemies," I said.

I could have sworn something like fear shone in her eyes. "Hybern is not our enemy," she said a tad breathlessly.

From her paleness as I left the tent, I knew my answering smile had done its job well.

+

Lucien and Tamlin showed the twins where the crack in the wall lay.

And as they had done with the first two, they spent hours surveying it, the surrounding land.

I kept close this time, watching them, my presence now deemed relatively unthreatening if not a nuisance. We'd played our little power games, established I could bite if I wished, but we'd tolerate each other.

"Here," Brannagh murmured to Dagdan, jerking her chin to the invisible divider. The only markings were the different trees: on our side, they were the bright, fresh green of spring. On the other, they were dark, broad, curling slightly with heat—the height of summer.

"The first one was better," Dagdan countered.

I sat atop a small boulder, peeling an apple with a paring knife.

"Closer to the western coast, too," he added to his twin.

"This is closer to the continent—to the strait."

I sliced deep into the flesh of the apple, carving out a hunk of white meat.

"Yes, but we'd have more access to the High Lord's supplies."

Said High Lord was currently off with Jurian, hunting for food more filling than the sandwiches we'd packed. Ianthe had gone to a nearby spring to pray, and I had no idea whatsoever where Lucien or the sentries were.

Good. Easier for me as I shoved the apple slice into my mouth and said around it, "I say go for this one."

They twisted toward me, Brannagh sneering and Dagdan's brows high. "What do you know of any of it?" Brannagh demanded.

I shrugged, cutting another piece of apple. "You two talk louder than you realize."

Shared accusatory glares between them. Proud, arrogant, cruel. I'd been taking their measure this fortnight. "Unless you want to risk the other courts having time to rally and intercepting you before you can cross to the strait, I'd pick this one."

Brannagh rolled her eyes.

I went on, rambling and bored, "But what do I know? You two have squatted on a little island for five hundred years. Clearly you know more about Prythian and moving armies than me."

Brannagh hissed, "This is not about armies, so I will trust you to keep that mouth *shut* until we have use for you."

I snorted. "You mean to tell me all of this nonsense hasn't been to find a place to break through the wall and use the Cauldron to *also* transport the mass of your armies here?"

She laughed, swinging her dark curtain of hair over a shoulder. "The Cauldron is not for transporting grunt armies. It is for remaking worlds. It is for bringing down this hideous wall and reclaiming what we were."

I merely crossed my legs. "I'd think that with an army of ten thousand you wouldn't need any magical objects to do your dirty work."

"Our army is ten times that, girl," Brannagh sneered. "And twice *that* number if you count our allies in Vallahan, Montesere, and Rask."

Two hundred thousand. Mother save us.

"You've certainly been busy all these years." I surveyed them, utterly nonplussed. "Why not strike when Amarantha had the island?"

"The king had not yet found the Cauldron, despite years of searching. It served his purposes to let her be an experiment for how we might break these people. And served as good motivation for our allies on the continent to join us, knowing what would await them."

I finished off my apple and chucked the core into the woods. They watched it fly like two hounds tracking a pheasant.

"So they're all going to converge here? I'm supposed to play hostess to so many soldiers?"

"Our own force will take care of Prythian before uniting with the others. Our commanders are preparing for it as we speak."

"You must think you stand a shot at losing if you're bothering to use the Cauldron to help you win."

"The Cauldron *is* victory. It will wipe this world clean again."

I lifted my brows in irreverent cynicism. "And you need this exact spot to unleash it?"

"This exact spot," Dagdan said, a hand on the hilt of his sword, "exists because a person or object of mighty power passed through it. The Cauldron will study the work they've already done—and magnify it until the wall collapses entirely. It is a careful, complex process, and one I doubt your mortal mind can grasp."

"Probably. Though this mortal mind did manage to solve Amarantha's riddle—and destroy her."

Brannagh merely turned back to the wall. "Why do you think Hybern let her live for so long in these lands? Better to have someone else do his dirty work."

⊹

I had what I needed.

Tamlin and Jurian were still off hunting, the royals were preoccupied, and I'd sent the sentries to fetch me more water, claiming that some of my bruises still ached and I wanted to make a poultice for them.

They'd looked positively murderous at that. Not at me—but at who had given me those bruises. Who had picked Ianthe over them—and Hybern over their honor and people.

I'd brought three packs, but I'd only need one. The one I'd carefully repacked with Alis's new supplies, now tucked beside everything I'd anticipated needing to get clear of them and go. The one I'd brought with me on every trip out to the wall, just in case. And now . . .

I had numbers, I had a purpose, I had a specific location, and the names of foreign territories.

But more than that, I had a people who had lost faith in their High Priestess. I had sentries who were beginning to rebel against their High Lord. And as a result of those things, I had Hybern royals doubting the strength of their allies here. I'd primed this court to fall. Not from outside forces—but its own internal warring.

And I had to be clear of it before it happened. Before the last sliver of my plan fell into place.

The party would return without me. And to maintain that illusion of strength, Tamlin and Ianthe would lie about it—where I'd gone.

And perhaps a day or two after that, one of these sentries would reveal the news, a carefully sprung trap that I'd coiled into his mind like one of my snares.

I'd fled for my life—after being nearly killed by the Hybern prince and princess. I'd planted images in his head of my brutalized body, the

83

markings consistent with what Dagdan and Brannagh had already revealed to be their style. He'd describe them in detail—describe how he helped me get away before it was too late. How I ran for my life when Tamlin and Ianthe refused to intervene, to risk their alliance with Hybern.

And when the sentry revealed the truth, no longer able to stomach keeping quiet when he saw how my sorry fate was concealed by Tamlin and Ianthe, just as Tamlin had sided with Ianthe the day he'd flogged that sentry . . .

When he described what Hybern had done to me, their Cursebreaker, their newly anointed Cauldron-blessed, before I'd fled for my life . . .

There would be no further alliance. For there would be no sentry or denizen of this court who would stand with Tamlin or Ianthe after this. After *me*.

I ducked into my tent to grab my pack, my steps light and swift. Listening, barely breathing, I scanned the camp, the woods.

A few seconds extra had me snatching Tamlin's bandolier of knives from where he'd left them inside his tent. They'd get in the way while using a bow and arrow, he'd explained that morning.

Their weight was considerable as I slung it across my chest. Illyrian fighting knives.

Home. I was going *home*.

I didn't bother to look back at that camp as I slipped into the northern tree line. If I winnowed without stopping between leaps, I'd be at the foothills in an hour—and would vanish through one of the caves not long after that.

I made it about a hundred yards into the cover of the trees before I halted.

I heard Lucien first.

"Back off."

A low female laugh.

Everything in me went still and cold at that sound. I'd heard it once before—in Rhysand's memory.

Keep going. They were distracted, horrible as it was.

Keep going, keep going, keep going.

"I thought you'd seek me out after the Rite," Ianthe purred. They couldn't be more than thirty feet through the trees. Far enough away not to hear my presence, if I was quiet enough.

"I was obligated to perform the Rite," Lucien snapped. "That night wasn't the product of desire, believe me."

"We had fun, you and I."

"I'm a mated male now."

Every second was the ringing of my death knell. I'd primed everything to fall; I'd long since stopped feeling any sort of guilt or doubt about my plan. Not with Alis now safely away.

And yet—and yet—

"You don't act that way with Feyre." A silk-wrapped threat.

"You're mistaken."

"Am I?" Twigs and leaves crunched, as if she was circling him. "You put your hands all over her."

I had done my job too well, provoked her jealousy too much with every instance I'd found ways to get Lucien to touch me in her presence, in Tamlin's presence.

"Do *not* touch me," he growled.

And then I was moving.

I masked the sound of my footfalls, silent as a panther as I stalked to the little clearing where they stood.

Where Lucien stood, back against a tree—twin bands of blue stone shackled around his wrists.

I'd seen them before. On Rhys, to immobilize his power. Stone hewn from Hybern's rotted land, capable of nullifying magic. And in this case . . . holding Lucien against that tree as Ianthe surveyed him like a snake before a meal.

She slid a hand over the broad panes of his chest, his stomach.

And Lucien's eyes shot to me as I stepped between the trees, fear and humiliation reddening his golden skin.

"That's enough," I said.

Ianthe whipped her head to me. Her smile was innocent, simpering. But I saw her note the pack, Tamlin's bandolier. Dismiss them. "We were in the middle of a game. Weren't we, Lucien?"

He didn't answer.

And the sight of those shackles on him, however she'd trapped him, the sight of her *hand* still on his stomach—

"We'll return to the camp when we're done," she said, turning to him again. Her hand slid lower, not for his own pleasure, but simply to throw it in my face that she *could*—

I struck.

Not with my knives or magic, but my mind.

I ripped down the shield I'd kept up around her to avoid the twins' control—and slammed myself into her consciousness.

A mask over a face of decay. That's what it was like to go inside that beautiful head and find such hideous thoughts inside it. A trail of males she'd used her power on or outright forced to bed, convinced of her entitlement to them. I pulled back against the tug of those memories, mastering myself. "Take your hands off him."

She did.

"Unshackle him."

Lucien's skin drained of color as Ianthe obeyed me, her face queerly vacant, pliant. The blue stone shackles thumped to the mossy ground.

Lucien's shirt was askew, the top button on his pants already undone.

The roaring that filled my mind was so loud I could barely hear myself as I said, "Pick up that rock."

Lucien remained pressed against that tree. And he watched in silence as Ianthe stooped to pick up a gray, rough rock about the size of an apple.

"Put your right hand on that boulder."

She obeyed, though a tremor went down her spine.

Her mind thrashed and struggled against me, like a fish snared on a line. I dug my mental talons in deeper, and some inner voice of hers began screaming.

"Smash your hand with the rock as hard as you can until I tell you to stop."

The hand she'd put on him, on so many others.

Ianthe brought the stone up. The first impact was a muffled, wet thud.

The second was an actual crack.

The third drew blood.

Her arm rose and fell, her body shuddering with the agony.

And I said to her very clearly, "You will never touch another person against their will. You will never convince yourself that they truly want your advances; that they're playing games. You will never know another's touch unless they initiate, unless it's desired by *both* sides."

Thwack; crack; thud.

"You will not remember what happened here. You will tell the others that you fell."

Her ring finger had shifted in the wrong direction.

"You are allowed to see a healer to set the bones. But not to erase the scarring. And every time you look at that hand, you are going to remember that touching people against their will has consequences, and if you do it again, everything you are will cease to exist. You will live with that terror every day, and never know where it originates. Only the fear of something chasing you, hunting you, waiting for you the instant you let your guard down."

Silent tears of pain flowed down her face.

"You can stop now."

The bloodied rock tumbled onto the grass. Her hand was little more than cracked bones wrapped in shredded skin.

"Kneel here until someone finds you."

Ianthe fell to her knees, her ruined hand leaking blood onto her pale robes.

"I debated slitting your throat this morning," I told her. "I debated it all last night while you slept beside me. I've debated it every single day since I learned you sold out my sisters to Hybern." I smiled a bit.

"But I think this is a better punishment. And I hope you live a long, long life, Ianthe, and never know a moment's peace."

I stared down at her for a moment longer, tying off the tapestry of words and commands I'd woven into her mind, and turned to Lucien. He'd fixed his pants, his shirt.

His wide eyes slid from her to me, then to the bloodied stone.

"The word you're looking for, Lucien," crooned a deceptively light female voice, "is *daemati*."

We whirled toward Brannagh and Dagdan as they stepped into the clearing, grinning like wolves.

CHAPTER
10

Brannagh ran her fingers through Ianthe's golden hair, clicking her tongue at the bloodied pulp cradled in her lap. "Going somewhere, Feyre?"

I let my mask drop.

"I have places to be," I told the Hybern royals, noting the flanking positions they were too casually establishing around me.

"What could be more important than assisting us? You are, after all, sworn to assist our king."

Time—biding their time until Tamlin returned from hunting with Jurian.

Lucien shoved off the tree, but didn't come to my side. Something like agony flickered across his face as he finally noted the stolen bandolier, the pack on my shoulders.

"I have no allegiance to you," I told Brannagh, even as Dagdan began to edge past my line of sight. "I am a free person, allowed to go where and when I will it."

"Are you?" Brannagh mused, sliding a hand to her sword at her hip. I pivoted slightly to keep Dagdan from slipping into my blind spot. "Such careful plotting these weeks, such skilled maneuvering. You didn't seem to worry that we'd be doing the same."

They weren't letting Lucien leave this clearing alive. Or at least with his mind intact.

He seemed to realize it at the same moment I did, understanding that there was no way they'd reveal this without knowing they'd get away with it.

"Take the Spring Court," I said, and meant it. "It's going to fall one way or another."

Lucien snarled. I ignored him.

"Oh, we intend to," Brannagh said, sword inching free of its dark sheath. "But then there's the matter of you."

I thumbed free two of the Illyrian fighting knives.

"Haven't you wondered at the headaches? How things seem a little muffled on certain mental bonds?"

My powers had tired so swiftly, had become weaker and weaker these weeks—

Dagdan snorted and finally observed to his sister, "I'd give her about ten minutes before the apple sets in."

Brannagh chuckled, toeing the blue stone shackle. "We gave the priestess the powder at first. Crushed faebane stone, ground so fine you couldn't see or scent or taste it in your food. She'd add a little at a time, nothing suspicious—not too much, lest it stifle all your powers at once."

Unease began to clench my gut.

"We've been daemati for a thousand years, girl," Dagdan sneered. "But we didn't even need to slip into her mind to get her to do our bidding. But you . . . what a valiant effort you put up, trying to shield them all from us."

Dagdan's mind speared for Lucien's, a dark arrow shot between them. I slammed up a shield between them. And my head—my very bones *ached*—

"What *apple*," I bit out.

"The one you shoved down your throat an hour ago," Brannagh said. "Grown and tended in the king's personal garden, fed a steady diet of water laced with faebane. Enough to knock out your powers for a few days straight, no shackles required. And here you are, thinking no one had noticed you planned to vanish today." She clicked her tongue again. "Our uncle would be most displeased if we allowed that to happen."

I was running out of borrowed time. I could winnow, but then I'd abandon Lucien to them if he somehow couldn't manage to himself with the faebane in his system from the food at the camp—

Leave him. I should and *could* leave him.

But to a fate perhaps worse than death—

His russet eye gleamed. "Go."

I made my choice.

I exploded into night and smoke and shadow.

And even a thousand years wasn't enough for Dagdan to adequately prepare as I winnowed in front of him and struck.

I sliced through the front of his leather armor, not deep enough to kill, and as steel snagged on its plates, he twisted expertly, forcing me to either expose my right side or lose the knife—

I winnowed again. This time, Dagdan went with me.

I was not fighting Hybern cronies unaware in the woods. I was not fighting the Attor and its ilk in the streets of Velaris. Dagdan was a Hybern prince—a commander.

He fought like one.

Winnow. Strike. Winnow. Strike.

We were a black whirlwind of steel and shadow through the clearing, and months of Cassian's brutal training clicked into place as I kept my feet under me.

I had the vague sense of Lucien gaping, even Brannagh taken aback by my show of skill against her brother.

But Dagdan's blows weren't hard—no, they were precise and swift, but he didn't throw himself into it wholly.

Buying time. Wearing me down until my body fully absorbed that apple and its power rendered me nearly mortal.

So I hit him where he was weakest.

Brannagh screamed as a wall of flame slammed into her.

Dagdan lost his focus for all of a heartbeat. His roar as I sliced deep into his abdomen shook the birds from the trees.

"You little bitch," he spat, dancing back from my next blow as the fire cleared and Brannagh was revealed on her knees. Her physical shield had been sloppy—she'd expected me to attack her mind.

She was shuddering, gasping with agony. The reek of charred skin now drifted to us, directly from her right arm, her ribs, her thigh.

Dagdan lunged for me again, and I brought up both of my knives to meet his blade.

He didn't pull the blow this time.

I felt its reverberation in every inch of my body.

Felt the rising, stifling silence, too. I'd felt it once before—that day in Hybern.

Brannagh surged to her feet with a sharp cry.

But Lucien was there.

Her focus wholly on me, on taking from me the beauty I'd burned from her, Brannagh did not see him winnow until it was too late.

Until Lucien's sword refracted the light of the sun leaking through the canopy. And then met flesh and bone.

A tremor shuddered through the clearing—like some thread between the twins had been snipped as Brannagh's dark head thudded onto the grass.

Dagdan screamed, launching himself at Lucien, winnowing across the fifteen feet between us.

Lucien had barely heaved his blade out of Brannagh's severed neck when Dagdan was before him, sword shoving forward to ram through his throat.

Lucien only had enough time to stumble back from Dagdan's killing blow.

I had enough time to stop it.

I parried Dagdan's blade aside with one knife, the male's eyes going wide as I winnowed between them—and punched the other into his eye. Right into the skull behind it.

Bone and blood and soft tissue scraped and slid along the blade, Dagdan's mouth still open with surprise as I yanked out the knife.

I let him fall atop his sister, the thud of flesh on flesh the only sound.

I merely looked at Ianthe, my power guttering, a hideous ache building in my gut, and made my last command, amending my earlier ones. "You tell them I killed them. In self-defense. After they hurt me so badly while you and Tamlin did *nothing*. Even when they torture you for the truth, you say that I fled after I killed them—to save this court from their horrors."

Blank, vacant eyes were my only answer.

"Feyre."

Lucien's voice was a hoarse rasp.

I merely wiped my two knives on Dagdan's back before going to reclaim my fallen pack.

"You're going back. To the Night Court."

I shouldered my heavy pack and finally looked at him. "Yes."

His tan face had paled. But he surveyed Ianthe, the two dead royals. "I'm going with you."

"No," was all I said, heading for the trees.

A cramp formed deep in my belly. I had to get away—had to use the last of my power to winnow to the hills.

"You won't make it without magic," he warned me.

I just gritted my teeth against the sharp pain in my abdomen as I rallied my strength to winnow to those distant foothills. But Lucien gripped my arm, halting me.

"I'm going with you," he said again, face splattered with blood as bright as his hair. "I'm getting my mate back."

There was no time for this argument. For the truth and debate and the answers I saw he desperately wanted.

Tamlin and the others would have heard the shouting by now.

"Don't make me regret this," I told him.

⊢

Blood coated the inside of my mouth by the time we reached the foothills hours later.

I was panting, my head throbbing, my stomach a twisting knot of aching.

Lucien was barely better off, his winnowing as shaky as my own before we halted amongst the rolling green and he doubled over, hands braced on his knees. "It's—gone," he said, gasping for breath. "My magic—not an ember. They must have dosed all of us today."

And given me a poisoned apple just to make sure it kept me down.

My power pulled away from me like a wave reeling back from the shore. Only there was no return. It just went farther and farther out into a sea of nothing.

I peered at the sun, now a hand's width above the horizon, shadows already thick and heavy between the hills. I took my bearings, sorting through the knowledge I'd compiled these weeks.

I stepped northward, swaying. Lucien gripped my arm. "You're taking a door?"

I slid aching eyes toward him. "Yes." The caves—doors, they called them—in those hollows led to other pockets of Prythian. I'd taken one straight Under the Mountain. I would now take one to get me home. Or as close to it as I could get. No door to the Night Court existed, here or anywhere.

And I would not risk my friends by bringing them here to retrieve me. No matter that the bond between Rhys and me . . . I couldn't so much as feel it.

A numbness had spread through me. I needed to get out—now.

"The Autumn Court portal is that way." Warning and reproach.

"I can't go into Summer. They'll kill me on sight."

Silence. He released my arm. I swallowed, my throat so dry I could barely do so. "The only other door here leads Under the Mountain. We sealed off all the other entrances. If we go there, we could wind up trapped—or have to return."

"Then we go to Autumn. And from there . . ." I trailed off before I finished. *Home*. But Lucien gleaned it anyway. And seemed to realize then—that's what the Night Court was. *Home*.

I could almost see the word in his russet eye as he shook his head. *Later*.

I gave him a silent nod. Yes—later, we'd have it all out. "The Autumn Court will be as dangerous as Summer," he warned.

"I just need somewhere to hide—to lie low until . . . until we can winnow again."

A faint buzzing and ringing filled my ears. And I felt my magic vanish entirely.

"I know a place," Lucien said, walking toward the cave that would take us to his home.

To the lands of the family who'd betrayed him as badly as this court had betrayed mine.

We hurried through the hills, swift and silent as shadows.

The cave to the Autumn Court had been left unguarded. Lucien looked at me over his shoulder as if to ask if I, too, had been responsible for the lack of guards who were always stationed here.

I gave him another nod. I'd slid into their minds before we'd left, making sure this door would be left open. Cassian had taught me to always have a second escape route. Always.

Lucien paused before the swirling gloom of the cave mouth, the blackness like a wyrm poised to devour us both. A muscle feathered in his jaw.

I said, "Stay, if you want. What's done is done."

For Hybern was coming—already here. I had debated it for weeks: whether it was better to claim the Spring Court for ourselves, or to let it fall to our enemies.

But it could not remain neutral—a barrier between our forces in the North and the humans in the South. It would have been easy to call in Rhys and Cassian, to have the latter bring in an Illyrian legion to claim the territory when it was weakest after my own maneuverings. Depending on how much mobility Cassian had retained—if he was still healing.

Yet then we'd hold one territory—with five other courts between us. Sympathy might have swayed for the Spring Court; others might have joined Hybern against us, considering our conquest here proof of our wickedness. But if Spring fell to Hybern . . . We could rally the other courts to us. Charge as one from the North, drawing Hybern in close.

"You were right," Lucien declared at last. "That girl I knew did die Under the Mountain."

I wasn't sure if it was an insult. But I nodded all the same. "At least we can agree on that." I stepped into the awaiting cold and dark.

Lucien fell into step beside me as we strode beneath the archway of carved, crude stone, our blades out as we left behind the warmth and green of eternal spring.

And in the distance, so faint I thought I might have imagined it, a beast's roar cleaved the land.

PART TWO

CURSEBREAKER

CHAPTER
11

The cold was what hit me first.

Brisk, crisp cold, laced with loam and rotting things.

In the twilight, the world beyond the narrow cave mouth was a latticework of red and gold and brown and green, the trees thick and old, the mossy ground strewn with rocks and boulders that cast long shadows.

We emerged, blades out, barely breathing beyond a trickle of air.

But there were no Autumn Court sentries guarding the entrance to Beron's realm—none that we could see or scent.

Without my magic, I was blind again, unable to sweep a net of awareness through the ancient, vibrant trees to catch any traces of nearby Fae minds.

Utterly helpless. That's how I'd been before. How I'd survived so long without it . . . I didn't want to consider.

We crept on cat-soft feet into the moss and stone and wood, our breath curling in front of us.

Keep moving, keep striding north. Rhys would have realized by now that our bond had gone dark—was likely trying to glean whether I had planned for that. Whether it was worth the risk of revealing our scheming to find me.

But until he did . . . until he could hear me, find me . . . I had to keep moving.

So I let Lucien lead the way, wishing I'd at least been able to shift my eyes to something that could pierce the darkening wood. But my magic was still and frozen. A crutch I'd become too reliant upon.

We picked our way through the forest, the chill deepening with each vanishing shaft of sunlight.

We hadn't spoken since we'd entered that cave between courts. From the stiffness of his shoulders, the hard angle of his jaw as he moved on silent, steady feet, I knew only our need for stealth kept his simmering questions at bay.

Night was fully overhead, the moon not yet risen, when he led us into another cave.

I balked at the entrance.

Lucien merely said, voice flat and as icy as the air, "It doesn't lead anywhere. It curves away in the back—it'll keep us out of sight."

I let him go inside first nonetheless.

Every limb and movement turned sluggish, aching. But I trailed him into the cave, and around the bend he'd indicated.

Flint struck, and I found myself gazing at a makeshift camp of sorts.

The candle Lucien had ignited sat on a natural stone ledge, and on the floor nearby lay three bedrolls and old blankets, crusted with leaves and cobwebs. A little fire pit lay in the sloped center of the space, the ceiling above it charred.

No one had been here in months. Years.

"I used to stay here while hunting. Before—I left," he said, examining a dusty, leather-bound book left on the stone ledge beside the candle. He set the tome down with a thump. "It's just for the night. We'll find something to eat in the morning."

I only lifted the closest bedroll and smacked it a few times, leaves and clouds of dust flying off before I laid it upon the ground.

"You truly planned this," he said at last.

I sat on the bedroll and began sorting through my pack, hauling out the warmer clothes, food, and supplies Alis herself had placed within. "Yes."

"That's all you have to say?"

I sniffed at the food, wondering what was laced with faebane. It could be in everything. "It's too risky to eat," I admitted, evading his question.

Lucien was having none of it. "I knew. I knew you were lying the moment you unleashed that light in Hybern. My friend at the Dawn Court has the same power—her light is identical. And it does not do whatever horseshit you lied about it doing."

I shoved my pack off my bedroll. "Then why not tell him? You were his faithful dog in every other sense."

His eye seemed to simmer. As if being in his own lands set that molten ore inside him rising to the surface, even with the damper on his power. "Glad to see the mask is off, at least."

Indeed, I let him see it all—didn't alter or shape my face into anything but coldness.

Lucien snorted. "I didn't tell him for two reasons. One, it felt like kicking a male already down. I couldn't take that hope away from him." I rolled my eyes. "Two," he snapped, "I knew if I was correct and called you on it, you'd find a way to make sure I never saw her."

My nails dug into my palms hard enough to hurt, but I remained seated on the bedroll as I bared my teeth at him. "And that's why you're here. Not because it's right and he's always been wrong, but just so you can get what *you* think you're owed."

"She is my *mate* and in my enemy's hands—"

"I've made no secret from the start that Elain is safe and cared for."

"And I'm supposed to believe you."

"Yes," I hissed. "You are. Because if I believed for one moment that my sisters were in danger, no High Lord or king would have kept me from going to save them."

He just shook his head, the candlelight dancing over his hair. "You have the gall to question my priorities regarding Elain—yet what was *your* motive where I was concerned? Did you plan to spare me from your path of destruction because of any genuine friendship, or simply for fear of what it might do to her?"

I didn't answer.

"Well? What *was* your grand plan for me before Ianthe interfered?"

I pulled at a stray thread in the bedroll. "You would have been fine," was all I said.

"And what about Tamlin? Did you plan to disembowel him before you left and simply not get the chance?"

I ripped the loose thread right out of the bedroll. "I debated it."

"But?"

"But I think letting his court collapse around him is a better punishment. Certainly longer than an easy death." I slung off Tamlin's bandolier of knives, leather scraping against the rough stone floor. "You're his emissary—surely you realize that slitting his throat, however satisfying, wouldn't win us many allies in this war." No, it'd give Hybern too many openings to undermine us.

He crossed his arms. Digging in for a good, long fight. Before he could do just that, I cut in, "I'm tired. And our voices echo. Let's have it out when it's not likely to get us caught and killed."

His gaze was a brand.

But I ignored it as I nestled down on the bedroll, the material reeking of dust and rot. I pulled my cloak over me, but didn't close my eyes.

I didn't dare sleep—not when he might very well change his mind. Yet just lying down, not moving, not thinking . . . Some of the tightness in my body eased.

Lucien blew out the candle and I listened to the sounds of him settling down as well.

"My father will hunt you for taking his power if he finds out," he said into the frigid dark. "And kill you for learning how to wield it."

"He can get in line," was all I said.

My exhaustion was a blanket over my senses as gray light stained the cave walls.

I'd spent most of the night shivering, jolting at every snap and sound in the forest outside, keenly aware of Lucien's movements on his bedroll.

From his own haggard face as he sat up, I knew he hadn't slept, either, perhaps wondering if I'd abandon him. Or if his family would find us first. Or mine.

We took each other's measure.

"What now," he rasped, scrubbing a broad hand over his face.

Rhys had not come—I had not heard a whisper of him down the bond.

I felt for my magic, but only ashes greeted me. "We head north," I said. "Until the faebane is out of our systems and we can winnow." Or I could contact Rhys and the others.

"My father's court lies due northward. We'll have to go to the east or west to avoid it."

"No. East takes us too close to the Summer Court border. And I won't lose time by going too far west. We go straight north."

"My father's sentries will easily spot us."

"Then we'll have to remain unseen," I said, rising.

I dumped the last of the contaminated food from my pack. Let the scavengers have it.

Walking through the woods of the Autumn Court felt like striding inside a jewel box.

Even with all that potentially hunted us now, the colors were so vivid it was an effort not to gawk and gape.

By midmorning, the rime had melted away under the buttery sun to reveal what was suitable for eating. My stomach growled with every step, and Lucien's red hair gleamed like the leaves above us as he scanned the woods for anything to fill our bellies.

His woods, by blood and law. He was a son of this forest, and here . . . He looked crafted from it. For it. Even that gold eye.

Lucien eventually stopped at a jade stream wending through a granite-flanked gully, a spot he claimed had once been rich with trout.

I was in the process of constructing a rudimentary fishing pole when he waded into the stream, boots off and pants rolled to his knees, and caught one with his bare hands. He'd tied his hair up, a few strands of it falling into his face as he swooped down again and threw a second trout onto the sandy bank where I'd been trying to find a substitute for fishing twine.

We remained silent as the fish eventually stopped flapping, their sides catching and gleaming with all the colors so bright above us.

Lucien picked them up by their tails, as if he'd done it a thousand times. He might very well have, right here in this stream. "I'll clean them while you start the fire." In the daylight, the glow of the flames wouldn't be noticed. Though the smoke . . . a necessary risk.

We worked and ate in silence, the crackling fire offering the only conversation.

⊹

We hiked north for five days, hardly exchanging a word.

Beron's seat was so vast it took us three days to enter, pass through, and clear it. Lucien led us through the outskirts, tense at every call and rustle.

The Forest House was a sprawling complex, Lucien informed me during the few times we risked or bothered to speak to each other. It had been built in and around the trees and rocks, and only its uppermost levels were visible above the ground. Below, it tunneled a few levels into the stone. But its sprawl generated its size. You might walk from one end of the House to the other and it would take you half the morning. There were layers and circles of sentries ringing it: in the trees, on the ground, atop the moss-coated shingles and stones of the House itself.

No enemies approached Beron's home without his knowledge. None left without his permission.

I knew we'd passed beyond Lucien's known map of their patrol routes and stations when his shoulders sagged.

Mine were slumped already.

I had barely slept, only letting myself do so when Lucien's breathing slid into a different, deeper rhythm. I knew I couldn't keep it up for long, but without the ability to shield, to sense any danger . . .

I wondered if Rhys was looking for me. If he'd felt the silence.

I should have gotten a message out. Told him I was going and how to find me.

The faebane—that was why the bond had sounded so muffled. Perhaps I should have killed Ianthe outright.

But what was done was done.

I was rubbing at my aching eyes, taking a moment's rest beneath our new bounty: an apple tree, laden with fat, succulent fruit.

I'd filled my bag with what I could fit inside. Two cores already lay discarded beside me, the sweet rotting scent as lulling as the droning of the bees gorging themselves on fallen apples. A third apple was already primed and poised for eating atop my outstretched legs.

After what the Hybern royals had done, I should have sworn off apples forever, but hunger had always blurred lines for me.

Lucien, sitting a few feet away, chucked his fourth apple into the bushes as I bit into mine. "The farmlands and fields are near," he announced. "We'll have to stay out of sight. My father doesn't pay well for his crops, and the land-workers will earn any extra coin they can."

"Even selling out the location of one of the High Lord's sons?"

"*Especially* that way."

"They didn't like you?"

His jaw tightened. "As the youngest of seven sons, I wasn't particularly needed or wanted. Perhaps it was a good thing. I was able to study for longer than my father allowed my brothers before shoving them out the door to rule over some territory within our lands, and I could train for as long as I liked, since no one believed I'd be dumb enough to kill my way up the long list of heirs. And when I grew bored with studying and fighting . . . I learned what I could of the land from its people. Learned about the people, too."

He eased to his feet with a groan, his unbound hair glimmering as the midday sun overhead set the blood and wine hues aglow.

"I'd say that sounds more High-Lord-like than the life of an idle, unwanted son."

A long, steely look. "Did you think it was mere hatred that prompted my brothers to do their best to break and kill me?"

Despite myself, a shudder rippled down my spine. I finished off the apple and uncoiled to my feet, plucking another off a low-hanging branch. "Would you want it—your father's crown?"

"No one's ever asked me that," Lucien mused as we moved on, dodging fallen, rotting apples. The air was sticky-sweet. "The bloodshed that would be required to earn that crown wouldn't be worth it. Neither would its festering court. I'd gain a crown—only to rule over a crafty, two-faced people."

"Lord of Foxes," I said, snorting as I remembered that mask he'd once worn. "But you never answered my question—about why the people here would sell you out."

The air ahead lightened, and a golden field of barley undulated toward a distant tree line.

"After Jesminda, they would."

Jesminda. He'd never spoken her name.

Lucien slid between the swaying, bobbing stalks. "She was one of them." The words were barely audible over the sighing barley. "And when I didn't protect her . . . It was a betrayal of their trust, too. I ran to some of their houses while fleeing my brothers. They turned me out for what I let happen to her."

Waves of gold and ivory rolled around us, the sky a crisp, unmarred blue.

"I can't blame them for it," he said.

᛭

We cleared the fertile valley by the late afternoon. When Lucien offered to stop for the night, I insisted we keep going—right into the steep foothills that leaped into gray, snowcapped mountains that marked the start of the shared range with the Winter Court. If we could get over the border in a day or two, perhaps my powers would have returned enough to contact Rhys—or winnow the rest of the way home.

The hike wasn't an easy one.

Great, craggy boulders made up the ascent, flecked with moss and long, white grasses that hissed like adders. The wind ripped at our hair, the temperature dropping the higher we climbed.

Tonight . . . We might have to risk a fire tonight. Just to stay alive.

Lucien was panting as we scaled a hulking boulder, the valley sprawling away behind, the wood a tangled river of color beyond it. There had to be a pass *into* the range at some point—out of sight.

"How are you not winded," he panted, hauling himself onto the flat top.

I shoved back the hair that had torn free of my braid to whip my face. "I trained."

"I gathered that much after you took on Dagdan and walked away from it."

"I had the element of surprise on my side."

"No," Lucien said quietly as I reached for a foothold in the next boulder. "That was all you." My nails barked as I dug my fingers into the rock and heaved myself up. Lucien added, "You had my back—with them, with Ianthe. Thank you."

The words hit something low in my gut, and I was glad for the wind that kept roaring around us, if only to hide the burning in my eyes.

✚

I slept—finally.

With the crackling fire in our latest cave, the heat and the relative remoteness were enough to finally drag me under.

And in my dreams, I think I swam through Lucien's mind, as if some small ember of my power was at last returning.

I dreamed of our cozy fire, and the craggy walls, the entire space barely big enough to fit us and the fire. I dreamed of the howling, dark night beyond, of all the sounds that Lucien so carefully sorted through while he kept watch.

His attention slid to me at one point and lingered.

I had never known how young, how human I looked when I slept. My braid was a rope over my shoulder, my mouth slightly parted, my face haggard with days of little rest and food.

I dreamed that he removed his cloak and added it over my blanket.

Then I ebbed away, flowing out of his head as my dreams shifted and sailed elsewhere. I let a sea of stars rock me into sleep.

✚

A hand gripped my face so hard the groaning of my bones jolted me awake.

"Look who we found," a cold male voice drawled.

I knew that face—the red hair, the pale skin, the smirk. Knew the faces of the other two males in the cave, a snarling Lucien pinned beneath them.

His brothers.

CHAPTER
12

"Father," the one now holding a knife to my throat said to Lucien, "is rather put out that you didn't stop by to say hello."

"We're on an errand and can't be delayed," Lucien answered smoothly, mastering himself.

That knife pressed a fraction harder into my skin as he let out a humorless laugh. "Right. Rumor has it you two have run off together, cuckolding Tamlin." His grin widened. "I didn't think you had it in you, little brother."

"He had it *in* her, it seems," one of the others sniggered.

I slid my gaze to the male above me. "You will release us."

"Our esteemed father wishes to see you," he said with a snake's smile. The knife didn't waver. "So you will come with us to his home."

"Eris," Lucien warned.

The name clanged through me. Above me, mere inches away . . . Mor's former betrothed. The male who had abandoned her when he found her brutalized body on the border. The High Lord's heir.

I could have sworn phantom talons bit into my palms.

A day or two more, and I might have been able to slash them across his throat.

But I didn't have that time. I only had now. I had to make it count.

Eris merely said to me, cold and bored, "Get up."

I felt it then—stirring awake as if some stick had poked it. As if being here, in this territory, amongst its blooded royals, had somehow sparked it to life, boiling past that poison. Turning that poison to steam.

With his knife still angled against my neck, I let Eris haul me to my feet, the other two dragging Lucien before he could stand on his own.

Make it count. Use my surroundings.

I caught Lucien's eye.

And he saw the sweat beading on my temple, my upper lip, as my blood heated.

A slight bob of his chin was his only sign of understanding.

Eris would bring us to Beron, and the High Lord would either kill us for sport, sell us to the highest bidder, or hold us indefinitely. And after what they had done to Lucien's lover, what they'd done to Mor . . .

"After you," Eris said smoothly, lowering that knife at last. He shoved me a step.

I'd been waiting. Balance, Cassian had taught me, was crucial to winning a fight.

And as Eris's shove caused him to get on uneven footing, I turned my propelled step on him.

Twisting, so fast he didn't see me get into his open guard, I drove my elbow into his nose.

Eris stumbled back.

Flame slammed into the other two, and Lucien hurtled out of the way as they shouted and fell deeper into the cave.

I unleashed every drop of the flame in me, a wall of it between us and them. Sealing his brothers inside the cave.

"*Run*," I gasped out, but Lucien was already at my side, a steadying hand under my arm as I burned that flame hotter and hotter. It wouldn't keep them contained for long, and I could indeed feel someone's power rising to challenge mine.

But there was another force to wield.

Lucien understood the same moment I did.

Sweat simmered on Lucien's brow as a pulse of flame-licked power slammed into the stones just above us. Dust and debris rained down.

I threw any trickle of magic into Lucien's next blow.

His next.

As Eris's livid face emerged from my net of flame, glowing like a new-forged god of wrath, Lucien and I brought down the cave ceiling.

Fire burst through the small cracks like a thousand flaming serpents' tongues—but the cave-in did not so much as tremble.

"Hurry," Lucien panted, and I didn't waste breath agreeing as we staggered into the night.

Our packs, our weapons, our food . . . all inside that cave.

I had two daggers on me, Lucien one. I'd been wearing my cloak, but . . . he'd indeed given me his. He shivered against the cold as we dragged and clawed our way up the mountain slope, and did not dare stop.

⊹

Had I still remained human, I would have been dead.

The cold was bone-deep, the screaming wind lashing us like burning whips. My teeth clacked against each other, my fingers so stiff I could scarcely grapple onto the icy granite with each mile we staggered through the mountains. Perhaps both of us were spared from an icy death by the kernel of flame that had just barely kindled inside our veins.

We didn't pause once, an unspoken fear that if we did, the cold would leech any lingering warmth and we'd never again move. Or Lucien's brothers would gain ground.

I tried, over and over, to shout down the bond to Rhys. To winnow. To grow wings and attempt to fly us out of the mountain pass we trudged through, the snow waist-deep and so densely packed in places we had to crawl over it, our skin scraped raw from the ice.

But the faebane's stifling grip still held the majority of my power in check.

We had to be close to the Winter Court border, I told myself as we squinted against a blast of icy wind through the other end of the narrow mountain pass. Close—and once we were over it, Eris and the others wouldn't dare set foot into another court's territory.

My muscles screamed with every step, my boots soaked through with snow, my feet perilously numb. I'd spent enough human winters in the forest to know the dangers of exposure—the threat of cold and wet.

Lucien, a step behind me, panted hard as the walls of rock and snow parted to reveal a bitter, star-flecked night—and more mountains beyond. I almost whimpered.

"We've got to keep going," he said, snow crusting the stray strands of his hair, and I wondered if the sound had indeed left me.

Ice tickled my frozen nostrils. "We can't last long—we need to get warm and rest."

"My brothers—"

"We will die if we continue." Or lose fingers and toes at the best. I pointed to the mountain slope ahead, a hazardous plunge down. "We can't risk that at night. We need to find a cave and try to make a fire."

"With *what?*" he snapped. "Do you see any wood?"

I only continued on. Arguing just wasted energy—and time.

And I didn't have an answer, anyway.

I wondered if we'd make it through the night.

⊹

We found a cave. Deep and shielded from wind or sight. Lucien and I carefully covered our tracks, making sure the wind blew in our favor, veiling our scents.

That was where our luck ran out. No wood to be found; no fire in either of our veins.

So we used our only option: body heat. Huddled in the farthest reaches of the cave, we sat thigh to thigh and arm to arm beneath my cloak, shuddering with cold and dripping wet.

I could scarcely hear the hollow scream of the wind over my chattering teeth. And his.

Find me, find me, find me, I tried shouting down that bond. But my mate's wry voice didn't answer.

There was only the roaring void.

"Tell me about her—about Elain," Lucien said quietly. As if the death that squatted in the dark beside us had drawn his thoughts to his own mate as well.

I debated not saying anything, shaking too hard to dredge up speech, but . . . "She loves her garden. Always loved growing things. Even when we were destitute, she managed to tend a little garden in the warmer months. And when—when our fortune returned, she took to tending and planting the most beautiful gardens you've ever seen. Even in Prythian. It drove the servants mad, because they were supposed to do the work and ladies were only meant to clip a rose here and there, but Elain would put on a hat and gloves and kneel in the dirt, weeding. She acted like a purebred lady in every regard but that."

Lucien was silent for a long moment. "Acted," he murmured. "You talk about her as if she's dead."

"I don't know what changes the Cauldron wrought on her. I don't think going home is an option. No matter how she might yearn to."

"Surely Prythian is a better alternative, war or no."

I steeled myself before saying, "She is engaged, Lucien."

I felt every inch of him go stiff beside me. "To whom."

Flat, cold words. With the threat of violence simmering beneath.

"To a human lord's son. The lord hates faeries—has dedicated his life and wealth to hunting them. Us. I was told that though it's a love match, her betrothed's father was keen to have access to her considerable dowry to continue his crusade against faerie-kind."

"Elain loves this lord's son." Not quite a question.

"She says she does. Nesta—Nesta thought the father and his obsession with killing faeries was bad enough to raise some alarms. She never voiced the concern to Elain. Neither did I."

"My mate is engaged to a human male." He spoke more to himself than to me.

"I'm sorry if—"

"I want to see her. Just once. Just—to know."

"To know what?"

He hitched my damp cloak higher around us. "If she is worth fighting for."

I couldn't bring myself to say she was, to give him that sort of hope when Elain might very well do everything in her power to hold to her engagement. Even if immortality had already rendered it impossible.

Lucien leaned his head back against the rock wall behind us. "And then I'll ask your mate how he survived it—knowing you were engaged to someone else. Sharing another male's bed."

I tucked my freezing hands under my arms, gazing toward the gloom ahead.

"Tell me when you knew," he demanded, his knee pressing into mine. "That Rhysand was your mate. Tell me when you stopped loving Tamlin and started loving *him* instead."

I chose not to answer.

"Was it going on before you even left?"

I whipped my head to him, even if I could barely make out his features in the dark. "I never touched Rhysand like that until months later."

"You kissed Under the Mountain."

"I had as little choice in that as I did in the dancing."

"And yet this is the male you now love."

He didn't know—he had no inkling of the personal history, the secrets, that had opened my heart to the High Lord of the Night Court. They were not my stories to tell.

"One would think, Lucien, that you'd be glad I fell in love with my mate, given that you're in the same situation Rhys was in six months ago."

"You *left* us."

Us. Not Tamlin. *Us.* The words echoed into the dark, toward the howling wind and lashing snow beyond the bend.

"I told you that day in the woods: you abandoned me long before I ever physically left." I shivered again, hating every point of contact, that I so desperately needed his warmth. "You fit into the Spring Court as little as I did, Lucien. You enjoyed its pleasures and diversions. But don't pretend you weren't made for something *more* than that."

His metal eye whirred. "And where, exactly, do you believe I will fit in? The Night Court?"

I didn't answer. I didn't have one, honestly. As High Lady, I could likely offer him a position, if we survived long enough to make it home. I'd do it mostly to keep Elain from ever going to the Spring Court, but I had little doubt Lucien would be able to hold his own against my friends. And some small, horrible part of me enjoyed the thought of taking one more thing away from Tamlin, something vital, something essential.

"We should leave at dawn," was my only reply.

⊹

We lasted the night.

Every part of me was stiff and aching when we began our careful trek down the mountain. Not a whisper or trace of Lucien's brothers— or any sort of life.

I didn't care, not when we at last passed over the border and into Winter Court lands.

Beyond the mountain, a great ice-plain sparkled into the distance. It would take days to cross, but it didn't matter: I'd awoken with enough power in my veins to warm us with a small fire. Slowly—so slowly, the effects of the faebane ebbed.

I was willing to wager that we'd be halfway across the ice by the time we could winnow out of here. If our luck held and no one else found us.

I ran through every lesson Rhys had taught me about the Winter Court and its High Lord, Kallias.

Towering, exquisite palaces, full of roaring hearths and bedecked in evergreens. Carved sleighs were the court's preferred method of transportation, hauled by velvet-antlered reindeer whose splayed hooves were ideal for the ice and snow. Their forces were well trained, but they often relied on the great, white bears that stalked the realm for any unwanted visitors.

I prayed none of them waited on the ice, their coats perfectly blended into the terrain.

The Night Court's relationship with Winter was fine enough, still tenuous, as all our bonds were, after Amarantha. After she'd butchered so many of them—including, I remembered with no small surge of nausea, dozens of Winter Court children.

I couldn't imagine it—the loss, the rage and grief. I'd never had the nerve to ask Rhys, in those months of training, who the children had belonged to. What the consequences had been. If it was considered the worst of Amarantha's crimes, or just one of countless others.

But despite any tentative bonds, Winter was one of the Seasonal Courts. It might side with Tamlin, with Tarquin. Our best allies remained the Solar Courts: Dawn and Day. But they lay far to the north—above the demarcation line between the Solar and Seasonal Courts. That slice of sacred, unclaimed land that held Under the Mountain. And the Weaver's cottage.

We'd be gone before we ever had to set foot in that lethal, ancient forest.

It was another day and night before we cleared the mountains entirely and set foot on the thick ice. Nothing grew, and I could only tell when we were on solid land by the dense snow packed beneath. Otherwise, too frequently, the ice was clear as glass—revealing dark, depthless lakes beneath.

At least we didn't encounter any of the white bears. But the real threat, we both quickly realized, was the utter lack of shelter: out on the ice, there was none to be found against the wind and cold. And if we lit a fire with our feeble magic, anyone nearby would spot it. No matter the practicality of lighting a fire atop a frozen lake.

The sun was just slipping above the horizon, staining the plain with gold, the shadows still a bruised blue, when Lucien said, "Tonight, we'll melt some of the ice pack enough to soften it—and build a shelter."

I considered. We were barely a hundred feet onto what seemed to be an endless lake. It was impossible to tell where it ended. "You think we'll be out on the ice for that long?"

Lucien frowned toward the dawn-stained horizon. "Likely, but who knows how far it extends?" Indeed, the snowdrifts hid much of the ice beneath.

"Perhaps there's some other way around . . . ," I mused, glancing back toward our abandoned little camp.

We looked at the same time. And both beheld the three figures now standing at the lake edge. Smiling.

Eris lifted a hand wreathed in flame.

Flame—to melt the ice on which we stood.

CHAPTER
13

"Run," Lucien breathed.

I didn't dare take my eyes off his brothers. Not as Eris lowered that hand to the frozen edge of the lake. "Run where, exactly?"

Flesh met ice and steam rippled. The ice went opaque, thawing in a line that shot for us—

We ran. The slick ice made for a treacherous sprint, my ankles roaring with the effort of keeping me upright.

Ahead, the lake stretched on forever. And with the sun barely awake, the dangers would be even harder to spot—

"Faster," Lucien ordered. "Don't look!" he barked as I began to turn my head to see if they'd followed. He lashed out a hand to grip my elbow, steadying me before I could even register that I'd stumbled.

Where would we go where would we go where would we go

Water splashed beneath my boots—thawed ice. Eris had to either be expending all his power to get through millennia of ice, or was just doing it slowly to torture us—

"Zag," Lucien panted. "We need to—"

He shoved me aside, and I staggered, arms wheeling.

Just as an arrow ricocheted off the ice where I'd been standing.

"*Faster*," Lucien snapped, and I didn't hesitate.

I hurtled into a flat-out sprint, Lucien and I weaving in and out of each other's paths as those arrows continued firing. Ice sprayed where they landed, and no matter how fast we ran, the ground beneath us melted and melted—

Ice. I had ice in my veins, and now that we were over the border of the Winter Court—

I didn't care if they saw it—my power. Kallias's power. Not when the alternatives were far worse.

I threw out a hand before us as a melting splotch began to spread, ice groaning.

A spray of ice shot from my palm, freezing the lake once more.

With each pump of my arms as I ran, I fired that ice from my palms, solidifying what Eris sought to melt ahead of us. Maybe—just maybe we could clear the lake, and if they were stupid enough to be atop it when we did . . . If I could form ice, I could certainly un-form it.

I crossed paths with Lucien again, meeting his wide eyes as we did, and opened my mouth to tell him my plan, when Eris appeared.

Not behind. Ahead.

But it was the other brother at his side, arrow aimed and already flying for me, who drew the shout from my throat.

I lunged to the side, rolling.

Not fast enough.

The arrow's edge sliced the shell of my ear, my cheek, leaving a stinging wake. Lucien shouted, but another arrow was flying.

It went clean through my right forearm this time.

Ice sliced into my face, my hands, as I went down, knees barking, arm shrieking in agony at the impact—

Behind, steps thudded on ice as the third brother closed in.

I bit my lip hard enough to draw blood as I ripped away the cloth of my jacket and shirt from my forearm, snapped the arrow in two, and tore the pieces from my flesh. My roar shattered and bounced across the ice.

Eris had taken one step toward me, smiling like a wolf, when I was up again, my last two Illyrian knives in my palms, my right arm screaming at the movement—

Around me, the ice began to melt.

"This can end with you going under, begging me to get you out once that ice instantly refreezes," Eris drawled. Behind him, cut off by his brothers, Lucien had drawn his own knife and now sized up the other two. "Or this can end with you agreeing to take my hand. But either way, you will be coming with me."

Already, the flesh in my arm was knitting together. Healing—from Dawn's powers reawakening in my veins—

And if that was working—

I didn't give Eris time to read my move.

I sucked in a sharp breath.

White, blinding light erupted from me. Eris swore, and I ran.

Not toward him, not when I was still too injured to wield my knives. But away—toward that distant shore. Half-blinded myself, I stumbled and staggered until I was clear of the treacherous, melting splotches, then sprinted.

I made it all of twenty feet before Eris winnowed in front of me and struck.

A backhanded blow to the face, so hard my teeth went through my lip.

He struck again before I could even fall, a punch to my gut that ripped the air from my lungs. Beyond me, Lucien had unleashed himself upon his two brothers. Metal and fire blasted and collided, ice spraying.

I'd no sooner hit the ice than Eris grabbed me by the hair, right at the roots, the grip so brutal tears stung my eyes. But he dragged me back toward that shore, back across the ice—

I fought against the blow to my gut, fought to get a wisp of air down my throat, into my lungs. My boots scraped against the ice as I feebly kicked, yet Eris held firm—

I think Lucien shouted my name.

I opened my mouth, but a gag of fire shoved its way between my lips. It didn't burn, but was hot enough to tell me it would if Eris willed it. Equal bands of flame wrapped around my wrists, my ankles. My throat.

I couldn't remember—couldn't remember what to do, how to move, how to *stop* this—

Closer and closer to the shore, to the awaiting party of sentries that winnowed in out of nowhere. *No, no, no*—

A shadow slammed into the earth before us, cracking the ice toward every horizon.

Not a shadow.

An Illyrian warrior.

Seven red Siphons glinted over his scaled black armor as Cassian tucked in his wings and snarled at Eris with five centuries' worth of rage.

Not dead. Not hurt. Whole.

His wings repaired and strong.

I loosed a shuddering sob over the burning gag. Cassian's Siphons flickered in response, as if the sight of me, at Eris's hand—

Another impact struck the ice behind us. Shadows skittered in its wake.

Azriel.

I began crying in earnest, some leash I'd kept on myself snapping free as my friends landed. As I saw that Azriel, too, was alive, was healed. As Cassian drew twin Illyrian blades, the sight of them like home, and said to Eris with lethal calm, "I suggest you drop my lady."

Eris's grip on my hair only tightened, wringing a whimper from me.

The wrath that twisted Cassian's face was world-ending.

But his hazel eyes slid to mine. A silent command.

He had spent months training me. Not just to attack, but to defend. Had taught me, over and over, how to get free of a captor's grasp. How to manage not only my body, but my mind.

As if he'd known that it was a very real possibility that this scenario would one day happen.

Eris had bound my limbs, but—I could still move them. Still use parts of my magic.

And getting him off balance long enough to let go, to let Cassian jump between us and take on the High Lord's son . . .

Towering over me, Eris didn't so much as glance down as I twisted, spinning on the ice, and slammed my bound legs up between his.

He lurched, bending over with a grunt.

Right into the fisted, bound hands I drove into his nose. Bone crunched, and his hand sprang free of my hair.

I rolled, scrambling away. Cassian was already there.

Eris hardly had time to draw his sword as Cassian brought his own down upon him.

Steel against steel rang out across the ice. Sentries on the shore unleashed arrows of wood and magic—only to bounce against a shield of blue.

Azriel. Across the ice, he and Lucien were engaging the other two brothers. That any of Lucien's siblings held out against the Illyrians was a testament to their own training, but—

I focused the ice in my veins on the gag in my mouth, the binds around my wrists and ankles. Ice to smother fire, to sing it to sleep . . .

Cassian and Eris clashed, danced back, clashed again.

Ropes of fire snapped free, dissolving with a hiss of steam.

I was on my feet again, reaching for a weapon I did not have. My daggers had been lost forty feet away.

Cassian got past Eris's guard with brutal efficiency. And Eris screamed as the Illyrian blade punched through his gut.

Blood, red as rubies, stained the ice and snow.

For a heartbeat, I saw how it would play out: three of Beron's sons dead at our hands. A temporary satisfaction for me, five centuries of satisfaction for Cassian, Azriel, and Mor, but if Beron still debated what side to support in this war . . .

I had other weapons to use.

"Stop," I said.

The word was a soft, cold command.

And Azriel and Cassian obeyed.

Lucien's other two brothers were back-to-back, bloody and gaping. Lucien himself was panting, sword still raised, as Azriel flicked the blood off his own blade and stalked toward me.

I met the hazel eyes of the shadowsinger. The cool face that hid such pain—and kindness. He had come. Cassian had come.

The Illyrians fell into place beside me. Eris, a hand pressed to his gut, was breathing wetly, glaring at us.

Glaring—then considering. Watching the three of us as I said to Eris, to his other two brothers, to the sentries on the shore, "You all deserve to die for this. And for much, much more. But I am going to spare your miserable lives."

Even with a wound through his gut, Eris's lip curled.

Cassian snarled his warning.

I only removed the glamour I'd kept on myself these weeks. With the sleeve of my jacket and shirt gone, there was nothing but smooth skin where that wound had been. Smooth skin that now became adorned with swirls and whorls of ink. The markings of my new title—and my mating bond.

Lucien's face drained of color as he strode for us, stopping a healthy distance from Azriel's side.

"I am High Lady of the Night Court," I said quietly to them all.

Even Eris stopped sneering. His amber eyes widened, something like fear now creeping into them.

"There's no such thing as a High Lady," one of Lucien's brothers spat.

A faint smile played on my mouth. "There is now."

And it was time for the world to know it.

I caught Cassian's gaze, finding pride glimmering there—and relief.

"Take me home," I ordered him, my chin high and unwavering.

Then to Azriel, "Take us both home." I said to the Autumn Court's scions, "We'll see you on the battlefield."

Let them decide whether it was better to be fighting beside us or against us.

I turned to Cassian, who opened his arms and tucked me in tight before launching us skyward in a blast of wings and power. Beside us, Azriel and Lucien did the same.

When Eris and the others were nothing but specks of black on white below, when we were sailing high and fast, Cassian observed, "I don't know who looks more uncomfortable: Az or Lucien Vanserra."

I chuckled, glancing over my shoulder to where the shadowsinger carried my friend, both of them making a point not to speak, look, or talk. "Vanserra?"

"You never knew his family name?"

I met those laughing, fierce hazel eyes.

Cassian's smile softened. "Hello, Feyre."

My throat tightened to the point of pain, and I threw my arms around his neck, embracing him tightly.

"I missed you, too," Cassian murmured, squeezing me.

⁜

We flew until we reached the border of the sacred, eighth territory. And when Cassian set us down in a snowy field before the ancient wood, I took one look at the blond female in Illyrian leathers pacing between the gnarled trees and launched into a sprint.

Mor held me as tightly as I gripped her.

"Where is he?" I asked, refusing to let go, to lift my head from her shoulder.

"He—it's a long story. Far away, but racing home. Right now." Mor pulled back enough to scan my face. Her mouth tightened at the lingering injuries, and she gently scraped away flecks of dried blood caked on my ear. "He picked up on you—the bond—minutes ago. The three of us were closest. I winnowed in Cassian, but with Eris and the others there . . ." Guilt dimmed her eyes. "Relations with the Winter Court are strained—we thought if I was out here on the border, it might keep Kallias's forces from looking south. At least long enough to get you." And to avoid an interaction with Eris that Mor was perhaps not ready for.

I shook my head at the shame still shadowing her usually bright features. "I understand." I embraced her again. "I understand."

Mor's answering squeeze was rib-crushing.

Azriel and Lucien landed, plumes of snow spraying in the former's wake. Mor and I released each other at last, my friend's face going grave as she sized up Lucien. Snow and blood and dirt coated him—coated us both.

Cassian explained to Mor, "He fought against Eris and the other two."

Mor's throat bobbed, noting the blood staining Cassian's hands— realizing it wasn't his own. Scenting it, no doubt, as she blurted, "Eris. Did you—"

"He remains alive," Azriel answered, shadows curling around the clawed tips of his wings, so stark against the snow beneath our boots. "So do the others."

Lucien was glancing between all of them, wary and quiet. What he knew of Mor's history with his eldest brother . . . I'd never asked. Never wanted to.

Mor tossed her mass of golden waves over a shoulder. "Then let's go home."

"Which one?" I asked carefully.

Mor swept her attention over Lucien once more. I almost pitied Lucien for the weight in her gaze, the utter judgment. The stare of the Morrigan—whose gift was pure truth.

Whatever she beheld in Lucien was enough for her to say, "The town house. You have someone waiting there for you."

CHAPTER
14

I had not let myself imagine it: the moment I'd again stand in the wood-paneled foyer of the town house. When I'd hear the song of the gulls soaring high above Velaris, smell the brine of the Sidra River that wended through the heart of the city, feel the warmth of the sunshine streaming through the windows upon my back.

Mor had winnowed us all, and now stood behind me, panting softly, as we watched Lucien survey our surroundings.

His metal eye whirred, while the other warily scanned the rooms flanking the foyer: the dining room and sitting room overlooking the little front yard and street; then the stairs to the second level; then the hallway beside it that led to the kitchen and courtyard garden.

Then finally to the shut front door. To the city waiting beyond.

Cassian took up a place against the banister, crossing his arms with an arrogance I knew meant trouble. Azriel remained beside me, shadows wreathing his knuckles. As if battling High Lords' sons was how they usually spent their days.

I wondered if Lucien knew that his first words here would either damn or save him. I wondered what my role in it would be.

No—it was my call.

High Lady. I—outranked them, my friends. It was my call to make whether Lucien was allowed to keep his freedom.

But their watchful silence was indication enough: let him decide his own fate.

At last, Lucien looked at me. At us.

He said, "There are children laughing in the streets."

I blinked. He said it with such . . . quiet surprise. As if he hadn't heard the sound in a long, long time.

I opened my mouth to reply, but someone else spoke for me.

"That they do so at all after Hybern's attack is testament to how hard the people of Velaris have worked to rebuild."

I whirled, finding Amren emerging from wherever she'd been sitting in the other room, the plush furniture hiding her small body.

She appeared exactly as she had the last time I'd seen her: standing in this very foyer, warning us to be careful in Hybern. Her chin-length, jet-black hair gleamed in the sunlight, her silver, unearthly eyes unusually bright as they met mine.

The delicate female bowed her head. As much of a gesture of obedience as a fifteen-thousand-year-old creature would make to a newly minted High Lady. And friend. "I see you brought home a new pet," she said, nose crinkling with distaste.

Something like fear had entered Lucien's eye, as if he, too, beheld the monster that lurked beneath that beautiful face.

Indeed, it seemed he had heard of her already. Before I could introduce him, Lucien bowed at the waist. Deeply. Cassian let out an amused grunt, and I shot him a warning glare.

Amren smiled slightly. "Already trained, I see."

Lucien slowly straightened, as if he were standing before the open maw of some great plains-cat he did not wish to startle with sudden movements.

"Amren, this is Lucien . . . Vanserra."

Lucien stiffened. "I don't use my family's name." He clarified to Amren with another incline of his head, "Lucien will do."

I suspected he'd ceased using that name the moment his lover's heart had stopped beating.

Amren was studying that metal eye. "Clever work," she said, then surveyed me. "Looks like someone clawed you up, girl."

The wound in my arm, at least, had healed, though a nasty red mark remained. I assumed my face wasn't much better. Before I could answer her, Lucien asked, "What is this place?"

We all looked at him. "Home," I said. "This is—my home."

I could see the details now sinking in. The lack of darkness. The lack of screaming. The scent of the sea and citrus, not blood and decay. The laughter of children that indeed continued.

The greatest secret in Prythian's history.

"This is Velaris," I explained. "The City of Starlight."

His throat bobbed. "And you are High Lady of the Night Court."

"Indeed she is."

My blood stopped at the voice that drawled from behind me.

At the scent that hit me, awoke me. My friends began smiling.

I turned.

Rhysand leaned against the archway into the sitting room, arms crossed, wings nowhere to be seen, dressed in his usual immaculate black jacket and pants.

And as those violet eyes met mine, as that familiar half smile faded . . .

My face crumpled. A small, broken noise cracked from me.

Rhys was instantly moving, but my legs had already given out. The foyer carpet cushioned the impact as I sank to my knees.

I covered my face with my hands while the past month crashed into me.

Rhys knelt before me, knee to knee.

Gently, he pulled my hands away from my face. Gently, he took my cheeks in his hands and brushed away my tears.

I didn't care that we had an audience as I lifted my head and beheld the joy and concern and love shining in those remarkable eyes.

Neither did Rhys as he murmured, "My love," and kissed me.

I'd no sooner slid my hands into his hair than he scooped me into his arms and stood in one smooth movement. I pulled my mouth from his, glancing toward a pallid Lucien, but Rhysand said to our companions without so much as looking at them, "Go find somewhere else to be for a while."

He didn't wait to see if they obeyed.

Rhys winnowed us up the stairs and launched into a steady, swift walk down the hallway. I peered down at the foyer in time to spy Mor grabbing Lucien's arm and nodding to the others before they all vanished.

"Do you want to go over what happened at the Spring Court?" I asked, voice raw, as I studied my mate's face.

No amusement, nothing but that predatory intensity, focused on my every breath. "There are other things I'd rather do first."

He carried me into our bedroom—once *his* room, now full of our belongings. It was exactly as I'd last seen it: the enormous bed that he now strode for, the two armoires, the desk by the window that overlooked the courtyard garden now bursting with purple and pink and blue amid the lush greens.

I braced myself to be sprawled on the bed, but Rhys paused halfway across the room, the door snicking shut on a star-kissed wind.

Slowly, he set me on the plush carpet, blatantly sliding me down his body as he did so. As if he was as powerless to resist touching me, as reluctant to let go as I was with him.

And every place where our bodies met, all of him so warm and solid and *real* . . . I savored it, my throat tight as I placed a hand on his sculpted chest, the thunderous heartbeat beneath his black jacket echoing into my palm. The only sign of whatever torrent coursed through him as he skimmed his hands up my arms in a lingering caress and gripped my shoulders.

His thumbs stroked a gentle rhythm over my filthy clothes as he scanned my face.

Beautiful. He was even more beautiful than I had remembered, dreamed of during those weeks at the Spring Court.

For a long moment, we only breathed in each other's air. For a long moment, all I could do was take the scent of him deep into my lungs, letting it settle inside me. My fingers tightened on his jacket.

Mate. My mate.

As if he'd heard it down the bond, Rhys finally murmured, "When the bond went dark, I thought . . ." Fear—genuine terror shadowed his eyes, even as his thumbs continued stroking my shoulders, gentle and steady. "By the time I got to the Spring Court, you'd vanished. Tamlin was raging through that forest, hunting for you. But you hid your scent. And even I couldn't—couldn't find you—"

The snag in his words was a knife to my gut. "We went to the Autumn Court through one of the doors," I said, setting my other hand on his arm. The corded muscles beneath shifted at my touch. "You couldn't find me because two Hybern commanders drugged my food and drink with faebane—enough to extinguish my powers. I—I still don't have full use."

Cold rage now flickered across that beautiful face as his thumbs halted on my shoulders. "You killed them."

Not entirely a question, but I nodded.

"Good."

I swallowed. "Has Hybern sacked the Spring Court?"

"Not yet. Whatever you did . . . it worked. Tamlin's sentries abandoned him. Over half his people refused to appear for the Tithe two days ago. Some are leaving for other courts. Some are murmuring of rebellion. It seems you made yourself quite beloved. Holy, even." Amusement at last warmed his features. "They were rather upset when they believed he'd allowed Hybern to terrorize you into fleeing."

I traced the faint silver whorl of embroidery on the breast of his jacket, and I could have sworn he shuddered beneath the touch. "I suppose they'll learn soon enough I'm well cared for." Rhys's hands tightened on my shoulders in agreement, as if he were about to show me just how well cared for I was, but I angled my head. "What about Ianthe—and Jurian?"

Rhysand's powerful chest heaved beneath my hand as he blew out a breath. "Reports are murky on both. Jurian, it seems, has returned to the hand that feeds him. Ianthe . . ." Rhys lifted his brows. "I assume *her* hand is courtesy of you, and not the commanders."

"She fell," I said sweetly.

"Must have been some fall," he mused, a dark smile dancing on those lips as he drifted even closer, the heat of his body seeping into me while his hands migrated from my shoulders to brush lazy lines down my back. I bit my lip, focusing on his words and not the urge to arch into the touch, to bury my face in his chest and do some exploring of my own. "She's currently convalescing after her ordeal, apparently. Won't leave her temple."

It was my turn to murmur, "Good." Perhaps one of those pretty acolytes of hers would get sick of her sanctimonious bullshit and smother Ianthe in her sleep.

I braced my hands on his hips, fully ready to slide beneath his jacket, *needing* to touch bare skin, but Rhys straightened, pulling back. Still close enough that one of his hands remained on my waist, but the other—

He reached for my arm, gently examining the angry welt where my skin had been torn by an arrow. Darkness rumbled in the corner of the room. "Cassian let me into his mind just now—to show me what happened on the ice." He stroked a thumb over the hurt, the touch feather-light. "Eris was always a male of limited days. Now Lucien might find himself closer to inheriting his father's throne than he ever expected to be."

My spine locked. "Eris is precisely as horrible as you painted him to be."

Rhys's thumb glided over my forearm again, leaving gooseflesh in its wake. A promise—not of the retribution he was contemplating, but of what awaited us in this room. The bed a few feet away. Until he murmured, "You declared yourself High Lady."

"Was I not supposed to?"

He released my arm to brush his knuckles across my cheek. "I've wanted to roar it from the rooftops of Velaris from the moment the priestess anointed you. How typical of you to upend my grand plans."

A smile tugged on my lips. "It happened less than an hour ago. I'm sure you could go crow from the chimney right now and everyone would give you credit for breaking the news."

His fingers threaded through my hair, tilting my face up. That wicked smile grew, and my toes curled in their boots. "There's my darling Feyre."

His head dipped, his gaze fixated on my mouth, hunger lighting those violet eyes—

"Where are my sisters?" The thought clanged through me, jarring as a pealing bell.

Rhys paused, hand slipping from my hair as his smile faded. "At the House of Wind." He straightened, swallowing—as if it somehow checked him. "I can—take you to them." Every word seemed to be an effort.

But he would, I realized. He'd shove down his need for me and take me to them, if that was what I wanted. My choice. It had always been my choice with him.

I shook my head. I wouldn't see them—not yet. Not until *I* was steady enough to face them. "They're well, though?"

His hesitation told me enough. "They're safe."

Not really an answer, but I wasn't going to fool myself into thinking my sisters would be thriving. I leaned my brow against his chest. "Cassian and Azriel are healed," I murmured against his jacket, breathing in the scent of him over and over as a tremor shuddered through me. "You told me that—and yet I didn't . . . it didn't sink in. Until now."

Rhys ran a hand down my back, the other sliding to grip my hip.

"Azriel healed within a few days. Cassian's wings . . . it was complex. But he's been training every day to regain his strength. The healer had to rebuild most of his wings—but he'll be fine."

I swallowed down the tightness in my throat and wrapped my arms around his waist, pressing my face wholly against his chest. His hand tightened on my hip in answer, the other resting at my nape, holding me to him as I breathed, "Mor said you were far away—that was why you weren't there."

"I'm sorry I wasn't."

"No," I said, lifting my head to scan his eyes, the guilt dampening them. "I didn't mean it like that. I just . . ." I savored the feel of him beneath my palms. "Where were you?"

Rhys stilled, and I braced myself as he said casually, "I couldn't very well let you do *all* the work to undermine our enemies, could I?"

I didn't smile. "Where. Were. You."

"With Az only recently back on his feet, I took it upon myself to do some of his work."

I clenched my jaw. "Such as?"

He leaned down, nuzzling my throat. "Don't you want to comfort your mate, who has missed you terribly these weeks?"

I planted a hand on his face and pushed him back, scowling. "I want my mate to tell me where the hell he was. *Then* he can get his *comfort.*"

Rhys nipped at my fingers, teeth snapping playfully. "Cruel, beautiful female."

I watched him beneath lowered brows.

Rhys rolled his eyes, sighing. "I was on the continent. At the human queens' palace."

I choked. "You were *where?*"

"Technically, I was flying above it, but—"

"You went *alone?*"

He gaped at me. "Despite what our mistakes in Hybern might have suggested, I *am* capable of—"

"You went to the human world, to our enemies' compound, *alone?*"

"I'd rather it be me than any of the others."

That had been his problem from the start. Always him, always sacrificing—

"Why," I demanded. "Why risk it? Is something happening?"

Rhys peered toward the window, as if he could see all the way to the mortal lands. His mouth tightened. "It's the quiet on their side of the sea that bothers me. No whisper of armies gathered, no other human allies summoned. Since Hybern, we've heard nothing. So I thought to see for myself why that is." He flicked my nose, tugging me closer again. "I'd just neared the edge of their territory when I felt the bond awaken again. I knew the others were closer, so I sent them."

"You don't need to explain."

Rhys rested his chin atop my head. "I wanted to be there—to get you. Find you. Bring you home."

"You do certainly enjoy a dramatic entrance."

He chuckled, his breath warming my hair as I listened to the sound rumble through his body.

Of course he would have been working against Hybern while I was away. Had I expected them all to be sitting on their asses for over a month? And Rhys, constantly plotting, always a step ahead . . . He would have used this time to his advantage. I debated asking about it, but right now, breathing him in, feeling his warmth . . . Let it wait.

Rhys pressed a kiss to my hair. "You're home."

A shuddering, small sound came out of me as I nodded, squeezing him tighter. Home. Not just Velaris, but wherever he was, our family was.

Ebony claws stroked along the barrier in my mind—in affection and request.

I lowered my shields for him, just as his own dropped. His mind curled around mine, as surely as his body now held me.

"I missed you every moment," Rhys said, leaning down to kiss the corner of my mouth. "Your smile." His lips grazed over the shell of my ear and my back arched slightly. "Your laugh." He pressed a kiss to my neck, right beneath my ear, and I tilted my head to give him access, biting down the urge to beg him to take more, to take faster as he murmured, "Your scent."

My eyes fluttered closed, and his hands coasted around my hips to cup my rear, squeezing as he bent to kiss the center of my throat. "The sounds you make when I'm inside you."

His tongue flicked over the spot where he'd kissed, and one of those sounds indeed escaped me. Rhys kissed the hollow of my collarbone, and my core went utterly molten. "My brave, bold, brilliant mate."

He lifted his head, and it was an effort to open my eyes. To meet his stare as his hands roved in lazy lines down my back, over my rear, then up again. "I love you," he said. And if I hadn't already believed him, felt it in my very bones, the light in his face as he said the words . . .

Tears burned my eyes again, slipping free before I could control myself.

Rhys leaned in to lick them away. One after another. As he'd once done Under the Mountain.

"You have a choice," he murmured against my cheekbone. "Either I lick every inch of you clean . . ." His hand grazed the tip of my breast, circling lazily. As if we had days and days to do this. "Or you can get into the bath that should be ready by now."

I pulled away, lifting a brow. "Are you suggesting that I smell?"

Rhys smirked, and I could have sworn my core pounded in answer. "Never. But . . ." His eyes darkened, the desire and amusement fading as he took in my clothes. "There is blood on you. Yours, and others'. I thought I'd be a good mate and offer you a bath before I ravish you wholly."

I huffed a laugh and brushed back his hair, savoring the silken, sable strands between my fingers. "So considerate. Though I can't believe you kicked everyone out of the house so you could take me to bed."

"One of the many benefits to being High Lord."

"What a terrible abuse of power."

That half smile danced on his mouth. "Well?"

"As much as I'd like to see you attempt to lick off a week's worth of dirt, sweat, and blood . . ." His eyes gleamed with the challenge, and I laughed again. "Normal bath, please."

He had the nerve to look vaguely disappointed. I poked him in the chest as I pushed away, aiming for the large bathing room attached to the bedroom. The massive porcelain tub was already filled with steaming water, and—

"Bubbles?"

"Do you have a moral objection to them?"

I grinned, unbuttoning my jacket. My fingers were near-black with dirt and caked blood. I cringed. "I might need more than one bath to get clean."

He snapped his fingers, and my skin was instantly pristine again. I blinked. "If you can do that, then what's the point of the bath?" He'd done it Under the Mountain for me a few times—that magical cleaning. I'd somehow never asked.

He leaned against the doorway, watching me peel off my torn and stained jacket. As if it were the most important task he'd ever been given. "The essence of the dirt remains." His voice roughened as he tracked each movement of my fingers while I unlaced my boots. "Like a layer of oil."

Indeed, my skin, while it looked clean, felt . . . unwashed. I kicked off the boots, letting them land on my filthy jacket. "So it's more for aesthetic purposes."

"You're taking too long," he said, jerking his chin toward the bath.

My breasts tightened at the slight growl lacing his words. He watched that, too.

And I smiled to myself, arching my back a bit more than necessary as I removed my shirt and tossed it to the marble floor. Sunlight streamed in through the steam rising from the tub, casting the space between us in gold and white. Rhys made a low noise that sounded vaguely like a whimper as he took in my bare torso. As he took in my breasts, now heavy and aching, badly enough that I had to swallow my plea to forget this bath entirely.

But I pretended not to notice as I unbuttoned my pants and let them fall to the floor. Along with my undergarments.

Rhys's eyes simmered.

I smirked, daring a look at his own pants. At the evidence of what, exactly, this was doing to him, pressing against the black material with impressive demand. I simply crooned, "Too bad there isn't room in the tub for two."

"A design flaw, and one I shall remedy tomorrow." His voice was rough, quiet—and it slid invisible hands down my breasts, between my legs.

Mother save me. I somehow managed to walk, to climb into the tub. Somehow managed to remember how to bathe myself.

Rhys remained leaning against the doorway the entire time, silently watching with that unrelenting focus.

I might have taken longer washing certain areas. And might have made sure he saw it.

He only gripped the threshold hard enough that the wood groaned beneath his hand.

But Rhys made no move to pounce, even when I toweled off and brushed out my tangled hair. As if the restraint . . . it was part of the game, too.

My bare toes curled on the marble floor as I set down my brush on the sink vanity, every inch of my body aware of where he stood in the doorway, aware of his eyes upon me in the mirror's reflection.

"All clean," I declared, my voice hoarse as I met his stare in the mirror. I could have sworn only darkness and stars swirled beyond his shoulders. A blink, and they were gone. But the predatory hunger on his face . . .

I turned, my fingers trembling slightly as I clutched my towel around me.

Rhys only extended a hand, his own fingers shaking. Even the towel was abrasive against my too-sensitive skin as I laid my hand on his, his calluses scraping as they closed over my fingers. I wanted them scraping all over me.

But he simply led me into the bedroom, step after step, the muscles of his broad back shifting beneath his jacket. And lower, the sleek, powerful cut of thighs, his ass—

I was going to devour him. From head to toe. I was going to *devour* him—

But Rhys paused before the bed, releasing my hand and facing me from the safety of a step away. And it was the expression on his face as he traced a still-tender spot on my cheekbone that checked the heat threatening to raze my senses.

I swallowed, my hair dripping on the carpet. "Is the bruise bad?"

"It's nearly gone." Darkness flickered in the room once more.

I scanned that perfect face. Every line and angle. The fear and rage and love—the wisdom and cunning and strength.

I let my towel drop to the carpet.

Let him look me over as I put a hand on his chest, his heart raging beneath my palm.

"Ready for ravishing." My words didn't come out with the swagger I'd intended.

Not when Rhys's answering smile was a dark, cruel thing. "I hardly know where to begin. So many possibilities."

He lifted a finger, and my breath came hard and fast as he idly circled one of my breasts, then the other. In ever-tightening rings. "I could start here," he murmured.

I clenched my thighs together. He noted the movement, that dark smile growing. And just before his finger reached the tip of my breast, just before he gave me what I was about to beg for, his finger slid upward—to my chest, my neck, my chin. Right to my mouth.

He traced the shape of my lips, a whisper of touch. "Or I could start here," he breathed, slipping the tip of his finger into my mouth.

I couldn't help myself from closing my lips around him, from flicking my tongue against the pad of his finger.

But Rhys withdrew his finger with a soft groan, making a downward path. Along my neck. Chest. Straight over a nipple. He paused there, flicking it once, then smoothed his thumb over the small hurt.

I was shaking now, barely able to keep standing as his finger continued past my breast.

He drew patterns on my stomach, scanning my face as he purred, "Or . . ."

I couldn't think beyond that single finger, that one point of contact as it drifted lower and lower, to where I wanted him. "Or?" I managed to breathe.

His head dipped, hair sliding over his brow as he watched—we both watched—his broad finger venture down. "Or I could start here," he said, the words guttural and raw.

I didn't care—not as he dragged that finger down the center of me. Not as he circled that spot, light and taunting. "Here would be nice," he observed, his breathing uneven. "Or maybe even here," he finished, and plunged that finger inside me.

I groaned, gripping his arm, nails digging into the muscles beneath— muscles that shifted as he pumped his finger once, twice. Then slid it out and drawled, brows rising. "Well? Where shall I begin, Feyre darling?"

I could barely form words, thoughts. But—I'd had enough of playing.

So I took that infernal hand of his, guiding it to my heart, and placed it there, half over the curve of my breast. I met his hooded gaze as I spoke the words that I knew would be his undoing in this little game, the words that were rising up in me with every breath. "You're mine."

It snapped the tether he'd kept on himself.

His clothes vanished—all of them—and his mouth angled over my own.

It wasn't a gentle kiss. Wasn't soft or searching.

It was a claiming, wild and unchecked—it was an unleashing. And the taste of him . . . the heat of him, the demanding stroke of his tongue against my own . . . Home. I was *home*.

My hands shot into his hair, pulling him closer as I answered each of his searing kisses with my own, unable to get enough, unable to touch and feel enough of him.

Skin to skin, Rhys nudged me toward the bed, his hands kneading my rear as I ran my own over the velvet softness of him, over every hard plane and ripple. His beautiful, mighty wings tore from his back, splaying wide before neatly tucking in.

My thighs hit the bed behind us, and Rhys paused, trembling. Giving me time to reconsider, even now. My heart strained, but I pulled my mouth from his. Held his gaze as I lowered myself onto the white sheets and inched back.

Further and further onto the bed, until I was bare before him. Until I took in the considerable, proud length of him and my core tightened in answer. "Rhys," I breathed, his name a plea on my tongue.

His wings flared, chest heaving as stars sparked in his eyes. And it was the longing there—beneath the desire, beneath the need—it was the longing in those beautiful eyes that made me glance to the mountains tattooed on his knees.

The insignia of this court—our court. The promise that he would kneel for no one and nothing but his crown.

And me.

Mine—he was *mine*. I sent the thought down the bond.

No playing, no delaying—I wanted him on me, in me. I *needed* to feel him, hold him, share breath with him. He heard the edge of desperation, felt it through the mating bond flowing between us.

His eyes did not leave mine as he prowled over me, every movement graceful as a stalking plains-cat. Interlacing our fingers, his breathing uneven, Rhys used a knee to nudge my legs apart and settle between them.

Carefully, lovingly, he laid our joined hands beside my head as he guided himself into me and whispered in my ear, "You're mine, too."

At the first nudge of him, I surged forward to claim his mouth.

I dragged my tongue over his teeth, swallowing his groan of pleasure as his hips rolled in gentle thrusts and he pushed in, and in, and in.

Home. This was *home*.

And when Rhys was seated to the hilt, when he paused to let me adjust to the fullness of him, I thought I might explode into moonlight and flame, thought I might die from the sheer force of what swept through me.

My pants were edged with sobs as I dug my fingers into his back, and Rhys withdrew slightly to study my face. To read what was there. "Never again," he promised as he pulled out, then thrust back in with excruciating slowness. He kissed my brow, my temple. "My darling Feyre."

Beyond words, I moved my hips, urging him deeper, harder. Rhys obliged me.

With every movement, every shared breath, every whispered endearment and moan, that mating bond I'd hidden so far inside myself grew brighter. Clearer.

And when it again shone as brilliantly as adamant, my release cascaded through me, leaving my skin glowing like a newborn star in its wake.

At the sight of it, right as I dragged a finger down the sensitive inside of his wing, Rhys shouted my name and found his pleasure.

I held him through every heaving breath, held him as he at last stilled, lingering inside me, and relished the feel of his skin on mine.

For long minutes, we remained there, tangled together, listening to our breathing even out, the sound of it finer than any music.

After a while, Rhys lifted his chest enough to take my right hand. To examine the tattoos inked there. He kissed one of the whorls of near-black blue ink.

His throat bobbed. "I missed you. Every second, every breath. Not just this," he said, shifting his hips for emphasis and dragging a groan from deep in my throat, "but . . . talking to you. Laughing with you. I missed having you in my bed, but missed having you as my friend even more."

My eyes burned. "I know," I managed to say, stroking a hand down his wings, his back. "I know." I kissed his bare shoulder, right over a whorl of Illyrian tattoo. "Never again," I promised him, and whispered it over and over as the sunlight drifted across the floor.

CHAPTER
15

My sisters had been living in the House of Wind since they'd arrived in Velaris.

They did not leave the palace built into the upper parts of a flat-topped mountain overlooking the city. They did not ask for anything, or anyone.

So I would go to them.

Lucien was waiting in the sitting room when Rhys and I came downstairs at last, my mate having given the silent order for them to return.

Unsurprisingly, Cassian and Azriel were *casually* seated in the dining room across the hall, eating lunch and marking every single breath Lucien emitted. Cassian smirked at me, brows flicking up.

I shot him a warning glare that dared him to comment. Azriel, thankfully, just kicked Cassian under the table.

Cassian gawked at Azriel as if to declare *I wasn't going to* say *anything* while I approached the open archway into the sitting room, Lucien rising to his feet.

I fought my cringe as I halted in the threshold. Lucien was still in his travel-worn, filthy clothes. His face and hands, at least, were clean, but . . . I should have gotten him something else. Remembered to offer him—

The thought rippled away into nothing as Rhys appeared at my side.

Lucien did not bother to hide the slight curling of his lip.

As if he could see the mating bond glowing between Rhys and me.

His eyes—both russet and golden—slid down my body. To my hand.

To the ring now on my finger, at the star sapphire sky-bright against the silver. A simple silver band sat on Rhysand's matching finger.

We'd slid them onto each other's hands before coming downstairs— more intimate and searing than any publicly made vows.

I'd told Rhys before we did so that I had half a mind to deposit his ring at the Weaver's cottage and make him retrieve it.

He'd laughed and said that if I truly felt it was necessary to settle the score between us, perhaps I could find some other creature for him to battle—one that wouldn't delight in removing *my* favorite part from his body. I'd only kissed him, murmuring about someone thinking rather highly of themselves, and had placed the ring he'd selected for himself, bought here in Velaris while I'd been away, onto his finger.

Any joy, any lingering laughter from that moment, those silent vows . . . It curled up like leaves in a fire as Lucien sneered at our rings. How close we stood. I swallowed.

Rhys noted it, too. It was impossible to miss.

My mate leaned against the carved archway and drawled to Lucien, "I assume Cassian or Azriel has explained that if you threaten anyone in this house, this territory, we'll show you ways to die you've never even imagined."

Indeed, the Illyrians smirked from where they lingered in the dining room threshold. Azriel was by far the more terrifying of the pair.

Something twisted in my gut at the threat—the smooth, sleek aggression.

Lucien was—had been—my friend. He wasn't my enemy, not entirely—

"But," Rhys continued, sliding his hands into his pockets, "I can understand how difficult this past month has been for you. I know Feyre explained we aren't exactly as rumor suggests . . ." I'd let him into my mind before we'd come down—shown him all that had occurred at the Spring Court. "But hearing it and seeing it are two different things." He shrugged with one shoulder. "Elain has been cared for. Her participation in life here has been entirely her choice. No one but us and a few trusted servants have entered the House of Wind."

Lucien remained silent.

"I was in love with Feyre," Rhys said quietly, "long before she ever returned the feeling."

Lucien crossed his arms. "How fortunate that you got what you wanted in the end."

I closed my eyes for a heartbeat.

Cassian and Azriel stilled, waiting for the order.

"I will only say this once," warned the High Lord of the Night Court. Even Lucien flinched. "I suspected Feyre was my mate before I ever knew she was involved with Tamlin. And when I learned of it . . . If it made her happy, I was willing to step back."

"You came to our house and stole her away on her wedding day."

"I was going to call the wedding off," I cut in, taking a step toward Lucien. "You knew it."

Rhysand went on before Lucien could snap a reply, "I was willing to lose my mate to another male. I was willing to let them marry, if it brought her joy. But what I was not willing to do was let her suffer. To let her fade away into a shadow. And the moment that piece of shit blew apart his study, the moment he *locked her in that house* . . ." His wings ripped from him, and Lucien started.

Rhys bared his teeth. My limbs turned light, trembling at the dark power curling in the corners of the room. Not fear—never fear of him. But at the shattered control as Rhys snarled at Lucien, "My mate may one day find it in herself to forgive him. Forgive you. But I will never forget how it felt to sense her *terror* in those moments." My cheeks heated, especially as Cassian and Azriel stalked closer, those hazel eyes now filled with a mix of sympathy and wrath.

I had never talked about it to them—what had gone on that day Tamlin had destroyed his study, or the day he'd sealed me inside the manor. I'd never asked Rhys if he'd informed them. From the fury rippling from Cassian, the cold rage seeping from Azriel . . . I didn't think so.

Lucien, to his credit, didn't back away a step. From Rhys, or me, or the Illyrians.

The Clever Fox Stares Down Winged Death. The painting flashed into my mind.

"So, again, I will say this only once," Rhys went on, his expression smoothing into lethal calm, dragging me from the colors and light and shadows gathering in my mind. "Feyre did not dishonor or betray Tamlin. I revealed the mating bond months later—and she gave me hell for it, don't worry. But now that you've found your mate in a similar situation, perhaps you will try to understand how it felt. And if you can't be bothered, then I hope you're wise enough to keep your mouth shut, because the next time you look at my mate with that disdain and disgust, I won't bother to explain it again, and I will rip out your fucking throat."

Rhys said it so mildly that the threat took a second to register. To settle in me like a stone plunked into a pool.

Lucien only shifted on his feet. Wary. Considering. I counted the heartbeats, debating how much I'd interfere if he said something truly stupid, when he at last murmured, "There is a longer story to be told, it seems."

Smart answer. The rage ebbed from Rhys's face—and Cassian's and Azriel's shoulders relaxed ever so slightly.

Just once, Lucien had said to me, during those days on the run. That was all he wanted—to see Elain only once.

And then . . . I'd have to figure out what to do with him. Unless my mate already had some plan in motion.

One look at Rhys, who lifted his brows as if to say *He's all yours*, told me it was my call. But until then . . . I cleared my throat.

"I'm going to see my sisters up at the House," I said to Lucien, whose eyes snapped to mine, the metal one tightening and whirring. I forced a grim smile to my face. "Would you like to come?"

Lucien weighed my offer—and the three males monitoring his every blink and breath.

He only nodded. Another wise decision.

We were gone within minutes, the quick walk up to the roof of the town house serving as Lucien's tour of my home. I didn't bother to point out the bedrooms. Lucien certainly didn't ask.

Azriel left us as we took to the skies, murmuring that he had some pressing business to attend to. From the glare Cassian gave him, I wondered if the shadowsinger had invented it to avoid carrying Lucien to the House of Wind, but Rhys's subtle nod to Azriel told me enough.

There were indeed matters afoot. Plans in motion, as they always were. And once I finished visiting my sisters . . . I'd get answers of my own.

So Cassian bore a stone-faced Lucien into the skies, and Rhys swept me into his arms, shooting us gracefully into the cloudless blue.

With every wing beat, with every deep inhale of the citrus-and-salt breeze . . . some tightness in my body uncoiled.

Even if every wing beat brought us closer to the House looming above Velaris. To my sisters.

+

The House of Wind had been carved into the red, sun-warmed stone of the flat-topped mountains that lurked over one edge of the city, with countless balconies and patios jutting to overhang the thousand-foot drop to the valley floor. Velaris's winding streets flowed right to the sheer wall of the mountain itself, and snaking through it wove the Sidra, a glittering, bright band in the midday sun.

As we landed on the veranda that edged our usual dining room, Cassian and Lucien alighting behind us, I let it sink in: the city and the river and the distant sea, the jagged mountains on the other side of Velaris and the blazing blue of the sky above. And the House of Wind, my other home. The grand, formal sister to the town house—our *public* home, I supposed. Where we would hold meetings and receive guests who weren't family.

A far more pleasant alternative to my other residence. The Court of Nightmares. At least there, I could stay in the moonstone palace high atop the mountain under which the Hewn City had been built. Though the people I'd rule over . . . I shut them from my thoughts as I adjusted my braid, tucking in strands that had been whipped free by the gentle wind Rhys had allowed through his shield while flying.

Lucien just walked to the balcony rail and stared out. I didn't quite blame him.

I glanced over a shoulder to where Rhys and Cassian now stood. Rhys lifted a brow.

Wait inside.

Rhys's smile was sharp. *So you won't have any witnesses when you push him over the railing?*

I gave him an incredulous look and strode for Lucien, Rhys's murmur to Cassian about getting a drink in the dining room the only indication of their departure. That, and the near-silent opening and closing of the glass doors that led into the dining room beyond. The same room where I'd first met most of them—my new family.

I came up beside Lucien, the wind ripping strands of his red hair free from where he'd tied it at his nape.

"This isn't what I expected," he said, taking in the sprawl of Velaris.

"The city is still rebuilding after the Hybern attack."

His eyes dropped to the carved balcony rail. "Even though we had no part in that . . . I'm sorry. But—that's not what I meant." He glanced behind us, to where Rhys and Cassian waited inside the dining room, drinks now in hand, leaning all too casually against the giant oak table in its center.

They became immensely interested in some spot or stain on the surface between them.

I scowled at them, but swallowed. And even though my sisters waited inside, even though the urge to see them was so tangible I wouldn't have been surprised to find a rope tugging me into the House, I said to Lucien, "Rhys saved my life on Calanmai."

So I told him. All of it—the story that perhaps would help him understand. And realize how truly safe Elain was—*he* now was. I eventually summoned Rhys to explain his own history—and he gave Lucien the barest details. None of the vulnerable, sorrowful bits that had reduced me to tears in that mountain cabin. But it painted a clear enough picture.

Lucien said nothing while Rhys spoke. Or when I continued with my tale, Cassian often chiming in with his own account of how it'd been to live with two mated-yet-un-mated people, to pretend Rhys wasn't courting me, to welcome me into their little circle.

I didn't know how long had passed when we finished, though Rhys and Cassian used the time to unabashedly sun their wings by the open balcony ledge. I left off our story at Hybern—at the day I'd gone back to the Spring Court.

Silence fell, and Rhys and Cassian again walked away, understanding the emotion swimming in Lucien's eye—the meaning of the long breath he blew out.

When we were alone, Lucien rubbed his eyes. "I've seen Rhysand do such . . . horrible things, seen him play the dark prince over and over. And yet you tell me it was all a lie. A mask. All to protect this place, these people. And I would have laughed at you for believing it, and yet . . . this city exists. Untouched—or until recently, I suppose. Even the Dawn Court's cities are nothing so lovely as this."

"Lucien—"

"And you love him. And he—he truly does love you." Lucien dragged a hand through his red hair. "And all these people I have spent my centuries hating, even fearing . . . They are your family."

"I think Amren would probably deny that she feels any affection for us—"

"Amren is a bedtime story they told us as younglings to make us behave. Amren was who would drink my blood and carry me to hell if I acted out of line. And yet there she was, acting more like a cranky old aunt than anything."

"We don't—we don't enforce protocol and rank here."

"Obviously. Rhys lives in a *town house*, by the Cauldron." He waved an arm to encompass the city.

I didn't know what to say, so I kept silent.

"I hadn't realized I was a villain in your narrative," Lucien breathed.

"You weren't." Not entirely.

The sun danced on the distant sea, turning the horizon into a glittering sprawl of light.

"She doesn't know anything about you. Only the basics that Rhys gave her: you are a High Lord's son, serving in the Spring Court. And you helped me Under the Mountain. Nothing else."

I didn't add that Rhys had told me my sister hadn't asked about him at all.

I straightened. "I would like to see them first. I know you're anxious—"

"Just do it," Lucien said, bracing his forearms on the stone rail of the veranda. "Come get me when she's ready."

I almost patted his shoulder—almost said something reassuring.

But words failed me again as I headed for the dim interior of the House.

Rhys had given Nesta and Elain a suite of connecting rooms, all with views overlooking the city and river and distant mountains beyond.

But it was in the family library that Rhys tracked down Nesta.

There was a coiled, razor-sharp tension in Cassian as the three of us strode down the stairways of the House, the red stone halls dim and echoing with the rustle of Cassian's wings and the faint howl of wind rattling at every window. A tension that grew more taut with every step toward the double doors of the library. I hadn't asked if they had seen each other, or spoken, since that day in Hybern.

Cassian volunteered no information.

And I might have asked Rhys down the bond had he not opened one of the doors.

Had I not immediately spied Nesta curled in an armchair, a book on her knees, looking—for once—very *un*-Nesta-like. Casual. Perhaps relaxed.

Perfectly content to be alone.

The moment my shoes scuffed against the stone floor, she shot straight up, back going stiff, closing her book with a muffled thud. Yet her gray-blue eyes didn't so much as widen as they beheld me.

As I took her in.

Nesta had been beautiful as a human woman.

As High Fae, she was devastating.

From the utter stillness with which Cassian stood beside me, I wondered if he thought the same thing.

She was in a pewter-colored gown, its make simple, yet the material fine. Her hair was braided over the crown of her head, accentuating her long, pale neck—a neck Cassian's eyes darted to, then quickly away from, as she sized us up and said to me, "You're back."

With her hair styled like that, it hid the pointed ears. But there was nothing to hide the ethereal grace as she took one step. As her focus again returned to Cassian and she added, "What do you want?"

I felt the blow like a punch to my gut. "At least immortality hasn't changed some things about you."

Nesta's look was nothing short of icy. "Is there a purpose to this visit, or may I return to my book?"

Rhys's hand brushed mine in silent comfort. But his face . . . hard as stone. And even less amused.

But Cassian sauntered over to Nesta, a half smile spreading across his face. She stood stiffly while he picked up the book, read the title, and chuckled. "I wouldn't have pegged you for a romance reader."

She gave him a withering glare.

Cassian leafed through the pages and drawled to me, "You haven't missed much while you were off destroying our enemies, Feyre. It's mostly been this."

Nesta whirled to me. "You—accomplished it?"

I clenched my jaw. "We'll see how it plays out. I made sure Ianthe suffered." At the hint of rage and fear that crept into Nesta's eyes, I amended, "Not enough, though."

I glanced at her hand—the one she'd pointed with at the King of Hybern. Rhys had mentioned no signs of special powers from either of my sisters. Yet that day in Hybern, when Nesta had opened her eyes . . . I had seen it. Seen something great and terrible within them.

"And, again, why are you here?" She snatched her book from Cassian, who allowed her to do so, but remained standing beside her. Watching every breath, every blink.

"I wanted to see you," I said quietly. "See how you were doing."

"See if I've accepted my lot and found myself grateful for becoming one of *them*?"

I steeled my spine. "You're my sister. I watched them hurt you. I wanted to see if you were all right."

A low, bitter laugh. But she turned to Cassian, looked him over as if she were a queen on a throne, and then declared to all of us, "What do I care? I get to be young and beautiful forever, and I never have to go back to those sycophantic fools over the wall. I get to do as I wish, since apparently no one here has any regard for rules or manners or our traditions. Perhaps I *should* thank you for dragging me into this."

Rhys put a hand on the small of my back before the words even struck their target.

Nesta snorted. "But it's not me you should be checking on. I had as little at stake on the other side of the wall as I do here." Hate rippled over her features—enough hate that I felt sick. Nesta hissed. "She will not leave her room. She will not stop crying. She will not eat, or sleep, or drink."

Rhys's jaw clenched. "I have asked you over and over if you needed—"

"Why should I allow any of *you*"—the last word was shot at Cassian with as much venom as a pit viper—"to get near her? It is no one's business but our own."

"Elain's mate is here," I said.

And it was the wrong thing to utter in Nesta's presence.

She went white with rage.

"He is no such thing to her," she snarled, advancing on me enough that Rhys slid a shield into place between us.

As if he, too, had glimpsed that mighty power in her eyes that day in Hybern. And did not know how it would manifest.

"If you bring that *male* anywhere near her, I'll—"

"You'll what?" Cassian crooned, trailing her at a casual pace as she stopped perhaps five feet from me. He lifted a brow as she whirled on him. "You won't join me for practice, so you sure as hell aren't going to hold your own in a fight. You won't talk about your powers, so you certainly aren't going to be able to wield them. And you—"

"Shut your mouth," she snapped, every inch the conquering empress. "I told you to stay the hell away from me, and if you—"

"You come between a male and his mate, Nesta Archeron, and you're going to learn about the consequences the hard way."

Nesta's nostrils flared. Cassian only gave her a crooked grin.

I cut in, "If Elain is not up for it, then she won't see him. I won't force the meeting on her. But he does wish to see her, Nesta. I'll ask on his behalf, but the decision will be hers."

"The male who sold us out to Hybern."

"It's more complicated than that."

"Well, it will certainly be more complicated when Father returns and finds us gone. What do you plan to tell *him* about all this?"

"Seeing as he hasn't sent word from the continent in months, I'll worry about that later," I sniped back. And thank the Cauldron for it— that he was off trading in some lucrative territory.

Nesta only shook her head, turning toward the chair and her book. "I don't care. Do what you want."

A stinging dismissal, if not admission that she still trusted me enough to consider Elain's needs first. Rhys jerked his chin at Cassian in a silent order to leave, and as I followed them, I said softly, "I'm sorry, Nesta."

She didn't answer as she sat stiffly in her chair, picked up her book, and dutifully ignored us. A blow to the face would have been better.

When I looked ahead, I found Cassian staring back at Nesta as well.

I wondered why no one had yet mentioned what now shone in Cassian's eyes as he gazed at my sister.

The sorrow. And the longing.

⊹

The suite was filled with sunlight.

Every curtain shoved back as far as it could go, to let in as much sun as possible.

As if any bit of darkness was abhorrent. As if to chase it away.

And seated in a small chair before the sunniest of the windows, her back to us, was Elain.

Where Nesta had been in contented silence before we found her, Elain's silence was . . . hollow.

Empty.

Her hair was down—not even braided. I couldn't remember the last time I'd seen it unbound. She wore a moon-white silk dressing robe.

She did not look, or speak, or even flinch as we entered.

Her too-thin arms rested on her chair. That iron engagement ring still encircled her finger.

Her skin was so pale it looked like fresh snow in the harsh light.

I realized then that the color of death, of sorrow, was white.

The lack of color. Of vibrancy.

I left Cassian and Rhys by the door.

Nesta's rage was better than this . . . shell.

This void.

My breath caught as I edged around her chair. Beheld the city view she stared so blankly at.

Then beheld the hollowed-out cheeks, the bloodless lips, the brown eyes that had once been rich and warm, and now seemed utterly dull. Like grave dirt.

She didn't so much as look at me as I said softly, "Elain?"

I didn't dare reach for her hand.

I didn't dare get too close.

I had done this. I had brought this upon them—

"I'm back," I added a bit limply. Uselessly.

All she said was, "I want to go home."

I closed my eyes, my chest unbearably tight. "I know."

"He'll be looking for me," she whispered.

"I know," I said again. Not Lucien—she wasn't talking about him at all.

"We were supposed to be married next week."

I put a hand on my chest, as if it'd stop the cracking in there. "I'm sorry."

Nothing. Not even a flicker of emotion. "Everyone keeps saying that." Her thumb brushed the ring on her finger. "But it doesn't fix anything, does it?"

I couldn't get enough air in. I couldn't—I couldn't *breathe*, looking at this broken, carved-out thing my sister had become. What I'd robbed her of, what I'd taken from her—

Rhys was there, an arm sliding around my waist. "Can we get you anything, Elain?" He spoke with such gentleness I could barely stand it.

"I want to go home," she repeated.

I couldn't ask her—about Lucien. Not now. Not yet.

I turned away, fully prepared to bolt and completely fall apart in another room, another section of the House. But Lucien was standing in the doorway.

And from the devastation on his face, I knew he'd heard every word. Seen and heard and felt the hollowness and despair radiating from her.

Elain had always been gentle and sweet—and I had considered it a different sort of strength. A better strength. To look at the hardness of the world and choose, over and over, to love, to be kind. She had been always so full of light.

Perhaps that was why she now kept all the curtains open. To fill the void that existed where all of that light had once been.

And now nothing remained.

CHAPTER
16

Rhysand silently led Lucien to the suite he'd be occupying at the opposite end of the House of Wind. Cassian and I trailed behind, none of us speaking until my mate opened a set of onyx doors to reveal a sunny sitting room carved from more red stone. Beyond the wall of windows, the city flowed far below, the view stretching to the distant jagged mountains and glittering sea.

Rhys paused in the center of a midnight-blue handwoven rug and gestured to the sealed doors on his left. "Bedroom." He waved a lazy hand toward the single door on the opposite wall. "Bathing room."

Lucien surveyed it all with cool indifference. What he felt about Elain, what he planned to do . . . I didn't want to ask.

"I assume you'll need clothes," Rhys went on, nodding toward Lucien's filthy jacket and pants—which he'd worn for the past week while we scrambled through territories. Indeed, that was . . . blood splattered in several spots. "Any preferences for attire?"

That drew Lucien's attention, the male shifting enough to take in Rhys—to note Cassian and me lurking in the doorway. "Is there a cost?"

"If you're trying to say that you have no money, don't worry—the clothes are complimentary." Rhys gave him a half smile. "If you're trying to ask if this is some sort of bribe . . ." A shrug. "You are a High Lord's son. It would be bad manners not to house and clothe you in your time of need."

Lucien bristled.

Stop baiting him, I shot down the bond.

But it's so fun, came the purred reply.

Something had rattled him. Rattled Rhys enough that taunting Lucien was an easy way to take the edge off. I stepped closer, Cassian remaining behind me as I told Lucien, "We'll be back for dinner in a few hours. Rest a while—bathe. If you need anything, pull that rope by the door."

Lucien stiffened—not at what I'd said, I realized, but at the tone. A hostess. But he asked, "What of—Elain?"

Your call, Rhys offered.

"I need to think about it," I answered plainly. "Until I figure out what to do with her, with Nesta, stay out of their way." I added perhaps too tightly, "This house is warded against winnowing, both from outside and within. There's one way out—the stairs to the city. It, too, is warded—and guarded. Please don't do anything stupid."

"So am I a prisoner?"

I could feel the response simmering in Rhys, but I shook my head. "No. But understand while you may be her mate, Elain is *my* sister. I'll do what I must to protect her from further harm."

"I would never hurt her."

A bleak sort of honesty in his words.

I simply nodded, loosening a breath, and met Rhysand's stare in silent urging.

My mate gave no indication of my wordless plea as he said, "You are free to wander where you wish, into the city itself if you feel like braving the stairs, but there are two conditions: you are not to take either sister, and you are not to enter their floor. If you require a book from the library, you will ask the servants. If you wish to speak to Elain or Nesta, you will also ask the servants, who will ask us. If you disregard those rules, I'll lock you in a room with Amren."

Then Rhys turned away, hands sliding into his pockets as he offered his hooked elbow to me. I looped my arm through his, but said to Lucien, "We'll see you in a few hours."

We were almost to the door, Cassian already in the hall, when Lucien said to me, "Thank you."

I didn't dare ask him for what.

⁜

We flew right to Amren's loft, more than a few people waving as we soared over the rooftops of Velaris. My smile wasn't faked when I waved back to them—my people. Rhys only held me a bit tighter while I did so, his own smile as bright as the sun on the Sidra.

Mor and Azriel were already waiting inside Amren's apartment, seated like scolded children on the threadbare divan against the wall while the dark-haired female flipped through the pages of books sprawled around her on the floor.

Mor gave me a grateful, relieved look as we entered, Azriel's own face revealing nothing while he stood, keeping a careful, too-casual distance from her side. But it was Amren who said from the floor, "You should kill Beron and his sons and set up the handsome one as High Lord of Autumn, self-imposed exile or no. It will make life easier."

"I'll take that into consideration," Rhys said, striding toward her while I remained with the others. If they were hanging back . . . Amren had to be in some mood.

I blew out a breath. "Who else thinks it's a terrible idea to leave the three of them up at the House of Wind?"

Cassian raised his hand as Rhys and Mor chuckled. The High Lord's general said, "I give him an hour before he tries to see her."

"Thirty minutes," Mor countered, sitting back down on the divan and crossing her legs.

I cringed. "I guarantee Nesta is now guarding Elain. I think she might honestly kill him if he so much as tries to touch her."

"Not without training she won't," Cassian grumbled, tucking in his wings as he claimed the seat beside Mor that Azriel had vacated. The shadowsinger didn't so much as look at it. No, Azriel just walked to the wall beside Cassian and leaned against the wood paneling.

But Rhys and the others remained quiet enough that I knew to proceed carefully as I asked Cassian, "Nesta spoke as if you've been up at the House . . . often. You've offered to train her?"

Cassian's hazel eyes shuttered as he crossed a booted ankle over another, stretching his muscled legs before him. "I go up there every other day. It's good exercise for my wings." Those wings shifted in emphasis. Not a scratch marred them.

"And?"

"And what you saw in the library is a pleasanter version of the conversation we always have."

Mor's lips pressed into a thin line, as if she was trying her best *not* to say anything. Azriel was trying *his* best to shoot a warning stare at Mor to remind her to indeed keep her mouth shut. As if they'd already discussed this. Many times.

"I don't blame her," Cassian said, shrugging despite his words. "She was—violated. Her body stopped belonging wholly to her." His jaw clenched. Even Amren didn't dare say anything. "And I am going to peel the King of Hybern's skin off his bones the next time I see him."

His Siphons flickered in answer.

Rhys said casually, "I'm sure the king will thoroughly enjoy the experience."

Cassian glowered. "I mean it."

"Oh, I have no doubt that you do." Rhys's violet eyes were dazzling in the dimness of the loft. "But before you lose yourself in plans for revenge, do remember that we have a war to plan first."

"Asshole."

A corner of my mate's mouth tugged upward. And—Rhys was goading him, working Cassian into a temper to keep that brittle edge of guilt from consuming him. The others letting him take on the task, likely having done it several times themselves these weeks. "I am most definitely that," Rhys said, "but the fact still remains that revenge is secondary to winning this war."

Cassian opened his mouth as if he'd keep arguing, but Rhys peered at the books scattered on the lush carpet. "Nothing?" he asked Amren.

"I don't know why you sent those two buffoons"—a narrowed glance toward Mor and Azriel—"to monitor me." So this was where Azriel had gone—right to the loft. To no doubt spare Mor from enduring Amren Duty alone. But Amren's tone . . . cranky, yes, but perhaps a bit of a front, too. To banish that too-fragile gleam in Cassian's eyes.

"We're not monitoring you," Mor said, tapping her foot on the carpet. "We're monitoring the Book."

And as she said it . . . I felt it. Heard it.

Amren had placed the Book of Breathings on her nightstand.

A glass of old blood atop it.

I didn't know whether to laugh or cringe. The latter won out as the Book murmured, *Hello, sweet-faced liar. Hello, princess with—*

"Oh, be quiet," Amren hissed toward the Book, who—shut up. "Odious thing," she muttered, and went back to the tome before her.

Rhys gave me a wry smile. "Since the two halves of the Book were joined back together, it has been . . . known to speak every now and then."

"What does it say?"

"Utter nonsense," Amren spat, scowling at the Book. "It just likes to hear itself talk. Like most of the people cramping up my apartment."

Cassian smirked. "Did someone forget to feed Amren again?"

She pointed a warning finger at him without so much as looking up. "Is there a reason, Rhysand, why you dragged your yapping pack into my home?"

Her home was little more than a giant, converted attic, but none of us dared argue as Mor, Cassian, and Azriel finally came closer, forming a small circle around Amren's sprawl in the center of the room.

Rhys said to me, "The information you got from Dagdan and Brannagh confirms what we've been gathering ourselves while you were gone. Especially Hybern's potential allies in other territories—on the continent."

"Vultures," Mor muttered, and Cassian looked inclined to agree.

But Rhys—Rhys had indeed been spying, while Azriel had been—

Rhys snorted. "I *can* stay hidden, mate."

I glared at him, but Azriel cut in. "Having Hybern's movements confirmed by you, Feyre, is what we needed."

"Why?"

Cassian crossed his arms. "We barely stand a chance of surviving Hybern's armies on our own. If armies from Vallahan, Montesere, and Rask join them . . ." He drew a line across his tan throat.

Mor elbowed him in the ribs. Cassian nudged her right back as Azriel shook his head at both of them, shadows coiling around the tips of his wings.

"Are those three territories . . . that powerful?" Perhaps it was a foolish question, showing how little I knew of the faerie lands on the continent—

"Yes," Azriel said, no judgment in his hazel eyes. "Vallahan has the numbers, Montesere has the money, and Rask . . . it is large enough to have both."

"And we have no potential allies amongst the other overseas territories?"

Rhys pulled at a stray thread on the cuff of his black jacket. "Not ones that would sail here to help."

My stomach turned. "What of Miryam and Drakon?" He'd once refused to consider, but— "You fought for Miryam and Drakon centuries ago," I said to Rhys. He'd done a great deal more than that, if Jurian was to be believed. "Perhaps it's time to call in that debt."

But Rhys shook his head. "We tried. Azriel went to Cretea." The island where Miryam, Drakon, and their unified human and Fae peoples had secretly lived for the past five centuries.

"It was abandoned," Azriel said. "In ruin. With no trace of what happened or where they went."

"You think Hybern——"

"There was no sign of Hybern, or of any harm," Mor cut in, her face taut. They had been her friends, too——during the War. Miryam, and Drakon, and the human queens who had gotten the Treaty signed. And it was worry——true, deep worry——that guttered in her brown eyes. In all their eyes.

"Then do you think they heard about Hybern and ran?" I asked. Drakon had a winged legion, Rhys had once told me. If there was any chance of finding them——

"The Drakon and Miryam I knew wouldn't have run——not from this," Rhys said.

Mor leaned forward, her golden hair spilling over her shoulders. "But with Jurian now a player in this conflict . . . Miryam and Drakon, whether they like it or not, have always been tied to him. I don't blame them for running, if he truly hunts them."

Rhys's face slackened for a heartbeat. "That is what the King of Hybern has on Jurian," he murmured. "Why Jurian works for him."

My brow furrowed.

"Miryam died——a spear through her chest during that last battle at the sea," Rhys explained. "She bled out while she was carried to safety. But Drakon knew of a sacred, hidden island where an object of great and terrible power had been concealed. An object made by the Cauldron itself, legend claimed. He brought her there, to Cretea—— used the item to resurrect her, make her immortal. As you were Made, Feyre."

Amren had said it——months ago. That Miryam had been *Made* as I was.

Amren seemed to remember it, too, as she said, "The King of

Hybern must have promised Jurian to use the Cauldron to track the item. To where Miryam and Drakon now live. Perhaps they figured that out—and left as fast as they could."

And for revenge, for that insane rage that hounded Jurian . . . he'd do whatever the King of Hybern asked. So he could kill Miryam himself.

"But where did they go?" I looked to Azriel, the shadowsinger still standing with preternatural stillness against the wall. "You found no trace at all of where they might have vanished to?"

"None," Rhys answered for him. "We've sent messengers back since—to no avail."

I rubbed at my face, sealing off that path of hope. "Then if they are not a possible ally . . . How do we keep those other territories on the continent from joining with Hybern—from sending their armies here?" I winced. "That's our plan—isn't it?"

Rhys smiled grimly. "It is. One we've been working on while you were away." I waited, trying not to pace as Amren's silver eyes seemed to glow with amusement. "I looked at Hybern first. At its people. As best I could."

He'd *gone* to Hybern—

Rhys smirked at the concern flaring across my face. "I'd hoped that Hybern might have some internal conflict to exploit—to get them to collapse from within. That its people might not want this war, might see it as costly and dangerous and unnecessary. But five hundred years on that island, with little trade, little opportunity . . . Hybern's people are hungry for change. Or rather . . . a change back to the old days, when they had human slaves to do their work, when there were no barriers keeping them from what they now perceive as their right."

Amren slammed shut the book she'd been perusing. "Fools." She shook her head, inky hair swaying, as she scowled up at me. "Hybern's wealth has been dwindling for centuries. Most of their trade routes before the War dealt with the South—with the Black Land. But once it went to the humans . . . We don't know if Hybern's king deliberately failed to establish new trade routes and opportunities for his people in order to one day fuel this war, or if he was just that shortsighted and let everything fall apart. But for centuries now, Hybern's people have been festering. Hybern *let* their resentment of their growing stagnation and poverty fester."

"There are many High Fae," Mor said carefully, "who believed before the War, and still believe now, that humans . . . that they are property. There were many High Fae who knew nothing but privilege thanks to those slaves. And when that privilege was ripped away from them, when they were forced to leave their homelands or forced to make room for other High Fae and re-form territories—create new ones— above that wall . . . They have not forgotten that anger, even centuries later. Especially not in places like Hybern, where their territory and population remained mostly untouched by change. They were one of the few who did not have to yield any land to the wall—and did not yield any land to the Fae territories now looking for a new home. Isolated, growing poorer, with no slaves to do their labor . . . Hybern has long viewed the days before the War as a golden era. And these centuries since as a dark age."

I rubbed at my chest. "They're all insane, to think that."

Rhys nodded. "Yes—they certainly are. But don't forget that their king has encouraged these limited world views. He did not expand their trade routes, did not allow other territories to take any of his land and bring their cultures. He considered where things went wrong for the Loyalists in the War. How they ultimately yielded not from being overwhelmed but because they began arguing amongst themselves. Hybern has had a long, long while to think on those mistakes. And how to avoid them at any cost. So he made sure his people are completely for this war, completely for the idea of the wall coming down, because they think it will somehow restore this . . . gilded vision of the past. Hybern's people see their king and their armies not as conquerors, but as liberators of High Fae and those who stand with them."

Nausea churned in my gut. "How can anyone *believe* that?"

Azriel ran a scarred hand through his hair. "That's what we've been learning. Listening in Hybern. And in territories like Rask and Montesere and Vallahan."

"We're to be made an example of, girl," Amren explained. "Prythian. We were among the fiercest defenders and negotiators of the Treaty. Hybern wants to claim Prythian not only to clear the path to the continent, but to make an example of what happens to High Fae territories that defend the Treaty."

"But surely other territories would protect it," I said, scanning their faces.

"Not as many as we'd hoped," Rhys admitted, wincing. "There are many—too many—who have also felt squashed and suffocated during these centuries. They want their old lands back beneath the wall, and the power and prosperity that came with it. Their vision of the past has been colored by five hundred years of struggling to adjust and thrive."

"Perhaps we did them a disservice," Mor mused, "in not sharing enough of our wealth, our territory. Perhaps we are to blame for allowing some of this to rot and fester."

"That remains to be discussed," Amren said, waving a delicate hand. "The point is that we are not facing an army hell-bent on destruction. They are hell-bent on what they believe is *liberation*. Of High Fae stifled by the wall, and what they believe still belongs to them."

I swallowed. "So how do the other territories play into it—the three Hybern claims will ally with them?" I looked between Rhys and Azriel. "You said you were . . . over there?"

Rhys shrugged. "Over there, in Hybern, in the other territories . . ." He winked at my gaping mouth. "I had to keep myself busy to avoid missing you."

Mor rolled her eyes. But it was Cassian who said, "We can't afford to let those three territories join with Hybern. If they send armies to Prythian, we're done."

"So what do we do?"

Rhys leaned against the carved post of Amren's bed. "We've been keeping them busy." He jerked his chin to Azriel. "We planted information—truth and lies and a blend of both—for them to find. And also scattered some of it among our old allies, who are now balking at supporting us." Azriel's smile was a slash of white. Lies and truth—the shadowsinger and his spies had sowed them in foreign courts.

My brow narrowed. "You've been playing the territories on the continent off each other?"

"We've been making sure that they're kept busy with each other," Cassian said, a hint of wicked humor glinting in his hazel eyes. "Making sure that longtime enemies and rival-nations of Rask, Vallahan, and Montesere have suddenly received information that has them worried about being attacked. And raising their own defenses. Which in turn has made Rask, Vallahan, and Montesere start looking toward their own borders and not our own."

"If our allies from the War are too scared to come here to fight," Mor said, folding her arms over her chest, "then as long as they're keeping the others occupied—keeping them from sailing *here*—we don't care."

I blinked at them. At Rhys.

Brilliant. Utterly brilliant, to keep them so focused and fearful of each other that they stayed away. "So . . . they won't be coming?"

"We can only pray," Amren said. "And pray we deal with this fast enough that they don't figure out we've played them all."

"What of the human queens, though?" I chewed on the tip of my thumb. "They have to be aware that no bargain with Hybern would ultimately work to their advantage."

Mor braced her forearms on her thighs. "Who knows what Hybern promised them—lied about? He already granted them immortality through the Cauldron in exchange for their cooperation. If they were foolish enough to agree to it, then I don't doubt they've already thrown open the gates to him."

"But we don't know that for certain," Amren countered. "And none of it explains why they've been so quiet—locked up in that palace."

Rhys and Azriel shook their heads in silent confirmation.

I surveyed them, their fading amusement. "It drives you mad, doesn't it, that no one has been able to get inside that palace."

A low growl from both of them before Azriel muttered, "You have no idea."

Amren just clicked her tongue, her upswept eyes settling on me. "Those Hybern commanders were fools to reveal their plans in regard to breaking the wall. Or perhaps they knew the information would return to us, and their master wants us to stew."

I angled my head. "You mean shattering the wall through the holes already in it?"

A bob of her sharp chin as she gestured to the books around her. "It's complex spell work—a loophole through the magic that binds the wall."

"And it implies," Mor said, frowning deeply, "that something might be amiss with the Cauldron."

I raised my brows, considering. "Because the Cauldron should be able to bring that wall down on its own, right?"

"Right," Rhysand said, striding to the Book on the nightstand. He didn't dare touch it. "Why bother seeking out those holes to help the Cauldron when he could unleash its power and be done with it?"

"Maybe he used too much of its power transforming my sisters and those queens."

"It's likely," Rhys said, stalking back to my side. "But if he's going to exploit those tears in the wall, we need to find a way to *fix* them before he can act."

I asked Amren, "Are there spells to patch it up?"

"I'm looking," she said through her teeth. "It'd help if *someone* dragged their ass to a library to do more research."

"We are at your disposal," Cassian offered with a mock bow.

"I wasn't aware you could read," Amren said sweetly.

"It could be a fool's errand," Azriel cut in before Cassian could voice the retort dancing in his eyes. "To get us to focus on the wall as a decoy—while he strikes from another direction."

I grimaced at the Book. "Why not just try to nullify the Cauldron again?"

"Because it nearly killed you the last time," Rhys said in a sort of calm, steady voice that told me enough: there was no way in hell he'd risk me attempting it again.

I straightened. "I wasn't prepared in Hybern. None of us were. If I tried again—"

Mor cut in. "If you tried again, it might very well kill you. Not to mention, we'd have to actually *get* to the Cauldron, which isn't an option."

"The king," Azriel clarified at my furrowed brow, "won't allow the Cauldron out of his sight. And he's rigged it with more spells and traps than the last time." I opened my mouth to object, but the shadowsinger added, "We looked into it. It's not a viable path."

I believed him—the stark honesty in those hazel eyes was confirmation enough that they'd weighed it thoroughly. "Well, if it's too risky to nullify the Cauldron," I mused, "then can *I* somehow fix the wall? If the wall was made *by* faeries coming together, and my very magic is a blend of so many . . ."

Amren considered in the silence that fell. "Perhaps. The relationship would be tenuous, but . . . yes, perhaps you could patch it up. Though your sisters, directly forged by the Cauldron itself, might bear the sort of magic we—"

"My sisters play no part in this."

Another beat of silence, interrupted only by the rustle of Azriel's wings.

"I asked them to help once—and look what happened. I won't risk them again."

Amren snorted. "You sound exactly like Tamlin."

I felt the words like a blow.

Rhys slid a hand against my back, having appeared so fast I didn't see him move. But before he could reply, Mor said quietly, "Don't you ever say that sort of bullshit again, Amren."

There was nothing on Mor's face beyond cold calm—fury.

I'd never seen her look so . . . terrifying. She had been furious with the mortal queens, but this . . . This was the face of the High Lord's third in command.

"If you're cranky because you're hungry, then tell us," Mor went on with that frozen quiet. "But if you say anything like that again, I will throw you in the gods-damned Sidra."

"I'd like to see you try."

A little smile was Mor's only answer.

Amren slid her attention to me. "We need your sisters—if not for this, then to convince others to join us, of the risk. Since any would-be ally might have some . . . difficulty believing us after so many years of lies."

"Apologize," said Mor.

"Mor," I murmured.

"*Apologize*," she hissed at Amren.

Amren said nothing.

Mor took a step toward her, and I said, "She's right."

They both looked to me, brows raised.

I swallowed. "Amren is right." I walked out of Rhys's touch—realizing he'd kept silent to let me sort it out. Let me figure out how to deal with both of them, as family, but mostly as their High Lady.

Mor's face tightened, but I shook my head. "I can—ask my sisters. See if they have any sort of power. See if they'd be willing to . . . talk to others about what they endured. But I won't force them to help, if they do not wish to participate. The choice will be theirs." I glanced at my mate—the male who had always presented me with a choice not as a gift, but as my own gods-given *right*. Rhys's violet eyes flickered in acknowledgment. "But I'll make our . . . desperation clear."

Amren huffed, hardly more than a bird of prey puffing its feathers.

"Compromise, Amren," Rhys purred. "It's called compromise."

She ignored him. "If you want to start convincing your sisters, get them out of the House. Being cooped up never helped anyone."

Rhys said smoothly, "I'm not entirely sure Velaris is prepared for Nesta Archeron."

"My sister's not some feral animal," I snapped.

Rhys recoiled a bit, the others suddenly finding the carpet, the divan, the books incredibly fascinating. "I didn't mean that."

I didn't answer.

Mor frowned in disapproval at Rhys, who I felt watching me carefully, but asked me, "What of Elain?"

I shifted slightly, pushing past the words still hanging between me and Rhys. "I can ask, but . . . she might not be ready to be around so many people." I clarified, "She was supposed to be married next week."

"So she keeps saying, over and over," Amren grumbled.

I shot her a glare. "Careful." Amren blinked up at me in surprise. But I went on, "So, we need to find a way to patch up the wall before Hybern uses the Cauldron to break it. And fight this war before any other territories join Hybern's assault. And eventually get the Cauldron itself. Anything else?"

Rhys said behind me, his own voice carefully casual, "That covers it. As soon as a force can be assembled, we take on Hybern."

"The Illyrian legions are nearly ready," Cassian said.

"No," Rhys said. "I mean a bigger force. A force not just from the Night Court, but from all of Prythian. Our only decent shot at finding allies in this war."

None of us spoke, none of us moved as Rhys said simply, "Tomorrow, invitations go out to every High Lord in Prythian. For a meeting in two weeks. It's time we see who stands with us. And make sure they understand the consequences if they don't."

CHAPTER
17

I let Cassian carry me to the House two hours later, just because he admitted he was still working to strengthen his wings and needed to push himself.

Heat rippled off the tiled roofs and red stone as we soared high over them, the sea breeze a cool kiss against my face.

We'd barely finished debating thirty minutes ago, only stopping when Mor's stomach had grumbled as loudly as a breaking thunderhead. We'd spent our time weighing the merits of where to meet, who to bring along to the meeting with the High Lords.

Invitations would go out tomorrow—but not specify the meeting place. There was no point in selecting one, Rhys said, when the High Lords would no doubt refuse our initial selection and counter with their own choice of where to gather. All we had chosen was the day and the time—the two weeks a cushion against the bickering that was sure to ensue. The rest . . . We'd just have to prepare for every possibility.

We'd quickly returned to the town house to change before heading back up to the House—and I'd found Nuala and Cerridwen waiting in my room, smiles on their shadowy faces.

I'd embraced them both, even if Rhys's hello had been less . . . enthusiastic. Not for dislike of the half-wraiths, but . . .

I'd snapped at him. In Amren's apartment. He hadn't seemed angry, and yet . . . I'd felt him carefully watching me these past few hours. It'd made it . . . strange to look at him. Strange enough that the appetite I'd been steadily building had gone a bit queasy. I'd challenged him before, but . . . not as High Lady. Not with the . . . tone.

So I didn't get to ask him about it as Nuala and Cerridwen helped me dress and he headed into the bathing room to wash up.

Not that there was much finery to bother with. I'd opted for my Illyrian leather pants and a loose, white shirt—and a pair of embroidered slippers that Cassian kept snorting at as we flew.

When he did so for the third time in two minutes, I pinched his arm and said, "It's hot. Those boots are stuffy."

His brows rose, the portrait of innocence. "I didn't say anything."

"You grunted. *Again.*"

"I've been living with Mor for five hundred years. I've learned the hard way not to question shoe choices." He smirked. "However stupid they may be."

"It's dinner. Unless there's some battle planned afterward?"

"Your sister will be there—I'd say that's battle aplenty."

I casually studied his face, noting how hard he worked to keep his features neutral, to keep his gaze fixed anywhere but on my own. Rhys flew nearby, far enough to remain out of earshot as I said, "Would you use her to see if she can somehow fix the wall?"

Hazel eyes shot to me, fierce and clear. "Yes. Not only for our sakes, but . . . she needs to get out of the House. She needs to . . ." Cassian's wings kept up a steady booming beat, the new sections only detectable by their lack of scarring. "She'll destroy herself if she stays cooped up in there."

My chest tightened. "Do . . ." I thought through my words. "The day she was changed, she . . . I felt something different with her." I fought against the tensing in my muscles as I recalled those moments. The screaming and the blood and the nausea as I watched my sisters taken against their will, as I could do nothing, as we—

I swallowed down the fear, the guilt. "It was like . . . everything she was, that steel and fire . . . It became magnified. Cataclysmic. Like . . . looking at a house cat and suddenly finding a panther standing there instead." I shook my head, as if it would clear away the memory of the predator, the rage simmering in those blue-gray eyes.

"I will never forget those moments," Cassian said quietly, scenting or sensing the memories wreaking havoc on me. "As long as I live."

"Have you seen any glimpse of it since?"

"Nothing." The House loomed, golden lights at the walls of windows and doorways beckoning us closer. "But I can feel it— sometimes." He added a bit ruefully, "Usually when she's pissed at me. Which is . . . most of the time."

"Why?" They'd always been at each other's throats, but this . . . yes, the dynamic between them had been different earlier. Sharper.

Cassian shook his dark hair out of his eyes, slightly longer than the last time I'd seen it. "I don't think Nesta will ever forgive me for what happened in Hybern. To her—but mostly to Elain."

"Your wings were shredded. You were barely alive." For that was guilt—ravaging and poisonous—in each of Cassian's words. What the others had been fighting against in the loft. "You were in no position to save anyone."

"I made her a promise." The wind ruffled Cassian's hair as he squinted at the sky. "And when it mattered, I didn't keep it."

I still dreamed of him trying to crawl toward her, reaching for her even in the semi-unconscious state the pain and blood loss had thrown him into. As Rhysand had once done for me during those last moments with Amarantha.

Perhaps only a few wing beats separated us from the broad landing veranda, but I asked, "Why do you bother, Cassian?"

His hazel eyes shuttered as we smoothly landed. And I thought he wouldn't answer, especially not as we heard the others already in the dining room beyond the veranda, especially not when Rhys gracefully landed beside us and strode in ahead with a wink.

But Cassian said quietly as we headed for the dining room, "Because I can't stay away."

✠

Elain, not surprisingly, didn't leave her room.

Nesta, surprisingly, did.

It wasn't a formal dinner by any means—though Lucien, standing near the windows and watching the sun set over Velaris, was wearing a fine green jacket embroidered with gold, his cream-colored pants showing off muscled thighs, and his knee-high black boots polished enough that the chandeliers of faelight reflected off them.

He'd always had a casual grace about him, but here, tonight, with his hair tied back and jacket buttoned to his neck, he truly looked the part of a High Lord's son. Handsome, powerful, a bit rakish—but well-mannered and elegant.

I aimed for him as the others helped themselves to the wine breathing in decanters on the ancient wood table, keenly aware that while my friends chatted, they kept one eye on us. Lucien ran *his* one eye over me—my casual attire, then the Illyrians in their leathers, and Amren in her usual gray, and Mor in her flowing red gown, and said, "What *is* the dress code?"

I shrugged, passing him the glass of wine I'd brought over. "It's . . . whatever we feel like."

That gold eye clicked and narrowed, then returned to the city ahead.

"What did you do with yourself this afternoon?"

"Slept," he said. "Washed. Sat on my ass."

"I could give you a tour of the city tomorrow morning," I offered. "If you like."

175

Never mind that we had a meeting to plan for. A wall to heal. A war to fight. I could set aside half a day. Show him *why* this place had become my home, why I had fallen in love with its ruler.

As if sensing my thoughts, Lucien said, "You don't need to waste your time convincing me. I get it. I get . . . I get that we were not what you wanted. Or needed. How small and isolated our home must have been for you, once you saw this." He jerked his chin toward the city, where lights were now sparking into view amid the falling twilight. "Who could compare?"

I almost said *Don't you mean* what *could compare?* but held my tongue.

His focus shifted behind me before he replied—and Lucien shut his mouth. His metal eye whirred softly.

I followed his glance, and tried not to tense as Nesta stepped into the room.

Yes, *devastating* was a good word for how lovely she'd become as High Fae. And in a long-sleeved, dark blue gown that clung to her curves before falling gracefully to the ground in a spill of fabric . . .

Cassian looked like someone had punched him in the gut.

But Nesta stared right at me, the faelight shimmering along the silver combs in her upswept hair. The others, she dutifully ignored, chin lifting as she strode for us. I prayed that Mor and Amren, their brows high, wouldn't say any—

"*Where* did that dress come from?" Mor said, red gown flowing behind her as she breezed toward Nesta. My sister drew up short, shoulders tensing, readying to—

But Mor was already there, fingering the heavy blue fabric, surveying every stitch. "I want one," she pouted. Her attempt, no doubt, to segue into an invitation to shop for a larger wardrobe with me. As High Lady, I'd need clothes—fancier ones. Especially for this meeting. My sisters, too.

Mor's brown eyes flicked to mine, and I had to fight the crushing gratitude that threatened to make my own burn as I approached them.

"I assume my mate dug it up somewhere," I said, throwing a glance over my shoulder at Rhys, who was perched on the edge of the dining table, flanked by Az and Cassian, all three Illyrians pretending that they weren't listening to every word as they poured the wine amongst themselves.

Busybodies. I sent the thought down the bond, and Rhys's dark laughter echoed in return.

"He gets all the credit for clothes," Mor said, examining the fabric of Nesta's skirt while my sister monitored like a hawk, "and he never tells me where he finds them. He still won't tell me where he found Feyre's dress for Starfall." She threw a glare over her shoulder. "Bastard."

Rhys chuckled. Cassian, however, didn't smile, every pore of him seemingly fixed on Nesta and Mor.

On what my sister would do.

Mor only examined the silver combs in Nesta's hair. "It's a good thing we're not the same size—or else I might be tempted to steal that dress."

"Likely right off her," Cassian muttered.

Mor's answering smirk wasn't reassuring.

But Nesta's face remained blank. Cold. She looked Mor up and down—noting the dress that exposed much of her midriff, back, and chest, then the flowing skirts with sheer panels that revealed glimpses of her legs. Scandalous, by human fashions. "Fortunately for you," Nesta said flatly, "I don't return the sentiment."

Azriel coughed into his wine.

But Nesta only walked to the table and claimed a seat.

Mor blinked, but confided to me with a wince, "I think we're going to need a lot more wine."

Nesta's spine stiffened. But she said nothing.

"I'll raid the collection," Cassian offered, disappearing through the inner hall doors too quickly to be casual.

Nesta stiffened a bit more.

Teasing my sister, poking fun at her . . . I snatched a seat at Nesta's side and murmured, "They mean well."

Nesta just ran a finger over her ivory-and-obsidian place setting, examining the silverware with vines of night-blooming jasmine engraved around the hilts. "I don't care."

Amren slid into the seat across from me, right as Cassian returned, a bottle in each hand, and cringed. Amren said to my sister, "You're a real piece of work."

Nesta's eyes flicked up. Amren idly swirled a goblet of blood, watching her like a cat with a new, interesting toy.

Nesta only said, "Why do your eyes glow?"

Little curiosity—just a blunt need for explanation.

And no fear. None.

Amren angled her head. "You know, none of these busybodies have ever asked me that."

Those busybodies were trying not to look too concerned. As was I.

Nesta only waited.

Amren sighed, her dark bob swaying. "They glow because it was the one part of me the containment spell could not quite get right. The one glimpse into what lurks beneath."

"And what is beneath?"

None of the others spoke. Or even moved. Lucien, still by the window, had turned the color of fresh paper.

Amren traced a finger along the rim of her goblet, her red-tinted nail gleaming as bright as the blood inside. "They never dared ask me that, either."

"Why."

"Because it is not polite to ask—and they are afraid."

Amren held Nesta's stare, and my sister did not balk. Did not flinch.

"We are the same, you and I," Amren said.

I wasn't sure I was breathing. Through the bond, I wasn't sure Rhys was, either.

"Not in flesh, not in the thing that prowls beneath our skin and bones . . ." Amren's remarkable eyes narrowed. "But . . . I see the kernel, girl." Amren nodded, more to herself than anyone. "You did not fit—the mold that they shoved you into. The path you were born upon and forced to walk. You tried, and yet you did not, *could* not, fit. And then the path changed." A little nod. "I know—what it is to be that way. I remember it, long ago as it was."

Nesta had mastered the Fae's preternatural stillness far more quickly than I had. And she sat there for a few heartbeats, simply staring at the strange, delicate female across from her, weighing the words, the power that radiated from Amren . . . And then Nesta merely said, "I don't know what you're talking about."

Amren's red lips parted in a wide, serpentine smile. "When you erupt, girl, make sure it is felt across worlds."

A shiver slithered down my skin.

But Rhys drawled, "Amren, it seems, has been taking drama lessons at the theater down the street from her house."

She shot him a glare. "I mean it, Rhysand—"

"I'm sure you do," he said, claiming the seat to my right. "But I'd prefer to eat *something* before you make us lose our appetites."

His broad hand warmed my knee as he clasped it beneath the table, giving me a reassuring squeeze.

Cassian took the seat on Amren's left, Azriel beside him, Mor grabbing the seat opposite him, leaving Lucien . . .

Lucien frowned at the remaining place setting at the head of the table, then at the blank, barren spot across from Nesta. "I—shouldn't you sit at the head?"

Rhys raised an eyebrow. "I don't care where you sit. I only care about eating something right"—he snapped his fingers—"now."

The food, prepared by cooks I made a point to go meet in the belly of the House, appeared across the table in platters and spreads and bowls. Roast meats, various sauces and gravies, rice and bread, steamed vegetables fresh from the surrounding farms . . . I nearly sighed at the smells curling around me.

Lucien slid into his seat, looking for all the world like he was perching atop a pincushion.

I leaned past Nesta to explain to Lucien, "You get used to it—the informality."

"You say that, Feyre darling, like it's a bad thing," Rhys said, helping himself to a platter of pan-fried trout before passing it to me.

I rolled my eyes, sliding a few crispy pieces onto my plate. "It took me by surprise that first dinner we all had, just so you know."

"Oh, I know." Rhys grinned.

Cassian sniggered.

"Honestly," I said to Lucien, who wordlessly stacked a pile of buttery green beans onto his plate but didn't touch it, perhaps marveling at the simple fare, so at odds with the overwrought dishes of Spring, "Azriel is the only polite one." A few cries of outrage from Mor and Cassian, but a ghost of a smile danced on the shadowsinger's mouth as he dipped his head and hauled a platter of roast beets sprinkled with goat cheese toward himself. "Don't even try to pretend that it's not true."

"Of course it's true," Mor said with a loud sigh, "but you needn't make us sound like *heathens*."

"I would have thought you'd find that term to be a compliment, Mor," Rhys said mildly.

Nesta was watching the volley of words as if it were a sporting match, eyes darting between us. She didn't reach for any food, so I took the liberty of dumping spoonfuls of various things onto her plate.

She watched that, too.

And when I paused, moving on to further fill my own plate, Nesta said, "I understand—what you meant about the food."

It took me a moment to recall—to remember that particular conversation back at our father's estate, when she and I had been at each other's throats over the differences between human and Fae food. It was the same in terms of *what* was served, but it just . . . *tasted* better above the wall.

"Is that a compliment?"

Nesta didn't return my smile as she speared some asparagus with her fork and dug in.

And I figured it was as good a time as any as I said to Cassian, "What time are we back in the training ring tomorrow?"

To his credit, Cassian didn't so much as glance at Nesta as he replied with a lazy smile, "I'd say dawn, but since I'm feeling rather grateful that you're back in one piece, I'll let you sleep in. Let's meet at seven."

"I'd hardly call that sleeping in," I said.

"For an Illyrian, it is," Mor muttered.

Cassian's wings rustled. "Daylight is a precious resource."

"We live in the *Night Court*," Mor countered.

Cassian only grimaced at Rhys and Azriel. "I told you that the moment we started letting females into our group, they'd be nothing but trouble."

"As far as I can recall, Cassian," Rhys countered drily, "you actually said you needed a reprieve from staring at our ugly faces, and that some *ladies* would add some much-needed prettiness for you to look at all day."

"Pig," Amren said.

Cassian gave her a vulgar gesture that made Lucien choke on his green beans. "I was a young Illyrian and didn't know better," he said, then pointed his fork at Azriel. "Don't try to blend into the shadows. You said the same thing."

"He did not," Mor said, and the shadows that Azriel had indeed been subtly weaving around himself vanished. "Azriel has never once said anything that awful. Only you, Cassian. Only you."

The general of the High Lord's armies stuck out his tongue. Mor returned the gesture.

Amren scowled at Rhys. "You'd be wise to leave *both* of them at home for the meeting with the others, Rhysand. They'll cause nothing but trouble."

I dared a peek at Lucien—just to gauge his reaction.

His face was indeed controlled, but—a hint of surprise twinkled there. Wariness, too, but . . . surprise. I risked another glance at Nesta, but she was watching her plate, dutifully ignoring the others.

Rhys said, "It remains to be seen if they'll be joining us." Lucien looked at him then, the curiosity in that one eye unmistakable. Rhys noted it and shrugged. "You'll find out soon enough, I suppose. Invitations are going out tomorrow, calling all the High Lords to gather to discuss this war."

Lucien's hand tightened on his fork. "All?"

I wasn't sure if he meant Tamlin or his father, but Rhys nodded nonetheless.

Lucien considered. "Can I offer my unsolicited advice?"

Rhys smirked. "I think that's the first time anyone at this table has ever asked such a thing."

Mor and Cassian now stuck out their tongues at him.

But Rhys waved a lazy hand at Lucien. "By all means, advise away."

Lucien studied my mate, then me. "I assume Feyre is going."

"I am."

Amren sipped from her glass of blood—the only sound in the room as Lucien considered again. "Are you planning to hide her powers?"

Silence.

Rhys at last said, "That was something I'd planned to discuss with my mate. Are you leaning one way or another, Lucien?"

There was still something sharp in his tone, something just a little vicious.

Lucien studied me again, and it was an effort not to squirm. "My father would likely join with Hybern if he thought he stood a chance of getting his power back that way—by killing you."

A snarl from Rhys.

"Your brothers saw me, though," I said, setting down my fork. "Perhaps they could mistake the flame as yours, but the ice . . ."

Lucien jerked his chin to Azriel. "That's the information you need to gather. What my father knows—if my brothers realized what she was doing. You need to start from there, and build your plan for this meeting accordingly."

Mor said, "Eris might keep that information to himself and convince the others to as well, if he thinks it'll be more useful that way." I wondered if Mor looked at that red hair, the golden-brown skin that was a few shades darker than his brothers', and still saw Eris.

Lucien said evenly, "Perhaps. But we need to find that out. If Beron or Eris has that information, they'll use it to their advantage in that meeting—to control it. Or control you. Or they might not show up at all, and instead go right to Hybern."

Cassian swore softly, and I was inclined to echo the sentiment.

Rhys swirled his wine once, set it down, and said to Lucien, "You and Azriel should talk. Tomorrow."

Lucien glanced toward the shadowsinger—who only nodded at him. "I'm at your disposal."

None of us were dumb enough to ask if he'd be willing to reveal details on the Spring Court. If he thought that Tamlin would arrive. That was perhaps a conversation best left for another time. With just him and me.

Rhys leaned back in his seat. Contemplating—something. His jaw tightened, then he let out a near-silent huff of air. Steeling himself.

For whatever he was about to reveal, whatever plans he had decided not to reveal until now. And even as my stomach tightened, some sort of thrill went through me at it—at that clever mind at work.

Until Rhys said, "There is another meeting that needs to be had—and soon."

CHAPTER
18

"Please don't say we need to go to the Court of Nightmares," Cassian grumbled around a mouthful of food.

Rhys lifted a brow. "Not in the mood to terrorize our friends there?"

Mor's golden face paled. "You mean to ask my father to fight in this war," she said to Rhys.

I reined in my sharp intake of breath.

"What is the Court of Nightmares?" Nesta demanded.

Lucien answered for us. "The place where the rest of the world believes the majority of the Night Court to be." He jerked his chin at Rhys. "The seat of his power. Or it was."

"Oh, it still is," Rhys said. "To everyone outside Velaris." He leveled a steady look at Mor. "And yes. Keir's Darkbringer legion is considerable enough that a meeting is warranted."

The last meeting had resulted in Keir's arm being shattered in so many places it had gone saggy. I doubted the male would be inclined to help us anytime soon—perhaps why Rhys wanted this meeting.

Nesta's brows narrowed. "Why not just order them? Don't they answer to you?"

Cassian set down his fork, food forgotten. "Unfortunately, there are protocols in place between our two subcourts regarding this sort of thing. They mostly govern themselves—with Mor's father their steward."

Mor's throat bobbed. Azriel watched her carefully, his mouth a tight line.

"The steward of the Hewn City is legally entitled to refuse to aid my armies," Rhys explained to Nesta, to me. "It was part of the agreement my ancestor made with the Court of Nightmares all those thousands of years ago. They would remain within that mountain, would not challenge or disturb us beyond its borders . . . and would retain the right to decide *not* to assist in war."

"And have they—refused?" I asked.

Mor nodded gravely. "Twice. Not my father." She nearly choked on the word. "But . . . there were two wars. Long, long ago. They chose not to fight. We won, but . . . barely. At great cost."

And with this war upon us . . . we would need every ally we could muster. Every army.

"We leave in two days," Rhys said.

"He'll say no," Mor countered. "Don't waste your time."

"Then I shall have to find a way to convince him otherwise."

Mor's eyes flashed. "What?"

Azriel and Cassian shifted in their seats, and Amren clicked her tongue at Rhys. Disapproval.

"He fought in the War," Rhys said calmly. "Perhaps we'll be lucky this time, too."

"I'll remind you that the Darkbringer legion was nearly as bad as the enemy when it came to their behavior," Mor said, pushing her plate away.

"There will be new rules."

"You will not be in a position to make rules, and you know it," Mor snapped.

Rhys only swirled his wine again. "We'll see."

I glanced to Cassian. The general shook his head subtly. *Stay out of this one. For now.*

I swallowed, nodding back with equal faintness.

Mor whipped her head toward Azriel. "What do *you* think?"

The shadowsinger held her stare, his face unreadable. Considering. I tried not to hold my breath. Defending the female he loved or siding with his High Lord . . . "It's not my call to make."

"That's a bullshit answer," Mor challenged.

I could have sworn hurt flickered in Azriel's eyes, but he only shrugged, his face again a mask of cold indifference. Mor's lips pursed.

"You don't need to come, Mor," Rhys said with that calm, even voice.

"Of course I'm coming. It'll make it worse if I'm not there." She drained her wine in one swift tilt of her head. "I suppose I have two days now to find a dress suitable to horrify my father."

Amren, at least, chuckled at that, Cassian rumbling a laugh as well.

But Rhys watched Mor for a long minute, some of the stars in his eyes winking out. I debated asking if there was some other way, some path to avoid *this* awfulness between us, but . . . Earlier, I had snapped at him. And with Lucien and my sister here . . . I kept my mouth shut.

Well, about that matter. In the silence that fell, I scrambled for any scrap of normalcy and turned again to Cassian. "Let's train at *eight* tomorrow. I'll meet you in the ring."

"Seven thirty," he said with a disarming grin—one that most of his enemies would likely run from. Lucien went back to picking at his food. Mor refilled her wineglass, Azriel monitoring every move she made, his fork clenched in his scarred hand.

"Eight," I countered with a flat look. I turned to Nesta, silent and watchful through all of this. "Care to join?"

"No."

The beat of silence was too pointed to be dismissed. But I gave my sister a casual shrug, reaching for the wine jug. Then I said to none of them in particular, "I want to learn how to fly."

Mor spewed her wine across the table, splattering it right across Azriel's chest and neck. The shadowsinger was too busy gawking at me to even notice.

Cassian looked torn between howling at Azriel and gaping.

My magic was still too weak to grow those Illyrian wings, but I gestured to the Illyrians and said, "I want you to teach me."

Mor blurted, "Really?" while Lucien—*Lucien*—said, "Well, that explains the wings."

Nesta leaned forward to appraise me. "What wings?"

"I can—shape-shift," I admitted. "And with the oncoming conflict," I declared to all of them, "knowing how to fly might be . . . useful." I jerked my chin toward Cassian, who now studied me with unnerving intensity—sizing me up. "I assume the battles against Hybern will include Illyrians." A shallow nod from the general. "Then I plan to fight with you. In the skies."

I waited for the objections, for Rhys to shut it down.

There was only the howling wind outside the dining room windows.

Cassian whooshed out a breath. "I don't know if it's technically even possible—time-wise. You'd have to learn not only how to fly, but how to bear the weight of your shield and weapons—and how to work within an Illyrian unit. It takes us decades to master that last part alone. We have months at best—weeks at worst."

My chest sank a bit.

"Then we'll teach her what we know until then," Rhys said. But the stars in his eyes turned stone-cold as he added, "I'll give her any shot at an advantage—at getting away if things go to shit. Even a day of training might make a difference."

Azriel tucked in his wings, his beautiful features uncharacteristically soft. Contemplative. "I'll teach you."

"Are you . . . certain?" I asked.

The unreadable mask slipped back over Azriel's face. "Rhys and Cass were taught how to fly so young that they barely remember it."

But Azriel, locked in his hateful father's dungeons like some criminal until he was eleven, denied the ability to fly, to fight, to do anything his Illyrian instincts screamed at him to do . . .

Darkness rumbled down the bond. Not anger at me, but . . . as Rhys, too, remembered what had been done to his friend. He'd never forgotten. None of them had. It was an effort not to look at the brutal scars coating Azriel's hands. I prayed Nesta wouldn't inquire about it.

"We've taught plenty of younglings the basics," Cassian countered.

Azriel shook his head, shadows twining around his wrists. "It's not the same. When you're older, the fears, the mental blocks . . . it's different."

None of them, not even Amren, said anything.

Azriel only said to me, "I'll teach you. Train with Cass for a few hours, and I'll meet you when you're through." He added to Lucien, who did not balk from those writhing shadows, "After lunch, we'll meet."

I swallowed, but nodded. "Thank you." And perhaps Azriel's kindness snapped some sort of tether in me, but I turned to Nesta. "The King of Hybern is trying to bring down the wall by using the Cauldron to expand the holes already in it." Her blue-gray eyes revealed nothing— only simmering rage at the king's name. "I might be able to patch up those holes, but you . . . being made of the Cauldron itself . . . if the Cauldron can widen those holes, perhaps you can close them, too. With training—in whatever time we have."

"I can show you," Amren clarified to my sister. "Or, in theory I can. If we start soon—tomorrow morning." She considered, then declared to Rhys, "When you go to the Court of Nightmares, we will go with you."

I whipped my head to Amren. "What?" The thought of Nesta in that place—

"The Hewn City is a trove of objects of power," Amren explained. "There may be opportunities to practice. Let the girl get a feel for what something like the wall or the Cauldron might be like." She added when Azriel seem poised to object, "*Covertly*."

Nesta said nothing.

I waited for her outright refusal, the cold shutdown of all hope.

But Nesta only asked, "Why not just kill the King of Hybern before he can act?"

Utter silence.

Amren said a bit softly, "If you want his killing blow, girl, it's yours."

Nesta's gaze drifted toward the open interior doors of the dining room. As if she could see all the way to Elain. "What happened to the human queens?"

I blinked. "What do you mean?"

"Were they made immortal?" This question went to Azriel.

Azriel's Siphons smoldered. "Reports have been murky and inconsistent. Some say yes, others say no."

Nesta examined her wineglass.

Cassian braced his forearms on the table. "Why?"

Nesta's eyes shot right to his face. She spoke quietly to me, to all of us, even as she held Cassian's gaze as if he were the only one in the room. "By the end of this war, I want them dead. The king, the queens—all of them. Promise me you'll kill them all, and I'll help you patch up the wall. I'll train with her"—a jerk of her chin to Amren—"I'll go to the Hewn City or whatever it is . . . I'll do it. But only if you promise me that."

"Fine," I said. "And we might need your assistance during the meeting with the High Lords—to provide testimony to other courts and allies of what Hybern is capable of. What was done to you."

"No."

"You don't mind fixing the wall or going to the Court of Nightmares, but speaking to people is where you draw your line?"

Nesta's mouth tightened. "No."

High Lady or sister; sister or High Lady . . . "People's lives might depend on your account of it. The success of this meeting with the High Lords might depend upon it."

She gripped the arms of her chair, as if restraining herself. "Don't talk down to me. My answer is no."

I angled my head. "I understand that what happened to you was horrible—"

"You have *no idea* what it was or was not. None. And I am not going to grovel like one of those Children of the Blessed, begging High Fae who would have gladly killed me as a mortal to help us. I'm not going to tell them *that* story—*my* story."

"The High Lords might not believe our account, which makes you a valuable witness—"

Nesta shoved her chair back, chucking her napkin on her plate, gravy soaking through the fine linen. "Then it is not my problem if you're unreliable. I'll help you with the wall, but I am not going to whore my story around to everyone on your behalf." She shot to her feet, color rising to her ordinarily pale face, and hissed, "And if you even *dare* suggest to Elain that she do such a thing, I will rip out your *throat*."

Her eyes lifted from mine to sweep over everyone—extending the threat.

None of us spoke as she left the dining room and slammed the door shut behind her.

I slumped in my chair, resting my head against the back.

Something thumped in front of me. A bottle of wine. "It's fine if you drink directly from it," was all Mor said.

⊹

"I'd say Nesta rivals Amren for sheer bloodthirstiness," Rhys mused hours later as he and I walked alone through the streets of Velaris. "The only difference is that Amren actually drinks it."

I snorted, shaking my head as we turned onto the broad street beside the Sidra and meandered along the star-flecked river.

So many scars still marred the lovely buildings of Velaris, streets gouged from fallen debris and claws. Most of it had been repaired, but some storefronts had been left boarded up, some homes along the river no more than mounds of rubble. We'd flown down from the House as soon as we'd finished dinner—well, the wine, I supposed. Mor had taken another bottle with her when she'd disappeared into the House, Azriel frowning after her.

Rhys and I hadn't invited anyone else with us. He'd only asked me through the bond, *Walk with me?* And I'd merely given him a subtle nod.

And here we were. We'd walked for over an hour now, mostly quiet, mostly . . . thinking. Of the words and information and threats shared today. Neither of us slowed our steps until we reached that little restaurant where we had all dined under the stars one night.

Something tight in my chest eased as I beheld the untouched building, the potted citrus plants sighing in the river breeze. And on that breeze . . . those delectable, rich spices, garlicky meat, simmering tomatoes . . . I leaned my back against the rail along the river walkway, watching the restaurant workers serve the packed tables.

"Who knows," I murmured, answering him at last. "Perhaps Nesta will take up the blood-drinking habit, too. I certainly believe her threat to rip out my throat. Maybe she'll enjoy the taste."

Rhys chuckled, the sound rumbling into my bones as he took up a spot beside me, his elbows braced on the rail, wings tucked in tight. I breathed in deeply, taking the citrus-and-sea scent of him into my lungs, my blood. His mouth grazed my neck. "Will you hate me if I say that Nesta is . . . difficult?"

I laughed softly. "I'd say this went fairly well, all things considered. She agreed to one thing, at least." I chewed on my lower lip. "I shouldn't have asked her in public. I made a mistake."

He remained silent, listening.

"With the others," I asked, "how do you find that balance—between High Lord and family?"

Rhys considered. "It isn't easy. I've made plenty of bad calls over the centuries. So I hate to tell you that tonight might only be the start of it."

I loosed a long sigh. "I should have considered that telling strangers what happened to her in Hybern might . . . might not be something she was comfortable with. My sister has been a private person her entire life, even amongst us."

Rhys leaned in to kiss my neck again. "Earlier today—at the loft," he said, pulling back to meet my eyes. Unflinching. Open. "I didn't mean to insult her."

"I'm sorry I snapped at you."

He lifted a dark brow. "Why in hell would you be? I insulted your sister; you defended her. You had every right to kick my ass for it."

"I didn't mean to . . . undermine you."

Shadows flickered in his eyes. "Ah." He twisted toward the Sidra, and I followed suit. The water meandered past, its dark surface rippling with golden faelights from the streetlamps and the bright jewels of the Rainbow. "That was why it was . . . strange between us this afternoon." He cringed and faced me fully. "Mother above, Feyre."

My cheeks heated and I interrupted before he could continue. "I get why, though. A solid, unified front is important." I scratched at the smooth wood of the rail with a finger. "Especially for us."

"Not amongst our family."

Warmth spread through me at the words—*our* family.

He took my hand, interlacing our fingers. "We can make whatever rules we want. You have every right to question me, push me—both in private and in public." A snort. "Of course, if you decide to truly kick my ass, I might request that it's done behind closed doors so I don't have to suffer centuries of teasing, but—"

"I won't undermine you in public. And you won't undermine me."

He remained quiet, letting me think, speak.

"We can question each other through the bond if we're around people other than our friends," I said. "But for now, for these initial years, I'd like to show the world a unified front . . . That is, if we survive."

"We'll survive." Uncompromising will in those words, that face. "But I want you to feel comfortable pushing me, calling me out—"

"When have I ever *not* done that?" He smiled. But I added, "I want you to do the same—for me."

"Deal. But amongst our family . . . call me on my bullshit all you want. I insist, actually."

"Why?"

"Because it's fun."

I nudged him with an elbow.

"Because you're my equal," he said. "And as much as that means having each other's backs in public, it also means that we grant each other the gift of honesty. Of truth."

I surveyed the bustling city around us. "Can I give you a bit of truth, then?"

He stilled, but said, "Always."

I blew out a breath. "I think you should be careful—working with Keir. Not for how despicable he is, but because . . . I think you could truly wound Mor if you don't play it right."

Rhys dragged a hand through his hair. "I know. I know."

"Is it worth it—whatever troops he can offer? If it means hurting her?"

"We've been working with Keir for centuries. She should be used to it by now. And yes—his troops are worth it. The Darkbringers are well trained, powerful, and have been idle too long."

I considered. "The last time we went to the Court of Nightmares, I played your whore."

He winced at the word.

"But I am now your High Lady," I went on, stroking a finger over the back of his hand. He tracked the movement. My voice dropped lower. "To get Keir to agree to aid us . . . Any tips on what mask I should wear to the Hewn City?"

"It's for you to decide," he said, still watching my finger trace idle circles on his skin. "You've seen how I am there—how we are. It is for you to decide how to play into that."

"I suppose I'd better decide soon—not just for this, but the meeting with the other High Lords in two weeks."

Rhys slid a sidelong glance to me. "Every court is invited."

"I doubt he'll come, given that he is Hybern's ally and knows we'd kill him."

The river breeze stirred his blue-black hair. "The meeting will occur with a binding spell that forces us all into cease-fire. If someone breaks it while the meeting occurs, the magic will demand a steep cost. Probably their life. Tamlin wouldn't be stupid enough to attack—nor us him."

"Why invite him at all?"

"Excluding him will only give him more ammunition against us. Believe me, I have little desire to see him. Or Beron. Who perhaps is higher on my kill list than Tamlin right now."

"Tarquin will be there. And *we* are pretty high on his kill list."

"Even with the blood rubies, he wouldn't be stupid enough to attack during the meeting." Rhys sighed through his nose.

"How many allies can we count on? Beyond Keir and the Hewn City, I mean." I glanced down the river walkway. The diners and revelers were too busy enjoying themselves to even note our presence, even with Rhys's recognizable wings. Still—perhaps not the best place for this conversation.

"I'm not sure," Rhys admitted. "Helion and his Day Court, probably. Kallias . . . maybe. Things have been strained with the Winter Court since Under the Mountain."

"I assume Azriel is going to be finding out more."

"He's already on the hunt."

I nodded. "Amren claimed she and Nesta needed help researching ways to repair the wall." I gestured to the city. "Point me toward the best library to find that sort of thing."

Rhys's brows lifted. "Right now? Your work ethic puts mine to shame."

I hissed, "*Tomorrow*, smartass."

He chuckled, wings flaring and tucking in tight. Wings . . . wings he'd allowed Lucien to see.

"You trust Lucien."

Rhys angled his head at the not-quite question. "I trust in the fact that we currently have possession of the one thing he wants above all else. And as long as that remains, he'll try to stay on our good side. But if that changes . . . His talent was wasted in the Spring Court. There was a reason he had that fox mask, you know." His mouth tugged to the side. "If he got Elain away, back to Spring or wherever . . . do you believe, deep down, that he wouldn't sell what he knows? Either for gain, or to ensure she stays safe?"

"You let him hear everything tonight, though."

"None of it is information that would let Hybern wreck us. The king likely already knows that we'll go for Keir's alliance—that we'll try to find a way to stop him from bringing down the wall. He wasn't subtle with Dagdan and Brannagh's searching. And he'll expect us to try to band the High Lords together. Which is why the meeting location will not be decided until later. Will I tell Lucien then? Bring him along?"

I considered his question: Did *I* trust Lucien? "I don't know, either," I admitted, and sighed. "I don't like that Elain is a pawn in this."

"I know. It's never easy."

He'd dealt with such things for centuries. "I want to wait—see what Lucien does over the next two weeks. How he acts, with us and Elain. What Azriel thinks of him." I frowned. "He's not a bad person—he's not evil."

"He certainly isn't."

"I just . . ." I met his calm, steady stare. "There is risk in trusting him without question."

"Did he discuss what he feels regarding Tamlin?"

"No. I didn't want to push on that. He was . . . remorseful about what happened with me, and Hybern, and Elain. Would he have felt that way without Elain in the mix? I don't know—maybe. I don't think he would have left, though."

Rhys brushed the hair from my face. "It's all part of the game, Feyre darling. Who to trust, when to trust them—what information to barter."

"Do you enjoy it?"

"Sometimes. Right now, I don't. Not when the risks are this high." His fingers grazed my brow. "When I have so much to lose."

I laid my palm on his chest, right over those Illyrian tattoos beneath his clothes, right over his heart. Felt the sturdy beat echoing into my skin and bones.

I forgot the city around us as he met my eyes, lips hovering over my skin, and murmured, "We will keep planning for the future, war or no war. *I* will keep planning for our future."

My throat burned, and I nodded.

"We deserve to be happy," he said, his eyes sparkling enough to tell me that he recalled the words I'd given him on the town house roof after the attack. "And I will fight with everything I have to ensure it."

"*We* will fight," I said hoarsely. "Not just you—not anymore."

Too much. He had given too much already, and still seemed to think it was not enough.

But Rhys only peered over his broad shoulder, to the cheerful restaurant behind us. "That first night we all came here," he said, and I followed his gaze, watching the workers set the tables with loving precision. "When you told Sevenda that you felt awake while eating her food . . ." He shook his head. "It was the first time you had looked . . . peaceful. Like you were indeed awake, *alive* again. I was so relieved I thought I'd puke right onto the table."

I recalled the long, strange look he'd given me when I'd finally spoken. Then the long walk we'd taken home, when we'd heard that music he'd sent to my cell Under the Mountain.

I pushed off the rail and tugged him toward the bridge that spanned the Sidra—the bridge to take us home. Let the debate over who'd give the most in this war rest for now. "Walk with me—through the Rainbow." The glittering, colorful jewel of the city, the beating heart that housed the artists' quarter. Vibrant and thrumming at this hour of the night.

I linked arms with him before saying, "You and this city helped wake me up—helped bring me back to life." His eyes flickered as I smiled up at him. "I will fight with everything I have, too, Rhys. Everything."

He only kissed the top of my head, tugging me closer as we crossed the Sidra under the starry sky.

CHAPTER
19

It was a good thing I'd insisted on meeting Cassian at eight, because even though I awoke at dawn, one look at Rhysand's sleeping face had me deciding to spend the morning slowly, sweetly waking him up.

I was still flushed by the time Rhys dropped me at the sparring ring atop the House of Wind, the space surrounded by a wall of red rock, the top open to the elements. He promised to meet me after lunch to show me the library for my researching, then gave me a roguish wink and kiss on the cheek before he shot back into the sky with a powerful flap of his wings.

Leaning against the wall beside the weapons rack, Cassian only said, "I hope you didn't exert yourself too much already, because this is *really* going to hurt."

I rolled my eyes, even as I tried to shut out the image of Rhysand laying me on my stomach, then kissing his way down my spine. Lower. Tried to shut out the feeling of his strong hands gripping my hips and lifting them up, up, until he lay beneath them and feasted on me, until I was quietly begging him and he rose behind me and I had to bite my pillow to keep from waking the whole house with my moaning.

Rhysand in the morning was . . . I didn't have words for what it was when he was unhurried and lazy and wicked, when his hair was still mussed with sleep and his eyes got that glazed, purely male gleam in them. They'd still had that lazy, satisfied glint a moment ago, and his mockingly chaste kiss on my cheek had sent a red-hot line through me.

Later. I'd torture him later.

For now . . . I strode to where Cassian stood, rotating my shoulders. "Two Illyrian males making me sweat in one morning. What's a female to do?"

Cassian barked a laugh. "At least you showed up with some spirit."

I grinned, bracing my hands on my hips as I surveyed the weapons rack. "Which one?"

"None." He jerked his chin toward the ring etched in white chalk behind us. "It's been a while since we trained. We're spending today going over the basics."

The words were laced with enough tightness that I said, "It hasn't been that long."

"It's been a month and a half."

I studied him, the wings tucked in tight, the shoulder-length dark hair. "What's wrong?"

"Nothing." He stalked past me to the ring.

"Is it Nesta?"

"Not everything in my life is about your sister, you know."

I kept my mouth shut on that front. "Is it something with the Court of Nightmares visit tomorrow?"

Cassian shucked off his shirt, revealing rippling muscles covered in beautiful, intricate tattoos. Illyrian markings for luck and glory. "It's nothing. Get into position."

I obeyed, even as I eyed him carefully. "You're . . . angry."

He refused to speak until I started my circuit of warm-ups: various lunges, kicks, and stretches designed to loosen my muscles. And only when we'd begun sparring, his hands wrapped against my onslaught of punching, did he say, "You and Rhys hid the truth from us. And we went into Hybern blind about it."

"About what?"

"That you're High Lady."

I jabbed at his raised hands in a one-two combination, breathing hard. "What difference would it have made?"

"It would have changed *everything*. None of it would have gone down like that."

"Perhaps that's why Rhys decided to keep it a secret."

"Hybern was a *disaster*."

I halted my punching. "You knew I was his mate when we went. I don't see how being High Lady alters anything."

"It does."

I put my hands on my hips, ignoring his motion to continue. "Why?"

Cassian dragged a hand through his hair. "Because . . . because as his mate, you were still . . . his to protect. Oh, don't get that look. He's yours to protect, too. I would have laid my life down for you as his mate—and as your friend. But you were still . . . his."

"And as High Lady?"

Cassian loosed a rough breath. "As High Lady, you are *mine*. And Azriel's, and Mor's and Amren's. You belong to all of us, and we belong to *you*. We would not have . . . put you in so much danger."

"Maybe that's why Rhys wanted to keep it a secret. It would have changed your focus."

"This is between you and me. And trust me, Rhys and I had . . . *words* about this."

I lifted a brow. "You're mad at me?"

He shook his head, eyes shuttering.

"Cassian."

He just held up his hands in a silent order to continue.

I sighed and began again. It was only after I'd gotten through fifteen repetitions and was panting heavily that Cassian said, "You didn't think you were essential. You saved our asses, yes, but . . . you didn't think you were essential here."

One-two, one-two, one-two. "I'm not." He opened his mouth, but I charged ahead, speaking around my gasps for breath. "You all have a . . . duty—you're all vital. Yes, I have my own abilities, but . . . You and Azriel were hurt, my sisters were . . . you know what happened to them. I did what I could to get us out. I'd rather it was me than any of you. I couldn't have lived with the alternative."

His upraised hands were unfaltering as I pummeled them. "Anything could have happened to you at the Spring Court."

I stopped again. "If Rhys isn't grilling me with the overprotective bullshit, then I don't see why *you*—"

"Don't for one moment think that Rhys wasn't beside himself with worry. Oh, he seems collected enough, Feyre, but I know him. And every moment you were gone, he was in a *panic*. Yes, he knew—we knew—you could handle yourself. But it doesn't stop us from worrying."

I shook out my sore hands, then rubbed my already-aching arms. "You were mad at him, too."

"If I hadn't been healing, I would have kicked his ass from one end of Velaris to the other."

I didn't reply.

"We were all terrified for you."

"I managed just fine."

"Of course you did. We knew you would. But . . ." Cassian crossed his arms. "Rhys pulled the same shit fifty years ago. When he went to that damned party Amarantha threw."

Oh. *Oh*.

"I'll never forget it, you know," he said, blowing out a breath. "The moment when he spoke to us all, mind to mind. When I realized what was happening, and that . . . he'd saved us. Trapped us here and tied our hands, but . . ." He scratched at his temple. "It went quiet—in my head. In a way it hadn't been before. Not since . . ." Cassian squinted at the cloudless sky. "Even with utter hell unleashing here, across our territory, I just went . . . quiet." He tapped the side of his head with a finger, and frowned. "After Hybern, the healer kept me asleep while she worked on my wings. So when I woke up two weeks later . . . that's when I heard. And when Mor told me what happened to you . . . It went quiet again."

I swallowed against the constriction of my throat. "You found me when I needed you most, Cassian."

"Pleased to be of service." He gave me a grim smile. "You can rely on us, you know. Both of you. He's inclined to do everything himself— to *give* everything of himself. He can't stand to let anyone else offer up anything." That smile faded. "Neither can you."

"And you can?"

"It's not easy, but yes. I'm general of his armies. Part of that includes knowing how to delegate. I've been with Rhys for over five hundred years and he still tries to do everything himself. Still thinks it's not enough."

I knew that—too well. And the thought of Rhys, in this war, trying to take on all that faced us . . . Nausea churned in my gut. "He gives orders all the time."

"Yes. And he's good at knowing what we excel at. But when it comes down to it . . ." Cassian adjusted the wrappings on his hands. "If the High Lords and Keir don't step up, he'll still face Hybern. And will take the brunt of it so we don't have to."

An unshakable, queasy sort of tightness pushed in on me. Rhys would survive—he wouldn't dare sacrifice everything to make sure we—

Rhys would. He had with Amarantha, and he'd do it again without hesitation.

I shut it out. Shoved it down. Focused on my breathing.

Something drew Cassian's attention behind me. And even as his body remained casual, a predatory gleam flickered in his eyes.

I didn't need to turn to know who was standing there.

"Care to join?" Cassian purred.

Nesta said, "It doesn't look like you're exercising anything other than your mouths."

I looked over my shoulder. My sister was in a dress of pale blue that turned her skin golden, her hair swept up, her back a stiff column. I scrambled to say something, to apologize, but . . . not in front of him. She wouldn't want this conversation in front of Cassian.

Cassian extended a wrapped hand, his fingers curling in a come-hither motion. "Scared?"

I wisely kept my mouth shut as Nesta stepped from the open doorway into the blinding light of the courtyard. "Why should I be scared of an oversized bat who likes to throw temper tantrums?"

I choked, and Cassian shot me a warning glare, daring me to laugh. But I felt for that bond in my mind, lowering my mental shields enough to say to Rhysand, wherever he was in the city, *Please come spare me from Cassian and Nesta's bickering.*

A heartbeat later, Rhys crooned, *Regretting becoming High Lady?*

I savored that voice—that humor. But I shoved that simmering panic down again as I countered, *Is this part of my duties?*

A sensual, dark laugh. *Why do you think I was so desperate for a partner? I've had almost five centuries to deal with this alone. It's only fair you have to endure it now.*

Cassian was saying to Nesta, "Seems like you're a little on edge, Nesta. And you left so abruptly last night . . . Any way I can help ease that tension?"

Please, I begged Rhys.

What will you give me?

I wasn't sure if I could *hiss* down the bond between us, but from the chuckle that echoed into my mind a heartbeat later, I knew the feeling had been conveyed. *I'm in a meeting with the governors of the Palaces. They might be a little pissy if I vanish.* I tried not to sigh.

Nesta picked at her nails. "Amren is coming to instruct me in a few—"

Shadow rippled across the courtyard, cutting her off. And it wasn't Rhysand who landed between us, but—

I sent another pretty face for you to admire, Rhys said. *Not as beautiful as mine, of course, but a close second.*

As the shadows wreathing him cleared, Azriel sized up Nesta and Cassian, then threw a vaguely sympathetic look in my direction. "I need to start our lesson early."

A piss-poor lie, but I said, "Right. No problem at all."

Cassian glowered at me, then Azriel. We both ignored him as I strode to the shadowsinger, unwrapping my hands as I went.

Thank you, I said down the bond.

You can make it up to me tonight.

I tried not to blush at the image Rhys sent into my head detailing precisely how I'd repay him, and slammed down my mental shields. On the other side of them, I could have sworn talon-tipped fingers trailed down the black adamant in a sensual, silent promise. I swallowed hard.

Azriel's wings spread, dark reds and golds shining through in the bright sun, and he opened his arms to me. "The pine forest will be good—the one by the lake."

"Why?"

"Because water is better to fall into than hard rock," Cassian replied, crossing his arms.

My stomach clenched. But I let Azriel scoop me up, his scent of night-chilled mist and cedar wrapping around me as he flapped his wings once, stirring the dirt of the courtyard.

I caught Cassian's narrowed gaze and grinned widely. "Good luck," I said, and Azriel, Cauldron bless him, shot into the cloudless sky.

Neither of us missed Cassian's barked, filthy curse, though we didn't deign to comment.

Cassian was a general—*the* general of the Night Court.

Surely Nesta wasn't anything he couldn't handle.

⊹

"I dropped Amren off at the House on my way in," Azriel told me as we landed at the shore of a turquoise mountain lake flanked by pines and granite. "I told her to get to the training ring immediately." A half smile. "After a few minutes, that is."

I snorted and stretched my arms. "Poor Cassian."

Azriel gave a huff of amusement. "Indeed."

I shifted on my feet, small gray rocks along the shore skittering beneath my boots. "So . . ."

Azriel's black hair seemed to gobble up the blinding sunlight. "In order to fly," he said drily, "you'll need wings."

Right.

My face heated. I rolled and cracked my wrists. "It's been a while since I summoned them."

His piercing stare didn't stray from my face, my posture. As immovable and steady as the granite this lake had been carved into. I might as well have been a flitting butterfly by comparison. "Do you need me to turn around?" He lifted a dark brow in emphasis.

I cringed. "No. But . . . it might take me a few tries."

"We started our lesson early—we've got plenty of time."

"I appreciate you making the effort to pretend that it wasn't because I was desperate to avoid Cassian and Nesta's early-morning bickering."

"I'd never let my High Lady suffer through that." He said it completely stone-faced.

I chuckled, rubbing at a sore spot on my shoulder. "Are you . . . ready to meet with Lucien this afternoon?"

Azriel angled his head. "*Should* I be preparing for it?"

"No. I just . . ." I shrugged. "When do you leave to gather information on the High Lords?"

"After I talk to him." His eyes were shining—lit with amusement. As if he knew I was buying time.

I blew out a breath. "Right. Here we go."

Touching that part of me, the part Tamlin had given me . . . Some vital piece of my heart recoiled. Even as something sharp and vicious in my gut preened at what I'd taken. All that I'd taken.

I shoved out the thoughts, focusing on those Illyrian wings. I'd summoned them that day in the Steppes from pure memory and fear. Creating them now . . . I let my mind slip into my recollections of Rhys's wings, how they felt and moved and weighed . . .

"The frame needs to be a bit thicker," Azriel offered as a weight began to drag at my back. "Strengthen the muscles leading to it."

I obeyed, my magic listening in turn. He provided more feedback, where to add and where to ease up, where to smooth and where to toughen.

I was rasping for breath, sweat sliding down my spine, by the time he said, "Good." He cleared his throat. "I know you're not Illyrian, but . . . amongst their kind, it is considered . . . inappropriate to touch someone's wings without permission. Especially females."

Their kind. Not his.

It took me a moment to realize what he was asking. "Oh—oh. Go ahead."

"I need to ascertain if they *feel* right."

"Right." I put my back to him, my muscles groaning as they worked to spread the wings. Everything—from my neck to my shoulders to my ribs to my spine to my ass—seemed to now control them, and was barking in protest at the weight and movement.

I'd only had them for a few seconds with Lucien in the Steppes—I hadn't realized how heavy they were, how complex the muscles.

Azriel's hands, for all their scarring, were featherlight as he grasped and touched certain areas, patting and tapping others. I gritted my teeth, the sensation like . . . like having the arch of my foot tickled and poked. But he made quick work of it, and I rolled my shoulders again as he stepped around me to murmur, "It's—amazing. They're the same as mine."

"I think the magic did most of the work."

A shake of the head. "You're an artist—it was your attention to detail."

I blushed a bit at the compliment, and braced my hands on my hips. "Well? Do we jump into the skies?"

"First lesson: don't let them drag on the ground."

I blinked. My wings were indeed resting on the rocks. "Why?"

"Illyrians think it's lazy—a sign of weakness. And from a practical standpoint, the ground is full of things that could hurt your wings. Splinters, shards of rock . . . They can not only get stuck and lead to infection, but also impact the way the wing catches the wind. So keep them off the ground."

Knife-sharp pain rippled down my back as I tried to lift them. I managed getting the left upright. The right just drooped like a loose sail.

"You need to strengthen your back muscles—and your thighs. And your arms. And core."

"So everything, then."

Again, that dry, quiet smile. "Why do you think Illyrians are so fit?"

"Why did no one warn me about this cocky side of yours?"

Azriel's mouth twitched upward. "Both wings up."

A quiet but unyielding demand.

I winced, contorting my body this way and that as I fought to get the right one to rise. No luck.

"Try spreading them, then tucking in, if you can't lift it up like that."

I obeyed, and hissed at the sharp pain along every muscle in my back as I flared the wings. Even the slightest breeze off the lake tickled and tugged, and I braced my feet apart on the rocky shore, seeking some semblance of balance—

"Now fold inward."

I did, snapping them shut—the movement so fast that I toppled forward.

Azriel caught me before I could eat stone, gripping me tightly under the shoulder and hauling me up. "Building your core muscles will also help with the balance."

"So, back to Cassian, then."

A nod. "Tomorrow. Today, focus on lifting and folding, spreading and lifting." Azriel's wings gleamed with red and gold as the sun gilded them. "Like this." He demonstrated, flaring his wings wide, tucking them in, flaring, angling, tucking them in. Over and over.

Sighing, I followed his movements, my back throbbing and aching. Perhaps flying lessons were a waste of time.

CHAPTER
20

"I've never been to a library before," I admitted to Rhys after lunch, as we strode down level after level beneath the House of Wind, my words echoing off the carved red stone. I winced with every step, rubbing at my back.

Azriel had given me a tonic that would help with the soreness, but I knew that by tonight, I'd be whimpering. If hours of researching any way to patch up those holes in the wall didn't make me start first.

"I mean," I clarified, "not counting the private libraries here and at the Spring Court, and my family had one as well, but not . . . Not a real one."

Rhys glanced sidelong at me. "I've heard that the humans have free libraries on the continent—open to anyone."

I wasn't sure if it was a question or not, but I nodded. "In one of the territories, they allow anyone in, regardless of their station or blood-line." I considered his words. "Did . . . were there libraries before the War?"

Of course there had been, but what I meant—

"Yes. Great libraries, full of cranky scholars who could find you tomes dating back thousands of years. But humans were not allowed inside—unless you were someone's slave on an errand, and even then you were closely watched."

"Why?"

"Because the books were full of magic, and things they wanted to keep humans from knowing." Rhys slid his hands into his pockets, leading me down a corridor lit only by bowls of faelight upraised in the hands of beautiful female statues, their forms High Fae and faerie alike. "The scholars and librarians refused to keep slaves of their own— some for personal reasons, but mainly because they didn't want them accessing the books and archives."

Rhys gestured down another curving stairwell. We must have been far beneath the mountain, the air dry and cool—and heavy. As if it had been trapped inside for ages. "What happened to the libraries once the wall was built?"

Rhys tucked in his wings as the stairs became tighter, the ceiling dropping. "Most scholars had enough time to evacuate—and were able to winnow the books out. But if they didn't have the time or the brute power . . ." A muscle ticked in his jaw. "They burned the libraries. Rather than let the humans access their precious information."

A chill snaked down my spine. "They'd rather have lost that information forever?"

He nodded, the dim light gilding his blue-black hair. "Prejudices aside, the fear was that the humans would find dangerous spells—and use them on us."

"But we—I mean, *they* don't have magic. Humans don't have magic."

"Some do. Usually the ones who can claim distant Fae ancestry. But some of those spells don't require magic from the wielder—only the right words, or use of ingredients."

His words snagged on something in my mind. "Could—I mean, obviously they did, but . . . Humans and Fae once interbred. What happened to the offspring? If you were half Fae, half human, where did you go once the wall went up?"

Rhys stepped into a hall at the foot of the stairs, revealing a wide passageway of carved red stone and a sealed set of obsidian doors, veins of silver running throughout. Beautiful—terrifying. Like some great beast was kept behind them.

"It did not go well for the half-breeds," he said after a moment. "Many were offspring of unwanted unions. Most usually chose to stay with their human mothers—their human families. But once the wall went up, amongst humans, they were a . . . reminder of what had been done, of the enemies lurking above the wall. At best, they were outcasts and pariahs, their children—if they bore the physical traits—as well. At worst . . . Humans were angry in those initial years, and that first generation afterward. They wanted someone to pay for the slavery, for the crimes against them. Even if the half-breed had done nothing wrong . . . It did not end well."

He approached the doors, which opened on a phantom wind, as if the mountain itself lived to serve him.

"And the ones above the wall?"

"They were deemed even lower than lesser faeries. Either they were unwanted everywhere they went, or . . . many found work on the streets. Selling themselves."

"Here in Velaris?" My words were a bare brush of air.

"My father was still High Lord then," Rhys said, his back stiffening. "We had not allowed any humans, slave or free, into our territory in centuries. He did not allow them in—either to whore or to find sanctuary."

"And once you were High Lord?"

Rhys halted before the gloom that spread beyond us. "By then, it was too late for most of them. It is hard to . . . offer refuge to someone without being able to explain *where* we were offering them a safe place. To get the word out about it while maintaining our illusion of ruthless cruelty." The starlight guttered in his eyes. "Over the years, we encountered a few. Some were able to make it here. Some were . . . beyond our help."

Something moved in the darkness beyond the doors, but I kept my focus on his face, on his tensed shoulders. "If the wall comes down, will . . . ?" I couldn't finish the words.

Rhys slid his fingers through mine, interlacing our hands. "Yes. If there are those, human or faerie, who need a safe place . . . this city will be open to them. Velaris has been closed off for so long—too long, perhaps. Adding new people, from different places, different histories and cultures . . . I do not see how that could be a bad thing. The transition might be more complex than we anticipate, but . . . yes. The gates to this city will be open for those who need its protection. To any who can make it here."

I squeezed his hand, savoring the hard-earned calluses on it. No, I would not let him bear the burden of this war, its cost, alone.

Rhys glanced to the open doors—to the hooded and cloaked figure patiently waiting in the shadows beyond them. Every aching sinew and bone locked up as I took in the pale robes, the hood crowned with a limpid blue stone, the panel that could be lowered over the eyes—

Priestess.

"This is Clotho," Rhys said calmly, releasing my hand to guide me toward the awaiting female. The weight of his hand on my lower back told me enough about how much he realized the sight of her would jar me. "She's one of the dozens of priestesses who work here."

Clotho lowered her head in a bow, but said nothing.

"I—I didn't know that the priestesses left their temples."

"A library is a temple of sorts," Rhys said with a wry smile. "But the priestesses here . . ." As we entered the library proper, golden lights flickered to life. As if Clotho had been in utter darkness until we'd entered. "They are special. Unique."

She angled her head in what might have been amusement. Her face remained in shadow, her slim body concealed in those pale, heavy robes. Silence—and yet life danced around her.

Rhys smiled warmly at the priestess. "Did you find the texts?"

And it was only when she bobbed her head in a sort of "so-so" motion that I realized either she could not or would not speak. Clotho gestured to her left—into the library itself.

And I dragged my eyes away from the mute priestess long enough to take in the library.

Not a cavernous room in a manor. Not even close.

This was . . .

It was as if the base of the mountain had been hollowed out by some massive digging beast, leaving a pit descending into the dark heart of the world. Around that gaping hole, carved into the mountain itself, spiraled level after level of shelves and books and reading areas, leading into the inky black. From what I could see of the various levels as I drifted toward the carved stone railing overlooking the drop, the stacks shot far into the mountain itself, like the spokes of a mighty wheel.

And through it all, fluttering like moth's wings, the rustle of paper and parchment.

Silent, and yet alive. Awake and humming and restless, some many-limbed beast at constant work. I peered upward, finding more levels rising toward the House above. And lurking far below . . . Darkness.

"What's at the bottom of the pit?" I asked as Rhys came up beside me, his shoulder brushing mine.

"I once dared Cassian to fly down and see." Rhys braced his hands on the railing, gazing down into the gloom.

"And?"

"And he came back up, faster than I've ever seen him fly, white as death. He never told me what he saw. The first few weeks, I thought it was a joke—just to pique my curiosity. But when I finally decided to see for myself a month later, he threatened to tie me to a chair. He said some things were better left unseen and undisturbed. It's been two hundred years, and he still won't tell me what he saw. If you even mention it, he goes pale and shaky and won't talk for a few hours."

My blood chilled. "Is it . . . some sort of monster?"

"I have no idea." Rhys jerked his chin toward Clotho, the priestess patiently waiting a few steps behind us, her face still in shadow. "They don't speak or write of it, so if they know . .*. They certainly won't tell me. So if it doesn't bother us, then I won't bother it. That is, if it's even an *it*. Cassian never said if he saw anything living down there. Perhaps it's something else entirely."

Considering the things I'd already witnessed . . . I didn't want to think about what lay at the bottom of the library. Or what could make Cassian, who had seen more dreadful and deadly parts of the world than I could ever imagine, so terrified.

Robes rustling, Clotho aimed for the sloping walkway into the library, and we fell into step behind her. The floors were red stone, like the rest of the place, but smooth and polished. I wondered if any of the priestesses had ever gone sledding down the spiraling path.

Not that I know of, Rhys said into my mind. *But Mor and I once tried when we were children. My mother caught us on our third level down, and we were sent to bed without supper.*

I clamped down on my smile. *Was it such a crime?*

It was when we'd oiled up the floor, and the scholars were falling on their faces.

I coughed to cover my laugh, lowering my head, even with Clotho a few steps ahead.

We passed stacks of books and parchment, the shelves either built into the stone itself or made of dark, solid wood. Hallways lined with both vanished into the mountain itself, and every few minutes, a little reading area popped up, full of tidy tables, low-burning glass lamps, and deep-cushioned chairs and couches. Ancient woven rugs adorned the floors beneath them, usually set before fireplaces that had been carved into the rock and kept well away from any shelves, their grates fine-meshed enough to retain any wandering embers.

Cozy, despite the size of the space; warm, despite the unknown terror lurking below.

If the others piss me off too much, I like to come down here for some peace and quiet.

I smiled slightly at Rhys, who kept looking ahead as we spoke mind to mind.

Don't they know by now that they can find you down here?

Of course. But I never go to the same spot twice in a row, so it usually takes them so long to find me that they don't bother. Plus, they know that if I'm here, it's because I want to be alone.

Poor baby High Lord, I crooned. *Having to run away to find solitude perfect for brooding.*

Rhys pinched my behind, and I clamped down on my lip to keep from yelping.

I could have sworn Clotho's shoulders shook with laughter.

But before I could bite off Rhys's head for the rippling pain my aching back muscles felt in the wake of the sudden movement, Clotho led us into a reading area about three levels down, the massive work-table laden with fat, ancient books bound in various dark leathers.

A neat stack of paper was set to one side, along with an assortment of pens, and the reading lamps were at full glow, merry and sparkling in the gloom. A silver tea service gleamed on a low-lying table between the two leather couches before the grumbling fireplace, steam curling from the arched spout of the kettle. Biscuits and little sandwiches filled the platter beside it, along with a fat pile of napkins that subtly hinted we use them before touching the books.

"Thank you," Rhys told the priestess, who only pulled a book off the pile she'd undoubtedly gathered and opened it to a marked page. The ancient velvet ribbon was the color of old blood—but it was her hand that struck me as it met the golden light of the lamps.

Her fingers were crooked. Bent and twisted at such angles I would have thought her born with them were it not for the scarring.

For a heartbeat, I was in a spring wood. For a heartbeat, I heard the crunch of stone on flesh and bone as I made another priestess smash her hand. Over and over.

Rhys put a hand on my lower back. The effort it must have taken Clotho to move everything into place with those gnarled hands . . .

But she looked toward another book—or at least her head turned that way—and it slid over to her.

Magic. Right.

She gestured with a finger that was bent in two different directions to the page she'd selected, then to the book.

"I'll look," Rhys said, then inclined his head. "We'll give a shout if we need anything."

Clotho bowed her head again and began striding away, careful and silent.

"Thank you," I said to her.

The priestess paused, looking back, and bowed her head, hood swaying.

Within seconds, she was gone.

I stared after her, even as Rhys slid into one of the two chairs before the piles of books.

"A long time ago, Clotho was hurt very badly by a group of males," Rhys said quietly.

I didn't need details to know what that had entailed. The edge in Rhys's voice implied enough.

"They cut out her tongue so she couldn't tell anyone who had hurt her. And smashed her hands so she couldn't write it." Every word was more clipped than the last, and darkness snarled through the small space.

My stomach turned. "Why not kill her?"

"Because it was more entertaining for them that way. That is, until Mor found her. And brought her to me."

When he'd undoubtedly looked into her mind and seen their faces.

"I let Mor hunt them." His wings tucked in tightly. "And when she finished, she stayed down here for a month. Helping Clotho heal as best as could be expected, but also . . . wiping away the stain of them."

Mor's trauma had been different, but . . . I understood why she'd done it, wanted to be here. I wondered if it had granted her any measure of closure.

"Cassian and Azriel were healed completely after Hybern. Nothing could be done for Clotho?"

"The males were . . . healing her as they hurt her. Making the injuries permanent. When Mor found her, the damage had been set. They hadn't finished her hands, so we were able to salvage them, give her some use, but . . . To heal her, the wounds would have needed to be ripped open again. I offered to take the pain away while it was done, but . . . She could not endure it—what having the wounds open again would trigger in her mind. Her heart. She has lived down here since then— with others like her. Her magic helps with her mobility."

I knew we should begin working, but I asked, "Are . . . all the priestesses in this library like her?"

"Yes."

The word held centuries of rage and pain.

"I made this library into a refuge for them. Some come to heal, work as acolytes, and then leave; some take the oaths to the Cauldron and Mother to become priestesses and remain here forever. But it belongs to them whether they stay a week or a lifetime. Outsiders are allowed to use the library for research, but only if the priestesses approve. And only if they take binding oaths to do no harm while they visit. This library belongs to them."

"Who was here before them?"

"A few cranky old scholars, who cursed me soundly when I relocated them to other libraries in the city. They still get access, but when and where is always approved by the priestesses."

Choice. It had always been about my choice with him. And for others as well. Long before he'd ever learned the hard way about it. The question must have been in my eyes because Rhys added, "I came here a great deal in those weeks after Under the Mountain."

My throat tightened as I leaned in to brush a kiss to his cheek. "Thank you for sharing this place with me."

"It belongs to you, too, now." And I knew he meant not just in terms of us being mates, but . . . in the ways it belonged to the other females here. Who had endured and survived.

I gave him a half smile. "I suppose it's a miracle that I can even stand to be underground."

But his features remained solemn, contemplative. "It is." He added softly, "I'm very proud of you."

My eyes burned, and I blinked as I faced the books. "And I suppose," I said with an effort at lightness, "that it's a miracle I can actually *read* these things."

Rhys's answering smile was lovely—and just a bit wicked. "I believe my little lessons helped."

"Yes, '*Rhys is the greatest lover a female can hope for*' is undoubtedly how I learned to read."

"I was only trying to tell you what you now know."

My blood heated a bit. "Hmmm," was all I said, pulling a book toward me.

"I'll take that *hmmm* as a challenge." His hand slid down my thigh, then cupped my knee, his thumb brushing along its side. Even through my leathers, the heat of him seeped to my very bones. "Maybe I'll haul you between the stacks and see how quiet you can be."

"Hmmm." I flipped through the pages, not seeing any of the text.

His hand began a lethal, taunting exploration up my thigh, his fingers grazing along the sensitive inside. Higher, higher. He leaned in to drag a book toward himself, but whispered in my ear, "Or maybe I'll spread you out on this desk and lick you until you scream loud enough to wake whatever is at the bottom of the library."

I whipped my head toward him. His eyes were glazed—almost sleepy.

"I was fully committed to that plan," I said, even as his hand stopped very, *very* close to the apex of my thighs, "until you brought in that *thing* down below."

A feline smile. He held my stare as his tongue brushed his bottom lip.

My breasts tightened beneath my shirt, and his gaze dropped—watching. "I would have thought," he mused, "that our bout this morning would be enough to tide you over until tonight." His hand slid between my legs, brazenly cupping me, his thumb pushing down on an aching spot. A low groan slipped from me, and my cheeks heated in its wake. "Apparently, I didn't do a good enough job sating you, if you're so easily riled after a few hours."

"Prick," I breathed, but the word was ragged. His thumb pressed down harder, circling roughly.

Rhys leaned in again, kissing my neck—that place right under my ear—and said against my skin, "Let's see what names you call me when my head is between your legs, Feyre darling."

And then he was gone.

He'd winnowed away, half the books with him. I started, my body foreign and cold, dizzy and disoriented.

Where the hell are you? I scanned around me, and found nothing but shadow and merry flame and books.

Two levels below.

And why *are you two levels below?* I shoved out of my chair, back aching in protest as I stormed for the walkway and rail beyond, then peered down into the gloom.

Sure enough, in a reading area two levels below, I could spy his dark hair and wings—could spy him leaning back in his chair before an identical desk, an ankle crossed over a knee. Smirking up at me. *Because I can't work with you distracting me.*

I scowled at him. I'm *distracting* you?

If you're sitting next to me, the last thing on my mind is reading dusty old books. Especially when you're in all that tight leather.

Pig.

His chuckle echoed up through the library amid the fluttering papers and scratching pens of the priestesses working throughout.

How can you winnow inside the House? I thought there were wards against it.

The library makes its own rules, apparently.

I snorted.

Two hours of work, he promised me, turning back to the table and flaring his wings—a veritable screen to block my view of him. And his view of me. *Then we can play.*

I gave him a vulgar gesture.

I saw that.

I did it again, and his laugh floated to me as I faced the books stacked before me and began to read.

⸙

We found a myriad of information about the wall and its forming. When we compared our notes two hours later, many of the texts were conflicting, all of them claiming absolute authority on the subject. But there were a few similar details that Rhys had not known.

He had been healing at the cabin in the mountains when they'd formed the wall, when they'd signed that Treaty. The details that emerged had been murky at best, but the various texts Clotho had dug up on the wall's formation and rules agreed on one thing: it had never been made to last.

No, initially, the wall had been a temporary solution—to cleave human and faerie until peace settled long enough for them to later reconvene. And decide how they were to live together—as one people.

But the wall had remained. Humans had grown old and died, and their children had forgotten the promises of their parents, their grandparents, their ancestors. And the High Fae who survived . . . it was a new world, without slaves. Lesser faeries stepped in to replace the missing free labor; territory boundaries had been redrawn to accommodate those displaced. Such a great shift in the world in those initial centuries, so many working to move past war, to heal, that the wall . . . the wall became permanent. The wall became legend.

"Even if all seven courts ally," I said as we plucked grapes from a silver bowl in a quiet sitting room in the House of Wind, having left the dim library for some much-needed sunshine, "even if Keir and the Court of Nightmares join, too . . . Will we stand a chance in this war?"

Rhys leaned back in the embroidered chair before the floor-to-ceiling window. Velaris was a glittering sprawl below and beyond—serene and lovely, even with the scars of battle now peppering it. "Army against army, the possibility of victory is slim." Blunt, honest words.

I shifted in my own identical chair on the other side of the low-lying table between us. "Could you . . . If you and the King of Hybern went head to head . . ."

"Would I win?" Rhys lifted a brow, and studied the city. "I don't know. He's been smart about keeping the extent of his power hidden. But he had to resort to trickery and threats to beat us that day in Hybern. He has thousands of years of knowledge and training. If he and I fought . . . I doubt he will let it come to that. He stands a better chance at sure victory by overwhelming us with numbers, in stretching us thin. If we fought one-on-one, if he'd even accept an open challenge from me . . . the damage would be catastrophic. And that's without him wielding the Cauldron."

My heart stumbled. Rhys went on, "I'm willing to take the brunt of it, if it means the others will at least *stand* with us against him."

I clenched the tufted arms of the chair.

"You shouldn't have to."

"It might be the only choice."

"I don't accept that as an option."

He blinked at me. "Prythian might need me as an option." Because with that power of his . . . He'd take on the king and his entire army. Burn himself out until he was—

"*I* need you. As an option. In *my* future."

Silence. And even with the sun warming my feet, a terrible cold spread through me.

His throat bobbed. "If it means giving you a future, then I'm willing to do—"

"You will do no such *thing*." I panted through my bared teeth, leaning forward in my chair.

Rhys only watched me, eyes shadowed. "How can you ask me not to give everything I have to ensure that you, that my family and people, survive?"

"You've given *enough*."

"Not enough. Not yet."

It was hard to breathe, to see past the burning in my eyes. "Why? Where does this *come* from, Rhys?"

For once, he didn't answer.

And there was something brittle enough in his expression, some long unhealed wound that glimmered there, that I sighed, rubbed my face, and then said, "Just—work with me. With all of us. *Together*. This isn't your burden alone."

He plucked another grape from its stem, chewed. His lips tilted in a faint smile. "So what do you propose, then?"

I could still see that vulnerability in his eyes, still feel it in that bond between us, but I angled my head. I sorted through all I knew, all that had happened. Considered the books I'd read in the library below. A library that housed—

"Amren warned us to never put the two halves of the Book together," I mused. "But we—*I* did. She said that older things might be . . . awoken by it. Might come sniffing."

Rhys crossed an ankle over a knee.

"Hybern might have the numbers," I said, "but what if we had the monsters? You said Hybern will see an alliance with all the courts coming—but perhaps not one with things wholly unconnected." I leaned forward. "And I'm not talking about the monsters roaming across the world. I am talking about one in particular—who has nothing to lose and everything to gain."

One that I would do everything in my power to use, rather than let Rhys face the brunt of this alone.

His brows rose. "Oh?"

"The Bone Carver," I clarified. "He and Amren have both been looking for a way back to their own worlds." The Carver had been insistent, relentless, in asking me that day in the Prison about where I had gone during death. I could have sworn Rhys's golden-brown skin paled, but I added, "I wonder if it's time to ask him what he'd give to go back home."

CHAPTER
21

The aching muscles along my back, core, and thighs had gone into complete revolt by the time Rhys and I parted ways, my mate heading off to track down Cassian—who would be my escort tomorrow morning to the Prison. If both of us had gone, it would perhaps look too . . . desperate, too vital. But if the High Lady and her general went to visit the Carver to pose some hypothetical questions . . .

It would still show our hand, but perhaps not quite how badly we needed any extra bit of assistance. And Cassian, unsurprisingly, knew more about the Carver than anyone thanks to some morbid fascination with all of the Prison's inmates. Especially since he was responsible for jailing some of them.

But while Rhys sought out Cassian, I had a task of my own.

I was wincing and hissing as I strode through the murky red halls of the House to find my sister and Amren. To see which of them was still standing after their first lesson. Among other things.

I found them in a quiet, forgotten workroom, coldly watching the other.

Books lay scattered on the table between them. A ticking clock by the dusty cabinets was the only sound.

"Sorry to interrupt your staring contest," I said, lingering in the doorway. I rubbed at a spot low in my back. "I wanted to see how the first lesson was going."

"Fine." Amren didn't take her eyes off my sister, a faint smile playing about her red mouth.

I studied Nesta, who gazed at Amren, utterly stone-faced.

"What are you doing?"

"Waiting," Amren said.

"For what?"

"For busybodies to leave us alone."

I straightened, clearing my throat. "Is this part of her training?"

Amren turned her head to me with exaggerated slowness, her chin-length, razor-straight hair shifting with the movement. "Rhys has his own method of training you. I have mine." Her white teeth flashed with every word. "We visit the Court of Nightmares tomorrow night—she needs *some* basic training before we do."

"Like what?"

Amren sighed at the ceiling. "Shielding herself. From prying minds and powers."

I blinked. I should have thought of that. That if Nesta were to join us, be at the Hewn City . . . she would need some defenses beyond what we could offer her.

Nesta at last looked to me, her face as cold as ever.

"Are you all right?" I asked her.

Amren clicked her tongue. "She's fine. Stubborn as an ass, but as you're related, I'm not surprised."

I scowled. "How am I supposed to know what your methods are? For all I know, you picked up some terrible techniques in that Prison."

Careful. So, so careful.

Amren hissed, "That place taught me plenty of things, but certainly not this."

I angled my head, the portrait of curiosity. "Did you ever interact with the others?"

The fewer people who knew about my trip tomorrow to see the Carver, the safer it was—the less chance of Hybern catching wind of it. Not for any fear of betrayal, but . . . there was always risk.

Azriel, now off hunting for information on the Autumn Court, would be told when he returned tonight. Mor . . . I'd tell her eventually. But Amren . . . Rhys and I had decided to wait to tell Amren. The last time we'd gone to the Prison, she'd been . . . testy. Telling her we planned to unleash one of her fellow inmates? Perhaps not the best thing to mention while we waited for her to find a way to heal that wall—and train my sister.

Impatience rippled across Amren's face, those silver eyes flaring. "I only spoke to them in whispers and echoes through rock, girl. And I was glad of it."

"What's the Prison?" Nesta asked at last.

"A hell entombed in stone," Amren said. "Full of creatures you should thank the Mother no longer walk the earth freely."

Nesta frowned deeply, but shut her mouth.

"Like who?" I asked. Any extra information she might have—

Amren bared her teeth. "I am giving a magic lesson, not a history one." She waved a dismissive hand. "If you want someone to gossip with, go find one of the dogs. I'm sure Cassian's still sniffing around upstairs."

Nesta's lips twitched upward.

Amren pointed at her with a slender finger ending in a sharp, mani-cured nail. "*Concentrate*. Vital organs *must* be shielded at all times."

I tapped a hand against the open doorway. "I'll keep looking for more information for you in the library, Amren." No response. "Good luck," I added.

"She doesn't need luck," Amren said. Nesta huffed a laugh.

I took that as the only farewell I'd get. Perhaps letting Amren and Nesta train together was . . . a bad choice. Even if the prospect of unleashing them upon the Court of Nightmares . . . I smiled a bit at the thought.

By the time Mor, Rhys, Cassian, and I gathered for dinner at the town house—Azriel still off spying—my muscles were so sore I could barely walk up the front stairs. Sore enough that any plans I had to visit Lucien up at the House after the meal vanished. Mor was testy and quiet throughout, no doubt in anticipation of the visit tomorrow night.

She'd had to work with Keir plenty throughout the centuries, and yet tomorrow . . . She'd only warned Rhys once while we ate that he should thoroughly consider any offer Keir might give him in exchange for his army. Rhys had shrugged, saying he'd think about it when the time came. A non-answer—and one that made Mor grit her teeth.

I didn't blame her. Long before the War, her family had brutalized her in ways I didn't let myself consider. Not a day before I was to meet with them again—ask *them* for help. Work with them.

Rhys, Mother bless him, had a bath waiting for me after the meal.

I'd need all my strength for tomorrow. For the monsters I was to face beneath two very different mountains.

☩

I had not visited this place for months. But the carved stone walls were just as I'd last seen them, the darkness still interrupted by bracketed torches.

Not the Prison. Under the Mountain.

But instead of Clare's mutilated body spiked high to the wall above me . . .

Her blue-gray eyes were still wide with terror. Gone was the haughty iciness, the queenly jut to her chin.

Nesta. They'd done precisely to her, wound for wound, what they'd done to Clare.

And behind me, screaming and pleading—

I turned, finding Elain, naked and weeping, tied to that enormous spit. What I had once been threatened to endure. Gnarled, masked faeries rotated the iron handles, turning her over—

I tried to move. Tried to lunge.

But I was frozen—utterly bound by invisible chains to the floor.

Feminine laughter flitted from the other end of that throne room. From the dais. Now empty.

Empty, because that was Amarantha, strutting into the gloom, down some hall that hadn't been there before but now stretched away into nothing.

Rhysand followed a step behind her. Going with her. To that bedroom.

He looked over his shoulder at me, only once.

Over his wings. His wings, which were out, which she'd see and destroy, right after she—

I was screaming for him to stop. Thrashing at those bonds. Elain's pleading rose, higher and higher. Rhys kept walking with Amarantha. Let her take his hand and tug him along.

I couldn't move, couldn't stop it, any of it—

✢

I was hauled out of the dream like a thrashing fish from a net cast deep into the sea.

And when I surfaced . . . I remained half there. Half in my body, half Under the Mountain, watching as—

"Breathe."

The word was an order. Laced with that primal command he so rarely wielded.

But my eyes focused. My chest expanded. I slipped a bit further back into my body.

"Again."

I did so. His face came into view, faelights murmuring to life inside their lamps and bowls in our bedroom. His wings were tucked in tight, framing his disheveled hair, his drawn face.

Rhys.

"Again," he only said. I obeyed.

My bones had turned brittle, my stomach a roiling mess. I closed my eyes, fighting the nausea. Rippling terror kept its talons buried deep. I could still see it: the way she'd led him down that hall. To—

I surged, rolling to the edge of the mattress and clamping down hard as my body tried to heave up its contents onto the carpet. His hand was instantly on my back, rubbing soothing circles. Utterly willing to let me vomit right over the side of the bed. But I focused on my breathing.

On closing down those memories, one by one. Memories repainted.

I lay half sprawled over the edge for uncounted minutes. He rubbed my back throughout.

When I could finally move, when the nausea had subsided . . . I twisted back over. And the sight of that face . . . I slid my arms around his waist, gripping tightly as he pressed a silent kiss to my hair, reminding myself over and over that we were out. We had survived. Never again— never again would I let someone hurt him like that. Hurt my sisters like that.

Never again.

CHAPTER
22

I felt Rhys's attention on me while we dressed the next morning, and throughout our hearty breakfast. Yet he didn't push, didn't demand to know what had dragged me into that screaming hell.

It had been a long while since those nightmares had hauled either of us from sleep. Blurred the lines.

It was only when we stood in the foyer, waiting for Cassian before we winnowed to the Prison, that Rhys asked from where he leaned against the stair banister, "Do you need to talk about it?"

My Illyrian leathers groaned as I turned toward him.

Rhys clarified, "With me—or anyone."

I answered him truthfully, tugging at the end of my braid. "With everything bearing down on us, everything at stake . . ." I let my braid drop. "I don't know. I think it's torn open some . . . part of me that was slowly repairing." Repairing thanks to both of us.

He nodded, no fear or reproach in his eyes.

So I told him. All of it. Stumbling over the parts that still made me ill. He only listened.

And when I was done, that shakiness remained, but . . . Speaking it, voicing it aloud to him . . .

The savage grip of those terrors lightened. Cleared away like dew in the sun. I freed a long breath, as if blowing those fears from me, letting my body loosen in its wake.

Rhys silently pushed off the banister and kissed me. Once. Twice.

Cassian stalked through the front door a heartbeat later and groaned that it was too early to stomach the sight of us kissing. My mate only snarled at him before he took us both by the hand and winnowed us to the Prison.

Rhys gripped my fingers tighter than usual as the wind ripped around us, Cassian now wisely keeping silent. And as we emerged from that black, tumbling wind, Rhys leaned over to kiss me a third time, sweet and soft, before the gray light and roaring wind greeted us.

Apparently, the Prison was cold and misty no matter the time of year.

Standing at the base of the mossy, rocky mountain under which the Prison was built, Cassian and I frowned up the slope.

Despite the Illyrian leathers, the chill seeped into my bones. I rubbed at my arms, lifting my brows at Rhys, who had remained in his usual attire, so out of place in this damp, windy speck of green in the middle of a gray sea.

The wind ruffled his black hair as he surveyed us, Cassian already sizing up the mountain like some opponent. Twin Illyrian blades were crossed over the general's muscled back. "When you're in there," Rhys said, the words barely audible over the wind and silver streams running down the mountainside, "you won't be able to reach me."

"Why?" I rubbed my already-freezing hands together before puffing a hot breath into the cradle of my palms.

"Wards and spells far older than Prythian," was all Rhys said. He jerked his chin to Cassian. "Don't let each other out of your sight."

It was the dead seriousness with which Rhys spoke that kept me from retorting.

Indeed, my mate's eyes were hard—unflinching. While we were

here, he and Azriel were to discuss what he'd found out about Autumn's leanings in this war. And then adjust their strategy for the meeting with the High Lords. But I could sense it, the urge to request he join us. Watch over us.

"Shout down the bond when you're out again," Rhys said with a mildness that didn't reach his gaze.

Cassian looked back over a shoulder. "Get back to Velaris, you mother hen. We'll be fine."

Rhys leveled another uncharacteristically hard stare at him. "Remember who you put in here, Cassian."

Cassian just tucked in his wings, as if every muscle shifted toward battle. Steady and solid as the mountain we were about to climb.

With a wink at me, Rhys vanished.

Cassian checked the buckles on his swords and motioned me to start the long trek up the hill. My gut tightened at the climb ahead. The shrieking hollowness of this place.

"Who did you put in here?" The mossy earth cushioned my steps.

Cassian put a scar-flecked finger to his lips. "Best left for another time."

Right. I fell into step beside him, my thighs burning with the steep hike. Mist chilled my face. Conserving his strength—Cassian wasn't wasting a drop of energy on shielding us from the elements.

"You really think unleashing the Carver will do the trick against Hybern?"

"You're the general," I panted, "you tell me."

He considered, the wind tossing his dark hair over his tan face. "Even if you promise to find a way to send him back to his own world with the Book, or give him whatever unholy thing he wants," Cassian mused, "I think you'd better find a way to control him in *this* world, or else we'll be fighting enemies on all fronts. And I know which one will hand our asses to us."

"The Carver's that bad."

"You're asking this right before we're to meet with him?"

I hissed, "I assumed Rhys would have put his foot down if it was *that* risky."

"Rhys has been known to hatch plans that make my heart stop dead," Cassian grumbled. "So, I wouldn't count on him to be the voice of reason."

I scowled at Cassian, earning a wolfish grin in return.

But Cassian scanned the heavy gray sky, as if hunting for spying eyes. Then the moss and grass and rocks beneath our boots for listening ears below. "There was life here," he said, answering my question at last, "before the High Lords took Prythian. Old gods, we call them. They ruled the forests and the rivers and the mountains—some *were* those things. Then the magic shifted to the High Fae, who brought the Cauldron and Mother along with them, and though the old gods were still worshipped by a select few, most people forgot them."

I grappled onto a large gray rock as I climbed over it. "The Bone Carver was an old god?"

He dragged a hand through his hair, the Siphon gleaming in the watery light. "That's what legend says. Along with whispers of being able to fell hundreds of soldiers with one breath."

A chill rippled down my skin that had nothing to do with the brisk wind. "Useful on a battlefield."

Cassian's golden-brown skin paled while his eyes churned with the thought. "Not without the proper precautions. Not without him being bound to obey us within an inch of his life." Which I'd have to figure out as well, I supposed.

"How did he wind up here—in the Prison?"

"I don't know. No one does." Cassian helped me over a boulder, his hand gripping mine tightly. "But *how* do you plan on freeing him from the Prison?"

I winced. "I suppose our friend would know, since she got out." Careful—we had to be careful when mentioning Amren's name here.

Cassian's face grew solemn. "She doesn't talk about how she did it, Feyre. I'd be careful how you push her." Since we still had not told Amren where we were today. What we were doing.

I thought about saying more, but ahead, far up the slope, the massive bone gates opened.

✥

I'd forgotten it—the weight of the air inside the Prison. Like wading through the unstirred air of a tomb. Like stealing a breath from the open mouth of a skull.

We both bore an Illyrian blade in one hand, the faelight bobbing ahead to show the way, occasionally dancing and sliding along the shining metal. Our other hands . . . Cassian clenched my fingers as tightly as I clutched his while we descended into the eternal blackness of the Prison, our steps crunching on the dry ground. There were no doors—none that we could see.

But behind that solid, black rock, I could still feel them. Could have sworn a faint scratching sound filled the passage. From the other side of that rock.

As if someone were running their nails down it. Something huge—and old. And quiet as the wind through a field of wheat.

Cassian kept utterly silent, tracking something—counting something.

"This could be . . . a very bad idea," I admitted, my grip tightening on his hand.

"Oh, it most certainly is," Cassian said with a faint smile as we continued down and down into the heavy black and thrumming silence. "But this is war. We don't have the luxury of good ideas—only picking between the bad ones."

✥

The Bone Carver's cell door swung open the moment I laid my palm to it.

234

"Worth the misery of being Rhys's mate," Cassian quipped as the white bone swung away into darkness.

A light chuckle within.

The amusement faded from Cassian's face at the sound—as we walked into the cell, still hand in hand.

The orb of faelight bobbed ahead, illuminating the stone-hewn cell.

Cassian growled at what it revealed. Who it revealed.

Wholly different, no doubt, from the same young boy who now smiled at me.

Dark-haired, with eyes of crushing blue.

I started at the child's face—what I had not noticed that first time. What I had not understood.

It was Rhysand's face. The coloring, the eyes . . . it was my mate's face.

But the Carver's full, wide mouth, curled into that hideous smile . . . That was my mouth. My father's mouth.

The hair on my arms rose. The Carver inclined his head in greeting—in greeting and in confirmation, as if he knew precisely what I realized. Who I had seen and was still seeing.

The High Lord's son. My son. *Our* son. Should we survive long enough to bear him.

Should I not fail in my task to recruit the Carver. Should we not fail to unify the High Lords and the Court of Nightmares. And keep that wall intact.

It was an effort to keep my knees from buckling. Cassian's face was pale enough that I knew whatever he was seeing . . . it wasn't a beautiful young boy.

"I was wondering when you'd return," the Carver said, that boy's voice sweet and yet dreadful—from the ancient creature that lurked beneath it. "High Lady," he added to me. "Please accept my congratulations on your union." A glance at Cassian. "I can smell the wind on you." Another little smile. "Have you brought me a gift?"

I reached into the pocket of my jacket and chucked a small shard of bone, no bigger than my hand, at the Carver's feet.

"This is all that's left of the Attor after I splattered him on the streets of Velaris."

Those blue eyes flared with unholy delight. I hadn't even known we'd kept this fragment. It had been stored until now—precisely for this sort of thing.

"So bloodthirsty, my new High Lady," the Carver purred, picking up the cracked bone and turning it over in those small, delicate hands. And then the Carver said, "I smell my sister on you, Cursebreaker."

My mouth went dry. His sister—

"Did you steal from her? Did she weave a thread of your life into her loom?"

The Weaver of the Wood. My heart thundered. No breathing could steady it. Cassian's hand tightened around mine.

The Carver purred to Cassian, "If I tell you a secret, warrior-heart, what will you give me?"

Neither of us spoke. Carefully—we'd have to phrase and do this so carefully.

The Carver stroked the shard of bone in his palm, attention fixed upon a stone-faced Cassian. "What if I tell you what the rock and darkness and sea beyond whispered to me, Lord of Bloodshed? How they shuddered in fear, on that island across the sea. How they trembled when *she* emerged. She took something—something precious. She ripped it out with her teeth."

Cassian's golden-brown face had drained of color, his wings tucking in tight.

"What did you wake that day in Hybern, Prince of Bastards?"

My blood went cold.

"What came out was not what went in." A rasping laugh as the Carver laid the shard of bone on the ground beside him. "How lovely she is—new as a fawn and yet ancient as the sea. How she calls to you.

A queen, as my sister once was. Terrible and proud; beautiful as a winter sunrise."

Rhys had warned me of the inmates' capacity to lie, to sell anything, to get free.

"Nesta," the Bone Carver murmured. "*Nes-ta.*"

I squeezed Cassian's hand. Enough. It was *enough* of this teasing and taunting. But he didn't look at me.

"How the wind moans her name. Can you hear it, too? Nesta. *Nesta. Nesta.*"

I wasn't sure Cassian was breathing.

"What did she do, drowning in the ageless dark? What did she *take?*"

It was the bite in the last word that snapped my tether of restraint. "If you wish to find out, perhaps you should stop talking long enough for us to explain."

My voice seemed to shake Cassian free of whatever trance he'd been in. His breathing surged, tight and fast, and he scanned my face—apology in his eyes.

The Carver chuckled. "I so rarely get company. Forgive me for wanting to make idle talk." He crossed an ankle over a foot. "And why have you sought my services?"

"We attained the Book of Breathings," I said casually. "There are . . . interesting spells inside. Codes within codes within codes. Someone we know cracked most of them. She is still looking for others. Spells that could . . . send someone like her home. Others like her, too."

The Carver's violet eyes flared bright as flame. "I'm listening."

CHAPTER
23

"War is upon us," I said to the Carver. "Rumor suggests you have . . . gifts that may be useful upon the battlefield."

A smile at Cassian, as if understanding why he'd joined me. "In exchange for a price," the Carver mused.

"Within reason," Cassian countered.

The Carver surveyed his cell. "And you think that I wish to go . . . back."

"Don't you?"

The Carver folded his legs beneath his small frame. "Where we came from . . . I do not believe it is now anything more than dust drifting across a plain. There is no home to return to. Not one that I desire."

For if he'd been here before even Amren had arrived . . . Tens of thousands of years—longer, perhaps. I shoved against the sinking sensation in my gut. "Then perhaps improving your . . . living conditions might entice you, if this world is where you wish to be."

"This cell, Cursebreaker, is where I wish to be." The Carver patted the dirt beside him. "Do you think I let them trap me without good reason?"

Cassian's entire body seemed to shift—seemed to go aware and focused. Ready to haul us out of there.

The Carver traced three overlapping, interlocked circles in the dirt. "You have met my sister—my twin. The Weaver, as you now call her. I knew her as Stryga. She, and our older brother, Koschei. How they delighted in this world when we fell into it. How those ancient Fae feared and worshipped them. Had I been braver, I might have bided my time—waited for their power to fade, for that long-ago Fae warrior to trick Stryga into diminishing her power and becoming confined to the Middle. Koschei, too—confined and bound by his little lake on the continent. All before Prythian, before the land was carved up and any High Lord was crowned."

Cassian and I waited, not daring to interrupt.

"Clever, that Fae warrior. Her bloodline is long gone now—though a trace still runs through some human line." He smiled, perhaps a bit sadly. "No one remembers her name. But I do. She would have been my salvation, had I not made my choice long before she walked this earth."

I waited and waited and waited, picking apart the story he laid out like crumbs of bread.

"She could not kill them in the end—they were too strong. They could only be contained." The Carver wiped a hand through the circles he'd drawn, erasing them wholly. "I knew that long before she ever trapped them—took it upon myself to find my way here."

"To spare the world from yourself?" Cassian asked, brows narrowing.

The Carver's eyes burned like the hottest flame. "To *hide* from my siblings."

I blinked. "Why?"

"They are death-gods, girl," the Carver hissed. "You are immortal—or long-lived enough to seem that way. But my siblings and I . . . We are different. And the two of them . . . Stronger. So much stronger than I ever was. My sister . . . she found a way to *eat* life itself. To stay young and beautiful forever thanks to the lives she steals."

The weaving—the threads inside that house, the roof made of hair . . . I made a note to throw Rhys in the Sidra for sending me into that cottage.

But the Carver himself . . . "If they are death-gods," I said, "then what are you?"

Death. He had asked me, over and over, about death. About what waited beyond it, what it felt like. Where I had gone. I'd thought it mere curiosity, but . . .

That boy's face crinkled with amusement. My son's face. The vision of the future that had once been shown to me all those months ago, as some sort of taunt or embodiment of what I hadn't dared yet admit to myself. What I was most uncertain of. And now . . . now that young boy . . . A different sort of taunt, for the future I now stood to lose.

"I am forgotten, that's what I am. And that's how I prefer to be." The Carver rested his head against the wall of rock behind him. "So you will find that I do not wish to leave. That I have no desire to remind my sister and brother that I am alive and in the world. Contained and diminished as they are, their influence remains . . . considerable."

"If Hybern wins this war," Cassian said roughly, "you might find the gates of this place blown wide open. And your sister and brother unleashed from their own territories—and interested in paying a visit."

"Even Hybern is not that foolish." A satisfied huff of air. "I'm sure there are other inmates here who will find your offer . . . tempting."

My blood roared. "You will not even consider assisting us." I waved a hand to the cell. "This is what you would prefer—for eternity?"

"If you knew my brother and sister, Cursebreaker, you would find this a much wiser and more comfortable alternative."

I opened my mouth, but Cassian squeezed my hand in warning. Enough. We'd said enough, revealed enough. Looking so desperate . . . It would help nothing.

"We should go," Cassian said to me, the very picture of unruffled calm. "The delights of the Hewn City await."

We'd indeed be late if we didn't leave now. I threw a glare at the

Carver by way of farewell, letting Cassian lead me toward the open cell door.

"You are going to the Hewn City," the Carver said—not entirely a question.

"I don't see how that is any business of yours," I said over my shoulder.

The Carver's beat of silence echoed around us. Made us pause on the threshold.

"One last attempt," the Carver mused, eyes skating over us, "to rally the entirety of the Night Court, I suppose."

"Again, it is none of your concern," I said coolly.

The Carver smiled. "You will be bargaining with him." A glance at the tattoo on my right hand. "I wonder what Keir's asking price will be." A low laugh. "Interesting."

Cassian let out a long-suffering sigh. "Out with it."

The Bone Carver again fell silent, toying with the shard of the Attor's bone in the dirt beside him. "The eddies of the Cauldron swirl in strange ways," he murmured, more to himself than us.

"We're going," I said, making to turn again, hauling Cassian with me.

"My sister had a collection of mirrors in her black castle," the Carver said.

We halted once more.

"She admired herself day and night in those mirrors, gloating over her youth and beauty. There was one mirror—the Ouroboros, she called it. It was old even when we were young. A window to the world. All could be seen, all could be told through its dark surface. Keir possesses it—an heirloom of his household. Bring it to me. That is my price. The Ouroboros, and I am yours to wield. If you can find a way to free me." A hateful smile.

I exchanged a glance with Cassian, and we both shrugged at the Carver. "We'll see," was all I said before we walked out.

✠

Cassian and I sat on a boulder overlooking a silver stream, breathing in the chill mists. The Prison loomed at our backs, a dreadful weight blocking out the horizon.

"You said that you knew the Carver was an old god," I mused softly. "Did you know he was a death-god?"

Cassian's face was taut. "I guessed." When I lifted a brow, he clarified, "He carves deaths into bones. Sees them. Enjoys them. It wasn't hard to figure out."

I considered. "Was it you or Rhys who suggested you come here with me?"

"I wanted to come. But Rhys . . . he guessed it, too."

Because what we'd seen in Nesta's eyes that day . . .

"Like calls to like," I murmured.

Cassian nodded tightly. "I don't think even the Carver knows what Nesta is. But I wanted to see—just in case."

"Why?"

"I want to help."

It was answer enough.

We fell into silence, the stream gurgling as it rushed by.

"Would you be frightened of her, if Nesta *was*—Death? Or if her power came from it?"

Cassian was quiet for a long moment.

He said at last, "I'm a warrior. I've walked beside Death my entire life. I would be more afraid *for* her, to have that power. But not afraid *of* her." He considered, and added after a heartbeat, "Nothing about Nesta could frighten me."

I swallowed, and squeezed his hand. "Thank you."

I wasn't sure why I even said it, but he nodded all the same.

I felt him before he appeared, a spark of star-kissed joy flaring through me right as Rhys stepped out of the air itself. "Well?"

Cassian hopped off the boulder, extending a hand to help me down. "You're not going to like his asking price."

Rhys held out both hands to winnow us back to Velaris. "If he wants the fancy dinner plates, he can have them."

Neither Cassian nor I could muster a laugh as we both reached for Rhys's outstretched hands. "You better bring your bargaining skills tonight," was all Cassian muttered to my mate before we vanished into shadow.

CHAPTER
24

When we returned to the town house in the height of summer after-noon heat, Cassian and Azriel drew sticks for who would remain in Velaris that night.

Both wanted to join us at the Hewn City, but someone had to guard the city—part of their long-held protocol. And someone had to guard Elain, though I certainly wasn't about to tell Lucien that. Cassian, swearing and pissy, got the short stick, and Azriel only clapped him on the shoulder before heading up to the House to prepare.

I followed after him a few minutes later, leaving Cassian to tell Rhys the rest of what the Carver had said. What he wanted.

There were two people I needed to see up at the House before we left. I should have checked in on Elain earlier, should have remem-bered that her would-have-been wedding was in a few days, but . . . I cursed myself for forgetting it. And as for Lucien . . . It wouldn't hurt, I told myself, to keep tabs on where he was. How that conversation with Azriel had gone yesterday. Make sure he remembered the rules we'd set.

But fifteen minutes later, I was trying not to wince as I walked down the halls of the House of Wind, grateful Azriel had gone ahead. I'd winnowed into the sky above the highest balcony—and since I figured now was as good a time as any to practice flying, I'd summoned wings.

And fallen twenty feet onto hard stone.

A rallied wind kept the fall from cracking any bones, but both my knees and my pride were significantly bruised by my graceless tumble through the air.

At least no one had witnessed it.

My stiff, limping steps, at least, had eased into a smoother gait by the time I found Elain in the family library.

Still staring at the window, but she was out of her room.

Nesta was reading in her usual chair, one eye on Elain, the other on the book spread in her lap. Only Nesta glanced my way as I slipped through the carved wooden doors.

I murmured, "Hello," and shut the doors behind me.

Elain didn't turn. She was wearing a pale pink gown that did little to complement her sallow skin, her brown-gold hair hanging in loose, heavy ringlets down her thin back.

"It's a fine day," I said to them.

Nesta arched an elegant eyebrow. "Where's your menagerie of friends?"

I leveled a steely look back at her. "Those friends have offered you shelter and comfort." And training—or whatever Amren was doing. "Are you ready for tonight?"

"Yes." Nesta merely resumed reading the book in her lap. Pure dismissal.

I let out a little snort that I knew would make her see red, and strode for Elain. Nesta monitored my every step, a panther readying to strike at the merest hint of danger.

"What are you looking at?" I asked Elain, keeping my voice soft. Casual.

Her face was wan, her lips bloodless. But they moved—barely—as she said, "I can see so very far now. All the way to the sea."

Indeed, the sea beyond the Sidra was a distant sparkle. "It takes some getting used to."

"I can hear your heartbeat—if I listen carefully. I can hear her heart-beat, too."

"You can learn to drown out the sounds that bother you." I had—entirely on my own. I wondered if Nesta had as well, or if they both suffered, hearing each other's heartbeats day and night. I didn't look to my other sister to confirm it.

Elain's eyes at last slid to mine. The first time she'd done so.

Even wasted away by grief and despair, Elain's beauty was remark-able. Hers was a face that could bring kings to their knees. And yet there was no joy in it. No light. No life.

She said, "I can hear the sea. Even at night. Even in my dreams. The crashing sea—and the screams of a bird made of fire."

It was an effort not to glance to Nesta. Even the town house was too far to hear anything from the nearby coast. And as for some fire-bird . . .

"There is a garden—at my other house," I said. "I'd like for you to come tend it, if you're willing."

Elain only turned toward the sunny windows again, the light dancing in her hair. "Will I hear the earthworms writhing through the soil? Or the stretching of roots? Will the bird of fire come to sit in the trees and watch me?"

I wasn't sure if I should answer. It was an effort to keep from shaking.

But I caught Nesta's eye, noting the glimmer of pain on my eldest sister's face before it was hidden beneath that cool mask. "There's a book I need you to help me find, Nesta," I said, giving a pointed stare to the stacks to my left.

Far enough away for privacy, but close enough to remain nearby should Elain need anything. Do anything.

Something in my chest cracked as Nesta's eyes also went to the windows before Elain.

To check, as I did, for whether they could be easily opened.

Mercifully, they were permanently sealed, likely to protect against some careless fool forgetting to close them and ruining the books. Likely Cassian.

Nesta wordlessly set down her book and followed me into the small labyrinth of stacks, both of us keeping an ear on the main sitting area.

When we were far enough away, I threw up a shield of hard wind around us. Keeping any sound inside. "How did you get her to leave her room?"

"I didn't," Nesta said, leaning against a shelf and crossing her slim arms. "I found her in here. She wasn't in bed when I awoke."

Nesta must have panicked upon finding her room empty—"Did she eat anything?"

"No. I managed to get her to drink some broth last night. She refused anything else. She's been talking in those half riddles all day."

I dragged a hand through my hair, freeing strands from my braid. "Did anything happen to trigger—"

"I don't know. I check on her every few hours." Nesta clenched her jaw. "I was gone for longer yesterday, though." While she trained with Amren. Rhys had informed me that by the end of it, Nesta's rudimentary shields were solid enough that Amren deemed my sister ready for tonight.

But there, beneath that cool demeanor—guilt. Panic.

"I doubt anything happened," I said quickly. "Maybe it's just . . . part of the recovery process. Her adjustment to being Fae."

Nesta didn't look convinced. "Does she have powers? Like mine."

And what, exactly, are those powers, Nesta? "I—don't know. I don't think so. Unless this is the first sign of something manifesting." It was an effort not to add, *If you'd talk about what went on in the Cauldron, perhaps we'd have a better understanding of it.* "Let's give her a day or two—see what happens. If she improves."

"Why not see now?"

"Because we're going to the Hewn City in a few hours. And you don't seem inclined to want us shoving into your business," I told her as evenly as I could. "I doubt Elain does, too."

Nesta stared me down, not a flicker of emotion on her face, and gave a curt nod. "Well, at least she left the room."

"And the chair."

We exchanged a rare, calm glance.

But then I said, "Why won't you train with Cassian?"

Nesta's spine locked up. "Why is it only Cassian that I may train with? Why not the other one?"

"Azriel?"

"Him, or the blond one who won't shut up."

"If you're referring to Mor—"

"And why must I train at all? I am no warrior, nor do I desire to be."

"It could make you strong—"

"There are many types of strength beyond the ability to wield a blade and end lives. Amren told me that yesterday."

"You said you wanted our enemies dead. Why not kill them yourself?"

She inspected her nails. "Why bother when someone else can do it for me?"

I avoided the urge to rub my temples. "We're—"

But the doors to the library opened, and I snapped my barrier of hard air down entirely at the thud of stalking footsteps, then their sudden halting.

I gripped Nesta's arm to keep her still just as Lucien's voice blurted, "You—you left your room."

Nesta bristled, teeth flashing. I gripped her harder, and threw a new wall of air around us—holding her there.

Weeks of cloistering Elain had done nothing to improve her state. Perhaps the half riddles were proof of that. And even if Lucien was currently breaking the rules we had set—

More steps—no doubt closer to where Elain stood at the window.

"Is . . . is there anything I can get for you?"

I'd never heard my friend's voice so soft. So tentative and concerned.

Perhaps it made me the lowest sort of wretch, but I cast my mind toward them. Toward him.

And then I was in his body, his head.

Too thin.

She must not be eating at all.

How can she even stand?

The thoughts flowed through his head, one after another. His heart was a raging, thunderous beat, and he didn't dare move from his position a mere five feet away. She hadn't yet turned toward him, but the ravages of her fasting were evident enough.

Touch her, smell her, taste her—

The instincts were a running river. He fisted his hands at his sides.

He hadn't expected her to be here. The other sister—the viper—was a possibility, but one he was willing to risk. Aside from talking to the shadowsinger yesterday—which had been just about as unnerving as he'd expected, though Azriel seemed like a decent enough male—he'd been cooped up in this wind-blasted House for two days. The thought of another one had been enough to make him risk Rhysand's wrath.

He just wanted a walk—and a few books. It had been an age since he'd even had free time to read, let alone do so for pleasure.

But there she was.

His mate.

She was nothing like Jesminda.

Jesminda had been all laughter and mischief, too wild and free to be contained by the country life that she'd been born into. She had teased him, taunted him—seduced him so thoroughly that he hadn't wanted anything but her. She'd seen him not as a High Lord's seventh son, but as a male. Had loved him without question, without hesitation. She had chosen him.

Elain had been . . . thrown at him.

He glanced toward the tea service spread on a low-lying table nearby. "I'm going to assume that one of those cups belongs to your sister." *Indeed, there was a discarded book in the viper's usual chair. Cauldron help the male who wound up shackled to her.*

"Do you mind if I help myself to the other?"

He tried to sound casual—comfortable. Even as his heart raced and raced, so swift he thought he might vomit on the very expensive, very old carpet. From Sangravah, if the patterns and rich dyes were any indication.

Rhysand was many things, but he certainly had good taste.

This entire place had been decorated with thought and elegance, with a penchant for comfort over stuffiness.

He didn't want to admit he liked it. Didn't want to admit that he found the city beautiful.

That the circle of people who now claimed to be Feyre's new family . . . It was what, long ago, he'd once thought life at Tamlin's court would be.

An ache like a blow to the chest went through him, but he crossed the rug. Forced his hands to be steady while he poured himself a cup of tea and sat in the chair opposite Nesta's vacated one.

"There's a plate of biscuits. Would you like one?"

He didn't expect her to answer, and he gave himself all of one more minute before he'd rise from this chair and leave, hopefully avoiding Nesta's return.

But sunlight on gold caught his eye—and Elain slowly turned from her vigil at the window.

He had not seen her entire face since that day in Hybern.

Then, it had been drawn and terrified, then utterly blank and numb, her hair plastered to her head, her lips blue with cold and shock.

Looking at her now . . .

She was pale, yes. The vacancy still glazing her features.

But he couldn't breathe as she faced him fully.

She was the most beautiful female he'd ever seen.

Betrayal, queasy and oily, slid through his veins. He'd said the same to Jesminda once.

But even as shame washed through him, the words, the sense chanted, Mine. You are mine, and I am yours. Mate.

Her eyes were the brown of a fawn's coat. And he could have sworn something sparked in them as she met his gaze.

"*Who are you?*"

He knew without demanding clarification that she was aware of what he was to her.

"*I am Lucien. Seventh son of the High Lord of the Autumn Court.*"

And a whole lot of nothing. He'd told the shadowsinger all he knew—of his surviving brothers, of his father. His mother . . . he'd kept some details, irrelevant and utterly personal, to himself. Everything else—his father's closest allies, the most conniving courtiers and lords . . . He'd handed it over. Granted, it was dated by a few centuries, but in his time as emissary, from the information he'd gathered, not much had changed. They'd all acted the same Under the Mountain, anyway. And after what had happened with his brothers a few days ago . . . There was no tinge of guilt when he told Azriel what he knew. None of what he felt when he looked toward the south— toward both of the courts he'd called home.

For a long moment, Elain's face did not shift, but those eyes seemed to focus a bit more. "*Lucien,*" *she said at last, and he clenched his teacup to keep from shuddering at the sound of his name on her mouth.* "*From my sister's stories. Her friend.*"

"*Yes.*"

But Elain blinked slowly. "*You were in Hybern.*"

"*Yes.*" *It was all he could say.*

"*You betrayed us.*"

He wished she'd shoved him out the window behind her. "*It—it was a mistake.*"

Her eyes went frank and cold. "*I was to be married in a few days.*"

He fought against the bristling rage, the irrational urge to find the male who'd claimed her and shred him apart. The words were a rasp as he instead said, "*I know. I'm sorry.*"

She did not love him, want him, need him. Another male's bride. A mortal man's wife. Or she would have been.

She looked away—toward the windows. "*I can hear your heart,*" *she said quietly.*

251

He wasn't sure how to respond, so he said nothing, and drained his tea, even as it burned his mouth.

"When I sleep," she murmured, "I can hear your heart beating through the stone." She angled her head, as if the city view held some answer. "Can you hear mine?"

He wasn't sure if she truly meant to address him, but he said, "No, lady. I cannot."

Her too-thin shoulders seemed to curve inward. "No one ever does. No one ever looked—not really." A bramble of words. Her voice strained to a whisper. "He did. He saw me. He will not now."

Her thumb brushed the iron ring on her finger.

Another male's ring, another marker that she was claimed—

It was enough. I had listened enough, learned enough. I pulled out of Lucien's mind.

Nesta was gaping at me, even as her face had leeched of color at every word uttered between them. "Have you ever gone into *my*—"

"No," I rasped.

How she knew what I had done, I didn't want to ask. Not as I dropped the shield around us and headed for the sitting area.

Lucien, no doubt having heard our steps, was flushed as he glanced between me and Nesta. No inkling whatsoever that I'd slid into his mind. Rifled through it like a bandit in the night. I shoved down the mild nausea.

My eldest sister merely said to him, "Get out."

I flashed Nesta a glare, but Lucien rose. "I came for a book."

"Well, find one and leave."

Elain only stared out the window, unaware—or uncaring.

Lucien didn't head for the stacks. He just went to the open doors. He paused right between them and said to me, to Nesta, "She needs fresh air."

"We'll judge what she needs."

I could have sworn his ruby hair gleamed like molten metal as his temper rose. But it faded, his russet eye fixing on me. "Take her to the sea. Take her to some garden. But get her out of this house for an hour or two."

Then he walked away.

I looked at my two sisters. Cloistered up here, high above the world.

"You're moving into the town house right now," I said to them. To Lucien, who paused in the dim hallway outside.

Nesta, to my shock, did not object.

✢

Neither did Rhys when I sent my order down the bond, asking him, Cassian, and Azriel to help move them. No, my mate just promised to assign two bedrooms to my sisters down the hall, on the other side of the stairs. And a third for Lucien—on our side of the hall. Well away from Elain's.

Thirty minutes later, Azriel carried Elain down, my sister silent and unresponsive in his arms.

Nesta had looked ready to walk off the balcony rather than let Cassian, already dressed and armed for guarding the town house tonight, hold her, so I nudged her toward Rhys, pushed Lucien toward Cassian, and flew myself back.

Or tried to—again. I soared for about half a minute, savoring the cleansing scream of the wind, before my wings wobbled, my back strained, and the fall became unbearably deadly. I winnowed the rest of the way to the town house, and adjusted vases and figurines in the sitting room while waiting for them.

Azriel arrived first, no shadows to be seen, my sister a pale, golden mass in his arms. He, too, wore his Illyrian armor, Elain's golden-brown hair snagging in some of the black scales across his chest and shoulders.

He set her down gently on the foyer carpet, having carried her in through the front door.

Elain peered up at his patient, solemn face.

Azriel smiled faintly. "Would you like me to show you the garden?"

She seemed so small before him, so fragile compared to the scales of his fighting leathers, the breadth of his shoulders. The wings peeking over them.

But Elain did not balk from him, did not shy away as she nodded—just once.

Azriel, graceful as any courtier, offered her an arm. I couldn't tell if she was looking at his blue Siphon or at his scarred skin beneath as she breathed, "Beautiful."

Color bloomed high on Azriel's golden-brown cheeks, but he inclined his head in thanks and led my sister toward the back doors into the garden, sunlight bathing them.

A moment later, Nesta was stomping through the front door, her face a remarkable shade of green. "I need—a toilet."

I met Rhys's stare as he prowled in behind her, hands in his pockets. *What did you do?*

His brows shot up. But I wordlessly pointed Nesta toward the powder room beneath the stairs, and she vanished, slamming the door behind her.

Me? Rhys leaned against the bottom post of the banister. *She complained that I was flying deliberately slow. So I went fast.*

Cassian and Lucien appeared, neither looking at the other. But Lucien's attention went right to the hallway toward the back, his nostrils flaring as he scented Elain's direction. And who she'd gone with.

A low snarl slipped out of him—

"Relax," Rhys said. "Azriel isn't the ravishing type."

Lucien cut him a glare.

Mercifully, or perhaps not, Nesta's retching filled the silence. Cassian gaped at Rhys. "What did you *do?*"

"I asked him the same thing," I said, crossing my arms. "He said he '*went fast.*'"

Nesta vomited again—then silence.

Cassian sighed at the ceiling. "She'll never fly again."

The doorknob twisted, and we tried—or at least Cassian and I did—not to seem like we'd been listening to her. Nesta's face was still greenish-pale, but . . . Her eyes burned.

There was no way of describing that burning—and even painting it might have failed.

Her eyes remained the same blue-gray as my own. And yet . . . Molten ore was all I could think of. Quicksilver set aflame.

She advanced a step toward us. All her attention fixed on Rhys.

Cassian casually stepped in her path, wings folded in tight. Feet braced apart on the carpet. A fighting stance—casual, but . . . his Siphons glimmered.

"Do you know," Cassian drawled to her, "that the last time I got into a brawl in this house, I was kicked out for a month?"

Nesta's burning gaze slid to him, still outraged—but hinted with incredulity.

He just went on, "It was Amren's fault, of course, but no one believed me. And no one dared banish *her*."

She blinked slowly.

But the burning, molten gaze became mortal. Or as mortal as one of us could be.

Until Lucien breathed, "What *are* you?"

Cassian didn't seem to dare take his focus off Nesta. But my sister slowly looked at Lucien.

"I made it give something back," she said with terrifying quiet. The Cauldron. The hairs along my arms rose. Nesta's gaze flicked to the carpet, then to a spot on the wall. "I wish to go to my room."

It took a moment to realize she'd spoken to me. I cleared my throat. "Up the stairs, on your right. Second door. Or the third—whichever suits you. The other is for Elain. We need to leave in . . ." I squinted at the clock in the sitting room. "Two hours."

A shallow nod was her only acknowledgment and thanks.

We watched as she headed up the steps, her lavender gown trailing after her, one slender hand braced on the rail.

"I'm sorry," Rhys called up after her.

Her hand tightened on the rail, the whites of her knuckles poking through her pale skin, but she didn't say anything as she continued on.

"Is that sort of thing even possible?" Cassian murmured when the door to her room had shut. "For someone to *take* from the Cauldron's essence?"

"It would seem so," Rhys mused, then said to Lucien, "The flame in her eyes was not of your usual sort, I take it."

Lucien shook his head. "No. It spoke to nothing in my own arsenal. That was . . . Ice so cold it burned. Ice and yet . . . fluid like flame. Or flame made of ice."

"I think it's death," I said quietly.

I held Rhys's gaze, as if it were again the tether that had kept me in this world. "I think the power is death—death made flesh. Or whatever power the Cauldron holds over such things. That's why the Carver heard it—heard about her."

"Mother above," Lucien said, dragging a hand through his hair.

Cassian gave him a solemn nod.

But Rhys rubbed his jaw, weighing, thinking. Then he said simply, "Only Nesta would not just conquer Death—but pillage it."

No wonder she didn't wish to speak to anyone about it—didn't wish to bear witness on our behalf. It had been mere seconds for us while she'd gone under.

I had never asked either of my sisters how long it had been for *them* inside that Cauldron.

⊹

"Azriel knows you're watching," Rhys drawled from where he stood before the mirror in our bedroom, adjusting the lapels of his black jacket.

The town house was a quiet flurry of activity as we prepared to leave. Mor and Amren had arrived half an hour ago, the former heading for the sitting room, the latter bearing a dress for my sister. I didn't dare ask Amren to see what she'd selected for Nesta.

Training, Amren had said days ago. There were magical objects in the Court of Nightmares that my sister could study tonight, while we were occupied with Keir. I wondered if the Ouroboros was one of them—and made a note to ask Amren what she knew of the mirror the Carver so badly desired. Which I'd somehow have to convince Keir to part with tonight.

Lucien had offered to make himself useful while we were gone by reading through some of the texts now piled on the tables throughout the sitting room. Amren had only grunted at the offer, which I told Lucien amounted to a yes.

Cassian was already on the roof, casually sharpening his blades. I'd asked him if *nine* swords were really necessary, and he merely told me that it didn't hurt to be prepared, and that if I had enough time to question him, then I should have enough time to do another workout. I'd quickly left, throwing a vulgar gesture his way.

My hair still damp from the bath I'd just taken, I slid my heavy earrings through my lobes and peered out our bedroom window, monitoring the garden below.

Elain sat silently at one of the wrought-iron tables, a cup of tea before her. Azriel was sprawled on the chaise longue across the gray stones, sunning his wings and reading what looked to be a stack of reports—likely information on the Autumn Court that he planned to present to Rhys once he'd sorted through it all. Already dressed for the Hewn City—the brutal, beautiful armor so at odds with the lovely garden. And my sister sitting within it.

"Why not make *them* mates?" I mused. "Why Lucien?"

"I'd keep that question from Lucien."

"I'm serious." I turned toward him and crossed my arms. "What decides it? *Who* decides it?"

Rhys straightened his lapels before plucking an invisible piece of lint from them. "Fate, the Mother, the Cauldron's swirling eddies . . ."

"*Rhys.*"

He watched me in the reflection of the mirror as I strode for my armoire, flinging open the doors to yank out the dress I'd selected. Scraps of shimmering black—a slightly more modest version of what I'd worn to the Court of Nightmares months ago. "You said your mother and father were wrong for each other; *Tamlin* said his own parents were wrong for each other." I peeled off my dressing robe. "So it can't be a perfect system of matching. What if"—I jerked my chin toward the window, to my sister and the shadowsinger in the garden— "*that* is what she needs? Is there no free will? What if Lucien wishes the union but she doesn't?"

"A mating bond can be rejected," Rhys said mildly, eyes flickering in the mirror as he drank in every inch of bare skin I had on display. "There is choice. And sometimes, yes—the bond picks poorly. Sometimes, the bond is nothing more than some . . . preordained guesswork at who will provide the strongest offspring. At its basest level, it's perhaps only that. Some natural function, not an indication of true, paired souls." A smile at me—at the rareness, perhaps, of what we had. "Even so," Rhys went on, "there will always be a . . . tug. For the females, it is usually easier to ignore, but the males . . . It can drive them mad. It is their burden to fight through, but some believe they are entitled to the female. Even after the bond is rejected, they see her as belonging to them. Sometimes they return to challenge the male she chooses for herself. Sometimes it ends in death. It is savage, and it is ugly, and it mercifully does not happen often, but . . . Many mated pairs will try to make it work, believing the Cauldron selected them for a reason. Only years later will they realize that perhaps the pairing was not ideal in spirit."

I scrounged up the jeweled, dark belt from an armoire drawer and slung it low over my hips. "So you're saying she could walk away—and Lucien would have free rein to kill whoever she wishes to be with."

Rhys turned from the mirror at last, his dark clothes pristine—cut perfectly to his body. No wings tonight. "Not free rein—not in my lands. It has been illegal in our territory for a long, long time for males to do that. Even before I was born. Other courts, no. On the continent, there are territories that believe the females literally *belong* to their mate. But not here. Elain would have our full protection if she rejects the bond. But it will still be a bond, however weakened, that will trail her for the rest of her existence."

"Do you think she and Lucien match well?" I pulled out a pair of sandals that laced up my bare thighs and jammed my feet into them before beginning work on the bindings.

"You know them better than I do. But I will say that Lucien is loyal—fiercely so."

"So is Azriel."

"Azriel," Rhys said, "has been preoccupied with the same female for the past five hundred years."

"Wouldn't the mating bond have snapped into place for them if it exists?"

Rhys's eyes shuttered. "I think that is a question Azriel has been asking himself every day since he met Mor." He sighed as I finished one foot and started on the other. "Am I allowed to request that you *not* play matchmaker? Let them sort it out."

I rose, bracing my hands on my hips. "I would never meddle in someone else's affairs!"

He only raised a brow in silent challenge. And I knew precisely what he referred to.

My gut tightened as I took a seat at the vanity and began braiding my hair into a coronet atop my head. Perhaps I was a coward, for not being able to ask it aloud, but I said down the bond, *Was it a violation— going into Lucien's mind like that?*

I can't answer that for you. Rhys came over and handed me a hairpin.

I slid it into a section of braid. *I needed to be sure—that he wasn't about to try to grab her, to sell us out.*

He handed me another. *And did you get an answer to that?*

We worked in unison, pinning my hair into place. *I think so. It wasn't just about what he thought—it was the . . . feeling. I sensed no ill will, no conniving. Only concern for her. And . . . sorrow. Longing.* I shook my head. *Do I tell him? What I did?*

Rhys pinned a hard-to-reach section of my hair. *You have to deem whether the cost is worth assuaging your guilt.*

The cost being Lucien's tentative trust in me, this place. *I crossed a line.*

But you did it to ensure the safety of people you love.

I didn't realize . . . I trailed off, shaking my head again.

He squeezed my shoulder. *Didn't realize what?*

I shrugged, slouching on the cushioned stool. *That it'd be so complicated.* My face warmed. *I know that sounds terribly naïve—*

It's always complicated, and it never gets easier, no matter how many centuries I've been doing it.

I pushed around the extra hairpins on the vanity. *It's the second time I've gone into his mind.*

Then say it's the last, and be done with it.

I blinked, lifting my head. I'd painted my lips in a shade of red so dark it was nearly black, and they now pressed into a thin line.

He clarified, *What's done is done. Agonizing over it won't change anything. You realized it was a line you didn't like crossing, and so you won't make that mistake again.*

I shifted in my seat. *Would you have done it?*

Rhys considered. *Yes. And I would have felt just as guilty afterward.*

Hearing that settled something, deep down. I nodded once—twice.

If you want to make yourself feel a little better, he added, *Lucien did technically violate the rules we set. So you were entitled to look into his mind, if only to ensure the safety of your sister. He crossed the line first.*

That thing deep in me eased a bit more. *You're right.*

And it was done.

I watched Rhys in the mirror as a dark crown appeared in his hands. The one of ravens' feathers that I'd seen him wear—or its feminine twin. A tiara—which he gently, reverently, set before the braid we'd pinned into place atop my head. The original crown . . . it appeared atop Rhys's head a moment later.

Together, we stared at our reflection. Lord and Lady Night.

"Ready to be wicked?" he purred in my ear.

My toes curled at the caress in that voice—at the memory of the last time we'd gone to the Court of Nightmares. How I'd sat in his lap—where his fingers had drifted.

I rose from the bench, facing him fully. His hands skimmed the bare skin along my ribs. Between my breasts. Down the outside of my thighs. Oh, he remembered, too.

"This time," I breathed, kissing the tendril of tattoo that peeked just above the collar of Rhys's black jacket, "I get to make Keir beg."

CHAPTER
25

Amren hadn't dressed Nesta in cobwebs and stardust, as Mor and I were clothed. And she hadn't dressed Nesta in her own style of loose pants and a cropped blouse.

She had kept it simple. Brutal.

A dress of impenetrable black flowed to the dark marble floors of the throne room of the Hewn City, tight through the bodice and sleeves, its neckline skimming the base of her pale throat. Nesta's hair had been swept into a simple style to reveal the panes of her face, the savage clarity of her eyes as she took in the assembled crowd, the towering carved pillars and the scaled beasts twined around them, the mighty dais and the throne atop it . . . and did not balk.

Indeed, Nesta's chin only lifted with each step we took toward that dais.

One throne, I realized—that mighty throne of those twined, scaly beasts.

Rhys realized it, too. Planned for it.

My sister and the others peeled away at the foot of the dais, taking flanking positions at its base. No fear, no joy, no light in their faces.

Azriel, at Mor's side, looked murderously calm as he surveyed those gathered. As he beheld Keir, waiting beside a golden-haired woman who had to be Mor's mother, sneering at us. *Promise them nothing*, Mor had warned me.

Rhys held out a hand for me to ascend the dais steps. I kept my head high, back straight, as I gripped his fingers and strode up the few stairs. Toward that solitary throne.

Rhys only winked as he gracefully escorted me right into that throne, the movement as easy and smooth as a dance.

The crowd murmured as I sat, the black stone bitingly cold against my bare thighs.

They outright gasped as Rhys simply perched on the arm of the throne, smirked at me, and said to the Court of Nightmares, "Bow."

For they had not. And with me seated on that throne . . .

Their faces were still a mixture of shock and disdain as they all dropped to their knees.

I avoided looking at Nesta while she had no choice but to follow suit.

But I made myself look at Keir, at the female beside him, at anyone who dared meet my gaze. Made myself remember what they had done to Mor, now bowing with a grin on her face, when she was barely more than a child. Some of the court averted their eyes.

"I will interpret the lack of two thrones to be due to the fact that this visit came upon you quickly," Rhys said with lethal calm. "And I will let you all escape without having your skin flayed from your bones as *my* mating gift to *you*. Our loyal subjects," he added, smiling faintly.

I traced a finger over the scaly coil of one of the beasts that made up the arms of the throne. Our court. Part of it.

And we needed them to fight with us. To agree to it—tonight.

The mouth I'd painted that dark, dark red parted into a lazy smile. Tendrils of power snaked toward the dais, but didn't dare venture past the first step. Testing me—what power I might have. But not getting close enough to offend Rhysand.

I let them creep closer, sniffing around, as I said to Rhys, to the throne room, "Surely, my love, they would like to stand now."

Rhys smiled down at me, then at the crowd. "Rise."

They did. And some of those tendrils of power dared climb up the first step.

I pounced.

Three gasps choked through the murmuring room as I slammed talon-sharp magic down upon those too-curious powers. Dug in deep and hard. A cat with a bird under its paw. Several of them.

"Do you wish to have this back?" I asked quietly to no one in particular.

Near the foot of the dais, Keir was scowling over a shoulder, his silver circlet glinting atop his golden hair. Someone whimpered in the back of the room.

"Don't you know," Rhys purred to the crowd, "that it's not polite to touch a lady without her permission?"

In answer, I sank those dark talons in further, the magic of whoever had dared try to test me thrashing and buckling. "Play nice," I crooned to the crowd.

And let go.

Three separate flurries of motion warred for my attention. Someone had winnowed outright, fleeing. Another had fainted. And a third was clinging to whoever stood beside them, trembling. I marked all their faces.

Amren and Nesta approached the foot of the dais. My sister was staring as if she'd never seen me before. I didn't dare break my mask of bemused coolness. Didn't dare ask if Nesta's shields were holding up—if someone had just tried to test her as well. Nesta's own imperious face yielded nothing.

Amren bowed her head to Rhys, to me. "By your leave, High Lord."

Rhys waved an idle hand. "Go. Enjoy yourselves." He jerked his chin to the watching crowd. "Food and music. Now."

He was obeyed. Instantly.

My sister and Amren vanished before the crowd could begin milling about, striding right through those towering doors and into the gloom. To go play with some of the magical trove kept here—to give Nesta some practice for whenever Amren figured out how to fix the wall.

A few heads turned in their direction—then quickly looked away as Amren noticed them.

Let some of the monster inside show.

We still had not told her of the Bone Carver—of the Prison visit. Something a bit like guilt coiled in my stomach. Though I supposed I had to get used to it as Rhys curled a finger toward Keir and said, "The council room. Ten minutes."

Keir's eyes narrowed at the order, the female beside him keeping her head down—the portrait of subservience. What Mor was supposed to have been.

My friend was indeed watching her parents, cold indifference on her face. Azriel kept a step away, monitoring everything.

I didn't let myself look too interested—too worried—as Rhys offered me a hand and we rose from the throne. And went to talk of war.

+

The council chamber of the Hewn City was nearly as large as the throne room. It was carved from the same dark rock, its pillars fashioned after those entangled beasts.

Far below the high, domed ceiling, a mammoth table of black glass split the room in two like a lightning strike, its corners left long and jagged. Sharp as a razor.

Rhys claimed a seat at the head of the table. I took the one at the opposite end. Azriel and Mor found seats on one side, and Keir settled into the seat on the other.

A chair beside him sat empty.

Rhys leaned back in his dark chair, swirling the wine that had been poured by a stone-faced servant a moment before. It had been an effort not to thank the male who'd filled my goblet.

But here, I did not thank anyone.

Here, I took what was mine, and offered no gratitude or apologies for it.

"I know why you're here," Keir said without any sort of preamble.

"Oh?" Rhys's eyebrow arched beautifully.

Keir surveyed us, distaste lingering on his handsome face. "Hybern is swarming. Your legions"—a sneer at Azriel, at the Illyrians he represented—"are gathering." Keir interlaced his long fingers and set them upon the dark glass. "You mean to ask for my Darkbringers to join your army."

Rhys sipped from his wine. "Well, at least you've spared me the effort of dancing around the subject."

Keir held his gaze without blinking. "I will confess that I find myself . . . sympathetic to Hybern's cause."

Mor shifted slightly in her seat. Azriel just pinned that icy, all-seeing stare on Keir.

"You would not be the only one," Rhys countered coolly.

Keir frowned up at the obsidian chandelier, fashioned after a wreath of night-blooming flowers—the center of each a twinkling silver faelight. "There are many similarities between Hybern's people and my own. Both of us trapped—stagnant."

"Last I checked," Mor cut in, "you have been free to do as you wish for centuries. Longer."

Keir didn't so much as look at her, earning a flicker of rage from Azriel at the dismissal. "Ah, but *are* we free here? Not even the entirety of this mountain belongs to us—not with your palace atop it."

"*All* of this belongs to me, I'll remind you," Rhys said wryly.

"It's that mentality that allows me to find Hybern's stifled people to be . . . kindred spirits."

"You want the palace upstairs, Keir, then it's yours." Rhys crossed his legs. "I didn't know you were lusting after it for so long."

Keir's answering smile was near-serpentine. "You must need my army rather desperately, Rhysand." Again, that hateful glance at Azriel. "Are the overgrown bats not up to snuff anymore?"

"Come train with them," Azriel said softly, "and you'll learn for yourself."

In his centuries of miserable existence, Keir had certainly mastered the art of sneering.

And the way he sneered at Azriel . . . Mor's teeth flashed in the dim light. It was an effort to keep myself from doing the same.

"I have no doubt," Rhys said, the portrait of glorious boredom, "that you've already decided upon your asking price."

Keir peered down the table—to me. Looked his fill as I held his stare. "I did."

My stomach turned at that gaze, the words.

Dark power rumbled through the chamber, setting the onyx chandelier tinkling. "Tread carefully, Keir."

Keir only smiled at me, then at Rhys. Mor had gone utterly still.

"What would you give me for a shot at this war, Rhysand? You whored yourself to Amarantha—but what about your mate?"

He had not forgotten how we'd treated him. How we'd humiliated him months ago.

And Rhys . . . there was only eternal, unforgiving death in his face, in the darkness gathering behind his chair. "The bargain our ancestors struck grants you the right to choose how and when your army assists my own. But it does not grant you the right to keep your life, Keir, when I grow tired of your existence."

As if in answer, invisible claws gouged deep marks in the table, the glass shrieking. I flinched. Keir blanched at the lines now inches from him.

"But I thought you might be . . . hesitant to assist me," Rhys went on. I'd never seen him so calm. Not calm—but filled with icy rage.

The sort I sometimes glimpsed in Azriel's eyes.

Rhys snapped his fingers and said to no one in particular, "Bring him in."

The doors opened on a phantom wind.

I didn't know where to look as a servant escorted in the tall male figure.

At Mor, whose face went white with dread. At Azriel, who reached for his dagger—Truth-Teller—his every breath alert, focused, but unsurprised. Not a hint of shock.

Or at Eris, heir to the Autumn Court, as he strolled into the room.

CHAPTER
26

That's who the final, empty seat was for.

And Rhys . . .

He remained sprawled in his chair, sipping from his wine. "Welcome back, Eris," he drawled. "It's been what—five centuries since you last set foot in here?"

Mor slid her eyes toward Rhys. Betrayal and—hurt. That was hurt flashing there.

For not warning us. For this . . . surprise.

I wondered if I schooled my features with any more success than my friend as Eris claimed the vacant seat at the table, not bothering to so much as nod to a wary-eyed Keir. "It has indeed been a while."

He'd healed since that day on the ice—not a sign of the gut-wound Cassian had given him. His red hair was unbound, a silken drape over his well-tailored cobalt jacket.

What is he doing here, I speared down the bond, not bothering to hide any of what coursed through me.

Making sure Keir agrees to help, was all Rhys said, the words tight and clipped. Restrained.

As if he were still holding the full might of his rage in check.

Shadows curled around Azriel's shoulders, whispering in his ear as he stared down Eris.

"You once wanted to build ties to Autumn, Keir," said Rhys, setting down his goblet of wine. "Well, here's your chance. Eris is willing to offer you a formal alliance—in exchange for your services in this war."

How the hell did you get him to agree to that?

Rhys didn't answer.

Rhysand.

Keir leaned back in his chair. "It is not enough."

Eris snorted, pouring himself a goblet of wine from the decanter in the center of the table. "I'd forgotten why I was so relieved when our bargain fell apart the last time."

Rhys shot him a warning look. Eris just drank deeply.

"What is it that you want, then, Keir?" Rhys purred.

I had the feeling if Keir suggested me again, he'd wind up splattered on the wall.

But Keir must have known, too. And said simply to Rhysand, "I want out. I want space. I want my people to be free of this mountain."

"You have every comfort," I finally said. "And yet it is not enough?"

Keir ignored me as well. As I'm sure he ignored most women in his life.

"You have been keeping secrets, High Lord," Keir said with a hateful smile, interlacing his hands and resting them on the mauled table. Right atop the nearest deep gouge. "I always wondered—where all of you *went* when you weren't here. Hybern answered the question at last—thanks to that attack on . . . what is its name? Velaris. Yes. On Velaris. The City of Starlight."

Mor went utterly still.

"I want access to the city," Keir said. "For me, and my court."

"No," Mor said. The word echoed off the pillars, the glass, the rock.

I was inclined to agree. The thought of these people, of Keir, in

Velaris . . . Tainting it with their presence, their hatred and small-mindedness, their disdain and cruelty . . .

Rhys did not refuse. Did not shoot down the suggestion.

You can't be serious.

Rhys only watched Keir as he answered down the bond, *I anticipated this—and I took precautions.*

I contemplated it. *The meeting with the Palace governors . . . That was tied to this?*

Yes.

Rhysand said to Keir, "There would be conditions."

Mor opened her mouth, but Azriel laid a scarred hand atop hers.

She snatched her hand back as if she'd been burned—burned as he had been.

Azriel's mask of cold didn't so much as waver at the rejection. Though Eris chuckled softly. Enough to make Azriel's hazel eyes glaze with rage as he settled them upon the High Lord's son. Eris only inclined his head to the shadowsinger.

"I want unrestricted access," Keir said to Rhys.

"You will not get it," Rhys said. "There will be limited stays, limited numbers allowed in. To be decided later."

Mor turned pleading eyes to Rhys. Her city—the place that she loved so much—

I could almost hear it. The crack I knew was about to sound amongst our own circle.

Keir looked to Mor at last—noted the despair and anger. And smiled.

He had no real desire to get out of here.

Only a desire to take something he'd undoubtedly gleaned that his daughter cherished.

I could have gladly shredded through his throat as Keir said, "Done."

Rhys didn't so much as smile. Mor was only staring and staring at him, that beseeching expression crumpling her face.

"There is one more thing," I added, squaring my shoulders. "One more request."

Keir deigned to acknowledge me. "Oh?"

"I have need of the Ouroboros mirror," I said, willing ice into my veins. "Immediately."

Interest and surprise flared in Keir's brown eyes. Mor's eyes.

"Who told you that I have it?" he asked quietly.

"Does it matter? I want it."

"Do you even know what the Ouroboros *is*?"

"Consider your tone, Keir," Rhys warned.

Keir leaned forward, bracing his forearms on the table. "The mirror . . ." He laughed under his breath. "Consider it my mating present." He added with sweet venom, "If you can take it."

Not a threat to face him, but— "What do you mean?"

Keir rose to his feet, smirking like a cat with a canary in its mouth. "To take the Ouroboros, to claim it, you must first look into it." He headed for the doors, not waiting to be dismissed. "And everyone who has attempted to do so has either gone mad or been broken beyond repair. Even a High Lord or two, if legend is true." A shrug. "So it is yours, if you dare to face it." Keir paused at the threshold as the doors opened on a phantom wind. He said to Rhys, perhaps the closest he'd come to asking for permission to leave, "Lord Thanatos is having . . . difficulties with his daughter again. He requires my assistance." Rhys only waved a hand, as if he hadn't just yielded our city to the male. Keir jerked his chin at Eris. "I will wish to speak with you—soon."

Once he was done gloating over his victory tonight. What we'd given.

And lost.

If the Ouroboros could not be retrieved, at least without such terrible risk . . . I shut out the thought, sealing it away for later, as Keir left. Leaving us alone with Eris.

The heir of Autumn just sipped his wine.

And I had the terrible sense that Mor had gone somewhere far, far away as Eris set down his goblet and said, "You look well, Mor."

"You don't speak to her," Azriel said softly.

Eris gave a bitter smile. "I see you're still holding a grudge."

"This arrangement, Eris," Rhys said, "relies solely upon you keeping your mouth shut."

Eris huffed a laugh. "And haven't I done an excellent job? Not even my father suspected when I left tonight."

I glanced between my mate and Eris. "How did this come about?"

Eris looked me over. The crown and dress. "You didn't think that I knew your shadowsinger would come sniffing around to see if I'd told my father about your . . . powers? Especially after my brothers so mysteriously *forgot* about them, too. I knew it was a matter of time before one of you arrived to take care of my memory as well." Eris tapped the side of his head with a long finger. "Too bad for you, I learned a thing or two about daemati. Too bad for my brothers that I never bothered to teach them."

My chest tightened. *Rhys.*

To keep me safe from Beron's wrath, to keep this potential alliance with the High Lords from falling apart before it began . . . *Rhys.*

It was an effort to keep my eyes from burning.

A gentle caress down the bond was his only answer.

"Of course I didn't tell my father," Eris went on, drinking from his wine again. "Why waste that sort of information on the bastard? His answer would be to hunt you down and kill you—not realizing how much shit we're in with Hybern and that you might be the key to stopping it."

"So he plans to join us, then," Rhys said.

"Not if he learns about your little secret." Eris smirked.

Mor blinked—as if realizing that Rhys's contact with Eris, his invitation here . . . The glance she gave me, clear and settled, told me enough. Hurt and anger still swirled, but understanding, too.

"So what's the asking price, Eris?" Mor demanded, leaning her bare arms on the dark glass. "Another little bride for you to torture?"

Something flickered in Eris's eyes. "I don't know who fed you those lies to begin with, Morrigan," he said with vicious calm. "Likely the bastards you surround yourself with." A sneer at Azriel.

Mor snarled, rattling the glasses. "You never gave any evidence to the contrary. Certainly not when you left me in those woods."

"There were forces at work that you have never considered," Eris said coldly. "And I am not going to waste my breath explaining them to you. Believe what you want about me."

"You hunted me down like an animal," I cut in. "I think we'll choose to believe the worst."

Eris's pale face flushed. "I was given an order. And sent to do it with two of my . . . brothers."

"And what of the brother you hunted down alongside me? The one whose lover you helped to execute before his eyes?"

Eris laid a hand flat on the table. "You know *nothing* about what happened that day. *Nothing*."

Silence.

"Indulge me," was all I said.

Eris stared me down. I stared right back.

"How do you think he made it to the Spring border," he said quietly. "I wasn't there—when they did it. Ask him. I refused. It was the first and only time I have denied my father anything. He punished me. And by the time I got free . . . They were going to kill him, too. I made sure they didn't. Made sure Tamlin got word—anonymously—to get the hell over to his own border."

Where two of Eris's brothers had been killed. By Lucien and Tamlin.

Eris picked at a stray thread on his jacket. "Not all of us were so lucky in our friends and family as you, Rhysand."

Rhys's face was a mask of boredom. "It would seem so."

And none of this entirely erased what he'd done, but . . . "What is the asking price," I repeated.

"The same thing I told Azriel when I found him snooping through my father's woods yesterday."

Hurt flared in Mor's eyes as she whipped her head toward the shadowsinger. But Azriel didn't so much as acknowledge her as he announced, "When the time comes . . . we are to support Eris's bid to take the throne."

Even as Azriel spoke, that frozen rage dulled his face. And Eris was wise enough to finally pale at the sight. Perhaps that was why Eris had kept knowledge of my powers to himself. Not just for this sort of bargaining, but to avoid the wrath of the shadowsinger. The blade at his side.

"The request still stands, Rhysand," Eris said, mastering himself, "to just kill my father and be done with it. I can pledge troops right now."

Mother above. He didn't even try to hide it—to look at all remorseful. It was an effort to keep my jaw from dropping to the table at his intent, the casualness with which he spoke it.

"Tempting, but too messy," Rhys replied. "Beron sided with us in the War. Hopefully he'll sway that way again." A pointed stare at Eris.

"He will," Eris promised, running a finger over one of the claw marks gouged into the table. "And will remain blissfully unaware of Feyre's . . . gifts."

A throne—in exchange for his silence. And sway.

"Promise Keir nothing you care about," Rhys said, waving a hand in dismissal.

Eris just rose to his feet. "We'll see." A frown at Mor as he drained his wine and set down the goblet. "I'm surprised you still can't control yourself around him. You had every emotion written right on that pretty face of yours."

"Watch it," Azriel warned.

Eris looked between them, smiling faintly. Secretly. As if he knew something that Azriel didn't. "I wouldn't have touched you," he said to Mor, who blanched again. "But when you fucked that other bastard—" A snarl ripped from Rhys's throat at that. And my own. "I knew why you did it." Again that secret smile that had Mor shrinking. *Shrinking*. "So I gave you your freedom, ending the betrothal in no uncertain terms."

"*And what happened next*," Azriel growled.

A shadow crossed Eris's face. "There are few things I regret. That is one of them. But . . . perhaps one day, now that we are allies, I shall tell you why. What it cost me."

"I don't give a shit," Mor said quietly. She pointed to the door. "Get out."

Eris gave a mocking bow to her. To all of us. "See you at the meeting in twelve days."

CHAPTER
27

We found Nesta and Amren waiting outside the throne room, both of them looking pissy and tired.

Well, that made six of us.

I didn't doubt Keir's claim about the mirror—and risking gazing into it . . . None of us could afford it. To be broken. Driven mad. None of us—not right now. Perhaps the Bone Carver had known that. Had sent me on a fool's errand to amuse himself.

We did not bother with good-byes to the whispering court as we winnowed to the town house. To Velaris—the peace and beauty that now felt infinitely more fragile.

Cassian had come off the roof at some point to join Lucien in the sitting room, the books from the wall spread on the low-lying table between them. Both got to their feet at the expressions on our faces.

Cassian was halfway to Mor when she whirled on Rhys and said, "*Why?*"

Her voice broke.

And something in my chest cracked, too, at the tears that began running down her face.

Rhys just stood there, staring down at her. His face unreadable.

Watching as she slammed her hands into his chest and shouted, "*Why?*"

He yielded a step. "Eris found Azriel—our hands were tied. I made the best of it." His throat bobbed. "I'm sorry."

Cassian was sizing them up, frozen halfway across the room. And I assumed Rhys was telling him mind to mind, assumed he was telling Amren and perhaps even Lucien and Nesta, from their surprised blinks.

Mor whirled on Azriel. "*Why didn't you say anything?*"

Azriel held her gaze unflinchingly. Didn't so much as rustle his wings. "Because you would have tried to stop it. And we can't afford to lose Keir's alliance—and face the threat of Eris."

"You're working with that prick," Cassian cut in, whatever catching-up now over, apparently. He moved to Mor's side, a hand on her back. He shook his head at Azriel and Rhys, disgust curling his lip. "You should have spiked Eris's fucking head to the front gates."

Azriel only watched them with that icy indifference. But Lucien crossed his arms, leaning against the back of the couch. "I have to agree with Cassian. Eris is a snake."

Perhaps Rhys had not filled him in on everything, then. On what Eris had claimed about saving his youngest brother in whatever way he could. Of his defiance.

"Your whole family is despicable," Amren said to Lucien from where she and Nesta lingered in the archway. "But Eris may prove a better alternative. If he can find a way to kill Beron off and make sure the power shifts to himself."

"I'm sure he will," Lucien said.

But Mor was still staring at Rhys, those silent tears streaming down her flushed cheeks. "It's not about Eris," she said, voice wobbling. "It's about *here*." She waved a hand to the town house, the city. "This is my *home*, and you are going to let Keir *destroy it*."

"I took precautions," Rhys said—an edge to his voice I had not heard in some time. "Many of them. Starting with meeting with the governors of the Palaces and getting them to agree never to serve, shelter, or entertain Keir or anyone from the Court of Nightmares."

Mor blinked. Cassian's hand moved to her shoulder and squeezed.

"They have been sending out the word to every business owner in the city," Rhys went on, "every restaurant and shop and venue. So Keir and his ilk may come here . . . But they will not find it a welcoming place. Or one where they can even procure lodgings."

Mor shook her head as she whispered, "He'll still destroy it."

Cassian slid his arm around her shoulders, his face harder than I'd ever seen it as he studied Rhys. Then Azriel. "You should have warned us."

"I should have," Rhys said—though he didn't sound sorry for it. Azriel just remained a foot away, wings tucked in tight and Siphons glimmering.

I stepped in at last. "We'll set limitations—on when and how often they come."

Mor shook her head, still not looking anywhere but at Rhys. "If Amarantha were alive . . ." The word slithered through the room, darkening the corners. "If she were alive and I offered to *work* with her— even if it was to save us all—how would you feel?"

Never—they had never come this close to discussing what had happened to him.

I approached Rhys's side, brushing my fingers against his. His own curled around mine.

"If Amarantha offered us a slim shot at survival," Rhys said, his gaze unflinching, "then I would not give a *shit* that she made me fuck her for all those years."

Cassian flinched. The entire *room* flinched.

"If Amarantha showed up at that door right now," Rhys snarled, pointing toward the foyer entry, "and said she could buy us a chance at defeating Hybern, at keeping all of *you* alive, *I would thank the fucking Cauldron.*"

Mor shook her head, tears slipping free again. "You don't mean that."

"I do."

Rhys.

But the bond, the bridge between us . . . it was a howling void. A raging, dark tempest.

Too far—this was pushing them both too far. I tried to catch Cassian's gaze, but he was monitoring them closely, his golden-brown skin unnaturally pale. Azriel's shadows gathered close, half veiling him from view. And Amren—

Amren stepped between Rhys and Mor. They both towered over her.

"I kept this unit from breaking for forty-nine years," Amren said, eyes flaring bright as lightning. "I am not going to let you rip it to shreds now." She faced Mor. "Working with Keir and Eris is not forgiving them. And when this war is over, I will hunt them down and butcher them with you, if that is what you wish." Mor said nothing—though she at last looked away from Rhys.

"My father will poison this city."

"I will not allow him to," Amren said.

I believed her.

And I think Mor did, too, for the tears that continued sliding free . . . they seemed to shift, somehow.

Amren turned to Rhys, whose face had now edged toward— devastation.

I slid my hand through his. *I see you,* I said, giving him the words I'd once whispered all those months ago. *And it does not frighten me.*

Amren said to him, "You're a sneaky bastard. You always have been, and likely always will be. But it doesn't excuse you, boy, from not warning us. Warning her, not where those two monsters are involved. Yes, you made the right call—played it well. But you also played it badly."

Something like shame dimmed his eyes. "I'm sorry."

The words—to Mor, to Amren.

Amren's dark hair swayed as she assessed them. Mor just shook her head at last—more acceptance than denial.

I swallowed, my voice rough as I said, "This is war. Our allies are few and already don't trust us." I met each of them in the eye—my sister, Lucien, Mor, and Azriel and Cassian. Then Amren. Then my mate. I squeezed his hand at the guilt now sinking its claws deep into him. "You all have been to war and back—when I've never even set foot on a battlefield. But . . . I have to imagine that we will not last long if . . . we cleave apart. From within."

Stumbling, near-incoherent words, but Azriel said at last, "She's right."

Mor didn't so much as look in his direction. I could have sworn guilt clouded Azriel's eyes, there and gone in a blink.

Amren stepped back to Nesta's side as Cassian asked me, "What happened with the mirror?"

I shook my head. "Keir says it's mine, if I dare to take it. Apparently, what you see inside will break you—or drive you insane. No one's ever walked away from it."

Cassian swore.

"Exactly," I said. It was a risk perhaps none of us were entirely prepared to face. Not when we were all needed—each one of us.

Mor added a bit hoarsely, straightening the ebony pleats and panels of her gossamer gown, "My father spoke true about that. I was raised with legends of the mirror. None were pleasant. Or successful."

Cassian frowned at me, at Rhys. "So what—"

"You are talking about the Ouroboros," Amren said.

I blinked. Shit. *Shit*—

"Why do you want that mirror?" Her voice had slipped to a low timbre.

Rhys slid his free hand into his pocket. "If honesty is the theme of the night . . . Because the Bone Carver requested it."

Amren's nostrils flared. "You went to the Prison."

"Your old friends say hello," Cassian drawled, leaning a shoulder against the sitting room archway.

Amren's face tightened, Nesta glancing between them—carefully. Reading us. Especially as Amren's quicksilver eyes swirled. "Why did you go."

I opened my mouth, but the gold of Lucien's eye caught my attention. Snared it.

My hesitation must have been indication enough of my wariness.

Jaw tight with a hint of frustration, Lucien excused himself to his room. Frustration—and perhaps disappointment. I blocked it out—what it did to my stomach.

"We had some questions for the Carver." Cassian gave Amren a slash of a smile when Lucien was gone. "And we have some for you."

Amren's smoke-filled eyes flared. "You are going to unleash the Carver."

I said simply, "Yes." A one-monster army.

"That is impossible."

"I'll remind you that *you*, sweet Amren, escaped," Rhys countered smoothly. "And have stayed free. So it can be done. Perhaps you could tell us how you did it."

Cassian had stationed himself by the doorway, I realized, to be closer to Nesta. To grab her if Amren decided she didn't particularly care for where this conversation was headed. Or for any of the furniture in this room.

Precisely why Rhys now placed himself on Amren's other side—to draw her attention away from me, and Mor behind us, every muscle in her lithe body on alert.

Cassian was staring at Nesta—hard enough that my sister at last twisted toward him. Met his gaze. His head tilted—slightly. A silent order.

Nesta, to my shock, obeyed. Drifted over to Cassian's side as Amren replied to Rhys, "No."

"It wasn't a request," Rhys said.

He'd once admitted that merely questioning Amren had been something she'd allowed him to do only in recent years. But giving her an
order, pushing her like this . . .

"Feyre and Cassian spoke to the Bone Carver. He wants the
Ouroboros in exchange for serving us—fighting Hybern for us. But we
need you to explain how to get him out." The bargain Rhys or I would
strike with him would suffice to hold him to our will.

"Anything else?" Her voice was too calm, too sweet.

"When we're done with all of this," Rhys said, "then my promise
from months ago still holds: use the Book to send yourself home, if you
want."

Amren stared up at him. It was so quiet that the clock on the sitting
room mantel could be heard. And beyond that—the fountain in the
garden—

"Call off your dog," Amren said with that lethal tone.

Because the shadow in the corner behind Amren . . . that was
Azriel. The obsidian hilt of Truth-Teller in his scarred hand. He'd
moved without my realizing it—though I had no doubt the others had
likely been aware.

Amren bared her teeth at him. Azriel's beautiful face didn't so much
as shift.

Rhys remained where he was as he asked Amren, "Why won't you
tell us?"

Cassian casually slid Nesta behind him, his fingers snagging in the
skirts of her black gown. As if to reassure himself that she wasn't in
Amren's direct path. Nesta only rose onto her toes to peer over his
shoulder.

"Because the stone beneath this house has ears, the wind has ears—
all of it listening," Amren said. "And if it reports back . . . They will
remember, Rhysand, that they have not caught me. And I will not let
them put me in that black pit again."

My ears hollowed out as a shield clicked into place. "No one will
hear beyond this room."

Amren surveyed the books lying forgotten on the low table in the sitting room.

Her brows narrowed. "I had to give something up. I had to give *me* up. To walk out, I had to become something else entirely, something the Prison would not recognize. So I—I bound myself into this body."

I'd never heard her stumble over a word before.

"You said someone else bound you," Rhys questioned carefully.

"I lied—to cover what I'd done. So none could know. To escape the Prison, I made myself mortal. Immortal as you are, but . . . mortal compared to—to what I was. And what I was . . . I did not feel, the way you do. The way I do now. Some things—loyalty and wrath and curiosity—but not the full spectrum." Again, that faraway look. "I was perfect, according to some. I did not regret, did not mourn—and pain . . . I did not experience it. And yet . . . yet I wound up *here*, because I was not quite like the others. Even as—as what I was, I was different. Too curious. Too questioning. The day the rip appeared in the sky . . . it was curiosity that drove me. My brothers and sisters fled. Upon the orders of our ruler, we had just laid waste to twin cities, smote them wholly into rubble on the plain, and yet they *fled* from that rip in the world. But I wanted to look. I *wanted*. I was not built or bred to feel such selfish things as *want*. I'd seen what happened to those of my kind who strayed, who learned to place their needs first. Who developed . . . feeling. But I went through the tear in the sky. And here I am."

"And you gave all that up to get out of the Prison?" Mor asked softly.

"I yielded my grace—my perfect immortality. I knew that once I did . . . I would feel pain. And regret. I would want, and I would burn with it. I would . . . fall. But I was—the time locked away down there . . . I didn't care. I had not felt the wind on my face, had not smelled the rain . . . I did not even remember what they felt like. I did not remember sunlight."

It was to Azriel that her attention drifted—the shadowsinger's darkness pulling away to reveal eyes full of understanding. *Locked away.*

"So I bound myself into this body. I shoved my burning grace deep into me. I gave up everything I was. The cell door just . . . unlocked. And so I walked out."

A burning grace . . . That still smoldered far within her, visible only through the smoke in her gray eyes.

"That will be the cost of freeing the Carver," Amren said. "You will have to bind him into a body. Make him . . . Fae. And I doubt he will agree to it. Especially without the Ouroboros."

We were silent.

"You should have asked me before you went," she said, that sharpness returning to her tone. "I would have spared you the visit."

Rhysand swallowed. "Can you be—unbound?"

"Not by me."

"What would happen if you were?"

Amren stared at him for a long while. Then me. Cassian. Azriel. Mor. Nesta. Finally back to my mate. "I would not remember you. I would not care for any of you. I would either smite you or abandon you. What I feel now . . . it would be foreign to me—it would hold no sway. Everything I am, this body . . . it would cease to be."

"What *were* you," Nesta breathed, coming around Cassian to stand at his side.

Amren toyed with one of her black pearl earrings. "A messenger—and soldier-assassin. For a wrathful god who ruled a young world."

I could feel the questions of the others brewing. Rhys's eyes were near-glowing with them.

"Was Amren your name?" Nesta asked.

"No." The smoke swirled in her eyes. "I do not remember the name I was given. I used Amren because—it's a long story."

I almost begged her to tell it, but soft footsteps thudded, and then— "Oh."

Elain started—enough so that I realized she couldn't hear us. Had no idea we were here, thanks to the shield that kept sound from escaping.

It instantly dropped. But my sister remained near the stairs. She'd covered her nightgown with a silk shawl of palest blue, her fingers grap-pling into the fabric as she held herself.

I went to her immediately. "Do you need anything?"

"No. I . . . I was sleeping, but I heard . . ." She shook her head. Blinked at our formal attire, the dark crown atop my head—and Rhysand's. "I didn't hear you."

Azriel stepped forward. "But you heard something else."

Elain seemed about to nod, but only backed away. "I think I was dreaming," she murmured. "I think I'm always dreaming these days."

"Let me get you some hot milk," I said, putting a hand on her elbow to guide her into the sitting room.

But Elain shook me off, heading back to the stairs. She said as she climbed the first steps, "I can hear her—crying."

I gripped the bottom post of the banister. "Who?"

"Everyone thinks she's dead." Elain kept walking. "But she's not. Only—different. Changed. As I was."

"Who," I pushed.

But Elain continued up the stairs, that shawl drooping down her back. Nesta stalked from Cassian's side to approach my own. We both sucked in a breath, to say what, I didn't know but—

"What did you see," Azriel said, and I tried not to flinch as I found him at my other side, not having seen him move. Again.

Elain paused halfway up the stairs. Slowly, she turned to look back at him. "I saw young hands wither with age. I saw a box of black stone. I saw a feather of fire land on snow and melt it."

My stomach dropped to the floor. One glance at Nesta confirmed that she felt it, too. Saw it.

Mad. Elain might very well have gone mad—

"It was angry," Elain said quietly. "It was so, so angry that some-thing was taken. So it took something from them as punishment."

We said nothing. I didn't know *what* to say—what to even ask or demand. If the Cauldron had done something to *her* as well . . .

I faced Azriel, exposing my palms to him. "What does that *mean*?"

Azriel's hazel eyes churned as he studied my sister, her too-thin body. And without a word, he winnowed away. Mor watched the space where he'd been standing long after he was gone.

＋

I waited until the others had left—Cassian and Rhys slipping away to ponder the possibilities or lack thereof of our would-be allies, Amren storming off to be rid of us entirely, and Mor striding out to enjoy what she deemed as her last few days of peace in this city, a brittleness still in her voice—before I cornered Nesta in the sitting room.

"What happened at the Hewn City—with you and Amren? You didn't mention it."

"It was fine."

I clenched my jaw. "What happened?"

"She brought me to a room full of treasure. Strange objects. And it . . ." She tugged at the tight sleeve of her gown. "Some of it wanted to *hurt* us. As if it were alive—aware. Like . . . like in all those stories and lies we were fed over the wall."

"Are you all right?" I couldn't find any signs of harm on either of them, and neither had said anything to suggest—

"It was a training exercise. With a form of magic designed to repel intruders." The words were recited. "As the wall will likely be. She wanted me to breach the defenses—find weaknesses."

"And repair them?"

"Just find the weaknesses. Repairing is another thing," Nesta said, her eyes going distant as she frowned at the still-open books on the low table before the fireplace.

I sighed. "So . . . that went right, at least."

Those eyes went razor-sharp again. "I failed. Every time. So, no. It did not go right."

I didn't know what to say. Sympathy would likely earn me a

tongue-lashing. So I opted for another route. "We need to do something about Elain."

Nesta stiffened. "And what solution do you propose, exactly? Letting your mate into her mind to scramble things around?"

"I'd never do that. I don't think Rhys can even . . . fix things like that."

Nesta paced in front of the darkened fireplace. "Everything has a cost. Maybe the cost of her youth and immortality was losing part of her sanity."

My knees wobbled enough that I took a seat on the deep-cushioned couch. "What was your cost?"

Nesta stopped moving. "Perhaps it was to see Elain suffer—while I got away unscathed."

I shot to my feet. "Nesta—"

"Don't bother." But I trailed her as she strode for the stairs. To where Lucien was now descending the steps—and winced at the sight of her approach.

He gave her a wide berth as she stormed past him. One look at his taut face had me bracing myself—and returning to the sitting room.

I slumped into the nearest armchair, surprised to find myself still in my black dress as the fabric scraped against my bare skin. How long had I been back from the Hewn City? Thirty minutes? Less? And had the Prison only been that morning?

It felt like days ago. I rested my head against the embroidered back of the chair and watched Lucien take a seat on the rolled arm of the nearest couch. "Long day?"

I grunted my response.

That metal eye tightened. "I thought the Prison was another myth."

"Well, it's not."

He weighed my tone, and crossed his arms. "Let me do something. About Elain. I heard—from my room. Everything that happened just now. It wouldn't hurt to have a healer look her over. Externally and internally."

I was tired enough that I could barely summon the breath to ask, "Do you think the Cauldron made her insane?"

"I think she went through something terrible," Lucien countered carefully. "And it wouldn't hurt to have your best healer do a thorough examination."

I rubbed my hand over my face. "All right." My breath snagged on the words. "Tomorrow morning." I managed a shallow nod, rallying my strength to rise from the chair. Heavy—there was an old heaviness in me. Like I could sleep for a hundred years and it wouldn't be enough.

"Please tell me," Lucien said when I crossed the threshold into the foyer. "What the healer says. And if—if you need me for anything."

I gave him one final nod, speech suddenly beyond me.

I knew Nesta still wasn't asleep as I walked past her room. Knew she'd heard every word of our conversation thanks to that Fae hearing. And I knew she heard as I listened at Elain's door, knocked once, and poked my head in to find her asleep—breathing.

I sent a request to Madja, Rhysand's preferred healer, to come the next day at eleven. I did not explain why or who or what. Then went into my bedroom, crawled onto the mattress, and cried.

I didn't really know why.

⁜

Strong, broad hands rubbed down my spine, and I opened my eyes to find the room wholly black, Rhysand perched on the mattress beside me. "Do you want anything to eat?" His voice was soft—tentative.

I didn't raise my head from the pillow. "I feel . . . heavy again," I breathed, voice breaking.

Rhys said nothing as he gathered me up into his arms. He was still in his jacket, as if he'd just come in from wherever he'd been talking with Cassian.

In the dark, I breathed in his scent, savored his warmth. "Are you all right?"

Rhys was quiet for a long minute. "No."

I slid my arms around him, holding him tightly.

"I should have found another way," he said.

I stroked my fingers through his silken hair.

Rhys murmured, "If she . . ." His swallow was audible. "If she showed up at this house . . ." I knew who he meant. "I would kill her. Without even letting her speak. I would kill her."

"I know." I would, too.

"You asked me at the library," he whispered. "Why I . . . Why I'd rather take all of this upon myself. Tonight is why. Seeing Mor *cry* is why. I made a bad call. Tried to find some other way around this shit-hole we're in." And had lost something—*Mor* had lost something—in the process.

We held each other in silence for minutes. Hours. Two souls, twining in the dark. I lowered my shields, let him in fully. His mind curled around mine.

"Would you risk looking into it—the Ouroboros?" I asked.

"Not yet," was all Rhys said, holding me tighter. "Not yet."

CHAPTER
28

I dragged myself out of bed by sheer will the next morning.

Amren had said the Carver wouldn't bind himself into a Fae body—had *claimed* that.

But it wouldn't hurt to try. If it gave us the slightest chance of holding out, of keeping Rhys from giving everything . . .

He was already gone by the time I awoke. I gritted my teeth as I dressed in my leathers and winnowed to the House of Wind.

I had my wings ready as I hit the wards protecting it, and managed a decent-enough glide into the open-air training ring on its flat top.

Cassian was already waiting, hands on his hips. Watching as I eased down, down . . .

Too fast. My feet skipped over the dirt, bouncing me up, up—

"*Backflap—*"

His warning was too late.

I slammed into a wall of crimson before I could get a face full of the ruddy rock, but—I swore, pride skinned as much as my palms as I staggered back, my wings unwieldy behind me. Cassian's shoulders shook as he reined in a laugh, and I gave him a vulgar gesture in return.

"If you go in for a landing that way, make sure you have room."

I scowled. "Lesson learned."

"Or space to bank and circle until you slow—"

"I get it."

Cassian held up his hands, but the amusement faded as he watched me dismiss the wings and stalk toward him. "You want to go hard today, or take it easy?"

I didn't think the others gave him enough credit—for noticing the shift in someone's emotional current. To command legions, I supposed, he needed to be able to read that sort of thing, judge when his soldiers or enemies were strong or breaking or broken.

I peered inside, to that place where I now felt like quicksand, and said, "Hard. I want to limp out of here." I peeled off the leather jacket and rolled up the sleeves of my white shirt.

Cassian swept an assessing stare over me. He murmured, "It helps me, too—the physical activity, the training." He rolled his shoulders as I began to stretch. "It's always helped me focus and center myself. And after last night . . ." He tied back his dark hair. "I definitely need it—this."

I held my leg folded behind me, my muscles protesting at the stretch. "I suppose there are worse methods of coping."

A lopsided grin. "Indeed there are."

⁜

Azriel's lesson afterward consisted of standing in a breeze and trying to memorize his instructions on currents and downdrafts, on how heat and cold could shape wind and speed. Throughout it, he was quiet— removed. Even by his standards.

I made the mistake of asking if he'd spoken to Mor since he'd left last night.

No, he had not. And that was that.

Even if he kept flexing his scarred hand at his side. As if recalling the sensation of the hand she'd whipped free of his touch during that meeting. Over and over. I didn't dare tell him that he'd made the right call—that perhaps he should talk to Mor, rather than let the guilt eat at him. The two of them had enough between them without me shoving myself into it.

I was indeed limping by the time I returned to the town house hours later, finding Mor at the dining table, munching on a giant pastry she'd grabbed from a bakery on her way in.

"You look like a team of horses trampled you," she said around her food.

"Good," I said, taking the pastry out of her hand and finishing it off. She squawked in outrage, but snapped her fingers, and a plate of carved melon from the kitchen down the hall appeared on the polished table before her.

Right atop the pile of what looked to be letters on various pieces of stationery. "What's that?" I said, wiping the crumbs from my mouth.

"The first of the High Lords' responses," she said sweetly, plucking up a slice of the green fruit and biting off a chunk. No hint of last night's rage and fear.

"That pleasant, hmm?"

"Helion's came first this morning. Between all the innuendo, I think he said he'd be willing to . . . join us."

I lifted my brows. "That's good—isn't it?"

A shrug. "Helion, we weren't worried about. The other two . . ." She finished off the melon, chewing wetly. "Thesan says he'll come, but won't do it unless it's in a truly neutral and safe location. Kallias . . . he doesn't trust any of us after . . . Under the Mountain. He wants to bring armed guards."

Day, Dawn, and Winter. Our closest allies. "No word from anyone else?" My gut tightened.

"No. Spring, Autumn, and Summer haven't sent a reply."

"We don't have much time until the meeting. What if they refuse to reply at all?" I didn't have the nerve to wonder aloud if Eris would be good to his word and make sure his father attended—and joined our cause. Not with the light back in her face.

Mor picked up another slice of melon. "Then we'll have to decide if Rhys and I will go drag them by their necks to this meeting, or if we'll have it without them."

"I'd suggest the second option." Mor furrowed her brows. "The first," I clarified, "doesn't sound conducive to actually forming an alliance."

Though I was surprised that Tarquin hadn't responded. Even with his blood feud with us . . . The male I'd met, whom I still admired so much . . . Surely he'd want to ally against Hybern. Unless he now wanted to ally *with* them to ensure Rhys and I were wiped off the map forever.

"We'll see," was all Mor said.

I blew out a breath through my nose. "About last night—"

"It's fine. It's nothing." The swiftness with which she spoke suggested anything but.

"It's not nothing. You're *allowed* to feel that way."

Mor fluffed her hair. "Well, it won't help us win this war."

"No. But . . . I'm not sure what to say."

Mor stared toward the window for a long moment. "I understand why Rhys did it. The position we were in. Eris is . . . You know what he is like. And if he was indeed threatening to sell information about your gifts to his father . . . Mother above, *I* would have made the same bargain with Eris to keep Beron from hunting you." Something in my chest eased at that. "It's just . . . My father knew—the second he heard of this place, he probably knew what it meant to me. There would have been no other asking price for my father's help in this war. None. Rhys knew that as well. Tried to bring Eris into it to sweeten the deal for my father—to possibly avoid this outcome with Velaris altogether."

I raised my brows in silent question.

"We talked—Rhys and I. This morning. While Cassian was kicking your ass."

I snorted. "What about Azriel?" So much for my decision to stay out of it.

Mor resumed picking at the melon. "Az . . . He had a tough call to make, when Eris found him. He . . ." She chewed on her lip. "I don't know why I expected him to side with me, why it caught me so off guard." I refrained from suggesting she tell him that. Mor shrugged. "It just . . . it all took me by surprise. And I will never be happy about any of these terms, but . . . My father wins, Eris wins, all the males like them *win* if I let it get to me. If I let it impact my joy, my life. My relationships with all of you." She sighed at the ceiling. "I hate war."

"Likewise."

"Not just for the death and awfulness," Mor went on. "But because of what it does to us. These decisions."

I nodded, even if I was only starting to understand. The choices and the costs.

I opened my mouth, but a knock on the front door sounded. I glanced to the clock in the sitting room across the foyer. Right. The healer.

I'd mentioned to Elain this morning that Madja was coming to see her at eleven, and I'd gotten a noncommittal response. Better than outright refusal, I supposed.

"Are you going to answer the door, or should I?"

I made a vulgar gesture at the sheer sass in Mor's question, but my friend gripped my hand as I rose from my chair.

"If you need anything . . . I'll be right here."

I gave Mor a small, grateful smile. "As will I."

She was still smiling at me as I took a deep breath before heading for the entry.

＋

The healer found nothing.

I believed her—if only because Madja was one of the few High Fae I'd seen whose dark skin was etched with wrinkles, her hair spindrift fine with age. Her brown eyes were still clear and kindled with an inner warmth, and her knobby hands remained steady as she passed them over Elain's body while my sister lay patiently, silently, on the bed.

Magic, sweet and cooling, had thrummed from the female, filling Elain's bedroom. And when she had gently laid her hands on either side of Elain's head and I'd started, Madja had only smiled wryly over her thin shoulder and told me to relax.

Nesta, sharp-eyed in the corner, had kept quiet.

After a long minute, Madja asked us to join her in fetching Elain a cup of tea—with a pointed glance to the door. We both took the invitation and left our sister in her sunlit room.

"What do you mean, *nothing* is wrong with her?" Nesta hissed under her breath as the ancient female braced a hand on the stair railing to help herself down. I kept beside the healer, a hand in easy reach of her elbow, should she need it.

Madja, I reminded myself, had healed Cassian and Azriel—and countless injuries beyond that. She'd healed Rhys's wings during the War. She looked ancient, but I had no doubt of her stamina—or sheer will to help her patients.

Madja didn't deign to answer Nesta until we were at the bottom of the steps. Lucien was already waiting in the sitting room, Mor still lingering in the dining room. Both of them rose to their feet, but remained in their respective rooms, flanking the foyer.

"What I mean," Madja said at last, sizing up Nesta, then me, "is that I can find nothing wrong with her. Her body is fine—too thin and in need of more food and fresh air, but nothing amiss. And as for her mind . . . I cannot enter it."

I blinked. "She has a shield?"

"She is Cauldron-Made," the healer said, again looking over Nesta. "You are not like the rest of us. I cannot pierce the places it left its mark most deeply." The mind. The soul. She shot me a warning glance. "And I would not try if I were you, Lady."

"But do you think there's something wrong, even if there are no signs?" Nesta pushed.

"I have seen the victims of trauma before. Her symptoms match well with many of those invisible wounds. But . . . she was also Made by something I do not understand. Is there something wrong with her?" Madja chewed over the words. "I do not like that word—*wrong*. Different, perhaps. Changed."

"Does she need further help?" Nesta said through her teeth.

The ancient healer jerked her chin toward Lucien. "See what he can do. If anyone can sense if something is amiss, it's a mate."

"How." The word was barely more than a barked command.

I braced myself to warn Nesta to be polite, but Madja said to my sister, as if she were a small child, "The mating bond. It is a bridge between souls."

The healer's tone made my sister stiffen, but Madja was already hobbling for the front door. She pointed at Lucien as she saw herself out. "Try sitting down with her. Just talking—sensing. See what you pick up. But don't push." Then she was gone.

I whirled on Nesta. "A little *respect*, Nesta—"

"Call another healer."

"Not if you're going to bark them out of the house."

"Call another healer."

Mor strode for us with deceptive calm, and Nesta gave her a withering glare.

I caught Lucien's eye. "Would you try it?"

Nesta snarled, "Don't you even *attempt*—"

"Be quiet," I snapped.

Nesta blinked.

I bared my teeth at her. "He will *try*. And if he doesn't find anything amiss, we'll consider bringing another healer."

"You're just going to drag her down here?"

"I'm going to invite her."

Nesta faced Mor, still watching from the archway. "And what will *you* be doing?"

Mor gave my sister a half smile. "I'll be sitting with Feyre. Keeping an eye on things."

Lucien muttered something about not needing to be monitored, and we all looked at him with raised brows.

He just lifted his hands, claimed he wanted to freshen up, and headed down the hall.

CHAPTER
29

It was the most uncomfortable thirty minutes I could recall.

Mor and I sipped chilled mint tea by the bay window, the replies of the three High Lords piled on the little table between our twin chairs, pretending to be watching the summer-kissed street beyond us, the children, High Fae and faerie, darting about with kites and streamers and all manner of toys.

Pretending, while Lucien and Elain sat in stilted silence by the dim fireplace, an untouched tea service between them. I didn't dare ask if he was trying to get into her head, or if he was feeling a bond similar to that black adamant bridge between Rhys's mind and my own. If a normal mating bond felt wholly different.

A teacup rattled and rasped against a saucer, and Mor and I glanced over.

Elain had picked up the teacup, and now sipped from it without so much as looking toward him.

In the dining room across the hall, I knew Nesta was craning her neck to look.

Knew, because Amren snapped at my sister to pay attention.

They were building walls—in their minds, Amren had told me as she ordered Nesta to sit at the dining room table, directly across from her.

Walls that Amren was teaching her to sense—to find the holes she'd laid throughout. And repair them. If the fell objects at the Court of Nightmares had not allowed my sister to grasp what must be done, then this was their next attempt—a different, invisible route. Not all magic was flash and glittering, Amren had declared, and then shooed me out.

But any sign of that power within my sister . . . I did not hear it or see it or feel it. And neither offered any explanation for what it was, exactly, that they were trying to coax from within her.

Outside the house, movement again caught our eye, and we found Rhys and Cassian strolling in through the low front gate, returning from their first meeting with Keir's Darkbringer army commanders—already rallying and preparing. At least that much had gone right yesterday.

Both of them spotted us in the window within a heartbeat. Stopped cold.

Don't come in, I warned him through the bond. *Lucien is trying to sense what's wrong with Elain. Through the bond.*

Rhys murmured what I'd said to Cassian, who now angled his head, much in the way I had no doubt Nesta had done, to peer beyond us.

Rhys said wryly, *Does Elain know this?*

She was invited down for tea. So we're having it.

Rhys muttered again to Cassian, who choked on a laugh and turned right around, heading into the street. Rhys lingered, sliding his hands into his pockets. *He's getting a drink. I'm inclined to join him. When can I return without fearing for my life?*

I gave him a vulgar gesture through the window. *Such a big, strong Illyrian warrior.*

Illyrian warriors know when to pick their battles. And with Nesta watching everything like a hawk and you two circling like vultures . . . I know who will walk away from that fight.

I made the gesture again, and Mor figured out enough of what was being said that she echoed the movement. Rhys laughed quietly and sketched a bow.

The High Lords sent replies, I said as he strolled away. *Day, Dawn, and Winter will come.*

I know, he said. *And I just received word from Cresseida that Tarquin is contemplating it.*

Better than nothing. I said as much.

Rhys smiled at me over his shoulder. *Enjoy your tea, you overbearing chaperone.*

I could have used a chaperone around you, you realize.

You had four *of them in this house.*

I smiled as he finally reached the low front gate where Cassian waited, apparently using the momentary delay to stretch out his wings, to the delight of the half-dozen children now gawking at them.

Amren hissed from the other room, "*Focus.*" The dining table rattled.

The sound seemed to startle Elain, who swiftly set down her teacup. She rose to her feet, and Lucien shot to his.

"I'm sorry," he blurted.

"What—what was that?"

Mor put a hand on my knee to keep me from rising, too.

"It—it was a tug. On the bond."

Amren snapped, "*Don't you*—wicked girl."

Then Nesta was standing in the threshold. "What did you do." The words were as sharp as a blade.

Lucien looked to her, then over to me. A muscle feathered in his jaw. "Nothing," he said, and again faced his mate. "I'm sorry—if that unsettled you."

Elain sidled toward Nesta, who seemed to be at a near-simmer. "It felt . . . strange," Elain breathed. "Like you pulled on a thread tied to a rib."

Lucien exposed his palms to her. "I'm sorry."

Elain only stared at him for a long moment. And any lucidity faded away as she shook her head, blinking twice, and said to Nesta, "Twin ravens are coming, one white and one black."

Nesta hid the devastation well. The frustration. "What can I get you, Elain?"

Only with Elain did she use that voice.

But Elain shook her head once more. "Sunshine."

Nesta cut me a furious stare before guiding our sister down the hall—to the sunny garden in the back.

Lucien waited until the glass door had opened and closed before he loosed a long breath.

"There's a bond—it's a real thread," he said, more to himself than us.

"And?" Mor asked.

Lucien ran both hands through his long red hair. His skin was darker—a deep golden-brown, compared to the paleness of Eris's coloring. "And I got to Elain's end of it when she ran off."

"Did you sense anything?"

"No—I didn't have time. I *felt* her, but . . ." A blush stained his cheek. Whatever he'd felt, it wasn't what we were looking for. Even if we had no idea what, precisely, that was.

"We can try again—another day," I offered.

Lucien nodded, but looked unconvinced.

Amren snapped from the dining room, "Someone go retrieve your sister. Her lesson isn't over."

I sighed. "Yes, Amren."

Lucien's attention slid behind me, to the various letters on different styles and makes of paper. That golden eye narrowed. As Tamlin's emissary, he no doubt recognized them. "Let me guess: they said yes, but picking the location is now going to be the headache."

Mor frowned. "Any suggestions?"

Lucien tied back his hair with a strap of brown leather. "Do you have a map?"

I supposed that left me to retrieve Nesta.

⁜

"That pine tree wasn't there a moment ago."

Azriel let out a quiet laugh from where he sat atop a boulder two days later, watching me pluck pine needles out of my hair and jacket. "Judging by its size, I'd say it's been there for . . . two hundred years at least."

I scowled, brushing off the shards of bark and my bruised pride.

That coldness, that aloofness that had been there in the wake of Mor's anger and rejection . . . It'd warmed. Either from Mor choosing to sit next to him at dinner last night—a silent offer of forgiveness—or simply needing time to recover from it. Even if I could have sworn some kernel of guilt had flickered every time Azriel had looked at Mor. What Cassian had thought of it, of his own anger toward Azriel . . . he'd been all smiles and lewd comments. Glad all was back to normal—for now at least.

My cheeks burned as I scaled the boulder he perched on, the drop at least fifteen feet to the forest floor below, the lake a sparkling sprawl peeking through the pine trees. Including the tree I'd collided with face-first on my latest attempt to leap off the boulder and simply *sail* to the lake.

I braced my hands on my hips, examining the drop, the trees, the lake beyond. "What did I do wrong?"

Azriel, who had been sharpening Truth-Teller in his lap, flicked his hazel eyes up to me. "Aside from the tree?"

The shadowsinger had a sense of humor. Dry and quiet, but . . . alone together, it came out far more often than it did amongst our group.

I'd spent these past two days either poring over ancient volumes for any hint on repairing the wall to hand over to Amren and Nesta, who continued to silently, invisibly build and mend walls within their minds, or debating with Rhys and the others about how to reply to the volley of letters now being exchanged with the other High Lords regarding where the meeting would take place. Lucien had indeed given us an initial location, and several more when those were struck down. But that was to be expected, Lucien had said, as if he'd arranged such things countless times. Rhys had only nodded in agreement—and approval.

And when I wasn't doing that . . . I was combing through *more* books, any and all Clotho could find me, all regarding the Ouroboros. How to master it.

The mirror was notorious. Every known philosopher had ruminated on it. Some had dared face it—and gone mad. Some had approached—and run away in terror.

I could not find an account of anyone who had mastered it. Faced what lurked within and walked away with the mirror in their possession.

Save for the Weaver in the Wood—who certainly seemed insane enough, perhaps thanks to the mirror she'd so dearly loved. Or perhaps whatever evil lurked in her had tainted the mirror, too. Some of the philosophers had suggested as much, though they hadn't known her name—only that a dark queen had once possessed it, cherished it. Spied on the world with it—and used it to hunt down beautiful young maidens to keep her eternally young.

I supposed Keir's family owning the Ouroboros for millennia suggested the success rate of walking away was low. It was not heartening. Not when all the texts agreed on one thing: there was no way around it. No loophole. Facing the terror within . . . that was the only route to claim it.

Which meant I perhaps had to consider alternatives—other ways to entice the Bone Carver to join us. When I found a moment.

Azriel sheathed his legendary fighting knife and examined the wings I'd spread wide. "You're trying to steer with your arms. The muscles are in the wings themselves—and in your back. Your arms are unnecessary—they're more for balancing than anything. And even that's mostly a mental comfort."

It was more words than I'd ever heard from him.

He lifted a brow at my gaping, and I shut my mouth. I frowned at the drop ahead. "Again?" I grumbled.

A soft laugh. "We can find a lower ledge to jump from, if you want."

I cringed. "You said *this* was low."

Azriel leaned back on his hands and waited. Patient, cool.

But I felt the bark tear into my palms, the thud of my knees into its rough side—

"You are immortal," he said quietly. "You are very hard to break." A pause. "That's what I told myself."

"Hard to break," I said glumly, "but it still *hurts*."

"Tell that to the tree."

I huffed a laugh. "I know the drop isn't far, and I know it won't kill me. Can't you just . . . *push* me?"

For it was that initial leap of utter faith, that initial lurch into motion that had my limbs locking up.

"No." A simple answer.

I still hesitated.

Useless—this fear. I had faced down the Attor, falling through the sky for a thousand feet.

And the rage at its memory, at what it had done with its miserable life, what more like it might do again, had me gritting my teeth and sprinting off the boulder.

I snapped my wings out wide, my back protesting as they caught the wind, but my lower half began to drop, my legs a dead weight as my core yielded—

The infernal tree rose up before me, and I swerved hard to the right.

Right into another tree.

Wings first.

The sound of bone and sinew on wood, then earth, hit me before the pain did. So did Azriel's soft curse.

A small noise came out of me. The stinging of my palms registered first—then in my knees.

Then my back—

"Shit," was all I could say as Azriel knelt before me.

"You're all right. Just stunned."

The world was still reordering itself.

"You banked well," he offered.

"Into another tree."

"Being aware of your surroundings is half of flying."

"You said that already," I snapped. He had. A dozen times just this morning.

Azriel only sat on his heels and offered me a hand up. My flesh burned as I gripped his fingers, a mortifying number of pine needles and splinters tumbling off me. My back throbbed enough that I lowered my wings, not caring if they dragged in the dirt as Azriel led me toward the lake edge.

In the blinding sun off the turquoise water, his shadows were gone, his face stark and clear. More . . . human than I had ever seen him.

"There's no chance that I'll be able to fly in the legions, is there?" I asked, kneeling beside him as he tended to my skinned palms with expert care and gentleness. The sun was brutal against his scars, hiding not one twisted, rippling splotch.

"Likely not," he said. My chest hollowed out at that. "But it doesn't hurt to practice until the last possible moment. You never know when any measure of training may be useful."

I winced as he fished out a large splinter from my palm, then washed it clean.

"It was very hard for me to learn how to fly," he said. I didn't dare respond. "Most Illyrians learn as toddlers. But . . . I assume Rhysand told you the particulars of my early childhood."

I nodded. He finished the one hand and started on the other. "Because I was so old, I had a fear of flying—and did not trust my instincts. It was an . . . embarrassment to be taught so late. Not just to me, but to all in the war-camp once I arrived. But I learned, often going off by myself. Cassian, of course, found me first. Mocked me, beat me to hell, then offered to train me. Rhys was there the next day. They taught me to fly."

He finished my other hand, and sat on the shore, the stones murmuring as they shifted beneath him. I sat beside him, bracing my sore palms faceup on my knees, letting my wings sag behind me.

"Because it was such an effort . . . A few years after the War, Rhys brought me back a story. It was a gift—the story. For me. He—he went to see Miryam and Drakon in their new home, the visit so secret even we hadn't known it was happening until he returned. We knew their people hadn't drowned in the sea, as everyone believed, as they wanted people to believe. You see, when Miryam freed her people from the queen of the Black Land, she led all of them—nearly fifty thousand of them—across the desert, all the way to the shores of the Erythrian Sea, Drakon's aerial legion providing cover. But they got to the sea and found the ships they'd arranged to transport them over the narrow channel to the next kingdom had been destroyed. Destroyed by the queen herself, who sent her lingering armies to drag her former slaves back.

"Drakon's people—the Seraphim—are winged. Like us, but their wings are feathered. And unlike us, their army and society allow women to lead, to fight, to rule. All of them are gifted with mighty magic of wind and air. And when they beheld that army charging after them, they knew their own force was too small to face them. So they cleaved the sea itself—made a path through the water, all the way through the channel, and ordered the humans to run.

"They did, but Miryam insisted on remaining behind until every last one of her people had crossed. Not one human would she leave behind. Not one. They were about halfway through the crossing when the army reached them. The Seraphim were spent—their magic could barely hold the sea passage. And Drakon knew that if they held it any longer . . . that army would make it across and butcher the humans on the other side. The Seraphim fought off the vanguard on the floor of the sea, and it was bloody and brutal and chaotic . . . And during the melee, they didn't see Miryam skewered by the queen herself. Drakon didn't see. He thought she made it out, carried by one of his soldiers. He ordered the parted sea to come down to drown the enemy force.

"But a young Seraphim cartographer named Nephelle saw Miryam go down. Nephelle's lover was one of Drakon's generals, and it was she who realized Miryam and Nephelle were missing. Drakon was frantic, but their magic was spent and no force in the world could hold back the sea as it barreled down, and no one could reach his mate in time. But Nephelle did.

"Nephelle, you see, was a cartographer because she'd been rejected from the legion's fighting ranks. Her wings were too small, the right one somewhat malformed. And she was slight—short enough that she'd be a dangerous gap in the front lines when they fought shield to shield. Drakon had let her try out for the legion as a courtesy to her lover, but Nephelle failed. She could barely carry the Seraphim shield, and her smaller wings hadn't been strong enough to keep up with the others. So she had made herself invaluable as a cartographer during the War, helping Drakon and her lover find the geographical advantages in their battles. And she became Miryam's dearest friend during those long months as well.

"And that day on the seafloor, Nephelle remembered that her friend had been in the back of the line. She returned for her, even as all others fled for the distant shore. She found Miryam skewered on the queen's spear, bleeding out. The sea wall started to come down—on the opposite shore. Killing the approaching army first—racing toward them.

"Miryam told Nephelle to save herself. But Nephelle would not abandon her friend. She picked her up and flew."

Azriel's voice was soft with awe.

"When Rhys spoke to Drakon about it years later, he still didn't have words to describe what happened. It defied all logic, all training. Nephelle, who had never been strong enough to hold a Seraphim shield, carried Miryam—triple the weight. And more than that . . . She *flew*. The sea was crashing down upon them, but Nephelle flew like the best of Seraphim warriors. The seafloor was a labyrinth of jagged rocks, too narrow for the Seraphim to fly through. They'd tried during their escape and crashed into them. But Nephelle, with her smaller wings . . . Had they been *one inch* wider, she would not have fit. And more than that . . . Nephelle soared through them, Miryam dying in her arms, as fast and skilled as the greatest of Seraphim. Nephelle, who had been passed over, who had been forgotten . . . She outraced death itself. There was not a foot of room between her and the water on either side of her when she shot up from the seafloor; not half of that rising up at her feet. And yet her too-small wingspan, that deformed wing . . . they did not fail her. Not once. Not for one wing beat."

My eyes burned.

"She made it. Suffice to say her lover made Nephelle her wife that night, and Miryam . . . well, she is alive today because of Nephelle." Azriel picked up a flat, white stone and turned it over in his hands. "Rhys told me the story when he returned. And since then we have privately adapted the Nephelle Philosophy with our own armies."

I raised a brow. Azriel shrugged. "We—Rhys, Cass, and I—will occasionally remind each other that what we think to be our greatest weakness can sometimes be our biggest strength. And that the most unlikely person can alter the course of history."

"The Nephelle Philosophy."

He nodded. "Apparently, every year in their kingdom, they have the Nephelle Run to honor her flight. On dry land, but . . . She and her wife crown a new victor every year in commemoration of what happened that day." He chucked the stone back amongst its brethren on the shore, the sound clattering over the water. "So we'll train, Feyre, until the last possible day. Because we never know if just one extra hour will make the difference."

I weighed his words, Nephelle's story. I rose to my feet and spread my wings. "Then let's try again."

✢

I groaned as I limped into our bedroom that night to find Rhys sitting at the desk, poring over more books.

"I warned you that Azriel's a hard bastard," he said without looking at me. He lifted a hand, and water gurgled in the adjacent bathing room.

I grumbled a thank-you and trudged toward it, gritting my teeth against the agony in my back, my thighs, my bones. Every part *hurt*, and since the muscles needed to re-form around the wings, I had to carry *them*, too. Their scraping along the wood and carpet, then wood again, was the only sound beyond my weary feet. I beheld the steaming bath that would require some balancing to get into and whimpered.

Even removing my clothes would entail using muscles that had nearly given out.

A chair scraped in the bedroom, followed by cat-soft feet, then—

"I'm sure you already know this, but you need to actually climb into a bath to get clean—not stare at it."

I didn't have the strength to even glare at him, and I managed all of one stumbling, stiff step toward the water when he caught me.

My clothes vanished, presumably to the laundry downstairs, and Rhys swept me into his arms, lowering my naked body into the water. With the wings, the fit was tight, and—

I groaned from deep in my throat at the glorious heat and didn't bother to do anything other than lean my head against the back of the tub.

"I'll be right back," he said, and left the bathroom, then the bedroom itself.

By the time he returned, I only knew I'd fallen asleep thanks to the hand he put on my shoulder. "Out," he said, but lifted me himself, toweled me off, and led me to the bed.

He lay me down belly-first, and I noted the oils and balms he'd set there, the faint odor of rosemary and—something I was too tired to notice but smelled lovely floating to me. His hands gleamed as he applied generous amounts to his palms, and then his hands were on me.

My groan was about as undignified as they came as he kneaded the aching muscles of my back. The sorer areas drew out rather pathetic-sounding whimpers, but he rubbed them gently, until the tension was a dull ache rather than sharp, blinding pain.

And then he started on my wings.

Relief and ecstasy, as muscles eased and those sensitive areas were lovingly, tauntingly grazed over.

My toes curled, and just as he reached the sensitive spot that had my stomach clenching, his hands slid to my calves. He began a slow progression, higher and higher, up my thighs, teasing strokes between them that left me panting through my nose. Rising up until he got to my backside, where his massaging was equally professional and sinful. And then up—up my lower back, to my wings.

His touch turned different. Exploring. Broad strokes and feather-light ones, arches and swirls and direct, searing lines.

My core heated, turning molten, and I bit down on my lip as he lightly scraped a fingernail so, so close to that inner, sensitive spot. "Too bad you're so sore from training," Rhys mused, making idle, lazy circles.

I could only manage a garbled strand of words that were both plea and insult.

He leaned in, his breath warming the space of skin between my wings. "Did I ever tell you that you have the dirtiest mouth I've ever heard?"

I muttered words that only offered more proof of that claim.

He chuckled and skimmed the edge of that sensitive spot, right as his other hand slid between my legs.

Brazenly, I lifted my hips in silent demand. But he just circled with a finger, as lazy as the strokes along my wing. He kissed my spine. "How shall I make love to you tonight, Feyre darling?"

I writhed, rubbing against the folds of the blankets beneath me, desperate for any sort of friction as he dangled me over that edge.

"So impatient," he purred, and that finger glided into me. I moaned, the sensation too much, too consuming, with his hand between my legs and the other stroking closer and closer to that spot on my wing, a predator circling prey.

"Will it ever stop?" he mused, more to himself than me as another finger joined the one sliding in and out of me with taunting, indolent strokes. "Wanting you—every hour, every breath. I don't think I can stand a thousand years of this." My hips moved with him, driving him deeper. "Think of how my productivity will plummet."

I growled something at him that was likely *not* very romantic, and he chuckled, slipping out both fingers. I made a little whining noise of protest.

Until his mouth replaced where his fingers had been, his hands gripping my hips to raise me up, to lend him better access as he feasted on me. I groaned, the sound muffled by the pillow, and he only delved deeper, taunting and teasing with every stroke.

A low moan broke from me, my hips rolling. Rhys's grip on them tightened, holding me still for his ministrations. "I never got to take you in the library," he said, dragging his tongue right up my center. "We'll have to remedy that."

"Rhys." His name was a plea on my lips.

"Hmmm," was all he said, a rumble of the sound against me . . . I panted, hands fisting in the sheets.

His hands drifted from my hips at last, and I again breathed his name, in thanks and relief and anticipation of him at last giving me what I wanted—

But his mouth closed around the bundle of nerves at the apex of my thighs while his hand . . . He went right to that damned spot at the inner edge of my left wing and stroked lightly.

My climax tore through me with a hoarse cry, sending me soaring out of my body. And when the shuddering ripples and starlight faded . . .

A bone-weary exhaustion settled over me, permanent and unending as the mating bond between us. Rhys curled into bed behind me, tucking my wings in so he could fold me against him. "That was a fun experiment," he murmured into my ear.

I could feel him against my backside, hard and ready, but when I made to reach for him, Rhys's arms only tightened around me. "Sleep, Feyre," he told me.

So I laid a hand on his forearm, savoring the corded strength beneath, and nestled my head back against his chest. "I wish I had days to spend with you—like this," I managed to say as my eyelids drooped. "Just me and you."

"We will." He kissed my hair. "We will."

CHAPTER
30

I was still sore enough the next day that I had to send word to Cassian I wasn't training with him. Or Azriel.

A mistake, perhaps, given that both of them showed up at the door to the town house within minutes, the former demanding what the hell was wrong with me, the latter bearing a tin of salve to help with the aches in my back.

I thanked Azriel for the salve and told Cassian to mind his own business.

And then asked him to fly Nesta up to the House of Wind for me, since I certainly couldn't fly her in—even for a few feet after winnowing.

My sister, it seemed, had found nothing in her books about repairing the wall—and since no one had yet shown her the library . . . I'd volunteered. Especially since Lucien had left before breakfast for a library across the city to look up anything in regard to fixing the wall, a task I'd been more than willing to hand over. I might have felt guilty for never giving him a proper tour of Velaris, but . . . he seemed eager. More than eager—he seemed to be itching to head into the city on his own.

The two Illyrians paused their inspection of me long enough to note my sisters finishing up breakfast, Nesta in a pale gray gown that brought out the steel in her eyes, Elain in dusty pink.

Both males went a bit still. But Azriel sketched a bow—while Cassian stalked for the dining table, reached right over Nesta's shoulder, and grabbed a muffin from its little basket. "Morning, Nesta," he said around a mouth of blueberry-lemon. "Elain."

Nesta's nostrils flared, but Elain peered up at Cassian, blinking twice. "He snapped your wings, broke your bones."

I tried to shut out the sound of Cassian's scream—the memory of the spraying blood.

Nesta stared at her plate. Elain, at least, was out of her room, but . . .

"It'll take more than that to kill me," Cassian said with a smirk that didn't meet his eyes.

Elain only said to Cassian, "No, it will not."

Cassian's dark brows narrowed. I dragged a hand over my face before going to Elain and touching her too-bony shoulder. "Can I set you up in the garden? The herbs you planted are coming in nicely."

"I can help her," said Azriel, stepping to the table as Elain silently rose. No shadows at his ear, no darkness ringing his fingers as he extended a hand.

Nesta monitored him like a hawk, but kept silent as Elain took his hand, and out they went.

Cassian finished the muffin, licking his fingers. I could have sworn Nesta watched the entire thing with a sidelong glance. He grinned at her as if he knew it, too. "Ready for some flying, Nes?"

"Don't call me that."

The wrong thing to say, from the way Cassian's eyes lit up.

I chose that moment to winnow to the skies above the House, chuckling as wind carried me through the world. Some sisterly payback, I supposed. For Nesta's general attitude.

Mercifully, no one saw my slightly better crash landing on the veranda, and by the time Cassian's dark figure appeared in the sky, Nesta's hair bright as bronze in the morning sun, I'd brushed off the dirt and dust from my leathers.

My sister's face was wind-flushed as Cassian gently set her down. Then she strode for the glass doors without a single look back.

"You're welcome," Cassian called after her, more than a bite to his voice. His hands clenched and slackened at his sides—as if he were trying to loosen the feel of her from his palms.

"Thank you," I said to him, but Cassian didn't bother saying farewell as he launched skyward and vanished into the clouds.

The library beneath the House was shadowed, quiet. The doors opened for us, the same way they'd opened when Rhys and I had first visited.

Nesta said nothing, only surveying every stack and alcove and dangling chandelier as I led her down to the level where Clotho had found those books. I showed her the small reading area where I'd been stationed, and gestured to the desk. "I know Cassian gets under your skin, *but* I'm curious, too. How *do* you know what to look for in regard to the wall?"

Nesta ran a finger over the ancient wood desk. "Because I just do."

"How."

"I don't know how. Amren told me to just . . . see if the information clicks." And perhaps that frightened her. Intrigued her, but frightened her. And she hadn't told Cassian not out of spite, but because she didn't wish to reveal that vulnerability. That lack of control.

I didn't push. Even as I stared at her for a long moment. I didn't know how—how to broach that subject, how to ask if she was all right, if I could help her. I had never been affectionate with her—I'd never held her. Kissed her cheek. I didn't know where to begin.

So I just said, "Rhys gave me a layout of the stacks. I think there might be more on the Cauldron and wall a few levels down. You can wait here, or—"

"I'll help you look."

We followed the sloping path in silence, the rustle of paper and occasional whisper of a priestess's robes along the stone floors the only sounds. I quietly explained to her who the priestesses were—why they were here. I explained that Rhys and I planned to offer sanctuary to any humans who could make it to Velaris.

She said nothing, quieter and quieter as we descended, that black pit on my right seeming to grow thicker the deeper we went.

But we reached a path of stacks that veered into the mountain in a long hall, faelights flickering into life within glass globes along the wall as we passed. Nesta scanned the shelves while we walked, and I read the titles—a bit more slowly, still needing a little time to process what was instinct for my sister.

"I didn't know you couldn't really read," Nesta said as she paused before a nondescript section, noticing the way I silently sounded out the words of a title. "I didn't know where you were in your lessons—when it all happened. I assumed you could read as easily as us."

"Well, I couldn't."

"Why didn't you ask us to teach you?"

I trailed a finger over the neat row of spines. "Because I doubted you would agree to help."

Nesta stiffened like I'd hit her, coldness blooming in those eyes. She tugged a book from a shelf. "Amren said Rhysand taught you to read."

My cheeks heated. "He did." And there, deep beneath the world, with only darkness for company, I asked, "Why do you push everyone away but Elain?" *Why have you always pushed* me *away?*

Some emotion guttered in her eyes. Her throat bobbed. Nesta shut her eyes for a moment, breathing in sharply. "Because—"

The words stopped.

I felt it at the same moment she did.

The ripple and tremor. Like . . . like some piece of the world shifted, like some off-kilter chord had been plucked.

We turned toward the illuminated path that we'd just taken through the stacks, then to the dark far, far beyond.

The faelights along the ceiling began to sputter and die. One by one. Closer and closer to us.

I only had an Illyrian knife at my side.

"What is that," Nesta breathed.

"Run," was all I said.

I didn't give her the chance to object as I grabbed her by the elbow and sprinted into the stacks ahead. Faelights flickered to life as we passed—only to be devoured by the dark surging for us.

Slow—my sister was so damned slow with her dress, her general lack of exercising—

Rhys.

Nothing.

If the wards around the Prison were thick enough to keep out communication . . . Perhaps the same applied here.

A wall approached—with a hall before it. A second slope: left rising, right plunging down—

Darkness slithered down from above. But the inky gloom leading deeper . . . fresh and open.

I went right. "Faster," I said to her. If we could lead whoever it was deep, perhaps we could cut back, right to the pit. I could winnow—

Winnow. I could winnow *now*—

I grabbed for Nesta's arm.

Right as the darkness behind us paused, and two High Fae stepped out of it. Both male.

One dark-haired, one light. Both in gray jackets embroidered with bone-white thread.

I knew their coat of arms on the upper right shoulder. Knew their dead eyes.

Hybern. Hybern was *here*—

I didn't move fast enough as one of them blew out a breath toward us.

As that blue faebane dust sprayed into my eyes, my mouth, and my magic died out.

Nesta's gasp told me she felt something similar.

But it was on my sister that the two focused as I staggered back, tears streaming the dust from my eyes, spitting out the faebane. I gripped her arm, trying to winnow. Nothing.

Behind them, a hooded priestess slumped to the ground.

"So easy to get into their minds once our master let us through the wards," said one of them—the dark-haired male. "To make them think we were scholars. We'd planned to come for you . . . But it seems you found us first."

All spoken to my sister. Nesta's face was near-white, though her eyes showed no fear. "Who are you."

The white-haired one smiled broadly as they approached. "We're the king's Ravens. His far-flying eyes and talons. And we've come to take you back."

The king—their master. He'd . . . Mother above.

Was the king here—in Velaris?

Rhys. I slammed a mental hand into the bond. Over and over. *Rhys.* Nothing.

Nesta's breath began to come quickly. Swords hung at their sides—two apiece. Their shoulders were broad, arms wide enough to indicate muscle filled those fine clothes.

"You're not taking her anywhere," I said, palming my knife. How had the king done it—arrived here unnoted, and fractured our wards? And if he was in Velaris . . . I shoved down my terror at the thought. At what he might be doing beyond this library, unseen and hidden—

"You're an unexpected prize, too," the black-haired one said to me. "But your sister . . ." A smile that showed all of his too-white teeth. "You took something from that Cauldron, girl. The king wants it back."

That was why the Cauldron couldn't shatter the wall. Not because its power was spent.

But because Nesta had stolen too much of it.

CHAPTER
31

I laid my options before me.

I doubted the king's Ravens were stupid enough to be kept talking long enough for my powers to return. And if the king was indeed here . . . I had to warn everyone. *Immediately*.

It left me with three choices.

Take them on in hand-to-hand combat with only a knife, when they were each armed with twin blades and were muscled enough to know how to use them.

Make a run for it, and try to get out of the library—and risk the lives and further trauma of the priestesses in the levels above.

Or . . .

Nesta was saying to them, "If he wants what I took, he can come get it himself."

"He's too busy to bother," the white-haired male purred, advancing another step.

"Apparently you're not."

I gripped Nesta's fingers in my free hand. She glanced at me.

I need you to trust me, I tried to convey to her.

Nesta read the emotion in my eyes—and gave the barest dip of her chin.

I said to them, "You made a grave mistake coming here. To *my* house."

They sniggered.

I gave them a returning smirk as I said, "And I hope it rips you into bloody ribbons."

Then I ran, hauling Nesta with me. Not toward the upper levels.

But down.

Down into the eternal blackness of the pit at the heart of the library.

And into the arms of whatever lurked inside it.

⁓

Around and down, around and down—

Shelves and paper and furniture and darkness, the smell turning musty and damp, the air thickening, the darkness like dew on my skin—

Nesta's breath was ragged, her skirts rustling with each sprinting step we took.

Time—only a matter of time before one of those priestesses contacted Rhys.

But even a minute might be too late.

There was no choice. None.

Faelights stopped appearing ahead.

Low, hideous laughter trickled behind us. "Not so easy, is it—to find your way in the dark."

"Don't stop," I panted to Nesta, flinging us farther into the dark.

A high-pitched scratching sounded. Like talons on stone. One of the Ravens crooned, "Do you know what happened to them—the queens?"

"Keep going," I breathed, gripping a hand against the wall to remain rooted.

Soon—we'd reach the bottom soon, and then . . . And then face some horror awful enough that Cassian wouldn't speak of it.

The lesser of two evils—or the worse of them.

"The youngest one—that pinched-faced bitch—went into the Cauldron first. Practically trampled the others to get in after it saw what it did to you and your sister."

"Don't stop," I repeated as Nesta stumbled. "If I go down, you *run.*"

That was a choice that I did not need to debate. That did not frighten me. Not for a heartbeat.

Stone screamed beneath twin sets of talons. "But the Cauldron . . . Oh, it *knew* that something had been taken from it. Not sentient, but . . . it knew. It was furious. And when that young queen went in . . ."

The Ravens laughed. Laughed as the slope leveled out and we found ourselves at the bottom of the library.

"Oh, it gave her immortality. It made her Fae. But since something had been taken from it . . . the Cauldron took what she valued most. Her youth." They sniggered again. "A young woman went in . . . but a withered crone came out."

And from the catacombs of my memory, Elain's voice sounded: *I saw young hands wither with age.*

"The other queens won't go into the Cauldron for terror of the same happening now. And the youngest one . . . Oh, you should hear how she talks, Nesta Archeron. The things *she* wants to do to you when Hybern is done . . ."

Twin ravens are coming.

Elain had known. *Sensed* it. Had tried to warn us.

There were ancient stacks down here. Or, at least I felt them as we bumped into countless hard edges in our blind sprint. Where was it, where *was* it—

Deeper into the dark, we ran.

"We're growing bored of this pursuit," one of them said. "Our master is waiting for us to retrieve you."

I snorted loudly enough for them to hear. "I'm shocked he could even muster the strength to break the wards—he seems to need a trove of magical objects to do his work for him."

The other one hissed, talons scratching louder, "Whose spell book do you think Amarantha stole many decades ago? Who suggested the amusement of sticking the masks to Spring's faces as punishment? Another little spell, the one he burned through today—to crack through your wards here. Only once could it be wielded—such a pity."

I studied the faint trickle of light I could make out—far away and high up. "Run toward the light," I breathed to Nesta. "I'll hold them off."

"No."

"Don't try to be noble, if that's what you're whispering about," one of the Ravens cawed from behind. "We'll catch you both anyway."

We didn't have time—for whatever was down here to find us. We didn't have time—

"*Run,*" I breathed. "Please."

She hesitated.

"*Please,*" I begged her, my voice breaking.

Nesta squeezed my hand once.

And between one breath and the next, she bolted to the side—toward the center of the pit. The light high above.

"What—" one of them snapped, but I struck.

Every bone in my body barked in pain as I slammed into one of the stacks. Then again. Again.

Until it teetered and fell, collapsing onto the one beside it. And the next. And the next.

Blocking the way Nesta had gone.

And any chance of my exit, too. Wood groaned and snapped, books thudded on stone.

But ahead . . .

I clawed and patted the wall as I plunged farther into the pit floor. My magic was a husk in my veins.

"We'll still catch her, don't worry," one of them crooned. "Wouldn't want dear sisters to be separated."

Where are you where are you where are you

I didn't see the wall in front of me.

My teeth sang as I collided face-first. I patted blindly, feeling for a break, a corner—

The wall continued on. Dead end. If it was a dead end—

"Nowhere to go down here, Lady," one of them said.

I kept moving, gritting my teeth, gauging the power still frozen inside me. Not even an ember to summon to light the way, to show where I was—

To show any holes ahead—

The terror of it had my bones locking up. No. No, keep moving, keep going—

I reached out, desperate for a bookshelf to grab. Surely they wouldn't put a shelf near a gaping hole in the earth—

Empty blackness met my fingers, slipped between them. Again and again.

I stumbled a step.

Leather met my fingers—solid leather. I fumbled, the hard spines of books meeting my palms, and bit down my sob of relief. A lifeline in a violent sea; I felt my way down the stack, running now. It ended too soon. I took another blind step forward, touched my way around a corner of another stack. Just as the Ravens hissed with displeasure.

The sound said enough.

They'd lost me—for a moment.

I inched along, keeping my back to a shelf, calming my heaving lungs until my breaths became near-silent.

"Please," I breathed into the dark, barely more than a whisper. "Please, help me."

In the distance, a *boom* shuddered through the ancient floor.

"High Lady of the Night Court," one of the Ravens sang. "What sort of cage shall our king build for you?"

Fear would get me killed, fear would—

A soft voice whispered in my ear, *You are the High Lady?*

The voice was both young and old, hideous and beautiful. "Y-yes," I whispered.

I could sense no body heat, detect no physical presence, but . . . I felt it behind me. Even with my back to the shelf, I felt the mass of it lurking behind me. Around me. Like a shroud.

"We can smell you," the other Raven said. "How your mate shall rage when he's found we've taken you."

"Please," I breathed to the thing crouched behind me, over me.

What shall you give me?

Such a dangerous question. Never make a bargain, Alis had once warned me before Under the Mountain. Even if the bargains I'd made . . . they'd saved us. And brought me to Rhys.

"What do you want?"

One of the Ravens snapped, "Who is she talking to?"

The stone and wind hear all, speak all. They whispered to me of your desire to wield the Carver. To trade.

My breath came hard and fast. "What of it?"

I knew him once—long ago. Before so many things crawled the earth.

The Ravens were close—far too close when one of them hissed, "What is she mumbling?"

"Does she know a spell, as the master did?"

I whispered to the lurking dark behind me, "What is your price?"

The Ravens' footsteps sounded so nearby they couldn't have been more than twenty feet away. "Who are you talking to?" one of them demanded.

Company. Send me company.

I opened my mouth, but then said, "To—eat?"

A laugh that made my skin crawl. *To tell me of* life.

The air ahead shifted—as the Hybern Ravens closed in. "There you are," one seethed.

"It's a bargain," I breathed. The skin along my left forearm tingled. The thing behind me . . . I could have sworn I felt it smile.

Shall I kill them?

"P-please do."

Light sputtered before me, and I blinked at the blinding ball of faelight.

I saw the twin Ravens first, that faelight at their shoulder—to illuminate me for their taking.

Their attention went to me. Then rose over my shoulder. My head.

Absolute, unfiltered terror filled their faces. At what stood behind me.

Close your eyes, the thing purred in my ear.

I obeyed, trembling.

Then all I heard was screaming.

High-pitched shrieking and pleading. Bones snapping, blood splattering like rain, cloth ripping, and screaming, screaming, *screaming*—

I squeezed my eyes shut so hard it hurt. Squeezed them shut so hard I was shaking.

Then there were warm, rough hands on me, dragging me away, and Cassian's voice at my ear, saying, "Don't look. *Don't look.*"

I didn't. I let him lead me away. Just as I felt Rhys arrive. Felt him land on the floor of the pit so hard the entire mountain shuddered.

I opened my eyes then. Found him storming toward us, night rippling off him, such fury on his face—

"Get them out."

The order was given to Cassian.

The screaming was still erupting behind us.

I lurched toward Rhys, but he was already gone, a plume of darkness spreading from him.

To shield the view of what he walked into.

Knowing I would look.

The screaming stopped.

In the terrible silence, Cassian hauled me out—toward the dim center of the pit. Nesta was standing there, arms around herself, eyes wide.

Cassian only stretched out an arm for her. As if in a trance, she walked right to his side. His arms tightened around both of us, Siphons flaring, gilding the darkness with bloodred light.

Then we launched skyward.

Just as the screaming began anew.

CHAPTER
32

Cassian gave us both a glass of brandy. A tall glass.

Seated in an armchair in the family library high above, Nesta drank hers in one gulp.

I claimed the chair across from her, took a sip, shuddered at the taste, and made to set it down on the low-lying table between us.

"Keep drinking," Cassian ordered. The wrath wasn't toward me.

No—it was toward whatever was below. What had happened.

"Are you hurt?" Cassian asked me. Each word was clipped—brutal.

I shook my head.

That he didn't ask Nesta . . . he must have found her first. Ascertained for himself.

I started, "Is the king—the city—"

"No sign of him." A muscle twitched in his jaw.

We sat in silence. Until Rhys appeared between the open doors, shadows trailing in his wake.

Blood coated his hands—but nothing else.

So much blood, ruby-bright in the midmorning sun.

Like he'd clawed through them with his bare hands.

His eyes were wholly frozen with rage.

But they dipped to my left arm, the sleeve filthy but still rolled up—

Like a slim band of black iron around my forearm, a tattoo now lay there.

It's custom in my court for bargains to be permanently marked upon flesh, Rhys had told me Under the Mountain.

"What did you give it." I hadn't heard that voice since that visit to the Court of Nightmares.

"It—it said it wanted company. Someone to tell it about life. I said yes."

"Did you volunteer *yourself.*"

"No." I drained the rest of the brandy at the tone, his frozen face. "It just said *someone.* And it didn't specify *when.*" I grimaced at the solid black band, no thicker than the width of my finger, interrupted only by two slender gaps near the side of my forearm. I tried to stand, to go to him, to take those bloody hands. But my knees still wobbled enough that I couldn't move. "Are the king's Ravens dead?"

"They nearly were when I arrived. It left enough of their minds functioning for me to have a look. And finish them when I was done."

Cassian was stone-faced, glancing between Rhys's bloody hands and his ice-cold eyes.

But it was to my sister that my mate turned. "Hybern hunts you because of what you took from the Cauldron. The queens want you dead for vengeance—for robbing them of immortality."

"I know." Nesta's voice was hoarse.

"What did you take."

"I don't know." The words were barely more than a whisper. "Even Amren can't figure it out."

Rhys stared her down. But Nesta looked to me—and I could have sworn fear shone there, and guilt and . . . some other feeling. "You told me to run."

"You're my sister," was all I said. She'd once tried to cross the wall to save me.

But she started. "Elain—"

"Elain is fine," Rhys said. "Azriel was at the town house. Lucien is headed back, and Mor is nearly there. They know of the threat."

Nesta leaned her head back against the armchair's cushion, going a bit boneless.

I said to Rhys, "Hybern infiltrated our city. Again."

"The prick held on to that fleeting spell until he really needed it."

"Fleeting spell?"

"A spell of mighty power, able to be wielded only once—to great effect. One capable of cleaving wards . . . He must have been biding his time."

"Are the wards here—"

"Amren is currently adapting them against such things. And will then begin combing through this city to find if the king also deposited any other cronies before he vanished."

Beneath the cold rage, there was a sharpness—honed enough that I said, *What's wrong?*

"What's wrong?" he replied—verbally, as if he could no longer distinguish between the two. "What's wrong is that those pieces of *shit* got into my house and attacked my *mate*. What's wrong is that my own damn wards worked against me, and you had to make a bargain with that *thing* to keep yourself from being taken. What's wrong—"

"Calm down," I said quietly, but not weakly.

His eyes glowed, like lightning had struck an ocean. But he inhaled deeply, blowing out the breath through his nose, and his shoulders loosened—barely.

"Did you see what it was—that thing down there?"

"I guessed enough about it to close my eyes," he said. "I only opened them when it had stepped away from their bodies."

Cassian's skin had turned ashen. He'd seen it. He'd seen it again. But he said nothing.

"Yes, the king got past our defenses," I said to Rhys. "Yes, things went badly. But we weren't hurt. And the Ravens revealed some key pieces of information."

Sloppy, I realized. Rhys had been sloppy in killing them. Normally, he would have kept them alive for Azriel to question. But he'd taken what he needed, quickly and brutally, and ended it. He'd shown more restraint about the Attor—

"We know why the Cauldron doesn't work at its full strength now," I went on. "We know that Nesta is more of a priority for the king than I am."

Rhys mulled it over. "Hybern showed part of his hand, in bringing them here. He has to have a sliver of doubt of his conquest if he'd risk it."

Nesta looked like she was going to be sick. Cassian wordlessly refilled her glass. But I asked, "How—how did you know that we were in trouble?"

"Clotho," Rhys said. "There's a spelled bell inside the library. She rang it, and it went out to all of us. Cassian got there first."

I wondered what had happened in those initial moments, when he'd found my sister.

As if he'd read my thoughts, Rhys sent the image to me, no doubt courtesy of Cassian.

Panic—and rage. That was all he knew as he shot down into the heart of the pit, spearing for that ancient darkness that had once shaken him to his very marrow.

Nesta was there—and Feyre.

It was the former he saw first, stumbling out of the dark, wide-eyed, her fear a tang that whetted his rage into something so sharp he could barely think, barely breathe—

She let out a small, animal sound—like some wounded stag—as she saw him. As he landed so hard his knees popped.

He said nothing as Nesta launched herself toward him, her dress filthy and disheveled, her arms stretching for him. He opened his own for her, unable to stop his approach, his reaching—

She gripped his leathers instead. "Feyre," she rasped, pointing behind her with a free hand, shaking him solidly with the other. Strength—such untapped strength in that slim, beautiful body. "Hybern."

That was all he needed to hear. He drew his sword—then Rhys was arrowing for them, his power like a gods-damned volcanic eruption. Cassian charged ahead into the gloom, following the screaming—

I pulled away, not wanting to see any further. See what Cassian had witnessed down there.

Rhys strode to me, and lifted a hand to brush my hair—but stopped upon seeing the blood crusting his fingers. He instead studied the tattoo now marring my left arm. "As long as we don't have to invite it to solstice dinner, I can live with it."

"*You* can live with it?" I lifted my brows.

A ghost of a smile, even with all that had happened, that now lay before us. "At least now if one of you misbehaves, I know the perfect punishment. Going down there to *talk* to that thing for an hour."

Nesta scowled with distaste, but Cassian let out a dark laugh. "I'll take scrubbing toilets, thank you."

"Your second encounter seemed less harrowing than the first."

"It wasn't trying to *eat* me this time." But shadows still darkened his eyes.

Rhys saw them, too. Saw them and said quietly, again with that High Lord's voice, "Warn whoever needs to know to stay indoors tonight. Children off the streets at sundown, none of the Palaces will remain open past moonrise. Anyone on the streets faces the consequences."

"Of what?" I asked, the liquor in my stomach now burning.

Rhys's jaw tightened, and he surveyed the sparkling city beyond the windows. "Of Amren on the hunt."

⊹

Elain was nestled beside a too-casual Mor on the sitting room couch when we arrived at the town house. Nesta strode past me, right to Elain, and took up a seat on her other side, before turning her attention to where we remained in the foyer. Waiting—somehow sensing the meeting that was about to unfold.

Lucien, stationed by the front window, turned from watching the street. Monitoring it. A sword and dagger hung from his belt. No humor, no warmth graced his face—only fierce, grim determination.

"Azriel's coming down from the roof," Rhys said to none of us in particular, leaning against the archway into the sitting room and crossing his arms.

And as if he'd summoned him, Azriel stepped out of a pocket of shadow by the stairs and scanned us from head to toe. His eyes lingered on the blood crusting Rhys's hands.

I took up a spot at the opposite doorway post while Cassian and Azriel remained between us.

Rhys was quiet for a moment before he said, "The priestesses will keep silent about what happened today. And the people of this city won't learn *why* Amren is now preparing to hunt. We can't afford to let the other High Lords know. It would unnerve them—and destabilize the image we have worked so hard to create."

"The attack on Velaris," Mor countered from her place on the couch, "already showed we're vulnerable."

"That was a surprise attack, which we handled quickly," Cassian said, Siphons flickering. "Az made sure the information came out portraying *us* as victors—able to defeat any challenge Hybern throws our way."

"We did that today," I said.

"It's different," Rhys said. "The first time, we had the element of their surprise to excuse us. This second time . . . it makes us look unprepared. Vulnerable. We can't risk that getting out before the meeting in ten days. So for all appearances, we will remain unruffled as we prepare for war."

Mor sagged against the couch cushions. "A war where we have no allies beyond Keir, either in Prythian or beyond it."

Rhys gave her a sharp look. But Elain said quietly, "The queen might come."

Silence.

Elain was staring at the unlit fireplace, eyes lost to that vague murkiness.

"What queen," Nesta said, more tightly than she usually spoke to our sister.

"The one who was cursed."

"Cursed by the Cauldron," I clarified to Nesta, pushing off the archway. "When it threw its tantrum after you . . . left."

"No." Elain studied me, then her. "Not that one. The other."

Nesta took a steadying breath, opening her mouth to either whisk Elain upstairs or move on.

But Azriel asked softly, taking a single step over the threshold and into the sitting room, "What other?"

Elain's brows twitched toward each other. "The queen—with the feathers of flame."

The shadowsinger angled his head.

Lucien murmured to me, eye still fixed on Elain, "Should we—does she need . . . ?"

"She doesn't need anything," Azriel answered without so much as looking at Lucien.

Elain was staring at the spymaster now—unblinkingly.

"We're the ones who need . . ." Azriel trailed off. "A seer," he said, more to himself than us. "The Cauldron made you a seer."

CHAPTER
33

Seer.

The word clanged through me.

She'd known. She'd *warned* Nesta about the Ravens. And in the chaos of the attack, that little realization had slipped from me. Slipped from me as reality and dream slipped and entwined for Elain. *Seer.*

Elain turned to Mor, who was now gaping at my sister from her spot beside her on the couch. "Is that what this is?"

And the words, the tone . . . they were so *normal*-sounding that my chest tightened.

Mor's gaze darted across my sister's face, as if weighing the words, the question, the truth or lie within.

Mor at last blinked, mouth parting. Like that magic of hers had at last solved some puzzle. Slowly, clearly, she nodded. Lucien silently slid into one of the chairs, before the window, that metal eye whirring as it roved over my sister.

It made sense, I supposed, that Azriel alone had listened to her. The male who heard things others could not . . . Perhaps he, too, had suffered as Elain had before he understood what gift he possessed. He asked Elain, "There is another queen?"

Elain squinted, as if the question required some inner clarification, some . . . path into looking the right way at whatever had addled and plagued her. "Yes."

"The sixth queen," Mor breathed. "The queen who the golden one said wasn't ill . . ."

"She said not to trust the other queens because of it," I added.

And as soon as the words left my mouth . . . It was like stepping back from a painting to see the entire picture. Up close, the words had been muddled and messy. But from a distance . . .

"You stole from the Cauldron," I said to Nesta, who seemed ready to jump between all of us and Elain. "But what if the Cauldron *gave* something to Elain?"

Nesta's face drained of color. "What?"

Equally ashen, Lucien seemed inclined to echo Nesta's hoarse question.

But Azriel nodded. "You knew," he said to Elain. "About the young queen turning into a crone."

Elain blinked and blinked, eyes clearing again. As if the under-standing, *our* understanding . . . it freed her from whatever murky realm she'd been in.

"The sixth queen is alive?" Azriel asked, calm and steady, the voice of the High Lord's spymaster, who had broken enemies and charmed allies.

Elain cocked her head, as if listening to some inner voice. "Yes."

Lucien just stared and stared at my sister, as if he'd never seen her before.

I whipped my face to Rhys. *A potential ally?*

I don't know, he answered. *If the others cursed her . . .*

"What sort of curse?" my mate asked before he'd even finished speaking to me.

Elain shifted her face toward him. Another blink. "They sold her—to . . . to some darkness, to some . . . sorcerer-lord . . ." She shook her head. "I can never see him. What he is. There is an onyx box that he possesses, more vital than anything . . . save for them. The girls. He keeps other girls—others so like her—but she . . . By day, she is one form, by night, human again."

"A bird of burning feathers," I said.

"Firebird by day," Rhys mused, "woman by night . . . So she's held captive by this sorcerer-lord?"

Elain shook her head. "I don't know. I hear her—her screaming. With rage. Utter rage . . ." She shuddered.

Mor leaned forward. "Do you know why the other queens cursed her—sold her to him?"

Elain studied the table. "No. No—that is all mist and shadow."

Rhys blew out a breath. "Can you sense where she is?"

"There is . . . a lake. Deep in—in the continent, I think. Hidden amongst mountains and ancient forests." Elain's throat bobbed. "He keeps them all at the lake."

"Other women like her?"

"Yes—and no. Their feathers are white as snow. They glide across the water—while she rages through the skies above it."

Mor said to Rhys, "What information do we have on this sixth queen?"

"Little," Azriel answered for him. "We know little. Young— somewhere in her mid-twenties. Scythia lies along the wall, to the east. It's smallest amongst the human queens' realms, but rich in trade and arms. She goes by Vassa, but I never got a report with her full name."

Rhys considered. "She must have posed a considerable threat to the queens if they turned on her. And considering their agenda . . ."

"If we can find Vassa," I cut in, "she could be vital in convincing the human forces to fight. And giving us an ally on the continent."

"*If* we can find her," Cassian countered, stepping up to Azriel's side, his wings flaring slightly. "It could take months. Not to mention, facing the male who holds her captive could be harder than expected. We can't afford all those potential risks. Or the time it'd take. We should focus on this meeting with the other High Lords first."

"But we could stand to gain much," Mor said. "Perhaps she has an army—"

"Perhaps she does," Cassian cut her off. "But if she's cursed, who will lead it? And if her kingdom is so far away . . . they have to travel the mortal way, too. You remember how slowly they moved, how quickly they died—"

"It's worth a try," Mor sniped.

"You're needed here," Cassian said. Azriel looked inclined to agree, even as he kept quiet. "I need you on a battlefield—not traipsing through the continent. The *human* half of it. If those queens have rallied armies to offer Hybern, they're no doubt standing between you and Queen Vassa."

"You don't give me orders—"

"No, but I do," Rhys said. "Don't give me that look. He's right—we need you here, Mor."

"Scythia," Mor said, shaking her head. "I remember them. They're horse people. A mounted cavalry could travel far faster—"

"No." Sheer will blazed in Rhys's eyes. The order was final.

But Mor tried again. "There is a reason why Elain is seeing these things. She was right about the other queen turning old, about the Ravens' attack—*why* is she being sent this image? *Why* is she hearing this queen? It must be vital. If we ignore it, perhaps we'll deserve to fail."

Silence. I surveyed them all. Vital. Each of them was vital *here*. But me . . .

I sucked in a breath.

"I'll go."

Lucien was staring at Elain as he spoke.

We all looked at him.

Lucien shifted his focus to Rhys, to me. "I'll go," he repeated, rising to his feet. "To find this sixth queen."

Mor opened and shut her mouth.

"What makes you think you could find her?" Rhys asked. Not rudely, but—from a commander's perspective. Sizing up the skills Lucien offered against the risks, the potential benefits.

"This eye . . ." Lucien gestured to the metal contraption. "It can see things that others . . . can't. Spells, glamours . . . Perhaps it can help me find her. And break her curse." He glanced at Elain, who was again studying her lap. "I'm not needed here. I'll fight if you need me to, but . . ." He offered me a grim smile. "I do not belong in the Autumn Court. And I'm willing to bet I'm no longer welcome at h—the Spring Court." *Home*, he had almost said. "But I cannot sit here and do *nothing*. Those queens with their armies—there is a threat in that regard, too. So use me. Send me. I will find Vassa, see if she can . . . bring help."

"You will be going into the human territory," Rhys warned. "I can't spare a force to guard you—"

"I don't need one. I travel faster on my own." His chin lifted. "I will find her. And if there's an army to bring back, or at least some way for her own story to sway the human forces . . . I'll find a way to do that, too."

My friends glanced to each other. Mor said, "It will be—very dangerous."

A half smile curved Lucien's mouth. "Good. It'd be boring otherwise."

Only Cassian returned the grin. "I'll load you up with some Illyrian steel."

Elain now watched Lucien warily. Blinking every now and then. She revealed no hint of whatever she might be seeing—sensing. None.

Rhys pushed off the archway. "I'll winnow you as close as we can get—to wherever you need to be to begin your hunt." Lucien had indeed been studying all those maps lately. Perhaps at the quiet behest of whatever force had guided us all. My mate added, "Thank you."

Lucien shrugged. And it was that gesture alone that made me say at last, "Are you sure?"

He only glanced at Elain, whose face was again a calm void while she traced a finger over the embroidery on the couch cushions. "Yes. Let me help in whatever way I can."

Even Nesta seemed relatively concerned. Not for him, no doubt, but the fact that if he were hurt, or killed . . . What would it do to Elain? The severing of the mating bond . . . I shut out the thought of what it'd do to me.

I asked Lucien, "When do you want to leave?"

"Tomorrow." I hadn't heard him sound so assertive in . . . a long time. "I'll prepare for the rest of today, and leave after breakfast tomorrow morning." He added to Rhys, "If that works for you."

My mate waved an idle hand. "For what you're about to do, Lucien, we'll make it work."

Silence fell once more. If he could find that missing queen and perhaps bring back some sort of human army, or at least sway the mortal forces from Hybern's thrall . . . If I could find a way to get the Carver to fight for us that did not involve using that terrible mirror . . . Would it be enough?

The meeting with the High Lords, it seemed, would decide that.

Rhys jerked his chin at Azriel, who took it as an order to vanish—to no doubt check in on Amren.

"Find out if Keir and his Darkbringers had any attacks," my mate ordered Mor and Cassian, who nodded and left as well. Alone with my sisters and Lucien, Rhys and I caught Nesta's eye.

And for once, my sister rose to her feet and came toward us, the three of us not so subtly heading upstairs. Leaving Lucien and Elain alone.

It was an effort not to linger atop the landing, to listen to what was said.

If anything was said at all.

But I made myself take Rhys's hand, flinching at the blood still caked on his skin, and led him to our bathing room. Nesta's bedroom door clicked shut down the hall.

Rhys wordlessly watched me as I turned on the bathtub faucet and grabbed a washcloth from the chest against the wall. I took up a seat at the edge of the tub, testing the water temperature against my wrist, and patted the porcelain rim beside me. "Sit."

He obeyed, his head drooping as he sat.

I took one of his hands, guided it to the gurgling stream of water, and held it beneath.

Red flowed off his skin, eddying in the water beneath. I plucked up the cloth and scrubbed gently, more blood flaking off, water splashing onto the still-immaculate sleeves of his jacket. "Why not shield your hands?"

"I wanted to feel it—their lives ending beneath my fingers."

Cold, flat words.

I scrubbed at his nails, the blood wedged into the cracks where it met his skin. The arcs beneath. "Why is it different this time?" Different from the Attor's ambush, Hybern's attack in the woods, the attack on Velaris . . . all of it. I'd seen him in a rage before, but never . . . never so detached. As if morality and kindness were things that lurked on a surface far, far above the frozen depths he'd plunged into.

I turned his palm into the spray, getting at the space between his fingers.

"What is the point of it," he said, "of all this power . . . if I can't protect those who are most vulnerable in my city? If it can't detect an incoming attack?"

"Even Azriel didn't learn of it—"

"The king used an archaic spell and walked in the *front door*. If I can't . . ." Rhys shook his head, and I lowered his now-clean hand and reached for the other. More blood stained the water. "If I can't protect them here . . . How can . . ." His throat bobbed. I lifted his chin with a hand. Icy rage had slipped into something a bit shattered and aching. "Those priestesses have endured enough. I failed them today. That library . . . it will no longer feel safe for them. The one place they've had to themselves, where they knew they were protected . . . Hybern took that away today."

And from him. He had gone to that library for his own need for healing—for safety.

He said, "Perhaps it's punishment for taking away Velaris from Mor—in granting Keir access here."

"You can't think like that—it won't end well." I finished washing his other hand, rinsed the cloth, then began swiping it along his neck, his temples . . . Soothing, warm presses, not to clean but to relax.

"I'm not angry about the bargain," he said, closing his eyes as I swiped the cloth over his brow. "In case you were . . . worried."

"I wasn't."

Rhys opened his eyes, as if he could hear the smile in my voice, and studied me while I chucked the cloth into the tub with a wet slap and turned off the faucet.

He was still studying me when I took his face in my damp hands. "What happened today was not your fault," I said, the words filling the sun-drenched bathing room. "None of it. It all lies on Hybern—and when we face the king again, we will remember these attacks, these injuries to our people. We forgot Amarantha's spell book—to our own loss. But we have a Book of our own—hopefully with the spell we need. And for now . . . for now, we will prepare, and we will face the consequences. For now, we move ahead."

He turned his head to kiss my palm. "Remind me to give you a salary raise."

I choked on a cough. "For what?"

"For the sage counsel—and the other vital services you provide me." He winked.

I laughed in earnest, and squeezed his face as I pressed a swift kiss to his mouth. "Shameless flirt."

The warmth returned to his eyes at last.

So I reached for an ivory towel and bundled his hands, now clean and warm, into the folds of soft fabric.

CHAPTER
34

Amren found no other Hybern assassins or spies during her long night of hunting through Velaris. How she sought them, how she distinguished friend from foe . . . Some people, Mor told me the next morning—after we *all* had a sleepless night—painted their thresholds in lamb's blood. A sort of offering to her. And payment to stay away. Some left cups of it on their doorsteps.

As if everyone in the city knew that the High Lord's Second, that small-boned female . . . she was the monster that defended them from the other horrors of the world.

Rhys had spent much of the previous day and night reassuring the priestesses of their safety, walking them through the new wards. The priestess who had let them in . . . for whatever reason, Hybern had left her alive. She allowed Rhys into her mind to see what had happened: once the king had sundered the wards with that fleeting spell, his Ravens had appeared as two old scholars to get the priestess to open the door, then forced their way into her mind so that she'd welcome them in without being vetted. The violation of that alone . . . Rhys had spent hours with those priestesses yesterday. Mor, too.

Talking, listening to the ones who *could* speak, holding the hands of the ones who couldn't.

And when they at last left . . . There was a peace between my mate and his cousin. Some lingering jagged edge that had somehow been soothed.

We didn't have long. I knew that. Felt it with every breath. Hybern wasn't coming; Hybern was *here*.

Our meeting with the High Lords was now over a week away—and still Nesta refused to join us.

But it was fine. We'd manage. I'd manage.

We didn't have another choice.

Which was why I found myself standing in the foyer the next morning, watching Lucien shoulder his heavy pack. He wore Illyrian leathers under a heavier jacket, along with layers of clothes beneath to help him survive in varying climates. He'd braided back his red hair, the length of it snaking across his back—right in front of the Illyrian sword strapped down his spine.

Cassian had given him free rein yesterday afternoon to loot his personal cache of weapons, though my friend had been economical about which ones he'd selected. The blade, plus a short sword, plus an assortment of daggers. A quiver of arrows and an unstrung bow were tied to his pack.

"You know precisely where you want Rhys to take you?" I asked at last.

Lucien nodded, glancing to where my mate now waited by the front door. He'd bring Lucien to the edge of the human continent—to wherever Lucien had decided would be the best landing spot. No farther, Azriel had insisted. His reports indicated it was too watched, too dangerous. Even for one of our own. Even for the most powerful High Lord in history.

I stepped forward, and didn't give Lucien time to step back as I hugged him tightly. "Thank you," I said, trying not to think about all the steel on him—if he'd need to use it.

"It was time," Lucien said quietly, giving me a squeeze. "For me to do something."

I pulled away, surveying his scarred face. "Thank you," I said again. It was all I could think of to say.

Rhys extended a hand to Lucien.

Lucien studied it—then my mate's face. I could nearly see all the hateful words they'd spoken. Dangling between them, between that outstretched hand and Lucien's own.

But Lucien took Rhys's hand. That silent offer of not only transportation.

Before that dark wind swept in, Lucien looked back.

Not to me, I realized—to someone behind me.

Pale and thin, Elain stood atop the stairs.

Their gazes locked and held.

But Elain said nothing. Did not so much as take one step downward.

Lucien inclined his head in a bow, the movement hiding the gleam in his eye—the longing and sadness.

And when Lucien turned to signal to Rhys to go . . . He did not glance back at Elain.

Did not see the half step she took toward the stairs—as if she'd speak to him. Stop him.

Then Rhys was gone, and Lucien with him.

When I turned to offer Elain breakfast, she'd already walked away.

⁜

I waited in the foyer for Rhys to return.

In the dining room to my left, Nesta silently practiced building those invisible walls in her mind—no sign of Amren since her hunt last night. When I asked if she was making any progress, my sister had only said, "Amren thinks I'm getting close enough to begin trying on something tangible."

And that was that. I left her to it, not bothering to ask if Amren had *also* come close to figuring out some sort of spell in the Book to repair that wall.

In silence, I counted the minutes, one by one.

Then a familiar dark wind swirled through the foyer, and I loosed a too-tight breath as Rhys appeared in the middle of the hall carpet. No indication of any sort of trouble, no sign of hurt or harm, but I slid my arms around his waist, needing to feel him, smell him. "Did everything go well?"

Rhys brushed a kiss to the top of my head. "As well as can be expected. He's now on the continent, heading eastward."

He marked Nesta studying at the dining table. "How's our new seer holding up?"

I pulled back to explain that I'd left Elain to her own thoughts, but Nesta said, "Don't call her that."

Rhys gave me an incredulous look, but Nesta just went back to flipping through a book, her face going vacant—while she practiced with whatever wall-building exercises Amren had ordered. I poked him in the ribs. *Don't provoke her.*

A corner of his mouth lifted—the expression full of wicked delight. *Can I provoke you instead?*

I clamped my lips to keep from smiling—

The front door blew open and Amren stormed in.

Rhys was instantly facing her. "What."

Gone was the slick amusement, the relaxed posture.

Amren's pale face remained calm, but her eyes . . . They swirled with rage.

"Hybern has attacked the Summer Court. They lay siege to Adriata as we speak."

CHAPTER
35

Hybern had made its grand move at last. And we had not anticipated it.

I knew Azriel would take the blame upon himself. One look at the
shadowsinger as he prowled through the front door of the town house
minutes later, Cassian on his heels, told me that he already did.

We stood in the foyer, Nesta lingering at the dining table behind me.

"Has Tarquin called for aid?" Cassian asked Amren.

None of us dared question how she knew.

Amren's jaw tightened. "I don't know. I got the message, and—
nothing else."

Cassian nodded once and turned to Rhys. "Did the Summer Court
have a mobile fighting force readied when you were there?"

"No," Rhys said. "His armada was scattered along the coast." A
glance at Azriel.

"Half is in Adriata—the other dispersed," the shadowsinger
supplied. "His terrestrial army was moved to the Spring Court
border . . . after Feyre. The closest legion is perhaps three days' march
away. Very few can winnow."

"How many ships?" Rhys asked.

"Twenty in Adriata, fully armed."

A calculating look at Amren. "Numbers on Hybern?"

"I don't know. Many. It—I think they are overwhelmed."

"What was the exact message?" Pure, unrelenting command laced every word.

Amren's eyes glittered like fresh silver. "It was a warning. From Varian. To prepare our own defenses."

Utter silence.

"Prince Varian sent you a warning?" Cassian asked a bit quietly.

Amren glared at him. "It is a thing that friends do."

More silence.

I met Rhys's stare, sensed the weight and dread and anger simmering behind the cool features. "We cannot leave Tarquin to face them alone," I said. Perhaps Hybern had sent the Ravens yesterday to distract us from looking beyond our own borders. To have our focus on Hybern, not our own shores.

Rhys's attention cut to Cassian. "Keir and his Darkbringer army are nowhere near ready to march. How soon can the Illyrian legions fly?"

+

Rhys immediately winnowed Cassian into the war-camps to give the orders himself. Azriel had vanished with them, going ahead to scout Adriata, taking his most trusted spies with him.

Nausea had churned in my gut as Cassian and Azriel tapped the Siphons atop their hands and that scaled armor unfurled across their body. As seven Siphons appeared on each. As the shadowsinger's scarred hands checked the buckles on his knife belts and his quiver, while Rhys summoned extra Illyrian blades for Cassian—two at his back, one at each side.

Then they were gone—stone-faced and steady. Ready for bloodshed.

Mor arrived moments later, heavily armed, her hair braided back and every inch of her thrumming with impatience.

But Mor and I waited—for the order to go. To join them. Cassian had positioned the Illyrian legions closer to the southern border the weeks I'd been away, but even so, they wouldn't be able to fly without a few hours of preparation. And it would require Rhys to winnow them in. *All* of them. To Adriata.

"Will you fight?"

Nesta was now standing a few steps up the staircase of the town house, watching as Mor and I readied. Soon—Azriel or Rhys would contact us soon with the all-clear to winnow to Adriata.

"We'll fight if it's required," I said, checking once more that the belt of knives was secure at my hips.

Mor wore Illyrian leathers as well, but the blades on her were different. Slimmer, lighter, some of their tips slightly curved. Like lightning given flesh. Seraphim blades, she told me. Gifted to her by Prince Drakon himself during the War.

"What do you know of battle?"

I couldn't tell if my sister's tone was insulting or merely inquisitive.

"We know plenty," Mor said tightly, arranging her long braid between the blades crossed over her back. Elain and Nesta would remain here, with Amren watching over them. And watching over Velaris, along with a small legion of Illyrians Cassian had ordered to camp in the mountains above the city. Mor had passed Amren on her way in, the small female apparently heading to the butcher to fill up on provisions before she'd return to stay here—for however long we'd be in Adriata. If we returned at all.

I met Nesta's gaze again. Only wary distance greeted me. "We'll send word when we can."

A rumble of midnight thunder brushed against the walls of my mind. A silent signal, speared over land and mountains. As if Rhys's concentration was now wholly focused elsewhere—and he did not dare break it.

My heart stumbled a beat. I gripped Mor's arm, the leather scales cutting into my palm. "They've arrived. Let's go."

Mor turned to my sister, and I had never seen her seem so . . . warriorlike. I'd known it lurked beneath the surface, but here was the Morrigan. The female who had *fought* in the War. Who knew how to end lives with blade and magic.

"It's nothing we can't handle," Mor said to Nesta with a cocky smile, and then we were gone.

Black wind roared and tore at me, and I clung to Mor as she winnowed us through the courts, her breath a ragged beat in my ear—

Then blinding light and suffocating heat and screams and thunderous booming and metal on metal—

I swayed, bracing my feet apart as I blinked. As I took in my surroundings.

Rhys and the Illyrians had already joined the fray.

Mor had winnowed us to the barren top of one of the hills flanking the half-moon bay of Adriata, offering perfect views of the island-city in its center and the city on the mainland below.

The waters of the bay were red.

Smoke rose in gnarled black columns from buildings and foundering ships.

People screamed, soldiers shouted—

So many.

I had not anticipated the scope of how many soldiers there would be. On either side.

I'd thought it would be neat lines. Not chaos everywhere. Not Illyrians in the skies above the city and the harbor, blasting their power and arrows into the Hybern army that rained hell upon the city. Ship after ship squatted toward the horizon, hemming either entrance to the bay. And in the bay . . .

"Those are Tarquin's ships," Mor said, her face taut as she pointed to the white sails colliding with terrible force against the gray sails of Hybern's fleet. Utterly outnumbered, and yet plumes of magic—water and wind and whips of vines—kept attacking any boat that neared. And those that broke through the magic faced soldiers armed with spears and bows and swords.

And ahead of them, pushing against the fleet . . . the Illyrian lines.

So many. Rhys had winnowed them in—all of them. The drain on his power . . .

Mor's throat bobbed. "No one else has come," she murmured. "No other courts."

No sign of Tamlin and the Spring Court on Hybern's side, either.

A thunderous boom of dark power blasted into Hybern's fleet, scattering ships—but not many. As if . . . "Rhys's power is either already nearly spent or . . . they've got something working against it," I said. "More of that faebane?"

"Hybern would be stupid not to use it." Her fingers curled and uncurled at her sides. Sweat beaded on her temple.

"Mor?"

"I knew it was coming," she murmured. "Another war, at some point. I knew battles would come for *this* war. But . . . I forgot how terrible it is. The sounds. The smells."

Indeed, even from the rocky outcropping so high above, it was . . . overwhelming. The tang of blood, the pleading and screaming . . . Getting into the midst of it . . .

Alis. Alis had left the Spring Court, fearing the hell I'd unleash there—only to come here. To *this*. I prayed she was not in the city proper, prayed she and her nephews were keeping safe.

"We're to go to the palace," Mor said, squaring her shoulders. I hadn't dared break Rhysand's concentration by opening up a channel in the bond, but it seemed he was still capable of giving orders. "Soldiers have reached its northern side, and their defenses are surrounded."

I nodded once, and Mor drew her slender, curving blade. It gleamed as brightly as Amren's eyes, that Seraphim steel.

I unsheathed my Illyrian blade from across my back, the metal dark and ancient by comparison to the living silver flame in her hand.

"We stick close—you don't get out of sight," Mor said, smoothly and precisely. "We don't go down a hall or stairwell without assessing first."

I nodded again, at a loss for words. My heart beat at a gallop, my palms turning sweaty. Water—I wished I'd had some water. My mouth had gone bone-dry.

"If you can't bring yourself to make the kill," she added without a hint of judgment, "then shield me from behind."

"I can do it—the . . . killing," I rasped. I'd done plenty of it that day in Velaris.

Mor assessed the grip I maintained on my blade, the set of my shoulders. "Don't stop, and don't linger. We press forward until I say we retreat. Leave the wounded to the healers."

None of them enjoyed this, I realized. My friends—they had gone to war and back and had not found it worthy of glorification, had not let its memory become rose-tinted in the centuries following. But they were willing to dive into its hell once again for the sake of Prythian.

"Let's go," I said. Every moment we wasted here could spell someone's doom in that gleaming palace in the bay.

Mor swallowed once and winnowed us into the palace.

+

She must have visited a few times throughout the centuries, because she knew where to arrive.

The middle levels of Tarquin's palace had been communal space between the lower floors that the servants and lesser faeries were shoved into and the shining residential quarters for the High Fae above. When I had last seen the vast greeting hall, the light had been clear and white, flitting off the seashell-encrusted walls, dancing along the running rivers built into the floor. The sea beyond the towering windows had been turquoise mottled with vibrant sapphire.

Now that sea was choked with mighty ships and blood, the clear skies full of Illyrian warriors swooping down upon them in determined, unflinching lines. Thick metal shields glinted as the Illyrians dove and rose, emerging each time covered in blood. If they returned to the skies at all.

But my task was here. This building.

We scanned the floor, listening.

Frantic murmurs echoed from the stairwells leading upward, along with heavy thudding.

"They're barricading themselves into the upper levels," Mor observed as my brows narrowed.

Leaving the lesser fae trapped below. With no aid.

"Bastards," I breathed.

The lesser fae did not have as much magic between them—not in the way the High Fae did.

"This way," Mor said, jerking her chin toward the descending stairs. "They're three levels down, and climbing. Fifty of them."

A ship's worth.

CHAPTER
36

The first and second kills were the hardest. I didn't waste physical strength on the cluster of five Hybern soldiers—High Fae, not Attor-like underlings—forcing their way into a barricaded room full of terrified servants.

No, even as my body hesitated at the kills, my magic did not.

The two soldiers nearest me had feeble shields. I tore through them with a sizzling wall of fire. Fire that then found its way down their throats and burned every inch of the way.

And then sizzled through skin and tendon and bone and severed the heads from their bodies.

Mor just killed the soldier nearest her with good old-fashioned beheading.

She whirled, the soldier's head still falling, and sliced off the head of the one just nearing us.

The fifth and final soldier stopped his assault on the battered door.

Looked between us with flat, hate-bright eyes.

"Do it, then," he said, his accent so like that of the Ravens.

His thick sword rose, blood sliding down the groove of the fuller.

Someone was sobbing in terror on the other side of that door.

The soldier lunged for us, and Mor's blade flashed.

But I struck first, an asp of pure water striking his face—stunning him. Then shoving down his open mouth, his throat, up his nose. Sealing off any air.

He slumped to the ground, clawing at his neck as if he'd free a passage for the water now drowning him.

We left him without looking back, the grunting of his choking soon turning to silence.

Mor slid me a sidelong glance. "Remind me not to get on your bad side."

I appreciated the attempt at humor, but . . . laughter was foreign. There was only the breath in my heaving lungs and the roiling of magic through my veins and the clear, unyielding crispness of my vision, assessing all.

We found eight more in the midst of killing and hurting, a dormitory turned into Hybern's own sick pleasure hall. I did not care to linger on what they did, and only marked it so that I knew how fast and easily to kill.

The ones merely slaughtering died fast.

The others . . . Mor and I lingered. Not much, but those deaths were slower.

We left two of them alive—hurt and disarmed but alive—for the surviving faeries to kill.

I gave them two Illyrian knives to do it.

The Hybern soldiers began screaming before we cleared the level.

The hallway on the floor below was splattered in blood. The din was deafening. A dozen soldiers in the silver-and-blue armor of Tarquin's court battled against the bulk of the Hybern force, holding the corridor.

They were nearly pushed back to the stairs we'd just exited, steadily overwhelmed by the solid numbers against them, the Hybern soldiers stepping over—stepping *on*—the bodies of the fallen Summer Court warriors.

Tarquin's soldiers were flagging, even as they kept swinging, kept fighting. The closest one beheld us—opened his mouth to order us to run. But then he noted the armor, the blood on us and our blades.

"Don't be afraid," Mor said—as I stretched out a hand and darkness fell.

Soldiers on both sides shouted, scrambling back, armor clanging.

But I shifted my eyes, made them night-seeing. As I had done in that Illyrian forest, when I had first drawn Hybern blood.

Mor, I think, was born able to see in the darkness.

We winnowed through the ebon-veiled corridor in short bursts.

I could see their terror as I killed them. But they could not see me.

Every time we appeared in front of Hybern soldiers, frantic in the impenetrable dark, their heads fell. One after another. Winnow; slash. Winnow; thump.

Until there were none left, only the mounds of their bodies, the puddles of their blood.

I banished the darkness from the corridor, finding the Summer Court soldiers panting and gaping. At us. At what we had done in a matter of a minute.

I didn't look too long at the carnage. Mor didn't, either.

"Where else?" was all I asked.

⊹

We cleared the palace to its lowest levels. Then we took to the city streets, the steep hill leading down to the water rampant with Hybern soldiers.

The morning sun rose higher, beating down on us, making our skin slick and swollen with sweat beneath our leathers. I stopped discerning the sweat on my palms from the blood coating it.

I stopped being able to feel a great many things as we killed and killed, sometimes engaging in outright combat, sometimes with magic, sometimes earning our own bruises and small wounds.

But the sun continued its arc across the sky, and the battle continued in the bay, the Illyrian lines battering the Hybern fleet from above while Tarquin's armada pushed from behind.

Slowly, we purged the streets of Hybern soldiers. All I knew was the sun baking the blood coating my skin, the coppery tang of it clinging to my nostrils.

We had just cleared a narrow street, Mor striding through the felled Hybern soldiers to make sure any survivors . . . stopped surviving. I leaned against a blood-bathed stone wall just outside the shattered front window of a clothier, watching Mor's quicksilver blade rise and fall in lightning-bright flashes.

Beyond us, all around us, the screams of the dying were like the never-ending pealing of the city's warning bells.

Water—I needed water. If only to wash the blood from my mouth.

Not my own blood, but that of the soldiers we'd cut down. Blood that had sprayed into my mouth, up my nose, into my eyes, when we'd ended them.

Mor reached the last of the dead, and terrified High Fae and faeries finally poked their heads out of the doorways and windows flanking the cobblestoned street. No sign of Alis, her nephews, or cousin—or anyone who looked like them, amongst the living or the fallen. A small blessing.

We had to keep moving. There were more—so many more.

As Mor began striding back to me, boots sloshing through puddles of blood, I reached a mental hand toward the bond. Toward Rhys— toward anything that was solid and familiar.

Wind and darkness answered me.

I became only half-aware of the narrow street and the blood and the sun as I peered down the bridge between us. *Rhys.*

Nothing.

I speared myself along it, stumbling blindly through that raging tempest of night and shadow. If the bond sometimes felt like a living band of light, it now had turned into a bridge of ice-kissed obsidian.

And rising up on its other end . . . his mind. The walls—his shields . . . They had turned into a fortress.

I laid a mental hand to the black adamant, my heart thundering. What was he facing—what was he *seeing* to have made his shields so impenetrable?

I couldn't feel him on the other side.

There was only the stone and the dark and the wind.

Rhys.

Mor had nearly reached me when his answer came.

A crack in the shield—so swift that I did not have time to do anything more than lunge for it before it had closed behind me. Sealing me inside with him.

The streets, the sun, the city vanished.

There was only here—only him. And the battle.

Looking through Rhysand's eyes as I once had that day Under the Mountain . . . I felt the heat of the sun, the sweat and blood sliding down his face, slipping beneath the neck of his black Illyrian armor— smelled the brine of the sea and the tang of blood all around me. Felt the exhaustion ripping at him, in his muscles and in his magic.

Felt the Hybern warship shudder beneath him as he landed on its main deck, an Illyrian blade in each hand.

Six soldiers died instantly, their armor and bodies turning into red-and-silver mist.

The others halted, realizing who'd landed amongst them, in the heart of their fleet.

Slowly, Rhys surveyed the helmeted heads before him, counted the weapons. Not that it mattered. All of them would soon be crimson mist or food for the beasts circling the waters around the clashing armada. And then this ship would be splinters on the waves.

Once he was done. It was not the common foot soldiers he'd sought out.

Because where power should have been thrumming from him, obliterating them . . . It was a muffled rumble. Stifled.

He'd tracked it here—that strange damper on his power, on the Siphons' power. As if some sort of spell had turned his power oily in his grip. Harder to wield.

It was why the battle had gone on so long. The clean, precise blow he'd intended to land upon arriving—the single shot that would have saved so many lives . . . It had slipped from his grasp.

So he'd hunted it down, that damper. Battled his way across Adriata to get to this ship. And now, exhaustion starting to rip at him . . . The armed soldiers around Rhysand parted—and he appeared.

Trapped within Rhysand's mind, his powers stifled and body weary, there was nothing I could do but watch as the King of Hybern stepped from belowdecks and smiled at my mate.

CHAPTER
37

Blood slid from the tips of Rhys's twin blades onto the deck. One drop—two. Three.

Mother above. The king—

The King of Hybern wore his own colors: slate gray, embroidered with bone-colored thread. Not a weapon on him. Not a speckle of blood.

Within Rhys's mind, there was no jagged breath for me to take, no heartbeat to thunder in my chest. There was nothing I could do but watch—watch and keep quiet, so I didn't distract him, didn't risk taking his focus away for one blink . . .

Rhys met the king's dark eyes, bright beneath heavy brows, and smiled. "Glad to see you're still not fighting your own battles."

The king's answering smile was a brutal slash of white. "I was waiting for more interesting quarry to find me." His voice was colder than the highest peak of the Illyrian mountains.

Rhys didn't dare look away from him. Not as his magic unfurled, sniffing out every angle to kill the king. A trap—it had been a trap to discover which High Lord hunted down the source of that damper first.

Rhys had known one of them—the king, his cronies—would be waiting here.

He'd known, and come. Known and not asked us to *help* him—

If I was smart, Rhys said to me, his voice calm and steady, *I'd find some way to take him alive, make Azriel break him—get him to yield the Cauldron. And make an example of him to the other bastards thinking of bringing down that wall.*

Don't, I begged him. *Just kill him—kill him and be done with it, Rhys. End this war before it can truly begin.*

A pause of consideration. *But a death here, quick and brutal . . . His followers would turn it against me, no doubt.*

If he could manage it. The king had not been fighting. Had not depleted his reserves of power. But Rhys . . .

I felt Rhys size up the odds alongside me. *Let one of us come to you. Don't face him alone—*

Because trying to take the king alive without full access to his power . . .

Information rippled into me, brimming with all Rhys had seen and learned. Taking the king alive depended on whether Azriel was in good enough shape to help. He and Cassian had taken a few blows themselves, but—nothing they couldn't handle. Nothing to spook the Illyrians still fighting under their command. Yet.

"Seems like the tide is turning," Rhys observed as the armada around them indeed pushed Hybern's forces out to sea. He had not seen Tarquin. Or Varian and Cresseida. But the Summer Court still fought. Still pushed Hybern back, back, back from the harbor.

Time. Rhys needed *time*—

Rhys lunged toward the king's mind—and met *nothing*. Not a trace, not a whisper. As if he were nothing but wicked thought and ancient malice—

The king clicked his tongue. "I'd heard that you were a charmer, Rhysand. Yet here you are, groping and pawing at me like a green youth."

A corner of Rhys's mouth twitched up. "Always a delight to disappoint Hybern."

"Oh, on the contrary," the king said, crossing his arms—muscle shifting beneath. "You've always been such a source of entertainment. Especially for my darling Amarantha."

I felt it—the thought that escaped Rhys.

He wanted to wipe that name from living memory. Perhaps one day he would. One day he'd erase it from every mind in this world, one by one, until she was no one and nothing.

But the king knew that. From that smile, he knew.

And everything he had done . . . All of it . . .

Kill him, Rhys. Kill him and be done with it.

It's not that easy, was his even reply. *Not without searching this ship, searching him for that source of the spell on our power, and breaking it.*

But if he lingered much longer . . . I had no doubt the king had some nasty surprise waiting. Designed to spring shut at any moment. I knew Rhys was aware of it, too.

Knew, because he rallied his magic, assessing and weighing, an asp readying to strike.

"The last report I received from Amarantha," the king went on, sliding his hands into his pockets, "she was still enjoying you." The soldiers laughed.

My mate was used to it—that laughter. Even if it made me want to roar at them, rend them to pieces. But Rhys didn't so much as grit his teeth, though the king gave him a smile that told me he was well aware of what sort of scars lingered. What my mate had done to keep Amarantha distracted. Why he'd done it.

Rhys smirked. "Too bad it didn't end so pleasantly for her." His magic slithered through the ship, hunting down that tether for the power holding back our forces . . .

Kill him—kill him now. The word was a chant in my blood, my mind.

In his, too. I could hear it, clear as my own thoughts.

"Such a remarkable girl—your mate," the king mused. No emotion, not so much as a bit of anger beyond that cold amusement. "First Amarantha, then my pet, the Attor . . . And then she broke past all the wards around my palace to aid your escape. Not to mention . . ." A low laugh. "My niece and nephew." Rage—that was rage starting to blacken in his eyes. "She savaged Dagdan and Brannagh—and for what reason?"

"Perhaps you should ask Tamlin." Rhys raised a brow. "Where is he, by the way?"

"Tamlin." Hybern savored the name, the sound of it. "He has plans for you, after what you and your mate did to him. His court. What a mess for him to clean up—though she certainly made it easier for me to plant more of my troops in his lands."

Mother above—Mother above, I'd *done* that—

"She'll be happy to hear that."

Too long. Rhys had lingered too long, and facing him now . . . Fight or run. Run or fight.

"Where did her gifts come from, I wonder? Or who?"

The king knew. What I was. What I possessed.

"I'm a lucky male to have her as my mate."

The king smiled again. "For the little time you have remaining."

I could have sworn Rhys blocked out the words.

The king went on casually, "It will take everything, you know. To try to stop me. Everything you have. And it still won't be enough. And when you have given everything and you are dead, Rhysand, when your mate is mourning over your corpse, I am going to take her."

Rhys didn't let a flicker of emotion show, sliding on that cool, amused mask over the roaring rage that surrounded me at the thought, the threat. That settled before me like a beast ready to lunge, to defend. "She defeated Amarantha and the Attor," Rhys countered. "I doubt you'll be much of an effort, either."

"We'll see. Perhaps I'll give her to Tamlin when I'm done."

Fury heated Rhys's blood. And my own.

Strike or flee, Rhys, I begged again. *But do it* now.

Rhys rallied his power, and I felt it rise within him, felt him grappling to sustain his grip on it.

"The spell will wear off," the king said, waving a hand. "Another little trick I picked up while rotting away in Hybern."

"I don't know what you're talking about," Rhys said mildly.

They only smiled at each other.

And then Rhys asked, "Why?"

The king knew what he meant.

"There was room at the table for everyone, you and your ilk claimed." The king snorted. "For humans, lesser faeries, for half-breeds. In this new world of yours, there was room at the table for everyone—so long as they thought like you. But the Loyalists . . . How you delighted in shutting us out. Looking down your noses at us." He gestured to the soldiers monitoring them, the battle in the bay. "You want to know why? Because we suffered—when you stifled us, when you shut us out." Some of his soldiers grunted their agreement. "I have no interest in spending another five centuries seeing my people bow before human pigs—seeing them claw out a living while you shield and coddle those mortals, granting them our resources and wealth in exchange for *nothing*." He inclined his head. "So we shall reclaim what is ours. What was always ours, and will always be ours."

Rhys offered him a sly grin. "You can certainly try."

My mate didn't bother saying more as he hurled a slender javelin of power at him, the shot as precise as an arrow.

And when it reached the king—

It went right through him.

He rippled—then steadied.

An illusion. A shade.

The king rumbled a laugh. "Did you think I'd appear at this battle

myself?" He waved a hand toward the soldiers still watching. "A taste—
this battle is only a taste for you. To whet your appetite."

Then he was gone.

The magic leaking from the boat, the oily sheen it'd laid over Rhys's
power . . . it vanished, too.

Rhys allowed the Hybern soldiers aboard the ship, aboard the ones
around him, the honor of at least lifting their blades.

Then he turned them all into nothing but red mist and splinters
floating on the waves.

CHAPTER
38

Mor was shaking me. I only knew it because Rhys threw me out of his mind the moment he unleashed himself upon those soldiers.

You were here too long, was all he said, caressing a dark talon down my face. Then I was out, stumbling down the bond, his shield slamming shut behind me.

"Feyre," Mor was saying, fingers digging into my shoulders through my leathers. "*Feyre*."

I blinked, the sun and blood and narrow street coming into focus.

Blinked—and then vomited all over the cobblestones between us.

People, shaken and petrified, only stared.

"This way," Mor said, and looped her arm around my waist as she led me into a dusty, empty alley. Far from watching eyes. I barely took in the city and bay and sea beyond—barely noticed that a mighty maelstrom of darkness and water and wind was now shoving Hybern's fleet back over the horizon. As if Tarquin's and Rhys's powers had been unleashed by the king's vanishing.

I made it to a pile of fallen stones from the half-wrecked building beside us when I vomited again. And again.

Mor put a hand on my back, rubbing soothing circles as I retched. "I did the same after my first battle. We all did."

It wasn't even a battle—not in the way I'd pictured: army against army on some unremarkable battlefield, chaotic and muddy. Even the real battle today had been out on the sea—where the Illyrians were now sailing inland.

I couldn't bear to start counting how many made the return trip.

I didn't know how Mor or Rhys or Cassian or Azriel could bear it.

And what I'd just seen . . . "The king was here," I breathed.

Mor's hand stilled on my back. "What?"

I leaned my brow against the sun-warmed brick of the building before me and told her—what I'd seen in Rhys's mind.

The king—he had been here and yet not here. Another trick—another spell. No wonder Rhys hadn't been able to attack his mind: the king hadn't been present to do so.

I closed my eyes as I finished, pressing my brow harder into the brick.

Blood and sweat still coated me. I tried to remember the usual fit of my soul in my body, the priority of things, my way of looking at the world. What to do with my limbs in the stillness. How did I usually position my hands without a blade between them? How did I *stop* moving?

Mor squeezed my shoulder, as if she understood the racing thoughts, the foreignness of my body. The War had raged for seven years. *Years.* How long would this one last?

"We should find the others," she said, and helped me straighten before winnowing us back to the palace towering high above.

I couldn't bring myself to send another thought down the bond. See where Rhys was. I didn't want him to see me—*feel* me—in such a state. Even if I knew he wouldn't judge.

He, too, had spilled blood on the battlefield today. And many others before it. All of my friends had.

And I could understand—just for a heartbeat, as the wind tore around us—why some rulers, human and Fae, had bowed before Hybern. Bowed, rather than face this.

It wasn't only the cost of life that ripped and devastated and sundered. It was the altering of a soul with it—the realization that I could perhaps go back home to Velaris, perhaps see peace achieved and cities rebuilt . . . but this battle, this war . . . *I* would be the thing forever changed.

War would linger with me long after it had ended, some invisible scar that would perhaps fade, but never wholly vanish.

But for my home, for Prythian and the human territory and so many others . . .

I would clean my blades, and wash the blood from my skin.

And I would do it again and again and again.

⊹

The middle level of the palace was a flurry of motion: blood-drenched Summer Court soldiers limped around healers and servants rushing to the injured being laid on the floor.

The stream through the center of the hall ran red.

More and more winnowed in, borne by wide-eyed High Fae.

A few Illyrians—just as bloody but eyes clear—hauled in their own wounded through the open windows and balcony doors.

Mor and I scanned the space, the throngs of people, the reek of death and screams of the injured.

I tried to swallow, but my mouth was too dry. "Where are—"

I recognized the warrior the same moment he spied me.

Varian, kneeling over an injured soldier with his thigh in ribbons, went utterly still as our eyes met. His brown skin was splattered in blood as bright as the rubies they'd sent to us, his white hair plastered to his head, as if he'd just chucked off his helmet.

He whistled through his teeth, and a soldier appeared at his side, taking up his position of tying a tourniquet around the hurt male's thigh. The Prince of Adriata rose to his feet.

I did not have any magic left in me to shield. After seeing Rhys with the king, there was only an empty pit where my fear had been a wild sea within me. But I felt Mor's power slide into place between us.

There was a death-promise on my head. From them.

Varian approached—slowly. Stiffly. As if his entire body ached. Though his handsome face revealed nothing. Only bone-weary exhaustion.

His mouth opened—then shut. I didn't have words, either.

So Varian rasped, his voice hoarse enough that I knew he'd been screaming for a long, long time, "He's in the oak dining room."

The one where I had first dined with them.

I just nodded at the prince and began easing my way through the crowd, Mor keeping close to my side.

I'd thought Varian meant Rhysand.

But it was Tarquin who stood in gore-flecked silver armor at the dining table, maps and charts before him, Summer Court Fae either blood-soaked or pristine filling the sunny chamber.

The High Lord of the Summer Court looked up from the table as we paused on the threshold. Took in me, then Mor.

The kindness, the consideration that I had last seen on the High Lord's face was gone. Replaced by a grim, cold thing that made my stomach turn.

Blood had clotted from a thick slice down his neck, the caked bits crumbling away as Tarquin glanced to the people in the room and said, "Leave us."

No one even dared glance twice at him as they filed out.

I had done a horrible thing the last time we were here. I had lied, and stolen. I had torn into his mind and tricked him into believing me innocent. Harmless. I did not blame him for the blood ruby he had sent. But if he sought to exact his vengeance now . . .

"I heard you two cleared the palace. And helped clear the island."

His words were low—lifeless.

Mor inclined her head. "Your soldiers fought bravely beside us."

Tarquin ignored her, his crushing turquoise eyes upon me. Taking in the blood, the wounds, the leathers. Then the mating band on my finger, the star sapphire dull, blood crusted between the delicate folds and arcs of metal.

"I thought you came to finish the job," Tarquin said to me.

I didn't dare move.

"I heard Tamlin took you. Then I heard the Spring Court fell. Collapsed from within. Its people in revolt. And you had vanished. And when I saw the Illyrian legion sweeping in . . . I thought you had come for me, too. To help Hybern finish us off."

Varian had not told him—of the message he'd snuck to Amren. Not a call for aid, but a frantic warning for Amren to save herself. Tarquin hadn't known that we'd be coming.

"We would never ally with Hybern," Mor said.

"I am talking to Feyre Archeron."

I'd never heard Tarquin use that tone. Mor bristled, but said nothing.

"Why?" Tarquin demanded, sunlight glinting on his armor—whose delicate, overlapping scales were fashioned after a fish's.

I didn't know what he meant. Why had we deceived and stolen from him? Why had we come to help? Why to both?

"Our dreams are the same," was all I could think to say.

A united realm, in which lesser faeries were no longer shoved down. A better world.

The opposite of what Hybern fought for. What his allies fought for.

"Is that how you justified stealing from me?"

My heart stumbled a beat.

Rhysand said from behind me, no doubt having winnowed in, "My mate and I had our reasons, Tarquin."

My knees nearly buckled at the evenness in his voice, at the blood-speckled face that still revealed no sign of great injury, at the dark armor—the twin to Azriel's and Cassian's—that had held intact despite a few deep scratches I could barely stand to note. *Cassian and Azriel?*

Fine. Overseeing the Illyrian injured and setting up camp in the hills.

Tarquin glanced between us. "Mate."

"Wasn't it obvious?" Rhysand asked with a wink. But there was an edge in his eyes—sharp and haunted.

My chest tightened. *Did the king leave some sort of trap to—*

He slid a hand against my back. *No. No—I'm all right. Pissed I didn't see that he was an illusion, but . . . Fine.*

Tarquin's face didn't so much as shift from that cold wrath. "When you went into the Spring Court and deceived Tamlin as well about your true nature, when you destroyed his territory . . . You left the door open for Hybern. They docked in his harbors." No doubt to wait for the wall to collapse and then sail south. Tarquin snarled, "It was an easy trip to my doorstep. You did this."

I could have sworn I felt Rhys flinch through the bond. But my mate said calmly, "We did nothing. Hybern chooses its actions, not us." He jerked his chin toward Tarquin. "My force shall remain camped in the hills until you've deemed the city secure. Then we will go."

"And do you plan to steal anything else before you do?"

Rhys went utterly still. Debating, I realized, whether to apologize. Explain.

I spared him from the choice. "Tend to your wounded, Tarquin."

"Don't give me orders."

The face of the former Summer Court admiral—the prince who had commanded the fleet in the harbor until the title was thrust upon him. I took in the weariness fogging his eyes, the anger and grief.

People had died. Many people. The city he had fought so hard to rebuild, the people who had tried to fight past the scars of Amarantha . . .

"We are at your disposal," I said to him, and walked out.

Mor kept close, and we emerged into the hall to find a cluster of his advisers and soldiers watching us carefully. Behind us, Rhys said to Tarquin, "I didn't have a choice. I did it to try to *avoid* this, Tarquin. To stop Hybern before he got this far." His voice was strained.

Tarquin only said, "Get out. And take your army with you. We can hold the bay now that they don't have surprise on their side."

Silence. Mor and I lingered just outside the open doors, not turning back, but both of us listening. Listening as Rhysand said, "I saw enough of Hybern in the War to tell you this attack is just a fraction of what the king plans to unleash." A pause. "Come to the meeting, Tarquin. We need you—Prythian needs you."

Another beat of quiet. Then Tarquin said, "Get out."

"Feyre's offer holds: we are at your disposal."

"Take your mate and leave. And I'd suggest warning her not to give High Lords orders."

I stiffened, about to whirl around, when Rhys said, "She is High Lady of the Night Court. She may do as she wishes."

The wall of Fae standing before us withdrew slightly. Now studying me, some gaping. A murmur rippled through them. Tarquin let out a low, bitter laugh. "You do love to spit on tradition."

Rhys didn't say anything more, his strolling footsteps sounding over the tiled floor until his hand warmed my shoulder. I looked up at him, aware of all who gawked at us. At me.

Rhys pressed a kiss to my sweaty, blood-crusted temple and we vanished.

CHAPTER
39

The Illyrian camp remained in the hills above Adriata.

Mostly because there were so many injured that we couldn't move them until they'd healed enough to survive it.

Wings shredded, guts dangling out, faces mauled . . .

I don't know how my friends were still standing as they tended to the wounded as much as they could. I barely saw Azriel, who had set up a tent to organize the information pouring in from his scouts: the Hybern fleet had retreated. Not to the Spring Court, but across the sea. No sign of any other forces waiting to strike. No whisper of Tamlin or Jurian.

Cassian, though . . . He limped through the injured laid out on the rocky, dry ground, offering kernels of praise or comfort to the soldiers who had not yet been tended. With the Siphons, he could do quick battlefield patching, but . . . nothing extensive. Nothing intricate.

His face, whenever we crossed paths as I fetched supplies for the healers working without rest, was grave. Gaunt. He still wore his armor, and though he'd rinsed the blood from his skin, it clung near the neck of his breastplate. The dullness in his hazel eyes was the same as that glazing my own. And Mor's.

But Rhys . . . His eyes were clear. Alert. His expression grim, but . . . It was to him the soldiers looked. And he was everything he should be: a High Lord confident in his victory, whose forces had smashed through the Hybern fleet and saved a city of innocents. The toll it had taken on his own soldiers was difficult, but a worthy cost for victory. He strolled through the camp—overseeing the wounded, the information Azriel handed him, checking in with his commanders—still in his Illyrian armor. But wings gone. They'd vanished before he'd appeared in Tarquin's chamber.

The sun set, leaving a blanket of darkness over the city lying below. So much darker than I'd last beheld it, alive and glittering with light. But this new darkness . . . We had seen it in Velaris after the attack—we now knew it too well.

Faelights bobbed over our camp, gilding the talons of all those Illyrian wings as they worked or lay injured. I knew many looked to me—their High Lady.

But I could not muster Rhys's ease. His quiet triumph.

So I kept fetching bowls of fresh water, kept hauling away the bloodied ones. Helped pin down screaming soldiers until my teeth clacked against each other with the force of their thrashing.

I sat down only when my legs could no longer keep me upright, upon an overturned bucket outside the healers' tent. Just a few minutes—I'd sit for just a few minutes.

I awoke inside another tent, laid upon a pile of furs, the faelight dim and soft.

Rhys sat beside me, legs crossed, his hair in unusual disarray. Streaked with blood—as if it had coated his hands when he dragged them through it.

"How long was I out?" My words were a rasp.

He lifted his head from where he'd been studying some array of papers spread on the fur before him. "Three hours. Dawn is still far off—you should sleep."

But I propped myself on my elbows. "You're not."

He shrugged, sipping from the water goblet set beside him. "I'm not the one who fell face-first off a bucket into the mud." His wry smile faded. "How are you feeling?"

I almost said *Fine*, but . . . "I'm still figuring out what to feel."

A careful nod. "Open war is like that . . . It takes a while to decide how to deal with everything that it brings. The costs."

I sat up fully, scanning the papers he'd laid out. Casualty lists. Only a hundred or so names on them, but . . . "Did you know them—the ones who died?"

His violet eyes shuttered. "A few. Tarquin lost many more than we did."

"Who tells their families?"

"Cassian. He'll send out lists once dawn arrives—when we see who survives the night. He'll visit their families if he knew them."

I remembered that Rhys had once told me he'd scanned casualty lists for his friends in the War—the dread they'd all felt, waiting to see if a familiar name was on them.

So many shadows clouded those violet eyes. I laid a hand on his own. He studied my fingers on his, the arcs of dirt beneath my fingernails.

"The king only came today," he said at last, "to taunt me. The library attack, this battle . . . It was a way to toy with me. Us."

I touched his jaw. Cold—his skin was cold, despite the warm summer night pressing on us. "You are not going to die in this war, Rhysand."

His attention snapped to me.

I cupped his face in both hands now. "Don't you listen to a word he says. He knows—"

"He knows about us. Our histories."

And that scared Rhys to death.

"He knew the library . . . He picked it for what it meant to *me*, not just to take Nesta."

"So we learn where to hit him, and strike hard. Better yet, we kill him before he can do any further harm."

Rhys shook his head slightly, removing his face from my hands. "If it was only the king to contend with . . . But with the Cauldron in his arsenal . . ."

And it was the way his shoulders began to curve in, the way his chin dipped ever so slightly . . . I grabbed his hand again. "We need allies," I said, my eyes burning. "We can't face the brunt of this war alone."

"I know." The words were heavy—weary.

"Move the meeting with the High Lords sooner. Three days from now."

"I will." I'd never heard that tone—that quiet.

And it was precisely because of it that I said, "I love you."

His head lifted, eyes churning. "There was a time when I dreamed of hearing that," he murmured. "When I never thought I'd hear it from you." He gestured to the tent—to Adriata beyond it. "Our trip here was the first time I let myself . . . hope."

To the stars who listen—and the dreams that are answered.

And yet today, with Tarquin . . .

"The world should know," I said. "The world should know how good you are, Rhysand—how wonderful all of you are."

"I can't tell if I should be worried that you're saying such nice things about me. Maybe the king's taunting *did* get to you."

I pinched his arm, and he let out a low laugh before raising my face to study my eyes. He angled his head. "*Should* I be worried?"

I put a hand to his cheek once more, the silken skin now warm. "You are selfless, and brave, and kind. You are more than I ever dreamed for myself, more than I . . ." The words choked off, and I swallowed, taking a deep breath. I wasn't sure if he needed to hear it after what the king had said, but *I* needed to say it. Starlight now danced in his eyes. But I went on, "At this meeting with the other High Lords, what role will you play?"

"The usual one."

I nodded, having anticipated his answer. "And the others will play their usual roles, too."

"And?"

I slid my hand from his face and put it over his heart. "I think the time has come for us to remove the masks. To stop playing the part."

He waited, hearing me out.

"Velaris is secret no longer. The king knows too much about us—who we are. What we are. And if we're to ally with the other High Lords . . . I think they need the truth. They will need the truth in order to trust us. The truth about who you really are—who Mor and Cassian and Azriel really are. Look at how poorly things went with Tarquin today. We can't—we can't let it continue like this. So no more masks, no more roles to play. We go as ourselves. As a family."

If anything, the king's taunting had told me that. Games were over. There would be no more disguises, no more lies. Perhaps he thought it'd drive us toward continuing to do such things. But to stand a chance . . . perhaps victory lay in the other direction. In honesty. With us standing together—as precisely who we were.

I waited for Rhys to tell me that I was young and inexperienced, that I knew nothing of politics and war.

Yet Rhys only brushed his thumb over my cheek. "They may be angry at the lies we've fed them over the centuries."

"Then we will make it clear that we understand their feelings—and make it clear that we had no alternative way to protect our people."

"We'll show them the Court of Dreams," he said quietly.

I nodded. We'd show them—and also show Keir, and Eris, and Beron. Show who we were to our allies—and our enemies.

Stars glimmered and burned out in those beautiful eyes. "And what of your powers?" The king had known of them, too—or guessed at it.

I knew from his cautious tone that he'd already formed an opinion. But the choice was mine—he'd face it at my side no matter what I decided.

And as I thought it through . . . "I think they'll see the revealing of our good sides as manipulative if it also comes out that your mate has stolen power from them all. If the king plans to use that information against us—we'll deal with that later."

"Technically, that power was *gifted*, but . . . you're right. We'll have to walk a fine enough line regarding how we show ourselves— spin it the right way so they don't think it's a trap or scheme. But when it comes to you . . ." Darkness blotted out the stars in his eyes. The darkness of assassins and thieves, the darkness of uncompromising death. "You could tip the scale in Hybern's favor if any of them are considering an alliance. Beron alone might try to kill you, with or without this war. I doubt even Eris could keep him from it."

I could have sworn the war-camp shuddered at the power that rumbled awake—the wrath. Voices outside the tent dropped to whispers. Or outright silence.

But I leaned over and kissed him lightly. "We'll deal with it," I said onto his mouth.

He pulled his mouth from mine, his face grave. "We keep all your powers but the ones I gave you hidden. As my High Lady, you will have been expected to have received some."

I swallowed hard, nodding, and took a long drink from his goblet of water. No more lies, no more deceptions—beyond my magic. Let Tarquin be the first and last casualty of our deceit.

I chewed on my lip. "What about Miryam and Drakon? Have you learned anything about where they might have gone?" *Along with that legion of aerial warriors?*

The question seemed to drag him up from wherever he'd gone while contemplating what now lay before us.

Rhys sighed, scanning those casualty lists again. The dark ink seemed to absorb the dim faelight. "No. Az's spies have found no trace of them in any of the surrounding territories." He rubbed his temple. "How do you vanish an entire people?"

I frowned. "I suppose Jurian's tactic to draw them out worked against him." Jurian—there hadn't been a whisper of him at the battle today.

"It would seem so." He shook his head, the light dancing in the raven-black locks of his hair. "I should have established protocols with them—centuries ago. Ways to contact them, for them to contact us, if we ever needed help."

"Why didn't you?"

"They wanted to be forgotten by the world. And when I saw how peaceful Cretea became . . . I did not want the world to intrude on them, either." A muscle flickered in his jaw.

"If we did somehow find them . . . would that be enough, though? If we can stop the wall from sundering first, I mean. Our forces and Drakon's, perhaps even Queen Vassa if Lucien can find her, against all of Hybern?" Against whatever gambits or spells the king still planned to unleash.

Rhys was quiet for a moment. "It might have to be."

It was the way his voice went hoarse, the way his eyes guttered, that made me press a kiss to his mouth as I laid a hand upon his chest and pushed him down upon the furs.

His brows rose, but a half smile appeared on his lips. "There's little privacy in a war-camp," he warned, some of the light coming back to his eyes.

I only straddled him, unfastening the button at the top of his dark jacket. The one below it. "Then I suppose you'll have to be quiet," I said, working my way down the front of the jacket until it gaped open to reveal the shirt beneath. I traced a finger of the whorl of tattoo peeking out near his neck. "When I saw you facing the king today . . ."

He brushed his fingers against my thighs. "I know. I felt you."

I tugged on the hem of his shirt, and he rose onto his elbows, helping me remove his jacket, then the shirt beneath. A bruise marred his ribs, an angry splotch—

"It's fine," he said before I could speak. "A lucky shot."

"With *what?*"

Again, that half smile. "A spear?"

My heart stopped. "A . . ." I delicately brushed the bruise, swallowing hard.

"Tipped in faebane. My shield blocked most of it—but not enough to avoid the impact."

Dread curled in my stomach. But I leaned down and brushed a kiss over the bruise.

Rhys loosed a long breath, his body seeming to settle. Calm.

So I kissed the bruise again. Moved lower. He drew idle circles on my shoulder, my back.

I felt his shield settle around our tent as I unbuttoned his pants. As I kissed my way across the muscled pane of his stomach.

Lower. Rhys's hands slid into my hair as the rest of his clothes vanished.

I stroked my hand over him once, twice—luxuriating in the feel of him, in knowing he was here, we were *both* here. Safe.

Then I echoed the movement with my mouth.

His growls of pleasure filled the tent, drowning out the distant cries of the injured and dying. Life and death—hovering so close, whispering in our ears.

But I tasted Rhys, worshipped him with my hands and mouth and then my body—and hoped that this shard of life we offered up, this undimming light between us, would drive death a bit further away. At least for another day.

⁜

Only a few more Illyrians died during the night. But high up in the hills, the screams and wails of Tarquin's people rose to us on plumes of smoke from the still-burning fires Hybern had set. They continued burning when we left in the early hours after dawn, winnowing back to Velaris.

Cassian and Azriel remained to lead the Illyrian legions to their new camp on our southern borders—and the former left from there to fly into the Steppes. To offer his condolences to a few of those families.

Nesta was waiting for us in the foyer of the town house, Amren seething in a chair before the unlit fireplace of the sitting room.

No sign of Elain, but before I could ask, Nesta demanded, "What happened?"

Rhys glanced to me, then to Amren, who had shot to her feet and was now watching us with the same expression as Nesta's. My mate said to my sister, "There was a battle. We won."

"We know that," Amren said, her small feet near-silent on the rugs as she strode for us. "What happened with Tarquin?"

Mor took a breath to say something about Varian that would likely not end well for any of us, so I cut in, "Well, he didn't try to slaughter us on sight, so . . . things went decently?"

Rhys gave me a bemused look. "The royal family remains alive and well. Tarquin's armada suffered losses, but Cresseida and Varian were unscathed."

Something tight in Amren's face seemed to relax at the words—his careful, diplomatic words.

But Nesta was glancing between us all, her back still stiff, mouth a thin line. "Where is he?"

"Who?" Rhys crooned.

"Cassian."

I didn't think I'd ever heard his name from her lips. Cassian had always been *him* or *that one*. And Nesta had been . . . pacing in the foyer.

As if she was worried.

I opened my mouth, but Mor beat me to it. "He's busy."

I'd never heard her voice so . . . sharp. Icy.

Nesta held Mor's stare. Her jaw tightened, then relaxed, then tightened—as if fighting some battle to keep questions in. Mor didn't drop her gaze.

Mor had never seemed ruffled by mention of Cassian's past lovers. Perhaps because they'd never meant much—not in the ways that counted. But if the Illyrian warrior no longer stood as a physical and emotional buffer between her and Azriel . . . And worse, if the person who caused that vacancy was Nesta . . .

Mor said flatly, "When he gets back, keep your forked tongue behind your teeth."

My heart leaped into a furious beat, my arms slack at my sides at the insult, the threat.

But Rhys said, "Mor."

She slowly—so slowly—looked at him.

There was nothing but uncompromising will in Rhys's face. "We now leave for the meeting in three days. Send out dispatches to the other High Lords to inform them. And I'm done debating where to meet. Pick a place and be done with it."

She stared him down for a heartbeat, then dragged her gaze back to my sister.

Nesta's face had not altered, the coldness limning it unbending. She was so still she seemed to barely be breathing. But she did not balk. She did not avert her eyes from the Morrigan.

Mor vanished with hardly a blink.

Nesta only turned and headed for the sitting room, where I noticed books had been laid on the low-lying table before the hearth.

Amren flowed in behind her, tossing a backward look over a shoulder at Rhys. The motion shifted her gray blouse enough that I caught the sparkle of red peeking beneath the fabric.

The necklace of rubies that she wore, hidden, beneath her shirt. Gifted from Varian.

But Rhys nodded to Amren, and the female asked my sister, "Where were we?"

Nesta sat in the armchair, holding herself tightly enough that the whites of her knuckles arced through her skin. "You were explaining how the territory lines were formed between courts."

The words were distant—brittle. And—*They've also taken up history lessons?*

I'm as shocked as you are that the house is still standing.

I swallowed my laugh, linking my arm through his and tugging him down the hall. It had been a while since I'd seen him so . . . dirty. We both needed a bath, but there was something I had to do first. Needed to do.

Behind us, Amren murmured to Nesta, "Cassian has gone to war many times, girl. He isn't general of Rhys's forces for nothing. This battle was a skirmish compared to what lies ahead. He's likely visiting the families of the fallen as we speak. He'll be back before the meeting."

Nesta said, "I don't care."

At least she was talking again.

I halted Rhys halfway down the hall.

With so many listening ears in the house, I said down the bond, *Take me to the Prison. Right now.*

Rhys asked no questions.

CHAPTER
40

I had no bone to bring with me. And though every step up that hillside and then down into the dark ripped and weighed on me, I kept moving. Kept planting one foot in front of the other.

I had the feeling Rhys did the same.

Standing before the Bone Carver two hours later, the ancient death-god still wearing my would-be son's skin, I said, "Find another object that you desire."

The Carver's violet eyes flared. "Why does the High Lord linger in the hall?"

"He has little interest in seeing you."

Partially true. Rhys had wondered if the blow to his pride would work in our favor.

"You reek of blood—and death." The Carver breathed in a great lungful of air. Of my scent.

"Pick another object than the Ouroboros," was all I said.

Hybern knew about our histories, our would-be allies. There remained a shred of hope that he would not see the Carver coming.

"I desire nothing else than my window to the world."

I avoided the urge to clench my hands into fists.

"I could offer you so many other things." My voice turned low, honeyed.

"You are afraid to claim the mirror." The Bone Carver angled his head. "Why?"

"You are not afraid of it?"

"No." A little smile. He leaned to the side. "Are you frightened of it, too, Rhysand?"

My mate didn't bother to answer from the hall, though he did come to lean against the threshold, crossing his arms. The Carver sighed at the sight of him—the dirt and blood and wrinkled clothes, and said, "Oh, I much prefer you bloodied up."

"Pick something else," I replied. *And not a fool's errand this time.*

"What would you give me? Riches do me no good down here. Power holds no sway over the stone." He chuckled. "What about your firstborn?" A secret smile as he gestured with that small boy's hand to himself.

Rhys's attention slid to me, surprise—surprise and something deeper, more tender—flickering on his face. *Not just any boy, then.*

My cheeks heated. *No. Not just any boy.*

"It is rude, Majesties, to speak when no one can hear you."

I sliced a glare toward the Carver. "There is nothing else, then." *Nothing else that won't break me if I so much as look upon it?*

"Bring me the Ouroboros and I am yours. You have my word."

I weighed the beatific expression on the Carver's face before I strode out.

"Where is my bone?" The demand cracked through the gloom.

I kept walking. But Rhys chucked something at him. "From lunch."

The Carver's hiss of outrage as a chicken bone skittered over the floor followed us out.

In silence, we began the trek up through the Prison. The mirror—I'd have to find some way to get it. After the meeting. Just in case it did indeed . . . destroy me.

What does he look like?

The question was soft—tentative. I knew who he meant.

I interlaced my fingers through Rhysand's and squeezed tightly. *Let me show you.*

And as we walked through the darkness, toward that distant, still-hidden light, I did.

✢

We were starving by the time we returned to the town house. And since neither of us felt like waiting for food to be prepared, Rhys and I headed right for the kitchen, passing by Amren and Nesta with little more than a wave.

My mouth was already watering as Rhys shouldered open the swinging door into the kitchen.

But we beheld what was within and halted.

Elain stood between Nuala and Cerridwen at the long worktable. All three of them covered in flour. Some sort of doughy mess on the surface before them.

The two handmaiden-spies instantly bowed to Rhys, and Elain—

There was a slight sparkle in her brown eyes.

As if she'd been enjoying herself with them.

Nuala swallowed hard. "The lady said she was hungry, so we went to make her something. But—she said she wanted to learn how, so . . ." Hands wreathed in shadows lifted in a helpless gesture, flour drifting off them like veils of snow. "We're making bread."

Elain was glancing between all of us, and as her eyes began to shutter, I gave her a broad smile and said, "I hope it'll be done soon—I'm starved."

Elain offered a faint smile in return and nodded.

She was hungry. She was . . . doing something. *Learning* something.

"We're going to bathe," I announced, even as my stomach grumbled. "We'll leave you to your baking."

I tugged Rhys into the hall before they'd finished saying good-bye, the kitchen door swinging shut behind us.

I put a hand on my chest, leaning against the wood panels of the stair wall. Rhys's hand covered my own a heartbeat later.

"That was what I felt," he said, "when I saw you smile that night we dined along the Sidra."

I leaned forward, resting my brow against his chest, right over his heart. "She still has a long way to go."

"We all do."

He stroked a hand over my back. I leaned into the touch, savoring his warmth and strength.

For long minutes, we stood there. Until I said, "Let's go find somewhere to eat—outside."

"Hmmm." He showed no sign of letting go.

I looked up at last. Found his eyes shining with that familiar, wicked light. "I think I'm hungry for something else," he purred.

My toes curled in my boots, but I lifted my brows and said coolly, "Oh?"

Rhys nipped at my earlobe, then whispered in my ear as he winnowed us up to our bedroom, where two plates of food now waited on the desk. "I owe you for last night, mate."

He gave me the courtesy, at least, of letting me pick what he consumed first: me or the food.

I picked wisely.

☩

Nesta was waiting at the breakfast table the next morning.

Not for me, I realized as her gaze slipped over me as if I were no more than a servant. But for someone else.

I kept my mouth shut, not bothering to tell her Cassian was still up at the war-camps. If she wouldn't ask . . . I wasn't getting in the middle of it.

Not when Amren claimed that my sister was close—so close—to grasping whatever skill was involved in potentially patching up the wall. If she would only *unleash* herself, Amren said. I didn't dare suggest that perhaps the world wasn't quite ready for that.

I ate my breakfast in silence, my fork scraping across the plate. Amren said she was close to finding what we needed in the Book, too— whatever spell my sister would wield. How Amren knew, I had no idea. It didn't seem wise to ask.

Nesta only spoke when I rose to my feet. "You're going to that meeting in two days."

"Yes."

I braced myself for whatever she intended to say.

Nesta glanced toward the front windows, as if still waiting, still watching.

"You went off into battle. Without a second thought. Why?"

"Because I had to. Because people needed help."

Her blue-gray eyes were near-silver in the trickle of morning light. But Nesta said nothing else, and after waiting for another moment, I left, winnowing up to the House for my flying lesson with Azriel.

CHAPTER
41

The next two days were so busy that the lesson with Azriel was the only time I trained with him. The spymaster had returned from dispatching the messages Mor had written about the meeting moving up. They had agreed on the date, at least. But Mor's declaration of the spot, despite her unyielding language, had been universally rejected. Thus continued the endless back-and-forth between courts.

Under the Mountain had once been their neutral meeting place.

Even if it hadn't been sealed, no one was inclined to meet there now.

So the debate raged about who would host the gathering of all the High Lords.

Well, six of them. Beron, at last, had deigned to join. But no word had come from the Spring Court, though we knew the messages had been received.

All of us would go—save Amren and Nesta, who the former insisted needed to practice more. Especially when Amren had found a passage in the Book last night that *might* be what we needed to fix the wall.

With only hours to spare the evening before, it was finally agreed that the meeting would take place in the Dawn Court. It was close enough to the middle of the land, and since Kallias, High Lord of Winter, would not allow anyone into his territory after the horrors Amarantha had wrought upon its people, it was the only other area flanking that neutral middle land.

Rhys and Thesan, High Lord of the Dawn Court, were on decent terms. Dawn was mostly neutral in any conflict, but as one of the three Solar Courts, their allegiance always leaned toward each other. Not as strong an ally as Helion Spell-Cleaver in the Day Court, but strong enough.

It didn't stop Rhys, Mor, and Azriel from gathering around the dining table at the town house the night before to go over every kernel of information they'd ever learned about Thesan's palace—about possible pitfalls and traps. And escape routes.

It was an effort not to pace, not to ask if perhaps the risks outweighed the benefits. So much had gone wrong in Hybern. So much was going wrong throughout the world. Every time Azriel spoke, I heard his roar of pain as that bolt went through his chest. Every time Mor countered an argument, I saw her pale-faced and backing away from the king. Every time Rhys asked for my opinion, I saw him kneeling in his friends' blood, begging the king not to sever our bond.

Nesta and Amren paused their practicing in the sitting room every so often so that the latter could chime in with some bit of advice or warning regarding the meeting. Or so that Amren could snap at Nesta to concentrate, to push harder. While she herself combed through the Book.

A few more days, Amren declared when Nesta at last went upstairs, complaining of a headache. A few more days, and my sister, through whatever mysterious power, might be able to *do* something. That is, Amren added, if *she* could crack that promising section of the Book in time. And with that, the dark-haired female bid us good night—to go read until her eyes were bleeding, she claimed.

Considering how awful the Book was, I wasn't entirely sure if she was joking.

The others weren't, either.

I barely touched my dinner. And I barely slept that night, twisting in the sheets until Rhys woke and patiently listened to me murmur my fears until they were nothing but shadows.

Dawn broke, and as I dressed, the morning unfurled into a sunny, dry day.

Though we would be going to the meeting as we truly were, our usual attire remained the same: Rhys in his preferred black jacket and pants, Azriel and Cassian in their Illyrian armor, all seven Siphons polished and gleaming. Mor had forgone her usual red gown for one of midnight blue. It was cut with the same revealing panels and flowing, gauzy skirts, but there was something . . . restrained in it. Regal. A princess of the realm.

The usual attire—except my own.

I had not found a new gown. For there was no other gown that could top the one I now wore as I stood in the foyer while the clock on the sitting room mantel struck eleven.

Rhys hadn't yet come downstairs, and there was no sign of Amren or Nesta to see us off. We'd gathered a few minutes earlier, but . . . I looked down at myself again. Even in the warm faelight of the foyer, the gown glittered and gleamed like a fresh-cut jewel.

We had taken my gown from Starfall and refashioned it, adding sheer silk panels to the back shoulders, the glittering material like woven starlight as it flowed behind me in lieu of a veil or cape. If Rhysand was Night Triumphant, I was the star that only glowed thanks to his darkness, the light only visible because of him.

I scowled up the stairs. That is, if he bothered to show up on time.

My hair, Nuala had swept into an ornate, elegant arc across my head, and in front of it . . .

I caught Cassian glancing at me for the third time in less than a minute and demanded, "What?"

His lips twitched at the corners. "You just look so . . ."

"Here we go," Mor muttered from where she picked at her red-tinted nails against the stair banister. Rings glinted at every knuckle, on every finger; stacks of bracelets tinkled against each other on either wrist.

"Official," Cassian said with an incredulous look in her direction. He waved a Siphon-topped hand to me. "*Fancy*."

"Over five hundred years old," Mor said, shaking her head sadly, "a skilled warrior and general, famous throughout territories, and complimenting ladies is still something he finds next to impossible. Remind me why we bring you on diplomatic meetings?"

Azriel, wreathed in shadows by the front door, chuckled quietly. Cassian shot him a glare. "I don't see *you* spouting poetry, brother."

Azriel crossed his arms, still smiling faintly. "I don't need to resort to it."

Mor let out a crow of laughter, and I snorted, earning a jab in the ribs from Cassian. I batted his hand away, but refrained from the shove I wanted to give him, only because it was the first I'd seen of him since Adriata and shadows still dimmed his eyes—and because of the precarious-feeling thing atop my head.

The crown.

Rhys had crowned me at each and every meeting and function we'd had, long before I was his mate, long before I was his High Lady. Even Under the Mountain.

I'd never questioned the tiaras and diadems and crowns that Nuala or Cerridwen wove into my hair. Never objected to them—even before things between us had been this way. But this one . . . I peered up the stairs as Rhys's strolling, unhurried footsteps thudded on the carpet.

This crown was heavier. Not unwelcome, but . . . strange. And as Rhys appeared at the top of the stairs, resplendent in that black jacket, his wings out and gleaming as if he'd polished them, I was again in that room he'd brought me to late last night, after I'd awoken him with my thrashing and twisting in bed.

It was contained a level above the library in the House of Wind, and warded with so many spells that it had taken him a few moments to work through them. Only he and I—and any future offspring, he added with a soft smile—were able to enter. Unless we brought guests.

The chamber was a cool, chill black—as if we'd stepped inside the mind of some sleeping beast. And within its round space gleamed glittering islands of light. Of jewels.

Ten thousand years' worth of treasure.

It was neatly organized, in podiums and open drawers and busts and racks.

"The family jewels," Rhys said with a devious grin. "Some of the pieces we don't like are kept at the Court of Nightmares, just so they don't get pissy and because we sometimes loan them to Mor's family, but these . . . these are for the family."

He led me past displays that sparkled like small constellations, the worth of each . . . Even as a merchant's daughter, I could not calculate the worth of any of it.

And toward the back of the chamber, shrouded in a heavier darkness . . .

I'd heard of catacombs on the continent, where skulls of beloved or infamous people were kept in little alcoves—dozens or hundreds of them to a wall.

The concept here was the same: carved into the rock was an entire wall of crowns. They each had their own resting place, lined with black velvet, each illuminated by—

"Glowworms," Rhys told me as the tiny, bluish globs crusted in the arches of each nook seemed to glitter like the entire night sky. In fact . . . What I'd taken for small faelights in the ceiling high above . . . It was all glowworms. Pale blue and turquoise, their light as silken as moonlight, illumining the jewels with their ancient, silent fire.

"Pick one," Rhys whispered in my ear.

"A glowworm?"

He nipped at my earlobe. "Smartass." He steered me back toward the wall of crowns, each wholly different—as individual as skulls. "Pick whichever crown you like."

"I can't just—take one."

"You most certainly can. They belong to you."

I lifted a brow. "They don't—not really."

"By law and tradition, this is all yours. Sell it, melt it, wear them—do whatever you want."

"You don't care about it?" I gestured to the trove worth more than most kingdoms.

"Oh, I have favorite pieces that I might convince you to spare, but . . . This is yours. Every last piece of it."

Our eyes met, and I knew he, too, recalled the words that I'd whispered to him months ago. That every piece of my still-healing heart belonged to him. I smiled, and brushed a hand down his arm before approaching the wall of crowns.

I had been terrified once, in Tamlin's court, of being given a crown. Had dreaded it. And I supposed that I indeed had never fretted over it when it came to Rhys. As if some small part of me had always known that this was where I was meant to be: at his side, as his equal. His queen.

Rhys inclined his head as if to say yes—he saw and understood and had always known.

Now striding down the town house stairs, Rhys's attention went right to that crown atop my head. And the emotion that rippled across his face was enough to make even Mor and Cassian look away.

I'd let the crown call to me. I hadn't picked it for style or comfort, but for the draw I felt to it, as if it were that ring in the Weaver's cottage.

My crown was crafted of silver and diamond, all fashioned into swirls of stars and various phases of the moon. Its arching apex held aloft a crescent moon of solid diamond, flanked by two exploding stars. And with the glittering dress from Starfall . . .

Rhys stepped off the stairs and took my hand.

Night Triumphant—and the Stars Eternal.

If he was the sweet, terrifying darkness, I was the glittering light that only his shadows could make clear.

"I thought you were leaving," Nesta's voice cut in from atop the stairs.

I braced myself, dragging my attention away from Rhys.

Nesta was in a gown of darkest blue, no jewelry to be seen, her hair swept up and unadorned as well. I supposed that with her stunning beauty, she needed no ornamentation. It would have been like putting jewelry on a lion. But for her to be dressed like that . . .

She strode down the stairs, and when the others were silent, I realized . . .

I tried not to look too obvious as I glanced at Cassian.

They had not seen each other since Adriata.

But the warrior only gave her a cursory once-over and turned toward Azriel to say something. Mor was watching both carefully—the warning she'd given my sister ringing silently between them. And Nesta, Mother damn it all, seemed to remember. Seemed to rein in whatever words she'd been about to spit and just approached me.

And nearly made my heart stop dead with shock as she said, "You look beautiful."

I blinked at her.

Mor said, "That, Cassian, was what you were attempting to say."

He grumbled something we chose not to hear. I said to Nesta, "Thank you. You do as well."

Nesta only shrugged.

I pushed, "Why *are* you dressed so nicely? Shouldn't you be practicing with Amren?"

I felt Cassian's attention slide to us, felt them all look as Nesta said, "I'm going with you."

CHAPTER
42

No one said anything.

Nesta only lifted her chin. "I . . ." I'd never seen her stumble for words. "I do not want to be remembered as a coward."

"No one would say that," I offered quietly.

"I would." Nesta surveyed us all, her gaze jumping past Cassian. Not to slight him, but . . . avoid answering the look he was giving her. Approval—more. "It was some distant thing," she said. "War. Battle. It . . . it's not anymore. I will help, if I can. If it means . . . telling them what happened."

"You've given enough," I said, my dress rustling as I braved a solitary step toward her. "Amren claimed you were close to mastering whatever skill you need. You should stay—focus on that."

"No." The word was steady, clear. "A day or two delay with my training won't make any difference. Perhaps by the time we return, Amren will have decoded that spell in the Book." She shrugged with a shoulder. "You went off to battle for a court you barely know—who barely see you as friends. Amren showed me the blood ruby. And when I asked you why . . . you said because it was the right thing. People needed help." Her throat bobbed. "No one is going to fight to save the humans beneath the wall. No one cares. But I do." She toyed with a fold in her dress. "I do."

Rhys stepped up to my side. "As High Lady, Feyre is no longer my emissary to the human world." He gave Nesta a tentative smile. "Want the job?"

Nesta's face yielded nothing, but I could have sworn some spark flared. "Consider this meeting a trial basis. And I'll make you pay through the teeth for my services."

Rhys sketched a bow. "I would expect nothing less of an Archeron sister." I poked him in the ribs, and he huffed a laugh. "Welcome to the court," he said to her. "You're about to have one hell of a first day."

And to my eternal shock, a smile tugged at Nesta's mouth.

"No going back now," Cassian said to Rhys, gesturing to his wings.

Rhys slid his hands into his pockets. "I figure it's time for the world to know who really has the largest wingspan."

Cassian laughed, and even Azriel smiled. Mor gave me a look that had me biting my lip to keep from howling.

"Twenty gold marks says there's a fight in the first hour," Cassian said, still not really looking at Nesta.

"Thirty, and I say within forty-five minutes," Mor said, crossing her arms.

"You do remember there are vows and wards of neutrality," Rhys said mildly.

"You lot don't need fists or magic to fight," Mor chirped.

Azriel said from the door, "Fifty, and I say within thirty minutes. Started by Autumn."

Rhys rolled his eyes. "Try *not* to look like you're all gambling on them. And no cheating by provoking fights." Their answering grins were anything but reassuring. Rhys sighed. "A hundred marks on a fight within fifteen minutes."

Nesta let out a soft snort. But they all looked to me, waiting.

I shrugged. "Rhys and I are a team. He can gamble away our money on this bullshit."

They all looked deeply offended.

Rhys looped his elbow through mine. "A queen in appearance—"

"Don't even finish that," I said.

He laughed. "Shall we?"

He'd winnow me in, Mor would now take Cassian *and* Nesta, and Azriel would carry himself. Rhys glanced toward the sitting room clock and gave the shadowsinger a nod.

Azriel instantly vanished. First to arrive—first to see if any trap awaited.

In silence, we waited. One minute. Two.

Then Rhys blew out a breath and said, "Clear." He threaded his fingers through mine, gripping tightly.

Mor sagged a bit, jewelry glinting with the movement, and went to take Cassian's arm.

But he'd at last approached Nesta. And as the world began to turn to shadows and wind, I saw Cassian tower over my sister, saw her chin lift defiantly, and heard him growl, "Hello, Nesta."

Rhys seemed to halt his winnowing as my sister said, "So you're alive."

Cassian bared his teeth in a feral grin, wings flaring slightly. "Were you hoping otherwise?"

Mor was watching—watching so closely, every muscle tense. She again reached for his arm, but Cassian angled out of reach, not tearing his eyes from Nesta's blazing gaze.

Nesta blurted, "You didn't come to—" She stopped herself.

The world seemed to go utterly still at that interrupted sentence, nothing and no one more so than Cassian. He scanned her face as if furiously reading some battle report.

Mor just watched as Cassian took Nesta's slim hand in his own, interlacing their fingers. As he folded in his wings and blindly reached his other hand back toward Mor in a silent order to transport them.

Cassian's eyes did not leave Nesta's; nor did hers leave his. There was no warmth, no tenderness on either of their faces. Only that raging intensity, that blend of contempt and understanding and fire.

Rhys began to winnow us again, and just as the dark wind swept in, I heard Cassian say to Nesta, his voice low and rough, "The next time, Emissary, I'll come say hello."

‡

I'd learned enough from Rhys about what to expect of the Dawn Court, but even the vistas he'd painted for me didn't do the sight justice.

It was the clouds I saw first.

Enormous clouds drifting in the cobalt sky, soft and magnanimous, still tinged by the rose remnants of sunrise, their round edges gilded with the golden light. The dewy freshness of morning lingered in the balmy air as we peered up at the mountain-palace spiraling into the heavens above.

If the palace above the Court of Nightmares had been crafted of moonstone, this was made from . . . sunstone. I didn't have a word for the near-opalescent golden stone that seemed to hold the gleaming of a thousand sunrises within it.

Steps and balconies and archways and verandas and bridges linked the towers and gilded domes of the palace, periwinkle morning glories climbing the pillars and neatly cut blocks of stone to drink in the gilded mists wafting by.

Wafting by, because the mountain on which the palace stood . . . There was a reason I beheld the clouds first.

The veranda that we'd appeared on was empty, save for Azriel and a slim-hipped attendant in the gold-and-ruby livery of Dawn. Light, loose robes—layered and yet flattering.

The male bowed, his brown skin smooth with youth and beauty. "This way, High Lord."

Even his voice was as lovely as the first glimmer of gold on the horizon. Rhys returned his bow with a shallow nod, and offered his arm to me.

Mor muttered behind us, falling into rank with Nesta at her side, "If you ever feel like building a new house, Rhys, let's use this one for inspiration."

Rhys threw her an incredulous look over a shoulder. Cassian and Azriel snorted softly.

I glanced to Nesta as the attendant led us not to the archway beyond the veranda, but the spiral stairs climbing upward—along the bare face of a tower.

Nesta seemed as out of place as all of us—save Mor—but . . .

That was awe on my sister's face.

Utter awe at the castle in the clouds, at the verdant countryside rippling away far below, speckled with red-roofed little villages and broad, sparkling rivers. A lush, eternal countryside, rich with the weight of summer upon it.

And I wondered if my face had appeared like that—the day I'd first seen Velaris. The mix of awe and anger and the realization that the world was large, and beautiful, and sometimes so overwhelming in its wonder that it was impossible to drink it down all at once.

There were other palaces within Dawn's territory—set in small cities that specialized in tinkering and clockwork and clever things. Here . . . beyond those little villages nestled in the country hills, there was no industry. Nothing beyond the palace and the sky and the clouds.

We ascended the spiral stairs, the drop off the too-near edge falling away into warm-colored rock peppered with clusters of pale roses and fluffy, magenta peonies. A beautiful, colorful death.

Every step had me bracing myself as we wound up and up the tower, Rhys's grip on my hand unwavering.

The wings remained out. He did not falter a single step.

His eyes slid to mine, amused and questioning. He said down the bond, *And do* you *think I need to redecorate our home?*

We passed open-air chambers full of fat, silk pillows and plush carpets, passed windows whose panes were arranged in colorful medleys, passed urns overflowing with lavender and fountains gurgling clearest water under the mild rays of the sun.

It's not a competition, I trilled to him.

His hand tightened on mine. *Well, even if Thesan has a prettier palace, I'm the only one blessed with a High Lady at my side.*

I couldn't help my blush.

Especially as Rhys added, *Tonight, I want you to wear that crown to bed. Only the crown.*

Scoundrel.

Always.

I smiled, and he leaned in smoothly to brush a kiss to my cheek.

Mor muttered a plea for mercy from mates.

Muted voices reached us from the open-air chamber atop the sunstone tower—some deep, some sharp, some lilting—before we finished the last rotation around it, the arched, glassless windows offering no barrier to the conversation within.

Three others are here already, Rhys warned me, and I had the feeling that was what Azriel was now murmuring to Mor and Cassian. *Helion, Kallias, and Thesan.*

The High Lords of Day, Winter, and our host, Dawn.

Meaning Autumn and Summer—Beron and Tarquin—had not arrived yet. Or Spring.

I still doubted Tamlin would come at all, but Beron and Tarquin . . . Perhaps the battle had changed Tarquin's mind. And Beron was awful enough to perhaps have sided with Hybern already, regardless of Eris's manipulating.

I caught the bob of Rhys's throat as we cleared the final steps to the open doorway. A long bridge connected the other half of the tower to the palace interior, its rails drooping with dawn-pale wisteria. I wondered if the others had been led up these stairs, or if it was somehow meant to be an insult.

Shields up? Rhys asked, but I knew he was aware mine had been raised since Velaris.

Just as I was aware that he'd put a shield, mental and physical, around all of us, terms of peace or no.

And though his face was calm, his shoulders thrown back, I said, *I see all of you, Rhys. And there is not one part that I do not love with everything that I am.*

His hand squeezed mine in answer before he laid my fingers on his arm, raising it enough that we must have painted a rather courtly portrait as we entered the chamber.

You bow to no one, was all he replied.

CHAPTER
43

The chamber was and was not what I expected. Deep-cushioned oak chairs had been arranged in a massive circle in the heart of the room— enough for all the High Lords and their delegates. Some, I realized, had been shaped to accommodate wings.

It seemed it was not unusual. For clustered around a beautiful, slender male who I immediately remembered from Under the Mountain were winged Fae. If the Illyrians had batlike wings, these . . . they were like birds.

The Peregryns are distantly related to Drakon's Seraphim people and provide Thesan with a small aerial legion, Rhys said to me of the muscular, golden-armored males and females gathered. *The male on his left is his captain and lover.* Indeed, the handsome male stood just a tad closer to his High Lord, one hand on the fine sword at his side. *No mating bond yet*, Rhys went on, *but I think Thesan didn't dare acknowledge it while Amarantha reigned. She delighted in ripping out their feathers—one by one. She made a dress out of them once.*

I tried not to wince as we stepped onto the polished marble floor, the stone warmed with the sun streaming through the open archways. The others had looked toward us, some murmuring at the sight of

Rhys's wings, but my attention went to the true gem of the chamber: the reflection pool.

Rather than a table occupying the space between that circle of chairs, a shallow, circular reflection pool was carved into the floor itself. Its dark water was laden with pink and gold water lilies, the pads broad and flat as a male's hand, and beneath them pumpkin-and-ivory fish lazily swam about.

This, I admitted to Rhys, *I might need to have.*

A wry pulse of humor down the bond. *I'll make a note of it for your birthday.*

More wisteria twined about the pillars flanking the space, and along the tables set against the few walls, bunches of wine-colored peonies unfurled their silken layers. Between the vases, platters and baskets of food had been laid—small pastries, cured meats, and garlands of fruit beckoned before sweating pewter ewers of some refreshment.

Then there were the three High Lords themselves.

We were not the only ones to have dressed well.

Rhys and I halted halfway through the space.

I knew them all—remembered them from those months Under the Mountain. Rhys had taught me their histories while we'd trained. I wondered if they sensed their power within me as their attention slid between us.

Thesan glided forward, his embroidered, exquisite shoes silent on the floor. His tunic was tight-fitting through his slender chest, but flowing pants—much like those Amren favored—whispered with movement as he approached. His brown skin and hair were kissed with gold, as if the sunrise had permanently gilded them, but his upswept eyes, the rich brown of freshly tilled fields, were his loveliest feature. He paused a few feet away, taking in Rhys and me, our entourage. The wings that Rhys kept folded behind him.

"Welcome," Thesan said, his voice as deep and rich as those eyes. His lover monitored our every breath from a few feet behind, no doubt realizing our own companions were doing the same behind us. "Or," Thesan mused, "since you've called this meeting, perhaps you should be doing the welcoming?"

A faint smile ghosted Rhys's perfect face, shadows twining between the strands of his hair. He'd loosened the damper on his power—just a bit. They all had. "I may have requested the meeting, Thesan, but you were the one gracious enough to offer up your beautiful residence."

Thesan gave a nod of thanks, perhaps deeming it impolite to inquire about Rhysand's newly revealed wings, then turned to me.

We stared at each other while my companions bowed behind me. As a High Lord's wife should have done with them.

Yet I simply stood. And stared.

Rhys did not interfere—not at this first test.

Dawn—the gift of healing. It was his gift that had allowed me to save Rhysand's life. That had sent me to the Suriel, that day I had learned the truth that would alter my eternity.

I offered Thesan a restrained smile. "Your home is lovely."

But Thesan's attention had gone to the tattoo. I knew he realized it the moment he noticed the ink covered the wrong hand. Then the crown atop my head. His brows flicked up.

Rhys only shrugged.

The other two High Lords had approached now.

"Kallias," Rhys said to the white-haired one, whose skin was so pale it looked frozen. Even his crushing blue eyes seemed like chips hewn from a glacier as he studied Rhys's wings and seemed to instantly dismiss them. He wore a jacket of royal blue embroidered with silver thread, its collar and sleeves dusted with white rabbit fur. I would have thought it too warm for the mild day, especially the fur-lined, knee-high brown boots, but given the utter iciness of his expression, perhaps his blood ran frozen. A trio of similarly colored High Fae remained in their seats, one of them a stunning young female who looked right at Mor—and grinned.

Mor returned the beam, hopping from one foot to another as Kallias opened his mouth—

And then my friend squealed.

Squealed.

Both females hurtled for each other, and Mor's squeal had turned to a quiet sob as she flung her arms around the slender stranger and hugged her tight. The female's own arms were shaking as she gripped Mor.

Then they were laughing and crying and dancing around each other, pausing to study each other's faces, to wipe away tears, and then embracing again.

"You look the same," the stranger was saying, beaming from ear to ear. "I think that's the same dress I saw you in—"

"*You* look the same! Wearing fur in the middle of summer—how utterly typical—"

"You brought the usual suspects, it seems—"

"Thankfully, the company has been improved by some new arrivals—" Mor waved me over. It had been ages since I'd seen her shining so brightly. "Viviane, meet Feyre. Feyre, meet Viviane—Kallias's wife."

I glanced at Thesan and Kallias, the latter of whom watched his wife and Mor with raised brows. "I tried to suggest she stay at home," Kallias said drily, "but she threatened to freeze my balls off."

Rhys let out a dark chuckle. "Sounds familiar."

I threw him a glare over a sparkling shoulder—just in time to see the smirk fade from Kallias's face as he truly took in Rhys. Not just the wings this time. My mate's own amusement dimmed, some thread of tension going taut between him and Kallias—

But I'd reached Mor and Viviane, and wiped the curiosity from my face as I shook the female's hand, surprised to find it warm.

Her silver hair glittered in the sun like fresh snow. "Wife," Viviane said, clicking her tongue. "You know, it still sounds strange to me. Every time someone says it, I keep looking over my shoulder as if it'll be someone else."

Kallias said to none of us in particular, from where he remained facing Rhys, stiff-backed, "I have yet to decide if I find it insulting. Since she says it every day."

Viviane stuck out her tongue at him.

But Mor gripped her shoulder and squeezed. "It's about time."

A blush stained Viviane's pale face. "Yes, well—everything was different after Under the Mountain." Her sapphire eyes slid to mine and she bowed her head. "Thank you—for returning my mate to me."

"Mates?" Mor fizzed, glancing between them. "Married *and* mates?"

"You two do realize that this is a serious meeting," Rhys said.

"And that the fish in the pool are very sensitive to high-pitched sounds," Kallias added.

Viviane gave them both a vulgar gesture that made me instantly like her.

Rhys looked to Kallias with what I assumed was some sort of long-suffering male expression. But the High Lord did not return it.

He only stared at Rhys, amusement again gone—that coldness settling in across his face.

There had been . . . tension with the Winter Court, Mor had explained when they'd rescued Lucien and me on the ice. A lingering anger over something that had occurred Under the Mountain—

But the third High Lord had at last approached from across the pool.

My father had once bought and traded a gold and lapis lazuli pendant that hailed from the ruins of an arid southeastern kingdom, where the Fae had ruled as gods amid swaying date palms and sand-swept palaces. I'd been mesmerized by the colors, the artistry, but more interested in the shipment of myrrh and figs that had come with it—a few of the latter my father had snuck to me while I loitered in his office. Even now, I could still taste their sweetness on my tongue, still smell that earthy scent, and I couldn't quite explain why, but . . . I remembered that ancient necklace and those exquisite delicacies as he prowled toward us.

His clothes had been formed from a single bolt of white fabric—not a robe, not a dress, but rather something in between, pleated and draped over his muscular body. A golden cuff of an upright serpent encircled one powerful bicep, offsetting his near-glowing dark skin, and a radiant crown of golden spikes—the rays of the sun, I realized—glistened atop his onyx hair.

The sun personified. Powerful, lazy with grace, capable of kindness and wrath. Nearly as beautiful as Rhysand. And somehow—somehow colder than Kallias.

His High Fae entourage was almost as large as ours, clad in similar robes of varying rich dyes—cobalt and crimson and amethyst—some with expertly kohl-lined eyes, all of them fit and gleaming with health.

But perhaps the physical power of them—of *him* was the sleight of hand.

For Helion's other title was Spell-Cleaver, and his one thousand libraries were rumored to contain the knowledge of the world. Perhaps all that knowledge had made him too aware, too cold behind those bright eyes.

Or perhaps that had come after Amarantha had looted some of those libraries for herself. I wondered if he'd reclaimed what she'd taken—or if he mourned what she'd burned.

Even Mor and Viviane halted their reunion as Helion stopped a wise distance away.

It was his power that had gotten my friends out of Hybern. His power that made me glow whenever Rhys and I were tangled in each other and every heartbeat ached with mirth.

Helion jerked his square chin to Rhys, the only one of them, it seemed, not surprised by my mate's wings. But his eyes—a striking amber—fell on me.

"Does Tamlin know what she is?"

His voice was indeed colder than Kallias's. And the question—so carefully worded.

Rhys drawled, "If you mean beautiful and clever, then yes—I think he does."

Helion leveled a flat look at him. "Does he know she is your mate—and High Lady?"

"*High Lady?*" Viviane squeaked, but Mor shushed her, drawing her away to whisper.

Thesan and Kallias took me in. Slowly.

Cassian and Azriel casually slid closer, no more than a night breeze.

"If he arrives," Rhys said smoothly, "I suppose we'll find out."

Helion let out a dark laugh. Dangerous—he was utterly lethal, this High Lord kissed by the sun. "I always liked you, Rhysand."

Thesan stepped forward, ever the good host. For that laugh indeed promised violence. His lover and the other Peregryns seemed to shift into defensive positions—either to guard their High Lord or simply to remind us that we were guests in their home.

But Helion's attention snagged on Nesta.

Lingered.

She only stared right back at him. Unruffled, unimpressed.

"Who is your guest?" the High Lord of Day asked a bit too quietly for my liking.

Cassian revealed nothing—not even a glimmer that he *knew* Nesta. But he didn't move an inch from his casual defensive position. Neither did Azriel.

"She is my sister, and our emissary to the human lands," I said at last to him, stepping to her side. "And she will tell her story when the others are here."

"She is Fae."

"No shit," Viviane muttered under her breath, and Mor's snort was cut off as Kallias raised his brows at them. Helion ignored them.

"Who Made her?" Thesan asked politely, angling his head.

Nesta surveyed Thesan. Then Helion. Then Kallias.

"Hybern did," she said simply. Not a flicker of fear in her eyes, in her upraised chin.

Stunned silence.

But I'd had enough of my sister being ogled. I linked elbows with her, heading toward the low-backed chairs that I assumed were for us. "They threw her in the Cauldron," I said. "Along with my other sister, Elain." I sat, placing Nesta beside me, and gazed at the three assembled High Lords without an inch of manners or niceness or flattery. "After the High Priestess Ianthe and Tamlin sold out Prythian and my family to them."

Nesta nodded her silent confirmation.

Helion's eyes blazed like a forge. "That is a heavy accusation to make—especially of your former lover."

"It is no accusation," I said, folding my hands in my lap. "We were all there. And now we're going to do something about it."

Pride flickered down the bond.

And then Viviane muttered to Kallias, jabbing him in the ribs, "Why can't *I* be High Lady as well?"

⸸

The others arrived late.

We took our seats around the reflection pool, Thesan's impeccably mannered attendants bringing us plates of food and goblets of exotic juices from the tables against the wall. Conversation halted and flowed, Mor and Viviane sitting next to each other to catch up on what seemed like fifty years' worth of gossip.

Viviane had not been Under the Mountain. As her childhood friend, Kallias had been protective of her to a fault over the years—had placed the sharp-minded female on border duty for decades to avoid the scheming of his court. He didn't let her near Amarantha, either. Didn't let anyone get a whiff of what he felt for his white-haired friend, who had no clue—not one—that he had loved her his entire life. And in those last moments, when his power had been ripped from him by that spell . . . Kallias had flung out the remnants to warn her. To tell Viviane he loved her. And then he begged her to protect their people.

So she had.

As Mor and my friends had protected Velaris, Viviane had veiled and guarded the small city under her watch, offering safe harbor to those who made it.

Never forgetting the High Lord and friend trapped Under the Mountain, never ceasing her hunt for finding a way to free him. Especially while Amarantha unleashed her horrors upon his court to break them, punish them. Yet Viviane held them together. And through that reign of terror—during all those years—she realized what Kallias was to her, what she felt for him in return.

The day he'd returned home, he'd winnowed right to her.

She'd kissed him before he could speak a word. He'd then knelt down and asked her to be his wife.

They went an hour later to a temple and swore their vows. And that night—*during the you-know*, Viviane grinned at Mor—the mating bond at last snapped into place.

The story occupied our time while we waited, since Mor wanted details. Lots of them. Ones that pushed the boundaries of propriety and left Thesan choking on his elderberry wine. But Kallias smiled at his wife and mate, warm and bright enough that despite his icy coloring, *he* should have been the High Lord of Day.

Not the sharp-tongued, brutal Helion, who watched my sister and me like an eagle. A great, golden eagle—with very sharp talons.

I wondered what his beast form was; if he grew wings like Rhysand. And claws.

If Thesan did, too—white wings like the watchful Peregryns who kept silent, his own fierce-eyed lover not uttering a word to anyone. Perhaps the High Lords of the Solar Courts all possessed wings beneath their skin, a gift from the skies that their courts claimed ownership of.

It was an hour before Thesan announced, "Tarquin is here."

My mouth went dry. An uncomfortable silence spread.

"Heard about the blood rubies." Helion smirked at Rhys, toying with the golden cuff on his bicep. "*That* is a story I want you to tell."

Rhys waved an idle hand. "All in good time." *Prick*, he said to me with a wink.

But then Tarquin cleared the top step into the chamber, Varian and Cresseida flanking him.

Varian glanced among us for someone who was not there—and glowered when he beheld Cassian, seated to Nesta's left. Cassian just gave him a cocky grin.

I wrecked one building, Cassian had said once of his last visit to the Summer Court. Where he was now *banned*. Apparently, even assisting them in battle hadn't lifted it.

Tarquin ignored Rhysand and me—ignored all of us, Rhys's wings included—as he made vague apologies for the tardiness, blaming it on the attack. Possibly true. Or he'd been deciding until the last minute whether to come, despite his acceptance of the invitation.

He and Helion were nearly as tense, and only Thesan seemed to be on decent terms with him. Neutral indeed. Kallias had become even colder—distant.

But the introductions were done, and then . . .

An attendant whispered to Thesan that Beron and *all* of his sons had arrived. The smile instantly vanished from Mor's mouth, her eyes.

From my own as well.

The violence simmering off my friends was enough to boil the pool at our toes as the High Lord of Autumn filed through the archway, his sons in rank behind him, his wife—Lucien's mother—at his side. Her russet eyes scanned the room, as if looking for that missing son. They settled instead on Helion, who gave her a mocking incline of his dark head. She quickly averted her gaze.

She had saved my life once—Under the Mountain. In exchange for my sparing Lucien's.

Did she wonder where her lost son was now? Had she heard the rumors I'd crafted, the lies I'd spun? I couldn't tell her that Lucien currently hunted the continent, dodging armies, for an enchanted queen. To find a scrap of salvation.

Beron—slender-faced and brown-haired—didn't bother to look anywhere but at the High Lords assembled. But his remaining sons sneered at us. Sneered enough that the Peregryns ruffled their feathers. Even Varian flashed his teeth in warning at the leer Cresseida earned from one of them. Their father didn't bother to check them.

But Eris did.

A step behind his father, Eris murmured, "Enough," and his younger brothers fell into line. All three of them.

Whether Beron noticed or cared, he did not let on. No, he merely stopped halfway across the room, hands folded before him, and scowled—as if we were a pack of mongrels.

Beron, the oldest among us. The most awful.

Rhys smoothly greeted him, though his power was a dark mountain shuddering beneath us, "It's no surprise that you're tardy, given that your own sons were too slow to catch my mate. I suppose it runs in the family."

Beron's lips curled slightly as he looked to me, my crown. "Mate—and High Lady."

I leveled a flat, bored stare at him. Turned it on his hateful sons. On—Eris.

Eris only smiled at me, amused and aloof. Would he wear that mask when he ended his father's life and stole his throne?

Cassian was watching the would-be High Lord like a hawk studying his next meal. Eris deigned a glance at the Illyrian general and inclined his head in invitation, subtly patting his stomach. Ready for round two.

Then Eris's attention shifted to Mor, sweeping over her with a disdain that made me see red. Mor only stared blankly at him. Bored.

Even Viviane was biting her lip. So she knew of what had been done to Mor—what Eris's presence would trigger.

Unaware of the meeting that had already occurred, the unholy alliance struck. Azriel was so still I wasn't sure he was breathing. Whether Mor noticed, whether she knew that though she'd tried to move past the bargain we'd made, the guilt of it still haunted Azriel, she didn't let on.

They sat—filling in the final seats.

Not one empty chair left.

It said enough about Tamlin's plans.

I tried not to sag in my chair as the attendants took care of the Autumn Court, as we all settled.

Thesan, as host, began. "Rhysand, you have called this meeting. Pushed us to gather sooner than we intended. Now would be the time to explain what is so urgent."

Rhys blinked—slowly. "Surely the invading armies landing on our shores explain enough."

"So you have called us to do what, exactly?" Helion challenged, bracing his forearms on his muscled, gleaming thighs. "Raise a unified army?"

"Among other things," Rhys said mildly. "We—"

It was almost the same—the entrance.

Almost the same as that night in my family's old cottage, when the door had shattered and a beast had charged in with the freezing cold and roared at us.

He did not bother with the landing balcony, or the escorts. He did not have an entourage.

Like a crack of lightning, vicious as a spring storm, he winnowed into the chamber itself.

And my blood went colder than Kallias's ice as Tamlin appeared, and smiled like a wolf.

CHAPTER
44

Absolute silence. Absolute stillness.

I felt the tremor of magic slide through the room as shield after shield locked into place around each High Lord and his retinue. The one Rhysand had already snapped around us, now reinforcing . . . Rage laced its essence. Wrath and rage. Even if my mate's face was bored—lazy.

I tried to school mine into the cold caution with which Nesta regarded him, or the vague distaste on Mor's. I tried—and failed utterly.

I knew his moods, his temper.

Here was the High Lord who had shredded those naga into bloody ribbons; here was the High Lord who had impaled Amarantha on Lucien's sword and ripped out her throat with his teeth.

All of it, gleaming in those green eyes as they fixed on me, on Rhys. Tamlin's teeth were white as crow-picked bones as he smiled broadly.

Thesan rose, his captain remaining seated beside him—albeit with a hand on his sword. "We were not expecting you, Tamlin." Thesan gestured with a slender hand toward his cringing attendants. "Fetch the High Lord a chair."

Tamlin did not tear his gaze from me. From us.

His smile turned subdued—yet somehow more unnerving. More vicious.

He wore his usual green tunic—no crown, no adornments. No sign of another bandolier to replace the one I'd stolen.

Beron drawled, "I will admit, Tamlin, that I am surprised to see you here." Tamlin didn't alter his focus from me. From every breath I took. "Rumor claims your allegiance now lies elsewhere."

Tamlin's gaze shifted—but down. To the ring on my finger. To the tattoo adorning my right hand, flowing beneath the glittering, pale blue sleeve of my gown. Then it rose—right to that crown I'd picked for myself.

I didn't know what to say. What to do with my body, my breathing.

No more masks, no more lies and deceptions. The truth, now sprawled bare and open before him. What I'd done in my rage, the lies I'd fed him. The people and land I'd laid vulnerable to Hybern. And now that I'd returned to my family, my mate . . .

My molten wrath had cooled into something sharp-edged and brittle.

The attendants hauled over a chair—setting it between one of Beron's sons and Helion's entourage. Neither looked thrilled about it, though they weren't stupid enough to physically recoil as Tamlin sat.

He said nothing. Not a word.

Helion waved a scar-flecked hand. "Let's get on with it, then."

Thesan cleared his throat. No one looked toward him.

Not as Tamlin surveyed the hand Rhys had resting on my sparkling knee.

The loathing in Tamlin's eyes practically simmered.

No one, not even Amarantha, had ever looked at me with such hatred.

No, Amarantha hadn't really known me—her loathing had been superficial, driven from a personal history that poisoned everything. Tamlin . . . Tamlin knew me. And now hated every inch of what I was.

He opened his mouth, and I braced myself.

"It would seem congratulations are in order."

The words were flat—flat and yet sharp as his claws, currently hidden beneath his golden skin.

I said nothing.

Rhys only held Tamlin's stare. Held it with a face like ice, and yet utter rage roiled beneath it. Cataclysmic rage, surging and writhing down the bond between us.

But my mate addressed Thesan, who had reclaimed his seat, yet seemed far from any sort of ease, "We can discuss the matter at hand later."

Tamlin said calmly, "Don't stop on my account."

The light in Rhysand's eyes guttered, as if a hand of darkness wiped away those stars. But he reclined in his chair, withdrawing his hand from my knee to trace idle circles on his seat's wooden arm. "I'm not in the business of discussing our plans with enemies."

Helion, across the reflection pool, grinned like a lion.

"No," Tamlin said with equal ease, "you're just in the business of fucking them."

Every thought and sound eddied out of my head.

Cassian, Azriel, and Mor were still as death—their fury rippling off them in silent waves. But whether Tamlin noticed or cared that three of the deadliest people in this room were currently contemplating his demise, he didn't let on.

Rhys shrugged, smiling faintly. "Seems a far less destructive alternative to war."

"And yet here you are, having started it in the first place."

Rhysand's blink was the only sign of his confusion.

A claw slid out of Tamlin's knuckle.

Kallias tensed, a hand drifting to the arm of Viviane's chair—as if he'd throw himself in front of it. But Tamlin only dragged that claw lightly down the carved arm of his own chair—as he'd once dragged them down my skin. He smiled as if he knew precisely what memory it triggered, but said to my mate, "If you hadn't stolen my bride away in the night, Rhysand, I would not have been forced to take such drastic measures to get her back."

417

I said quietly, "The sun was shining when I left you."

Those green eyes slid to me, glazed and foreign. He let out a low snort, then looked away again.

Dismissal.

Kallias asked, "Why are you here, Tamlin?"

Tamlin's claw dug into the wood, puncturing deep even as his voice remained mild. I had no doubt that gesture was meant for me, too. "I bartered access to my lands to get back the woman I love from a sadist who plays with minds as if they are toys. I meant to fight Hybern—to find a way around the bargain I made with the king once she was back. Only Rhysand and his cabal had turned her into one of them. And she delighted in ripping open my territory for Hybern to invade. All for a petty grudge—either her own or her . . . master's."

"You don't get to rewrite the narrative," I breathed. "You don't get to spin this to your advantage."

Tamlin only angled his head at Rhys. "When you fuck her, have you ever noticed that little noise she makes right before she climaxes?"

Heat stained my cheeks. This wasn't outright battle, but a steady, careful shredding of my dignity, my credibility. Beron beamed, delighted—while Eris carefully monitored.

Rhys turned his head, looking me over from head to toe. Then back to Tamlin. A storm about to be unleashed.

But it was Azriel who said, his voice like cold death, "Be careful how you speak about my High Lady."

Surprise flashed in Tamlin's eyes—then vanished. Vanished, swallowed by pure fury as he realized what that tattoo coating my hand was for. "It was not enough to sit at my side, was it?" A hateful smile curled his lips. "You once asked me if you'd be my High Lady, and when I said no . . ." A low laugh. "Perhaps I underestimated you. Why serve in my court, when you could rule in his?"

Tamlin at last faced the other gathered High Lords and their retinues. "They peddle tales of defending our land and peace. And yet *she* came to my lands and laid them bare for Hybern. *She* took my High Priestess and warped her mind—after she shattered her bones for spite. And if you are asking yourself what happened to that human girl who went Under the Mountain to save us . . . Look to the male sitting beside her. Ask what he stands to gain—what *they* stand to gain from this war, or lack of it. Would we fight Hybern, only to find ourselves with a Queen and King of Prythian? She's proved her ambition—and you saw how he was more than happy to serve Amarantha to remain unscathed."

It was an effort not to snarl, not to grip the arms of my chair and roar at him.

Rhys let out a dark laugh. "Well played, Tamlin. You're learning."

Ire contorted Tamlin's face at the condescension. But he faced Kallias. "You asked why I'm here? I might ask the same of you." He jerked his chin at the High Lord of Winter, at Viviane—the few other members of their retinue who had remained silent. "You mean to tell me that after Under the Mountain, you can stomach working with him?" A finger flung in Rhysand's direction.

I wanted to rip that finger right off Tamlin's hand. And feed it to the Middengard Wyrm.

The silvery glow about Kallias dulled.

Even Viviane seemed to dim. "We came here to decide that for ourselves."

Mor was staring at her friend in quiet question. Viviane, for the first time since we'd arrived, did not look toward her. Only at her mate.

Rhys said softly to them, to everyone, "I had no involvement in that. None."

Kallias's eyes flared like blue flame. "You stood beside her throne while the order was given."

I watched, stomach twisting, as Rhys's golden skin paled. "I tried to stop it."

"Tell that to the parents of the two dozen younglings she butchered," Kallias said. "That you *tried*."

I had forgotten. Forgotten that bit of Amarantha's despicable history. It had happened while I was still at the Spring Court—a report one of Lucien's contacts at the Winter Court managed to smuggle out. Of two dozen children killed by the "blight." By Amarantha.

Rhys's mouth tightened. "There is not one day that passes when I don't remember it," he said to Kallias, to Viviane. To their companions. "Not one day."

I hadn't known.

He had told me once, all those months ago, that there were memories he could not bring himself to share—even with me. I had assumed it was only in regard to what Amarantha had done to him. Not . . . what he might have been forced to witness, too. Forced to endure, bound and trapped.

And standing by, leashed to Amarantha, while she ordered the murder of those children—

"Remembering," Kallias said, "doesn't bring them back, does it?"

"No," Rhys said plainly. "No, it doesn't. And I am now fighting to make sure it never happens again."

Viviane glanced between her husband and Rhys. "I was not present Under the Mountain. But I would hear, High Lord, how you tried to—stop her." Pain tightened her face. She, too, had been unable to prevent it while she guarded her small slice of the territory.

Rhys said nothing.

Beron snorted. "Finally speechless, Rhysand?"

I put a hand on Rhys's arm. I had no doubt Tamlin marked it. And I didn't care. I said to my mate, not bothering to keep my voice down, "I believe you."

"Says the woman," Beron countered, "who gave an innocent girl's name in her stead—for Amarantha to butcher as well."

I blocked out the words, the memory of Clare.

Rhys swallowed. I tightened my grip on his arm.

His voice was rough as he said to Kallias, "When your people rebelled . . ." They had, I recalled. Winter had rebelled against Amarantha. And the children . . . that had been Amarantha's answer. Her punishment for the disobedience. "She was furious. She wanted you dead, Kallias."

Viviane's face drained of color.

Rhys went on, "I . . . convinced her that it would serve little purpose."

"Who knew," Beron mused, "that a cock could be so persuasive?"

"Father." Eris's voice was low with warning.

For Cassian, Azriel, Mor, and I had fixed our gazes upon Beron. And none of us were smiling.

Perhaps Eris would be High Lord sooner than he planned.

But Rhys went on to Kallias, "She backed off the idea of killing you. Your rebels were dead—I convinced her it was enough. I thought it was the end of it." His breathing hitched slightly. "I only found out when you did. I think she viewed my defense of you as a warning sign—she didn't tell me any of it. And she kept me . . . confined. I tried to break into the minds of the soldiers she sent, but her damper on my power was too strong to hold them—and it was already done. She . . . she sent a daemati with them. To . . ." He faltered. The children's minds—they'd been shattered. Rhys swallowed. "I think she wanted you to suspect me. To keep us from ever allying against her."

What he must have witnessed within those soldiers' minds . . .

"Where did she confine you?" The question came from Viviane, her arms wrapped around her middle.

I wasn't entirely ready for it when Rhys said, "Her bedroom."

My friends did not hide their rage, their grief at the details he'd kept even from them.

"Stories and words," Tamlin said, lounging in his chair. "Is there any proof?"

"*Proof*—" Cassian snarled, half rising in his seat, wings starting to flare.

"No," Rhys cut in as Mor blocked Cassian with an arm, forcing him to sit. Rhys added to Kallias, "But I swear it—upon my mate's life." His hand at last rested atop mine.

For the first time since I'd known him, Rhys's skin was clammy.

I reached down the bond, even as Rhys held Kallias's stare. I did not have any words. Only myself—only my soul, as I curled up against his towering shields of black adamant.

He'd known what coming here, presented just as we were, would cost him. What he might have to reveal beyond the wings he loved so dearly.

Tamlin rolled his eyes. It took every scrap of restraint to keep me from lunging for him—from ripping out those eyes.

But whatever Kallias read in Rhys's face, his words . . . He pinned Tamlin with a hard stare as he asked again, "Why are you *here*, Tamlin?"

A muscle flickered in Tamlin's jaw. "I am here to help you fight against Hybern."

"Bullshit," Cassian muttered.

Tamlin glowered at him. Cassian, folding his wings in neatly as he leaned back in his chair once more, just offered a crooked grin in return.

"You will forgive us," Thesan interrupted gracefully, "if we are doubtful. And hesitant to share any plans."

"Even when I have information on Hybern's movements?"

Silence. Tarquin, across the pool, watched and listened—either because he was the youngest of them, or perhaps he knew some advantage lay in letting us battle it out ourselves.

Tamlin smiled at me. "Why do you think I invited them to the house? Into my lands?" He let out a low snarl, and I felt Rhys tensing as Tamlin said to me, "I once told you I would fight against tyranny, against that sort of evil. Did you think *you* were enough to turn me from that?" His teeth shone white as bone. "It was so *easy* for you to call me a monster, despite all I did for you, for your family." A sneer toward Nesta, who was frowning with distaste. "Yet you witnessed all that *he* did Under the Mountain, and still spread your legs for him. Fitting, I suppose. He whored for Amarantha for decades. Why shouldn't you be his whore in return?"

"Watch your mouth," Mor snapped. I was having difficulty swallowing—breathing.

Tamlin ignored her wholly and waved a hand toward Rhysand's wings. "I sometimes forget—what you are. Have the masks come off now, or is this another ploy?"

"You're beginning to become tedious, Tamlin," Helion said, propping his head on a hand. "Take your lovers' spat elsewhere and let the rest of us discuss this war."

"You'd be all too happy for war, considering how well you made out in the last one."

"No one says war can't be lucrative," Helion countered. Tamlin's lip curled in a silent snarl that made me wonder if he'd gone to Helion to break my bargain with Rhys—if Helion had refused.

"Enough," Kallias said. "We have our opinions on how the conflict with Hybern should be dealt with." Those glacial eyes hardened as he again took in Tamlin. "Are you here as an ally of Hybern or Prythian?"

The mocking, hateful gleam faded into granite resolve. "I stand against Hybern."

"Prove it," Helion goaded.

Tamlin lifted his hand, and a stack of papers appeared on the little table beside his chair. "Charts of armies, ammunition, caches of faebane . . . Everything carefully gleaned these months."

All of this directed at me, as I refused to so much as lower my chin. My back ached from keeping it so straight, a twinge of pain flanking either side of my spine.

"Noble as it sounds," Helion went on, "who is to say that information is correct—or that you aren't Hybern's agent, trying to mislead us?"

"Who is to say that Rhysand and his cronies are not agents of Hybern, all of this a ruse to get you to yield without realizing it?"

Nesta murmured, "You can't be serious." Mor gave my sister a look as if to say that he certainly was.

"If we need to ally against Hybern," Thesan said, "you are doing a good job of convincing us not to band together, Tamlin."

"I am simply warning you that they might present the guise of honesty and friendship, but the fact remains that *he* warmed Amarantha's bed for fifty years, and only worked against her when it seemed the tide was turning. I'm warning you that while he claims his own city was attacked by Hybern, they made off remarkably well—as if they'd been anticipating it. Don't think he wouldn't sacrifice a few buildings and lesser faeries to lure you into an alliance, into thinking you had a common enemy. Why is it that only the Night Court got word about the attack on Adriata—and were the only ones to arrive in time to play savior?"

"They received word," Varian cut in coolly, "because *I* warned them of it."

Tarquin whipped his head to his cousin, brows high with surprise.

"Perhaps you're working with them, too," Tamlin said to the Prince of Adriata. "You're next in line, after all."

"You're insane," I breathed to Tamlin as Varian bared his teeth. "Do you hear what you're *saying*?" I pointed toward Nesta. "Hybern turned my sisters into Fae—after *your* bitch of a priestess sold them out!"

"Perhaps Ianthe's mind was already in Rhysand's thrall. And what a tragedy to remain young and beautiful. You're a good actress—I'm sure the trait runs in the family."

Nesta let out a low laugh. "If you want someone to blame for all of this," she said to Tamlin, "perhaps you should first look in the mirror."

Tamlin snarled at her.

Cassian snarled right back, "*Watch it*."

Tamlin looked between my sister and Cassian—his gaze lingering on Cassian's wings, tucked in behind him. Snorted. "Seems like other preferences run in the Archeron family, too."

My power began to rumble—a behemoth rising up, yawning awake.

"What do you want?" I hissed. "An apology? For me to crawl back into your bed and play nice, little wife?"

"Why should I want spoiled goods returned to me?"

My cheeks heated.

Tamlin growled, "The moment you let him fuck you like an—"

One heartbeat, the poisoned words were spewing from his mouth—where fangs lengthened.

Then they stopped.

Tamlin's mouth simply stopped emitting *sounds*. He shut his mouth, opened it—tried again.

No sound, not even a snarl, came out.

There was no smile on Rhysand's face, not a glint of that irreverent amusement as he rested his head against the back of his chair. "The gasping-fish look is a good one for you, Tamlin."

The others, who had been watching with disdain and amusement and boredom, now turned to my mate. Now possessed a shadow of fear in their eyes as they realized who and what, exactly, sat amongst them.

Brethren, and yet not. Tamlin was a High Lord, as powerful as any of them.

Except for the one at my side. Rhys was as different from them as humans were to Fae.

They forgot it, sometimes—how deep that well of power went. What manner of power Rhys bore.

But as Rhysand ripped away Tamlin's ability to speak, they remembered.

CHAPTER
45

Only my friends didn't seem surprised.

Tamlin's eyes were green flame, golden light flickering around him as his magic sought to wrest free from Rhysand's control. As he tried and tried to speak.

"If you want proof that we are not scheming with Hybern," Rhysand said blandly to them all, "consider the fact that it would be far less time-consuming to slice into your minds and make you do my bidding."

Only Beron was stupid enough to scoff. Eris was just angling his body in his chair—blocking the path to his mother.

"Yet here I am," Rhysand went on, not deigning to give Beron a glance of acknowledgment. "Here we all are."

Absolute silence.

Then Tarquin, silent and watchful, cleared his throat.

I waited for it—for the blow that would surely doom us. We were thieves who had deceived him, we had come to his house in peace and stolen from him, had ripped into their minds to ensure our success.

But Tarquin said to me, to Rhysand, "Despite Varian's unsanctioned warning . . ." A glare at his cousin, who didn't so much as look sorry about it, "You were the only ones who came to help. The only ones. And yet you asked for nothing in return. Why?"

Rhys's voice was a bit hoarse as he asked, "Isn't that what friends do?"

A subtle, quiet offer.

Tarquin took him in. Then me. And the others. "I rescind the blood rubies. Let there be no debts between us."

"Don't expect Amren to return hers," Cassian muttered. "She's grown attached to it."

I could have sworn a smile tugged on Varian's mouth.

But Rhys faced Tamlin, whose own mouth remained shut. His eyes still livid. And my mate said to him, "I believe you. That you will fight for Prythian."

Kallias didn't appear so convinced. Neither did Helion.

Rhys loosened his grasp on Tamlin's voice. I only knew because a low snarl slipped from him. But Tamlin made no move to attack, to even speak.

"War is upon us," Rhysand declared. "I have no interest in wasting energy arguing amongst ourselves."

The better man—male. His restraint, his choice of words . . . All of it a careful portrayal of reason and power. But Rhysand . . . I knew he meant what he said. Even if Tamlin had been a part of killing his own family, even if he had played his part in Hybern . . . For our home, for Prythian, he'd set it aside. A sacrifice that would harm no one but his own soul.

But Beron said, "You may be inclined to believe him, Rhysand, but as someone who shares a border with his court, I am not so easily swayed." A wry look. "Perhaps my errant son can clarify. Pray, where is he?"

Even Tamlin looked toward us—toward me.

"Helping to guard our city," was all I said. Not a lie, not entirely.

Eris snorted and surveyed Nesta, who stared back at him with steel in her face. "Pity you didn't bring the other sister. I hear our little brother's mate is quite the beauty."

If they knew Elain was Lucien's mate . . . It was now another avenue, I realized with no small amount of horror. Another way to strike at the youngest brother they hated so fiercely, so unreasonably. Eris's bargain with us had not included protection of Lucien. My mouth went dry.

But Mor replied smoothly, "You still certainly like to hear yourself talk, Eris. Good to know some things don't change over the centuries."

Eris's mouth curled into a smile at the words, the careful game of pretending that they had not seen each other in years. "Good to know that after five hundred years, you still dress like a slut."

One moment, Azriel was seated.

The next, he'd blasted through Eris's shield with a flare of blue light and tackled him backward, wood shattering beneath them.

"Shit," Cassian spat, and was instantly there—

And met a wall of blue.

Azriel had sealed them in, and as his scarred hands wrapped around Eris's throat, Rhys said, "Enough."

Azriel squeezed, Eris thrashing beneath him. No physical brawling—there had been a rule against that, but Azriel, with whatever power those shadows gave him . . .

"*Enough*, Azriel," Rhys ordered. Perhaps those shadows that now slid and eddied around the shadowsinger *hid* him from the wrath of the binding magic. The others made no move to interfere, as if wondering the same.

Azriel dug his knee—and all his weight—into Eris's gut. He was silent, utterly silent as he ripped the air from Eris's body. Beron's flames struck the blue shield, over and over, but the fire skittered off and fizzled out on the water. Any that escaped were torn to shreds by shadows.

"Call off your overgrown bat," Beron ordered Rhys.

Rhys was enjoying it, bargain with Eris or no—could have ended it seconds ago. He gave me a glance as if to say so. And an invitation.

I rose on surprisingly steady knees.

Felt all of them tense, Tamlin's gaze like a brand as I walked toward the shadowsinger, my sparkling gown hissing along the floor behind me. As I put a tattooed hand on the hard, near-invisible curve of the shield and said, "Come, Azriel."

Azriel stopped.

Eris gasped for air as those scarred hands loosened. As Azriel turned his face toward me—

The frozen rage there rooted me to the spot.

But beneath it, I could almost see the images that haunted him: the hand Mor had yanked away, her weeping, distraught face as she had screamed at Rhys.

And now, behind us, Mor was shaking in her chair. Pale and shaking.

I only offered my hand to Azriel. "Come sit beside me."

Nesta had already moved her seat, and an extra chair appeared beside mine.

I didn't let my hand tremble as I kept it extended. And waited.

Azriel's eyes slid to Eris, the High Lord's son panting beneath him. And the shadowsinger leaned down to whisper something in his ear that made Eris blanch further.

But the shield dropped. The shadows lightened into sunshine.

Beron struck—only for his fire to bounce off a hard barrier of my own. I lifted my gaze to the High Lord of Autumn. "That's twice now we've handed you your asses. I'd think you'd be sick of the humiliation."

Helion laughed. But my attention returned to Azriel, who took my still-offered hand and rose. The scars were rough against my fingers, but his skin was like ice. Pure ice.

Mor opened her mouth to say something to Azriel, but Cassian put a hand on her bare knee and shook his head. I led the shadowsinger to the empty chair beside mine—then walked to the table myself to pour him a glass of wine.

No one spoke until I offered it to him and sat down.

"They are my family," I said at the raised brows I received for my waiting on him. Tamlin just shook his head in disgust and finally slid that claw back into his hand. But I met Eris's fuming gaze, my voice as cold as Azriel's face as I said, "I don't care if we are allies in this war. If you insult my friend again, I won't stop him the next time."

Only Eris knew how far that alliance went—information that could damn this meeting if either side revealed it. Information that could get him wiped off the earth by his father.

Mor was staring and staring at Azriel, who refused to look at her, who refused to do anything but give Eris that death-gaze.

Eris, wisely, averted his eyes. And said, "Apologies, Morrigan."

His father actually gawked at the words. But something like approval shone on the Lady of Autumn's face as her eldest son settled himself once more.

Thesan rubbed his temples. "This does not bode well."

But Helion smirked at his retinue, crossing an ankle over a knee and flashing those powerful, sleek thighs. "Looks like you owe me ten gold marks."

It seemed like we weren't the only ones who'd placed bets. Even if not one of Helion's entourage answered his mocking smile with one of their own.

Helion waved a hand, and the stacks of papers Tamlin had compiled drifted over to him on a phantom wind. With a snap of his fingers— scar-flecked from swordplay—other stacks appeared before every chair in the room. Including my own. "Replicas," he said without looking up as he leafed through the documents.

A handy trick—for a male whose trove was not in gold, but in knowledge.

No one made any move to touch the papers before us.

Helion clicked his tongue. "If all of this is true," he announced, Tamlin snarling at the haughty tone, "then I'd suggest two things: first, destroying Hybern's caches of faebane. We won't last long if they've made them into so many versatile weapons. It's worth the risk to destroy them."

Kallias arched a brow. "How would you suggest we do that?"

"We'll handle it," Tarquin offered. Varian nodded. "We owe them for Adriata."

Thesan said, "There is no need."

We all blinked at him. Even Tamlin. The High Lord of Dawn just folded his hands in his lap. "A master tinkerer of mine has been waiting for the past several hours. I would like for her to now join us."

Before anyone could reply, a High Fae female appeared at the edge of the circle. She bowed so quickly that I barely glimpsed more than her light brown skin and long, silken black hair. She wore clothes similar to Thesan's, and yet—her sleeves had been rolled up to the forearms, the tunic unbuttoned to her chest. And her hand—

I guessed who she was before she rose. Her right hand was solid gold—mechanical. The way Lucien's was. It clicked and whirred quietly, drawing the eye of every immortal in the room as she faced her High Lord. Thesan smiled in warm welcome.

But her face . . . I wondered if Amren had modeled her own features after a similar bloodline when she'd bound herself into her Fae body: the sharp chin, round cheeks, and stunning uptilted eyes. But where Amren's were that unholy silver, this female's were dark as onyx. And aware—utterly aware of us gawking at her hand, her arrival—as she said to Thesan, "My Lord."

Thesan gestured to the female standing tall before the assembled group. "Nuan is one of my most skilled craftspeople."

Rhys leaned back in his seat, brows rising with recognition at the name, and jerked his chin to Beron, to Eris. "You might know her as the person responsible for granting your . . . errant son, as you called him, the ability to use his left eye after Amarantha removed it."

Nuan nodded once in confirmation, her lips pressing into a thin line as she took in Lucien's family. She didn't so much as turn in Tamlin's direction—and he certainly didn't bother to acknowledge her, regardless of the past binding them, their mutual friend.

"And what has this to do with the faebane?" Helion demanded.

Thesan's lover seethed at the High Lord of Day's tone, but one glance from Thesan had the male relaxing.

Nuan turned, her dark hair slipping over a shoulder as she studied Helion. And did not seem impressed. "Because I found a solution for it."

Thesan waved a hand. "We heard rumors of faebane being used in this war—used in the attack on your city, Rhysand. We thought to look into the issue before it became a deadly weakness for all of us." He nodded to Nuan. "Beyond her unparalleled tinkering, she is a skilled alchemist."

Nuan crossed her arms, the sun glinting off her metal hand. "Thanks to samples attained after the attack in Velaris, I was able to create an . . . antidote, of sorts."

"How did you get those samples?" Cassian demanded.

A flush crept over Nuan's cheeks. "I—heard the rumors and assumed Lucien Vanserra would be residing there after . . . what happened." She still didn't look at Tamlin, who remained silent and brooding. "I managed to contact him a few days ago—asked him to send samples. He did—and did not tell you," she added quickly to Rhysand, "because he did not want to raise your hopes. Not until I'd found a solution."

No wonder he'd been so eager to head alone into Velaris that day he'd gone to help us research. I shot a look at Rhys. *Seems like Lucien can still play the fox.*

Rhys didn't look at me, though his lips twitched as he replied, *Indeed.*

Nuan went on, "The Mother has provided us with everything we need on this earth. So it has been a matter of finding what, exactly, she gave us in Prythian to combat a material from Hybern capable of wiping out our powers."

Helion shifted with impatience, that glistening, white fabric slipping over his muscled chest.

Thesan read that impatience, too, and said, "Nuan has been able to quickly create a powder for us to ingest in drink, food, however you please. It grants immunity from the faebane. I already have workers in three of my cities manufacturing as much of it as possible to hand out to our unified armies."

Even Rhys seemed impressed at the stealth, the unveiling. *I'm surprised you didn't have a grand reveal of your own today*, I quipped down the bond.

Cruel, beautiful High Lady, he purred, eyes twinkling.

Tarquin asked, "But what of physical objects made from faebane? They possessed gauntlets at the battle to smash through shields." He jerked his chin to Rhys. "And when they attacked your own city."

"Against that," Nuan said, "you only have your wits to protect you." She did not break Tarquin's stare, and he straightened, as if surprised she did so. "The compound I've made will only protect you—your powers—from being rendered void by the faebane. Perhaps if you are pierced with a weapon tipped in faebane, having the compound in your system will negate its impact."

Quiet fell.

Beron said, "And we are supposed to trust you"—a look at Thesan, then at Nuan—"with this . . . substance we're to blindly ingest."

"Would you rather face Hybern without any power?" Thesan demanded. "My master alchemists and tinkerers are no fools."

"No," Beron said, frowning, "but where did she come from? *Who* are you?" The last bit directed at Nuan.

"I am the daughter of two High Fae from Xian, who moved here to give their children a better life, if that is what you are demanding to know," Nuan answered tightly.

Helion demanded of Beron, "What does this have to do with anything?"

Beron shrugged. "If her family is from Xian—which I'll have you remember fought for the Loyalists—then whose interests does she serve?"

Helion's amber eyes flashed.

Thesan cut in sharply, "I will have *you* remember, Beron, that my own mother hailed from Xian. And a large majority of my court did as well. Be careful what you say."

Before Beron could hiss a retort, Nuan said to the Lord of Autumn, her chin high, "I am a child of Prythian. I was born here, on this land, as your sons were."

Beron's face darkened. "Watch your tone, girl."

"She doesn't have to watch anything," I cut in. "Not when you fling that sort of horseshit at her." I looked to the alchemist. "I will take your antidote."

Beron rolled his eyes.

But Eris said, "Father."

Beron lifted a brow. "You have something to add?"

Eris didn't flinch, but he seemed to choose his words very, very carefully. "I have seen the effects of faebane." He nodded toward me. "It truly renders us unable to tap our power. If it's wielded against us in war or beyond it—"

"If it is, we shall face it. I will not risk my people or family in testing out a *theory*."

"It is no theory," Nuan said, that mechanical hand clicking and whirring as it curled into a fist. "I would not stand here unless it had been proved without a doubt."

A female of pride and hard work.

Eris said, "I will take it."

It was the most . . . decent I'd ever heard him sound. Even Mor blinked at it.

Beron studied his son with a scrutiny that made some small, small part of me wonder if Eris might have grown to be a good male if he'd had a different father. If one still lurked there, beneath centuries of poison.

Because Eris . . . What had it been like for him, Under the Mountain? What games had he played—what had he endured? Trapped for forty-nine years. I doubted he would risk such a thing happening again. Even if it set him in opposition to his father—or perhaps because of that.

Beron only said, "No, you will not. Though I'm sure your brothers will be sorry to hear it."

Indeed, the others seemed rather put-out that their first barrier to the throne wasn't about to risk his life in testing Nuan's solution.

Rhys said simply, "Then don't take it. I will. My entire court will, as will my armies." He gave a thankful nod to Nuan.

Thesan did the same—in thanks and dismissal—and the master tinkerer bowed once more and left.

"At least you have armies to give it to," Tamlin said mildly, breaking his roiling silence. A smile at me. "Though perhaps that was part of the plan. Disable my force while your own swept in. Or was it just to see my people suffer?"

A headache was beginning to pound at my right temple.

Those claws poked through his knuckles again. "Surely you knew that when you turned my forces on me, it would leave my people defenseless against Hybern."

I said nothing. Even as I blocked the images from my mind.

"You primed my court to fall," Tamlin said with venomous quiet. "And it did. Those villages you wanted so badly to help rebuild? They're nothing more than cinders now."

I shut out that, too. He'd said they'd remain untouched, that Hybern had *promised*—

"And while you've been making antidotes and casting yourselves as saviors, I've been piecing together my forces—regaining their trust, their numbers. Trying to gather my people in the East—where Hybern has not yet marched."

Nesta said drily, "So you won't be taking the antidote, then."

Tamlin ignored her, even as his claws sank into the arm of his chair. But I believed him—that he'd moved as many of his people as he could to the eastern edge of the territory. He'd said as much long before I'd returned home.

Thesan cleared his throat and said to Helion, "You said you had two suggestions based on the information you analyzed."

Helion shrugged, the sun catching in the embroidered gold thread of his tunic. "Indeed, though it seems Tamlin is already ahead of me.

The Spring Court must be evacuated." His amber eyes darted between Tarquin and Beron. "Surely your northern neighbors will welcome them."

Beron's lip curled. "We do not have the resources for such a thing."

"Right," Viviane said, "because everyone's too busy polishing every jewel in that trove of yours."

Beron threw her a glare that had Kallias tensing. "Wives were invited as a courtesy, not as consultants."

Viviane's sapphire eyes flared as if struck by lightning. "If this war goes poorly, we'll be bleeding out right alongside you, so I think we damn well get a say in things."

"Hybern will do far worse things than kill you," Beron countered coolly. "A young, pretty thing like you especially."

Kallias's snarl rippled the water in the reflection pool, echoed by Mor's own growl.

Beron smiled a bit. "Only three of us were present for the last war." A nod to Rhys and Helion, whose face darkened. "One does not easily forget what Hybern and the Loyalists did to captured females in their war-camps. What they reserved for High Fae females who either fought for the humans or had families who did." He put a heavy hand on his wife's too-thin arm. "Her two sisters bought her time to run when Hybern's forces ambushed their lands. The two ladies did not walk out of that war-camp again."

Helion was watching Beron closely, his stare simmering with reproach.

The Lady of the Autumn Court kept her focus on the reflection pool. Any trace of color drained from her face. Dagdan and Brannagh flashed through my mind—along with the corpses of those humans. What they'd done to them before and after they'd died.

"We will take your people," Tarquin cut in quietly to Tamlin. "Regardless of your involvement with Hybern . . . your people are innocent. There is plenty of room in my territory. We will take all of them, if need be."

A curt nod was Tamlin's only acknowledgment and gratitude.

Beron said, "So the Seasonal Courts are to become the charnel houses and hostels, while the Solar Courts remain pristine here in the North?"

"Hybern has focused its efforts on the southern half," Rhys said. "To be close to the wall—and human lands."

At this, Nesta and I exchanged looks.

Rhys went on, "Why bother to go through the northern climes—through faerie territories on the continent, when you could claim the South and use it to go directly to the human lands of the continent?"

Thesan asked, "And you believe the human armies there will bow to Hybern?"

"Its queens sold us out," Nesta said. She lifted her chin, poised as any emissary. "For the gift of immortality, the human queens will allow Hybern in to sweep away any resistance. They might very well hand over control of their armies to him." Nesta looked to me, to Rhys. "Where do the humans on our island go? We cannot evacuate them to the continent, and with the wall intact . . . Many might rather risk waiting than cross over the wall anyway."

"The fate of the humans below the wall," Beron cut in, "is none of our concern. Especially in a spit of land with no queen, no army."

"It is my concern," I said, and the voice that came out of me was not Feyre the huntress or Feyre the Cursebreaker, but Feyre the High Lady. "Humans are nearly defenseless against our kind."

"So go waste your own soldiers defending them," Beron said. "I will not send my own forces to protect chattel."

My blood heated, and I took a breath to cool it, to cool the magic crackling at the insult. It did nothing. If it was this impossible to get all of them to ally against Hybern . . .

"You're a coward," I breathed to the High Lord of Autumn. Even Rhys tensed.

Beron just said, "The same could be claimed of you."

My stomach churned. "I don't need to explain myself to you."

"No, but perhaps to that girl's family—but they're dead, too, aren't they? Butchered and burned to death in their own beds. Funny, that you should now seek to defend humans when you were all too happy to offer them up to save yourself."

My palms heated, as if twin suns built and swirled beneath them. *Easy*, Rhys purred. *He's a cranky old bastard.*

But I could barely hear the words behind the tangle of images: Clare's mutilated body nailed to the wall; the cinders of the Beddors' house staining the snow like wisps of shadow; the smile of the Attor as it hauled me through those stone halls Under the Mountain—

"As my lady said," Rhys drawled, "she does not need to explain herself to you."

Beron leaned back in his chair. "Then I suppose I don't need to explain my motivations, either."

Rhys lifted a brow. "Your staggering generosity aside, *will* you be joining our forces?"

"I have not yet decided."

Eris went so far as to give his father a look bordering on reproach. From genuine alarm or for what that refusal might mean for our *own* covert alliance, I couldn't tell.

"Armies take time to raise," Cassian said. "You don't have the luxury of sitting on your ass. You need to rally your soldiers now."

Beron only sneered. "I don't take orders from the bastards of lesser fae whores."

My heartbeat was so wild I could hear it in every corner of my body, feel it pounding in my arms, my gut. But it was nothing compared to the wrath on Cassian's face—or the icy rage on Azriel's and Rhys's. And the disgust on Mor's.

"That bastard," Nesta said with utter coolness, though her eyes began to burn, "may wind up being the only person standing in the way of Hybern's forces and your people."

She didn't so much as look at Cassian as she said it. But he stared at her—as if he'd never seen her before.

This argument was pointless. And I didn't care who they were or who I was as I said to Beron, "Get out if you're not going to be helpful."

At his side, Eris had the wits to actually look worried. But Beron continued to ignore his son's pointed stare and hissed at me, "Did you know that while your *mate* was warming Amarantha's bed, most of our people were locked beneath that mountain?"

I didn't deign responding.

"Did you know that while he had his head between her legs, most of us were fighting to keep our families from becoming the nightly entertainment?"

I tried to shut out the images. The blinding fury at what had been done, what he'd done to keep Amarantha distracted—the secrets he still kept from shame or disinterest in sharing, I didn't know. Cassian was now trembling two seats down—with restraint. And Rhys said nothing.

Tarquin murmured, "That's enough, Beron."

Tarquin, who had guessed at Rhysand's sacrifice, his motives.

Beron ignored him. "And now Rhysand wants to play hero. Amarantha's Whore becomes Hybern's Destroyer. But if it goes badly . . ." A cruel, cold smile. "Will he get on his knees for Hybern? Or just spread his—"

I stopped hearing the words. Stopped hearing anything other than my heart, my breathing.

Fire exploded out of me.

Raging, white-hot flame that blasted into Beron like a lance.

CHAPTER
46

Beron shielded barely fast enough to block me, but the wake singed Eris's arm—right through the cloth. And the pale, lovely arm of Lucien's mother.

The others shouted, shooting to their feet, but I couldn't think, couldn't hear *anything* but Eris's words, see those moments Under the Mountain, see that nightmare of Amarantha leading Rhys down the hall, what Rhys had endured—

Feyre.

I ignored it as I stood. And sent a wave of water from the reflection pond to encircle Beron and his chair. A bubble without air.

Flame pounded against it, turning water to steam, but I pushed harder.

I'd kill him. Kill him and gladly be done with it.

Feyre.

I couldn't tell if Rhysand was yelling it, if he was murmuring it down the bond. Maybe both.

Beron's flame barrier slammed into my water, hard enough that ripples began to form, steam hissing amongst them.

So I bared my teeth and sent a fist of white light punching into that fiery shield—the white light of Day. Spell-breaker. Ward-cleaver.

Beron's eyes widened as his shields began to fray. As that water pushed in.

Then hands were on my face. And violet eyes were before mine, calm and yet insistent. "You've proved your point, my love," Rhys said. "Kill him, and horrible Eris will take his place."

Then I'll kill all of them.

"As interesting an experiment as that might be," Rhys crooned, "it would only complicate the matters at hand."

Into my mind he whispered, *I love you. The words of that hateful bastard don't mean anything. He has nothing of joy in his life. Nothing good. We do.*

I began to hear things—the trickling water of the pool, the crackle of flames, the quick breathing of those around us, the cursing of Beron trapped in that tightening cocoon of light and water.

I love you, Rhys said again.

And I let go of my magic.

Beron's flames exploded like an unfurling flower—and bounced harmlessly off the shield Rhys had thrown around us.

Not to shield against Beron.

But the other High Lords were now on their feet.

"That was how you got through my wards," Tarquin murmured.

Beron was panting so hard he looked like he might spew fire.

But Helion rubbed his jaw as he sat down once more. "I wondered where it went—that little bit. So small—like a fish missing a single scale. But I still felt whenever something brushed against that empty spot." A smirk at Rhys. "No wonder you made her High Lady."

"I made her High Lady," Rhys said simply, lowering his hands from my face but not leaving my side, "because I love her. Her power was the last thing I considered."

I was beyond words, beyond basic feelings. Helion asked Tamlin, "You knew of her powers?"

Tamlin was only watching me and Rhys, my mate's declaration hanging between us. "It was none of your business," was all Tamlin said to Helion. To all of them.

"The power belongs to *us*. I think it is," Beron seethed.

Mor leveled a look at Beron that would have sent lesser males running.

The Lady of Autumn was clutching her arm, angry red splattered along the moon-white skin. No glimmer of pain on that face, though. I said to her as I reclaimed my seat, "I'm sorry."

Her eyes lifted toward mine, round as saucers.

Beron spat, "Don't talk to her, you human filth."

Rhys shattered through Beron's shield, his fire, his defenses.

Shattered through them like a stone hurled into a window, and slammed his dark power into Beron so hard he rocked back in his seat. Then that seat disintegrated into black, sparkling dust beneath him.

Leaving Beron to fall on his ass.

Glittering ebony dust drifted away on a phantom wind, staining Beron's crimson jacket, clinging like clumps of ash to his brown hair.

"Don't ever," Rhys said, hands sliding into his pockets, "speak to my mate like that again."

Beron shot to his feet, not bothering to brush off the dust, and declared to no one in particular, "This meeting is over. I hope Hybern butchers you all."

But Nesta rose from her chair. "This meeting is *not* over."

Even Beron paused at her tone. Eris sized up the space between my sister and his father.

She stood tall, a pillar of steel. "You are all there is," she said to Beron, to all of us. "You are all that there is between Hybern and the end of everything that is good and decent." She settled her stare on Beron, unflinching and fierce. "You fought against Hybern in the last war. Why do you refuse to do so now?"

Beron did not deign to answer. But he did not leave. Eris subtly motioned his brothers to sit.

Nesta marked the gesture—hesitated. As if realizing she indeed held their complete attention. That every word mattered. "You may hate us. I don't care if you do. But I do care if you let innocents suffer and die. At least stand for them. Your people. For Hybern will make an example of them. Of all of us."

"And you know this how?" Beron sneered.

"I went into the Cauldron," Nesta said flatly. "It showed me his heart. He will bring down the wall, and butcher those on either side of it."

Truth or lie, I could not tell. Nesta's face revealed nothing. And no one dared contradict her.

She looked to Kallias and Viviane. "I am sorry for the loss of those children. The loss of one is abhorrent." She shook her head. "But beneath the wall, I witnessed children—entire families—starve to death." She jerked her chin at me. "Were it not for my sister . . . I would be among them."

My eyes burned, but I blinked it away.

"Too long," Nesta said. "For too long have humans beneath the wall suffered and died while you in Prythian thrived. Not during that— queen's reign." She recoiled, as if hating to even speak Amarantha's name. "But long before. If you fight for anything—fight now, to protect those you forgot. Let them know they're not forgotten. Just this once."

Thesan cleared his throat. "While a noble sentiment, the details of the Treaty did not demand we provide for our human neighbors. They were to be left alone. So we obeyed."

Nesta remained standing. "The past is the past. What I care about is the road ahead. What I care about is making sure no children—Fae or human—are harmed. You have been entrusted with protecting this land." She scanned the faces around her. "How can you not fight for it?"

She looked to Beron and his family as she finished. Only the Lady and Eris seemed to be considering—impressed, even, by the strange, simmering woman before them.

I didn't have the words in me—to convey what was in my heart. Cassian seemed the same.

Beron only said, "I shall consider it." A look at his family, and they vanished.

Eris was the last to winnow, something conflicted dancing over his face, as if this was not the outcome he'd planned for. Expected.

But then he, too, was gone, the space where they'd been empty save for that black, glittering dust.

Slowly, Nesta sat, her face again cold—as if it were a mask to conceal whatever raged in her at Beron's disappearance.

Kallias asked me quietly, "Did you master the ice?"

I gave a shallow nod. "All of it."

Kallias scrubbed at his face as Viviane set a hand on his arm. "Does it make a difference, Kal?"

"I don't know," he admitted.

That fast, this alliance unraveled. That fast—because of my lack of control, my—

It either would have been this or something else, Rhys said from where he stood beside my chair, one hand toying with the glittering panels on the back of my gown. *Better now than later. Kallias won't break—he just needs to sort it through on his own.*

But Tarquin said, "You saved us Under the Mountain. Losing a kernel of power seems a worthy payment."

"It seems she took far more than that," Helion argued, "if she could be within seconds of drowning Beron despite the wards." Perhaps I'd gotten around them simply by being Made—outside anything the wards knew to recognize.

Helion's power, warm and clear, brushed against the shield, trawling through the air between us. As if testing for a tether. As if I were some parasite, leeching power from him. And he'd gladly sever it.

Thesan declared, "What's done is done. Short of killing her"—
Rhys's power roiled through the room at the words—"there is nothing
we can do."

It wasn't entirely placating, his tone. Words of peace, yet the tone
was terse. As if, were it not for Rhys and his power, he'd consider tying
me down on an altar and cutting me open to see where his power was—
and how to take it back.

I stood, looking Thesan in the eye. Then Helion. Tarquin. Kallias.
Exactly as Nesta had done. "I did not take your power. You gave it to
me, along with the gift of my immortal life. I am grateful for both. But
they are mine now. And I will do with them what I will."

My friends had risen to their feet, now in rank behind me, Nesta at
my left. Rhys stepped up to my right, but did not touch me. Let me
stand on my own, stare them all down.

I said quietly, but not weakly, "I will use these powers—*my*
powers—to smash Hybern to bits. I will burn them, and drown them,
and freeze them. I will use these powers to heal the injured. To shatter
through Hybern's wards. I have done so already, and I will do so again.
And if you think that my possession of a kernel of your magic is your
biggest problem, then your priorities are *severely* out of order."

Pride flickered down the bond. The High Lords and their retinues
said nothing.

But Viviane nodded, chin high, and rose. "I will fight with you."

Cresseida stood a heartbeat later. "As will I."

Both of them looked to the males in their court.

Tarquin and Kallias rose.

Then Helion, smirking at me and Rhys.

And finally Thesan—Thesan and Tamlin, who did not so much as
breathe in my direction, had barely moved or spoken these past few
minutes. It was the least of my concerns, so long as they all were standing.

Six out of seven. Rhys chuckled down the bond. *Not bad, Cursebreaker.*
Not bad at all.

CHAPTER
47

Our alliance did not begin well.

Even though we talked for a good two hours afterward . . . the bickering, the back-and-forth, continued. With Tamlin there, none would declare what numbers they had, what weapons, what weaknesses.

As the afternoon slipped into evening, Thesan pushed back his chair. "You are all welcome to stay the night and resume this discussion in the morning—unless you wish to return to your own homes for the evening."

We're staying, Rhysand said. *I need to talk to some of the others alone.*

Indeed, the others seemed to have similar thoughts, for all decided to stay.

Even Tamlin.

We were shown toward the suites appointed for us—the sunstone turning a deep gold in the late-afternoon sun. Tamlin was escorted away first, by Thesan himself and a trembling attendant. He had wisely chosen not to attack Rhys or me during the debating, though his refusal to even acknowledge us did not go unnoticed. And as he left, back stiff and steps clipped, he did not say a word. Good.

Then Tarquin was led out, then Helion. Until only Kallias's party and our own waited.

Rhys rose from his seat and dragged a hand through his hair. "That went well. It would seem *none* of us won our bet about who'd fight first."

Azriel stared at the floor, stone-faced. "Sorry." The word was emotionless—distant.

He had not spoken, had barely moved, since his savage attack. It had taken Mor thirty minutes after it to stop shaking.

"He had it coming," Viviane said. "Eris is a piece of shit."

Kallias turned to his mate with high brows.

"What?" She put a hand on her chest. "He is."

"Be that as it may," Kallias said with cool humor, "the question remains about whether Beron will fight with us."

"If all the others are allying," Mor said hoarsely, her first words in hours, "Beron will join. He's too smart to risk siding with Hybern and losing. And I'm sure if things go badly, he'll easily switch over."

Rhys nodded, but faced Kallias. "How many troops do you have?"

"Not enough. Amarantha did her job well." Again, that ripple of guilt that pulsed down the bond. "We've got the army that Viv commanded and hid, but not much else. You?"

Rhys didn't reveal a whisper of the tension that tightened in me, as if it were my own. "We have sizable forces. Mostly Illyrian legions. And a few thousand Darkbringers. But we'll need every soldier who can march."

Viviane walked to where Mor remained seated, still pale, and braced her hands on my friend's shoulders. "I always knew we'd fight alongside each other one day."

Mor dragged her brown eyes up. But she glanced toward Kallias, who seemed to be trying his best not to appear worried. Mor gave the High Lord a look as if to say *I'll take care of her* before she smiled at Viviane. "It's almost enough to make me feel bad for Hybern."

"Almost." Viviane grinned wickedly. "But not quite."

⊹

We were led to a suite built around a lavish sitting area and private dining room. All of it carved from that sunstone, bedecked in jewel-toned fabrics, broad cushions clumped along the thick carpets, and overlooked by ornate golden cages filled with birds of all shapes and sizes. I'd spied peacocks parading about the countless courtyards and gardens as we'd walked through Thesan's home, some preening in the shade beneath potted fig trees.

"How did Thesan keep Amarantha from trashing this place?" I asked Rhys as we surveyed the sitting room that opened to the hazy sprawl of countryside far, far below.

"It's his private residence." Rhys dismissed his wings and slumped onto a pile of emerald cushions near the darkened fireplace. "He likely shielded it the same way Kallias and I did."

A decision that would weigh heavily on them for many centuries, I had no doubt.

But I looked to Azriel, currently leaning against the wall beside the floor-to-ceiling window, shadows fluttering around him. Even the birds in their cages nearby remained silent.

I said down the bond, *Is he all right?*

Rhys tucked his hands behind his head, though his mouth tightened. *Likely not, but if we try to talk to him about it, it'll only make it worse.*

Mor was indeed sprawled on a couch—one wary eye on Azriel. Cassian sat beside her, holding her feet in his lap. He'd taken the spot closer to Azriel—right between them. As if he'd leap into their path if need be.

You handled it beautifully, Rhys added. *All of it.*

Despite my explosion?

Because *of your explosion.*

I met his stare, sensing the emotions swirling beneath as I claimed a seat in an overstuffed chair near my mate's pillow-mound. *I knew that you were powerful. But I didn't realize that you had such an advantage on the others.*

Rhys's eyes shuttered, even as he gave me a half smile. *I'm not sure* even *Beron knew until today. Suspected, maybe, but . . . He'll now be wishing he'd found a way to kill me in the cradle.*

A shiver skittered down my spine. *He knows about Elain being Lucien's mate. He makes a move to harm or take her, and he's dead.*

Uncompromising will swept over the stars in his eyes. *I'll kill him myself if he does. Or hold him long enough for you to do the job. I think I'd enjoy watching you.*

I'll keep it in mind for your next birthday. I drummed my fingers on the polished arm of the chair, the wood as smooth as glass. *Do you really believe Tamlin's claim that he's been working for our side?*

Yes. A beat of silence down the bond. *And perhaps we did him a disservice by not even considering the possibility. Perhaps even I started to think him some warrior brute.*

I felt tired—in my bones, my breath. *Does it change anything, though?*

In some ways, yes. In others . . . Rhys surveyed me. *No. No, it does not.*

I blinked, realizing I'd been lost in the bond, but found Azriel still by the window, Cassian now rubbing Mor's feet. Nesta had retired to her own room without a word—and remained there. I wondered if Beron's leaving despite her words . . . Perhaps it had thrown her.

I got to my feet, straightening the folds of my shimmering gown. *I should check on Nesta. Talk to her.*

Rhys nestled deeper into his spread of pillows, tucking his hands behind his head. *She did well today.*

Pride fluttered at the praise as I crossed the room. But I got as far as the foyer archway when a knock thudded on the door that opened into the sunny hallway. I halted, the sheer panels of my dress swaying, sparkling like pale blue fire in the golden light.

"Don't open it," Mor warned from her spot on the couch. "Even with the shield, don't open it."

Rhys uncoiled to his feet. "Wise," he said, prowling past me to the front door, "but unnecessary." He opened the door, revealing Helion—alone.

Helion braced a hand on the door frame and grinned. "How'd you convince Thesan to give you the better view?"

"He finds my males to be prettier than yours, I think."

"I think it's a wing fetish."

Rhys laughed and opened the door wider, beckoning him in. "You've really mastered the swaggering prick performance, by the way. Expertly done."

Helion's robe swayed with his graceful steps, brushing his powerful thighs. He spied me standing by the round table in the center of the foyer and bowed. Deeply.

"Apologies for the bastard act," he said to me. "Old habits and all."

Here it was—the amusement and joy in his amber eyes. The lightness that led to my own glow when lost to pure bliss. Helion frowned at Rhys. "*You* were on unnaturally nice behavior today. I was betting Beron would be dead by the end of it—you can't imagine my shock that he walked out alive."

"My mate suggested it would be in our favor to appear as we truly are."

"Well, now I look as bad as Beron." He strode straight past me with a wink, stalking into the sitting room. He grinned at Azriel. "You handing Eris's ass to him will be my new fantasy at night, by the way."

Azriel didn't so much as bother to look over his shoulder at the High Lord. But Cassian snorted. "I was wondering when the come-ons would begin."

Helion threw himself onto the couch across from Cassian and Mor. He'd ditched that radiant crown somewhere, but kept that gold armband of the upright serpent. "It's been what—four centuries now, and you three still haven't accepted my offer."

Mor lolled her head to the side. "I don't like to share, unfortunately."

"You never know until you try," Helion purred.

The three of them in bed . . . with him? I must have been blinking like a fool because Rhys said to me, *Helion favors both males and females.*

Usually together in his bed. And has been hounding after that trio for centuries.

I considered—Helion's beauty and the others . . . *Why the hell haven't they said yes?*

Rhys barked a laugh that had all of them looking at him with raised brows.

My mate just came up behind me and slid his arms around my waist, pressing a kiss to my neck. *Would you like someone to join us in bed, Feyre darling?*

My skin stretched tight over my bones at the tone, the suggestion. *You're incorrigible.*

I think you'd like two males worshipping you.

My toes curled.

Mor cleared her throat. "Whatever you're saying mind to mind, either share it or go to another room so we don't have to sit here, stewing in your scents."

I stuck out my tongue. Rhys laughed again, kissing my neck once more before saying, "Apologies for offending your delicate sensibilities, cousin."

I pushed out of his embrace, out of the touch that still made me dizzy enough that basic thought became difficult, and claimed a chair adjacent to Mor and Cassian's couch.

Cassian said to Helion, "Are your forces ready?"

Helion's amusement faded—reshaping into that hard, calculating exterior. "Yes. They'll rendezvous with yours in the Myrmidons."

The mountain range we shared at our border. He'd refused to divulge such information earlier.

"Good," Cassian said, rubbing at the arch of Mor's foot. "We'll push south from there."

"With the final encampment being where?" Mor asked, withdrawing her foot from Cassian's hands and tucking both feet beneath her. Helion traced the curve of her bare leg, his amber eyes a bit glazed as he met hers.

Mor didn't balk from the heated look. And a keen sort of awareness seemed to overtake her—like every nerve in her body shook awake. I didn't dare look toward Azriel.

There must have been multiple shields around the room, around every crack and opening where spying eyes and ears might be waiting, because Cassian said, "We join Thesan's forces, then eventually make camp along Kallias's southwestern border—near the Summer Court."

Helion drew his gaze from Mor long enough to ask Rhys, "You and pretty Tarquin had a moment today. Do you truly think he'll join us?"

"If you mean in bed, definitely not," Rhys said with a wry smile as he again sprawled on his spread of cushions. "But if you mean in this war . . . Yes. I believe he means to fight. Beron, on the other hand . . ."

"Hybern is focusing on the South," Helion said. "And regardless of what *you* think Tamlin's up to, the Spring Court is now mostly occupied. Beron has to realize his court will be a battleground if he doesn't join us to push southward—especially if Summer has joined us."

Meaning the Spring Court and human lands would see the brunt of the battles.

"Will Beron choose to listen to reason, though?" Mor mused.

Helion tapped a finger against the carved arm of his couch. "He played games in the War and it cost him—dearly. His people still remember those choices—those losses. His own damn wife remembers."

Helion had looked at the Lady of Autumn repeatedly during the meeting. I asked, carefully and casually, "What do you mean?"

Mor shook her head—not at what I'd said, but at whatever had occurred.

Helion fixed his full attention upon me. It was an effort not to flinch at the weight of that focus, the simmering intensity. The muscled body was only a mask—to hide that cunning mind beneath. I wondered if Rhys had picked that up from him.

Helion folded an ankle over a knee. "The Lady of the Autumn

Court's two older sisters were indeed . . ." He searched for a word. "Butchered. Tormented, and then butchered, during the War."

I shut out Nesta's screaming, shut out Elain's sobbing as she was hauled toward that Cauldron.

Lucien's aunts. Dead before he'd ever existed. Had his mother ever told him this story?

Rhys explained to me, "Hybern's forces had swarmed our lands by that point."

Helion's jaw clenched. "The Lady of the Autumn Court was sent to stay with her sisters, her younger children packed off to other relatives. To spread out the bloodline." He dragged a hand through his sable hair. "Hybern attacked their estate. Her sisters bought her time to run. Not because she was married to Beron, but because they loved each other. Fiercely. She tried to stay, but they convinced her to go. So she did— she ran and ran, but Hybern's beasts were still faster. Stronger. They cornered her at a ravine, where she became trapped atop a ledge, the beasts snapping at her feet."

He didn't speak for a long moment.

Too many details. He knew so many details.

I said quietly, "You saved her. You found her, didn't you?"

A coronet of light seemed to flicker over that thick black hair. "I did."

There was enough weight, anger, and something else in those two words that I studied the High Lord of Day.

"What happened?"

Helion didn't break my stare. "I tore the beasts apart with my bare hands."

A chill slid down my spine. "Why?"

He could have ended it a thousand other ways. Easier ways. Cleaner ways.

Rhys's bloody hands after the Ravens' attack flashed through my mind.

Helion didn't so much as shift in his chair. "She was still young—though she'd been married to that delightful male for nearly two decades. Married too young, the marriage arranged when she was twenty."

The words were clipped. And twenty—so young. Nearly as young as Mor had been when her own family tried to marry her to Eris.

"So?" A dangerous, taunting question.

And how his eyes burned at that, flaring bright as suns.

But it was Mor who said coolly, "I heard a rumor once, Helion, that she waited before agreeing to that marriage. For a certain someone who had met her by chance at an equinox ball the year before."

I tried not to blink, not to let any of my rising interest surface.

The fire banked to embers and Helion threw a half smile in Mor's direction. "Interesting. I heard her family wanted internal ties to power, and that they didn't give her a choice before they sold her to Beron."

Sold her. Mor's nostrils flared. Cassian ran a hand down the back of her hair. Azriel didn't so much as turn from his vigil at the window, though I could have sworn his wings tucked in a bit tighter.

"Too bad they're just rumors," Rhys cut in smoothly, "and can't be confirmed by anyone."

Helion merely toyed with the gold cuff on his sculpted arm, twisting the serpent to the center of his bicep. But I furrowed my brows. "Does Beron know you saved his wife in the War?" He hadn't mentioned anything during the meeting.

Helion let out a dark laugh. "Cauldron, no." There was enough wry, knowing humor that I straightened.

"You had—an affair after you rescued her?"

The amusement only grew, and Helion pushed a finger against his lips in mock warning. "Careful, High Lady. Even the birds report to Thesan here."

I frowned at the birds in cages throughout the room, still silent in Azriel's shadowy presence.

I threw shields around them, Rhys said down the bond.

"How long did the affair last?" I asked. That withdrawn female . . . I couldn't imagine it.

Helion snorted. "Is that a polite question for a High Lady to be asking?" But the way he spoke, that smile . . .

I only waited, using silence to push him instead.

Helion shrugged. "On and off for decades. Until Beron found out. They say the lady was all brightness and smiles before that. And after Beron was through with her . . . You saw what she is."

"What did he do to her?"

"The same things he does now." Helion waved a hand. "Belittle her, leave bruises where no one but him will see them."

I clenched my teeth. "If you were her lover, why didn't you stop it?"

The wrong thing to say. Utterly wrong, by the dark fury that rippled across Helion's face. "Beron is a High Lord, and she is his wife, mother of his brood. She chose to stay. *Chose*. And with the protocols and rules, *Lady*, you will find that most situations like the one you were in do *not* end well for those who interfere."

I didn't back down, didn't apologize. "You barely even looked at her today."

"We have more important matters at hand."

"Beron never called you out for it?"

"To publicly do so would be to admit that his *possession* made a fool of him. So we continue our little dance, these centuries later." I somehow doubted that beneath that roguish charm and irreverence, Helion felt it was a dance at all.

But if it had ended centuries ago, and she'd never seen him again, had let Beron treat her so abominably . . .

Whatever you've just figured out, Rhys said, *you'd better stop looking so shocked by it.*

I forced a smile to my face. "You High Lords really do love your melodrama, don't you?"

Helion's own smile didn't reach his eyes. But Rhys asked, "In your libraries, have you ever encountered a mention of how the wall might be repaired?"

Helion began asking why we wanted to know, what Hybern was doing with the Cauldron . . . and Rhys fed him answers, easily and smoothly.

While we spoke, I said down the bond, *Helion is Lucien's father.*

Rhys was silent. Then—

Holy burning hell.

His shock was a shooting star between us.

I let my gaze dart through the room, half paying attention to Helion's musing on the wall and how to repair it, then dared study the High Lord for a heartbeat. *Look at him. The nose is the same, the smile. The voice. Even Lucien's skin is darker than his brothers'.* A golden brown compared to their pale coloring.

It would explain why his father and brothers detest him so much—why they have tormented him his entire life.

My heart squeezed at that. *And why Eris didn't want him dead. He wasn't a threat to Eris's power—his throne.* I swallowed. *Helion has no idea, does he?*

It would seem not.

The Lady of Autumn's favorite son—not only from Lucien's goodness. But because he was the child she'd dreamed of having . . . with the male she undoubtedly loved.

Beron must have discovered the affair when she was pregnant with Lucien.

He likely suspected, but there was no way to prove it—not if she was sharing his bed, too. Rhys's disgust was a tang in my mouth. *I have no doubt Beron debated killing her for the betrayal, and even afterward. When Lucien could be passable as his own offspring—just enough to make him doubt who had sired his last son.*

I wrapped my head around it. Lucien not Beron's son, but Helion's. *His power is flame, though. They've mused Beron's title could go to him.*

His mother's family is strong—that was why Beron wanted a bride from their line. The gift could be hers.

You never suspected?

Not once. I'm mortified I didn't even consider it.

What does this mean, though?

Nothing—ultimately nothing. Other than the fact that Lucien might be Helion's sole heir.

And that . . . it changed nothing in this war. Especially not with Lucien on the continent, hunting that enchanted queen. A bird of flame . . . and a lord of fire. I wondered if they'd found each other yet.

A door opened and shut in the foyer beyond, and I braced myself as Nesta appeared. Helion paused his debating the wall to survey her carefully, as he had done earlier.

Spell-Cleaver. That was his title.

She surveyed *him* with her usual disdain.

But Helion gave her the same bow he'd offered me—though his smile was edged with enough sensuality that even my heart raced a bit. No wonder the Lady of Autumn hadn't stood a chance. "I don't think we were introduced properly earlier," he crooned to Nesta. "I'm—"

"I don't care," Nesta said with a snap of her wrist, striding right past him and up to my side. "I'd like a word," she said. "Now."

Cassian was biting his knuckle to keep from laughing—at the utter surprise and shock on Helion's face. It wasn't every day, I supposed, that anyone of either sex dismissed him so thoroughly. I threw the High Lord a semi-apologetic glance and led my sister out of the room.

"What is it?" I asked when Nesta and I had entered her bedroom, the space bedecked in pink silk and gold, accents of ivory scattered throughout. The lavishness of it indeed put our various homes to shame.

"We need to leave," Nesta said. "Right now."

Every sense went on alert. "Why?"

"It feels wrong. Something feels wrong."

I studied her, the clear sky beyond the towering, drape-framed windows. "Rhys and the others would sense it. You're likely just picking up on all the power gathered here."

"Something is *wrong*," Nesta insisted.

"I'm not doubting you feel that way but . . . If none of the others are picking it up—"

"I am not *like* the others." Her throat bobbed. "We need to leave."

"I can send you back to Velaris, but we have things to discuss here—"

"I don't care about me, I—"

The door opened, and Cassian stalked in, face grave. The sight of the wings, the Illyrian armor in this opulent, pink-filled room planted itself in my mind, the painting already taking form, as he said, "What's wrong."

He studied every inch of her. As if there were nothing and no one else here, anywhere.

But I said, "She senses something is off—says we need to leave right away."

I waited for the dismissal, but Cassian angled his head. "What, precisely, feels wrong?"

Nesta stiffened, mouth pursing as she weighed his tone. "It feels like there's this . . . dread. This sense that . . . that I forgot something but can't remember what."

Cassian stared at her for a moment longer. "I'll tell Rhys."

And he did.

Within moments, Rhys, Cassian, and Azriel had vanished, leaving Mor and Helion in alert silence. I waited with Nesta. Five minutes. Ten. Fifteen.

Thirty minutes later, they returned, shaking their heads. Nothing.

Not in the palace, not in the lands around it, not in the skies above or the earth below. Not for miles and miles. Nothing. Rhys even checked with Amren, and found nothing amiss in Velaris—Elain, mercifully, safe and sound.

None of them, however, were stupid enough to suggest that Nesta had made it up. Not with that otherworldly power in her veins. Or that perhaps the dread was a lingering effect of her time in Hybern. Like the crushing panic that I'd struggled to face down, that still stalked me some nights.

So we stayed. We ate in our private dining room, Helion joining us, no sign of Tarquin or Thesan—certainly not Tamlin.

Kallias and Viviane appeared midway through the meal, and Mor kicked Cassian out of his seat to make space for her friend. They chatted and gossiped—even though Mor kept glancing at Helion.

And the High Lord of Day kept glancing at her.

Azriel barely spoke, those shadows still perched on his shoulders. Mor barely looked at him.

But we dined and drank for hours, until night was overhead. And though Rhys and Kallias were tense, careful around each other . . . By the end of the meal, they were at least talking.

Nesta was the first to leave the table, still wary and on edge. The others made one final check of the grounds before we tumbled into the silk sheets of our cloud-soft beds.

Rhys and I left Mor and Helion talking knee to knee on the sitting room cushions, Viviane and Kallias long returned to their suite. I had no idea where Azriel went off to—or Cassian, for that matter.

And when I emerged from washing up in the ivory-and-gold bathing room and Helion's deep murmur and Mor's sultry laugh flitted in from the hall—when it moved past our door and then *her* door creaked open and closed . . .

Rhysand's wings were folded in tightly as he surveyed the stars beyond the bedroom windows. Quieter and smaller here, somehow.

"Why?"

He knew what I meant.

"Mor gets spooked. And what Az did today scared the shit out of her."

"The violence?"

"The violence as a result of what he feels, lingering guilt over the deal with Eris—and what neither of them will face."

"Don't you think it's been long enough? And that taking Helion to bed is likely the *worst* possible thing to do?"

But I had no doubt Helion needed a distraction as much as Mor did. From thinking too long about the people they loved—who they could not have.

"Mor and Azriel have both taken lovers throughout the centuries," he said, wings shifting slightly. "The only difference here is the close proximity."

"You sound remarkably fine with this."

Rhys glanced over a shoulder to where I lingered by the foot of the massive ivory bed, its carved headboard fashioned after overlapping waterlilies. "It's their life—their relationship. They have both had plenty of opportunities to confess what they feel. Yet they have not. Mor especially. For private reasons of her own, I'm sure. My meddling isn't going to make it any better."

"But—but he *loves* her. How can he sit idly by?"

"He thinks she's happier without him." His eyes shone with the memory—of his own choice to sit back. "He thinks he's unworthy of her."

"It seems like an Illyrian trait."

Rhys snorted, returning to the stars. I came up to his side and slid my arm around his waist. He opened his arm to me, cupping my shoulder as I rested my head against that soft spot where his own shoulder met his chest. A heartbeat later, his wing curved around me, too, enveloping me in his shadowed warmth. "There will come a day when Azriel has to decide if he is going to fight for her or let her go. And it won't be because some other male insults her or beds her."

"And what about Cassian? He's entangled—and enabling this nonsense."

A wry smile. "Cassian is going to have to decide some things, too. In the near future, I think."

"Are he and Nesta . . . ?"

"I don't know. Until the bond snaps into place, it can be hard to detect." Rhys swallowed once, gaze fixed on the stars. I simply waited. "Tamlin still loves you, you know."

"I know."

"That was an ugly encounter."

"All of it was ugly," I said. What Beron and Tamlin had brought up with Amarantha, what Rhys had been forced to reveal . . . "Are you all right?" I could still feel the clamminess of his hand upon mine as he spoke of what Amarantha had done.

He brushed a thumb down my shoulder. "It wasn't . . . easy." He amended, "I thought I'd vomit all over the floor."

I squeezed him a little tighter. "I'm sorry you had to share those things—sorry you . . . sorry for all of it, Rhys." I breathed in his scent, taking it deep into my lungs. Out—we had made it out. "And I know it likely means nothing, but . . . I'm proud of you. That you were brave enough to tell them."

"It doesn't mean nothing," he said softly. "That you feel that way about me—about today." He kissed my temple, and warmth flickered along the bond. "It means . . ." His wing curved closer around me. "I don't have the words to tell you what it means." But as that love, that joy and light shimmered through the bond . . . I understood.

He peered down at me. "And are you . . . all right?"

I nestled my head further into his chest. "I just feel . . . tired. Sad. Sad that it turned so awful—and yet . . . yet *furious* about everything that happened to me, to my sisters. I . . ." I blew out a long breath. "When I was back at the Spring Court . . ." I swallowed. "I looked—for their wings."

Rhys went utterly still, and I took his hand, squeezing hard as he only said, "Did you find them?" The words were barely a brush of air.

I shook my head, but said before the grief on his face could grow, "I learned that he burned them—long ago."

Rhys said nothing for a lingering moment, his attention returning to the stars. "Thank you for even thinking—for risking to look for them."

The only trace—the horrific remnants—of his mother and sister. "I didn't . . . I'm glad he burned them," Rhys admitted. "I could happily kill him, for so many things, and yet . . ." He rubbed his chest. "I'm glad he offered them that peace, at least."

I nodded. "I know." I ran my thumb over the back of his hand. And perhaps because of the raw, stark quiet, I confessed, "It feels strange, to share a room, a bed, with you under the same roof as him."

"I can imagine."

For somewhere in this palace, Tamlin *was* lying in bed—well aware that I was about to enter this one with Rhysand. The past tangled and snarled, and I whispered, "I don't think—I don't think I can have sex here. With him so close." Rhys remained quiet. "I'm sorry if—"

"You don't need to apologize. Ever."

I looked up, finding his gaze on me—not angry or frustrated, but . . . sad. Knowing. "I want to share this bed with you, though," I breathed. "I want you to hold me."

Stars flickered to life in his eyes. "Always," he promised, kissing my brow, his wings now enveloping me completely. "Always."

CHAPTER
48

Helion slipped from Mor's room before we were awake—though I certainly heard them throughout the night. Enough so that Rhys put a shield around our room. Azriel and Cassian didn't return at all.

Mor didn't look like a female who had been tumbling with a gorgeous High Lord, however, as she picked at her breakfast. There was something vacant in her brown eyes, a paleness to her ordinarily golden skin.

Cassian strutted in at last, greeting Mor with a chipper, "You look terrible—Helion keep you up all night?"

She threw her spoon at him. Then her porridge.

Cassian caught the first and shielded against the other, his Siphon blazing like an awakening ember. Porridge slid to the floor.

"Helion wanted you to join," she mildly replied, refilling her tea. "Quite badly."

"Maybe next time," Cassian said, dropping into the seat beside me. "How's your sister?"

"She seemed fine—still worried." I didn't ask where he and Azriel had been all night. If only because I wasn't sure Mor wanted to hear the answer.

Cassian served himself from the platters of fruits and pastries, frowning at the lack of meat. "Ready for another day full of arguing and plotting?"

Mor and I grumbled. Rhys strode in, hair still damp from his bath, and grinned. "That's the spirit."

Despite the fraught day ahead, I smiled at my mate.

He'd held me all night, tucked against his chest, his wing draped over me. A different sort of intimacy than the sex—deeper. Our souls entwined, holding tight.

I'd awoken to his wing still over me, his breath tickling my ear. My throat had closed up as I'd studied his sleeping face, my chest tightening to the point of pain. I was well aware how wildly I loved him, but looking at him then . . . I felt it in every pore of my body, felt it as if it might crush me, consume me. And the next time someone insulted him . . .

The thought was still prowling through my mind as we finished breakfast, dressed, and returned to that chamber atop the palace. To begin forming the backbone of this alliance.

I kept the crown from yesterday, but swapped my Starfall gown for one of glittering black, the dress made up of solid ebony silk overlaid with shimmering obsidian gossamer. Its skirts flowed behind me, the tight sleeves tapered to points that brushed the center of my hand, looped into place around my middle finger with an attached onyx ring. If I was a fallen star yesterday, today Rhys's mysterious clothier had made me into the Queen of the Night.

The rest of my companions had dressed accordingly.

Yesterday, we had been ourselves—open and friendly and caring. Today we showed the other courts what we'd unleash upon our enemies. What we were capable of if provoked.

Helion was back to his edged, swaggering aloofness, lounging in his chair as we entered that lovely chamber atop one of the palace's many gilded towers. He gave Mor an extra glance, lips curving in sensual amusement. He was resplendent today in robes of cobalt edged in gold that offset his gleaming brown skin, golden sandals upon his feet. Azriel, shadows wafting from his shoulders and trailing at his feet, ignored him as he passed. The shadowsinger hadn't shown a flicker of emotion, however, to Mor when he'd met us in the foyer.

She hadn't asked where he'd been all night and morning, and Azriel had volunteered nothing. But he didn't seem inclined to ignore her, at least. No, he'd just settled back into his usual watchful quiet, and Mor had been content to let him, slumping a bit in relief as soon as he'd turned to lead us to the meeting, likely having already scouted the walk minutes ago.

Thesan was the only person who bothered to greet us when we passed through that wisteria-draped archway, but he took one look at our attire, our faces, and muttered a prayer to the Cauldron. His lover, clad in his captain's armor once more, sized us up, his wings flaring slightly, but kept seated with the other Peregryns.

Tamlin arrived last, raking his gaze over all of us as he sat. I didn't bother to acknowledge him.

And Helion didn't wait for Thesan to beckon to begin. He merely crossed an ankle over a knee and said, "I thoroughly reviewed the charts and figures you've compiled, Tamlin."

"And?" Tamlin bit out. Today would go *incredibly* well, then.

"And," Helion said simply, no trace of the laughing, easy male of the night before, "if you can rally your forces quickly, you and Tarquin might be able to hold the front line long enough for those of us above the Middle to bring the larger hosts."

"It's not that easy," Tamlin said through his teeth. "I have a third of them left." A seething look toward me. "After Feyre destroyed their faith in me."

I had done that—in my rage, my need for vengeance . . . I had not thought long-term. Had not considered that perhaps we would *need* that army. But—

Nesta let out a breathy, sharp noise and surged from her chair.

I lunged for her, nearly tripping over the skirts of my dress as she staggered back, a hand clutching at her chest.

Another step would have taken her stumbling into the reflection pool, but Mor sprang forward, gripping her. "What's wrong?" Mor demanded, holding my sister upright as her face contorted in what looked to be—pain. Confusion and pain.

Sweat beaded on Nesta's brow, though her face went deathly pale. "Something . . ." The word was cut off by a low groan. She sagged, and Mor caught her fully, scanning Nesta's face. Cassian was instantly there, his hand at her back, teeth bared at the invisible threat.

"Nesta," I said, reaching for her.

Nesta seized—then twisted past Cassian to empty her stomach into the reflection pool.

"Poison?" Kallias asked, pushing Viviane behind him. She merely stepped around his arm. Tamlin remained seated, his jaw a hard line, monitoring us all.

But Helion and Thesan strode forward, grim and focused. Helion's power flickered around him like blindingly bright fireflies, darting to my sister, landing on her gently.

Thesan, glowing gold and rosy, laid a hand on Nesta's arm. Healing.

"Nothing," they said together.

Nesta rested her head against Mor's shoulder, her breathing ragged. "Something is wrong," she managed to say. "Not with me. Not me."

But with the Cauldron.

Rhys was having some sort of silent conversation with Azriel and Cassian, the latter monitoring every breath my sister took. But the two Illyrians nodded to Rhys, and began stalking for the open windows—to fly out.

Nesta moaned, body tensing as if she'd vomit again. But then we felt it.

A shuddering through the earth. Through air and stone and green, growing things.

As if some great god blew a breath across the land.

Then the impact came.

Rhys threw himself over me so fast I didn't register wholly that the mountain itself *shook*, that the building *swayed*. We hit the stones as debris rained, and I felt him readying to winnow—

Then it stopped.

Screaming rose up from the valley below. But silence reigned in the palace. Amongst us.

Nesta vomited again, and Mor let her sag to the floor this time.

"What in *hell*—" Helion began.

But Rhys hauled his body off mine, his tan face draining of color. His lips going bloodless as he stared southward. Far, far southward.

I felt his magic spear from him, a shooting star across the land.

And when he looked back at us, his eyes went right to me. It was the fear in them—the sorrow and fear—that made my mouth go wholly dry. That made my blood run cold.

Rhys swallowed. Once. Twice. Then he declared hoarsely, "The King of Hybern just used the Cauldron to attack the wall."

Murmuring—some gasps.

Rhys swallowed a third time, and the ground slid out from under me as he clarified, "The wall is gone. Shattered. Across Prythian, and on the continent." He said again, as if convincing himself, "We were too late—too slow. Hybern just destroyed the wall."

CHAPTER
49

Nesta's connection to the Cauldron, Rhys mused as we gathered around the dining table in the town house, had allowed her to sense that the King of Hybern was rallying its power.

The same way I was able to wield the connection to the High Lords to track their traces of power, and to find the Book and Cauldron, Nesta's own power—own immortality—was so closely bound to the Cauldron that its dreadful presence, when awoken, brushed through her, too.

That was why he hunted her. Not just for the power she'd taken . . . but for the fact that Nesta was a warning bell.

We'd all departed the Dawn Court within minutes, Thesan promising large shipments of faebane antidote to every High Lord and army within two days, and that his Peregryns would begin readying themselves under his captain's command—to join the Illyrians in the skies.

Kallias and Helion swore their own terrestrial armies would march as soon as possible. Only Tamlin, whose southern border covered the entire wall, was unaccounted for—his armies in shambles. Helion just said to Tamlin before the latter left, "Get your people out. Bring whatever host you can muster." Whatever remained after me.

Tarquin echoed the sentiment, along with his promise to offer safe harbor for the Spring Court. Tamlin didn't reply to either of them. Didn't confirm that he would be bringing forces before he winnowed—without a glance at me. A small relief, since I hadn't decided whether to demand his sworn help or spit on him.

Good-byes were brief. Viviane had embraced Mor tightly—then me, to my surprise. Kallias only clasped Rhys's hand, a taut, tentative gesture, and vanished with his mate. Then Helion, with a wink at all of us. Tarquin was the last to go, Varian and Cresseida flanking him. His armada, they'd decided, would be left to guard his own cities while the bulk of his soldiers would march on land.

Tarquin's crushing blue eyes flared as his power rallied to winnow them. But Varian said—to me, to Rhys—"Tell her thank you." He put a hand on his chest, the fine gold-and-silver thread of his teal jacket glinting in the morning sun. "Tell her . . ." The Prince of Adriata shook his head. "I'll tell her myself the next time I see her." It seemed like more of a promise—that Varian *would* see Amren again, war or no. Then they were gone.

No word arrived from Beron before we uttered our farewells and gratitude to Thesan. Not a whisper that Beron might have changed his mind. Or that Eris might have persuaded him.

But that was not my concern. Or Nesta's.

If the wall had come down . . . Too late. We'd been too late. All of that research . . . I should have insisted that if Amren deemed Nesta nearly ready, then we should have gone directly to the wall. Seen what she could do, spell from the Book or no.

Perhaps it was my fault, for wanting to shelter her, build her strength, for letting her remain withdrawn. But if I had pushed and pushed . . .

Even now, seated around the town house dining table in Velaris, I hadn't decided whether the potential of breaking my sister permanently was worth the cost of saving lives. I didn't know how Rhys and the others had made such decisions—for years. Especially during Amarantha's reign.

"We should have evacuated months ago," Nesta said, her plate of roast chicken and vegetables untouched. It was the first words any of us had spoken in minutes while we'd all picked at our food.

Elain had been told—by Amren. She now sat at the table, more straight-backed and clear-eyed than I'd seen her. Had she beheld this, in whatever wanderings that new, inner sight granted her? Had the Cauldron whispered of it while we'd been away? I hadn't the heart to ask her.

Rhys was saying to Nesta, "We can go to your estate tonight—evacuate your household and bring them back here."

"They will not come."

"Then they will likely die."

Nesta straightened her fork and knife beside her plate. "Can't you spirit them away somewhere south—far from here?"

"That many people? Not without first finding a safe place, which would take time we don't have." Rhys considered. "If we get a ship, they can sail—"

"They will demand their families and friends come."

A beat of silence. Not an option. Then Elain said quietly, "We could move them to Graysen's estate."

We all faced her at the evenness of her voice.

She swallowed, her slender throat so pale, and explained, "His father has high walls—made of thick stone. With space for plenty of people and supplies." All of us made a point *not* to look at that ring she still wore. Elain went on, "His father has been planning for something like this for . . . a long time. They have defenses, stores . . ." A shallow breath. "And a grove of ash trees, with a cache of weapons made from them."

A snarl from Cassian. Despite their power, their might . . . However those trees had been created, something in the ash wood cut right through Fae defenses. I'd seen it firsthand—killed one of Tamlin's sentinels with an arrow through the throat.

"If the faeries who attack possess magic," Cassian said, and Elain recoiled at the harsh tone, "then thick stone won't do much."

"There are escape tunnels," Elain whispered. "Perhaps it is better than nothing."

A glance between the Illyrians. "We can set up a guard—" Cassian began.

"No," Elain interrupted, her voice louder than I'd heard in months. "They . . . Graysen and his father . . ."

Cassian's jaw tightened. "Then we cloak—"

"They have hounds. Bred and trained to hunt you. Detect you."

A stiff silence as my friends contemplated how, exactly, those hounds had been trained.

"You can't mean to leave their castle undefended," Cassian tried a shade more gently. "Even with the ash, it won't be enough. We'd need to set wards at the very minimum."

Elain considered. "I can speak to him."

"No," I said—at the same moment Nesta did.

But Elain cut us off. "If—if you and . . . they"—a glance at Rhys, my friends—"come with me, your Fae scents might distract the dogs."

"You're Fae, too," Nesta reminded her.

"Glamour me," Elain said—to Rhys. "Make me look human. Just long enough to convince him to open his gates to those seeking sanctuary. Perhaps even let you set those wards around the estate."

And with our scents to confuse the hounds . . . "This could end very badly, Elain."

She brushed her thumb over the iron-and-diamond engagement ring. "It's already ended badly. Now it's just a matter of deciding how we meet the consequences."

"Wisely said," Mor offered, smiling softly at Elain. She looked to Cassian. "You need to move the Illyrian legions today."

Cassian nodded, but said to Rhys, "With the wall down, we need you to make a few things clear to the Illyrians. I need you at the camp with me—to give one of your pretty speeches before we go."

Rhys's mouth twitched toward a smile. "We can all go—then head to the human lands." He surveyed us, the town house. "We have an hour to prepare. Meet back here—then we leave."

Mor and Azriel instantly winnowed out, Cassian striding for Rhys to ask him about the Court of Nightmares soldiers and their preparation.

Nesta and I aimed for Elain, both of us speaking at once. "Are you sure?" I demanded at the same time Nesta said, "I can go—let me talk to him."

Elain only rose to her feet. "He doesn't know you," she said to me. Then she faced Nesta with a frank, bemused look. "And he hates you."

Some rotten part of me wondered if their broken engagement was for the best, then. Or if Elain had somehow suggested this visit, right after Lucien had left Prythian, for some chance to . . . I didn't let myself finish the thought.

I said, watching the space where my friends had vanished from the town house, "I need you to understand, Elain, that if this goes badly . . . if he tries to harm you, or any of us . . ."

"I know. You will defend your own."

"I will defend *you*."

The vacancy fogged over her eyes. But Elain lifted her chin. "No matter what, don't kill him. Please."

"We'll try—"

"*Swear it.*" I'd never heard that tone from her. Ever.

"I can't make that promise." I wouldn't back down, not on this. "But I will do everything in my power to avoid it."

Elain seemed to realize it, too. She peered down at herself, at the simple blue gown she wore. "I need to dress."

"I'll help you," Nesta offered.

But Elain shook her head. "Nuala and Cerridwen will help me."

Then she was gone—shoulders a little squarer.

Nesta's throat bobbed. I murmured, "It wasn't your fault—that the wall came down before we could stop it."

Steel-filled eyes cut to me. "If I had stayed to practice—"

"Then you just would have been here while you waited for us to return from the meeting."

Nesta smoothed a hand down her dark dress. "What do I do now?"

A purpose, I realized. Assigning her the task of finding a way to repair the holes in the wall . . . it had given my sister what perhaps our human lives had never granted her: a bearing.

"You come with us—to Graysen's estate, and then travel with the army. If you're connected with the Cauldron, then we'll need you close. Need you to tell us if it's being wielded again."

Not quite a mission, but Nesta nodded all the same.

Right as Cassian clapped Rhys on the shoulder and prowled toward us. He paused a foot away, and frowned. "Dresses aren't good for flying, ladies."

Nesta didn't reply.

He lifted a brow. "No barking and biting today?"

But Nesta didn't rise to meet him, her face still drained and sallow. "I've never worn pants," was all she said.

I could have sworn concern flashed across Cassian's features. But he brushed it aside and drawled, "I have no doubt you'd start a riot if you did."

No reaction. Had the Cauldron—

Cassian stepped in Nesta's path when she tried to walk past him. Put a tan, callused hand on her forehead. She shook off the touch, but he gripped her wrist, forcing her to meet his stare. "Any one of those human pricks makes a move to hurt you," he breathed, "and you kill them."

He wouldn't be coming—no, he'd be mustering the full might of the Illyrian legions. Azriel would be joining us, though.

Cassian pressed one of his knives into Nesta's hand. "Ash can kill you now," he said with lethal quiet as she stared down at the blade. "A scratch can make you queasy enough to be vulnerable. Remember where the exits are in every room, every fence and courtyard—mark them when you go in, and mark how many men are around you. Mark where Rhys and the others are. Don't forget that you're stronger and faster. Aim for the soft parts," he added, folding her fingers around the hilt. "And if someone gets you into a hold . . ." My sister said nothing as Cassian showed her the sensitive areas on a man. Not just the groin, but the inside of the foot, pinching the thigh, using her elbow like a weapon. When he finished, he stepped back, his hazel eyes churning with some emotion I couldn't place.

Nesta surveyed the fine dagger in her hand. Then lifted her head to look at him.

"I told you to come to training," Cassian said with a cocky grin, and strode off.

I studied Nesta, the dagger, her quiet, still face.

"Don't even start," she warned me, and headed for the stairs.

⁜

I found Amren in her apartment, cursing at the Book.

"We're leaving within the hour," I said. "Do you have everything you need here?"

"Yes." Amren lifted her head, those uptilted silver eyes swirling with ire. Not at me, I realized with no small relief. At the fact that Hybern had beaten us to the wall. Beaten *her*.

That wasn't my problem.

Not as the words of that meeting with the High Lords eddied. Not as I again saw Beron walk out, no soldiers or help promised. Not as I heard Rhys and Cassian discussing how few soldiers the others possessed compared to Hybern's forces.

The king's taunt to Rhys had been roiling through my mind for days now.

Hybern expected him to give everything—*everything*—to stop them. Had claimed only that would give us a fighting shot. And I knew my mate. Perhaps better than I knew myself. I knew Rhys would spend all of himself, destroy himself, if it meant a chance at winning. At survival.

The other High Lords . . . I couldn't afford to risk counting on them. Helion, strong as he was, wouldn't even step in to save his own lover. Tarquin, perhaps. But the others . . . I didn't know them. Didn't have time to. And I would not gamble their tentative allegiance. I would not gamble Rhys.

"What do you want?" Amren snapped when I remained staring at her.

"There is a creature beneath the library. Do you know it?"

Amren shut the Book. "Its name is Bryaxis."

"What is it."

"You do not want to know, girl."

I shoved back the arm of my ebony dress, the finery so at odds with the loft, its messiness. "I made a bargain with it." I showed her the band of tattoo around my forearm. "So I suppose I do."

Amren stood, brushing dust off her gray pants. "I heard about that. Foolish girl."

"I had no choice. And now we are bound to each other."

"And what of it?"

"I want to ask it for another bargain. I need you to examine the wards holding it down there—and to explain things." I didn't bother to look pleasant. Or desperate. Or grateful. I didn't bother to wipe the cold, hard mask from my face as I added, "You're coming with me. Right now."

CHAPTER
50

There was no priestess waiting to lead us into the black pit at the heart of the library. And Amren, for once, kept quiet.

We reached that bottom level, that impenetrable dark, our steps the only sound.

"I want to talk to you," I said into the blackness beckoning beyond the end of the light leaking down from high above.

One does not summon me.

"I summon you. I'm here to offer you company. As part of our bargain."

Silence.

Then I felt it, snaking and curling around us, gobbling up the light. Amren swore softly.

You brought—what is it you brought?

"Someone like you. Or you could be like them."

You speak in riddles.

A cool, insubstantial hand brushed against my nape and I tried not to inch back toward the light. "Bryaxis. Your name is Bryaxis. And someone locked you down here a long time ago."

The darkness paused.

"I'm here to offer you another bargain."

Amren remained still and silent, as I'd told her to, offering me a single nod of confirmation. She could indeed sever the wards holding Bryaxis down here—when the time was right.

"There is a war," I said, fighting to keep my voice steady. "A terrible war about to break across the land. If I can free you, will you fight for me? For me and my High Lord?"

The thing—Bryaxis—did not reply.

I nudged Amren with my elbow.

She said, her voice as young and old as the creature's, "We will offer you freedom from this place in exchange for it."

A bargain. A simple, powerful magic. As great as any the Book could muster.

This is my home.

I considered. "Then what is it you want in exchange?"

Silence.

Sunlight. And moonlight. The stars.

I opened my mouth to say I wasn't entirely sure that even as High Lady of the Night Court I could promise such things, but Amren stepped on my foot and murmured, "A window. High above."

Not a mirror, as the Carver wanted. But a window in the mountain. We'd have to carve far, far up, but—

"That's it?"

Amren stomped on my foot this time.

Bryaxis whispered in my ear, *Will I be able to hunt without restraint on the battlefields? Drink in their fear and dread until I am sated?*

I felt slightly bad for Hybern as I said, "Yes—only Hybern. And only until the war is over." One way or another.

A beat of silence. *What would you have me do, then?*

I gestured to Amren. "She will explain. She will disable the wards— when we need you."

Then I will wait.

"Then it's a bargain. You will obey our orders in this war, fight for us until we no longer need you, and in exchange . . . we shall bring the sun and moon and stars to you. In your home." Another prisoner who had come to love its cell. Perhaps Bryaxis and the Carver should meet. An ancient death-god and the face of nightmares. The painting, dreadful yet alluring, began to creep roots deep within my mind.

I kept my shoulders loose, posture as casual as I could summon while the darkness slid around me, winding between me and Amren, and whispered into my ear, *It is a bargain.*

⁜

I made the hour count. When we all gathered in the town house foyer once more to winnow to the Illyrian camp, I'd changed into my fighting leathers, my new tattoo concealed beneath.

No one asked where I'd gone. Though Mor looked me over and said, "Where's Amren?"

"Still poring over the Book," I answered just as Rhys winnowed into the town house. Not a lie. Amren would stay here—until we needed her at the battlefields.

Rhys angled his head. "Looking for what? The wall is gone."

"For anything," I said. "For another way to nullify the Cauldron that doesn't involve the insides of my head leaking out through my nose."

Rhys cringed and opened his mouth to object, but I cut him off. "There must be another way—Amren thinks there *must* be another way. It doesn't hurt to look. And have her hunt for any other spell that might stop the king."

And when Amren was not doing that . . . she'd bring down those complex wards containing Bryaxis beneath the library—to be severed only when I called for Bryaxis. Only when the might of Hybern's army was fully upon us. If I could not get the Ouroboros for the Carver . . . then Bryaxis was better than nothing.

I wasn't entirely certain why I didn't mention it to the others.

Rhys's eyes flickered, no doubt warring with the idea of what role any other route would require of me in regard to the Cauldron, but he nodded.

I interlaced my fingers with his, and he squeezed once.

Behind me, Mor took Nesta and Cassian by the hand, readying to winnow them to the camp, while shadows gathered around Azriel, Elain at his side, wide-eyed at the spymaster's display.

But we hesitated—all of us. And I allowed myself one last time to drink it in, the furniture and the wood and the sunlight. To listen to the sounds of Velaris, the laughing of children in the streets, the song of the gulls.

In the silence, I knew my friends were, too.

Rhys cleared his throat, and nodded to Mor. Then she was gone, Cassian and Nesta with her. Then Azriel, gently taking Elain's hand in his own, as if afraid his scars would hurt her.

Alone with Rhys, I savored the buttery sunshine leaking in from the windows of the front door. Breathed in the smell of the bread Nuala and Cerridwen had baked that morning with Elain.

"The creature in the library," I murmured. "Its name is Bryaxis."

Rhys lifted a brow. "Oh?"

"I offered it a bargain. To fight for us."

Stars danced in those violet eyes. "And what did Bryaxis say?"

"Only that it wants a window—to see the stars and moon and sun."

"You did explain that we need it to slaughter our enemies, didn't you?"

I nudged him with a hip. "The library is its home. It only wanted some adjustments made to it."

A crooked smile tugged on Rhys's mouth. "Well, I suppose if I now have to redecorate my own lodgings to match Thesan's splendor, I might as well add a window for the poor thing."

I elbowed him in the ribs that time. He still wore his finery from the meeting. Rhys chuckled. "So our army grows by one. Poor Cassian will never recover when he sees his newest recruit."

"With any luck, Hybern won't, either."

"And the Carver?"

"He can rot down there. I don't have time for his games. Bryaxis will have to be enough."

Rhys glanced at my arm, as if he could see the new, second band beside the first one. He lifted our joined hands and pressed a kiss to the back of my palm.

Again, we silently looked around the town house, taking in every last detail, the quiet that now lay like a layer of dust upon it.

Rhys said softly, "I wonder if we'll see it again."

I knew he wasn't just talking about the house. But I rose up on my toes and kissed his cheek. "We will," I promised as a dark wind gathered to sweep us to the Illyrian war-camp. I held tightly to him as I added, "We'll see it all again."

And when that night-kissed wind winnowed us away, away into war, away into untold danger . . . . I prayed that my promise held true.

PART THREE

HIGH LADY

CHAPTER
51

Even at the height of summer, the Illyrian mountain-camp was damp. Brisk. There were some truly lovely days, Rhys assured me when I scowled as we winnowed in, but cooler weather was better anyway, when an army was involved. Heat made tempers rise. Especially when it was too hot to sleep comfortably. And considering the Illyrians were a testy lot to begin with . . . It was a blessing that the sky was cloudy and the wind mist-kissed.

But even the weather wasn't enough to make the greeting party look pleasant.

I only recognized one of the muscle-bound Illyrians in full armor waiting for us. Lord Devlon. The sneer was still on his face—though milder compared to the outright contempt contorting the features of a few. Like Azriel and Cassian, they possessed dark hair and eyes of assorted hazel and brown. And like my friends, their skin was rich shades of golden brown, some flecked with bone-white scars of varying severity.

But unlike my friends, one or two Siphons adorned their hands. The seven Azriel and Cassian wore seemed almost vulgar by comparison.

But the gathered males only looked at Rhys, as if the two Illyrians flanking him were little more than trees. Mor and I remained on either side of Nesta, who had changed into a dark blue, practical dress and now surveyed the camp, the winged warriors, the sheer *size* of the host assembled in the camp around us . . .

We kept Elain half-hidden behind the wall of our bodies. Considering the backward view of the Illyrians toward females, I'd suggested we remain a step away on this meeting—literally. There were only a few female fighters in the legion . . . Now was not the time to test the tolerance of the Illyrians. Later—later, if we won this war. If we survived.

Devlon was speaking, "It's true, then. The wall came down."

"A temporary failure," Rhys crooned. He was still wearing his fine jacket and pants from the meeting with the High Lords. For whatever reason, he hadn't chosen to wear the Illyrian leathers. Or the wings.

It's because they already know I trained with them, am one of them. They need to remember that I'm also their High Lord. And I have no intention of loosening the leash.

The words were a silk-covered scrape of nails down my mind.

Rhys began giving unwavering, cold instructions about the impending push southward. The voice of the High Lord—the voice of a warrior who had fought in the War and had no intention of losing this one. Cassian frequently added his own orders and clarifications.

Azriel—Azriel just stared them all down. He had not wanted to come to the camp months ago. Disliked being back here. Hated these people, his heritage.

The other lords kept glancing to the shadowsinger in dread and rage and disgust. He only leveled that lethal gaze back at them.

On and on they went, until Devlon looked over Rhys's shoulder—to where we stood.

A scowl at Mor. A frown at me—wisely subdued. Then he noticed Nesta.

"What is *that*," Devlon asked.

Nesta merely stared at him, one hand clamping the edges of her gray cloak together at her chest. One of the other camp-lords made some sign against evil.

"*That*," Cassian said too quietly, "is none of your concern."

"Is she a witch."

I opened my mouth, but Nesta said flatly, "Yes."

And I watched as nine full-grown, weathered Illyrian warlords flinched.

"She may act like one sometimes," Cassian clarified, "but no—she is High Fae."

"She is no more High Fae than we are," Devlon countered.

A pause that went on for too long. Even Rhys seemed at a loss for words. Devlon had complained when we'd first met that Amren and I were *Other*. As if he possessed some sense for such things. Devlon muttered, "Keep her away from the females and children."

I clutched Nesta's free hand in silent warning to remain quiet.

Mor let out a snort that made the Illyrians stiffen. But she shifted, revealing Elain behind her. Elain was just blinking, wide-eyed, at the camp. The army.

Devlon let out a grunt at the sight of her. But Elain wrapped her own blue cloak around herself, averting her eyes from all of those towering, muscled warriors, the army camp bustling toward the horizon . . . She was a rose bloom in a mud field. Filled with galloping horses.

"Don't be afraid of them," Nesta said beneath lowered brows.

If Elain was a blooming flower in this army camp, then Nesta . . . she was a freshly forged sword, waiting to draw blood.

Take them into our war tent, Rhys said silently to me. *Devlon honestly might throw a hissy fit if he has to face Nesta for another minute.*

I'd pay good money to see that.

So would I.

I hid my smile. "Let's find something warm to drink," I said to my sisters, beckoning Mor to join. We aimed for the largest of the tents in the camp, a black banner sewn with a mountain and three silver stars flapping from its apex. Warriors and females laboring around the fires silently monitored us. Nesta stared them all down. Elain kept her focus on the dry, rocky ground.

The tent's interior was simple yet luxurious: thick carpets covered the low wooden platform on which the tent had been erected to keep out the damp; braziers of faelights flickered throughout, chairs and a few chaise longues were scattered around, covered in thick furs. A massive desk with several chairs occupied one half of the main space. And behind a curtain in the back . . . I assumed our bed waited.

Mor flung herself onto the nearest chaise. "Welcome to an Illyrian war-camp, ladies. Try to keep your awe contained."

Nesta drifted toward the desk, the maps atop it. "What is the difference," she asked none of us in particular, "between a faerie and a witch?"

"Witches amass power beyond their natural reserve," Mor answered with sudden seriousness. "They use spells and archaic tools to harness more power to them than the Cauldron allotted—and use it for whatever they desire, good or ill."

Elain silently surveyed the tent, head tipping back. Her mass of heavy brown-gold hair shifted with the movement, the faelight dancing among the silken strands. She'd left it half-up, the style arranged to hide her ears should the glamours fail at Graysen's estate. Tamlin's hadn't worked on Nesta—perhaps Graysen and his father would have a similar immunity to such things.

Elain at last slid into the chair near Mor's, her dawn-pink dress— finer than the ones she usually wore—crinkling beneath her. "Will— will many of these soldiers die?"

I cringed, but Nesta said, "Yes." I could almost see the unspoken words Nesta reined in. *Your mate might die sooner than them, though.*

Mor said, "Whenever you're ready, Elain, I'll glamour you."

"Will it hurt?" Elain asked.

"It didn't when Tamlin glamoured your memories," Nesta said, leaning against the desk.

Mor still said, "No. It might . . . tingle. Just act as you would as a human."

"It's the same as how I act now." Elain began wringing her slender fingers.

"Yes," I said, "but . . . try to keep the vision-talk . . . to yourself. While we're there." I added quickly, "Unless it's something that you can't—"

"I can," Elain said, squaring her slim shoulders. "I will."

Mor smiled tightly. "Deep breath."

Elain obeyed. I blinked, and it was done.

Gone was the faint glow of immortal health; the face that had become a bit sharper. Gone were the pointed ears, the grace. Muted. Drab—or in the way that someone as beautiful as Elain could be drab. Even her hair seemed to have lost its luster, the gold now brassy, the brown mousy.

Elain studied her hands, turning them over. "I hadn't realized . . . how ordinary it looked."

"You're still lovely," Mor said a bit gently.

Elain offered a half smile. "I suppose that war makes wanting things like that unimportant."

Mor was quiet for a heartbeat. "Perhaps. But you should not let war steal it from you regardless."

+

Elain's palm was clammy in mine as Rhys winnowed us into the human lands, Mor taking Azriel and Nesta. And though her face was calm when we found ourselves blinking at the heat and sunshine of a full mortal summer, her grip on my hand was as strong as the iron ring around her finger.

The heat lay heavy over the estate we now faced—the stone guardhouse the only opening I could see in either direction.

The only opening in the towering stone wall rising up before us, solid as some mammoth beast, so high I had to crane my neck back to spy the spikes jutting from its top.

The guards at the thick iron gates . . .

Rhys slid his hands into his pockets, a shield already around us. Mor and Azriel took up defensive positions at our sides.

Twelve guards at this gate. All armed, faces hidden beneath thick helmets, despite the heat. Their bodies were equally covered in plated armor, right down to their boots.

Any of us could end their lives without lifting a hand. And the wall they guarded, the gates they held . . . I did not think they would last long, either.

But . . . if we could place wards here, perhaps set up a bastion of Fae warriors . . . Through those open gates, I glimpsed sprawling lands—fields and pastures and groves and a lake . . . And beyond it . . . a solid, bulky fortress of dark brown stone.

Nesta had been right. It was like a prison, this place. Its lord had prepared to weather the storm from inside, a king over these resources. But there was room. Plenty of room for people.

And the would-be mistress of this prison . . . Head high, Elain said to the guards, to the dozen arrows now pointed at her slender throat, "Tell Graysen that his betrothed has come for him. Tell him . . . tell him that Elain Archeron begs for sanctuary."

CHAPTER
52

We waited outside the gates while a guard mounted a horse and galloped down the long, dusty road to the fortress itself. A second curtain wall lay around the bulky building. With our Fae sight, we could see as *those* gates opened, then another pair.

"How did you even *meet* him," I murmured to Elain as we lingered beneath the shade of the looming oaks outside the gate, "if he's locked up in here?"

Elain stared and stared at the distant fortress. "At a ball—his father's ball."

"I've been to funerals that were merrier," Nesta muttered.

Elain cut her a look. "This house has needed a woman's touch for years."

Neither of us said that it didn't seem likely she would be the one.

Azriel kept a few steps away, little more than the shade of one of the oaks behind us. But Mor and Rhys . . . they monitored everything. The guards whose fear . . . the salty, sweaty tang of it grated on every nerve.

But they held firm. Held those ash-tipped arrows at us.

Long minutes passed. Then finally a yellow flag was raised at the distant fortress gates. We braced ourselves.

But one of the guards before us grunted, "He'll come out to see you."

✠

We were not to be allowed within the keep. To see their defenses, their resources.

The guardhouse was as far as they'd allow us.

They led us inside, and though we tried to keep our otherness to a minimum . . . The hounds leashed to the walls within snarled. Viciously enough that the guards led them out.

The main room of the guardhouse was stuffy and cramped, more so with all of us in there, and though I offered Elain a seat by the sealed window, she remained standing—at the front of our company. Staring at the shut iron door.

I knew Rhys was listening to every word the guards uttered outside, his tendrils of power waiting to sense any turn in their intentions. I doubted the stone and iron of the building could hold any of us, certainly not together, but . . . Letting them shut us in here to wait . . . It rubbed against some nerve. Made my body restless, a cold sweat breaking out. Too small, not enough air—

It's all right, Rhys soothed. *This place cannot hold you.*

I nodded, though he hadn't spoken, trying to swallow the feeling of the walls and ceiling pushing on me.

Nesta was watching me carefully. I admitted to her, "Sometimes . . . I have problems with small spaces."

Nesta studied me for a long moment. And then she said with equal quiet, though we could all hear, "I can't get into a bathtub anymore. I have to use buckets."

I hadn't known—hadn't even thought that bathing, submerging in water . . .

I knew better than to touch her hand. But I said, "When we get home, we'll install something else for you."

I could have sworn there was gratitude in her eyes—that she might have said something else when horses approached.

"Two dozen guards," Azriel murmured to Rhys. A glance at Elain. "And Lord Graysen and his father, Lord Nolan."

Elain went still as a doe as footsteps crunched outside. I caught Nesta's eye, read the understanding there, and nodded.

Any attempt to hurt Elain . . . I did not care what I had promised my sister. I'd leave Nesta to shred him. Indeed, my eldest sister's fingers had curled—as if invisible talons crowned them.

But the door banged open, and—

The panting young man was so . . . human-looking.

Handsome, brown-haired, blue-eyed, but . . . human. Solidly built beneath his light armor, tall—perhaps a mortal ideal of a knight who would swoop a beautiful maiden onto his horse and ride off into the sunset.

So at odds from the savage strength of the Illyrians, the cultivated lethalness of Mor and Amren. From my own clawing and shredding— and Nesta's.

But a small sound came out of Elain as she beheld Graysen. As he gasped for breath, scanning her from head to toe. He staggered toward her a step—

A broad, scar-flecked hand gripped the back of Graysen's armor, hauling him to a stop.

The man who held the young lord fully entered the cramped room.

Tall and thin, hawk-nosed and gray-eyed . . . "What is the meaning of this."

We all stared at him beneath lowered brows.

Elain was shaking. "Sir—Lord Nolan . . ." Words failed her as she again looked at her betrothed, who had not taken his earnest blue eyes from her, not for a heartbeat.

"The wall has come down," Nesta said, stepping to Elain's side.

Graysen looked to Nesta at that. Shock flared at what he beheld: the ears, the beauty, the . . . otherworldly power that thrummed around her. "How," he said, his voice low and raspy.

"I was kidnapped," Nesta answered coolly, not one flicker of fear in her eyes. "I was taken by the army invading these lands and turned against my will."

"How," Nolan echoed.

"There is a Cauldron—a weapon. It grants its owner power to . . . do such things. I was a test." Nesta then launched into a sharp, short explanation of the queens, of Hybern, of why the wall had fallen.

When she finished Lord Nolan only demanded, "And who are your companions?"

It was a gamble—we knew it was. To say who we were, when we knew full well the terror of *any* Fae, let alone High Lords . . .

But I stepped forward. "My name is Feyre Archeron. I am High Lady of the Night Court. This is Rhysand, my—husband." I doubted *mate* would go over well as a term.

Rhys came to my side. Some of the guards shifted and murmured with terror. Some flinched at the hand Rhys lifted—to gesture behind him. "Our third in command, Morrigan. And our spymaster, Azriel."

Lord Nolan, to his credit, did not blanch. Graysen did, but remained steady. "Elain," Graysen breathed. "Elain—why are you *with* them?"

"Because she is our sister," Nesta answered, her fingers still curled with those invisible talons. "And there is no safer place for her during this war than with us."

Elain whispered, "Graysen—we've come to beg you . . ." A pleading glance at his father. "Both of you . . . Open your gates to any humans who can get here. To families. With the wall down . . . We—they believe . . . There is not enough time for an evacuation. The queens will not send aid from the continent. But here—they might stand a chance."

Neither man responded, though Graysen now looked at Elain's engagement ring. His blue eyes rippled with pain. "I would be inclined to believe you," he said quietly, "if you were not lying to me with your every breath."

Elain blinked. "I—I am not, I—"

"Did you think," Lord Nolan said, and Nesta and I closed ranks around Elain as he took a step toward us, "that you could come to *my* house and deceive me with your faerie magic?"

Rhys said, "We don't care what you believe. We only come to ask you to help those who cannot defend themselves."

"At what gain? What risk of your own?"

"You have an arsenal of ash weapons," I said. "I'd think the risk to us is apparent."

"And to your sister as well," Nolan spat toward Elain. "Don't forget to include her."

"Any weapon can hurt a mortal," Mor said blandly.

"But she isn't a mortal, is she?" Nolan sneered. "No, I have it on good authority that it was Elain Archeron who was turned Fae first. And who now has a High Lord's son as a *mate*."

"And who, exactly, told you this?" Rhys said with a lift of the brow, not showing one ounce of ire, of surprise.

Steps sounded.

But we all went for our weapons as Jurian strolled into the guard-house and said, "I did."

CHAPTER
53

Jurian held up his tanned hands, new calluses dotting his palms and fingers. New—for the remade body he'd had to train to handle weapons these months.

"I came alone," Jurian said. "You can stop snarling."

Elain began shaking—either at the truth revealed, or the memories that pelted her, pelted Nesta, at the sight of him. Jurian inclined his head to my sisters. "Ladies."

"They are no ladies," Lord Nolan sneered.

"Father," Graysen warned.

Nolan ignored him. "Upon his arrival, Jurian explained what had been done to you—*both* of you. What the queens on the continent desire."

"And what is that?" Rhys asked, his voice a deceptive croon.

"Power. Youth," Jurian said with a shrug. "The usual things."

"Why are you *here*," I demanded. Kill him—we should kill him *now* before he could hurt us any further, kill him for that bolt he'd put through Azriel's chest and the threat he'd made to Miryam and Drakon, perhaps causing them to vanish and leave us to fight this war on our own—

"The queens are snakes," Jurian said, leaning against the edge of a table shoved by the wall. "They deserve to be butchered for their treachery. It took no effort on my part when Hybern sent me to woo them to our cause. Only one of them was noble enough to play the game—to know we'd been dealt a shitty hand and to play it the best she could. But when she helped you, the others found out. And they gave her to the Attor." Jurian's eyes gleamed bright—not with madness, I realized.

But clarity.

And I had the sense of the world sliding out from beneath my feet as Jurian said, "He resurrected me to turn them to his cause, believing I had gone mad during the five hundred years Amarantha trapped me. So I was reborn, and found myself surrounded by my old enemies—faces I had once marked to kill. I found myself on the wrong side of a wall, with the human realm poised to shatter beneath it."

Jurian looked right to Mor, whose mouth was a tight line. "You were my friend," he said, voice straining. "We fought back-to-back during some battles. And yet you believed me at first sight—believed that I'd ever let them *turn* me."

"You went mad with—with Clythia. It was *madness*. It destroyed you."

"And I was glad to do it," Jurian snarled. "I was *glad* to do it, if it bought us an edge in that war. I didn't *care* what it did to me, what it broke in me. If it meant we could be *free*. And I have had five hundred years to think about it. While being held prisoner by my enemy. Five hundred years, Mor." The way he said her name, so familiar and knowing—

"You played the villain convincingly enough, Jurian," Rhys purred.

Jurian snapped his face toward Rhys. "You should have looked. I expected you to *look* into my mind, to see the truth. Why didn't you?"

Rhys was quiet for a long moment. Then he said softly, "Because I didn't want to see her."

See any trace of Amarantha.

"You mean to imply," Mor pushed, "that you've been working to help *us* during this?"

"Where better to plot your enemy's demise, to learn their weaknesses, than at their side?"

We were silent, Lord Graysen and his father watching—or the latter did. Graysen and Elain were just staring at each other.

"Why this obsession to find Miryam and Drakon?" Mor asked.

"It's what the world expects of me. What Hybern expects. And if he grants my asking price to find them . . . Drakon has a legion capable of turning the tide in battle. It was why I allied with him during the War. I don't doubt Drakon still has it trained and ready. Word will have reached him by now. Especially that I am looking for them."

A warning. The only way Jurian could send one—by making himself the hunter.

I said to Jurian, "You don't want to kill Miryam and Drakon."

There was stark honesty in Jurian's eyes as he shook his head once. "No," he said roughly. "I want to beg their forgiveness."

I looked to Mor. But tears lined her eyes, and she blinked them furiously away.

"Miryam and Drakon have vanished," Rhys said. "Their people with them."

"Then find them," Jurian said. He jerked his chin to Azriel. "Send the shadowsinger, send whomever you trust, but *find* them."

Silence.

"Look into my head," Jurian said to Rhys. "Look, and see for yourself."

"Why now," Rhys said. "Why here."

Jurian held his stare. "Because the wall came down, and now I can move freely—to warn the humans here. Because . . ." He loosed a long breath. "Because Tamlin ran right back to Hybern after your meeting ended this morning. Right to their camp in the Spring Court, where Hybern now plans to launch a land assault on Summer tomorrow."

CHAPTER
54

Jurian was not my enemy.

I couldn't wrap my mind around it. Even as Rhys and I *both* looked.

I didn't linger for long.

The pain and guilt and rage, what he had seen and endured . . .

But Jurian spoke true. Laid himself bare to us.

He knew the spot they planned to attack. Where and when and how many.

Azriel vanished without a glance at any of us—to warn Cassian and move the legion.

Jurian was saying to Mor, "They didn't kill the sixth queen. Vassa. She saw through me—or thought she did—from the start. Warned them against this. Told them that if I was reborn, it was a bad sign, and to rally their armies to face the threat before it grew too large. But Vassa is too brash, too young. She didn't play the game the way the golden one, Demetra, did. Didn't see the lust in their eyes when I told them of the Cauldron's powers. Didn't know that from the moment I began to spin Hybern's lies . . . they became her enemies. They couldn't kill Vassa—the next in line to her throne is far more willful. So they found an old death-lord above the wall, with a penchant for enslaving young women. He cursed her, and stole her away . . . The entire world believes she's been sick these past months."

"We know," Mor said, and none of us dared glance at Elain. "We learned about it."

And even with the truth laid bare . . . none of us told him that Lucien had gone after her.

Elain seemed to remember, though. Who was hunting for that missing queen. And she said to Graysen, stone-faced and sorrowful through all of this, "I did not mean to deceive you."

His father answered, "I find I have trouble believing that."

Graysen swallowed. "Did you think you could come back here—live with me as this . . . lie?"

"No. Yes. I—I don't know what I wanted—"

"And you are bound to some . . . Fae male. A High Lord's son."

A different High Lord's heir, likely, I wanted to say.

"His name is Lucien." I wasn't certain if I'd ever heard his name from her lips.

"I don't care what his name is." The first sharp words from Graysen. "You are his *mate*. Do you even know what that means?"

"It means *nothing*," Elain said, her voice breaking. "It means *nothing*. I don't *care* who decided it or why they did—"

"You belong to *him*."

"I belong to *no one*. But my heart belongs to *you*."

Graysen's face hardened. "I don't want it."

He would have been better off hitting her, that's how deep the hurt in her eyes went. And seeing her face crumple . . .

I stepped close, pushing her behind me. "Here is what is going to happen. You are going to take in any people who can make it here. We will supply these walls with wards."

"We don't need them," sneered Nolan.

"Shall I demonstrate for you," I said, "how wrong you are? Or shall you take my word for it that I could reduce this wall to rubble with half a thought? And that is to say nothing of my friends. You will find, Lord Nolan, that you *want* our wards, and our help. All in exchange for taking in whatever humans need the safety."

"I don't want riffraff wandering through here."

"So only the rich and chosen will walk through the gates?" Rhys asked, arching a brow. "I can't imagine the aristocracy being content to work your land and fish in your lake or butcher your meat."

"We have plenty of workers here to do that."

It was happening again. Another fight with narrow-minded, hateful people . . .

But Jurian said to the lords, "I fought beside your ancestor. And he would be ashamed if you locked out those who needed it. You would spit on his grave to do so. I hold a position of trust with Hybern. One word from me, and I will make sure his legion takes a visit here. To you."

"You'll threaten to bring the very enemy you seek to protect us from?"

Jurian shrugged. "I can also convince Hybern to steer clear. He trusts me that much. You let in those people . . . I will do my best to keep his armies far away."

He gave Rhys a look, daring him to doubt it.

We were still too stunned to even try to look neutral.

But then Nolan said, "I do not pretend to have a large army. Only a considerable unit of soldiers. If what you say is true . . ." A glance at Graysen. "We will take them. Whoever can make it."

I wondered if the elder lord might be the one who could actually be reasoned with. Especially as Graysen said to Elain, "Take that ring off."

Elain's fingers curved into a fist. "No."

Ugly. This was about to get ugly in the worst way—

"Take. It. Off."

It was Nolan's turn to murmur a warning to his son. Graysen ignored him. Elain did not move.

"*Take it off!*" The roared words barked over the stones.

"That's enough," Rhys said, his voice lethally calm. "The lady keeps the ring, if she wants it. Though none of us will be particularly sad to see it go. Females tend to prefer gold or silver to iron."

Graysen leveled a seething look at Rhysand. "Is this the start of it? You Fae *males* will come to take our women? Are your own not fuckable enough?"

"Watch your tongue, boy," his father said. Elain turned white at the coarse language.

Graysen only said to her, "I am not marrying you. Our engagement is over. I will take whatever people occupy your lands. But not you. Never *you*."

Tears began sliding down Elain's face, their scent filling the room with salt.

Nesta stepped forward. Then another step. And another.

Until she was in front of Graysen, faster than anyone could see.

Until Nesta smacked him hard enough that his head snapped to the side.

"You never deserved her," Nesta snarled into the stunned silence as Graysen cupped his face and swore, bending over. Nesta only looked back at me. Rage, unfiltered and burning, roiled in her eyes. But her voice was stone-cold as she said to me, "I assume we're done here."

I gave her a wordless nod. And proud as any queen, Nesta took Elain's arm and led her from the guardhouse. Mor trailed behind, guarding their backs as they entered the veritable field of weapons and snarling hounds waiting outside.

The two lords saw themselves out without so much as a good-bye.

Alone, Jurian said, "Tell the shadowsinger I'm sorry about the arrow to the chest."

Rhys shook his head. "What's the next move, then? I assume you're doing more than warning humans to flee or hide."

Jurian pushed off the table. "The next move, Rhysand, is me going back to that Hybern war-camp and throwing a fit that my search for

Miryam and Drakon's whereabouts wasn't fruitful. My step after that is to take another trip to the continent and sow the seeds of discord amongst the queens' courts. To let some *vital* things slip about their agenda. Who they really support. What they really want. It will keep them busy—too worried about their own internal conflict to consider sailing here. And once that's done . . . who knows? Perhaps I'll join you on the battlefield."

Rhys rubbed his brows with a thumb and forefinger, the locks of his hair sliding forward as he dipped his head. "I wouldn't believe a word, except I looked into that head of yours."

Jurian tapped a hand on the door frame. "Tell Cassian to hammer the left flank hard tomorrow. Hybern is putting his untrained nobles there for some seasoning—they're spoiled and untested. Buckle the ranks there, and it'll spook the grunts. Hit them with everything you've got, and fast—don't give them time to rally or find their courage." Jurian gave me a grim smile. "I never congratulated you for slaughtering Dagdan and Brannagh. Good riddance."

"I did it for those Children of the Blessed," I said. "Not for glory."

"I know," Jurian said, flicking up his brows. "Why do you think I decided to trust you?"

CHAPTER
55

"I'm too old for these sorts of surprises," Mor groused as the war-tent groaned in the howling mountain wind at the northern border of the Winter Court, the Illyrian army settling down for the night. To wait for the attack tomorrow. They'd flown all day, the location remote enough to keep even an army of our size hidden. Until tomorrow, at least.

We'd warned Tarquin—and dispatched messages to Helion and Kallias to join if they could make it in time. But come the hour before dawn, the Illyrian legion would take to the skies and fly hard for that southern battlefield. They would land, hopefully, before it began. Right as Keir and his commanders winnowed in the Darkbringer legion from the Night Court.

And then the slaughter would begin. On either side.

If what Jurian claimed was true. Cassian had choked when we'd told him Jurian's battle advice. A milder reaction, Azriel said, than his initial response.

I asked Mor from where I sat at the foot of the fur-covered chaise we currently shared, "You never suspected Jurian might be . . . good?"

She swigged from her wine and leaned back against the cushions piled before the rolled headrest. My sisters were in another tent, not quite as big but equally luxurious, their lodgings flanked by Cassian's and Azriel's tents, and Mor's before it. No one would get to them without my friends knowing. Even if Mor was currently here with me.

"I don't know," she said, hauling a heavy wool throw blanket over her legs. "I was never as close to Jurian as I was to some of the others, but . . . we did fight together. Saved each other. I just assumed Amarantha broke him."

"Parts of him are broken," I said, shuddering to recall those memories I'd seen, the feelings. I pulled some of her blanket over my lap.

"We're all broken," Mor said. "In our own ways—in places no one might see."

I angled my head to inquire, but she asked, "Is Elain . . . all right?"

"No," was all I said. Elain was not all right.

She had quietly cried while we winnowed here. And in the hours afterward, while the army arrived and the camp was rebuilt. She did not take off her ring. She only lay on the cot in her tent, nestled among the furs and blankets, and stared at nothing.

Any bit of good, any advancement . . . gone. I debated returning to smash every bone in Graysen's body, but resisted—if only because it would give Nesta license to unleash herself upon him. And death at Nesta's hands . . . I wondered if they'd have to invent a new word for *killing* when she was done with Graysen.

So Elain silently cried, the tears so unending that I wondered if it was some sign of her heart bleeding out. Some sliver of hope that had shattered today. That Graysen would still love her, still marry her—and that love would trump even a mating bond.

A final tether had been snapped—to her life in the human lands.

Only our father, wherever he was, remained as any sort of connection.

Mor read whatever was on my face and set down the wine on the small wood table beside the chaise. "We should sleep. I don't even know why I'm drinking."

"Today was . . . unexpected."

"It's so much harder," she said, groaning as she chucked the rest of the blanket into my lap and rose to her feet. "When enemies turn into friends. And the opposite, I suppose. What didn't I see? What did I overlook or dismiss? It always makes me reassess *myself* more than them."

"Another joy of war?"

She snorted, heading for the tent flaps. "No—of life."

☩

I barely slept that night.

Rhys didn't come to the tent—not once.

I slipped from our bed when the darkness was just starting to yield to gray, following the tug of the mating bond as I had done that day Under the Mountain.

He stood atop a rocky outcropping crusted with patches of ice, watching the stars fade away one by one over the still-slumbering camp.

I wordlessly slid my arm around his waist, and he shifted his wings to fold me into his side.

"A lot of soldiers are going to die today," he said quietly.

"I know."

"It never gets easier," he whispered.

The strong panes of his face were taut, and silver lined his eyes as he studied the stars. Only here, only now, would he show that grief—that worry and pain. Never before his armies; never before his enemies.

He loosed a long breath. "Are you ready?" I would stay near the back of the lines with Mor to get a feel for battle. The flow and terror and structure. My sisters would remain here until it was safe to winnow them afterward. If things didn't go to hell first.

"No," I admitted. "But I have no other choice than to be ready."

Rhys kissed the top of my head, and we stared at the dying stars in silence.

"I'm grateful," he said after a while, as the camp beneath us stirred in the building light. "To have you at my side. I don't know if I ever told you that—how grateful I am to have you stand with me."

I blinked back the burning in my eyes and took his hand. I laid it over my heart, letting him feel its beating while I kissed him one final time, the last of the stars vanishing as the army below us awoke to do battle.

CHAPTER
56

Jurian was right.

We'd seen inside his head, yet we'd still doubted. Still wondered if we'd arrive to find Hybern had changed their position, or attacked elsewhere.

But Hybern's horde was precisely where Jurian claimed they'd be.

And as the Illyrian army swept for them while they marched over the Spring border and into Summer . . . Hybern's forces certainly seemed shocked.

Rhys had cloaked our forces—all of them. Sweat had slid down his temple at the strain, at keeping the mass of us hidden from sight and sound and scent as we flew mile after mile. My wings weren't strong enough—so Mor winnowed us through the sky, keeping pace with them.

But we arrived together. And as Rhys ripped the sight shield away, revealing battle-hungry Illyrians spearing from the skies in neat, precise lines . . . As he revealed the legion of Keir's Darkbringers charging on foot, swathed in wisps of night and armed with star-bright steel . . . It was hard not to be smug at the panic that rippled over the marching mass of Hybern.

But Hybern's army . . . It stretched far—deep and long. Meant to sweep away everything in its path.

"*SHIELDS,*" Cassian bellowed at the front line.

One by one by one, shields of red and blue and green flickered into life around the Illyrians and their weapons, overlapping like the scales of a fish. Overlapping like the solid metal shields they each bore on their left arms, locking into place from ankle to shoulder.

Below, Keir's troops rippled with shadowy shields flaring into place before them.

Mor winnowed us to the tree-covered hill that overlooked the field Cassian had deemed would be the best place to hit them based on Azriel's scouting. There was a slope to the grass—in our advantage. We held the high ground; a narrow, shallow river lay not too far back from Hybern's army. Success in battle, Cassian had told me that morning over a swift breakfast, was often decided not by numbers, but by picking where to fight.

The Hybern army seemed to realize their disadvantage within moments.

But the Illyrians had landed beside Keir's soldiers. Cassian, Azriel, and Rhys spread out amongst the front line, all clad in that black Illyrian armor, all armed as the other winged soldiers were: shield gripped in the left hand, Illyrian blade in the right, an assortment of daggers on them, and helmets.

The helmets were the only markers of who they were. Unlike the smooth domes of the others, Rhys, Azriel, and Cassian wore black helmets whose cheek-guards had been fashioned and swept upward like ravens' wings. Albeit razor-sharp ravens' wings that jutted up on either side of the helmet, right above the ear, but . . . The effect, I admitted, was terrifying. Especially with the two other swords strapped across their backs, the gauntlets that covered every inch of their hands, and the Siphons gleaming amongst Cassian's and Azriel's ebony armor.

Rhys's own power roiled around him, readying to hammer the right flank while Cassian aimed for the left. Rhys was to conserve his power—in case the king arrived. Or worse—the Cauldron.

This army, however huge . . . It did not seem that the king was even there to lead it. Or Tamlin. Or Jurian. Merely an invading harbinger of the force to come, but sizable enough that the damage . . . We could easily spy the damage behind the army, the plumes of smoke staining the cloudless summer sky.

Mor and I said little in the hours that followed.

I did not have it in me for words, for any sort of coherent speech as we watched. Either through our surprise or pure luck, there was no sign of that faebane. I was inclined to thank the Mother for that.

Even if every soldier in our camp this morning had mixed Nuan's antidote into their gruel, it would do nothing against *blocking* weapons tipped in faebane from shattering shields. Only stop against the stifling of magic, should it come into contact either through that damned powder . . . or by being impaled by a weapon tipped in it. Lucky—so lucky it was not in use today.

Because seeing the carnage, the fine line of control . . . There was no place for me on those front lines, where the Illyrians fought by the strength of their sword, their power, and their trust in the male on either side of them. Even Keir's soldiers fought as one—obedient and unfaltering, lashing out with shadows and steel. I would have been a fissure in that impenetrable armor—and what Cassian and the Illyrians unleashed upon Hybern . . .

Cassian slammed into that left flank. Siphons unleashed bursts of power that sometimes bounced off shields, sometimes found their mark and shredded flesh and bone.

But where Hybern's magic shields held out . . . Rhys, Azriel, and Cassian sent out blasts of their own power to shatter them. Leaving them vulnerable to those Siphons—or pure Illyrian steel. And if that did not fell them . . . Keir and his Darkbringers cleaned up the rest. Precisely. Coolly.

The field became a blood-drenched mud pit. Bodies gleamed in the morning sun, light bouncing off their armor. Hybern panicked at the unbreakable Illyrian lines that pushed and pushed them back. That battered them.

And as that left flank broke apart, as its nobles fell or turned and fled . . . The other Hybern soldiers began descending into panic, too.

There was one mounted commander who did not go easily. Who didn't turn his horse toward that river behind them to flee.

Cassian selected him as his opponent.

Mor gripped my hand tight enough to hurt as Cassian stepped out of that impenetrable front line of shields and swords, the soldiers around him immediately closing the gap. Mud and blood splattered Cassian's dark helmet, his armor.

He ditched his tall shield for a round one strapped across his back, crafted from the same ebony metal.

And then he launched into a run.

I could have sworn even Rhys paused on the other end of the battlefield to watch as Cassian cut his way through those enemy soldiers, aiming for the mounted Hybern commander. Who realized what and who was coming for him and started to search for a better weapon.

Cassian had been born for this—these fields, this chaos and brutality and calculation.

He didn't stop moving, seemed to know where every opponent fought both ahead and behind, seemed to breathe in the flow of the battle around him. He even let his Siphons' shield drop—to get close, to *feel* the impact of the arrows that he took in that ebony shield. If he slammed that shield into a soldier, his other arm was already swinging his sword at the next opponent.

I'd never seen anything like it—the skill and precision. It was like a dance.

I must have said it aloud because Mor replied, "For him, that's what battle is. A symphony."

Her eyes did not stray from Cassian's death-dance.

Three soldiers were brave or stupid enough to try to charge him. Cassian had them down and dying with four maneuvers.

"Holy Mother," I breathed.

That was who had been training me. Why Fae trembled at his name.

Why the high-born Illyrian warriors had been jealous enough to want him dead.

But there Cassian was, no one between him and the commander.

The commander had found a discarded spear. He threw it.

Fast and sure, I skipped a heartbeat as it spiraled for Cassian.

His knees bent, wings tucked in tight, shield twisting—

He took the spear in the shield with an impact I could have sworn I heard, then sliced off the shaft and kept running.

Within a heartbeat, Cassian had sheathed both shield and sword across his back.

And I would have asked why but he'd already picked up another fallen spear.

Already hurled it, his entire body going into the throw, the movement so perfect that I knew I'd one day paint it.

Both armies seemed to stop at the throw.

Even with the distance, Cassian's spear hit home.

It went right through the commander's chest, so hard it knocked the male clean off his horse.

By the time he was done falling, Cassian was there.

His sword caught the sunlight as it lifted and plunged down.

Cassian had picked his mark well. Hybern fled now. Outright turned and fled for the river.

But Hybern found Tarquin's army waiting on its opposite bank, exactly where Cassian had ordered it to appear.

Trapped with the Illyrians and Keir's Darkbringers at their backs and Tarquin's two thousand soldiers on the other side of the narrow river . . .

It was harder to watch—that slaughter.

Mor said to me, "It's over."

The sun was high in the sky, heat rising with every minute.

"You don't need to see this," she added.

Because some of the Hybern soldiers were surrendering. On their knees.

As it was Tarquin's territory, Rhys yielded the decision about what to do with prisoners.

From the distance, I picked out Tarquin from his armor—more ornate than Rhysand's, but still brutal. Fish fins and scales seemed to be the motif, and his azure cloak flowed through the mud behind him as he stepped over fallen bodies to get to the few hundred surviving enemy.

Tarquin stared at where the enemy had knelt, his helmet masking his features.

Nearby, Rhys, Cassian, and Azriel monitored, speaking to Keir and the Illyrian captains. I did not see many wings amongst the fallen on the field. A mercy.

The only mercy, it seemed, as Tarquin made a motion with his hand.

Some of the Hybern soldiers began screaming for clemency, their offers to sell information ringing out, even to us.

Tarquin pointed at a few of them, and they were hauled away by his soldiers. To be questioned. And I doubted it would be pleasant.

But the others . . .

Tarquin stretched out his hand toward them.

It took me a heartbeat to realize why the Hybern soldiers were thrashing and clawing at themselves, some trying to crawl away. But then one of them collapsed, and sunlight caught on his face. And even with the distance, I could tell—could tell it was water now bubbling out of his lips.

Out the lips of all the Hybern soldiers as Tarquin drowned them on dry land.

✠

I didn't see Rhys or the others for hours—not when he gave the order that the Illyrian war-camp was to be moved from the border of the Winter Court and rebuilt at the edge of the battlefield. So Mor and I winnowed to and from the camps as the exodus began. We brought my sisters last, waiting until many of the bodies had been turned to black dust by Rhysand. The blood and mud remained, but the camp maintained too good a position to yield—or waste time finding another one.

Elain didn't seem to care. Didn't seem to even notice that we winnowed her. She just went from her tent to Mor's arms, then into the same tent rebuilt in the new camp.

Nesta, however . . . I told her upon arriving that everyone was fine. But when we winnowed to the battlefield . . . She stared at that bloody, muddy plain. At the weapons soldiers of both courts were plundering from the fallen enemy.

Nesta listened to the low-level Illyrian soldiers whispering about how Cassian had thrown that spear, how he'd cut down soldiers like stalks of wheat, how he'd fought like Enalius—their most ancient warrior-god and the first of the Illyrians.

It had been a while, it seemed, since they had seen Cassian in open battle. Since they'd realized that he'd been young in the War, and now . . . the looks they gave Cassian as he passed . . . they were the same as those the High Lords had given Rhys upon seeing his power. Like them, and yet Other.

Nesta watched, and listened to it all, while the camp was built around us.

She did not ask where the bodies had gone before her arrival. She wholly ignored the camp Keir and his Darkbringers built beside ours— the ebony-armored soldiers who sneered at her, at me, at the Illyrians. No, Nesta only made sure that Elain was dozing in her tent, and then offered to help cut up linen for bandages.

We were doing just that around the early-evening fire when Rhys and Cassian approached, still in their armor, Azriel nowhere to be found.

Rhys took a seat on the log I was perched atop of, armor thudding, and silently pressed a kiss to my temple. He reeked of metal and blood and sweat.

His helmet clunked on the ground at our feet. I silently handed him a pitcher of water, and made to grab a glass when Rhys just lifted the pewter container and drank right from it. It sloshed over the sides, water pinging against the black metal coating his thighs, and when he at last set it down, he looked . . . tired. In his eyes, Rhys seemed weary.

But Nesta had jolted to her feet, staring at Cassian, at the helmet he had tucked into the crook of his arm, the weapons still poking above his shoulder, in need of cleaning. His dark hair hung limp with sweat, his face was mud-splattered where even the helmet had not kept it out.

But she surveyed his seven Siphons, the dim red stones. And then she said, "You're hurt."

Rhys snapped to attention at that.

Cassian's face was grim—his eyes glassy. "It's fine." Even the words were laced with exhaustion.

But she reached for his arm—his shield arm.

Cassian seemed to hesitate, but offered it to her, tapping the Siphon atop his palm. The armor slid back a fraction over his forearm, revealing—

"You know better than to walk around with an injury," Rhys said a bit tensely.

"I was busy," Cassian said, not taking his focus off Nesta as she studied the swollen wrist. How she'd detected it through the armor . . . She must have read it in his eyes, his stance.

I hadn't realized she'd been observing the Illyrian general enough to notice his tells.

"And it'll be fixed by morning," Cassian added, daring Rhys to say otherwise.

But Nesta's pale fingers gently probed his golden-brown skin, and he hissed through his teeth.

"How do I fix it?" she asked. Her hair had been tied in a loose knot atop her head earlier in the day, and in the hours that we'd worked to ready and distribute supplies to the healers, through the heat and humidity, stray tendrils had come free to curl about her temple, her nape. Faint color had stained her cheeks from the sun, and her forearms, bare beneath the sleeves she'd rolled up, were flecked with mud.

Cassian slowly sat on the log where she'd been perched a moment before, groaning softly—as if even that movement taxed him. "Icing it usually helps, but wrapping it will just lock it in place long enough for the sprain to repair itself—"

She reached for the basket of bandages she'd been preparing, then for the pitcher at her feet.

I was too tired to do anything other than watch as she washed his wrist, his hand, her own fingers gentle. Too tired to ask if she possessed the magic to heal it herself. Cassian seemed too weary to speak as well while she wrapped bandages around his wrist, only grunting to confirm if it was too tight or too loose, if it helped at all. But he watched her—didn't take his eyes off her face, the brows bunched and lips pursed in concentration.

And when she'd tied it neatly, his wrist wrapped in white, when Nesta made to pull back, Cassian gripped her fingers in his good hand. She lifted her gaze to his. "Thank you," he said hoarsely.

Nesta did not yank her hand away.

Did not open her mouth for some barbed retort.

She only stared and stared at him, at the breadth of his shoulders, even more powerful in that beautiful black armor, at the strong column of his tan neck above it, his wings. And then at his hazel eyes, still riveted to her face.

Cassian brushed a thumb down the back of her hand.

Nesta opened her mouth at last, and I braced myself—

"You're hurt?"

At the sound of Mor's voice, Cassian snatched his hand back and pivoted toward Mor with a lazy smile. "Nothing for you to cry over, don't worry."

Nesta dragged her stare from his face—down to her now-empty hand, her fingers still curled as if his palm lay there. Cassian didn't look at Nesta as she rose, snatching up the pitcher, and muttered something about getting more water from inside the tent.

Cassian and Mor fell into their banter, laughing and taunting each other about the battle and the ones ahead.

Nesta didn't come back out again for some time.

╬

I helped with the wounded long into the night, Mor and Nesta working alongside me.

A long day for all of us, yes, but the others . . . They had fought for hours. From the tight angle of Mor's jaw as she tended to injured Darkbringers and Illyrians alike, I knew the various recountings of the battle wore on her—not for the tales of glory and gore, but for the sole fact that she had not been there to fight beside them.

But between the Darkbringer forces and the Illyrians . . . I wondered where she'd fight. Whom she'd command or answer to. Definitely not Keir, but . . . I was still chewing it over when I at last slipped between the warm sheets of my bed and curled my body into Rhys's.

His arm instantly slid over my waist, tugging me in closer. "You smell like blood," he murmured into the dimness.

"Sorry," I said. I'd washed my hands and forearms before sliding into bed, but a full bath . . . I had barely managed the walk through the camp moments ago.

He stroked a hand over my waist, down to my hip. "You must be exhausted."

"And *you* should be sleeping," I chided, shifting closer, letting his warmth and scent wrap around me.

"Can't," he admitted, his lips brushing over my temple.

"Why?"

His hand drifted to my back, and I arched into the long, trailing strokes along my spine. "It takes a while—to settle myself after battle." It had been hours and hours since the fighting had ceased. Rhys's lips began a journey from my temple down my jaw.

And even with the weight of exhaustion pressing on me, as his mouth grazed over my chin, as he nipped at my bottom lip . . . I knew what he was asking.

Rhys sucked in a breath as I traced the contours of his muscled stomach, as I marveled at the softness of his skin, the strength of the body beneath it.

He pressed a featherlight kiss to my lips. "If you're too tired," he began, even as he went wholly still while my fingers continued their journey, past the sculpted muscles of his abdomen.

I answered him with a kiss of my own. Another. Until his tongue slid over the seam of my lips and I opened for him.

Our joining was fast, and hard, and I was clawing at his back before the end shattered through both of us, dragging my hands over his wings.

For long minutes afterward, we remained there, my legs thrown over his shoulders, the rise and fall of his chest pushing into mine in a lingering echo of our bodies' movements.

Then he withdrew, gently lowering my legs from his shoulders. He kissed the inside of each of my knees as he did so, setting them on either side of him as he rose up to kneel before me.

The tattoos on his knees were nearly obscured by the rumpled sheets, the design stretched with the position. But I traced my fingers over the tops of those mountains, the three stars inked atop them, as he remained kneeling between my legs, gazing down at me.

"I thought about you every moment I was on that battlefield," he said softly. "It focused me, centered me—let me get through it."

I stroked those tattoos on his knees again. "I'm glad. I think . . . I think some part of me was down there on that battlefield with you, too." I glanced to his suit of armor, cleaned and displayed on a dummy near the small dressing area. His winged helmet shone like a dark star in the dimness. "Seeing that battle today . . . It felt different from the one in Adriata." Rhys only listened, those star-flecked eyes patient. "In Adriata, I didn't . . ." I struggled for the words. "The chaos of the battle in Adriata was easier, somehow. Not *easy*, I mean—"

"I know what you meant."

I sighed, sitting up so that we were knee-to-knee and face-to-face. "What I'm trying and failing miserably to explain is that attacks like the one in Adriata, in Velaris . . . I can fight in those. There are people to defend, and the disorder of it . . . I can—I'll gladly fight in those battles. But what I saw today, that sort of warfare . . ." I swallowed. "Will you be ashamed of me if I admit that I'm not sure if I'm ready for that sort of battling?" Line against line, swinging and stabbing until I didn't know up from down, until mud and gore blurred the line between enemy and foe, relying as much upon the warriors beside me as my own skill set. And the closeness of it, the sounds and sheer scale of the bloodbath . . .

He took my face in his hands, kissing me once. "Never. I can never be ashamed of you. Certainly not over this." He kept his mouth close to mine, sharing breath. "Today's battle *was* different from Adriata, and Velaris. If we had more time to train you with a unit, you could easily fight amongst the lines and hold your own. But only if you wanted to. And for now, these initial battles . . . Being down in that slaughterhouse is not something I'd wish upon you." He kissed me again. "We are a pair," he said against my lips. "If you ever wish to fight by my side, it will be my honor."

I pulled my head back, frowning at him. "I feel like a coward now."

He stroked a thumb over my cheek. "No one would ever think that of you—not with all you have done, Feyre." A pause. "War is ugly, and messy, and unforgiving. The soldiers doing the fighting are only a fraction of it. Don't underestimate how far it goes for them to see you here—to see you tending to the wounded and participating in these meetings and councils."

I considered, letting my fingers drift across the Illyrian tattoos over his chest and shoulders.

And perhaps it was the afterglow of our joining, perhaps it was the battle today, but . . . I believed him.

⛧

Tarquin's army didn't blend into ours as Keir's did, but rather camped beside it. Azriel led team after team of scouts to find the rest of Hybern's host, discover their next movement . . . But nothing.

I wondered if Tamlin was with them—if he'd whispered to Hybern everything that had been discussed in that meeting. The weaknesses between courts. I didn't dare ask anyone.

But I did dare to question Nesta about whether she felt the Cauldron's power stirring. Mercifully, she reported feeling nothing amiss. Even so . . . I knew Rhys was frequently checking with Amren in Velaris— asking if she had made any discoveries with the Book.

And even if she found some alternative way to stop that Cauldron . . . We needed to know where the king was hiding the rest of his army first. And not so we could face it—not alone. No, so we could bring others to finish the job.

But only once we knew where the rest of Hybern's army was— where I was to unleash Bryaxis. It would do no good to have Hybern learn of Bryaxis's existence and adjust its plans. No, only when that full army was upon us . . . Only then would I set it upon them.

The first three days after the battle, the armies healed their wounded and rested. By the fourth, Cassian ordered them to do menial tasks to stave off any restlessness and chances for dangerous grumbling. His first order: dig a trench around the entire camp.

But the fifth day, the trench halfway finished . . . Azriel appeared, panting, in the middle of our war-tent.

Hybern had somehow skirted us entirely, and sent a force marching up the seam between the Autumn and Summer Courts. Heading for the Winter Court border.

We couldn't glean a reason why. Azriel hadn't discovered one, either. They were half a day's flight from us. He'd already sent warnings to Kallias and Viviane.

Rhys, Tarquin, and the others debated for hours, weighing the possibilities. Abandon this spot by the border, and we could be playing into Hybern's plans. But leave that northward army unattended and it could keep going north as far as it pleased. We could not afford to split our own army in two—there weren't enough soldiers to spare.

Until Varian came up with an idea.

He dismissed all the captains and generals, Keir and Devlon looking none too pleased at the order as they stormed out, dismissed everyone but his sister, Tarquin, and my own family.

"We march north—*and* we stay."

Rhys lifted a brow. Cassian frowned.

But Varian jabbed a finger on the map spread on the table we'd gathered around. "Spin a glamour—a good one. So that if anyone walks by here, they see and hear and smell an army. Put whatever spells in place to repel them from actually coming up to it. But let Hybern's eyes report that we are still here. That we choose to stay here."

"While we march north under a sight shield," Cassian murmured, rubbing his jaw. "It could work." He added with a grin to Varian, "You ever get sick of all that sunshine, you can come play with us in Velaris."

Though Varian frowned, something glinted in his eye.

But Tarquin said to Rhys, "You could make such a deception?"

Rhys nodded and winked at me. "With assistance from my mate."

I prayed that I'd rested enough as they all looked to me.

⊹

I was nearly drained by the time Rhys and I were finished that night. I followed his instructions, marking faces and details, willing that shape-shifting magic to craft them out of thin air, to give them life of their own.

It was like . . . applying a thin film over all those living in the camp, that would then separate when we moved out—separate and grow into its own entity that walked and talked and did all manner of things here. While we marched to intercept Hybern's army, hidden from sight by Rhys.

But it worked. Cresseida, skilled with glamours herself, worked personally on the Summer Court soldiers. She and I were both panting and sweaty hours later, and I nodded my thanks as she handed me a skein of water. She was not a trained warrior like her brother, but she was a solid, needed presence amongst the army—the soldiers looked to her for guidance and stability.

We moved out again, a far larger beast than the one that had flown down here. The Summer Court soldiers and Keir's legion could not fly, but Tarquin dug deep into his reservoirs and winnowed them along with us. He'd be wholly empty by the time we reached the enemy, but he insisted he was better at fighting with steel anyway.

We found the Hybern army at the northern edge of the mighty forest that stretched along the Summer Court's eastern border.

Azriel had scouted the land ahead for Cassian, laid it out in precise detail. It was late enough in the afternoon that Hybern was readying to settle down for the night.

Cassian had let our army rest all day, anticipating that. Knowing that at the end of a long day of marching, Hybern's forces would be exhausted, muddled. Another rule of war, he told me. Knowing *when* to pick your battles could be equally as important as where you fought them.

With rain-heavy clouds sweeping in from the east and the sun sinking toward the trees behind us—sycamores and oaks that towered high—we landed. Rhys ripped off the glamour surrounding us.

He wanted word to get out—wanted word to spread amongst Hybern's forces *who* was meeting them at every turn. Slaughtering them.

But they already knew.

Again, I watched from the camp itself, atop a broad rim leading into the grassy little valley where Hybern had planned to rest. Elain ducked into her tent the moment the Illyrian warriors built it for her. Only Nesta strode toward the edge of the tents to watch the battle on the valley floor below. Mor joined her, then me.

Nesta did not flinch at the clash and din of battle. She only stared toward one black-armored figure, leading the lines, his occasional order to *push* or to *hold that flank* barking across the battle.

Because this battle . . . Hybern had been ready. And the appearance they'd given, of a tired army ready to rest for the night . . . It had been a ruse, as our own had been.

Keir's soldiers started going down first, shadows sputtering out. Their front lines buckling.

Mor watched it, stone-faced. I had no doubt she was half hoping her father joined the dead now piling up. Even as Keir managed to rally the Darkbringers, reassembled that front line—only after Cassian had roared at him to fix it. And on the other side of the field . . .

Rhys and Tarquin were drained enough that they were actually battling sword to sword against soldiers. And again, no sign of the king or Jurian or Tamlin.

Mor was hopping from one foot to another, glancing at me every now and then. The bloodshed, the brutality—it sang to some part of her. Being up here with me . . . It was not where she wished to be.

But this . . . this running after armies, scrambling to stay ahead . . .

It would not provide a solution. Not for long.

The skies opened up, and the battle turned into outright muddy slaughter. Siphons flared, soldiers died. Hybern wielded its own magic upon our forces, arrows tipped in faebane finally making an appearance, along with clouds of it, that mercifully didn't last long in the rain. And did not impact us—not one bit—with Nuan's antidote in our systems. Only those arrows, which were skillfully avoided with shields or outright destruction to their shafts, leaving the stone to fall harmlessly from the sky.

Still Cassian, Azriel, and Rhys kept fighting, kept killing. Tarquin and Varian held their own—spreading out their soldiers to aid Keir's once-again foundering line.

Too late.

From the distance, through the rain, we could see perfectly as the dark line of Keir's soldiers caved to an onslaught of Hybern cavalry.

"Shit," Mor breathed, gripping my arm tight enough to bruise, warm summer rain soaking our clothes, our hair. "*Shit.*"

Like a burst dam, Hybern's soldiers poured through, cleaving Keir's force in half. Cassian's bellowing was audible even from the hilltop—then he was soaring, dodging arrows and spears, his Siphons so dim they barely guarded him against it. I could have sworn Rhys roared some order to him—that Cassian disregarded as he landed in the middle, the *middle* of those enemy forces sundering our lines, and unleashed himself.

Nesta inhaled in a sharp, high gasp.

More and more—Hybern spread us farther and farther apart. Rhys's power slammed into the flank of them, trying to shove them back. But his power was drained, exhausted from last night. Dozens fell to those snapping shadows, rather than hundreds.

"Re-form the lines," Mor was muttering, releasing me to pace, rain sluicing down her face. "Re-form the damned lines!"

Cassian was trying. Azriel had lunged into the fray, nothing more than shadows edged in blue light, battling his way toward where Cassian fought, utterly surrounded.

"Mother above," Nesta said softly. Not in awe. No—no, that was dread in her voice.

And within my own as I said, "They can fix this." Or I prayed they could.

Even if this battle . . . this was not all that Hybern had to offer against us.

This was not all they had to offer, and yet we were being pushed back, back, back—

Red flared in the heart of that battle like an exploding ember. A circle of soldiers died.

But more of Hybern's soldiers pushed in around Cassian. Even Azriel could not get to his side. My stomach turned, over and over.

Hybern had hidden the majority of its force somewhere. Our scouts could not find it. *Azriel* could not find it. And Elain . . . She could not see that mighty army, she'd said. In her dreams awake and asleep.

I knew little of war, of battle. But this . . . it felt like patching up holes in a boat while it sank.

As the rain drenched us, as Mor paced and swore at the slaughter, the bodies starting to pile up on our side, the foundering lines . . . I realized what I had to do, if I could not be down there, fighting.

Who I had to hunt down—and ask about the location of Hybern's true army.

The Suriel.

CHAPTER
57

"Absolutely not," Mor said when I pulled her a few feet away from Nesta, the din of battle and rain drowning out our voices. "*Absolutely not.*"

I jerked my head toward the valley below. "Go join them. You're wasted here. They need you." It was true. "Cassian and Az *need* you to push back the front lines." For Cassian's Siphons were beginning to sputter.

"Rhys will *kill* me if I leave you here."

"Rhys will do no such thing, and you know it. He's got wards around this camp, and I'm not entirely defenseless, you know."

I wasn't *lying*, exactly, but . . . The Suriel might very well not appear if Mor was there. And if I told her where I was going . . . I had no doubt she *would* insist on coming with me.

We didn't have the luxury of waiting for Jurian to give us information. About many things. I needed to leave—now.

"Go fight. Make those Hybern pricks scream a bit."

Nesta drew her attention away from the slaughter enough to add, "Help them."

For that was Cassian, making another charge toward a Hybern commander. Hoping to spook the soldiers again.

Mor frowned deeply, bounced once on her toes. "Just—be on your guard. Both of you."

I gave her a wry look—right before she rushed for her tent. I waited until she'd emerged again, buckling on weapons, and saluted me before she winnowed away. To the battlefield.

Right to Azriel's side—just as a soldier nearly landed a blow to his back.

Mor punched her sword through the soldier's throat before he could land that strike.

And then Mor began cutting a path toward Cassian, toward the broken front line beyond him, her damp golden hair a ray of sunshine amid the mud and dark armor.

Soldiers began screaming. Screamed some more when Azriel, blue Siphons flaring, fell into place beside her. Together, they plowed a path to Cassian—or tried to.

They made it perhaps ten feet before they were swarmed again. Before the press of bodies made even Mor's hair vanish in mud and rain.

Nesta laid a hand against her bare, rain-slick throat. Cassian began another assault on a Hybern captain—slower this time than he'd been.

Now. I had to go now—quickly. I took a step away from the outlook.

My sister narrowed her brows at me. "You're leaving?"

"I'll be back soon," was all I said. I didn't dare wonder how much of our army would be left when I did.

By the time I strode away, Nesta had already faced the battle once more, rain plastering her hair to her head. Resuming her unending vigil of the general battling on the valley floor below.

⊹

I had to track the Suriel.

And even though Elain could not see the Hybern host . . . It was worth a try.

525

Her tent was dim, and quiet—the sounds of slaughter far away, dreamlike.

She was awake, staring blankly at the canvas ceiling.

"I need you to find something for me," I said, dripping water everywhere as I laid a map across her thighs. Perhaps not as gentle as I should have been, but she at least sat up at my tone. Blinked at the map of Prythian.

"It's called the Suriel—it's one of many who bear that name. But . . . but it looks like this," I said, and reached for her hand to show her. I hesitated. "*May* I show it to you?"

My sister's brown eyes were glazed.

"Plant the image in your mind," I clarified. "So you know where to look."

"I don't know how to look," Elain mumbled.

"You can try." I should have asked Amren to train her, too.

But Elain studied me, the map, then nodded.

She had no mental shields, no barriers. The gates to her mind . . . Solid iron, covered in vines of flowers—or it would have been. The blossoms were all sealed, sleeping buds tucked into tangles of leaves and thorns.

I took a step beyond them, just into the antechamber of her mind, and planted the image of the Suriel there, trying to infuse it with safety—the truth that it looked terrifying, but had not harmed me.

Still, Elain shuddered when I pulled out. "Why?"

"It has answers I need. Immediately." Or else we might not have much of an army *left* to fight that entire Hybern host once I located it.

Elain again glanced at the map. At me. Then closed her eyes.

Her eyes shifted beneath her lids, the skin so delicate and colorless that the blue veins beneath were like small streams. "It moves . . . ," she whispered. "It moves through the world like . . . like the breath of the western wind."

"Where is it headed?"

Her finger lifted, hovering over the map, the courts.

Slowly, she set it down.

"There," she breathed. "It is going there. Now."

I looked at where she had laid her finger and felt the blood rush from my face.

The Middle.

The Suriel was headed to that ancient forest in the Middle. Just south—miles, perhaps . . .

From the Weaver of the Wood.

⊹

I winnowed in five leaps. I was breathless, my power nearly drained thanks to the glamouring I'd done yesterday, the summoned flame I'd used to dry myself off, and the winnowing that had taken me from the battle and right into the heart of that ancient wood.

The heavy, ripe air was as awful as I remembered, the forest thick with moss that choked the gnarled beeches and the gray stones scattered throughout. Then there was the silence.

I wondered if I should have indeed brought Mor with me as I listened. As I felt with my lingering magic for any sign of it.

The moss cushioned my steps as I eased into a walk. Scanning, listening. How far away, how small, that battle to the south felt.

My swallow was loud in my ears.

Things other than the Weaver prowled these woods. And the Weaver herself . . . Stryga, the Bone Carver had called her. His sister. Both siblings to an awful, male creature lurking in another part of the world.

I drew my Illyrian blade, the metal singing in the thick air.

But an ancient, rasping voice asked behind me, "Have you come to kill me, or to beg for my help once again, Feyre Archeron?"

CHAPTER

58

I turned, but did not sheath my blade across my back.

The Suriel was standing a few feet away, clad not in the cloak I had given it months ago, but a different one—heavier and darker, the fabric already torn and shredded. As if the wind it traveled on had ripped through it with invisible talons.

Only a few months since I had last seen it—when it had told me that Rhys was my mate. It might as well have been a lifetime ago.

Its over-large teeth clacked faintly. "Thrice now, we have met. Thrice now, you have hunted for me. This time, you sent the trembling fawn to find me. I did not expect to see those doe-eyes peering at me from across the world."

"I'm sorry if it was a violation," I said as steadily as I could. "But it's an urgent matter."

"You wish to know where Hybern is hiding its army."

"Yes. And other things. But let's start with that."

A hideous, horrific smile. "Even I cannot see it."

My stomach tightened. "You can see everything but that?"

The Suriel angled its head in a way that reminded me it was indeed a predator. And there was no snare this time to hold it back.

"He uses magic to cloak it—magic far older than I."

"The Cauldron."

Another awful smile. "Yes. That mighty, wicked thing. That bowl of death and life." It shivered with what I could have sworn was delight. "You have one already who can find Hybern."

"Elain says she cannot see it—see past his magic."

"Then use the other to track it."

"Nesta. Use *Nesta* to track the Cauldron?"

"Like calls to like. The King of Hybern does not travel without the Cauldron. So where it is, he and his army shall be. Tell the beautiful thief to find it."

The hair on my arms rose. "How?"

It angled its head, as if listening. "If she is unskilled . . . bones will do the talking for her."

"Scrying—you mean scrying with bones?"

"Yes." Those tattered robes flitted in a phantom wind. "Bones and stones."

I swallowed again. "Why did the Cauldron not react when I joined the Book and spoke the spell to nullify its power?"

"Because you did not hold on for long enough."

"It was killing me."

"Did you think you could leash its power without a cost?"

My heart stuttered. "I need to—to die for it to be stopped?"

"So dramatic, human-heart. But yes—yes, that spell would have drained the life from you."

"Is there—is there another spell to use instead? To nullify its powers."

"If there were such a thing, you would still have to get close enough to the Cauldron to do it. Hybern will not make that mistake twice."

I swallowed. "Even if we nullify the Cauldron . . . will it be enough to stop Hybern?"

"It depends on your allies. If they survive long enough to battle afterward."

"Would the Bone Carver make a difference?" *And Bryaxis.*

The Suriel had no eyelids. But its milky eyes flared with surprise. "I cannot see—not him. He is not . . . born of this earth. His thread has not been woven in." Its twisted mouth tightened. "You wish to save Prythian so much that you would risk unleashing him."

"Yes." The moment I located that army, I'd unleash Bryaxis upon it. But as for the Carver . . . "He wanted a—gift. In exchange. The Ouroboros."

The Suriel let out a sound that might have been a gasp—delight or horror, I did not know. "The Mirror of Beginnings and Endings."

"Yes—but . . . I cannot retrieve it."

"You are afraid to look. To see what is within."

"Will it drive me—mad? Break me?"

It was an effort not to flinch at that monstrous face, at the milky eyes and lipless mouth. All focused upon me. "Only you can decide what breaks you, Cursebreaker. Only you." Not an answer—not really. Certainly not enough to risk retrieving the mirror. The Suriel again listened to that phantom wind. "Tell the silver-eyed messenger that the answer lies on the second and penultimate pages of the Book. Together they hold the key."

"The key to *what*?"

The Suriel clicked its bony fingers together, like the many-jointed limbs of a crustacean, tip-tapping against each other. "The answer to what you need to stop Hy—"

It took me a heartbeat to register what happened.

To identify the wooden thing that burst through the Suriel's throat as an ash arrow. To realize that what sprayed in my face, landing on my tongue and tasting like soil, was black blood.

To realize that the thudding before the Suriel could even scream . . . more arrows.

The Suriel stumbled to its knees, a choking sound coming out of that mouth.

It had been afraid of the naga that day in the woods. Had known it could be killed.

I surged toward it, palming a knife with my left hand, sword angling up.

Another arrow fired, and I ducked behind a gnarled tree.

The Suriel let out a scream at the impact. Birds scattered into flight, and my ears rang—

And then its labored, wet breathing filled the wood. Until a lilting female voice crooned, "Why does it talk to you, Feyre, when it would not even deign to speak with me?"

I knew that voice. That laughter beneath the words.

Ianthe.

Ianthe was here. With two Hybern soldiers behind her.

CHAPTER
59

Concealed behind the tree, I took in my surroundings. I was exhausted, but . . . I could winnow. I could winnow and be gone. The ash arrows they'd put into the Suriel, however . . .

I met its eyes as it lay there, bleeding out on the moss.

The same ash arrows that had brought down Rhys. But my mate's had been carefully placed to disable him.

These had been aimed to kill.

That mouth of too-big teeth formed a silent word. *Run.*

"It took the King of Hybern *days* to unravel what you did to me," Ianthe purred, her voice drawing closer. "I still can't use most of my hand."

I didn't reply. Winnow—I should winnow.

Black blood dribbled out of the Suriel's neck, that arrow tip vulgar as it jutted up from its thick skin. I couldn't heal it—not with those ash arrows still in its flesh. Not until they were out.

"I'd heard from Tamlin how you captured this one," Ianthe went on, coming closer and closer. "So I adapted your methods. And it would not tell me *anything*. But since you have made contact so many times, the robe *I* gave it . . ." I could hear the smile in her voice. "A simple tracking spell, a gift from the king. To be triggered in your presence. If you should come calling again."

Run, the Suriel mouthed once more, blood dribbling past its withered lips.

That was pain in its eyes. Real pain, as mortal as any creature. And if Ianthe took it alive to Hybern . . . The Suriel knew it was a possibility. It had begged me for freedom once . . . yet it was willing to be taken. For me to run.

Its milky eyes narrowed—in pain and understanding. *Yes*, it seemed to say. *Go*.

"The king built shields in my mind," Ianthe prattled on, "to keep you from harming me again when I found you."

I peered around the tree to spy her standing at the edge of the clearing, frowning at the Suriel. She wore her pale robes, that blue stone crowning her hood. Only two guards with her. Even after all this time . . . She still underestimated me.

I ducked back around before she could spot me. Met the Suriel's stare one more time.

And I let it read every one of the emotions that solidified in me with absolute clarity.

The Suriel began to shake its head. Or tried to.

But I gave it a smile of farewell. And stepped into the clearing.

"I should have slit your throat that night in the tent," I said to the priestess.

One of the guards shot an arrow at me.

I blocked it with a wall of hard air that instantly buckled. Drained— mostly drained. And if it took another hit from an ash arrow . . .

Ianthe's face tightened. "You'll find you want to reconsider how you speak to me. I'll be your best advocate in Hybern."

"I suppose you'll have to catch me first," I said coolly—and ran.

✛

I could have sworn that ancient forest moved to make room for me.

Could have sworn it, too, read my final thoughts to the Suriel, and cleared the way.

But not for them.

I hurled every scrap of strength into my legs, into keeping upright, as I sprinted through the trees, leaping over rocks and streams, dodging moss-coated boulders.

Yet those guards, yet *Ianthe*, managed to keep close behind, even as they swore at the snapping trunks that seemed to shift into their way, the rocks that went loose beneath their feet. I only had to outrun them for so long.

Only for a few miles. Draw them away from the Suriel, buy it time to flee.

And make sure they *paid* for what they had done. All of it.

I opened my senses, letting them lead the way. The forest did the rest.

Perhaps she was waiting for me. Perhaps she had ordered the woods to open a path.

The Hybern guards gained on me. My feet flew beneath me, swift as a deer.

I began to recognize the trees, the rocks. There, I had stood with Rhys—there, I had flirted with him. There, he had lounged atop a branch while waiting for me.

The air behind me parted—an arrow.

I veered left, nearly slamming into a tree. The arrow went wide.

The light shifted ahead—brighter. The clearing.

I let out a whimper of relief that I made sure they heard.

I broke from the tree line in a leap, knees popping as I flew over the stones leading to that hair-thatched cottage.

"*Help me*," I breathed, making sure they heard that, too.

The wooden door was already half-open. The world slowed and cleared with each step, each heartbeat, as I hurtled over the threshold.

And into the Weaver's cottage.

CHAPTER
60

I gripped the door handle as I passed the threshold, digging in my heels and throwing every scrap of strength into my arms to keep that door from shutting. From locking me in.

Invisible hands shoved against it, but I gritted my teeth and braced a foot against the wall, iron biting into my hands.

The room behind me was dark. "Thief," intoned a lovely voice in the blackness.

"You do know," Ianthe tittered from outside the cottage, her steps slowing into a walk, "that we'll have to kill whoever is inside there with you. Selfish of you, Feyre."

I panted, holding the door open, making sure they couldn't see me on the other side.

"You have seen my twin," the Weaver hissed softly—with a hint of wonder. "I smell him on you."

Outside, Ianthe and the guard grew closer. Closer and closer.

Somewhere deep in the room, I *felt* her move. Felt her stand. And take a step toward me.

"What are you," the Weaver breathed.

"Feyre, you can be quite tedious," Ianthe said. Right outside. I could barely make out her pale robes through the crack between the door and threshold. "Do you think you can ambush us in there? I saw your shield. You're drained. And I do not think your *glowing* trick will help."

The Weaver's dress rustled as she crept closer in the gloom. "Who did you bring, little wolf? Who did you bring to me?"

Ianthe and her two guards stepped over the threshold. Then another step. Past the open door. They didn't see me in the shadows behind it.

"Dinner," I said to the Weaver, whirling around the door—to its outside face. And let go of the handle.

Just as the door slammed shut hard enough to rattle the cottage, I saw the ball of faelight that Ianthe lifted to illuminate the room.

Saw the horrible face of the Weaver, that mouth of stumped teeth opening wide with delight and unholy hunger. A death-god of old—starved for life. With a beautiful priestess before her.

I was already hurtling for the trees when the guards and Ianthe began screaming.

⁜

Their unending screams followed me for half a mile. By the time I reached the spot where I'd seen the Suriel fall, they'd faded.

Sprawled out, the Suriel's bony chest heaved unevenly, its breaths few and far between.

Dying.

I slid to my knees before it, sinking into the bloody moss. "Let me help you. I can heal you."

I'd do it the same way I'd helped Rhysand. Remove those arrows—and offer it my blood.

I reached for the first one, but a dry, bony hand settled on my wrist. "Your magic . . . ," it rasped, "is spent. Do not . . . waste it."

"I can save you."

It only gripped my wrist. "I am already gone."

"What—what can I do?" The words turned thin—brittle.

"Stay . . . ," it breathed. "Stay . . . until the end."

I took its hand in mine. "I'm sorry." It was all I could think to say. I had done this—I had brought it here.

"I knew," it gasped, sensing my shift in thoughts. "The tracking . . . I knew of it."

"Then why come at all?"

"You . . . were kind. You . . . fought your fear. You were . . . kind," it said again.

I began crying.

"And you were kind to me," I said, not brushing away the tears that fell onto its bloodied, tattered robe. "Thank you—for helping me. When no one else would."

A small smile on that lipless mouth. "Feyre Archeron." A labored breath. "I told you—to stay with the High Lord. And you did."

Its warning to me that first time we'd met. "You—you meant Rhys." All this time. All this time—

"Stay with him . . . and live to see everything righted."

"Yes. I did—and it was."

"No—not yet. *Stay with him.*"

"I will." I always would.

Its chest rose—then fell.

"I don't even know your name," I whispered. The Suriel—it was a title, a name for its kind.

That small smile again. "Does it matter, Cursebreaker?"

"Yes."

Its eyes dimmed, but it did not tell me. It only said, "You should go now. Worse things—worse things are coming. The blood . . . draws them."

I squeezed its bony hand, the leathery skin growing colder. "I can stay a while longer."

I had killed enough animals to know when a body neared death. Soon, now—it would be a matter of breaths.

"Feyre Archeron," the Suriel said again, gazing at the leafy canopy, the sky peeking through it. A painful inhale. "A request."

I leaned close. "Anything."

Another rattling breath. "Leave this world . . . a better place than how you found it."

And as its chest rose and stopped altogether, as its breath escaped in one last sigh, I understood why the Suriel had come to help me, again and again. Not just for kindness . . . but because it was a dreamer.

And it was the heart of a dreamer that had ceased beating inside that monstrous chest.

Its sudden silence echoed into my own.

I laid my head on its chest, on that now-silent vault of bone, and wept.

I wept and wept, until there was a strong hand at my shoulder.

I didn't know the scent, the feel of that hand. But I knew the voice as Helion said softly to me, "Come, Feyre. It is not safe here. Come."

I lifted my head. Helion was there, features grim, his brown skin ashen.

"I can't leave it here like this," I said, refusing to let go of its hand. I didn't care how Helion had found me. Why he'd found me.

He looked to the fallen creature, mouth tightening. "I'll take care of it."

Burn it—with the power of the sun.

I let him help me to my feet. Let him extend a hand toward that body—

"Wait."

Helion obeyed.

"Give me your cloak. Please."

Brows narrowing, Helion unfastened the rich crimson cloak pinned at each shoulder.

I didn't bother to explain as I covered the Suriel's body with the fine fabric. Far finer than the hateful rags Ianthe had given it. I tucked the High Lord's cloak gently around its broad shoulders, its bony arms.

"Thank you," I said one last time to the Suriel, and stepped away.

Helion's flame was a pure, blinding white.

It burned the Suriel into ashes within a heartbeat.

"Come," Helion said again, extending a hand. "Let's get you to the camp."

It was the kindness in his voice that cracked my chest. But I took Helion's hand.

As warm light whisked us away, I could have sworn that the pile of ashes was stirred by a phantom wind.

CHAPTER
61

Helion winnowed me into the camp. Right into Rhys's war-tent.

My mate was pale. Blood-splattered and filthy, from his skin to his armor to his hair.

I opened my mouth—to ask how the battle had gone, to say what had happened, I don't know.

But Rhys just reached for me, folding me into his chest.

And at the smell and warmth and solidity of him . . . I began weeping again.

I didn't know who was in the tent. Who had survived the battle. But they all left.

Left, while my mate held me, rocking me gently, as I cried and cried.

⊹

He only told me what had happened when my tears had quieted. When he'd washed the Suriel's black blood from my hands, my face.

I was out of the tent a heartbeat later, charging through the mud, dodging exhausted and weary soldiers. Rhys was a step behind me, but said nothing as I shoved through flaps of another tent and took stock of what and who was before me.

Mor and Azriel were standing before the cot, monitoring every move the healer sitting beside it made.

As she held her glowing hands over Cassian.

I understood then—the quiet Cassian had once mentioned to me.

It was now in my head as I looked at his muddy, pained face— pained, even in unconsciousness. As I heard his labored, wet breathing.

As I beheld the slice curving up from his navel to the bottom of his sternum. The split flesh. The blood—mostly just a trickle.

I swayed—only for Rhys to grip me beneath the elbows.

The healer didn't turn to look at me as her brow bunched in concentration, hands flaring with white light. Beneath them—slowly, the lips of the wound reached toward each other.

If it was this bad now—

"How," I rasped. Rhys had told me three things a moment ago:

We'd won—barely. Tarquin had again decided what to do with any survivors. And Cassian had been gravely injured.

"Where were you," was all Mor said to me. She was soaked, bloody, and coated in mud. Azriel was, too. No sign of injuries beyond minor cuts, mercifully.

I shook my head. I'd let Rhys into my mind while he held me. Showed him everything—explained Ianthe and the Suriel and the Weaver. What it had told me. Rhys's eyes had gone distant for a moment, and I knew Amren was on her way, the Book in tow. To help Nesta track that Cauldron—or try to. He could explain to Mor.

He'd only known I was gone after the battle stopped—when he realized Mor had been fighting. And that I was not at the camp anymore. He'd just reached Elain's tent when Helion sent word he'd found me. Using whatever gift he possessed that allowed him to sense such things. And was bringing me back. Vague, brief details.

"Is he—is he going to—" I couldn't finish the rest. Words had become as foreign and hard to reach as the stars.

"No," the healer said without looking at me. "He'll be sore for a few days, though."

Indeed, she'd gotten either side of the wound to touch—to now start weaving together.

Bile surged up my throat at the sight of that raw flesh—

"How," I asked again.

"He wouldn't wait for us," Mor said flatly. "He kept charging—trying to re-form the line. One of their commanders engaged him. He wouldn't turn away. By the time Az got there, he was down."

Azriel's face was stone-cold, even as his hazel eyes fixed unrelentingly upon that knitting wound.

Mor said again, "Where did you *go*?"

"If you're about to fight," the healer said sharply, "take it outside. My patient doesn't need to hear this."

None of us moved.

Rhys brushed a hand down my arm. "You are, as always, free to go wherever and whenever you wish. But what I think Mor is saying is . . . try to leave a note the next time."

The words were casual, but that was panic in his eyes. Not—not the controlling fear Tamlin had once succumbed to, but . . . genuine terror of not knowing where I was, if I needed help. Just as I would want to know where he was, if he needed help, if he vanished when our enemies surrounded us. "I'm sorry," I said. To him, to the others.

Mor didn't so much as look at me.

"You have nothing to be sorry for," Rhys replied, hand sliding to cup my cheek. "You decided to take things into your own hands, and got us valuable information in the process. But . . ." His thumb stroked over my cheekbone. "We have been lucky," he breathed. "Keeping a step ahead—keeping out of Hybern's claws. Even if today . . . today wasn't so fortunate on the battlefield. But the cynic in me wonders if our luck is about to expire. And I would rather it not end with you."

They all had to think me young and reckless.

No, Rhys said through the bond, and I realized I'd left my shields open. *Believe me, if you knew half of the shit Cassian and Mor have pulled, you'd get why we don't. I just . . . Leave a note. Or tell me the next time.*

Would you have let me go if I had?

I do not let you do anything. He tilted my face up, Mor and Azriel looking away. *You are your own person, you make your own choices. But we are mates—I am yours, and you are mine. We do not let each other do things, as if we dictate the movements of each other. But . . . I might have insisted I go with you. More for my own mental well-being, just to know you were safe.*

You were occupied.

A slash of a smile. *If you were hell-bent on going into the Middle, I would have unoccupied myself from battle.*

I waited for him to chide me about not waiting until they were done, about all of it, but . . . he angled his head. "I wonder if the Weaver forgives you now," he mused aloud.

Even the healer seemed to start at the name—the words.

A shiver ran down my spine. "I don't want to know."

Rhys let out a low laugh. "Then let's never find out."

But the amusement faded as he again surveyed Cassian. The wound that was now sealed over.

The Suriel wasn't your fault.

I loosed a breath as Cassian's eyelids began to shift and flutter. *I know.*

I'd already added its death to my ever-growing list of things I'd soon make Hybern pay for.

Long minutes passed, and we stood in silence. I did not ask where Nesta was. Mor barely acknowledged me. And Rhys . . .

He perched on the foot of the cot as Cassian's eyes at last opened, and the general let out a groan of pain.

"That's what you get," the healer chided, gathering her supplies, "for stepping in front of a sword." She frowned at him. "Rest tonight and tomorrow. I know better than to insist on a third day after that, but try *not* to leap in front of blades anytime soon."

Cassian just blinked rather dazedly at her before she bowed to Rhys and me and left.

"How bad," he asked, his voice hoarse.

"How bad was your injury," Rhys said mildly, "or how badly did we have our asses kicked?"

Cassian blinked again. Slowly. As if whatever sedative he'd been given still held sway.

"To answer the second question," Rhys went on, Mor and Azriel backing away a step or two as something sharpened in my mate's voice, "we managed. Keir took heavy hits, but . . . we won. Barely. To answer the first . . ." Rhys bared his teeth. "Don't you *ever* pull that kind of shit again."

The glaze wore off Cassian's eyes as he heard the challenge, the anger, and tried to sit up. He hissed, scowling down at the red, angry slice down his chest.

"Your guts were hanging out, you stupid prick," Rhys snapped. "Az held them in for you."

Indeed, the shadowsinger's hands were caked in blood—Cassian's blood. And his face . . . cold with—anger.

"I'm a soldier," Cassian said flatly. "It's part of the job."

"I gave you an order to *wait*," Rhys growled. "You ignored it."

I glanced to Mor, to Azriel—a silent question of whether we should remain. They were too busy watching Rhys and Cassian to notice.

"The line was breaking," Cassian retorted. "Your order was bullshit."

Rhys braced his hands on either side of Cassian's legs and snarled in his face, "I am your *High Lord*. You don't get to disregard orders you don't like."

Cassian sat up this time, swearing at the pain lingering in his body. "Don't you pull rank because you're pissed off—"

"You and your damned theatrics on the battlefield nearly got you *killed*." And even as Rhys spat the words—that was panic, again, in his eyes. His voice. "I'm not pissed. I'm *furious*."

"So you're allowed to be mad about our choices to protect *you*—and we're not allowed to be furious with you for *your* self-sacrificing bullshit?"

Rhys just stared at him. Cassian stared right back.

"You could have died," was all Rhys said, his voice raw.

"So could you."

Another beat of silence—and in its wake, the anger shifted.

Rhys said quietly, "Even after Hybern . . . I can't stomach it."

Seeing him hurt. Any of us hurt.

And the way Rhys spoke, the way Cassian leaned forward, wincing again, and gripped Rhys's shoulder . . .

I strode out of the tent. Left them to talk. Azriel and Mor followed behind me.

I squinted at the watery light—the very last before true dark. When my vision adjusted . . . Nesta stood by the nearest tent, an empty water bucket between her feet. Her hair a damp mess atop her mud-flecked head. Watching us emerge, grim-faced—

"He's fine. Healed and awake," I said quickly.

Nesta's shoulders sagged a bit.

She'd saved me the trouble of hunting her down to ask her about tracking the Cauldron. Better to do it now, with some privacy. Especially before Amren arrived.

But Mor said coldly, "Shouldn't you be refilling that bucket?"

Nesta went stiff. Sized up Mor. But Mor didn't flinch from that look.

After a moment, Nesta picked up her bucket, mud caked up to her shins, and continued on, steps squelching.

I turned, finding Azriel striding for the commanders' tent, but Mor—

Livid. She was absolutely *livid* as she faced me. "She didn't bother to tell anyone that you left."

Hence the anger. "Nesta is many things, but she's certainly loyal."

Mor didn't smile. Not as she said, "You lied."

She stormed for her own tent, and with *that* comment . . . I had no choice but to follow her in.

The space was mostly occupied with her bed and a small desk littered with weapons and maps. "I didn't *lie*," I said, wincing. "I just . . . didn't tell you what I planned to do."

She gaped at me. "You nudged me to *leave you*, insisting you would be safe *at the camp*."

"I'm sorry," I said.

"Sorry? *Sorry?*" She splayed her arms. Bits of mud flew off.

I didn't know what to do with my own—how to even look her in the eye. I'd seen her mad before, but never . . . never at me. I'd never had a friend to quarrel with—who cared enough.

"I know everything you're about to say, every excuse for why I couldn't go with you," Mor snapped. "But none of it excuses you for *lying* to me. If you'd explained, I would have let you go—if you'd *trusted* me, I would have let you go. Or maybe talked you out of an idiotic idea that nearly got you *killed*. They are *hunting* for you. They want to get their hands on you and *use you. Hurt you.* You've only seen a *taste* of what Hybern can do, what they delight in. And to break you to his will, the king will do *anything*."

I didn't know what to say other than, "We needed this information."

"Of course we did. But do you know what it felt like to look Rhys in the eye and tell him I had *no idea* where you were? To realize—for myself—that you had *vanished*, and likely duped me into enabling it?" She scrubbed at her filthy face, smearing the mud and gore further. "I thought you were smarter than that. *Better* than that sort of thing."

The words sent a line of fire searing across my vision, burning down my spine. "I'm not going to listen to this."

I turned to leave, but Mor was already there, gripping my arm. "Oh, yes, you are. Rhys might be all smiles and forgiveness, but you still have *us* to answer to. You are my *High Lady*. Do you understand what it means when you imply you don't trust us to help you? To respect your wishes if you want to do something alone? When you *lie* to us?"

"You want to talk about lying?" I didn't even know what came out of my mouth. I wished I'd killed Ianthe myself, if only to get rid of the rage that writhed along my bones. "How about the fact that you lie to yourself and all of us *every single day*?"

She went still, but didn't loosen her hold on my arm. "You don't know what you're talking about."

"Why haven't you ever made a move for Azriel, Mor? Why did you invite Helion to your bed? You clearly found no pleasure in it—I saw the way you looked the next day. So before you accuse me of being a liar, I'd suggest you look long and hard at *yourself*—"

"That's enough."

"Is it? Don't like someone pushing you about it? About *your* choices? Well, neither do I."

Mor dropped my arm. "Get out."

"Fine."

I didn't glance back as I left. I wondered if she could hear my thunderous heartbeat with every storming step I took through the muddy camp.

Amren found me within twenty steps, a wrapped bundle in her arms. "Every time you lot leave me at home, *someone* manages to get gutted."

CHAPTER
62

I couldn't bring myself to smile at Amren. I could barely keep my chin high.

She peered behind me, as if she could see the path I'd taken from Mor's tent, smell the fight on me. "Be careful," Amren warned as I fell into step beside her, heading for our tent again, "of how you push her. There are some truths that even Morrigan has not herself faced."

The hot anger was swiftly slipping into something cold and queasy and heavy.

"We all fight from time to time, girl," Amren said. "Both of you should cool your heels. Talk tomorrow."

"Fine."

Amren shot me a sharp look, her hair swinging with the motion, but we'd reached my tent.

Rhys and Azriel were holding Cassian between them as they gently set him into a chair at the paper-strewn desk. The general's face was still grayish, but someone had found a shirt for him—and washed off the blood. From the way Cassian sagged in that seat . . . He must have insisted he come. And from the way Rhys lightly mussed his hair as he strode to the other side of the desk . . . That wound, too, had been patched up.

Rhys lifted a brow as I entered, still stomping a bit. I shook my head. *I'll tell you later.*

A caress of claws down my innermost barrier—a comforting touch.

Amren laid the Book onto the desk with a thud that echoed in the earth beneath our feet.

"The second and penultimate pages," I said, trying not to flinch at the power of the Book slithering through the tent. "The Suriel claimed the key you were looking for is there. To nullify the Cauldron's power."

I assumed Rhys had told Amren what had occurred—and assumed that he'd told someone to fetch Nesta, since she pushed through the heavy flaps a moment later.

"Did you bring them?" Rhys asked Amren as Nesta silently approached the table.

Still coated in mud up to her shins, my sister paused on the other side—away from where Cassian now sat. Looked him over. Her face revealed nothing, yet her hands . . . I could have sworn a faint tremor rippled through her fingers before she balled them into fists and faced Amren. Cassian watched her for a moment longer before turning his head toward Amren as well. How long had Nesta stood atop that hill, watching the battle? Had she seen him fall?

Amren reached into the pocket of her pewter cloak and chucked a black velvet bag onto the desk. It clacked and thunked as it hit the wood. "Bones and stones."

Nesta only angled her head at the sight of the bag.

Your sister came immediately when I explained what we needed, Rhys said. *I think seeing Cassian hurt convinced her not to pick a fight today.*

Or convinced my sister to pick a fight with someone else entirely.

Nesta lifted the bag. "So, I scatter these like some backstreet charlatan and it'll find the Cauldron?"

Amren let out a low laugh. "Something like that."

Arcs of mud lay beneath Nesta's nails. She didn't seem to notice as she untied the small pouch and dumped out its contents. Three stones, four bones. The latter were brown and gleamed with age; the former were white as the moon and smooth as glass, each marked with a thin, reedy letter I did not recognize.

"Three stones for the faces of the Mother," Amren said upon seeing Nesta's raised brows. "Four bones . . . for whatever reason the *charlatans* came up with that I can't be bothered to remember."

Nesta snorted. Rhys echoed the sentiment. My sister said, "So what—I just shake them around in my hands and chuck them? How am I to make sense of any of it?"

"We can figure it out," Cassian said, his voice rough and weary. "But start with holding them in your hands and thinking—about the Cauldron."

"Don't just *think* about it," Amren corrected. "You must cast your mind *toward* it. Find the bond that links you."

Even I paused at that. And Nesta, stones and bones now in hand . . . She made no move to close her eyes. "I—am I to . . . touch it?"

"No," Amren warned. "Just come close. Find it, but do not interact."

Nesta still didn't move. She could not use the bathtub, she'd told me. Because the memories it dragged up—

Cassian said to her, "Nothing can harm you here." He sucked in a breath, groaning softly, and rose to his feet. Azriel tried to stop him, but Cassian brushed him off and strode for my sister's side. He braced a hand on the desk when he at last stopped. "Nothing can harm you," he repeated.

Nesta was still looking at him when she finally shut her eyes. I shifted, and the angle allowed me to see what I hadn't detected before.

Nesta stood before the map, a fist of bones and stones clenched over it. Cassian remained at her side—his other hand on her lower back.

And I marveled at the touch she allowed—marveled at it as much as I did the mud-splattered hand she held out. The concentration that settled over her face.

Her eyes shifted beneath their lids, as if scanning the world. "I don't see anything."

"Go deeper," Amren urged. "Find that tether between you."

She stiffened, but Cassian stepped closer, and she settled again.

A minute went by. Then another.

A muscle twitched on Nesta's brow. Her hand bobbed.

Her breath then came fast and hard, her lips curling back as she panted through her teeth.

"Nesta," Cassian warned.

"Quiet," Amren snapped.

A small noise came out of her—one of terror.

"Where is it, girl," Amren coaxed. "Open your hand. Let us see."

Nesta's fingers only clutched tighter, the whites of her knuckles as stark as the stones held within them.

Too deep—whatever she had done—

I lunged for her. Not physically, but with my mind.

If Elain's mental gates were those of a sleeping garden, Nesta's . . . They belonged to an ancient fortress, sharp and brutal. The sort I imagined they once impaled people upon.

But they were open wide. And inside . . .

Dark.

Dark like I had never known, even with Rhysand.

Nesta.

I took a step into her mind.

The images slammed into me.

One after one after one, I saw them.

The army that stretched into the horizon. The weapons, the hate, the sheer size.

I saw the king standing over a map in a war-tent, flanked by Jurian and several commanders, the Cauldron squatting in the center of the room behind them.

And there was Nesta.

Standing in that tent, watching the king, the Cauldron.

Frozen in place.

With undiluted fear.

"Nesta."

She did not seem to hear me as she stared at them.

I reached for her hand. "You found it. I see—I see where it is."

Nesta's face was bloodless. But she at last dragged her attention to me. "Feyre."

Surprise lit her terror-wide eyes.

"Let's go back," I said.

She nodded, and we turned. But we felt it—we both did.

Not the king or the commanders plotting with him. Not Jurian as he played his deadly game of deception. But the Cauldron. As if some great sleeping beast opened an eye.

The Cauldron seemed to sense us watching. Sense us *there*.

I felt it stir—like it would lunge for Nesta. I grabbed my sister and ran.

"Open your fist," I ordered her as we sprinted for the iron gates to her mind. "Open it *now*."

She only panted, and that monstrous force swelled behind us, a black wave rising up.

"Open it *now*, or it will get in here. Open it *now*, Nesta!"

I heard the words as I threw myself out of her mind—heard them because I'd been shouting in that tent.

With a gasp, Nesta's fingers splayed wide, scattering stones and bones over the map.

Cassian caught her with an arm around the waist as she swayed. He hissed in pain at the movement. "What the *hell*—"

"Look," Amren breathed.

There was no throw that could have done it—save for one blessed by magic.

The stones and bones formed a perfect, tight circle around a spot on the map.

Nesta and I went pale. I had seen the size of that army—we both had. While Hybern had been driving us northward, letting us chase them in these two battles . . .

The king had amassed his host along the western edge of the human territory.

Perhaps no more than a hundred miles from our family's estate.

⁜

Rhys called in Tarquin and Helion to show them what we'd discovered.

Too few. We had too few soldiers, even with three armies here, to take on that host. I'd shown Rhysand what I'd seen—and he'd shown it to the others.

"Kallias will arrive soon," Helion said, dragging his hands through his onyx hair.

"He'd have to bring forty thousand soldiers," Cassian said. "I doubt he has half that."

Rhys was staring and staring at that cluster of stones and bones on the map. I could feel the wrath rippling off him—not just at Hybern, but himself for not thinking Hybern might be deliberately toying with us. Positioning us here.

We'd won the high ground these two battles—Hybern had won the high ground in this war.

He knew what waited in the Middle.

And Hybern had now forced us to gather here—in this spot—so that he and his behemoth army could drive us northward. A clean sweep from the south, eventually pushing us into the Middle or forcing us to break apart to avoid the lethal tangle of trees and denizens.

And if we took the battle to them . . . We might court death.

None of us were foolish enough to risk building any plans around Jurian, regardless of where his true allegiance lay. Our best chance was in buying time for other allies to arrive. Kallias. Thesan.

Tamlin had chosen who to back in this war. And even if he'd picked Prythian, he would have been left with the problem of mustering a Spring Court force after I'd destroyed their faith in him.

And Miryam and Drakon . . . *Not enough time*, Rhys said to me. *To hunt for them—find them, and bring back their army. We could return to find Hybern has wiped our own off the map.*

But there was the Carver—if I dared risk retrieving his prize. I didn't mention it, didn't offer it. Not until I could know for certain—once I wasn't about to faint from exhaustion.

"We'll rest on it," Tarquin said, blowing out a breath. "Meet at dawn tomorrow. Making a decision after a long day never helped anyone."

Helion agreed, and saw himself out. It was hard not to stare, not to compare his features to Lucien's. Their nose was the same—eerily identical. How had no one ever called him out for it?

I supposed it was the least of my worries. Tarquin frowned at the map one last time and declared, "We'll find a way to face this."

Rhys nodded, while Cassian's mouth quirked to the side. He'd slid back into his chair for the discussion, and now nursed a cup of some healing brew Azriel had fetched for him.

Tarquin turned from the table, just as the tent flaps parted for a pair of broad shoulders—

Varian. He didn't so much as look at his High Lord, his focus going right to where Amren sat at the head of the table. As if he'd sensed she was here—or someone had reported. And he'd come running.

Amren's eyes flicked up from the Book as Varian halted. A coy smile curved her red lips.

There was still blood and dirt splattered on Varian's brown skin, coating his silver armor and close-cropped white hair. He didn't seem to notice or care as he strode for Amren.

And none of us dared to speak as Varian dropped to his knees before Amren's chair, took her shocked face in his broad hands, and kissed her soundly.

CHAPTER
63

None of us lasted long after dinner.

Amren and Varian didn't even bother to join us.

No, she'd just wrapped her legs around his waist, right there in front of us, and he'd stood, lifting her in one swift movement. I wasn't entirely sure how Varian managed to walk them out of the tent while still kissing her, Amren's hands dragging through his hair, letting out noises that were unnervingly like purring as they vanished into the camp.

Rhys had let out a low laugh as we all gawked in their wake. "I suppose that's how Varian decided he'd tell Amren he was feeling rather grateful she ordered us to go to Adriata."

Tarquin cringed. "We'll alternate who has to deal with them on holidays."

Cassian chuckled hoarsely, and looked to Nesta, who remained pale and quiet. What she'd seen, what *I'd* seen in her mind . . .

The size of that army . . .

"Eat or bed?" Cassian had asked Nesta, and I honestly couldn't tell if he'd meant it as some invitation. I debated telling him he was in no shape.

Nesta only said, "Bed." And there was certainly *no* invitation in the exhausted reply.

Rhys and I managed to eat, quietly discussing what we'd seen. Exhaustion weighted my every breath, and I'd barely finished my plate of roast mutton before I crawled into bed and passed out atop the blankets. Rhys woke me only to tug off my boots and jacket.

Tomorrow morning. We'd figure out how to deal with everything tomorrow morning. I'd talk to Amren about finally mustering Bryaxis to help us wipe out that army.

Maybe there was something else we weren't seeing. Some additional shot at salvation beyond that nullifying spell.

My dreams were a tangled garden, thorns snagging on me as I stumbled through them.

I dreamed of the Suriel, bleeding out and smiling. I dreamed of the Weaver's open mouth ripping into Ianthe while she still screamed. I dreamed of Lord Graysen—so mortal and young—standing at the edge of the camp, beckoning to Elain. Telling her he'd come for her. To come home with him. That he'd found a way to undo what had been done to her—to make her human again.

I dreamed of that Cauldron in the King of Hybern's war-tent, so dark and slumbering . . . Awakening as Nesta and I stood there, invisible and unseen.

How it had watched back. *Known* us.

I could feel it watching me, even then. In my dreams. Feel it extend an ancient, black tendril toward me—

I jolted awake.

Rhys's naked body was wrapped around mine, his face softened with sleep. In the blackness of the tent, I listened.

Crackling fires outside. The drowsy murmurs of the soldiers on watch. The wind sighing along the canvas tents, snapping at the banners crowning them.

I scanned the dark, listening.

The skin on my arms pebbled.

"Rhys."

He was instantly awake—sitting upright. "What is it?"

"Something . . ." I listened so hard my ears strained. "Something is here. Something is wrong."

He moved, hauling on his pants and knife-belt. I followed suit, still trying to listen, fingers stumbling over the buckles. "I dreamed," I whispered. "I dreamed about the Cauldron . . . that it was *watching* again."

"*Shit*." The word was a hiss of breath.

"I think we opened a door," I breathed, shoving my feet into my boots. "I think . . . I think . . ." I couldn't finish the sentence as I hurried for the tent flaps, Rhys at my heels. Nesta. I had to find Nesta—

Gold-brown hair flashed in the firelight, and she was already there, hurrying for me, still in her nightgown. "You hear it, too," she panted.

Hear—I couldn't hear, but just *feel*—

Amren's small figure darted around a tent, wearing what looked to be Varian's shirt. It came down to her knees, and its owner was indeed behind her, bare-chested as Rhys was, and wide-eyed.

Amren's bare feet were splattered in mud and grass. "It came here— its power. I can feel it—slithering around. *Looking*."

"The Cauldron," Varian said, brows narrowing. "But—it's *aware*?"

"We pried too deep," Amren said. "Battle aside, it knows where we are as much as we now know its location."

Nesta raised a hand. "*Listen*."

And I heard it then.

It was a song and invitation, a cluster of notes sung by a voice that was male and female, young and old, haunting and alluring and—

"I can't hear anything," Rhys said.

"You were not Made," Amren snapped. But we were. The three of us . . .

Again, the Cauldron sang its siren song.

My very bones recoiled. "What does it *want*?"

I felt it pulling away—felt it sliding off into the night.

Azriel stepped out of a shadow. "What *is* that," he hissed.

My brows rose. "You hear it?"

A shake of the head. "No—but the shadows, the wind . . . They recoil."

The Cauldron sang again.

Distant—withdrawing.

"I think it's leaving," I whispered.

Cassian stumbled and staggered for us a moment later, a hand braced on his chest, Mor on his heels. She did not so much as look at me, nor I her, as Rhys told them. Standing together in the dead of night—

The Cauldron sang one final note—then went silent.

The presence, the weight . . . vanished.

Amren loosed a sigh. "Hybern knows where we are by now. The Cauldron likely wanted to have a look for itself. After we taunted it."

I rubbed at my face. "Let's pray that's the last we see of it."

Varian angled his head. "So you three . . . because you were *Made*, you can hear it? Sense it?"

"It would appear so," Amren said, looking inclined to tug him back to wherever they'd been, to finish what they'd no doubt still been in the middle of doing.

But Azriel asked softly, "What about Elain?"

Something cold went through me. Nesta was just staring at Azriel. Staring and staring—

Then she broke into a run.

Her bare feet slid through the mud, splattering me as we charged for our sister's tent.

"Elain—" Nesta shoved open the tent.

She stopped short so fast I slammed into her. The tent—the tent was empty.

Nesta flung herself inside, tossing away blankets, as if Elain had somehow sunk into the ground. *"Elain!"*

I whirled into the camp, scanning the tents nearby. One look at Rhys conveyed what we'd found inside. An Illyrian blade appeared in his hand just before he winnowed.

Azriel stalked to my side, right into the tent where Nesta had now come to her feet. He tucked his wings in tightly as he squeezed through the narrow space, ignoring Nesta's snarl of warning, and knelt at the cot.

He ran a scarred hand over the rumpled blankets. "They're still warm."

Outside, Cassian was barking orders, the camp rousing.

"The Cauldron," I breathed. "The Cauldron was fading away—going somewhere—"

Nesta was already moving, sprinting for where we'd heard that voice. *Luring* Elain out.

I knew how it had done it.

I'd dreamed of it.

Graysen standing on the edge of camp, calling to her, promising her love and healing.

We reached the copse of trees at the edge of the camp, just as Rhys appeared out of the night, his blade now sheathed across his back. There was something in his hands. No emotion on his carefully neutral face.

Nesta let out a sound that might have been a sob as I realized what he'd found at the edge of the forest. What the Cauldron had left behind in its haste to return to Hybern's war-camp. Or as a mocking gift.

Elain's dark blue cloak, still warm from her body.

CHAPTER
64

Nesta sat with her head in her hands inside my tent. She did not speak, did not move. Coiled in on herself, clinging to stay whole—that's how she looked. How I felt.

Elain—taken to Hybern's army.

Nesta had stolen something vital from the Cauldron. And in those moments Nesta had hunted it down for us . . . The Cauldron had learned what was vital to *her*.

So the Cauldron had stolen something in return.

"We'll get her back," Cassian rasped from where he perched on the rolled arm of the chaise longue across the small sitting area, watching her carefully. Rhys, Amren, and Mor were meeting with the other High Lords, informing them what had been done. Seeing if they knew anything. Had any way of helping.

Nesta lowered her hands, lifting her head. Her eyes were red-rimmed, lips thin. "No, you will not." She pointed to the map on the table. "I saw that army. Its size, who is in it. I *saw* it, and there is no chance of *any* of you getting into its heart. Even you," she added when Cassian opened his mouth again. "*Especially* not when you're injured."

And what Hybern would do to Elain, might already be doing—

From the shadows near the entrance to the tent, Azriel said, as if in answer to some unspoken debate, "I'm getting her back."

Nesta slid her gaze to the shadowsinger. Azriel's hazel eyes glowed golden in the shadows.

Nesta said, "Then you will die."

Azriel only repeated, rage glazing that stare, "I'm getting her back."

With the shadows, he might stand a chance of slipping in. But there were wards to consider, and ancient magic, and the king with those spells and the Cauldron . . .

For a moment, I saw that set of paints Elain had once bought me with the extra money she'd saved. The red, yellow, and blue I'd savored, used to paint that dresser in our cottage. I had not painted in years at that point, had not dared spend the money on myself . . . But Elain had.

I stood. Met Azriel's wrathful stare.

"I'm going with you," I said.

Azriel only nodded.

"You'll never get far enough into the camp," Cassian warned.

"I'm going to walk right in."

And as they narrowed their brows, I shifted myself. Not a glamour, but a true changing of features.

"Shit," Cassian breathed when I was done.

Nesta rose to her feet. "They might already know she's dead."

For it was Ianthe's face, her hair, that I now possessed. It nearly drained what was left of my depleted magic. Anything more . . . I might not have enough left to keep her features in place. But there were other ways. Routes. For the rest of what I needed.

"I need one of your Siphons," I said to Azriel. The blue was slightly deeper, but at night . . . they might not notice the difference.

He held out his palm, a round, flat blue stone appearing in it, and chucked it to me. I wrapped my fingers around the warm stone, its power throbbing in my veins like an unearthly heartbeat as I looked to Cassian. "Where is the blacksmith."

╬

The camp blacksmith did not ask any questions when I handed over the silver candlesticks from my tent and Azriel's Siphon. When I asked him to craft that circlet. Immediately.

A mortal blacksmith might have taken a while—days. But a Fae one . . .

By the time he finished, Azriel had gone to the camp priestess and retrieved a spare set of her robes. Perhaps not identical to Ianthe's, but close enough. As High Priestess, none would dare look too closely at her. Ask questions.

I had just set the circlet atop my hood when Rhys prowled into our tent. Azriel was honing Truth-Teller with relentless focus, Cassian sharpening the weapons I was to fasten beneath the robe—atop the Illyrian leathers.

"He'll sense your power," I said to Rhys before he could speak.

"I know," Rhys said hoarsely. And I realized—realized the other High Lords had come up empty.

My hands began shaking. I knew the odds. Knew what I'd face in there. I'd seen it in Nesta's mind hours ago.

Rhys closed the distance between us, clutching my hands. Gazing at *me*, and not Ianthe's face, as if he could see the soul beneath. "There are wards around the camp. You can't winnow. You have to walk in—and out. Then you can make the jump back here."

I nodded.

He brushed a kiss to my brow. "Ianthe sold out your sisters," he said, his voice turning sharp and hard. "It's only fitting that you use her to get Elain back."

He gripped the sides of my face, bringing us nose to nose.

"Do not get distracted. Do not linger. You are a warrior, and warriors know when to pick their fights."

I nodded, our breath mingling.

Rhys growled. "They took what is ours. And we do not allow those crimes to go unpunished."

His power rippled and swirled around me.

"You do not fear," Rhys breathed. "You do not falter. You do not yield. You go in, you get her, and you come out again."

I nodded again, holding his stare.

"Remember that you are a wolf. And you cannot be caged."

He kissed my brow one more time, my blood thrumming and boiling in me, howling to draw blood.

I began to buckle on the weapons Cassian had lined up in neat rows on the table, Rhys helping me with the straps and loops, positioning them so that they wouldn't be visible beneath my robe. The only one I couldn't fit was the Illyrian blade—no way to hide it and be able to easily draw it. Cassian gave me an extra dagger to make up for its absence.

"You get them in and out again, shadowsinger," Rhys said to Azriel as I walked to the spymaster's side, getting a feel for the weight of the weapons and the flow of the heavy robe. "I don't care how many of them you have to kill to do it. They both come out."

Azriel gave a grave, steady nod. "I swear it, High Lord."

Formal words, formal titles.

I gripped Azriel's scarred hand, the weight of his Siphon pressing on my brow through the hood. We looked to Rhys, to Cassian and Nesta, to Mor—right as she appeared, breathless, between the tent flaps. Her eyes went to me, then the shadowsinger, and flared with shock and fear—

But we were gone.

Azriel's dark breeze was different from Rhys's. Colder. Sharper. It cut through the world like a blade, spearing us toward that army camp.

Night was still overhead, dawn perhaps two hours away, when he landed us in a thick forest on a hilltop that overlooked the outskirts of the mighty camp.

The king had used the same spells that Rhys had put around Velaris and our own forces. Spells to hide it from sight, and dispel people who got too close.

We'd landed inside of them, thanks to Nesta's specifics. With a perfect view of the city of soldiers that sprawled away into the night.

Campfires burned, as numerous as the stars. Beasts snapped and snarled, yanking on leashes and chains. On and on and on that army went, a squatting terror drinking the life from the earth.

Azriel silently faded into blackness—until he was my own shadow and nothing more.

I fluffed out the priestess's pale robe, adjusted the circlet atop my head, and began to pick my way down the hill.

Into the heart of Hybern's army.

CHAPTER
65

The first test would be the most dangerous—and informative.

Passing through the guards stationed at the edge of the camp—and learning if they'd heard of Ianthe's demise. Learning what sort of power Ianthe truly wielded here.

I kept my features in that beatific, pretty mask she'd always plastered on her face, head held just so, my mating ring turned facedown and put onto my other hand, a few silver bracelets Azriel had borrowed from the camp priestess dangling at my wrists. I let them jangle loudly, as she had, like a cat with a bell on its collar.

A pet—I supposed Ianthe was no more than a pet of the king.

I couldn't see Azriel, but I could feel him, as if the Siphon parading itself as Ianthe's jewel was a tether. He dwelled in every pocket of shadow, darting ahead and behind.

The six guards flanking the camp entrance monitored Ianthe, strutting out of the dark, with unmasked distaste. I steadied my heart, *became* her, preening and coy, vain and predatory, holy and sensual.

They did not stop me as I walked past them and onto the long avenue that cut through the endless camp. Did not look confused or expectant.

I didn't dare let my shoulders slump, or even heave a sigh of utter relief. Not as I headed down the broad artery lined by tents and forges, fires and—and things I did not look at, did not even turn toward as the sounds coming out of them charged at me.

This place made the Court of Nightmares seem like a human sitting room filled with chaste maidens embroidering pillows.

And somewhere in this hell-pit . . . Elain. Had the Cauldron presented her to the king? Or was she in some in-between, trapped in whatever dark world the Cauldron occupied?

I'd seen the king's tent in Nesta's scrying. It had not seemed as far away as it did now, rising like a gargantuan, spiny beast from the center of the camp. Entrance to it would present another set of obstacles.

If we made it that far without being noticed.

The time of night worked to our advantage. The soldiers who were awake were either engaged in activities of varying awfulness, or were on guard and wishing they could be. The rest were asleep.

It was strange, I realized with each bouncing step and jangle of jewelry toward the heart of camp, to consider that Hybern actually needed rest.

I'd somehow assumed they were beyond it—mythic, unending in their strength and rage.

But they, too, tired. And ate. And slept.

Perhaps not as easily or as much as humans, but, with two hours until dawn, we were lucky. Once the sun chased away the shadows, though . . . Once it made some gaps in my costume all too clear . . .

It was hard to scan the tents we passed, hard to focus on the sounds of the camp while pretending to be someone wholly used to it. I didn't even know if Ianthe *had* a tent here—if she was allowed near the king whenever she wished.

I doubted it—doubted we'd be able to stroll right into his personal tent and find wherever the hell Elain was.

A massive bonfire smoldered and crackled near the center of camp, the sounds of revelry reaching us long before we got a good visual.

I knew within a few heartbeats that most of the soldiers were *not* sleeping.

They were here.

Celebrating.

Some danced in wicked circles around the fire, their contorted shapes little more than twisted shadows flinging through the night. Some drank from enormous oak barrels of beer I recognized—right from Tamlin's stores. Some writhed with each other—some merely watched.

But through the laughter and singing and music, over the roar of the fire . . . Screaming.

A shadow gripped my shoulder, reminding me not to run.

Ianthe would not run—would not show alarm.

My mouth went dry as that scream sounded again.

I couldn't bear it—to let it go on, to see what was being done—

Azriel's shadow-hand grasped my own, tugging me closer. His rage rippled off his invisible form.

We made a lazy circuit of the revelry, other parts of it becoming clear. The screaming—

It was not Elain.

It was not Elain who hung from a rack near a makeshift dais of granite.

It was one of the Children of the Blessed, young and slender—

My stomach twisted, threatening to surge up my throat. Two others were chained up beside her. From the way they sagged, the injuries on their naked bodies—

Clare. It was like Clare, what had been done to them. And like Clare, they had been left there to rot, left for the crows surely to arrive at dawn.

This one had held out for longer.

I couldn't. I couldn't—couldn't *leave* her there—

But if I lingered too long, they'd see. And drawing attention to myself . . .

Could I live with it? I'd once killed two innocents to save Tamlin and his people. I'd be as good as killing her if I left her there in favor of saving my sister . . .

Stranger. She was a *stranger*—

"He's been looking for you," drawled a hard male voice.

I pivoted to find Jurian striding from between two tents, buckling his sword-belt. I glanced at the dais. And as if an invisible hand wiped away the smoke . . .

There sat the King of Hybern. He lounged in his chair, head propped on a fist, face a mask of vague amusement as he surveyed the revelry, the torture and torment. The adulation of the crowd that occasionally turned to toast or bow to him.

I willed my voice to soften, adapted that lilt. "I have been busy with my sisters."

Jurian stared at me for a long moment, eyes sliding to the Siphon atop my head.

I knew the moment he realized who I was. Those brown eyes flared—barely.

"Where is she," was all I breathed.

Jurian gave a cocky grin. Not directed at me, but anyone watching us. "You've been lusting after me for weeks now," he purred. "Act like it."

My throat constricted. But I laid a hand on his forearm, batting my eyelashes at him as I stepped closer.

A bemused snort. "I have trouble believing that's how you won his heart."

I tried not to scowl. "*Where* is she."

"Safe. Untouched."

My chest caved in at the word.

"Not for long," Jurian said. "It gave him a shock when she appeared before the Cauldron. He had her contained. Came here to brood over what to do with her. And how to make you pay for it."

I ran a hand up his arm, then rested it over his heart. "Where. Is. She."

Jurian leaned in as if he'd kiss me, and brought his mouth to my ear. "Were you smart enough to kill her before you took her skin?"

My hands tightened on his jacket. "She got what she deserved."

I could feel Jurian's smile against my ear. "She's in his tent. Chained with steel and a little spell from his favorite book."

Shit. *Shit.* Perhaps I should have gotten Helion, who could break almost any—

Jurian caught my chin between his thumb and forefinger. "Come to my tent with me, Ianthe. Let me see what that pretty mouth can do."

It was an effort not to recoil, but I let Jurian put a hand on my lower back. He chuckled. "Seems like you've already got some steel in you. No need for mine."

I gave him a pretty, sunshine smile. "What of the girl on the rack?"

Darkness flickered in those eyes. "There have been many before her, and many will come after."

"I can't leave her here," I said through my teeth.

Jurian led me into the labyrinth of tents, heading for that inner circle. "Your sister or her—you won't be able to take two out."

"Get her to me, and I'll make it happen."

Jurian muttered, "Say you would like to pray before the Cauldron before we retire."

I blinked, and realized there were guards—guards and that giant, bone-colored tent ahead of us. I clasped my hands before me and said to Jurian, "Before we . . . retire, I should like to pray before the great Cauldron. To give thanks for today's bounty."

Jurian glowered—a man ready for rutting who had been delayed. "Make it quick," he said, jerking his chin to the guards on either side of the tent flaps. I caught the look he gave them—male to male. They didn't bother to hide their leering as I passed.

And since I was *Ianthe* . . . I gave them each a sultry smile, sizing them up for conquest of a different kind than the one they'd come to Prythian to do.

The one on the right's answering grin told me he was mine for the taking.

Later, I willed my eyes to say. *When I'm done with the human.*

He adjusted his belt a bit as I slipped into the tent.

Dim—cold. Like the sky before dawn, that's how the tent felt.

No crackling braziers, no faelights. And in the center of the massive tent . . . a darkness that devoured the light. The Cauldron.

The hair on my arms rose.

Jurian whispered in my ear, "You have five minutes to get her out. Take her to the western edge—there's a cliff overlooking the river. I'll meet you there."

I blinked at him.

Jurian's grin was a slash of white in the gloom. "If you hear screaming, don't panic." His diversion. He smirked toward the shadows. "I hope you can carry three, shadowsinger."

Azriel did not confirm that he was there, that he'd heard.

Jurian studied me for a heartbeat longer. "Save a dagger for your own heart. If they catch you alive, the king will—" He shook his head. "Don't let them catch you alive."

Then he was gone.

Azriel emerged from the deep shadows in the corner of the tent a heartbeat later. He jerked his chin toward the curtains in the back. I began intoning one of Ianthe's many prayers, a pretty speech I'd heard her say a thousand times at the Spring Court.

We rushed across the rugs, dodging tables and furniture. I chanted her prayers all the while.

Azriel slid back the curtain—

Elain was in her nightgown. Gagged, wrists wrapped in steel that glowed violet. Her eyes went wide as she saw us—Azriel and *me*—

I shifted my face back into my own, raising a hand to my lips as Azriel knelt before her. I kept up my litany of praying, beseeching the Cauldron to make my womb fruitful, on and on—

Azriel gently removed the gag from her mouth. "Are you hurt?"

She shook her head, devouring the sight of him as if not quite believing it. "You came for me." The shadowsinger only inclined his head.

"Hurry," I whispered, then resumed my prayer. We had until it ran out.

Azriel's Siphons flared, the one atop my head warming.

The magic did nothing when it came into contact with those bonds. Nothing.

Only a few more verses of my prayer left to chant.

Her wrists and ankles were bound. She couldn't run out of here with them on.

I reached a hand toward her, scrambling for a thread of Helion's power to unravel the king's spell on the chains. But my magic was still depleted, in shambles—

"We don't have time," Azriel murmured. "He's coming."

The screaming and shouting began.

Azriel scooped up Elain, looping her bound arms around his neck. "Hold tight," he ordered her, "and don't make a sound."

Barking and baying rent the night. I drew off the robe, and pocketed Azriel's Siphon before palming two knives. "Out the back?"

A nod. "Get ready to run."

My heart thundered. Elain glanced between us, but did not tremble. Did not cringe.

"Run, and don't stop," he told me. "We sprint for the western edge—the cliff."

"If Jurian's not there with the girl in time—"

"Then you will go. I'll get her."

I blew out a breath, steadying myself.

The barking and growling grew louder—closer.

"Now," Azriel hissed, and we ran.

His Siphons blazed, and the canvas of the back of the tent melted into nothing. We bolted through it before the guards nearby noticed.

They didn't react to us. Only peered at the hole.

Azriel had made us invisible—shadow-bound.

We sprinted between tents, feet flying over the grass and dirt. "Hurry," he whispered. "The shadows won't last long."

For in the east, behind us . . . the sun was beginning to rise.

A piercing howl split the dying night. And I knew they'd realized what we'd done. That we were *here*. And even if they couldn't see us . . . the King of Hybern's hounds could scent us.

"*Faster*," Azriel snarled.

The earth shuddered behind us. I didn't dare look behind.

We neared a rack of weapons. I sheathed my knives, freeing my hands as we hurtled past and I snatched a bow and quiver of arrows from their stand. *Ash* arrows.

The arrows clacked as I slung the quiver over a shoulder. As I nocked an arrow into place.

Azriel cut right, swerving around a tent.

And with the angle . . . I turned and fired.

The nearest hound—it was not a hound, I realized as the arrow spiraled for its head.

But some cousin of the naga—some monstrous, scaled thing that thundered on all fours, serpentine face snarling and full of bone-shredding white teeth—

My arrow went right through its throat.

It went down, and we rounded the tent, hurtling for that still-dim western horizon.

I nocked another arrow.

Three others. Three more behind us, gaining with every clawed step—

I could feel them around us—Hybern commanders, racing along

with the hounds, tracking the beasts because they still could not see us. That arrow I'd fired had told them enough about the distance. But the moment the hounds caught up . . . those commanders would appear. Kill us or drag us away.

Row after row of tents, slowly awakening at the ruckus in the center of the camp.

The air rippled, and I looked up to see the rain of ash arrows unleashed from behind, so many they were a blind attempt to hit *any* target—

Azriel's blue shield shuddered at the impact, but held. Yet our shadows shivered and faded.

The hounds closed in, two breaking away—to cut to the side. To herd us.

For that was a *cliff* at the other edge of the camp. A cliff with a very, *very* long drop, and unforgiving river below.

And standing at its end, huddled in a dark cloak . . .

That was the girl.

Jurian had left her there—for us. Where he'd gone . . . I saw no sign of him.

But behind us, filling the air as if he'd used magic to do so . . . The king spoke.

"What intrepid thieves," he drawled, the words everywhere and nowhere. "How shall I punish you?"

I had no doubt the wards ended just beyond the cliff's edge. It was confirmed by the snarls of the hounds, who seemed to know that their prey would escape in less than a hundred yards. If we could jump far enough to be clear of them.

"*Get her out, Azriel,*" I begged him, panting. "I'll get the other."

"We're *all*—"

"*That's an order.*"

A clean shot, an unimpeded path right to that cliff's edge, and to freedom beyond—

"You need to—" My words were cut off.

I felt the impact before the pain. The searing, *burning* pain that erupted through my shoulder. An ash arrow—

My feet snagged beneath me, blood spraying, and I hit the rocky ground so hard my bones groaned. Azriel swore, but with Elain in his arms, fighting—

The hounds were there in a second.

I fired an arrow at one, my shoulder screaming with the movement. The hound fell, clearing the view behind.

Revealing the king striding down the line of tents, unhurried and assured of our capture, a bow dangling from his hand. The bow that had delivered the arrow now piercing through my body.

"Torturing you would be so dull," the king mused, voice still magnified. "At least, the traditional sort of torture." Every step was slow, intentional. "How Rhysand shall rage. How he shall panic. His mate, at last come to see me."

Before I could warn Azriel to hurry, the other two hounds were on me.

One leaped right for me. I lifted my bow to intercept its jaws.

The hound snapped it in two, hurling the wood away. I grabbed for a knife, just as the second one leaped—

A roar deafened me, made my head ring. Just as one of the hounds was thrown off me.

I knew that roar, knew—

A golden-furred beast with curling horns tore into the hounds.

"Tamlin," I got out, but his green eyes narrowed. *Run*, he seemed to say.

That was who had been running alongside us. Trying to find us.

He ripped and shredded, the hounds launching themselves wholly on him. The king paused, and though he remained far off, I could clearly make out the surprise slackening his face.

Now. I had to go *now*—

I scrambled to my feet, whipping the arrow out with a swallowed scream. Azriel was already there, no more than a few heartbeats having passed—

Azriel gripped me by the collar, and a web of blue light fastened itself at my shoulder. Holding the blood in, a bandage until a healer—

"You need to fly," he panted.

Six more hounds closed in. Tamlin still fought the others, gaining ground—holding the line.

"We need to get airborne," Azriel said, one eye now on the king as he resumed his mockingly slow approach. "Can you make it?"

The young woman was still standing at the edge of the cliff. Watching us with wide eyes, black hair whipping over her face.

I'd never made a running takeoff before. I'd barely been able to keep in the skies.

Even if Azriel took the girl in his free arm . . .

I didn't let myself consider the alternative. I *would* get airborne. Only long enough to sail over that cliff, and winnow out when we'd passed the wards' edge.

Tamlin let out a yelp of what sounded like pain, followed by another earth-shuddering roar. The rest of the hounds had reached him. He did not falter, did not yield an inch to them—

I summoned the wings. The drag and weight of them . . . Even with the Siphon-bandage, pain razed my senses at the tug on my muscles.

I panted through my gritted teeth as Azriel plunged ahead, wings beginning to flap. Not enough space on the jutting ledge for us to do this side by side. I gobbled down details of his takeoff, the beating of his wings, the shifting angle of his body.

"Grab onto him!" Elain ordered the wide-eyed human girl as Azriel thundered toward her. The girl looked like a doe about to be run down by a wolf.

The girl did not open her arms as they neared.

Elain screamed at her, *"If you want to live, do it now!"*

The girl dropped her cloak, opened her arms wide.

Her black hair streamed behind Azriel, catching amongst his wings as he practically tackled her into the sky. But I saw, even as I ran, Elain's pale hands lurch—gripping the girl by her neck, holding her as tightly as she could.

And just in time.

One of the hounds broke free from Tamlin in a mighty leap. I ducked, bracing for impact.

But it was not aiming for me. Two bounding strides down the stone ledge and another leap—

Azriel's roar echoed off the rocks as the hound slammed into him, dragging those shredding talons down his spine, his wings—

The girl screamed, but Elain moved. As Azriel battled to keep them airborne, keep his grip on them, my sister sent a fierce kick into the beast's face. Its eye. Another. Another.

It bellowed, and Elain slammed her bare, muddy foot into its face again. The blow struck home.

With a yelp of pain, it released its claws—and plunged into the ravine.

So fast. It happened so fast. And blood—blood sprayed from his back, his wings—

But Azriel remained in the air. Blue light splayed over the wounds. Staunching the blood, stabilizing his wings. I was still running for the cliff as he whirled, revealing a pain-bleached face, while he gripped the two women tightly.

But he beheld what charged after me. The sprint ahead. And for the first time since I had known him, there was terror in Azriel's eyes as he watched me make that run.

I flapped my wings, an updraft hauling my feet up, then crashing them down onto the rock. I stumbled, but kept running, kept flapping, back screaming—

Another one of the hounds broke past Tamlin's guard. Came barreling down that narrow stretch of rock, claws gouging the stone beneath. I could have sworn the king laughed from behind.

"Faster!" Azriel roared, blood oozing with each wing beat. I could see the dawn through the shreds in the membrane. *"Push up!"*

The stone echoed with the thunderous steps of the hound at my heels.

The end of the rock loomed. Freefall lay beyond. And I knew the hound would leap with me. The king would have it retrieve me by any means necessary, even if my body was broken on the river far, far below. This high, I would splatter like an egg dropped from a tower.

And he'd keep whatever was left of me, as Jurian had been kept, alive and aware.

"Hold them high!"

I stretched my wings as far as they would go. Thirty steps between me and the edge.

"Legs up!"

Twenty steps. The sun broke over the eastern horizon, gilding Azriel's bloody armor with gold.

The king fired another arrow—two. One for me, one soaring for Elain's exposed back. Azriel slammed both away with a blue shield. I didn't look to see if that shield extended to Tamlin.

Ten steps. I beat my wings, muscles screaming, blood sliding past even that Siphon's bandage. Beat them as I sent a wave of wind rising up beneath me, air filling the flexible membrane, even as the bone and sinews strained to snapping.

My feet lifted from the ground. Then hit again. I pushed with the wind, flapping like hell. The hound gained on me.

Five steps. I knew—I knew that whatever force had compelled me to learn to fly . . . Somehow, it had known. That this moment was coming. All of it—all of it, for this moment.

And with barely three steps to the edge of that cliff . . . A warm wind, kissed with lilac and new grass, blasted up from beneath me. A wind of—spring. Lifting me, filling my wings.

My feet rose. And rose. And rose.

The hound leaped after me.

"Bank!"

I threw my body sideways, wings swinging me wide. The rising dawn and drop and sky tilted and spun before I evened out.

I looked behind to see that naga-hound snap at where my heels had been. And then plunge down, down, down into the ravine and river below.

The king fired again, the arrow tipped with glimmering amethyst power. Azriel's shield held—barely. Whatever magic the king had wrapped around it—Azriel grunted in pain.

But he snarled, *"Fly,"* and I veered toward the way I'd come, back trembling with the effort to keep my body upright. Azriel turned, the girl moaning in terror as he lost a few feet to the sky—before he leveled out and soared beside me.

The king barked a command, and a barrage of arrows arced up from the camp—rained down upon us.

Azriel's shield buckled, but held solid. I flapped my wings, back shrieking.

I pressed a hand to my wound, just as the wards pushed against me. Pushed as if they tried and tried to contain me, to hold Azriel where he now flapped like hell against them, blood spraying from those wounded wings, sliding down his shredded back—

I unleashed a flare of Helion's white light. Burning, singeing, melting.

A hole ripped through the wards. Barely wide enough.

We didn't hesitate as we sailed through, as I gasped for breath. But I looked back. Just once.

Tamlin was surrounded by the hounds. Bleeding, panting, still in that beast form.

The king was perhaps thirty feet away, livid—utterly livid as he beheld the hole I'd again ripped through his wards. Tamlin made the most of his distraction.

He did not glance toward us as he made a break for the cliff edge.

He leaped far—far and wide. Farther than any beast or Fae should be able to. That wind he'd sent my way now bolstering him, guiding him toward that hole we'd swept through.

Tamlin cleared it and winnowed away, still not looking at me as I gripped Azriel's hand and we vanished as well.

⚜

Azriel's power gave out on the outskirts of our camp.

The girl, despite the burns and lashings on her moon-white skin, was able to walk.

The gray light of morning had broken over the world, mist clinging to our ankles as we headed into that camp, Azriel still cradling Elain to his chest. He dripped blood behind him the entire time—a trickle compared to the torrent that should be leaking out. Contained only by the patches of power he'd slapped on it. Help—he needed a healer immediately.

We both did. I pressed a hand against the wound in my shoulder to keep the bleeding minimal. The girl went so far as to even offer to use her lingering scraps of clothing to bind it.

I didn't have the breath to explain that I was Fae, and there had been ash in my skin. I needed to see a healer before it set and sealed in any splinters. So I just asked for her name.

Briar, she said, her voice raw from screaming. Her name was Briar.

She did not seem to mind the mud that squelched under her feet and splattered her bare shins. She only gazed at the tents, the soldiers who stumbled out. One saw Azriel and shouted for a healer to hurry for the spymaster's tent.

Rhys winnowed into our path before we'd made it past the first line of tents. His eyes went right to Azriel's wings, then the wound in my shoulder, the paleness of my face. To Elain, then Briar.

"I couldn't leave her," I said, surprised to find my own voice raw.

Running steps approached, and then Nesta rounded a tent, skidding to a halt in the mud.

She let out a sob at the sight of Elain, still in Azriel's arms. I'd never heard a sound like that from her. Not once.

She isn't hurt, I said to her, into that chamber in her mind. Because words . . . I couldn't form them.

Nesta broke into another sprint. I reached for Rhysand, his face taut as he stalked for us—

But Nesta got there first.

I swallowed my shout of pain as Nesta's arms went around my neck and she embraced me so hard it snatched my breath away.

Her body shook—shook as she sobbed and said over and over and over, "Thank you."

Rhys lunged for Azriel, taking Elain from him and gently setting my sister down. Azriel rasped, swaying on his feet, "We need Helion to get these chains off her."

Yet Elain didn't seem to notice them as she rose up on her toes and kissed the shadowsinger's cheek. And then walked to me and Nesta, who pulled back long enough to survey Elain's clean face, her clear eyes.

"We need to get you to Thesan," Rhys said to Azriel. "Right now."

Before I could turn back, Elain threw her arms around me. I did not remember when I began to cry as I felt those slender arms hold me, tight as steel.

I did not remember the healer who patched me up, or how Rhys bathed me. How I told him what happened with Jurian, and Tamlin, Nesta hovering around Elain as Helion came to remove her chains, cursing the king's handiwork, even as he admired its quality.

But I did remember lying down on the bearskin rug once it was done. How I felt Elain's slim body settle next to mine and curl into my side, careful not to touch the bandaged wound in my shoulder. I had not realized how cold I was until her warmth seeped into me.

A moment later, another warm body nestled on my left. Nesta's scent drifted over me, fire and steel and unbending will.

Distantly, I heard Rhys usher everyone out—to join him in checking on Azriel, now under Thesan's care.

I didn't know how long my sisters and I lay there together, just like we had once shared that carved bed in that dilapidated cottage. Then— back then, we had kicked and twisted and fought for any bit of space, any breathing room.

But that morning, as the sun rose over the world, we held tight. And did not let go.

CHAPTER
66

Kallias and his army arrived by noon.

It was only the sound of it that woke me from where my sisters and I dozed on the floor. That, and a thought that clanged through me.

Tamlin.

His actions would cover Jurian's betrayal. I had no doubt Tamlin hadn't gone back to Hybern's army after the meeting to betray us—but to play spy.

Though after last night . . . it was unlikely he'd get close to Hybern again. Not when the king himself had witnessed everything.

I didn't know what to make of it.

That he'd saved me—that he'd given up his deception to do so. Where had he gone to when he'd winnowed? We hadn't heard anything about the Spring Court forces.

And that wind he'd sent . . . I'd never seen him use such a power.

The Nephelle Philosophy indeed. The weakness that had transformed into a strength hadn't been my wings, my flying. But Tamlin. If he hadn't interfered . . . I didn't let myself consider.

Elain and Nesta were still dozing on the bearskin rug when I eased out from their tangle of limbs. Washed my face in the copper basin set near my bed. A glimpse in the mirror above it revealed I'd seen better days. Weeks. Months.

I peeled back the neck of my white shirt to frown at the wound bandaged at my shoulder. I winced, rotating the joint—marveling at how much it had already healed. My back, however . . .

Aching pain jolted and rippled all along it. In my abdomen, too. Muscles I'd pushed to the breaking point to get airborne. Frowning at the mirror, I braided my hair and shrugged on my jacket, hissing at the movement in my shoulder. Another day or two, and the pain might be minimal enough to wield a sword. Maybe.

I prayed Azriel would be in better shape. If Thesan himself had been healing him, perhaps he was. If we were lucky.

I didn't know how Azriel had managed to stay aloft—stay conscious during those minutes in the sky. I didn't let myself think about how and when and why he'd learned to manage pain like that.

I quietly asked the nearest camp-mother to dig up some platters of food for my sisters. Elain was likely starving, and I doubted Nesta had eaten anything during the hours we'd been gone.

The winged matron only asked if *I* needed anything, and when I told her I was fine, she just clicked her tongue and said she'd make sure food found its way to me, too.

I didn't have the nerve to request she find some of Amren's preferred food as well. Even if I had no doubt Amren would need it—after her . . . activities with Varian last night. Unless he'd—

I didn't let myself think about that as I aimed for her tent. We'd found Hybern's army. And having seen it last night . . . I'd offer Amren any help I could in decoding that spell the Suriel had pointed her toward. Anything, if it meant stopping the Cauldron. And when we'd picked our final battlefield . . . then, only then, would I unleash Bryaxis upon Hybern.

I was nearly to her tent, offering grim smiles in exchange for the nods and wary glances the Illyrian warriors gave me, when I spied the commotion just near the edge of camp. A few extra steps had me staring out across a thin demarcation line of grass and mud—to the Winter Court camp now nearly constructed in its full splendor.

Kallias's army was still winnowing in supplies and units of warriors, his court made up of High Fae with either his snow-white hair or hair of blackest night, skin ranging from moon pale to rich brown. The lesser fae . . . he'd brought more lesser faeries than any of us, if you excluded the Illyrians. It was an effort not to gawk as I lingered at the edge of where their camp began.

Long-limbed creatures like shards of ice given form stalked past, tall enough to plant the cobalt-and-silver banners atop various tents; wagons were hauled by sure-footed reindeer and lumbering white bears in ornate armor, some so keenly aware when they ambled by that I wouldn't have been surprised if they could talk. White foxes scuttled about underfoot, bearing what looked to be messages strapped to their little embroidered vests.

Our Illyrian army was brutal, basic—few frills and sheer rank reigned. Kallias's army—or, I suppose, the army that Viviane had held together during Amarantha's reign—was a complex, beautiful, teeming thing. Orderly, and yet thrumming with life. Everyone had a purpose, everyone seemed keen on doing it efficiently and proudly.

I spotted Mor walking with Viviane and a stunningly beautiful young woman who looked like either Viviane's twin or sister. Viviane was beaming, Mor perhaps more subdued for once, and as she twisted—

My brows rose. The human girl—Briar—was with them. Now tucked beneath Viviane's arm, face still bruised and swollen in spots, but . . . smiling timidly at the Winter Court ladies.

Viviane began to lead Briar away, chattering merrily, and Mor and Viviane's possible-sister lingered to watch them. Mor said something to the stranger that made her smile—well, slightly.

It was a restrained smile, and it faded quickly. Especially as a High

Fae soldier strode past, grinned at her with some teasing remark, and then continued on. Mor watched the female's face carefully—and swiftly looked away as she turned back to her, clapped Mor on the shoulder, and strode off after her possible-sister and Briar.

I remembered our argument the moment Mor turned toward me. Remembered the words we'd left unsaid, the ones I probably shouldn't have spoken. Mor flipped her hair over a shoulder and headed right for me.

I spoke before she could get the first word out, "You gave Briar over to them?"

We fell into step back toward our own camp. "Az explained the state you found her in. I didn't think being exposed to battle-ready Illyrians would do much to soothe her."

"And the Winter Court army is much better?"

"They've got fuzzy animals."

I snorted, shaking my head. Those enormous bears were indeed fuzzy—if you ignored the claws and teeth.

Mor glanced sidelong at me. "You did a very brave thing in saving Briar."

"Anyone would have done it."

"No," she said, adjusting her tight Illyrian jacket. "I'm not sure . . . I'm not sure even *I* would have tried to get her. If I would have deemed the risk worth it. I've made enough calls like that where it went badly that I . . ." She shook her head.

I swallowed. "How's Azriel?"

"Alive. His back is fine. But Thesan hasn't healed many Illyrian wings, so the healing is . . . slow. Different from repairing Peregryn wings, apparently. Rhys sent for Madja." The healer in Velaris. "She'll be here either later today or tomorrow to work on him."

"Will he—fly again?"

"Considering Cassian's wings were in worse shape, I'd say yes. But . . . perhaps not in battle. Not anytime soon."

My stomach tightened. "He won't be happy about that."

"None of us are."

To lose Azriel on the field . . .

Mor seemed to read what I was thinking and said, "Better than being dead." She dragged a hand through her golden hair. "It would have been so easy—for things to have gone wrong last night. And when I saw you two vanish . . . I had this thought, this terror, that I might not get to see you again. To make things right."

"I said things I didn't really mean to—"

"We both did." She led me up to the tree line at the border of both our camps, and I knew from that alone . . . I knew she was about to tell me something she didn't wish anyone overhearing. Something worth delaying my meeting with Amren for a little while.

She leaned against a towering oak, foot tap-tapping on the ground. "No more lies between us."

Guilt tugged on my gut. "Yes," I said. "I—I'm sorry about deceiving you. I just . . . I made a mistake. And I'm sorry."

Mor rubbed her face. "You were right about me, though. You were . . ." Her hand shook as she lowered it. She gnawed on her lip, throat bobbing. Her eyes at last met mine—bright and fearful and anguished. Her voice broke as she said, "I don't love Azriel."

I remained perfectly still. Listening.

"No, that's not true, either. I—I do love him. As my family. And sometimes I wonder if it can be . . . more, but . . . I do not love him. Not the way he—he feels for me." The last words were a trembling whisper.

"Have you ever loved him? That way?"

"No." She wrapped her arms around herself. "No. I don't . . . You see . . ." I'd never seen her at such a loss for words. She closed her eyes, fingers digging into her skin. "I *can't* love him like that."

"Why?"

"Because I prefer females."

For a heartbeat, only silence rippled through me. "But—you sleep with males. You slept with Helion . . ." And had looked terrible the next day. Tortured and not at all sated.

Not just because of Azriel, but . . . because it wasn't what she wanted.

"I do find pleasure in them. In both." Her hands were shaking so fiercely that she gripped herself even tighter. "But I've known, since I was little more than a child, that I prefer females. That I'm . . . attracted to them more over males. That I connect with them, care for them more on that soul-deep level. But at the Hewn City . . . All they care about is breeding their bloodlines, making alliances through marriage. Someone like me . . . If I were to marry where my heart desired, there would be no offspring. My father's bloodline would have *ended* with me. I knew it—knew that I could never tell them. Ever. People like me . . . we're reviled by them. Considered selfish, for not being able to pass on the bloodline. So I never breathed a word of it. And then . . . then my father betrothed me to Eris, and . . . And it wasn't just the prospect of marriage to *him* that scared me. No, I knew I could survive his brutality, his cruelty and coldness. I was—I *am* stronger than him. It was . . . It was the idea of being bred like a prize mare, of being forced to give up that one part of me . . ." Her mouth wobbled, and I reached for her hand, prying it off her arm. I squeezed gently as tears began sliding down her flushed face.

"I slept with Cassian because I knew it would mean little to him, too. Because I knew doing it would buy me a shot at freedom. If I had told my parents that I preferred females . . . You've met my father. He and Beron would have tied me to that marriage bed for Eris. Literally. But sullied . . . I knew my shot at freedom lay there. And I saw how Azriel looked at me . . . knew how he felt. And if I'd chosen him . . ." She shook her head. "It wouldn't have been fair to him. So I slept with Cassian, and Azriel thought I deemed him unsuitable, and then everything happened and . . ." Her fingers tightened on mine. "After Azriel found me with that note nailed to my womb . . . I tried to explain. But he started to confess what he felt, and I panicked, and . . . and to get him to *stop*, to keep him from saying he loved me, I just turned and left, and . . . and I couldn't face explaining it after that. To Az, to the others."

She loosed a shuddering breath. "I sleep with males in part because I enjoy it, but . . . also to keep people from looking too closely."

"Rhys wouldn't care—I don't think anyone in Velaris would."

A nod. "Velaris is . . . a haven for people like me. Rita's . . . the owner is like me. A lot of us go there—without anyone really ever picking up on it."

No wonder she practically lived at the pleasure hall.

"But this part of me . . ." Mor wiped at her tears with her free hand. "It didn't matter as much, when my family disowned me. When they called me a whore and a piece of trash. When they hurt me. Because those things . . . they weren't part of me. Weren't true, and weren't . . . intrinsic. They couldn't break me because . . . because they never touched that innermost part of me. They never even guessed. But I hid it . . . I've hidden it because . . ." She tilted back her head, looking skyward. "Because I live in terror of my family finding out—and shaming me, *hurting* me about this one thing that has remained wholly mine. This one part of me. I won't let them . . . won't let them destroy it. Or try to. So I've rarely . . . During the War, I finally took my first— female lover."

She was quiet for a long moment, blinking away tears. "It was Nephelle and her lover—now her wife, I suppose—who made me dare to try. They made me so jealous. Not of them personally, but just . . . of what they had. Their openness. That they lived in a place, with a people who thought nothing of it. But with the War, with the traveling across the world . . . No one from home was with me for months at a time. It was safe, for once. And one of the human queens . . ."

The friends she had so passionately mentioned, had known so intimately.

"Her name was Andromache. And she was . . . so beautiful. And kind. And I loved her . . . so much."

Human. Andromache had been human. My eyes burned.

"But she was human. And a queen—who needed to continue her royal line, especially during such a tumultuous time. So I left—went home after the last battle. And when I realized what a mistake it was, that I didn't care if I only had sixty more years with her . . . The wall went up that day." A small sob came out of her.

"And I could not . . . I was not allowed or able to cross it. I tried. For three years, I tried over and over. And by the time I managed to find a hole to cross . . . She had married. A man. And had an infant daughter—with another on the way. I didn't set foot inside her castle. Didn't even try to see her. I just turned around and went home."

"I'm so sorry," I breathed, my voice breaking.

"She bore five children. And died an old woman, safe in her bed. And I saw her spirit again—in that golden queen. Her descendant."

Mor closed her eyes, breath rippling past her shaking lips. "For a while, I mourned her. Both while she lived and after she died. For a few decades, there were no lovers—of any kind. But then . . . one day I woke up, and I wanted . . . I don't know what I wanted. The opposite of her. I found them—female, male. A few lovers over these past centuries, the females always secret—and I think that's why it wore on them, why they always ended it. I could never be . . . open about it. Never be seen with them. And as for the males . . . it never went as deep. The bond, I mean. Even if I did still crave—you know, every now and then." A huff of a laugh that I echoed. "But all of them . . . It wasn't the same as Andromache. It doesn't feel the same—in here," she breathed, putting a hand over her heart.

"And the male lovers I took . . . it became a way to keep Azriel from wondering why—why I wouldn't notice him. Make that move. You see—you see how marvelous he is. How special. But if I slept with him, even once, just to *try* it, to make sure . . . I think after all this time, he'd think it was a culmination—a happy ending. And . . . I think it might shatter him if I revealed afterward that . . . I'm not sure I can give my entire heart to him that way. And . . . and I love him enough to want him to find someone who can truly love him like he deserves. And I love myself . . . I love myself enough to not want to settle until I find that person, too." A shrug. "If I can even work up the courage to tell the world first. My gift is truth—and yet I have been living a lie my entire existence."

I squeezed her hand once more. "You'll tell them when you're ready. And I'll stand by you no matter what. Until then . . . Your secret is safe. I won't tell anyone—even Rhys."

"Thank you," she breathed.

I shook my head. "No—thank you for telling me. I'm honored."

"I wanted to tell you; I realized I wanted to tell you the moment you and Azriel winnowed to Hybern's camp. And the thought of not being able to tell you . . ." Her fingers tightened around mine. "I promised the Mother that if you made it back safely, I would tell you."

"It seemed she was happy to take the bargain," I said with a smile.

Mor wiped at her face and grinned. It faded almost instantly. "You must think I'm horrible for stringing along Azriel—and Cassian."

I considered. "No. No, I don't." So many things—so many things now made sense. How Mor had looked away from the heat in Azriel's eyes. How she'd avoided that sort of romantic intimacy, but had been fine to defend him if she felt his physical or emotional well-being was at stake.

Azriel loved her, of that I had no doubt. But Mor . . . I'd been blind not to see. Not to realize that there was a damn good reason why five hundred years had passed and Mor had not accepted what Azriel so clearly offered to her.

"Do you think Azriel suspects?" I asked.

Mor drew her hand from mine and paced a few steps. "Maybe. I don't know. He's too observant not to, but . . . I think it confuses him whenever I take a male home."

"So the thing with Helion . . . Why?"

"He wanted a distraction from his own problems, and I . . ." She sighed. "Whenever Azriel makes his feelings clear, like he did with Eris . . . It's stupid, I know. It's so *stupid* and cruel that I do this, but . . . I slept with Helion just to remind Azriel . . . Gods, I can't even say it. It sounds even worse saying it."

"To remind him that you're not interested."

"I should tell him. I *need* to tell him. Mother above, after last night, I should. But . . ." She twisted her mass of golden hair over a shoulder. "It's gone on for so long. So long. I'm petrified to face him—to tell him he's spent five hundred years pining for someone and something that won't ever exist. The potential fallout . . . I like things the way they are. Even if I can't . . . can't really be *me*, I . . . things are good enough."

"I don't think you should settle for 'good enough,' " I said quietly. "But I understand. And, again . . . when you decide the time is right, whether it's tomorrow or in another five hundred years . . . I'll have your back."

She blinked away tears again. I turned toward the camp, and a faint smile bloomed on my mouth.

"What?" she asked, coming to my side.

"I was just thinking," I said, smile growing, "that whenever you're ready . . . I was thinking about how much fun I'm going to have playing matchmaker for you."

Mor's answering grin was brighter than the entirety of the Day Court.

⁜

Amren had secluded herself in a tent, and would not let anyone in. Not me, or Varian, or Rhysand.

I certainly tried, hissing as I pushed against her wards, but even Helion's magic could not break them. And no matter how I demanded and coaxed and pleaded, she did not answer. Whatever the Suriel had told me to suggest to her about the Book . . . she'd deemed it more vital, it seemed, than even why I'd come to speak to her: to join me in retrieving Bryaxis. I could likely do it without her since she'd already disabled the wards to contain Bryaxis, but . . . Amren's presence would be . . . welcome. On my end, at least.

Perhaps it made me a coward, but facing Bryaxis on my own, to bind it into a slightly more tangible body and summon it here at last to smash through Hybern's army . . . Amren would be better—at the talking, the ordering.

But since I wasn't about to start shouting about my plans in the middle of that camp . . . I cursed Amren soundly and stormed back to my war-tent.

Only to find that my plans were to be upended anyway. For even if I brought Bryaxis to Hybern's army . . . That army was no longer where it was supposed to be.

Standing beside the enormous worktable in the war-tent, every side flanked with High Lords and their commanders, I crossed my arms as Helion slid an unnerving number of figures across the lower half of Prythian's map. "My scouts say Hybern is on the move as of this afternoon."

Azriel, perched on a stool, his wings and back heavily bandaged and face still grayish with blood loss, nodded once. "My spies say the same." His voice was still hoarse from screaming.

Helion's blazing amber eyes narrowed. "He shifted directions, though. He'd planned to move that army north—drive us back that way. Now he marches due east."

Rhys braced his hands on the table, his sable hair sliding forward as he studied the map. "So he's now heading straight across the island—to what end? He would have been better off sailing around. And I doubt he's changed his mind about meeting us in battle. Even with Tamlin now revealed as an enemy." They'd all been quietly shocked, some relieved, to hear it. Though we'd had no whisper of whether Tamlin would be now marching his small force to us. And nothing from Beron, either.

Tarquin frowned. "Losing Tamlin won't cost him many troops, but Hybern could be going to meet another ally on the eastern coast—to rendezvous with the army of those human queens from the continent."

Azriel shook his head, wincing at the movement and what it surely did to his back. "He sent the queens back to their homes—and there they remain, their armies not even raised. He'll wait to wield that host until he arrives on the continent."

Once he was done annihilating us. And if we failed tomorrow . . . would there be anyone at all to challenge Hybern on the continent? Especially once those queens rallied their human armies to his banner—

"Perhaps he's leading us on another chase," Kallias mused with a frown, Viviane peering at the map beside him.

"Not Hybern's style," Mor said. "He doesn't establish patterns—he knows we're onto his first method of stretching us thin. Now he'll try another way."

As she spoke, Keir—standing with two silent Darkbringer captains—studied her closely. I braced myself for any sort of sneer, but the male merely resumed examining the map. These meetings had been the only place where she'd bothered to acknowledge her father's role in this war—and even then, even now, she barely glanced his way.

But it was better than outright hostility, though I had no doubt Mor was wise enough not to lay into Keir when we still needed his Darkbringers. Especially after Keir's legion had suffered so many losses at that second battle. Whether Keir was furious about those casualties, he had not let on—neither had any of his soldiers, who did not speak with anyone outside their own ranks beyond what was necessary. Silence, I supposed, was far preferable. And Keir's sense of self-preservation no doubt kept his mouth shut in these meetings—and bade him take whatever orders were sent his way.

"Hybern is delaying the conflict," Helion murmured. "Why?"

I glanced over at Nesta, sitting with Elain by the faelight braziers. "He still doesn't have the missing piece. Of the Cauldron's power."

Rhys angled his head, studying the map, then my sisters. "Cassian." He pointed to the massive river snaking inland through the Spring Court. "If we were to cut south from where we are now—to head right down to the human lands . . . would you cross that river, or go west far enough to avoid it?"

Cassian lifted a brow. Gone was yesterday's pallid face and pain. A small mercy.

On the opposite side of the table, Lord Devlon seemed inclined to open his mouth to give his opinion. Unlike Keir, the Illyrian commander had no such qualms about making his disdain for us known. Especially in regard to Cassian's command.

But before Devlon could shove his way in, Cassian said, "A river crossing like that would be time-consuming and dangerous. The river's too wide. Even with winnowing, we'd have to construct boats or bridges to get across. And an army this size . . . We'd have to go west, then cut south—"

As the words faded, Cassian's face paled. And I looked at where Hybern's army was now marching eastward, below that mighty river. From where we were now—

"He wanted us exhausting ourselves on winnowing armies around," Helion said, picking up the thread of Cassian's thought. "On fighting those battles. So that when it counted, we would not have the strength to winnow past that river. We'd have to go on foot—and take the long way around to avoid the crossing."

Tarquin swore now. "So he could march south, knowing we're days behind. And enter the human lands with no resistance."

"He could have done that from the start," Kallias countered. My knees began to shake. "Why now?"

It was Nesta who said from her seat across the room beside the faelight brazier, "Because we insulted him. Me—and my sisters."

All eyes went to us.

Elain put a hand on her throat. She breathed, "He's going to march on the human lands—butcher them. To spite us?"

"I killed his priestess," I murmured. "You took from his Cauldron," I said to Nesta. "And you . . ." I examined Elain. "Stealing you back was the final insult."

Kallias said, "Only a madman would wield the might of his army just to get revenge on three women."

Helion snorted. "You forget that some of us fought in the War. We know firsthand how unhinged he can be. And that something like this would be exactly his style."

I caught Rhys's eye. *What do we do?*

Rhys's thumb brushed down the back of my hand. "He knows we'll come."

"I'd say he's assuming quite a lot about how much we care for humans," Helion said. Keir looked inclined to agree, but wisely remained silent.

Rhys shrugged. "He'll have seen our prioritizing of Elain's safety as proof that the Archeron sisters hold sway here. He thinks they'll convince us to haul our asses down there, likely to a battlefield with few advantages, and be annihilated."

"So we're not going to?" Tarquin frowned.

"Of course we're going to," Rhys said, straightening to his full height and lifting his chin. "We will be outnumbered, and exhausted, and it will not end well. But this has nothing to do with my mate, or her sisters. The wall is down. It is gone. It is a new world, and we must decide how we are to end this old one and begin it anew. We must decide if we will begin it by allowing those who cannot defend themselves to be slaughtered. If that is the sort of people we are. Not individual courts. We, as a Fae *people*. Do we let the humans stand alone?"

"We'll all die together, then," Helion said.

"Good," Cassian said, glancing at Nesta. "If I end my life defending those who need it most, then I will consider it a death well spent." Lord Devlon, for once, nodded his approval. I wondered if Cassian noticed it—if he cared. His face revealed nothing, not as his focus remained wholly on my sister.

"So will I," Tarquin said.

Kallias looked to Viviane, who was smiling sadly up at him. I could see the regret there—for the time they had lost. But Kallias said, "We'll need to leave by tomorrow if we are to stand a chance at staunching the slaughter."

"Sooner than that," Helion said, flashing a dazzling smile. "A few hours." He jerked his chin at Rhys. "You realize humans will be slaughtered before we can get there."

"Not if we can act faster," I said, rotating my shoulder. Still stiff and sore, but healing fast.

They all raised their brows.

"Tonight," I said. "We winnow—those of us who can. To human homes—towns. And we winnow out as many of them as we can before dawn."

"And where will we put them?" Helion demanded.

"Velaris."

"Too far," Rhys murmured, scanning the map before us. "To do all that winnowing."

Tarquin tapped a finger on the map—on his territory. "Then bring them to Adriata. I will send Cresseida back—let her oversee them."

"We'll need all the strength we have to fight Hybern," Kallias said carefully. "Wasting it on winnowing humans—"

"It is no waste," I said. "One life may change the world. Where would you all be if someone had deemed saving my life to be a waste of time?" I pointed to Rhys. "If *he* had deemed saving my life Under the Mountain a waste of time? Even if it's only twenty families, or ten . . . They are not a waste. Not to me—or to you."

Viviane was giving her mate a sharp, reproachful glare, and Kallias had the good sense to mumble an apology.

Then Amren said from behind us, striding through the tent flaps, "I hope you all voted to face Hybern in battle."

Rhys arched a brow. "We did. Why?"

Amren set the Book upon the table with a thump. "Because we will need it as a distraction." She smiled grimly at me. "We need to get to the Cauldron, girl. *All* of us."

And I knew she didn't mean the High Lords.

But rather the four of us—who had been Made. Me, Amren . . . and my sisters.

"You found another way to stop it?" Tarquin asked.

Amren's sharp chin bobbed in a nod. "Even better. I found a way to stop his entire army."

CHAPTER
67

We'd need access to the Cauldron—be able to touch it. Together.

Alone, it had nearly killed me. But split amongst others who were Made . . . We could withstand its lethal power.

If we got it under our control, in one fell swoop we could harness its might to bind the king and his army. And wipe them off the earth.

Amren had found the spell to do it. Right where the Suriel had claimed it'd be encoded in the Book. Rather than nullify the Cauldron's powers . . . we would nullify the person controlling it. *And* his entire host.

But we had to attain the Cauldron first. And with the two armies poised to fight . . .

We would move only when the carnage was at its peak. When Hybern might be distracted in the chaos. Unless he planned to wield that Cauldron on the killing field.

Which was a high possibility.

There was no chance we'd infiltrate that army camp again—not after we'd stolen Elain. So we would have to wait until we walked into the trap he'd set for us. Wait until we took up disadvantageous positions on that battlefield he'd selected, and arrive exhausted from the battles before it, the trek there. Exhausted from winnowing those human families out of his path.

Which we did. That night, any of us who could winnow . . .

I went to my old village with Rhysand.

I went to the houses where I had once left gold as a mortal woman.

At first, they did not recognize me.

Then they realized what I was.

Rhys held their minds gently, soothing them, as I explained. What had happened to me, what was coming. What we needed to do.

They did not have time to pack more than a few things. And they were all trembling as we swept them across the world, to the warmth of a lush forest just outside Adriata, Cresseida already waiting with food and a small army of servants to help and organize.

The second family did not believe us. Thought it was some faerie trick. Rhys tried to hold their minds, but their panic was too deep, their hatred too tangible.

They wanted to stay.

Rhys didn't give them a choice after that. He winnowed their entire family, all of them screaming. They were still shrieking when we left them in that forest, more humans around them, our companions winnowing in new arrivals for Cresseida to document and soothe.

So we continued. House to house. Family to family. Anyone in Hybern's path.

All night. Every High Lord in our army, any commander or noble with the gift and strength.

Until we were panting. Until there was a small city of humans huddled together in that summer-ripe forest. Until even Rhys's strength flagged and he could barely winnow back to our tent.

He passed out before his head had hit the pillow, his wings splayed across the bed.

Too much strain, too much relying on his power.

I watched him sleep, counting his breaths.

We knew—all of us did. We knew that we wouldn't walk away from that battlefield.

Maybe it would inspire others to fight, but . . . We knew. My mate, my family . . . they would fight, buy us time with their lives while Amren and my sisters and I tried to stop that Cauldron. Some would go down before we could reach it.

And they were willing to do it. If they were afraid, none of them let on.

I brushed Rhys's sweat-damp hair back from his brow.

I knew he'd give everything before any of us could offer it. Knew he'd try.

It was as much a part of him as his limbs, this need to sacrifice, to protect. But I wouldn't let him do it—not without trying myself.

Amren had not mentioned Bryaxis in our talks earlier. Had seemed to have forgotten it. But we still had a battle to wage tomorrow. And if Bryaxis could buy my friends, could buy Rhys, any extra time while I hunted down that Cauldron . . . If it could buy them the slimmest shot of survival . . . Then the Bone Carver could as well.

I didn't care about the cost. Or the risk. Not as I looked at my sleeping mate, exhaustion lining his face.

He had given enough. And if this broke me, drove me mad, ripped me apart . . . All Amren would need was my presence, my body, tomorrow with the Cauldron. Anything else . . . if it was what I had to give, my own cost to buy them any sliver of survival . . . I would gladly pay it. Face it.

So I rallied the dregs of my power and winnowed away—winnowed north.

To the Court of Nightmares.

There was a winding stair, deep within the mountain. It led to only one place: a chamber near the uppermost peak. I had learned as much from my research.

I stood at the base of that stairwell, peering up into the impenetrable gloom, my breath clouding in front of me.

A thousand stairs. That was how many steps stood between me and the Ouroboros. The Mirror of Beginnings and Endings.

Only you can decide what breaks you, Cursebreaker. Only you.

I kindled a ball of faelight over my head and began my ascent.

CHAPTER
68

I did not expect the snow.

Or the moonlight.

The chamber must have lain beneath the palace of moonstone—shafts in the rough rock leading outside, welcoming in snowdrifts and moonlight.

I gritted my teeth against the bitter cold, the wind howling through the cracks like wolves raging along the mountainside beyond.

The snow glittered over the walls and floor, slithering over my boots with the wind gusts. Moonlight peered in, bright enough that I vanished my ball of faelight, bathing the entire chamber in blues and silvers.

And there, against the far wall of the chamber, snow crusting its surface, its bronze casing . . .

The Ouroboros.

It was a massive, round disc—as tall as I was. Taller. And the metal around it had been fashioned after a massive serpent, the mirror held within its coils as it devoured its own tail.

Ending and beginning.

From across the room, with the snow . . . I could not see it. What lay within.

I forced myself to take a step forward. Another.

The mirror itself was black as night—yet . . . wholly clear.

I watched myself approach. Watched the arm I had upraised against the wind and snow, the pinched expression on my face. The exhaustion.

I stopped three feet away. I did not dare touch it.

It only showed me myself.

Nothing.

I scanned the mirror for any signs of . . . *something* to push or touch with my magic. But there was only the devouring head of the serpent, its maw open wide, frost sparkling on its fangs.

I shuddered against the cold, rubbing my arms. My reflection did the same.

"Hello?" I whispered.

There was nothing.

My hands burned with cold.

Up close, the surface of the Ouroboros was like a gray, calm sea. Undisturbed. Sleeping.

But in its upper corner—movement.

No—not movement in the mirror.

Behind me.

I was not alone.

Crawling down the snow-kissed wall, a massive beast of claws and scales and fur and shredding teeth inched toward the floor. Toward me.

I kept my breathing steady. Did not let it scent a tendril of my fear— whatever it was. Some guardian of this place, some creature that had crawled in through the cracks—

Its enormous paws were near-silent on the floor, the fur on them a blend of black and gold. Not a beast designed to hunt in these mountains. Certainly not with the ridge of dark scales down its back. And the large, shining eyes—

I didn't have time to remark on those blue-gray eyes as the beast pounced.

I whirled, Illyrian dagger in my freezing hand, ducking low and aiming up—for the heart.

But no impact came. Only snow, and cold, and wind.

There was nothing before me. Behind me.

No paw prints in the snow.

I whirled to the mirror.

Where I had been standing . . . that beast now sat, scaled tail idly swishing through the snow.

Watching me.

No—not watching.

Gazing back at me. My reflection.

Of what lurked beneath my skin.

My knife clattered to the stones and snow. And I looked into the mirror.

✛

The Bone Carver was sitting against the wall as I entered his cell.

"No escort this time?"

I only stared at him—that boy. My son.

And for once, the Carver seemed to go very still and quiet.

He whispered, "You retrieved it."

I looked toward a corner of his cell. The Ouroboros appeared, snow and ice still crusting it. Mine to summon, wherever and whenever I wished.

"How."

Words were still foreign, strange things.

This body that I had returned to . . . it was strange, too.

My tongue was dry as paper as I said, "I looked."

"What did you see?" The Carver got to his feet.

I sank a little further back into my body. Just enough to smile slightly. "That is none of your concern." For the mirror . . . it had shown me. So many things.

I did not know how long had passed. Time—it had been different inside the mirror.

But even a few hours might have been too many—

I pointed to the door. "You have your mirror. Now uphold your end. Battle awaits."

The Bone Carver glanced between me and the mirror. And he smiled. "It would be my pleasure."

And the way he said it . . . I was wrung dry, my soul new and trembling, and yet I asked, "What do you mean?"

The Carver simply straightened his clothes. "I have little need for that thing," he said, gesturing to the mirror. "But you did."

I blinked slowly.

"I wanted to see if you were worth helping," the Carver went on. "It's a rare person to face who they truly are and not run from it—not be broken by it. That's what the Ouroboros shows all who look into it: who they are, every despicable and unholy inch. Some gaze upon it and don't even realize that the horror they're seeing is *them*—even as the terror of it drives them mad. Some swagger in and are shattered by the small, sorry creature they find instead. But you . . . Yes, rare indeed. I could risk leaving here for nothing less."

Rage—blistering rage started to fill in the holes left by what I'd beheld in that mirror. "You wanted to see if I was *worthy*?" That innocent people were *worthy* of being helped.

A nod. "I did. And you are. And now I shall help you."

I debated slamming that cell door in his face.

But I only said quietly, "Good." I walked over to him. And I was not afraid as I grabbed the Bone Carver's cold hand. "Then let's begin."

CHAPTER
69

Dawn broke, gilding the low-lying mists snaking over the plains of the mortal land.

Hybern had razed everything from the Spring Court down to the few miles before the sea.

Including my village.

There was nothing left but smoking cinders and crumbled stone as we marched past.

And my father's estate . . . One-third of the house remained standing, the rest wrecked. Windows shattered, walls cracked down to the foundation.

Elain's garden was trampled, little more than a mud pit. That proud oak near the edge of the property—where Nesta had liked to stand in the shade and overlook our lands . . . It had been burned into a skeletal husk.

It was a personal attack. I knew it. We all did. The king had ordered our livestock killed. I'd gotten the dogs and horses out the night before—along with the servants and their families. But the riches, the personal touches . . . Looted or destroyed.

That Hybern had not lingered to decimate what was left standing of the house, Cassian told me, suggested he did not want us gaining too much on him. He'd establish his advantage—pick the right battlefield. We had no doubt that finding the empty villages along the way whetted the king's rage. And there were enough towns and villages that we had not reached in time that we hurried.

An easier feat in theory than in practice, with an army of our size and made up of so many differently trained soldiers, with so many leaders giving orders about what to do.

The Illyrians were testy—yanking at the leash, even under Lord Devlon's strict command. Annoyed that we had to wait for the others, that we couldn't just fly ahead and intercept Hybern, stop them before they could select the battlefield.

I watched Cassian lay into two different captains within the span of three hours—watched him reassign the grumbling soldiers to hauling carts and wagons of supplies, pulling some off the honor of being on the front lines. As soon as the others saw that he meant every word, every threat . . . the complaining ceased.

Keir and his Darkbringers watched Cassian, too—and were wise enough to keep any discontent off their tongues, their faces. To keep marching, their dark armor growing muddier with every passing mile.

During the brief midday break in a large meadow, Nesta and I climbed inside one of the supply caravan's covered wagons to change into Illyrian fighting leathers. When we emerged, Nesta even buckled a knife at her side. Cassian had insisted, yet he'd admitted that since she was untrained, she was just as likely to hurt herself as she was to hurt someone else.

Elain . . . She'd taken one look at us in the swaying grasses outside that wagon, the legs and assets on display, and turned crimson. Viviane stepped in, offering a Winter Court fashion that was far less scandalous: leather pants, but paired with a thigh-length blue surcoat, white fur trimming the collar. In the heat, it'd be miserable, but Elain was thankful enough that she didn't complain when we again emerged from the covered wagon and found our companions waiting. She refused the knife Cassian handed her, though.

Went white as death at the sight of it.

Azriel, still limping, merely nudged aside Cassian and extended another option.

"This is Truth-Teller," he told her softly. "I won't be using it today—so I want you to."

His wings had healed—though long, thin scars now raked down them. Still not strong enough, Madja had warned him, to fly today.

The argument with Rhys this morning had been swift and brutal: Azriel insisted he *could* fly—fight with the legions, as they'd planned. Rhys refused. Cassian refused. Azriel threatened to slip into shadow and fight anyway. Rhys merely said that if he so much as tried, he'd chain Azriel to a tree.

And Azriel . . . It was only when Mor had entered the tent and begged him—*begged* him with tears in her eyes—that he relented. Agreed to be eyes and ears and nothing else.

And now, standing amongst the sighing meadow grasses in his Illyrian armor, all seven Siphons gleaming . . .

Elain's eyes widened at the obsidian-hilted blade in Azriel's scarred hand. The runes on the dark scabbard.

"It has never failed me once," the shadowsinger said, the midday sun devoured by the dark blade. "Some people say it is magic and will always strike true." He gently took her hand and pressed the hilt of the legendary blade into it. "It will serve you well."

"I—I don't know how to use it—"

"I'll make sure you don't have to," I said, grass crunching as I stepped closer.

Elain weighed my words . . . and slowly closed her fingers around the blade.

Cassian gawked at Azriel, and I wondered how often Azriel had lent out that blade—

Never, Rhys said from where he finished buckling on his own weapons against the side of the wagon. *I have never once seen Azriel let another person touch that knife.*

Elain looked up at Azriel, their eyes meeting, his hand still lingering on the hilt of the blade.

I saw the painting in my mind: the lovely fawn, blooming spring vibrant behind her. Standing before Death, shadows and terrors lurking over his shoulder. Light and dark, the space between their bodies a blend of the two. The only bridge of connection . . . that knife.

Paint that when we get home.

Busybody.

I peered over my shoulder to Rhys, who stepped up to our little circle in the grass. His face remained more haggard than usual, lines of strain bracketing his mouth. And I realized . . . I would not get that last night with him. Last night—*that* had been the final night. We'd spent it winnowing—

Don't think like that. Don't go into this battle thinking you won't walk off again. His gaze was sharp. Unyielding.

Breathing became difficult. *This break is the last time we'll all be here—talking.*

For this final leg of the march we were about to embark on . . . It would take us right to the battlefield.

Rhys lifted a brow. *Would you like to go into that wagon for a few minutes, then? It's a little cramped between the weapons and supplies, but I can make it work.*

The humor—as much for me as it was for him. I took his hand, realizing the others were talking quietly, Mor having sauntered over in full, dark armor, Amren . . . Amren was in Illyrian leathers, too. So small—they must have been built for a child.

Don't tell her, but they were.

My lips tugged toward a smile. But Rhys stared at all of us, somehow assembled here in the sun-drenched open grasses without being given the order. Our family—our court. The Court of Dreams.

They all quieted.

Rhys looked them each in the eye, even my sisters, his hand brushing the back of my own.

"Do you want the inspiring talk or the bleak one?" he asked.

"We want the real one," Amren said.

Rhys pushed his shoulders back, elegantly folding his wings behind him. "I believe everything happens for a reason. Whether it is decided by the Mother, or the Cauldron, or some sort of tapestry of Fate, I don't know. I don't really care. But I am grateful for it, whatever it is. Grateful that it brought you all into my life. If it hadn't . . . I might have become as awful as that prick we're going to face today. If I had not met an Illyrian warrior-in-training," he said to Cassian, "I would not have known the true depths of strength, of resilience, of honor and loyalty." Cassian's eyes gleamed bright. Rhys said to Azriel, "If I had not met a shadowsinger, I would not have known that it is the family you make, not the one you are born into, that matters. I would not have known what it is to truly hope, even when the world tells you to despair." Azriel bowed his head in thanks.

Mor was already crying when Rhys spoke to her. "If I had not met my cousin, I would never have learned that light can be found in even the darkest of hells. That kindness can thrive even amongst cruelty." She wiped away her tears as she nodded.

I waited for Amren to offer a retort. But she was only waiting.

Rhys bowed his head to her. "If I had not met a tiny monster who hoards jewels more fiercely than a firedrake . . ." A quiet laugh from all of us at that. Rhys smiled softly. "My own power would have consumed me long ago."

Rhys squeezed my hand as he looked to me at last. "And if I had not met my mate . . ." His words failed him as silver lined his eyes.

He said down the bond, *I would have waited five hundred more years for you. A thousand years. And if this was all the time we were allowed to have . . . The wait was worth it.*

He wiped away the tears sliding down my face. "I believe that everything happened, exactly the way it had to . . . so I could find you." He kissed another tear away.

And then he said to my sisters, "We have not known each other for long. But I have to believe that you were brought here, into our family, for a reason, too. And maybe today we'll find out why."

He surveyed them all again—and held out his hand to Cassian. Cassian took it, and held out his other for Mor. Then Mor extended her other to Azriel. Azriel to Amren. Amren to Nesta. Nesta to Elain. And Elain to me. Until we were all linked, all bound together.

Rhys said, "We will walk onto that field and only accept Death when it comes to haul us away to the Otherworld. We will fight for life, for survival, for our futures. But if it is decided by that tapestry of Fate or the Cauldron or the Mother that we do not walk off that field today . . ." His chin lifted. "The great joy and honor of my life has been to know you. To call you my family. And I am grateful—more than I can possibly say—that I was given this time with you all."

"We are grateful, Rhysand," Amren said quietly. "More than you know."

Rhys gave her a small smile as the others murmured their agreement.

He squeezed my hand again as he said, "Then let's go make Hybern very *un*grateful to have known us, too."

⁜

I could smell the sea long before we beheld the battlefield. Hybern had chosen well.

A vast, grassy plain stretched to the shore. A mile inland, he had planted his army.

It rippled away, a dark mass spreading to the eastern horizon. Rocky foothills arose at his back—some of his army also stationed atop them. Indeed, even the plain seemed to slope upward to the east.

I lingered at Rhysand's side atop a broad knoll overlooking the plain, my sisters, Azriel, and Amren close behind. At the distant front lines far ahead, Helion, resplendent in golden armor and a rippling red cape, gave the order to halt. Armies obeyed, shifting into the positions they'd sorted out.

The host we faced, though . . . they were waiting. Poised.

So many. I knew without counting that we were vastly outnumbered.

Cassian landed from the skies, stone-faced, all of his Siphons smoldering as he crossed the flat-topped knoll in a few steps. "The prick took every inch of high ground and advantage he could find. If we want to rout them, we'll have to chase them up into those hills. Which I have no doubt he's already calculated. Likely set with all kinds of surprises." In the distance, those naga-hounds began snarling and howling. With hunger.

Rhys only asked, "How long do you think we have?"

Cassian clenched his jaw, glancing at my sisters. Nesta was watching him keenly; Elain monitored the army from our minor elevation, face white with dread. "We have five High Lords, and there's only one of him. You all could shield us for a while. But it might not be in our interest to drain every one of you like that. He'll have shields, too—and the Cauldron. He's been careful not to let us see the full extent of his power. I have no doubt we're about to, though."

"He'll likely be using spells," I said, remembering that he'd trained Amarantha.

"Make sure Helion is on alert," Azriel offered, limping to Rhys's side. "And Thesan."

"You didn't answer my question," Rhys said to Cassian.

Cassian sized up Hybern's unending army, then our own. "Let's say it goes badly. Shields shattered, disarray, he uses the Cauldron . . . A few hours."

I closed my eyes. During that time, I'd have to get across the battlefield before us, find wherever he kept the Cauldron, and stop it.

"My shadows are hunting for it," Azriel said to me, reading my face as I opened my eyes. His jaw clenched at the words. He was supposed to have been searching for it himself. He flared and settled his wings, as if testing them. "But the wards are strong—no doubt reinforced by the king after you shredded through his at the camp. You might have to go on foot. Wait until the slaughter starts getting sloppy."

Cassian dipped his head and said to Amren, "You'll know when."

She nodded sharply, crossing her arms. I wondered if she'd said good-bye to Varian.

Cassian clapped Rhys on the shoulder. "On your command, I'll get the Illyrians into the skies. We advance on your signal after that."

Rhys nodded distantly, attention still fixed on that overwhelming army.

Cassian took a step away, but looked back at Nesta. Her face was hard as granite. He opened his mouth, but seemed to decide against whatever he was about to say. My sister said nothing as Cassian shot into the sky with a powerful thrust of his wings. Yet she tracked his flight until he was hardly more than a dark speck.

"I can fight on foot," Azriel said to Rhys.

"No." There was no arguing with that tone.

Azriel seemed like he was debating it, but Amren shook her head in warning and he backed down, shadows coiling at his fingers.

In silence, we watched our army settle into neat, solid lines. Watched the Illyrians lift into the skies at whatever silent command Rhys sent to Cassian, forming mirror lines above. Siphons glinted with color, and shields locked into place, both magical and metal. The ground itself shook with each step toward that demarcation line.

Rhys said into my mind, *If Hybern has a lock on my power, he will sense me sneaking across the battlefield.*

I knew what he was implying. *You're needed here. If we both disappear, he'll know.*

A pause. *Are you afraid?*

Are you?

His violet eyes caught mine. So few stars now shone within them. "Yes," he breathed. *Not for myself. For all of you.*

Tarquin barked an order far ahead, and our unified army came to a halt, like some mighty beast pausing. Summer, Winter, Day, Dawn, and Night—each court's forces clearly marked by the alterations in color and armor. In the faeries who fought alongside the High Fae, ethereal and deadly. A legion of Thesan's Peregryns flapped into rank beside the Illyrians, their golden armor gleaming against the solid black of our own.

No sign of Beron or Eris—not a whisper of Autumn coming to assist us. Or Tamlin.

But Hybern's army did not advance. They might as well have been statues. The stillness, I knew, was more to unnerve us.

"Magic first," Amren was explaining to Nesta. "Both sides will try to bring down the shields around the armies."

As if in answer, they did. My magic writhed in response to the High Lords unleashing their might—all but Rhysand.

He was saving his power for once the shields came down. I had no doubt Hybern himself was doing the same across the plain.

Shields faltered on either side. Some died. Not many, but a few. Magic against magic, the earth shuddering, the grass between the armies withering and turning to ash.

"I forgot how boring this part is," Amren muttered.

Rhys shot her a dry look. But he prowled to the edge of our little outlook, as if sensing the stalemate was soon to break. He'd deliver a mighty, devastating blow to the army the moment their shield buckled. A veritable tidal wave of night-kissed power. His fingers curled at his sides.

To my left, Azriel's Siphons glowed—readying to unleash blasts to echo Rhysand's. He might not be able to fight, but he would wield his power from here.

I came to Rhys's side. Ahead, both shields were wobbling at last.

"I never got you a mating present," I said.

Rhys monitored the battle ahead. His power rumbled beneath us, surging from the shadowy heart of the world.

Soon. A matter of moments. My heart thundered, sweat beading my brow—not just from the summer heat now thick across the field.

"I've been thinking and thinking," I went on, "about what to get you."

Slowly, so slowly, Rhys's eyes slid to mine. Only a chasm of power lay within them—blotting out those stars.

I smiled at him, bathing in that power, and sent an image into his mind.

Of the column of my spine, now inked from my base to my nape with four phases of the moon. And a small star in the middle of them.

"But, I'll admit," I said as his eyes flared, "this mating gift is probably for *both* of us."

Hybern's shield came crashing down. My magic snapped from me, cleaving through the world. Revealing the glamour I'd had in place for hours.

Before our front line . . . A cloud of darkness appeared, writhing and whirling on itself.

"Mother above," Azriel breathed. Right as a male figure appeared beside that swirling ebony smoke.

Both armies seemed to pause with surprise.

"You retrieved the Ouroboros," Rhys whispered.

For standing before Hybern were the Bone Carver and the living nest of shadows that was Bryaxis, the former contained and freed in a Fae body by myself last night. Both bound to obey by the simple bargain now inked onto my spine. "I did."

He scanned me from head to toe, the wind stirring his blue-black hair as he asked softly, "What did you see?"

Hybern was stirring, frantically assessing what and who now stood before them. The Carver had chosen the form of an Illyrian soldier in his prime. Bryaxis remained within the darkness roiling around it, the living tapestry it would use to reveal the nightmares of its victims.

"Myself," I said at last. "I saw myself."

It was, perhaps, the one thing I would never show him. Anyone. How I had cowered and raged and wept. How I had vomited, and screamed, and clawed at the mirror. Slammed my fists into it. And then curled up, trembling at every horrific and cruel and selfish thing I'd beheld within that monster—within me. But I had kept watching. I did not turn from it.

And when my shaking stopped, I studied it. All of those wretched things. The pride and the hypocrisy and the shame. The rage and the cowardice and the hurt.

Then I began to see other things. More important things—more vital.

"And what I saw," I said quietly to him as the Carver raised a hand. "I think—I think I loved it. Forgave it—me. All of it." It was only in that moment when I knew—I'd understood what the Suriel had meant. Only I could allow the bad to break me. Only I could own it, embrace it. And when I'd learned that . . . the Ouroboros had yielded to me.

Rhys arched a brow, even as awe crept across his face. "You loved all of it—the good and the bad?"

I smiled a bit. "Especially the bad." The two figures seemed to take a breath—a mighty inhale that had Bryaxis's dark cloud contracting. Readying to spring. I inclined my head to my mate. "Here's to a long, happy mating, Rhys."

"Seems like you beat me to it."

"To what?"

With a wink, Rhys pointed toward Bryaxis and the Carver. Another figure appeared.

The Carver stumbled back a step. And I knew—from the slim, female figure, the dark, flowing hair, the once-again beautiful face . . . I knew who she was.

Stryga—the Weaver.

And atop the Weaver's dark hair . . . A pale blue jewel glittered.

Ianthe's jewel. A blood trophy as the Weaver smiled at her twin, gave him a mocking bow, and faced the host before them. The Carver halted his slow retreat, stared at his sister for a long moment, then turned to the army once more.

"You're not the only one who can offer bargains, you know," Rhys drawled with a wicked smile.

The Weaver. Rhys had gotten the *Weaver* to join us— "How?"

He angled his neck, revealing a small, curling tattoo behind his ear. "I sent Helion to bargain on my behalf—that was why he was in the Middle that day he found you. To offer to break the containment spell on the Weaver . . . in exchange for her services today."

I blinked at my mate. Then grinned, not bothering to hide the savagery within it. "Hybern has no idea about the hell that's about to rain down upon them, do they."

"Here's to family reunions," was all Rhys said.

Then the Weaver, the Carver, and Bryaxis unleashed themselves upon Hybern.

CHAPTER
70

"You actually did it," Amren murmured, gaping as the three immortals slammed into Hybern's lines, and the screaming began.

Bodies fell before them; bodies were left in their wake—some mere husks encased in armor. Drained by the Carver and Stryga. Some fled from what they beheld in Bryaxis—the face of their deepest fears.

Rhys was still smiling at me as he extended a hand toward Hybern's army, now trying to adjust to the rampant havoc.

His fingers pointed.

Obsidian power erupted from him.

A massive chunk of Hybern's army just . . .

Misted.

Red mist, and metal shavings lay where they had been.

Rhys panted, his eyes a bit wild. The hit had been well placed. Splitting the army in two.

Azriel unleashed a second blast—blue light slamming into the now-exposed flank. Driving them farther apart.

The Illyrians moved. That had been Rhys's signal.

They shot down from the skies—just as a legion rose up from Hybern teeming with things like the Attor. Hidden amongst Hybern's ranks. Siphons flared, locking shields into place—and the Illyrians rained arrows with deadly accuracy.

But the Attor legion was well prepared. And when they answered with a volley of their own . . . Ash shafts, but arrowheads made from faebane. Even with Nuan's antidote in our soldiers' veins, it did not extend to their magic—and it was no defense against the stone itself. Faebane arrows pierced Siphon-shields as easily as butter. The king had adapted—improved—his arsenal.

Some Illyrians went down quickly. The others realized the threat and used their metal shields, unhooking them from across their backs.

On land, Tarquin's, Helion's, and Kallias's soldiers began to charge. Hybern unleashed its hounds—and other beasts.

And as those two sides barreled for each other . . . Rhys sent another blast, followed by a wave of power from Tarquin. Splitting and shoving Hybern's lines into uneven groups.

And through it all, Bryaxis . . . All I could make of it was a blur of ever-changing claws and fangs and wings and muscle, shifting and whirling within that dark cloud that struck and smothered. Blood sprayed wherever it plunged into screaming soldiers. Some seemed to die of pure terror.

The Bone Carver fought near Bryaxis. No weapons to be seen beyond a scimitar of ivory—of bone—in that male's hands. He swept it before himself, as if he were threshing wheat.

Soldiers dropped dead before it—with barely a blow laid upon them. Even that Fae body of his could not contain that lethal power—stifle it.

Hybern fled before him. Before the Weaver. For on the other side of the Carver, leaving husks of corpses in her wake . . . Stryga shredded through Hybern in a tangle of black hair and white limbs.

Our own soldiers, mercifully, did not balk as they ran for the enemy lines. And I sent a roaring order down that two-pronged bond that now linked me to the Carver and Bryaxis, reminding them, my teeth gritted, that our soldiers were *not* fair game. Only Hybern and its allies.

Both raged against the order, yanking at the leash.

I rallied every scrap of night and starlight and snarled at them to *obey*.

I could have sworn an otherworldly, ungodly sense of *self* grumbled about it in response.

But they listened. And did not turn on our soldiers who at last intercepted Hybern's lines.

The sound as both armies collided . . . I didn't have words for it. Elain covered her ears, cringing.

My friends were down there. Mor fought with Viviane, keeping an eye on her as she'd promised Kallias, while he released his power in sprays of skin-shredding ice. Cassian—I couldn't even spot him beyond the blazing flare of his Siphons near the front lines, crimson glowing amid the vicious shadows of Keir's Darkbringers as they wielded them to their advantage: blinding swaths of Hybern soldiers in sudden darkness . . . then blinding them doubly when they ripped those shadows away and left nothing but glaring sunlight. Left nothing but their awaiting blades.

"It's already getting messy," Amren said, even though our lines— especially the Illyrians and Thesan's Peregryns—held.

"Not yet," Rhys said. "Much of the army isn't yet engaged past the front lines. We need Hybern's focus elsewhere."

Starting with Rhys setting foot on that battlefield.

My guts twisted up. Hybern's army began to move, pressing ahead. The Weaver, Carver, and Bryaxis plunged deep into the ranks, but Hybern's soldiers quickly stepped up to staunch the holes in the lines.

Helion bellowed at our front lines to hold steady. Arrows rose and fell on either side. The ones tipped in faebane found their mark. Over and over again. As if the king had spelled them to hunt their targets.

"This will be over before we can even walk down this hill," Amren snapped.

Rhys growled at her. "*Not yet*—"

A horn sounded—to the north.

Both armies seemed to pause to look.

And Rhys only breathed to me, "Now. You have to go *now*."

Because the army that broke over the northern horizon . . .

Three armies. One bearing the burnt-orange flag of Beron.

The other the grass-green flag of the Spring Court.

And one . . . one of mortal men in iron armor. Bearing a cobalt flag with a striking badger. Graysen's crest.

Out of a rip in the world, Eris appeared atop our knoll, clad head to toe in silver armor, a red cape spilling from his shoulders. Rhys snarled a warning, too far gone in his power to bother controlling himself.

Eris just rested a hand on the pommel of his fine sword and said, "We thought you might need some help."

Because Tamlin's small army, and Beron's, and Graysen's . . . Now they were running and winnowing and blasting for Hybern's ranks. And leading that human army . . .

Jurian.

But Beron. *Beron* had come.

Eris registered our shock at that, too, and said, "Tamlin made him. Dragged my father out by his neck." A half smile. "It was delightful."

They had come—and Tamlin had managed to rally that force I'd so gleefully destroyed—

"Tamlin wants orders," Eris said. "Jurian does, too."

Rhys's voice was rough—low. "And what of your father?"

"We're taking care of a problem," was all Eris said, and pointed toward his father's army.

For those were his brothers approaching the front line, winnowing in bursts through the host. Right past the front lines and to the enemy wagons scattered throughout Hybern's ranks.

Wagons full of faebane, I realized as they crackled with blue fire and then turned to ash without even a trace of smoke. His brothers winnowed to every cache, every arsenal. Flames exploded in their path.

Destroying that supply of deadly faebane. Burning it into nothing.

As if someone—Jurian or Tamlin—had told them precisely where each would be.

Rhys blinked, his only sign of surprise. He looked to me, then Amren, and nodded. *Go. Now.*

While Hybern was focused on the approaching army—trying to calculate the risks, to staunch the chaos Beron and his sons unleashed with their targeted attacks. Trying to figure out what the hell Jurian was doing there, and how many weaknesses Jurian had learned. And would now exploit.

Amren ushered my sisters forward, even as Elain let out a low sob at the sight of the Graysen coat of arms. "Now. Quick and quiet as shadows."

We were going down—into *that*. Bryaxis and the Carver were still shredding, still slaughtering in their little pockets past the enemy lines. And the Weaver . . . Where was the Weaver—

There. Slowly plowing a slim path of carnage. As Rhys had instructed her moments before.

"This way," I said to them, keeping an eye on Stryga's path of horror. Elain was shaking, still gazing toward that human army and her betrothed in it. Nesta monitored the Illyrian legions soaring past overhead, their lines unfaltering.

"I assume we'll be following the path of bodies," Amren muttered to me. "How does the Weaver know how to find the Cauldron?"

Rhys seemed to be listening, even as we turned away, his fingers brushing mine in silent farewell. I just said, "Because she appears to have an unnaturally good sense of smell."

Amren snorted, and we fell into flanking positions around my sisters. A glamour of invisibility would hopefully allow us to skirt the southern edge of the battlefield—along with Azriel's shadows as he monitored from behind. But once we got behind enemy lines . . .

I looked back as we neared the edge of the knoll. Just once. At Rhys, where he now stood talking to Azriel and Eris, explaining the plan to relay to Tamlin, Beron, and Jurian. Eris's brothers made it back behind their father's lines—fires now burning throughout Hybern's army. Not enough to stop them, but . . . at least the faebane had been dealt with. For now.

Rhys's attention slid to me. And even with the battle around us, hell unleashing everywhere . . . For a heartbeat, we were the only two people on this plain.

I opened up my mental barriers to speak to him. Just one more farewell, one more—

Nesta inhaled a shuddering gasp. Stumbled, and took down Amren with her when she tried to keep her upright.

Rhys was instantly there, before the understanding dawned upon me. The Cauldron.

Hybern was rousing the Cauldron.

Amren squirmed out from beneath Nesta, whirling toward the battlefield. "*Shields—*"

Eris winnowed away—to warn his father, no doubt.

Nesta pushed herself onto her elbows, hair shaking free of her braid, lips bloodless. She heaved into the grass.

Rhys's magic shot out of him, arcing around our entire army, his breathing a wet rasp—

Nesta's hands grappled into the grass as she lifted her head, scanning the horizon.

Like she could see right to where the Cauldron was now about to be unleashed.

Rhys's power flowed and flowed out of him, bracing for impact. Azriel's Siphons flashed, a sprawling shield of cobalt locking over Rhysand's, his breathing just as heavy as my mate's—

And then Nesta began screaming. Not in pain. But a name. Over and over.

"*CASSIAN.*"

Amren reached for her, but Nesta roared, "*CASSIAN!*"

She scrambled to her feet, as if she'd leap into the skies.

Her body lurched, and she went down, heaving again.

A figure shot from the Illyrian ranks, spearing for us, flapping hard, red Siphons blazing—

Nesta moaned, writhing on the ground.

The earth seemed to shudder in response.

No—not in response to her. In terror of the thing that erupted from Hybern's army.

I understood why the king had claimed those rocky foothills. Not to make us charge uphill if we should push them so far. But to position the Cauldron.

For it was from the rocky outcropping that a battering ram of death-white light hurled for our army. Just about level with the Illyrian legion in the sky—as the Attor's legion dropped to the earth, and ducked for cover. Leaving the Illyrians exposed.

Cassian was halfway to us when the Cauldron's blast hit the Illyrian forces.

I saw him scream—but heard nothing. The force of that power . . .

It shredded Azriel's shield. Then Rhysand's. And then shredded any Siphon-made ones.

It hollowed out my ears and seared my face.

And where a thousand soldiers had been a heartbeat before . . .

Ashes rained down upon our foot soldiers.

Nesta had known. She gaped up at me, terror and agony on her face, then scanned the sky for Cassian, who flapped in place, as if torn between coming for us and charging back to the scattering Illyrian and Peregryn ranks. She'd known where that blast was about to hit.

Cassian had been right in the center of it.

Or would have been, if she hadn't called him away.

Rhys was looking at her like he knew, too. Like he didn't know whether to scold her for the guilt Cassian would no doubt feel, or thank her for saving him.

Nesta's body went stiff again, a low moan breaking from her.

I felt Rhys cast out his power—a silent warning signal.

The other High Lords raised shields this time, backing the one he rallied.

But the Cauldron did not hit the same spot twice. And Hybern was willing to incinerate part of his own army if it meant wiping out a strength of ours.

Cassian was again hurtling for us, for Nesta sprawled on the ground, as the light and unholy heat of the Cauldron were unleashed again.

Right into its own lines. Where the Bone Carver was gleefully shredding apart soldiers, draining the life from them in sweeps and gusts of that deadly wind.

An unearthly, female shriek broke from deep in the Hybern forces. A sister's warning—and pain. Just as that white light slammed into the Bone Carver.

But the Carver . . . I could have sworn he looked toward me as the Cauldron's power crashed into him. Could have sworn he smiled— and it was not a hideous thing at all.

There—and gone.

The Cauldron wiped him away without any sign of effort.

CHAPTER
71

I could barely hear, barely think in the wake of the Cauldron's power.

In the wake of the empty, blasted bit of plain where the Carver had been. The sudden cold that shuddered down my spine—as if erasing the tattoo inked upon it.

And then the silence—silence in some pocket of my mind as a section of that two-pronged leash of control faded into darkness without end. Leaving nothing behind.

I wondered who would carve his death in the Prison.

If he had perhaps already carved it for himself on the walls of that cell. If he had wanted to make sure I was worthy not to taunt me, but because he wanted his end . . . he wanted his end to be worth carving.

And as I gazed at that decimated part of the plain, the ashes of the Illyrians still raining down . . . I wondered if the Carver had made it. To wherever he had been so curious about going.

I sent up a quiet prayer for him—for all the soldiers who had been there and were now ash on the wind . . . sent up a prayer that they found it everything they'd hoped it would be.

It was the Illyrians who drew me out of the quiet, the ringing in my ears. Even as our army began to panic in the wake of the Cauldron's might, the remaining bulk of the Illyrian legions re-formed their lines and charged ahead, Thesan's Peregryns wholly interspersed with them now.

Jurian's human army, made up of Graysen's men and others . . . To their credit, they did not falter. Did not break, even as they went down one by one.

If the Cauldron dealt another blow . . .

Nesta had her brow in the grass as Cassian landed so hard the ground shuddered. He was reaching for her as he panted, "What is it, what—"

"It's gone quiet again," Nesta breathed, letting Cassian haul her into a sitting position as he scanned her face. Devastation and rage lay in his own. Did he know? That she had screamed for him, knowing he'd come . . . That she'd done it to save him?

Rhys only ordered him, "Get back in line. The soldiers need you there."

Cassian bared his teeth. "What the *hell* can we do against that?"

"I'm going in," Azriel said.

"No," Rhys snapped. But Azriel was spreading his wings, the sunlight so stark on the new, slashing scars down the membrane.

"Chain me to a tree, Rhys," Azriel said softly. "Go ahead." He began checking the buckles on his weapons. "I'll rip it out of the ground and fly with it on my damned back."

Rhys just stared at him—the wings. Then the decimated Illyrian forces.

Any chance we had of victory . . .

Nesta wasn't going anywhere. She could barely stay sitting. And Elain . . . Amren was holding Elain upright as she vomited in the grass. Not from the Cauldron. But pure terror.

But if we did not stop the Cauldron before it refilled again . . . We'd be gone within a few more strikes. I met Amren's gaze. *Can it be done—with just me?*

Her eyes narrowed. *Maybe.* A pause. *Maybe. It never specified how many. Between the two of us . . . it could be enough.*

I eased to my feet. The view of the battle was so much worse standing.

Helion, Tarquin, and Kallias struggled to hold our lines. Jurian, Tamlin, and Beron still battered the northern flank, while the Illyrians and Peregryns slammed back the aerial legion; Keir's Darkbringers now little more than wisps of shadow amid the chaos, but . . .

But it was not enough. And Hybern's sheer size . . . It was beginning to push us back.

Beginning to overwhelm us.

Even by the time Amren and I crossed the miles of battlefield . . . What would be left?

Who would be left?

There was another horn, then.

I knew it did not belong to any ally.

Just as I knew Hybern had not only picked this battlefield for its physical advantages . . . but geographical ones.

Because toward the sea, sailing out of the west, out of Hybern . . .

An armada appeared.

So many ships. All teeming with soldiers.

I caught the look between Cassian, Azriel, and Rhys as they beheld the other army sailing in—at our backs.

Not another army. The *rest* of Hybern's army.

We were trapped between them.

Amren swore. "We might need to run, Rhysand. Before they make landfall."

We could not fight both armies. Couldn't even fight one.

Rhys turned to me. *If you can get across that battlefield in time, then do it. Try to stop the army. The king. But if you can't, when it all goes to hell . . . When there are none of us left . . .*

Don't, I begged him. *Don't say it.*

I want you to run. I don't care what it costs. You run. Get far away, and live to fight another day. You don't look back.

I began to shake my head. *You said no good-byes.*

"Azriel," Rhys said quietly. Hoarsely. "You lead the remaining Illyrians on the northern flank." Guilt—guilt and fear rippled in my mate's eyes at the command. Knowing that Azriel was not fully healed—

Azriel didn't give Rhys a chance to reconsider. Didn't say good-bye to any of us. He shot into the sky, those still-healing wings beating hard as they carried him toward the scrambling northern flank.

That armada sailed nearer. Hybern, sensing their reinforcements were soon to make landfall, cheered and pushed. Hard. So hard the Illyrian lines buckled. Azriel sailed closer and closer to them, Siphons trailing tendrils of blue flame in his wake.

Rhys watched him for a moment, throat bobbing, before he said, "Cassian, you take the southern flank."

This was it. The last moments . . . the last time I would see them all.

I wouldn't run. If it all went to hell, I would make it count and use my own last breath to get that army and king wiped off the earth. But right now . . .

Hybern's armada sailed directly for the distant beach. If I didn't go now, I'd have to charge right through them. The Weaver was already slowing on the eastern front, her death-dance hindered by too many enemies. Bryaxis continued to shred through the lines, swaths of the dead in its wake. But it was still not enough. All that planning . . . it was still not enough.

Cassian said to Rhys, to me, to Nesta, "I'll see you on the other side."

I knew he didn't mean the battlefield.

His wings shifted, readying to lift him.

A horn blast cleaved the world.

A dozen horns, lifted in perfect, mighty harmony.

Rhys went still.

Utterly still at the sound of those horns from the distance. From the east—from the sea.

He whipped his head to me, grabbed me by the waist, and hauled me into the sky. A heartbeat later, Cassian was beside us, Nesta in his arms—as if she'd demanded to see.

And there . . . sailing over the eastern horizon . . .

I did not know where to look.

At the winged soldiers—thousands upon thousands of them—flying straight toward us, high above the ocean. Or the armada of ships stretching away beneath them. More than Hybern's armada. Far, far more.

I knew who they were the moment the aerial host's white, feathered wings became clear.

The Seraphim.

Drakon's legion.

And in those ships below . . . So many different ships. A thousand ships from countless nations, it seemed. Miryam's people. But the other ships . . .

Out of the clouds, a tan-skinned, dark-haired Seraphim warrior soared for us. And Rhys's choked laugh was enough to tell me who it was. Who now flapped before us, grinning broadly.

"You could have asked for aid, you know," drawled the male—*Drakon*. "Instead of letting us hear of all this through the rumor mill. Seems we arrived just in time."

"We came looking for you—and found you gone," Rhys said—but those were tears in his eyes. "Makes it hard to ask someone for aid."

Drakon snorted. "Yes, we realized that. Miryam figured it out—why we hadn't heard from you yet." His white wings were almost blindingly bright in the sun. "Three centuries ago, we had some trouble on our borders and set up a glamour to keep the island shielded. Tied to—you know. So that anyone who approached would only see a ruin and be inclined to turn around." He winked at Rhys. "Miryam's idea—she got it from you and your city." Drakon winced a bit. "Turns out, it worked *too* well, if it kept out both enemies *and* friends."

"You mean to tell me," Rhys said softly, "that you've been on Cretea this entire time."

Drakon grimaced. "Yes. Until . . . we heard about Hybern. About Miryam being . . . hunted again." By Jurian. The prince's face tightened with rage, but he surveyed me, then Nesta and Cassian, with a sharp-eyed scrutiny. "Shall we assist you, or just flap here, talking?"

Rhys inclined his head. "At your leisure, Prince." He glanced to the armada now aiming for Hybern's forces. "Friends of yours?"

Drakon's mouth quirked to the side. "Friends of yours, I think." My heart stopped. "Some of Miryam's boats are down there, she with them, but most of that came for you."

"What," Nesta said sharply, not quite a question.

Drakon pointed to the ships. "We met up with them on the flight here. Saw them crossing the channel and decided to join ranks. It's why we're a little late—though we gave them a bit of a push across." Indeed, wind was now whipping at their white sails, propelling those boats faster and faster toward that Hybern armada.

Drakon rubbed his jaw. "I can't even begin to explain the convoluted story they told me, but . . ." He shook his head. "They're led by a queen named Vassa."

I began crying.

"Who apparently was found by—"

"Lucien," I breathed.

"Who?" Drakon's brows narrowed. "Oh, the male with the eye. No. He met up with them later on—told them where to go. To come *now*, actually. So pushy, you Prythian males. Good thing we, at least, were already on our way to see if you needed help."

"Who found Vassa," Nesta said with that same flat tone. As if she somehow already knew.

Closer, those human ships sailed. So many—so, so many, bearing a variety of different flags that I could just start to make out, thanks to my Fae sight.

"He calls himself the Prince of Merchants," Drakon said. "Apparently, he discovered the human queens were traitors months ago, and has been gathering an independent human army to face Hybern ever since. He managed to find Queen Vassa—and together they rallied this army." Drakon shrugged. "He told me that he's got three daughters who live here. And that he failed them for many years. But he would not fail them this time."

The ships at the front of the human armada became clear, along with the gold lettering on their sides.

"He named his three personal ships after them," Drakon said with a smile.

And there, sailing at the front . . . I beheld the names of those ships.

The *Feyre*.

The *Elain*.

And leading the charge against Hybern, flying over the waves, unyielding and without an ounce of fear . . .

The *Nesta*.

With my father . . . our father at the helm.

CHAPTER
72

The wind whipped away the tears rolling down Nesta's face at the sight of our father's ships.

At the sight of the ship he'd chosen to sail into battle, for the daughter who had hated him for not fighting for us, who had hated him for our mother dying, for the poverty and the despair and years lost.

Drakon said drily, "I take it you're acquainted?"

Our father—gone for months and months with no word.

He had left, my sisters had once said, to attend a meeting regarding the threat above the wall. At that meeting, had it become clear that we had been betrayed by our own kind? And had he then departed, under such secrecy he would not risk the messages to us falling into the wrong hands, to find help?

For us. For me, and my sisters.

Rhys said to Drakon, "Meet Nesta. And my mate, Feyre."

Neither of us looked to the prince. Only at our father's fleet—at the ships he'd named in honor of us.

"Speaking of Vassa," Rhys said to Drakon, "was her curse—ended?"

The human armada and the Hybern host neared, and I knew the

impact would be lethal. Saw Hybern's magic shields go up. Saw the Seraphim raise their own. "See for yourself," Drakon said.

I blinked at what began to shoot between the human boats. What soared over the water, fast as a shooting star. Spearing for Hybern. Red and gold and white—vibrant as molten metal.

I could have sworn Hybern's fleet began to panic as it broke from the lines of the human armada and closed the gap between them.

As it spread its wings wide, trailing sparks and embers across the waves, and I realized what—*who*—now flew at that enemy host.

A firebird. Burning as hot and furious as the heart of a forge.

Vassa—the lost queen.

╬

Rhys kissed away the tears sliding down my own face as that firebird queen slammed into Hybern's fleet. Burning husks of ships were left in her wake.

Our father and the human army spread wide. To pick off the others. Rhys said to Drakon, "Get your legion on land."

A slim chance—a fool's chance of winning this thing. Or staunching the slaughter.

Drakon's eyes went glazed in a way that told me he was conveying orders to someone far away. I wondered if Nephelle and her wife were in that legion—if the last time they had drawn swords was that long-ago battle at the bottom of the sea.

Rhys seemed to be thinking of the past, too. Because he muttered to Drakon over the din exploding off the sea and the battle below, "Jurian is here."

The casual, cocky grace of the prince vanished. Cold rage hardened his features into something terrifying. And his brown eyes . . . they went wholly black.

"He fights for us."

Drakon didn't look convinced, but he nodded. He jerked his chin to

Cassian. "I assume you're Cassian." The general's chin dipped. I could already see the shadows in his eyes—at the loss of those soldiers. "My legion is yours. Command them as you like."

Cassian scanned our foundering host, the northern flank that Azriel was reassembling, and gave Drakon a few terse orders. Drakon flapped those white wings, so stark against his honey-brown skin, and said to Rhys, "Miryam's furious with you, by the way. Three hundred fifty-one years since you last visited. If we survive, expect to do some groveling."

Rhys rasped a laugh. "Tell that witch it goes both ways."

Drakon grinned, and with a powerful sweep of his wings, he was gone.

Rhys and Cassian looked after him, then at the armadas now engaged in outright bloodshed. Our father was down there—our father, who I had never seen wield a weapon in his *life*—

The firebird rained hell upon the ships. Literally. Burning, molten hell as she slammed into them and sent their panicking soldiers to the bottom of the sea.

"Now," I said to Rhys. "Amren and I need to go *now*."

The chaos was complete. With a battle raging in every direction . . . Amren and I could make it. Perhaps the king would be preoccupied.

Rhys made to shoot me back down to the ground, where Amren and Elain were still waiting. Nesta said, "Wait."

Rhys obeyed.

Nesta stared toward that armada, toward our father fighting in it. "Use me. As bait."

I blinked at the same moment Cassian said, "No."

Nesta ignored him. "The king is probably waiting beside that Cauldron. Even if you get there, you'll have him to contend with. Draw him out. Draw him far away. To me."

"How," Rhys said softly.

"It goes both ways," Nesta murmured, as if my mate's words

moments before had triggered the idea. "He doesn't know how much I took. And if . . . if I make it seem like I'm about to use his power . . . He'll come running. Just to kill me."

"He *will* kill you," Cassian snarled.

Her hand clenched on his arm. "That's—that's where you come in."

To guard her. Protect her. To lay a trap for the king.

"No," Rhys said.

Nesta snorted. "You're not my High Lord. I may do as I wish. And since he'll sense that you're with me . . . You need to go far away, too."

Rhys said to Cassian, "I'm not letting you throw your life away for this."

I was inclined to agree.

Cassian surveyed the depleted Illyrian lines, now holding strong as Azriel rallied them. "Az has control of the lines."

"I said *no*," Rhys snapped. I'd never heard him use that tone with Cassian, with any of them.

Cassian said steadily, "It's the only shot we have of a diversion. Luring him away from that Cauldron." His hands tightened on Nesta. "You gave everything, Rhys. You went through that *hell* for us, for *fifty years*." He'd never addressed it—not fully. "You think I don't know what happened? I know, Rhys. We all do. And we know you did it to save us, spare us." He shook his head, sunlight glinting off that dark, winged helmet. "Let us return the favor. Let us repay the debt."

"There is no debt to repay." Rhys's voice broke. The sound of it cracked my heart.

Cassian's own voice broke as he said, "I never got to repay your mother—for her kindness. Let me do it this way. Let me buy you time."

"I can't."

I wasn't sure if in the entire history of Illyria, there had ever been such a discussion.

"You can," Cassian said gently. "You can, Rhys." He gave a lazy grin. "Save some of the glory for the rest of us."

"Cassian—"

But Cassian asked Nesta, "Do you have what you need?"

Nesta nodded. "Amren showed me enough. What to do to rally the power to me."

And if Amren and I could control the Cauldron between us . . . That distraction they'd offer . . .

Nesta looked down to Elain—our sister monitoring the bloodbath ahead. Then to me. She said quietly, "Tell Father—thank you."

She wrapped her arms tightly around Cassian, those gray-blue eyes bright, then they were gone.

Rhys's body strained with the effort of not going after them as they soared for a copse of trees far behind the battlefield. "He might survive," I said softly.

"No," Rhys said, flying us down to Amren and Elain. "He won't."

I had Rhys move Elain to the farthest reaches of our camp. And when he returned, my mate only pressed a kiss to my mouth before he took to the skies, spearing for the heart of the battle—the heaviest fighting. I could barely stand to look—to see where he landed.

Alone with Amren, she said to me, "Shield us from sight, and run as fast as you can. Don't stop; try not to kill. It'll leave a trail."

I nodded, checking my weapons. The Seraphim were soaring overhead now, wings bright as the sun on snow. I settled a glamour around us, veiling us and muffling our sounds.

"Quickly," Amren repeated, silver eyes churning like thunderclouds. "Don't look back."

So I didn't.

CHAPTER
73

The Cauldron had been nestled in a craggy overlook.

The Weaver had done her job well. Key guards and posts were little more than wet, red piles of bone and sinew. And I knew that when I saw her again . . . she would be even more blindingly beautiful.

Amren's power flared again and again, breaking through wards in our path until we reached Stryga's wake. Whatever spells the king had laid . . . Amren was prepared for them. *Hungry* for them. She shattered them all with a savage smile.

But the gray hill was crawling with Hybern commanders, content to let their underlings fight. Waiting until the killing field had sorted the grunts from the true warriors. I could hear them hissing about who on our side they wanted to personally take on.

Helion and Tarquin were two of the most frequent wishes.

Tamlin was the other. Tamlin, for his two-faced lying. And Jurian. How they would suffer.

Varian. Azriel. Cassian. Kallias and Viviane. Mor. They said the names of my friends like they were horses at a race. Who would last long enough for them to face off. Who would haul the pretty mate of the Lord of Winter back here. Who would break the Morrigan at last.

Who would bring home Illyrian wings to pin on the wall. My blood was boiling, even as my bones quaked. I hoped Bryaxis devoured them all—and made them wet themselves in terror before it did.

But I dared look behind us once.

Mor and Viviane weren't coming to this camp anytime soon. They held off an entire cluster of Hybern soldiers, flanked by that white-haired female I'd seen in the Winter camp and a unit of those mighty bears that shredded apart soldiers with swipes of their enormous paws.

Amren hissed in warning, and I faced forward as we began to scale the quiet side of the gray hill. No sign of Stryga, though she had stopped here, at the base of the hill atop which the Cauldron squatted. I could already feel its terrible presence—the beckoning.

Amren and I climbed slowly. Listening after every step.

The battle raged behind us. In the skies and on the earth and in the sea.

I did not think . . . even with Drakon and the human army . . . I did not think it was going well.

My hands bit into the sharp gray rock of the hill's cliff face, body straining as I hauled myself up, Amren climbing with ease. Nesta had to lure the king away soon, or we'd be face-to-face with him.

Movement at the base of the rock caught my attention.

I went still as death.

A beautiful, dark-haired young woman stood there. Staring up at us, squinting and sniffing.

A smile bloomed on her red—her *bloody* mouth. She smiled in my general direction. Revealing blood-coated teeth.

Stryga. The Weaver had waited. Hiding here. Until we arrived.

She brushed a snow-white hand over the tattoo of a crescent moon now on her forearm. Rhys's bargain-mark. A reminder—and warning.

To go. To hurry.

She faced the rocky path half-visible to our left, Ianthe's jewel splattered with blood where it sat atop her head. Strode right to the guards stationed there, who we'd been climbing the cliff face to avoid. Some of them jolted. Stryga smiled once—a hateful, awful smile—and leaped upon them.

A diversion.

Amren shuddered, but we launched into motion once more. The guards were focused on her slaughtering, sprinting from their posts up the hill to meet her.

Faster—we didn't have much time. I could feel the Cauldron rallying—

No. Not the Cauldron.

That power . . . it came from *behind*.

Nesta.

"Good girl," Amren muttered under her breath. Just before she grabbed me by the back of my jacket and slammed me face-first into the stone, ducking low.

Right as a pair of boots strolled down the narrow path. I knew the sound of his footsteps. They haunted my dreams.

The King of Hybern walked right past us. Focused on Stryga, on Nesta's distant rumble of power.

The Weaver paused as she beheld who approached. Smiled, blood dripping off her chin.

"How beautiful you are," he murmured, his voice a seductive croon. "How magnificent, ancient one."

She brushed her dark hair over a slim shoulder. "You may bow, king. As it was once done."

The King of Hybern walked right up to her. Smiled down at Stryga's exquisite face.

Then he took that face in his broad hands, faster than she could move, and snapped her neck.

It might not have killed her. The Weaver was a death-god—her very existence defied our own. So it might not have killed her, that cracking of her spine. Had the king not tossed her body down to the two naga-hounds snarling at the foot of the hill.

They ripped into the Weaver's limp body without hesitation.

Even Amren let out a sound of dismay.

But the king was staring northward. Toward Nesta.

That power—*her* power—surged again. Beckoning, as the Cauldron atop this rock now called to me.

He gazed toward the sea—the battle raging there.

I could have sworn he was smiling as he winnowed away.

"Now," Amren breathed.

I couldn't move. Cassian and Nesta—even Rhys thought there was no shot of survival.

"You make it count," Amren snapped, and that was true grief shining in her eyes. She knew what was about to happen. The window that we'd been bought.

I swallowed my despair, my terror, and charged up the hill—to the crag.

To where the Cauldron sat. Unguarded. Waiting for us.

The Book appeared in Amren's small hands. The Cauldron was nearly as tall as she was. A looming black pit of hate and power.

I could stop this. Right now. Stop this army—and the king before he killed Nesta and Cassian. Amren opened the Book. Looked at me expectantly.

"Put your hand on the Cauldron," she said quietly. I obeyed.

The Cauldron's endless power slammed into me, a wave threatening to sweep me under, a storm with no end.

I could barely keep one foot in this world, barely remember my name. I clung to what I had seen in the Ouroboros—clung to every reflection and memory I had faced and owned, the good and wicked and the gray. Who I was, who I was, who I was—

Amren watched me for a long moment. And did not read from the Book. Did not put it in my hands. She shut the gold pages and shoved it behind her with a kick.

Amren had lied. She did not plan to leash the king or his army with the Cauldron and the Book.

And whatever trap she had set . . . I had fallen right into it.

CHAPTER
74

I gripped my sense of self in the face of the black maw of the Cauldron. Gripped it with everything I had.

Amren only said, "I'm sorry I lied to you."

I could not remove my hand. Could not pry my fingers away. I was being shredded apart, slowly, thoroughly.

I flung my magic out, desperate for any chain to this world to save me, keep me from being devoured by the eternal, awful *thing* that now tried to drag me into its embrace.

Fire and water and light and wind and ice and night. All rallied. All failed me.

Some tether slipped, and my mind slid closer to the Cauldron's outstretched arms.

I felt it *touch* me.

And then I was half gone.

Half there, standing silently next to the Cauldron, hand glued to the black rim.

Half . . . elsewhere.

Flying through the world. Searching. The Cauldron now hunted for that power that had come so close . . . And now taunted it.

Nesta.

The Cauldron searched for her, searched for her as the king now sought her.

It skimmed across the battlefield like an insect over the surface of a pond.

We were losing. Badly. Seraphim and Illyrians were bloodied and being hauled out of the sky. Azriel had been forced to the ground, his wings dragging in the bloody mud as he fought sword to sword against the endless onslaught. Our foot soldiers had broken the lines in places, Keir screaming at his Darkbringers to get back into position, plumes of shadows flaring from him.

I saw Rhysand. In the thick of those breaking lines. Blood-splattered, fighting beautifully.

I saw him assess the field ahead—and transform.

The talons came first. Replacing fingers and feet. Then dark scales or perhaps feathers, I couldn't get a look at them, covered his legs, his arms, his chest. His body contorted, bones and muscles growing and shifting.

The beast form Rhys had kept hidden. Never liked to unleash.

Unless it was dire enough to do so.

Before the Cauldron swept me away, I beheld what happened to his head, his face.

It was a thing of nightmares. Nothing human or Fae in it. It was a creature that lived in black pits and only emerged at night to hunt and feast. The face . . . it was those creatures that had been carved into the rock of the Court of Nightmares. That made up his throne. The throne not only a representation of his power . . . but of what lurked within. And with the wings . . .

Hybern soldiers began fleeing.

Helion beheld what happened and ran, too—but toward Rhys.

Shifting as well.

If Rhys was a flying terror crafted from shadows and cold moonlight, Helion was his daytime equivalent.

Gold feathers and shredding claws and feathered wings—

Together, my mate and the High Lord of Day unleashed themselves upon Hybern.

Until they paused. Until a slim, short male walked out of the ranks toward them—one of Hybern's commanders, no doubt. Rhys's snarl shook the earth. But it was Helion, glowing with white light, who stepped forward to face the male, claws sinking deep into the mud.

The commander didn't so much as wear a sword. Only fine gray clothes and a vaguely amused expression on his face. Amethyst light swirled around him. Helion growled at Rhys—an order.

And my mate nodded, gore dripping from his maw, before he lunged back into the fray.

Leaving the commander and Helion Spell-Cleaver to go head-to-head. Spell to spell.

Soldiers on either side began fleeing.

But the Cauldron whipped me away as Helion unleashed a blast of light toward the commander, its quarry not to be found on that battlefield.

Come, Nesta's power seemed to sing. *Come.*

The Cauldron caught her scent and hurtled us onward.

We arrived before the king did.

The Cauldron seemed to skid to a halt at the clearing. Seemed to coil and reel back, a snake poised to strike.

Nesta and Cassian stood there, his sword out, Nesta's eyes blazing with that inner, unholy fire. "Get ready," she breathed. "He's coming."

The power Nesta was holding back . . .

She'd kill the King of Hybern.

Cassian was the distraction—while her blow found its mark.

Time seemed to slow and warp. The dark power of the king speared toward us. Toward that clearing where I was neither seen nor heard, where I was nothing but a scrap of soul carried on a black wind.

The King of Hybern winnowed right in front of them.

Nesta's power rallied—then vanished.

Cassian did not move. Did not dare.

For the King of Hybern held my father before him, a sword to his throat.

⁜

That was why he had looked to the sea. He'd known Nesta would land that killing blow the moment he appeared, and the only way to stop it . . .

A human shield. One she'd think twice about allowing to die.

Our father was blood-splattered, leaner than the last time I'd seen him. "Nesta," he breathed, noting the ears, the Fae grace. The power sputtering out in her eyes.

The king smiled. "What a loving father—to bring an entire *army* to save his daughters."

Nesta did not say anything. Cassian's attention darted through the clearing, sizing up every advantage, every angle.

Save him, I begged the Cauldron of my father. *Help him.*

The Cauldron did not answer. It had no voice, no consciousness save some base need to take back that which had been stolen.

The King of Hybern tilted his head to peer at my father's bearded and weather-tanned face. "So many things have changed since you were last home. Three daughters, now Fae. One of them married *quite* well."

My father only gazed at my sister. Ignored the monster behind him and said to her, "I loved you from the first moment I held you in my arms. And I am . . . I am so sorry, Nesta—my Nesta. I am so sorry, for all of it."

"Please," Nesta said to the king. Her only word, guttural and hoarse. "Please."

"What will you give me, Nesta Archeron?"

Nesta stared and stared at my father, who was shaking his head. Cassian's hand twitched, the blade rising. Trying to get a good shot.

"Will you give back what you took?"

"Yes."

"Even if I have to carve it out of you?"

Our father snarled, "Don't you lay your filthy hands on my daughter—"

I heard the crack before I realized what happened.

Before I saw the way my father's head twisted. Saw the light freeze in his eyes.

Nesta made no sound. Showed no reaction as the King of Hybern snapped our father's neck.

I began screaming. Screaming and thrashing inside the Cauldron's grip. Begging it to stop it—to bring him back, to end it—

Nesta looked down at my father's body as it crumpled to the forest floor.

And as the king had predicted . . . Nesta's power flickered out.

But Cassian's had not.

Arrows of blinding red shot for the King of Hybern, a shield locking around Nesta as Cassian launched himself forward.

And as Cassian took on the king, who laughed and seemed willing to engage in a bit of swordplay . . . I stared at my father on that ground. At his open, unseeing eyes.

Cassian pushed the king away from my father's body, swords and magics clashing. Not for long. Only long enough to hold him off—for Nesta to perhaps run.

For me to finish what I had let my family give their lives for. But the Cauldron still held me there.

Even as I tried to come back to that hill where Amren had betrayed me, had used me for whatever purpose of her own—

Nesta knelt before our father, her face a void. She gazed into his still-open eyes.

Closed them gently. Hands steady as stone.

Cassian had shoved the king deeper into the trees. His shouts rang out.

Nesta leaned forward to press a kiss to our father's blood-splattered brow.

And when she lifted her head . . .

The Cauldron thrashed and roiled.

For in Nesta's eyes, limning her skin . . . Uncut power.

She gazed toward the king and Cassian. Just as Cassian's bark of pain cut toward us.

The power around her shuddered. Nesta got to her feet.

Then Cassian screamed. I looked toward him. Away from my father.

Not twenty feet away, Cassian was on the ground. Wings—snapped in spots. Blood leaking from them.

Bone jutted from his thigh. His Siphons were dull. Empty.

He'd already drained them before coming here. Was exhausted.

But he had come—for her. For us.

He was panting, blood dribbling from his nose. Arms buckling as he tried to rise.

The King of Hybern stood over him, and extended a hand.

Cassian arched off the ground, bellowing in pain. A bone cracked somewhere in his body.

"Stop."

The king looked over a shoulder as Nesta stepped forward. Cassian mouthed at her to run, blood escaping from his lips and onto the moss beneath him.

Nesta took in his broken body, the pain in Cassian's eyes, and angled her head.

The movement was not human. Not Fae.

Purely animal.

Purely predator.

And when her eyes lifted to the king again . . . "I am going to kill you," she said quietly.

"Really?" the king asked, lifting a brow. "Because I can think of *far* more interesting things to do with you."

Not again. I could not watch this play out again. Standing by, idle, while those I loved suffered.

The Cauldron crept along with Nesta, a hound at her side.

Nesta's fingers curled.

The king snorted. And brought his foot down upon Cassian's nearest wing.

Bone snapped. And his scream—

I thrashed against the Cauldron's grip. Thrashed and clawed.

Nesta exploded.

All of that power, all at once—

The king winnowed out of the way.

Her power blasted the trees behind him to cinders. Blasted across the battlefield in a low arc, then landed right in the Hybern ranks. Taking out hundreds before they knew what happened.

The king appeared perhaps thirty feet away and laughed at the smoking ruins behind him. "Magnificent," he said. "Barely trained, brash, but magnificent."

Nesta's fingers curled again, as if rallying that power.

But she'd spent it all in one blow. Her eyes were blue-gray once more.

"Go," Cassian managed to breathe. "*Go*."

"This seems familiar," the king mused. "Was it him or the other bastard who crawled toward you that day?"

Cassian was indeed now crawling toward her, broken wings and leg dragging, leaving a trail of blood over the grass and roots.

Nesta rushed to him, kneeling.

Not to comfort.

But to pick up his Illyrian blade.

Cassian tried to stop her as she stood. As Nesta lifted that sword before the King of Hybern.

She said nothing. Only held her ground.

The king chuckled and angled his own blade. "Shall I see what the Illyrians taught you?"

He was upon her before she could lift the sword higher.

Nesta jumped back, clipping his sword with her own, eyes flaring wide. The king lunged again, and Nesta again dodged and retreated through the trees.

Leading him away—away from Cassian.

She managed to draw him another few feet before the king grew bored.

In two movements, he had her disarmed. In another, he struck her across the face, so hard she went down.

Cassian cried out her name, trying again to crawl to her.

The king only sheathed his sword, towering over her as she pushed off the ground. "Well? What else do you have?"

Nesta turned over, and threw out a hand.

White, burning power shot out of her palm and slammed into his chest.

A ploy. To get him close. To lower his guard.

Her power sent him flying back, trees snapping under him. One after another after another.

The Cauldron seemed to settle. All that was left—that was it. All that was left of her power.

Nesta surged to her feet, staggering across the clearing, blood at her mouth from where he'd hit her, and threw herself to her knees before Cassian. "Get up," she sobbed, hauling at his shoulder. "*Get up.*"

He tried—and failed.

"You're too heavy," she pleaded, but still tried to raise him, fingers scrabbling in his black, bloodied armor. "I can't—he's coming—"

"Go," Cassian groaned.

Her power had stopped hurling the king across the forest. He now stalked toward them, brushing off splinters and leaves from his jacket—taking his time. Knowing she would not leave. Savoring the awaiting slaughter.

Nesta gritted her teeth, trying to haul Cassian up once more. A broken sound of pain ripped from him. "*Go!*" he barked at her.

"I can't," she breathed, voice breaking. "I *can't.*"

The same words Rhys had given him.

Cassian grunted in pain, but lifted his bloodied hands—to cup her face. "I have no regrets in my life, but this." His voice shook with every word. "That we did not have time. That I did not have time with *you*, Nesta."

She didn't stop him as he leaned up and kissed her—lightly. As much as he could manage.

Cassian said softly, brushing away the tear that streaked down her face, "I will find you again in the next world—the next life. And we will have that time. I promise."

The King of Hybern stepped into that clearing, dark power wafting from his fingertips.

And even the Cauldron seemed to pause in surprise—surprise or some . . . *feeling* as Nesta looked at the king with death twining around his hands, then down at Cassian.

And covered Cassian's body with her own.

Cassian went still—then his hand slid over her back.

Together. They'd go together.

I will offer you a bargain, I said to the Cauldron. *I will offer you my soul. Save them.*

"Romantic," the king said, "but ill-advised."

Nesta did not move from where she shielded Cassian's body.

The king raised his hand, power whirling like a dark galaxy in his palm.

I knew they'd both die the moment that power hit them.

Anything, I begged the Cauldron. *Anything—*

The king's hand began to drop.

And then halted. A choking noise came out of him.

For a moment, I thought the Cauldron had answered my pleas.

But as a black blade broke through the king's throat, spraying blood, I realized someone else had.

Elain stepped out of a shadow behind him, and rammed Truth-Teller to the hilt through the back of the king's neck as she snarled in his ear, "*Don't you touch my sister.*"

CHAPTER
75

The Cauldron purred in Elain's presence as the King of Hybern slumped to his knees, clawing at the knife jutting through his throat. Elain backed away a step.

Choking, blood dribbling from his lips, the king gaped at Nesta. My sister lunged to her feet.

Not to go to Elain. But to the king.

Nesta wrapped her hand around Truth-Teller's obsidian hilt.

And slowly, as if savoring every bit of effort it took . . . Nesta began to twist the blade. Not a rotation of the blade itself—but a rotation *into* his neck.

Elain rushed to Cassian, but the warrior was panting—smiling grimly and panting—as Nesta twisted and twisted the blade into the king's neck. Severing flesh and bone and tendon.

Nesta looked down at the king before she made the final pass, his hands still trying to rise, to claw the blade free.

And in Nesta's eyes . . . it was the same look, the same gleam that she'd had that day in Hybern. When she pointed her finger at him in a death-promise. She smiled a little—as if she remembered, too.

And then she pushed the blade, like a worker heaving the spoke of a mighty, grinding wheel.

The king's eyes flared—then his head tumbled off his shoulders.

"Nesta," Cassian groaned, trying to reach for her.

The king's blood sprayed her leathers, her face.

Nesta didn't seem to care as she bent over. As she took up his fallen head and lifted it. Lifted it in the air and stared at it—into Hybern's dead eyes, his gaping mouth.

She did not smile. She only stared and stared and stared.

Savage. Unyielding. Brutal.

"Nesta," Elain whispered.

Nesta blinked, and seemed to realize it, then—whose head she was holding.

What she and Elain had done.

The king's head rolled from her bloodied hands.

The Cauldron seemed to realize what she'd done, too, as his head thumped onto the mossy ground. That Elain . . . Elain had defended this thief. Elain, who it had gifted with such powers, found her so lovely it had wanted to give her *something* . . . It would not harm Elain, even in its hunt to reclaim what had been taken.

It retreated the moment Elain's eyes fell on our dead father lying in the adjacent clearing.

The moment the scream came out of her.

No. I lunged for them, but the Cauldron was too fast. Too strong.

It whipped me back, back, back—across the battlefield.

No one seemed to know the king was dead. And our armies . . .

Rhys and the other High Lords had given themselves wholly to the monsters that lurked under their skins, swaths of enemy soldiers dying in their wake, shredded or gutted or rent in two. And Helion—

The High Lord of Day was bloodied, his golden fur singed and torn, but he still battled against the Hybern commander. The commander remained unmarred. His face unruffled. As if he knew—he might very well win against Helion Spell-Cleaver today.

We arced away, across the field. To Bryaxis—still fighting. Holding the line for Graysen's men. A black cloud that cut a path for them, shielded them. Bryaxis, Fear itself, guarding the mortals.

We passed Drakon and a black-haired woman with skin like dark honey, both squaring off against—

Jurian. They were fighting Jurian. Drakon had an ancient score to settle—and so did Miryam.

We whisked by so quickly I couldn't hear what was said, couldn't see if Jurian was indeed fighting back or trying to fend them off while he explained. Mor joined the fray, bloodied and limping, shouting at them—it was the least of our problems.

Because our armies . . .

Hybern was overwhelming us. Without the king, without the Cauldron, they'd still do it. The fervor the king had roused in them, their belief that they had been wronged and forgotten . . . They'd keep fighting. No solution would ever appease them beyond the complete reclaiming of what they still believed they were entitled to—*deserved*.

There were too many. So many. And we were all drained.

The Cauldron hurtled away, withdrawing toward itself.

There was a roar of pain—a roar I recognized, even with the different, harrowing form.

Rhys. *Rhys*—

He was faltering, he needed *help*—

The Cauldron sucked back into itself, and I was again atop that rock.

Again staring at Amren, who was slapping my face, shouting my name.

"*Stupid girl*," she barked. "*Fight it!*"

Rhys was hurt. Rhys was being overwhelmed—

I snapped back into my body. My hand remained atop the Cauldron.

A living bond. But with the Cauldron settled into itself . . . I blinked. I *could* blink.

Amren blew out a breath. "What in *hell*—"

"The king is dead," I said, my voice cold and foreign. "And you're going to be soon, too."

I'd kill her for this, for betraying us for whatever reason—

"I know," Amren said quietly. "And I need you to help me do it."

I almost let go of the Cauldron at the words, but she shook her head. "Don't break it—the contact. I need you to be . . . a conduit."

"I don't understand."

"The Suriel—it gave you a message. For me. Only me."

My brows narrowed.

Amren said, "The answer in the Book was no spell of control. I lied about that. It was . . . an unbinding spell. For me."

"What?"

Amren looked to the carnage, the screams of the dying ringing us. "I thought I'd need your sisters to help you control the Cauldron, but after you faced the Ouroboros . . . I knew you could do it. Just you. And just me. Because when you unbind me with the Cauldron's power, in my real form . . . I will wipe that army away. Every last one of them."

"Amren—"

But a male voice pleaded from behind, "*Don't.*"

Varian appeared from the rocky path, gasping for breath, splattered with blood.

Amren smirked. "Like a hound on a scent."

"Don't," was all Varian said.

"Unleash me," Amren said, ignoring him. "Let me end this."

I began shaking my head. "You—you will be *gone*. You said you won't remember us, won't be *you* anymore if you're freed."

Amren smiled slightly—at me, at Varian. "I watched them for so many eons. Humans—in my world, there were humans, too. And I watched them love, and hate—wage senseless war and find precious peace. Watched them build lives, build *worlds*. I was . . . I was never allowed such things. I had not been designed that way, had not been ordered to do so. So I watched. And that day I came here . . . it was the first selfish thing I had done. For a long, long while I thought it was punishment for disobeying my Father's orders, for *wanting*. I thought this world was some hell he'd locked me into for disobedience."

Amren swallowed.

"But I think . . . I wonder if my Father knew. If he saw how I watched them love and hate and build, and opened that rip in the world not as punishment . . . but as a gift." Her eyes gleamed. "For it has been a gift. This time—with you. With all of you. It has been a gift."

"Amren," Varian said, and sank onto his knees. "I am *begging* you—"

"Tell the High Lord," she said softly, "to leave out a cup for me."

I did not think I had it in my heart for another ounce of sorrow. I gripped the Cauldron a little harder my throat thick. "I will."

She looked to Varian, a wry smile on her red mouth. "I watched them most—the humans who loved. I never understood it—*how* it happened. *Why* it happened." She paused a step away from the Cauldron. "I think I might have learned with you, though. Perhaps that was a last gift, too."

Varian's face twisted with anguish. But he made no further move to stop her.

She turned to me. And spoke the words into my head—the spell I must think and feel and *do*. I nodded.

"When I am free," Amren said to us, "do not run. It will attract my attention."

She lifted a steady hand toward my arm.

"I am glad we met, Feyre."

I smiled at her, bowing my head. "Me too, Amren. Me too."

Amren grabbed my wrist. And swung herself into the Cauldron.

⊹

I fought. I fought with every breath to get through the spell, my arm half-submerged in the Cauldron as Amren went under the dark water that had filled it. I said the words with my tongue, said them with my heart and blood and bones. Screamed them.

Her hand vanished from my arm, melting away like dew under the morning sun.

The spell ended, shuddering out of me, and I snapped back, losing my hold on the Cauldron. Varian caught me before I fell, and gripped me hard as we gazed at the black mass of the Cauldron, the still surface.

He breathed, "Is she——"

It started far, far beneath us. As if she had gone to the earth's core.

I let Varian haul me a few steps away as the ripple thundered up through the ground, spearing for us, the Cauldron.

We had only enough time to throw ourselves behind the nearest rock when it hit us.

The Cauldron shattered into three pieces, peeling apart like a blossoming flower—and then she came.

She exploded from that mortal shell, light blinding us. Light and fire.

She was roaring—in victory and rage and pain.

And I could have sworn I saw great, burning wings, each feather a simmering ember, spread wide. Could have sworn a crown of incandescent light floated just above her flaming hair.

She paused. The thing that was inside Amren paused.

Looked at us—at the battlefield and all of our friends, our family still fighting on it.

As if to say, *I remember you.*

And then she was gone.

She spread those wings, flame and light rippling to encompass her, no more than a burning behemoth that swept down upon Hybern's armies.

They began running.

Amren came down on them like a hammer, raining fire and brimstone.

She swept through them, burning them, drinking in their death. Some died at the mere whisper of her passing.

I heard Rhys bellowing—and the sound was the same as hers. Victory and rage and pain. And warning. A warning not to run from her.

Bit by bit, she destroyed that endless Hybern army. Bit by bit, she wiped away their taint, their threat. The suffering they had brought.

She shattered through that Hybern commander, poised to strike Helion a deathblow. Shattered through that commander as if he were made of glass. She left only ashes behind.

But that power—it was fading. Vanishing ember by ember.

Yet Amren went to the sea, where my father and Vassa's army battled alongside Miryam's people. Entire boats full of Hybern soldiers fell still after she passed.

As if she had inhaled the life right out of them. Even while her own life sputtered out.

Amren reached the final boat—the very last ship of our enemy— and was no more than a flame on the breeze.

And when that ship, too, fell silent . . .

There was only light. Bright, clean light, dancing on the waves.

CHAPTER
76

Tears slid down Varian's blood-flecked skin as we watched that spot on the sea where Amren had vanished.

Below, beyond, our forces were beginning to cry out with victory—with joy.

Up on the rock . . . utter quiet.

I looked at last toward the broken thirds of the Cauldron.

Perhaps I had done it. In unbinding her, I had unbound the Cauldron. Or perhaps Amren in her unleashed power . . . even that had been too great for the Cauldron.

"We should go," I said to Varian. The others would be looking for us.

I had to get my father. Had to bury him. Help Cassian.

Had to see who else was among the dead—or living.

Hollow—I was so tired and hollow.

I managed to stand. To take one step before I felt it.

The . . . *thing* in the Cauldron. Or lack of it.

It was lack and substance, absence and presence. And . . . it was leaking into the world.

I dared a step toward it. And what I beheld in those ruins of the Cauldron . . .

It was a void. But also *not* a void—a growth.

It did not belong here. Belong anywhere.

There were hands at my face, turning me, touching me. "Are you hurt, are you—"

Rhys's face was battered—bloody. His hands were still tipped in talons, his canines still elongated. Barely out of that beast form. "You—you freed her—"

He was stammering. Shaking. I wasn't entirely sure how he was even standing.

I didn't know where to begin. How to explain.

I let him into my mind, his presence gentle—and as exhausted as I was, I let him see my father. Nesta and Cassian. The king. And Amren.

All of it.

Including that *thing* behind us. That hole.

Rhys folded me into his arms—just for a moment.

"We have a problem," Varian murmured, pointing behind us.

We followed the line of his finger. To where that fissure in the world within the shards of the Cauldron . . . It was growing.

The Cauldron could never be destroyed, we had been warned. Because our very *world* was bound to it.

If the Cauldron were destroyed . . . we would be, too.

"What have I done," I breathed. I had saved our friends—only to damn us all.

Made. Made and un-Made.

I had broken it. I could remake it again.

I ran for the Book, flinging open the pages.

But the gold was engraved with symbols only one being on this earth knew how to read, and she was gone. I hurled the damn thing into the void inside the Cauldron.

It vanished and did not appear again.

"Well, that's one way to try," Rhys said.

I whirled at the humor, but his face was hard. Grim.

"I don't know what to do," I whispered.

Rhys studied the ruins. "Amren said you were a conduit." I nodded. "So be one again."

"What?"

He looked at me like *I* was the insane one as he said, "Remake the Cauldron. Forge it anew."

"With *what* power?"

"My own."

"You're—you're drained, Rhys. So am I. We all are."

"Try. Humor me."

I blinked, that edge of panic dulling a bit. Yes—yes, with him, with my mate . . .

I thought through the spell Amren had shown me. If I changed one small thing . . . It was a gamble. But it might work.

"Better than nothing," I said, blowing out a breath.

"That's the spirit." Humor danced in his eyes.

The dead lay around us for miles, cries of the wounded and grieving starting to rise up, but . . . We had stopped Hybern. Stopped the king.

Perhaps in this . . . in this we would be lucky, too.

I reached for him—with my hand, my mind.

His shields were up—solid walls he'd erected during battle. I brushed a hand along one, but it remained. Rhys smiled down at me, kissed me once. "Remind me to never get on Nesta's bad side."

That he could even *joke*—no, it was a form of enduring. For both of us. Because the alternative to laughter . . . Varian's devastated face, watching us silently, was the alternative. And with this thing before us, this final task . . .

So I managed a laugh.

And I was still smiling, just a bit, when I again laid my hand on the broken shards of the Cauldron.

⊹

It was a hole. Airless. No life could exist here. No light.

It was . . . it was what had existed at the beginning. Before all things had exploded from it.

It did not belong here. Maybe one day, when the earth had grown old and died, when the stars had vanished, too . . . maybe then, we would return to this place.

Not today. Not now.

I was both form and nothing.

And behind me . . . Rhys's power was a tether. An unending lightning strike that surged from me into this . . . place. To be shaped as I willed it.

Made and un-Made.

From a distant corner of my memory, my human mind . . . I remembered a mural I had seen at the Spring Court. Tucked away in a dusty, unused library. It told the story of Prythian.

It told the story of a Cauldron. *This* Cauldron.

And when it was held by female hands . . . All life flowed from it.

I reached mine out, Rhys's power rippling through me.

United. Joined as one. Ask and answer.

I was not afraid. Not with him there.

I cupped my hands as if the cracked thirds of the Cauldron could fit into them. The entire universe into the palm of my hand.

I began to speak that last spell Amren had found us. Speak and think and feel it. Word and breath and blood.

Rhys's power flowed through me, out of me. The Cauldron appeared.

Light danced along the fissures where the broken thirds had come together. There—there I would need to forge. To weld. To *bind*.

I put a hand against the side of the Cauldron. Raw, brutal power cascaded out of me.

I leaned back into him, unafraid of that power, of the male who held me.

It flowed and flowed, a burst dam of night.

The cracks fizzled and blurred.

That void began to slither back in.

More. We needed more.

He gave it to me. Rhys handed over everything.

I was a bearer, a vessel, a link.

I love you, he whispered into my mind.

I only leaned back into him, savoring his warmth, even in this non-place.

Power shuddered through him. Wrapped around the Cauldron. I recited the spell over and over and over.

The first crack healed.

Then the second.

I felt him tremble behind me, heard his wet rasp of breath. I tried to turn—

I love you, he said again.

The third and final crack began to heal over.

His power began to sputter. But it kept flowing out.

I threw mine into it, sparks and snow and light and water. Together, we threw everything in. We gave every last drop.

Until that Cauldron was whole. Until the thing it contained . . . it was in there. Locked away.

Until I could feel the sun again warming my face. And saw that Cauldron squatting before me—beneath my hand.

I eased my fingers from the icy iron rim. Gazed down into the inky depths.

No cracks. Whole.

I loosed a shuddering breath. We had done it. We had done—

I turned.

It took me a moment to grasp it. What I saw.

Rhys was sprawled on the rocky ground, wings draped behind him.

He looked like he was sleeping.

But as I breathed in—

It wasn't there.

That thing that rose and fell with each breath. That echoed each heartbeat.

The mating bond.

It wasn't there. It was gone.

Because his own chest . . . it was not moving.

And Rhys was dead.

CHAPTER
77

I had only silence in my head. Only silence, as I began screaming.

Screaming and screaming and screaming.

The emptiness in my chest, my *soul* at the lack of that bond, that *life*—

I was shaking him, screaming his name and shaking him, and my body stopped being my body and just became this *thing* that held me and this *lack* of him, and I could not stop screaming and screaming—

Then Mor was there. And Azriel, swaying on his feet, an arm hooked around Cassian—just as bloody and barely standing thanks to the blue, webbed Siphon-patches all over him. Over them both.

They were saying things, but all I could hear was that last *I love you*, which had not been a declaration but a good-bye.

And he had known. He had *known* he had nothing left, and stopping it would take everything. It would *cost* him everything. He'd kept his shields up so I wouldn't see, because I wouldn't have said yes, I would have rather the world *ended* than this, this *thing* he had done and this *emptiness* where he was, where we were—

Someone was trying to haul me away from him, and I let out a sound that might have been a snarl or another scream, and they let go.

SARA J. MAAS

I couldn't live with this, couldn't endure this, couldn't *breathe*—

There were hands—unknown hands on his throat. Touching him—

I lunged for them, but someone held me back. "He's seeing if there's anything to be done," Mor said, voice raw.

He—him. Thesan. High Lord of the Dawn. And of healing. I lunged again, to beg him, to plead—

But he shook his head. At Mor. At the others.

Tarquin was there. Helion. Panting and battered. "He . . . ," Helion rasped, then shook his head, closing his eyes. "Of course he did," he said, more to himself than anyone.

"Please," I said, and wasn't sure who I was speaking to. My fingers scraped against Rhys's armor, trying to get to the heart beneath.

The Cauldron—maybe the Cauldron—

I did not know those spells. How to put him in and make sure *he* came back out—

Hands wrapped around my own. They were blood-splattered and cut up, but gentle. I tried to pull away, but they held firm as Tarquin knelt beside me and said, "I'm sorry."

It was those two words that shattered me. Shattered me in a way I didn't know I could still be broken, a rending of every tether and leash.

Stay with the High Lord. The Suriel's last warning. *Stay . . . and live to see everything righted*.

A lie. A *lie*, as Rhys had lied to me. *Stay with the High Lord*.

Stay.

For there . . . the torn scraps of the mating bond. Floating on a phantom wind inside me. I grasped at them—tugged at them, as if he'd answer.

Stay. Stay, stay, stay.

I clung to those scraps and remnants, clawing at the void that lurked beyond.

Stay.

I looked up at Tarquin, lip curling back from my teeth. Looked at

Helion. And Thesan. And Beron and Kallias, Viviane weeping at his side. And I snarled, "*Bring him back*."

Blank faces.

I screamed at them, "*BRING HIM BACK*."

Nothing.

"You did it for me," I said, breathing hard. "*Now do it for him*."

"You were a human," Helion said carefully. "It is not the same—"

"I don't care. Do it." When they didn't move, I rallied the dregs of my power, readying to rip into their minds and force them, not caring what rules or laws it broke. I wouldn't care, only if—

Tarquin stepped forward. He slowly extended his hand toward me.

"For what he gave," Tarquin said quietly. "Today and for many years before."

And as that seed of light appeared in his palm . . . I began crying again. Watched it drop onto Rhys's bare throat and vanish into the skin beneath, an echo of light flaring once.

Helion stepped forward. That kernel of light in his hand flickered as it fell onto Rhys's skin.

Then Kallias. And Thesan.

Until only Beron stood there.

Mor drew her sword and laid it on his throat. He jerked, having not even seen her move. "I do not mind making one more kill today," she said.

Beron gave her a withering glare, but shoved off the sword and strode forward. He practically chucked that fleck of light onto Rhys. I didn't care about that, either.

I didn't know the spell, the power it came from. But I was High Lady.

I held out my palm. Willing that spark of life to appear. Nothing happened.

I took a steadying breath, remembering how it had looked. "Tell me how," I growled to no one.

Thesan coughed and stepped forward. Explaining the core of power and on and on and I didn't care, but I listened, until—

There. Small as a sunflower seed, it appeared in my palm. A bit of me—my life.

I laid it gently on Rhys's blood-crusted throat.

And I realized, just as he appeared, what was missing.

Tamlin stood there, summoned by either the death of a fellow High Lord or one of the others around me. He was splattered in mud and gore, his new bandolier of knives mostly empty.

He studied Rhys, lifeless before me. Studied all of us—the palms still out.

There was no kindness on his face. No mercy.

"Please," was all I said to him.

Then Tamlin glanced between us—me and my mate. His face did not change.

"*Please*," I wept. "I will—I will give you *anything*—"

Something shifted in his eyes at that. But not kindness. No emotion at all.

I laid my head on Rhysand's chest, listening for any kind of heartbeat through that armor.

"Anything," I breathed to no one in particular. "Anything."

Steps scuffed on the rocky ground. I braced myself for another set of hands trying to pull me away, and dug my fingers in harder.

The steps remained behind me for long enough that I looked.

Tamlin stood there. Staring down at me. Those green eyes swimming with some emotion I couldn't place.

"Be happy, Feyre," he said quietly.

And dropped that final kernel of light onto Rhysand.

⊹

I had not witnessed it—when it had been done to me.

So all I did was hold on to him. To his body, to the tatters of that bond.

Stay, I begged. *Stay*.

Light glowed beyond my shut eyelids.

Stay.

And in the silence . . . I began to tell him.

About that first night I'd seen him. When I'd heard that voice beckoning me to the hills. When I couldn't resist its summons, and now . . . now I wondered if I had heard him calling for me on Calanmai. If it had been his voice that brought me there that night.

I told him how I had fallen in love with him—every glance and passed note and croak of laughter he coaxed from me. I told him of everything we'd done, and what it had meant to me, and all that I still wanted to do. All the *life* still left before us.

And in return . . . a thud sounded.

I opened my eyes. Another thud.

And then his chest rose, lifting my head with it.

I couldn't move, couldn't breathe—

A hand brushed my back.

Then Rhys groaned, "If we're all here, either things went very, very wrong or very right."

Cassian's broken laugh cracked out of him.

I couldn't lift my head, couldn't do anything but hold him, savoring every heartbeat and breath and the rumble of his voice as Rhys rasped, "You lot will be pleased to know . . . My power remains my own. No thieving here."

"You do know how to make an entrance," Helion drawled. "Or should I say exit?"

"You're horrible," Viviane snapped. "That's not even remotely funny—"

I didn't hear what else they said. Rhys sat up, lifting me off him. He brushed away the hair clinging to my damp cheeks.

"*Stay with the High Lord*," he murmured.

I hadn't believed it—until I looked into that face. Those star-flecked eyes.

Hadn't let myself believe it wasn't anything but some delusion—

"It's real," he said, kissing my brow. "And—there's another surprise."

He pointed with a healed hand toward the Cauldron. "Someone fish out dear Amren before she catches a cold."

Varian whirled toward us. But Mor was sprinting for the Cauldron, and her cry as she reached in—

"How?" I breathed.

Azriel and Varian were there, helping Mor heave a waterlogged form out of the dark water.

Her chest rose and fell, her features the same, but . . .

"She was there," Rhys said. "When the Cauldron was sealing. Going . . . wherever we go."

Amren sputtered water, vomiting onto the rocky ground. Mor thumped her back, coaxing her through it.

"So I reached out a hand," Rhys went on quietly. "To see if she might want to come back."

And as Amren opened her eyes, as Varian let out a choked sound of relief and joy—

I knew—what she had given up to come back. High Fae—and just that.

For her silver eyes were solid. Unmoving. No smoke, no burning mist in them.

A normal life, no trace of her powers to be seen.

And as Amren smiled at me . . . I wondered if that had been her last gift.

If it all . . . if it all had been a gift.

CHAPTER
78

Amongst the sprawling field of corpses and wounded, there was one body I wanted to bury.

Only Nesta, Elain, and I returned to that clearing, once Azriel had given the all-clear that the battle was well and truly over.

Letting Rhys out of my sight to wrangle our scattered armies, sort through the living and dead, and figure out some semblance of order was an effort in self-control.

I nearly begged Rhys to come with us, so I didn't have to let go of his hand, which I had not stopped clutching since those moments I'd heard his beautiful, solid heartbeat echoing into his body once more.

But this task, this farewell . . . I knew, deep down, that it was only for my sisters and me.

So I released Rhys's hand, kissing him once, twice, and left him in the war-camp to help Mor haul a barely standing Cassian to the nearest healer.

Nesta was watching them when I reached her and Elain at the tree-lined outskirts. Had she done some healing, somehow, in those moments after she'd severed the king's head? Or had it been Cassian's immortal blood and Azriel's battlefield patching that had already healed him enough to manage to stand, even with the wing and leg? I didn't ask my sister, and she supplied no answer as she took the water bucket dangling from Elain's still-bloody hands, and I followed them both through the trees.

The King of Hybern's corpse lay in the clearing, crows already picking at it.

Nesta spat on it before we approached our father. The crows barely scattered in time.

The screams and moaning of the wounded was a distant wall of sound—another world away from the sun-dappled clearing. From the blood still fresh on the moss and grass. I blocked out the coppery tang of it—Cassian's blood, the king's blood, Nesta's blood.

Only our father had not bled. He hadn't been given the chance to. And through whatever small mercy of the Mother, the crows hadn't started on him.

Elain quietly washed his face. Combed out his hair and beard. Straightened his clothes.

She found flowers—somewhere. She laid them at his head, on his chest.

We stared down at him in silence.

"I love you," Elain whispered, voice breaking.

Nesta said nothing, face unreadable. There were such shadows in her eyes. I had not told her what I'd seen—had let them tell me what they wanted.

Elain breathed, "Should we—say a prayer?"

We did not have such things in the human world, I remembered. My sisters had no prayers to offer him. But in Prythian . . .

"Mother hold you," I whispered, reciting words I had not heard since that day Under the Mountain. "May you pass through the gates; may you smell that immortal land of milk and honey." Flame ignited at my fingertips. All I could muster. All that was left. "Fear no evil. Feel no pain." My mouth trembled as I breathed, "May you enter eternity."

Tears slid down Elain's pallid cheeks as she adjusted an errant flower on our father's chest, white-petaled and delicate, and then backed away to my side with a nod.

Nesta's face did not shift as I sent that fire to ignite our father's body.

He was ash on the wind in a matter of moments.

We stared at the burned slab of earth for long minutes, the sun shifting overhead.

Steps crunched on the grass behind us.

Nesta whirled, but—

Lucien. It was Lucien.

Lucien, haggard and bloody, panting for breath. As if he'd run from the shore.

His gaze settled on Elain, and he sagged a little. But Elain only wrapped her arms around herself and remained at my side.

"Are you hurt?" he asked, coming toward us. Spying the blood speckling Elain's hands.

He halted short as he noticed the King of Hybern's decapitated head on the other side of the clearing. Nesta was still showered with his blood.

"I'm fine," Elain said quietly. And then asked, noticing the gore on him, the torn clothes and still-bloody weapons, "Are you—"

"Well, I never want to fight in another battle as long as I live, but . . . yes, I'm in one piece."

A faint smile bloomed on Elain's lips. But Lucien noticed that scorched patch of grass behind us and said, "I heard—what happened. I'm sorry for your loss. All of you."

I just strode to him and threw my arms around his neck, even if it wasn't the embrace he was hoping for. "Thank you—for coming. With the battle, I mean."

"I've got one hell of a story to tell you," he said, squeezing me tightly. "And don't be surprised if Vassa corners you as soon as the ships are sorted. And the sun sets."

"Is she really—"

"Yes. But your father, ever the negotiator . . ." A sad, small smile toward that burnt grass. "He managed to cut a deal with Vassa's *keeper* to come here. Temporarily, but . . . better than nothing. But yes—queen by night, firebird by day." He blew out a breath. "Nasty curse."

"The human queens are still out there," I said. Maybe I'd hunt them down.

"Not for long—not if Vassa has anything to do with it."

"You sound like an acolyte."

Lucien blushed, glancing at Elain. "She's got a foul temper and a fouler mouth." He cut me a wry look. "You'll get along just fine."

I nudged him in the ribs.

But Lucien again looked at that singed grass, and his blood-splattered face turned solemn. "He was a good man," he said. "He loved you all very much."

I nodded, unable to form the words. The thoughts. Nesta didn't so much as blink to indicate she'd heard. Elain just wrapped her arms tighter around herself, a few more tears streaking free.

I spared Lucien the torment of debating whether to touch her, and linked my arm through his as I began to walk away, letting my sisters decide to follow or remain—if they wanted a moment alone with that burnt grass.

Elain came.

Nesta stayed.

Elain fell into step beside me, peering at Lucien. He noticed it. "I heard you made the killing blow," he said.

Elain studied the trees ahead. "Nesta did. I just stabbed him."

Lucien seemed to fumble for a response, but I said to him, "So where now? Off with Vassa?" I wondered if he'd heard of Tamlin's role—the help he'd given us. A look at my friend showed me he had. Someone, perhaps my mate, had informed him.

Lucien shrugged. "First—here. To help. Then . . ." Another glance at Elain. "Who knows?"

I nudged Elain, who blinked at me, then blurted, "You could come to Velaris."

He saw all of it, but nodded graciously. "It would be my pleasure."

As we strode back to the camp, Lucien told us of his time away—how he'd hunted for Vassa, how he'd found her already with my father, an army marching westward. How Miryam and Drakon had found them on their own journey to help us.

I was still mulling over all he said when I slipped into my tent to finally change out of my leathers, leaving him and Elain to go find a place to wash up. And talk—perhaps.

But as I strode through the flaps, sound greeted me within—talking. Many voices, one of them belonging to my mate.

I got one step inside and knew I wouldn't be changing my clothes anytime soon.

For seated in a chair before the brazier was Prince Drakon, Rhys sprawled and still bloody on the cushions across from him. And on the pillows beside Rhys sat a lovely female, her dark hair tumbling down her back in luscious curls, already smiling at me.

Miryam.

CHAPTER
79

Miryam's smiling face was more human than High Fae. But Miryam, I remembered as she and Drakon rose to their feet to greet me, was only half Fae. She bore the delicately pointed ears, but . . . there was something still human about her. In that broad smile that lit up her brown eyes.

I instantly liked her. Mud splattered her own leathers—a different make than the Illyrians', but obviously designed by another aerial people to keep warm in the skies—and a few speckles of blood coated the honey-brown skin along her neck and hands, but she didn't seem to notice. Or care. She held out her hands to me. "High Lady," Miryam said, her accent the same as Drakon's. Rolling and rich.

I took her hands, surprised to find them dry and warm. She squeezed my fingers tightly while I managed to say, "I've heard so much about you—thank you for coming." I cast a look at where Rhys still remained sprawled on the cushions, watching us with raised brows. "For someone who was just dead," I said tightly, "you seem remarkably relaxed."

Rhys smirked. "I'm glad you're bouncing back to your usual spirits, Feyre darling."

Drakon snorted, and took my hands, squeezing them as tightly as his mate had. "What he doesn't want to tell you, my lady, is that he's so damn old he *can't* stand up right now."

I whirled to Rhys. "Are you——"

"Fine, fine," Rhys said, waving a hand, even as he groaned a bit. "Though perhaps now you see why I didn't bother visiting these two for so long. They're terribly cruel to me."

Miryam laughed, plopping down on the cushions again. "Your mate was in the middle of telling us *your* story, as it seems you've already heard ours."

I had, but even as Prince Drakon gracefully returned to his seat and I slid into the chair beside his, just watching the two of them . . . I wanted to know the entire thing. One day——not tomorrow or the day after, but . . . one day, I wanted to hear their tale in full. But for now . . .

"I——saw you two. Battling Jurian." Drakon instantly stiffened, Miryam's eyes going shuttered as I asked, "Is he . . . Is he dead?"

"No," was all Drakon said.

"Mor," Miryam cut in, frowning, "wound up convincing us not to . . . settle things."

They would have. From the expression on Drakon's face, the prince still didn't seem convinced. And from the haunted gleam in Miryam's eyes, it seemed as if far more had occurred during that fight than they let on. But I still asked, "Where is he?"

Drakon shrugged. "After we didn't kill him, I have no idea where he slithered off to."

Rhys gave me a half smile. "He's with Lord Graysen's men——seeing to the wounded."

Miryam asked carefully, "Are you——friends with Jurian?"

"No," I said. "I mean——I don't think so. But . . . every word he said was true. And he did help me. A great deal."

Neither of them so much as nodded as they exchanged a long glance, unspoken words passing between them.

Rhys asked, "I thought I saw Nephelle during the battle——any chance I'll get to say hello, or is she too important now to bother with me?" Laughter—beautiful laughter—danced in his eyes.

I straightened, smiling. "She's here?"

Drakon lifted a dark brow. "You know Nephelle?"

"Know *of* her," I said, and glanced toward the tent flaps as if she'd come striding right in. "I—it's a long story."

"We have time to hear it," Miryam said, then added, "Or . . . a bit of time, I suppose."

For there were indeed many, many things to sort out. Including—

I shook my head. "Later," I said to Miryam, to her mate. The proof that a world could exist without a wall, without a Treaty. "There's something . . ." I relayed my thought down the bond to Rhys, earning a nod of approval before I said, "Is your island still secret?"

Miryam and Drakon exchanged a guilty look. "We do apologize for that," Miryam offered. "It seems that the glamour worked *too* well, if it kept well-meaning messengers away." She shook her head, those beautiful curls moving with her. "We would have come sooner—we left the moment we realized what trouble you all were in."

"No," I said, shaking my own head, scrambling for the words. "No—I don't blame you. Mother above, we owe you . . ." I blew out a breath. "We are in your debt." Drakon and Miryam objected to that, but I went on, "What I mean is . . . If there was an object of terrible power that now needed to be hidden . . . Would Cretea remain a good place to conceal it?"

Again that look between them, a look between mates. "Yes," Drakon said.

Miryam breathed, "You mean the Cauldron."

I nodded. It had been hauled into our camp, guarded by whatever Illyrians could still stand. None of the other High Lords had asked—for now. But I could see the debate that would rage, the war we might start internally over who, exactly, got to keep the Cauldron. "It needs to disappear," I said softly. "Permanently." I added, "Before anyone remembers to lay claim to it."

Drakon and Miryam considered, some unspoken conversation passing between them, perhaps down their own mating bond. "When we leave," Drakon said at last, "one of our ships might find itself a little heavier in the water."

I smiled. "Thank you."

"When are you, exactly, planning to leave?" Rhys asked, lifting a brow.

"Kicking us out already?" Drakon said with a half smile.

"A few days," Miryam cut in wryly. "As soon as the injured are ready."

"Good," I said.

They all looked to me. I swallowed. "I mean . . . Not that I'm glad for you to go . . ." The amusement in Miryam's eyes spread, twinkling. I smiled myself. "I want you here. Because I'd like to call a meeting."

┿

A day later . . . I didn't know how it'd come together so quickly. I'd merely explained what I wanted, what we *needed* to do, and . . . Rhys and Drakon made it happen.

There was no proper space to do it—not with the camps in disarray. But there was one place—a few miles off.

And as the sun set and my family's half-ruined estate became filled with High Lords and princes, generals and commanders, humans and Fae . . . I still didn't have the words to really express it. How we could all gather in the giant sitting room, the only usable space in my family's old estate, and actually have . . . this meeting.

I'd slept through the night, deep and undisturbed, Rhys in bed beside me. I hadn't let go of him until dawn had leaked into our tent. And then . . . the war-camps were too full of blood and injured and the dead. And there was this meeting to arrange between various armies and camps and peoples.

It took all day, but by the end of it, I found myself in the wrecked foyer, Rhys and the others beside me, the chandelier a broken mass behind us on the cracked marble floor.

The High Lords arrived first. Starting with Beron.

Beron, who did not so much as glance at his son-who-was-not-his-son. Lucien, standing on my other side, didn't acknowledge Beron's existence, either. Or Eris's, as he strode a step behind his father.

Eris was bruised and cut up enough to indicate he must have been in terrible shape after the fighting ceased yesterday, sporting a brutal slice down his cheek and neck—barely healed. Mor let out a satisfied grunt at the sight of it—or perhaps a sound of disappointment that the wound had not been fatal.

Eris continued by as if he hadn't heard it, but didn't sneer at least. Rather—he just nodded at Rhys.

It was silent promise enough: soon. Soon, perhaps, Eris would finally take what he desired—and call in our debt.

We did not bother to nod back. None of us.

Especially not Lucien, who continued dutifully ignoring his eldest brother.

But as Eris strode by . . . I could have sworn there was something like sadness—like regret, as he glanced to Lucien.

Tamlin crossed the threshold moments later.

He had a bandage over his neck, and one over his arm. He came, as he had to that first meeting, with no one in tow.

I wondered if he knew that this wrecked house had been purchased with the money he'd given my father. With the kindness he'd shown them.

But Tamlin's attention didn't go to me.

It went to the person just to my left. To Lucien.

Lucien stepped forward, head high, even as that metal eye whirred. My sisters were already within the sitting room, ready to guide our guests to their predetermined spots. We'd planned those carefully, too.

Tamlin paused a few feet away. None of us said a word. Not as Lucien opened his mouth.

"Tamlin—"

But Tamlin's attention had gone to the clothes Lucien now wore. The Illyrian leathers.

He might as well have been wearing Night Court black.

It was an effort to keep my mouth shut, to not explain that Lucien didn't have any other clothes with him, and that they weren't a sign of his allegiance—

Tamlin just shook his head, loathing simmering in his green eyes, and walked past. Not a word.

I looked at Lucien in time to see the guilt, the devastation, flicker in that russet eye. Rhys had indeed told Lucien everything about Tamlin's covert assistance. His help in dragging Beron here. Saving me at the camp. But Lucien remained standing with us as Tamlin found his place in the sitting room to our right. Did not glance at his friend even once.

Lucien wasn't foolish enough to beg for forgiveness.

That conversation, that confrontation—it would take place at another time. Another day, or week, or month.

I lost track of who filed in afterward. Drakon and Miryam, along with a host of their people. Including—

I started at the slight, dark-haired female who entered on Miryam's right, her wings much smaller than the other Seraphim.

I glanced to where Azriel stood on Rhys's other side, bandaged all over and wings in splints after he'd worked them too hard yesterday. The shadowsinger nodded in confirmation. Nephelle.

I smiled at the legendary warrior-scribe when she noticed my stare as she passed by. She grinned right back at me.

Kallias and Viviane flowed in, along with that female who was indeed her sister. Then Tarquin and Varian. Thesan and his battered Peregryn captain—whose hand he tightly held.

Helion was the last of the High Lords to arrive. I didn't dare look through the ruined doorway to where Lucien now stood in the sitting room, close to Elain's side as she and my sister silently kept against the wall by the intact bay of windows.

Beron, wisely, didn't approach—and Eris only looked over every now and then. To watch.

Helion was limping, flanked by a few of his captains and generals, but still managed a grim smile. "Better enjoy this while it lasts," he said to me and Rhys. "I doubt we'll be so unified when we walk out of here."

"Thank you for the words of encouragement," I said tightly, and Helion chuckled as he eased inside.

More and more people filled that room, the tense conversation broken up by bursts of laughter or greeting. Rhys at last told our family to head into the room—while he and I waited.

Waited and waited, long minutes.

It'd take them longer to arrive, I realized. Since they could not winnow or move as quickly through the world.

I was about to turn into the room to begin without them when two male figures filled the night-darkened doorway.

Jurian. And Graysen.

And behind them . . . a small contingent of other humans.

I swallowed hard. Now the difficult part would begin.

Graysen looked inclined to turn around, the fresh cut down his cheek crinkling as he scowled, but Jurian nudged him in. A black eye bloomed on the left side of Jurian's face. I wondered if Miryam or Drakon had given it to him. My money was on the former.

Graysen only gave us a tight nod. Jurian smirked at me.

"I put you on opposite ends of the room," I said.

From both Miryam and Drakon. And from Elain.

Neither man responded, and only strode, proud and tall, into that room full of Fae.

Rhys kissed my cheek and strode in behind them. Which left—

As Lucien had promised, with darkness now overhead, Vassa found me.

The last to arrive—the last piece of this meeting. She stormed over the threshold, breathless and unfaltering, and paused only a foot away.

Her unbound hair was a reddish gold, thick dark lashes and brows framing the most stunningly blue eyes I'd ever seen. Beautiful, her freckled skin golden-brown and gleaming. Only a few years older than me, but . . . young-feeling. Coltish. Fierce and untamed, despite her curse.

Vassa said in a lilting accent, "Are you Feyre Cursebreaker?"

"Yes," I said, sensing Rhys listening wryly from the other room, where the rest were now beginning to quiet themselves. To wait for me.

Vassa's full mouth tightened. "I am sorry—about your father. He was a great man."

Nesta, striding out of the sitting room, halted at the words. Looked Vassa up and down.

Vassa returned the favor. "You are Nesta," Vassa declared, and I wondered how my father had described her so that Vassa would know. "I am sorry for your loss, too."

Nesta simply regarded her with that cool indifference.

"I heard you slew the King of Hybern," Vassa said, those dark brows narrowing as she again surveyed Nesta, searching for any sign of a warrior beneath the blue dress she wore. Vassa only shrugged to herself when Nesta didn't reply and said to me, "He was a better father to me than my own. I owe much to him, and will honor his memory as long as I live."

The look Nesta was giving the queen was enough to wither the grass beyond the shattered front door. It didn't get any better as Vassa said, "Can you break the curse on me, Feyre Archeron?"

"Is that why you agreed to come so quickly?"

A half smile. "Partly. Lucien suggested you had gifts. And other High Lords do as well."

Like his father—his true one. Helion.

She went on before I could answer. "I do not have much time left— before I must return to the lake. To him."

To the death-lord who held her leash. "Who is he?" I breathed.

Vassa only shook her head, waving a hand as her eyes darkened, and repeated, "Can you break my curse?"

"I—I don't know how to break those kinds of spells," I admitted. Her face fell. I added, "But . . . we can try."

She considered. "With the healing of our armies, I won't be able to leave for some time. Perhaps it will give me a . . . loophole, as Lucien called it, to remain longer." Another shake of the head. "We shall discuss this later," she declared. "Along with the threat my fellow queens pose."

My heart stumbled a beat.

A cruel smile curved Vassa's mouth. "They will try to intervene," she said. "With any sort of peace talks. Hybern sent them back before this battle, but I have no doubt they were smart enough to encourage that. Not to waste their armies here."

"But they will elsewhere?" Nesta demanded.

Vassa tossed her smooth sheet of hair over a shoulder. "We shall see. And you will think of ways to help me."

I waited until she headed for the sitting room before I flicked my brows up at the order. Either she didn't know or didn't care that I was *also* a queen in my right.

Nesta smirked. "Good luck with *that*."

I scowled, shoving down the worry already blooming in my gut, and said, "Where are you going? The meeting is starting."

"Why should I be in there?"

"You're the guest of honor. You killed the king."

Shadows flickered in her face. "So what."

I blinked. "You're our emissary as well. You should be here for this."

Nesta looked toward the stairs, and I noticed the object she clutched in her fist.

The small, wooden carving. I couldn't make out what manner of animal it was, but I knew the wood. Knew the work.

One of the little carvings our father had crafted during those years he—he hadn't done much of anything at all. I looked at her face before she could notice my attention.

Nesta said, "Do you think it will work—this meeting?"

With so many Fae ears in the room beyond, I didn't dare give any answer but the truth. "I don't know. But I'm willing to try." I offered my hand to my sister. "I want you here for this. With me."

Nesta considered that outstretched hand. For a moment, I thought she'd walk away.

But she slid her hand into mine, and together we walked into that room crammed with humans and Fae. Both parts of this world. *All* parts of this world.

High Fae from every court. Miryam and Drakon and their retinue. Humans from many territories.

All watching me and Nesta as we entered, as we strode to where Rhys and the others waited, facing the gathered room. I tried not to cringe at the shattered furniture that had been sorted through for any possible seats. At the ripped wallpaper, the half-dangling curtains. But it was better than nothing.

I supposed the same could be said of our world.

Silence settled. Rhys nudged me forward, a hand brushing the small of my back as I took a step past him. I lifted my chin, scanning the room. And I smiled at them, the humans and Fae assembled here—in peace.

My voice was clear and unwavering. "My name is Feyre Archeron. I was once human—and now I am Fae. I call both worlds my home. And I would like to discuss renegotiating the Treaty."

CHAPTER
80

A world divided was not a world that could thrive.

That first meeting went on for hours, many of us short-tempered with exhaustion, but . . . channels were made. Stories were exchanged. Tales narrated of either side of the wall.

I told them my story.

All of it.

I told it to the strangers who did not know me, I told it to my friends, and I told it to Tamlin, hard-faced by the distant wall. I explained the years of poverty, the trials Under the Mountain, the love I had found and let go, the love that had healed and saved me. My voice did not quaver. My voice did not break. Nearly everything I had seen in the Ouroboros—I let them see it, too. Told them.

And when I was done, Miryam and Drakon stepped forward to tell their own story.

Another glimmer of proof—that humans and Fae could not only work together, live together, but become so much more. I listened to every word of it—and did not bother to brush away my tears at times. I only clutched Rhys's hand, and did not let go.

There were several others with tales. Some that went counter to our own. Relations that had not gone so well. Crimes committed. Hurts that could not be forgiven.

But it was a start.

There was still much work to be done, trust to build, but the matter of crafting a new wall . . .

It remained to be seen whether we could agree on that. Many of us were against it. Many of the humans, rightfully so, were wary. There were still other Fae territories to contend with—those who had found Hybern's promises appealing. Seductive.

The High Lords quarreled the most about the possibility of a new wall. And with every word of it, just as Helion said, that temporary allegiance frayed and snapped. Court lines were redrawn.

But at least they stayed until the end—until the early hours of the morning when we finally decided that the rest would be discussed on another day. At another place.

It would take time. Time, and healing, and trust.

And I wondered if the road ahead—the road to true peace—would perhaps be the hardest and longest one yet.

The others left, winnowing or flying or striding off into the darkness, already peeling back into their groups and courts and war-bands. I watched them go from the open doorway of the estate until they were only shadows against the night.

I'd seen Elain staring out the window earlier—watching Graysen leave with his men without so much as a look back at her. He had meant every word that day at his keep. Whether he noticed that Elain still wore his engagement ring, that Elain stared and stared at him as he walked off into the night . . . I didn't know. Let Lucien deal with that—for now.

I sighed, leaning my head against the cracked stone door frame. The grand wooden door had been shattered completely, the splinters still scattered on the marble entry behind me.

I recognized his scent before I heard his easy steps approach.

"Where do you go now?" I asked without looking over my shoulder as Jurian paused beside me and stared into the darkness. Miryam and Drakon had left quickly, needing to tend to their wounded—and to spirit away the Cauldron to one of their ships before the other High Lords had a moment to consider its whereabouts.

Jurian leaned against the opposite door frame. "Queen Vassa offered me a place within her court." Indeed, Vassa still remained inside, chatting with Lucien animatedly. I supposed that if she only had until dawn before turning back into that firebird, she wanted to make every minute count. Lucien, surprisingly, was chuckling, his shoulders loose and his head angled while he listened.

"Are you going to accept?"

Jurian's face was solemn—tired. "What sort of court can a cursed queen have? She's bound to that death-lord—she has to go back to his lake on the continent at some point." He shook his head. "Too bad the king was so spectacularly beheaded by your sister. I bet he could have found a way to break that curse of hers."

"Too bad indeed," I muttered.

Jurian grunted his amusement.

"Do you think we stand a chance?" I asked, motioning to the human figures still walking, far away, back toward the camp. "Of peace between all of us?"

Jurian was silent for a long moment. "Yes," he said softly. "I do."

And I didn't know why, but it gave me comfort.

⊹

I was still mulling over Jurian's words days later, when that war-camp was at last dismantled. When we said our final good-byes, and made promises—some more sincere than others—to see each other again.

When my court, my family, winnowed back to Velaris.

Sunlight still leaked in through the windows of the town house. The scent of citrus and the sea and baked bread still filled every room.

And distantly . . . Children were still laughing in the streets.

Home. Home was the same—home was untouched.

I squeezed Rhys's hand so tightly I thought he'd complain, but he only squeezed right back.

And even though we had all bathed, as we stood there . . . there was a grime to us. Like the blood hadn't entirely washed off.

And I realized that home was indeed the same, but we . . . perhaps we were not.

Amren muttered, "I suppose I shall have to eat real food now."

"A monumental sacrifice," Cassian quipped.

She gave him a vulgar gesture, but her eyes narrowed at the sight of his still-bandaged wings. Her eyes—normal silver eyes—slid to Nesta, holding herself by the stair rail, as if she'd retreat to her room.

My sister had barely spoken, barely eaten these past few days. Had not visited Cassian in his healing bed. Still had not talked to me about what had happened.

Amren said to her, "I'm surprised you didn't take the king's head back to have stuffed and hung on your wall."

Nesta's eyes shot to her.

Mor clicked her tongue. "Some would consider that joke to be in bad taste, Amren."

"I saved your asses. I'm entitled to say what I want."

And with that Amren stalked out of the house and into the city streets.

"The new Amren is even crankier than the old one," Elain said softly.

I burst out laughing. The others joined me, and even Elain smiled—broadly.

All but Nesta, who stared at nothing.

When the Cauldron had broken . . . I didn't know if it had broken that power in her, too. Severed its bond. Or if it still lived, somewhere within her.

"Come on," Mor said, slinging her arm around Azriel's shoulders, then one carefully around Cassian's and leading them toward the sitting room. "We need a drink."

"We're opening the fancy bottles," Cassian called over his shoulder to Rhys, still limping on that barely healed leg.

My mate sketched a subservient bow. "Save a bit for me, at least."

Rhys glanced at my sisters, then winked at me. The shadows of battle still lingered, but that wink . . . I was still shaky with terror that it wasn't real. That it was all some fever dream inside the Cauldron.

It is real, he purred into my mind. *I'll prove it to you later. For hours.*

I snorted, and watched as he made an excuse to no one in particular about finding food and sauntered down the hall, hands in his pockets.

Alone in the foyer with my sisters, Elain still smiling a bit, Nesta stone-faced, I took a breath.

Lucien had remained behind to help with any of the human wounded still needing Fae healing, but had promised to come here when he finished. And as for Tamlin . . .

I had not spoken to him. Had barely seen him after he'd told me to be happy, and given me back my mate. He'd left the meeting before I could say anything.

So I gave Lucien a note to hand to him if he saw him. Which I knew—I knew he would. There was a stop that Lucien had to make before he came here, he'd said. I knew where he meant.

My note to Tamlin was short. It conveyed everything I needed to say.

Thank you.

I hope you find happiness, too.

And I did. Not just for what he'd done for Rhys, but . . . Even for an immortal, there was not enough *time* in life to waste it on hatred. On feeling it and putting it into the world.

So I wished him well—I truly did, and hoped that one day . . . One day, perhaps he would face those insidious fears, that destructive rage rotting away inside him.

"So," I said to my sisters. "What now?"

Nesta just turned and went up the stairs, each step slow and stiff. She shut her door with a decisive click once she got to her bedroom.

"With Father," Elain whispered, still staring up those steps, "I don't think Nesta—"

"I know," I murmured. "I think Nesta needs to sort through . . . a lot of it."

Too much of it.

Elain faced me. "Do we help her?"

I fiddled with the end of my braid. "Yes—but not today. Not tomorrow." I loosed a breath. "When—when she's ready." When *we* were ready, too.

Elain nodded, smiling up at me, and it was tentative joy—and *life* that shone in her eyes. A promise of the future, gleaming and sweet.

I led her into the sitting room, where Cassian had a bottle of amber-colored liquor in each hand, Azriel was already rubbing his temples, and Mor was grabbing fine-cut crystal glasses off a shelf.

"What now?" Elain mused, at last answering my question from moments ago as her attention drifted to the windows facing the sunny street. That smile grew, bright enough that it lit up even Azriel's shadows across the room. "I would like to build a garden," she declared. "After all of this . . . I think the world needs more gardens."

My throat was too tight to immediately reply, so I just kissed my sister's cheek before I said, "Yes—I think it does."

CHAPTER
81

Rhysand

Even from the kitchen, I could hear all of them. The lapping of what was surely the oldest bottle of liquor I owned, then the clink of those equally ancient crystal glasses against each other.

Then the laughter. The deep rumble—that was Azriel. Laughing at whatever Mor had said that prompted her into a fit of it as well, the sound cackling and merry.

And then another laugh—silvery and bright. More beautiful than any music played at one of Velaris's countless halls and theaters.

I stood at the kitchen window, staring at the garden in full summer splendor, not quite seeing the blooms Elain Archeron had tended these weeks. Just staring—and listening to that beautiful laugh. My mate's laugh.

I rubbed a hand over my chest at that sound—the joy in it.

Their conversation flitted past, falling back into old rhythms and yet . . . Close. We had all come so close to not seeing it again. This place. Each other. And I knew that the laughter . . . it was in part because of that, too. In defiance and gratitude.

"You coming to drink, or are you just going to stare at the flowers all day?" Cassian's voice cut through the melody of sounds.

I turned, finding him and Azriel in the kitchen doorway, each with a drink in hand. A second lay in Azriel's other scarred hand—he floated it over to me on a blue-tinged breeze.

I clasped the cool, heavy crystal tumbler. "Sneaking up on your High Lord is ill-advised," I told them, drinking deeply. The liquor burned its way down my throat, warming my stomach.

"It's good to keep you on edge in your old age," Cassian said, drinking himself. He leaned against the doorway. "Why are you hiding in here?"

Azriel shot him a look, but I snorted, taking another sip. "You really did open the fancy bottles."

They waited. But Feyre's laugh sounded again, followed by Elain's and Mor's. And when I dragged my gaze back to my brothers, I saw the understanding on their faces.

"It's real," Azriel said softly.

Neither laughed or commented on the burning in my eyes. I took another drink to wash away the tightness in my throat, and approached them. "Let's not do this again for another five hundred years," I said a bit hoarsely, and clinked my glass against theirs.

Azriel cracked a smile as Cassian lifted a brow. "And what are we going to do until then?"

Beyond brokering peace, beyond those queens who were sure to be a problem, beyond healing our fractured world . . .

Mor called for us, demanding we bring them a spread of food. An *impressive* one, she added. *With extra bread.*

I smiled. Smiled wider as Feyre's laugh sounded again—as I *felt* it down the bond, sparkling brighter than the entirety of Starfall.

"Until then," I said to my brothers, slinging my arms around their shoulders and leading them back to the sitting room. I looked ahead, toward that laugh, that light—and that vision of the future Feyre had shown me, more beautiful than anything I could have ever wished for—anything I *had* wished for, on those long-ago, solitary nights with only the stars for company. A dream still unanswered—but not forever. "Until then, we enjoy every heartbeat of it."

CHAPTER
82
Feyre

Rhysand was on the roof, the stars bright and low, the tiles beneath my bare feet still warm from the day's sun.

He sat in one of those small iron chairs, no light, no bottle of liquor—just him, and the stars, and the city.

I slid into his lap and let him wrap his arms around me.

We sat in silence for a long time. We'd barely had a moment alone in the aftermath of the battle, and had been too tired to do anything but sleep. But tonight . . . His hand ran down my thigh, bared with the way my nightgown had hitched.

He startled when he actually looked at me, then huffed a laugh against my shoulder.

"I should have known."

"The shop ladies gave it to me for free. As thanks for saving them from Hybern. Maybe I should do it more often, if it gets me free lingerie."

For I indeed wore that pair of red, lacy underthings—beneath a matching red nightgown that was so scandalously sheer it showed them off.

"Hasn't anyone told you? You're disgustingly rich."

"Just because I have money doesn't mean I need to spend it."

He squeezed my knee. "Good. We need someone with a head for money around here. I've been bleeding out gold left and right thanks to our Court of Dreams taking advantage of my ridiculous generosity."

A laugh rumbled deep in my throat as I leaned my head back against his shoulder. "Is Amren still your Second?"

"Our Second."

"Semantics."

Rhys traced idle circles on my bare skin, along my knee and lower thigh. "If she wants it, it's hers."

"Even if she doesn't have her powers anymore?"

"She's now High Fae. I'm sure she'll discover some hidden talent to terrorize us with."

I laughed again, savoring the feel of his hand on my skin, the warmth of his body around me.

"I heard you," he said softly. "When I was—gone."

I began to tense at the lingering terror that had driven me from sleep these past few nights—the terror I doubted I'd soon recover from. "Those minutes," I said once he began making long, soothing strokes down my thigh. "Rhys . . . I never want to feel that again."

"Now you know how I felt Under the Mountain."

I craned my neck to look up at him. "*Never* lie to me again. Not about that."

"But about other things?"

I pinched his arm hard enough that he laughed and batted away my hand. "I couldn't let all you *ladies* take the credit for saving us. Some male had to claim a bit of glory so you don't trample us until the end of time with your bragging."

I punched his arm this time.

But he wrapped his arm around my waist and squeezed, breathing me in. "I heard you, even in death. It made me look back. Made me stay—a little longer."

Before going to that place I had once tried to describe to the Carver.

"When it's time to go there," I said quietly, "we go together."

"It's a bargain," he said, and kissed me gently.

I murmured back onto his lips, "Yes, it is."

The skin on my left arm tingled. A lick of warmth snaked down it.

I looked down to find another tattoo there—the twin to the one that had once graced it, save for that black band of the bargain I'd made with Bryaxis. He'd modified this one to fit around it, to be seamlessly integrated amid the whorls and swirls.

"I missed the old one," he said innocently.

On his own left arm, the same tattoo flowed. Not to his fingers the way mine did, but rather from his wrist to his elbow.

"Copycat," I said tartly. "It looks better on me."

"Hmmm." He traced a line down my spine, then poked two spots along it. "Sweet Bryaxis has vanished. Do you know what that means?"

"That I have to go hunt it down and put it back in the library?"

"Oh, you most certainly do."

I twisted in his lap, looping my arms around his neck as I said, "And will you come with me? On this adventure—and all the rest?"

Rhys leaned forward and kissed me. "Always."

The stars seemed to burn brighter in response, creeping closer to watch. His wings rustled as he shifted us in the chair and deepened the kiss until I was breathless.

And then I was flying.

Rhys gathered me up in his arms, shooting us high into the starry night, the city a glimmering reflection beneath.

Music flitted out from the riverfront cafés. People laughed as they walked arm in arm down the streets and across the bridges spanning the Sidra. Dark spots still stained some of the glimmering expanse—piles of rubble and ruined buildings—but even some of those had been lit up with small lights. Candles. Defiant and lovely against the blackness.

We would need more of that in the days to come—on the long road ahead. To a new world. One I would leave a better place than how I'd found it.

But for now . . . this moment, with the city below us, the world around us, savoring that hard-won peace . . . I savored it, too. Every heartbeat. Every sound and smell and image that planted itself in my mind, so many that it would take me a lifetime—several of them—to paint.

Rhys leveled out, sent a thought into my mind, and grinned broadly as I summoned wings.

He let go of me and I swept smoothly out of his arms, basking in the warm wind caressing every inch of me, drinking in the air laced with salt and citrus. It took me a few flaps to get it right—the feel and rhythm. But then I was steady, even.

Then I was flying. Soaring.

Rhys fell into flight beside me, and when he smiled at me again as we sailed through the stars and the lights and the sea-kissed breeze, when he showed me all the wonders of Velaris, the glittering Rainbow a living river of color beneath us . . . When he brushed his wing against mine, just because he could, because he wanted to and we'd have an eternity of nights to do this, to see everything together . . .

A gift.

All of it.

ACKNOWLEDGMENTS

Even after nine books, it never gets any easier to express my tremendous gratitude to the people in my life, both personally and professionally, who make my world brighter just by being in it.

To Josh: Every moment with you is a gift. Long ago, when I looked up at the stars and wished, it was for someone like you to be in my life. I truly believe those stars listened, because getting to share this wild adventure with you has been a dream answered. I love you more than words can convey.

To Annie: Thank you for the cuddles, the sass, and the constant demands for more treats that keep me on my toes. I love you forever and ever and ever, baby pup (and no matter what anyone says, I swear you *can* read this).

To my agent, Tamar, who works so tirelessly and is the fiercest badass I know: none of this would be possible without you, and I will never stop being grateful for it. Thank you for everything.

To Cat Onder: Working with you was such an enormous privilege and joy. Thank you for being such a creative, caring, and insightful editor, and for all the years of friendship.

To the genius team at Bloomsbury worldwide: Cindy Loh, Cristina Gilbert, Kathleen Farrar, Nigel Newton, Rebecca McNally, Sonia Palmisano, Emma Hopkin, Ian Lamb, Emma Bradshaw, Lizzy Mason, Courtney Griffin, Erica Barmash, Emily Ritter, Grace Whooley, Eshani Agrawal, Emily Klopfer, Alice Grigg, Elise Burns, Jenny Collins, Beth Eller, Kerry Johnson, Kelly de Groot, Ashley Poston, Lucy Mackay-Sim, Hali Baumstein, Melissa Kavonic, Diane Aronson, Linda Minton, Christine Ma, Donna Mark, John Candell, Nicholas Church, and the entire foreign rights team—thank you for the hard work to make these books a reality and for being the best damn global publishing team *ever*. To Jon Cassir and the team at CAA: thank you for championing me and my books.

To Cassie Homer, assistant extraordinaire: thank you for all of your help and for being such a delight to work with!

To my parents: thank you for the fairy tales and folklore, for the adventures around the world, and for the weekend mornings with bagels and lox from Murray's. To Linda and Dennis: you raised such a spectacular son, and I will be forever grateful for it. To my family: I'm so lucky to have all of you in my life.

To Roshani Chokshi, Lynette Noni, and Jennifer Armentrout: thank you for being such bright lights and wonderful friends—and for all your invaluable feedback with this book. To Renée Ahdieh, Steph Brown, and Alice Fanchiang: I adore you.

A massive thank-you to Sasha Alsberg, Vilma Gonzalez, Alexa Santiago, Rachel Domingo, Jessica Reigle, Kelly Grabowski, Jennifer Kelly, Laura Ashforth, and Diyana Wan for being supremely awesome and lovely people. To the marvelous Caitie Flum: thank you *so* much for taking the time to read this book and for providing such valuable feedback. To Louisse Ang: thank you, thank you, thank you for all of your remarkable kindness, infectious joy, and astounding generosity.

To Charlie Bowater, who is not only a brilliant artist, but also a magnificent human being: thank you for the art that has moved and inspired me, and for all of your hard and phenomenal work on the coloring book. It's an honor to work with you.

And lastly, to *you*, dear reader: thank you from the bottom of my heart for coming with me and Feyre on this journey. Your heartfelt letters and incredible art, your lovely music and clever cosplays . . . all of it means more than I can possibly say. I'm truly blessed to have you as readers, and can't wait to share more of this world with you in the next book!

FEYRE NAVIGATES HER
FIRST WINTER SOLSTICE
AS HIGH LADY IN . . .

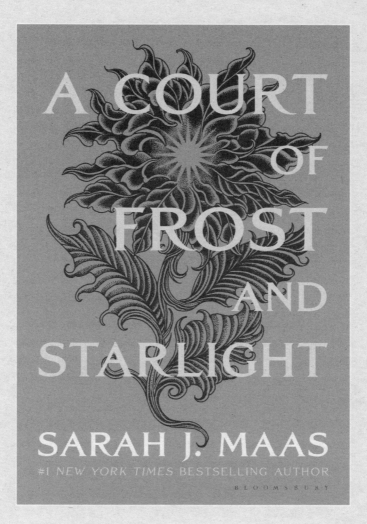

READ ON FOR A SNEAK PEEK AT THE NEXT
BOOK IN THIS ELECTRIFYING SERIES.

Feyre

The first snow of winter had begun whipping through Velaris an hour earlier.

The ground had finally frozen solid last week, and by the time I'd finished devouring my breakfast of toast and bacon, washed down with a heady cup of tea, the pale cobblestones were dusted with fine, white powder.

I had no idea where Rhys was. He hadn't been in bed when I'd awoken, the mattress on his side already cold. Nothing unusual, as we were both busy to the point of exhaustion these days.

Seated at the long cherrywood dining table at the town house, I frowned at the whirling snow beyond the leaded glass windows.

Once, I had dreaded that first snow, had lived in terror of long, brutal winters.

But it had been a long, brutal winter that had brought me so deep into the woods that day nearly two years ago. A long, brutal winter that had made me desperate enough to kill a wolf, that had eventually led me here—to this life, this . . . happiness.

The snow fell, thick clumps plopping onto the dried grass of the tiny front lawn, crusting the spikes and arches of the decorative fence beyond it.

Deep inside me, rising with every swirling flake, a sparkling, crisp power stirred. I was High Lady of the Night Court, yes, but also one blessed with the gifts of all the courts. It seemed Winter now wanted to play.

Finally awake enough to be coherent, I lowered the shield of black adamant guarding my mind and cast a thought down the soul-bridge between me and Rhys. *Where'd you fly off to so early?*

My question faded into blackness. A sure sign that Rhys was nowhere near Velaris. Likely not even within the borders of the Night Court. Also not unusual—he'd been visiting our war allies these months to solidify our relationships, build trade, and keep tabs on their post-wall intentions. When my own work allowed it, I often joined him.

I scooped up my plate, draining my tea to the dregs, and padded toward the kitchen. Playing with ice and snow could wait.

Nuala was already preparing for lunch at the worktable, no sign of her twin, Cerridwen, but I waved her off as she made to take my dishes. "I can wash them," I said by way of greeting.

Up to the elbows in making some sort of meat pie, the half-wraith gave me a grateful smile and let me do it. A female of few words, though neither twin could be considered shy. Certainly not when they worked—spied—for both Rhys and Azriel.

"It's still snowing," I observed rather pointlessly, peering out the kitchen window at the garden beyond as I rinsed off the plate, fork, and cup. Elain had already readied the garden for winter, veiling the more delicate bushes and beds with burlap. "I wonder if it'll let up at all."

Nuala laid the ornate lattice crust atop the pie and began pinching the edges together, her shadowy fingers making quick, deft work of it. "It'll be nice to have a white Solstice," she said, voice lilting and yet hushed. Full of whispers and shadows. "Some years, it can be fairly mild."

Right. The Winter Solstice. In a week. I was still new enough to being High Lady that I had no idea what my formal role was to be. If we'd have a High Priestess do some odious ceremony, as Ianthe had done the year before—

A year. Gods, nearly a year since Rhys had called in his bargain, desperate to get me away from the poison of the Spring Court, to save me from my despair. Had he been only a minute later, the Mother knew what would have happened. Where I'd now be.

Snow swirled and eddied in the garden, catching in the brown fibers of the burlap covering the shrubs.

My mate—who had worked so hard and so selflessly, all without hope that I would ever be with him.

We had both fought for that love, bled for it. Rhys had died for it.

I still saw that moment, in my sleeping and waking dreams. How his face had looked, how his chest had not risen, how the bond between us had shredded into ribbons. I still felt it, that hollowness in my chest where the bond had been, where *he* had been. Even now, with that bond again flowing between us like a river of star-flecked night, the echo of its vanishing lingered. Drew me from sleep; drew me from a conversation, a painting, a meal.

Rhys knew exactly why there were nights when I would cling tighter to him, why there were moments in the bright, clear sunshine that I would grip his hand. He knew, because *I* knew why his eyes sometimes turned distant, why he occasionally just blinked at all of us as if not quite believing it and rubbed his chest as if to ease an ache.

Working had helped. Both of us. Keeping busy, keeping focused—I sometimes dreaded the quiet, idle days when all those thoughts snared me at last. When there was nothing but me and my mind, and that memory of Rhys lying dead on the rocky ground, the King of Hybern snapping my father's neck, all those Illyrians blasted out of the sky and falling to earth as ashes.

Perhaps one day, even the work wouldn't be a battlement to keep the memories out.

Mercifully, plenty of work remained for the foreseeable future. Rebuilding Velaris after the attacks from Hybern being only one of many monumental tasks. For other tasks required doing as well—both in Velaris and beyond it: in the Illyrian Mountains, in the Hewn City, in the vastness of the entire Night Court. And then there were the other courts of Prythian. And the new, emerging world beyond.

But for now: Solstice. The longest night of the year. I turned from the window to Nuala, who was still fussing over the edges of her pie. "It's a special holiday here as well, right?" I asked casually. "Not just in Winter and Day." And Spring.

"Oh, yes," Nuala said, stooping over the worktable to examine her pie. Skilled spy—trained by Azriel himself—and master cook. "We love it dearly. It's intimate, warm, lovely. Presents and music and food, sometimes feasting under the starlight . . ." The opposite of the enormous, wild, days-long party I'd been subjected to last year. But—presents.

I had to buy presents for all of them. Not had to, but *wanted* to.

Because all my friends, now my family, had fought and bled and nearly died as well.

I shut out the image that tore through my mind: Nesta, leaning over a wounded Cassian, the two of them prepared to die together against the King of Hybern. My father's corpse behind them.

I rolled my neck. We could use something to celebrate. It had become so rare for all of us to be gathered for more than an hour or two.

Nuala went on, "It's a time of rest, too. And a time to reflect on the darkness—how it lets the light shine."

"Is there a ceremony?"

The half-wraith shrugged. "Yes, but none of us go. It's more for those who wish to honor the light's rebirth, usually by spending the entire night sitting in absolute darkness." A ghost of a smirk. "It's not quite such a novelty for my sister and me. Or for the High Lord."

I tried not to look too relieved that I wouldn't be dragged to a temple for hours as I nodded.

Setting my clean dishes to dry on the little wooden rack beside the sink, I wished Nuala luck on lunch, and headed upstairs to dress. Cerridwen had already laid out clothes, but there was still no sign of Nuala's twin as I donned the heavy charcoal sweater, the tight black leggings, and fleece-lined boots before loosely braiding back my hair.

A year ago, I'd been stuffed into fine gowns and jewels, made to parade in front of a preening court who'd gawked at me like a prized breeding mare.

Here . . . I smiled at the silver-and-sapphire band on my left hand. The ring I'd won for myself from the Weaver in the Wood.

My smile faded a bit.

I could see her, too. See Stryga standing before the King of

Hybern, covered in the blood of her prey, as he took her head in his hands and snapped her neck. Then threw her to his beasts.

I clenched my fingers into a fist, breathing in through my nose, out through my mouth, until the lightness in my limbs faded, until the walls of the room stopped pressing on me.

Until I could survey the blend of personal objects in Rhys's room—our room. It was by no means a small bedroom, but it had lately started to feel . . . tight. The rosewood desk against one wall was covered in papers and books from both of our own dealings; my jewelry and clothes now had to be divided between here and my old bedroom. And then there were the weapons.

Daggers and blades, quivers and bows. I scratched my head at the heavy, wicked-looking *mace* that Rhys had somehow dumped beside the desk without my noticing.

I didn't even want to know. Though I had no doubt Cassian was somehow behind it.

We could, of course, store everything in the pocket between realms, but . . . I frowned at my own set of Illyrian blades, leaning against the towering armoire.

If we got snowed in, perhaps I'd use the day to organize things. Find room for everything. Especially that mace.

It would be a challenge, since Elain still occupied a bedroom down the hall. Nesta had chosen her own home across the city, one that I opted to not think about for too long. Lucien, at least, had taken up residence in an elegant apartment down by the river the day after he'd returned from the battlefields. And the Spring Court.

I hadn't asked Lucien any questions about that visit—to Tamlin.

Lucien hadn't explained the black eye and cut lip, either. He'd only asked Rhys and me if we knew of a place to stay in Velaris, since he did not wish to inconvenience us further by staying at the town house, and did not wish to be isolated at the House of Wind.

He hadn't mentioned Elain, or his proximity to her. Elain had not asked him to stay, or to go. And whether she cared about the bruises on his face, she certainly hadn't let on.

But Lucien had remained, and found ways to keep busy, often gone for days or weeks at a time.

Yet even with Lucien and Nesta staying in their own apartments, the town house was a bit small these days. Even more so if Mor, Cassian, and Azriel stayed over. And the House of Wind was too big, too formal, too far from the city proper. Nice for a night or two, but . . . I loved this house.

It was my home. The first I'd really had in the ways that counted.

And it'd be nice to celebrate the Solstice here. With all of them, crowded as it might be.

I scowled at the pile of papers I had to sort through: letters from other courts, priestesses angling for positions, and kingdoms both human and faerie. I'd put them off for weeks now, and had finally set aside this morning to wade through them.

High Lady of the Night Court, Defender of the Rainbow and the . . . Desk.

I snorted, flicking my braid over a shoulder. Perhaps my Solstice gift to myself would be to hire a personal secretary. Someone to read and answer those things, to sort out what was vital and what could be put aside. Because a little extra time to myself, for *Rhys* . . .

I'd look through the court budget that Rhys never really cared to follow and see what could be moved around for the possibility of such a thing. For him and for me.

I knew our coffers ran deep, knew we could easily afford it and not make so much as a dent in our fortune, but I didn't mind the work. I loved the work, actually. This territory, its people—they were as much my heart as my mate. Until yesterday, nearly every waking hour had been packed with helping them. Until I'd been politely, graciously, told to *go home and enjoy the holiday.*

In the wake of the war, the people of Velaris had risen to the challenge of rebuilding and helping their own. Before I'd even come up with an idea of *how* to help them, multiple societies had been created to assist the city. So I'd volunteered with a handful of them for tasks ranging from finding homes for those displaced by the destruction to visiting families affected during the war to helping those without shelter or belongings ready for winter with new coats and supplies.

All of it was vital; all of it was good, satisfying work. And yet . . . there was more. There was *more* that I could do to help. Personally. I just hadn't figured it out yet.

It seemed I wasn't the only one eager to assist those who'd lost so much. With the holiday, a surge of fresh volunteers had arrived, cramming the public hall near the Palace of Thread and Jewels, where so many of the societies were headquartered. *Your help has been crucial, Lady,* one charity matron had said to me yesterday. *You have been here nearly every day—you have worked yourself to the bone. Take the week off. You've earned it. Celebrate with your mate.*

I'd tried to object, insisting that there were still more coats to hand out, more firewood to be distributed, but the faerie had just motioned to the crowded public hall around us, filled to the brim with volunteers. *We have more help than we know what to do with.*

When I'd tried objecting again, she'd shooed me out the front door. And shut it behind me.

Point taken. The story had been the same at every other organization I'd stopped by yesterday afternoon. *Go home and enjoy the holiday.*

So I had. At least, the first part. The *enjoying* bit, however . . .

Rhys's answer to my earlier inquiry about his whereabouts finally flickered down the bond, carried on a rumble of dark, glittering power. *I'm at Devlon's camp.*

It took you this long to respond? It was a long distance to the Illyrian Mountains, yes, but it shouldn't have taken minutes to hear back.

A sensual huff of laughter. *Cassian was ranting. He didn't take a breath.*

My poor Illyrian baby. We certainly do torment you, don't we?

Rhys's amusement rippled toward me, caressing my innermost self with night-veiled hands. But it halted, vanishing as quickly as it had come. *Cassian's getting into it with Devlon. I'll check in later.* With a loving brush against my senses, he was gone.

I'd get a full report about it soon, but for now . . .

I smiled at the snow waltzing outside the windows.

Rhysand

It was barely nine in the morning, and Cassian was already pissed.

The watery winter sun tried and failed to bleed through the clouds looming over the Illyrian Mountains, the wind a boom across the gray peaks. Snow already lay inches deep over the bustling camp, a vision of what would soon befall Velaris.

It had been snowing when I departed at dawn—perhaps there would be a good coating already on the ground by the time I returned. I hadn't had a chance to ask Feyre about it during our brief conversation down the bond minutes ago, but perhaps she would go for a walk with me through it. Let me show her how the City of Starlight glistened under fresh snow.

Indeed, my mate and city seemed a world away from the hive of activity in the Windhaven camp, nestled in a wide, high mountain pass. Even the bracing wind that swept between the peaks, belying the camp's very name by whipping up dervishes of snow, didn't deter the Illyrians from going about their daily chores.

For the warriors: training in the various rings that opened onto a sheer drop to the small valley floor below, those not present out on patrol. For the males who hadn't made the cut: tending to various trades, whether merchants or blacksmiths or cobblers. And for the females: drudgery.

They didn't see it as such. None of them did. But their required tasks, whether old or young, remained the same: cooking, cleaning, child-rearing, clothes-making, laundry . . . There was honor in such tasks—pride and good work to be found in them. But not when every single one of the females here was *expected* to do it. And if they shirked those duties, either one of the half-dozen camp-mothers or whatever males controlled their lives would punish them.

So it had been, as long as I'd known this place, for my mother's people. The world had been reborn during the war months before, the wall blasted to nothingness, and yet some things did not alter. Especially here, where change was slower than the melting glaciers scattered amongst these mountains. Traditions going back thousands of years, left mostly unchallenged.

Until us. Until now.

Drawing my attention away from the bustling camp beyond the edge of the chalk-lined training rings where we stood, I schooled my face into neutrality as Cassian squared off against Devlon.

"The girls are busy with preparations for the Solstice," the camp-lord was saying, his arms crossed over his barrel chest. "The wives need all the help they can get, if all's to be ready in time. They can practice next week."

I'd lost count of how many variations of this conversation we'd had during the decades Cassian had been pushing Devlon on this.

The wind whipped Cassian's dark hair, but his face remained hard as granite as he said to the warrior who had begrudgingly trained us, "The girls can help their mothers *after* training is done for the day. We'll cut practice down to two hours. The rest of the day will be enough to assist in the preparations."

Devlon slid his hazel eyes to where I lingered a few feet away. "Is it an order?"

I held that gaze. And despite my crown, my power, I tried not to fall back into the trembling child I'd been five centuries ago, that first day Devlon had towered over me and then hurled me into the sparring ring. "If Cassian says it's an order, then it is."

It had occurred to me, during the years we'd been waging this same battle with Devlon and the Illyrians, that I could simply rip into his mind, all their minds, and make them agree. Yet there were some lines I could not, would not cross. And Cassian would never forgive me.

Devlon grunted, his breath a curl of steam. "An hour."

"Two hours," Cassian countered, wings flaring slightly as he held a hard line that I'd been called in this morning to help him maintain.

It had to be bad, then, if my brother had asked me to come. Really damn bad. Perhaps we needed a permanent presence out here, until the Illyrians remembered things like consequences.

Don't miss
any of the bestselling
Court of Thorns and Roses series:

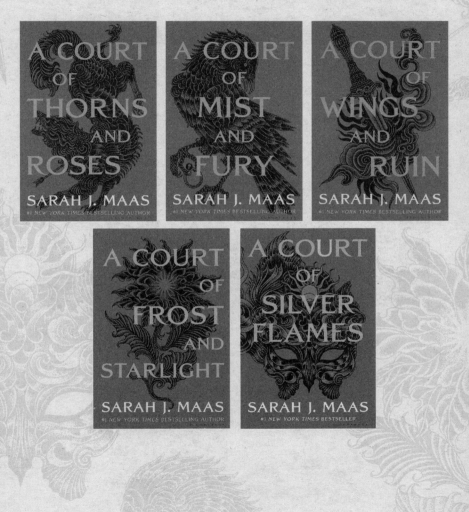

BOUND BY BLOOD.
TEMPTED BY DESIRE.
UNLEASHED BY DESTINY.

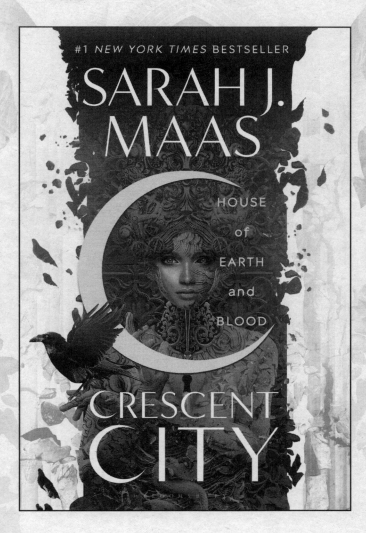

#1 *NEW YORK TIMES* **BESTSELLER**

SARAH J. MAAS

HOUSE

of

EARTH

and

BLOOD

CRESCENT CITY

THE FIRST NOVEL IN THE
EPIC NEW SERIES.